THE PENGUIN CLASSICS

FOUNDER EDITOR (1944–64): E. V. RIEU

EDITORS: ROBERT BALDICK (1966–72)

BETTY RADICE

ALESSANDRO MANZONI was born in 1785 on his father's estate near Lake Como, Italy. From the age of five he was packed off to boarding-school, where his mother never visited him. When he was seven, she left his father and went off to live in Paris with a wealthy Milanese liberal. As a young man Manzoni subscribed to the ideals of the French Revolution, and in 1801 he wrote a poem which contained harsh anti-Christian views. He joined his mother in Paris in 1805, and in 1808 married Henriette Blondel, a Swiss Protestant girl. The marriage was a very happy one, except for a few tensions over religion which were resolved when they both became practising Catholics. Manzoni took his family to Milan in 1810. The next few years saw the publication of a series of odes, largely on religious subjects. Manzoni also studied Italian history, and wrote several historical plays in verse during the years following 1818. He began work on *I Promessi Sposi* (The Betrothed) in 1821, and published it in 1827; it was an instant success, and ran to nine editions in four years. Manzoni rewrote the book completely for a definitive, Tuscanized edition, which appeared in 1840 and virtually marked the end of his creative life. He lived another thirty-three years, but they were not particularly happy ones. He had long suffered from a nervous disorder, which now grew worse. Henriette had died in 1833, his second wife also died many years before him, and only two of his nine children survived him. When he died in 1873 he was given a state funeral, and Verdi wrote his famous *Requiem* for the first anniversary of Manzoni's death.

BRUCE PENMAN is a versatile linguist who has a good reading knowledge of ten languages and speaks four of them fluently. He is the export market-research manager of a large industrial firm, and follows the same system for translating books that Trollope used for writing them – a long, regular daily stint before breakfast. His other translations include works of travel and of ancient history, besides seven of the *novelle* in the *Penguin Book of Italian Short Stories*.

Alessandro Manzoni

The Betrothed

Translated with an introduction
by Bruce Penman

Penguin Books

Penguin Books Ltd, Harmondsworth, Middlesex, England
Penguin Books Inc., 7110 Ambassador Road, Baltimore, Maryland 21207, U.S.A.
Penguin Books Australia Ltd, Ringwood, Victoria, Australia

—

This translation first published 1972
Copyright © Bruce Penman, 1972

—

Made and printed in Great Britain
by Richard Clay (The Chaucer Press), Ltd
Bungay, Suffolk
Set in Linotype Granjon

Contents

Introduction

ALESSANDRO MANZONI's mother was the beautiful and brilliant daughter of Cesare Beccaria, a distinguished writer on penal reform who enjoyed considerable fame not only in his native Lombardy, but also in liberal literary circles in pre-revolutionary Paris. By the time Giulia Beccaria was nineteen she had formed a friendship with Giovanni Verri, a member of another prominent Milanese liberal family, which was compromising for both of them; for Verri was a Knight of Malta and consequently stood to lose both his position and his income if he married. His family, rather than hers, took the initiative in regularizing the situation by marrying her off in 1782 at the age of twenty to someone else. This was Don Pietro Manzoni, a solemn, religious, conservative widower of forty-seven, with estates in the beautiful country near Lake Como which was to be described so well in *I Promessi Sposi* (*The Betrothed*). On 7 March 1785 the author was born, and put straight out to nurse. Seven years later his mother left her husband and went off to Paris with Carlo Imbonati, a wealthy Milanese liberal, with whom she lived happily and devotedly until his death. They had considerable social success in literary circles in the French capital.

There has been some controversy about Alessandro's true paternity.

Alessandro clearly did not have a happy childhood. After a long time out at nurse and a short time back at home, he had been sent off at the age of five to boarding-school, where his mother never visited him, even before her elopement. A series of boarding-schools followed, none of which he enjoyed, though he studied well and acquired a good knowledge of Latin. His holidays were spent largely on the family estates near Lake Como, and his lasting love for that countryside clearly dates

From 1812 to 1822 a fair amount of his time was taken up in the composition of a series of lengthy hymns (we would perhaps call them odes) on the various major festivals of the church.

These were historically eventful years – the years of Napoleon's defeat, downfall and death, and of the collapse of the political structure Bonaparte had set up in Italy, which led to Austrian rule returning to Lombardy in an even harsher form than before. Though liberation – and subsequent administration – by the French had been a very mixed blessing, Manzoni was profoundly shocked by Napoleon's downfall. Many of the events of those years are celebrated in his secular poetry, and the ugly riots of 1814 in Milan provided him with materials for the riot described in chapter 12 and 13 of *The Betrothed*.

In 1816 we first hear of a nervous disorder which was to dog him for the rest of his life – a feeling of faintness and causeless anxiety which came on in the open air, and made him unable to go out of doors alone.

At about this time he began an intensive study of Italian history, which led on to the publication in 1819 of his verse tragedy *Il Conte di Carmagnola*. He stopped work on this play in the middle to write a work of Christian apologetics, at the suggestion of his spiritual adviser. From the time of his conversion on he was much under the influence of spiritual advisers, who sometimes tried to direct his literary efforts as well as his conscience. His historical studies continued, and he became especially absorbed in the period of the early seventeenth century.

Some time about 1820 it must have occurred to him that a historical novel would provide an ideal means of bringing his principal interests together into a single literary work. It could include a historically accurate picture – into which a deeply religious strand would naturally be woven – of the extraordinary and fascinating society of the early seventeenth century. It could show the evils of authoritarian rule and of foreign domination – still at that time the curse of Italy and the natural preoccupation of an Italian liberal. It could provide an outlet for his dramatic talents – and for a vein of gently ironical humour which had so far only found expression in his letters. He began to write the first draft of what was to be *The Betrothed* in 1821. He finished it in 1823, having published a number of other works in the intervening two years, including the best of his hymns and a fine ode on the death of Napoleon. After much revision the novel was published in 1827. It was an instant and overwhelming success, hailed as a masterpiece both in Italy and abroad. Some of the warmest praise came from Goethe and Lamartine. It ran through nine editions in Italian, one in French, two in German and one in English in the first four years.

Thoroughly as the work had been revised before publication, there was still one more major revision to come, which was the most important of all. It played a highly significant part in the *'questione della lingua'* – that interminable controversy about the foundation on which standard Italian ought to rest. Should the written language be based on the dialect used by most of the great Italian writers of the past, which was Tuscan, or on a synthesis of all the dialects, or what? There were various schools of thought, holding mutually incompatible views, and the resulting uncertainty caused the written language to become more and more remote from all forms of the spoken word.

Shortly after the first edition of Manzoni's great novel had been published, he became a whole-hearted convert to the Tuscanizing school. He conscientiously mastered the Tuscan idiom, and slowly and painstakingly rewrote the book in it. The new version finally appeared thirteen years after the first edition – long after the book had won European fame as the great Italian novel. And the new version was unmistakably and undeniably a great improvement on the old.

This gave a most tremendous boost to the Tuscanizers' cause. Though it cannot be said to have settled the *'questione della lingua'* finally in their favour, it undoubtedly had a lasting and beneficial effect in lessening what had been an excessive gap between the written and spoken languages.

Manzoni's productive life as an author virtually ended with the production of the final version of *The Betrothed* in 1840. He lived on for another thirty-three years, a deeply revered but unhappy figure, dogged by ill-health and bad luck. His beloved Henriette had died in 1833. He made a reasonably happy second marriage a few years later, but his second wife did not get on with her step-children, and she too died many years before his own life drew to a close. Some of his nine children turned out badly, and only two of them survived him. He took little active part in politics, though he welcomed the final struggle to free Italy from foreign rule, and was indeed regarded as in some ways a symbol of it. The death of his favourite son, in April 1873, was probably the immediate cause of his own final illness During his last days he was much troubled by the thought that his sins might be too great for forgiveness. But he died with all the comforts of the Church, and was given a splendid State funeral. Verdi's famous Requiem was written for the first anniversary of his death.

If Dickens had written only one novel, and there had been no Fielding or Thackeray; if his novel had foreshadowed the theme of a successful national liberation movement and had had a profound, lasting and beneficial effect on the English language; then we would have a book that would stand out in our literature in the same way that *The Betrothed* does in Italy.

I Promessi Sposi is in fact a national institution – a splendid situation, but one which inevitably entails some disadvantages. But the English reader need not be discouraged by the fact that some Italians have heard so much about the book at school that it has been spoilt for them; nor by the fact that others have felt impelled to include it in a revolt against national institutions in general.

Attempts have been made to find the origin of Manzoni's book in various earlier plays and novels; but all these analogies are pretty far-fetched. The origins of the historical parts of the book – the wars, the famine, the bread riots, the plague, the administrative and social background – are in history. The Nun of Monza, the Unnamed and Cardinal Federigo Borromeo are historical characters too. Manzoni says that the story of Renzo and Lucia was suggested to him by the text of the historically authentic edict which Dr Quibbler shows to Renzo in chapter 3,[1] and there is no reason to doubt him.

The question of a more general debt to Scott, some of whose works were undoubtedly known to Manzoni before he started writing his own novel, is more difficult to resolve. But the only one of Scott's books with a plot resembling that of the Italian novel was written after it. To the extent that Scott had shown that it was possible to achieve literary success with a historical novel (then a new genre), he clearly must count as a precursor of Manzoni. In one important respect, however, Manzoni was ahead of Scott – he did not put pseudo-archaic dialogue into the mouths of his characters, but made them speak the colloquial Italian of his own day, without anachronisms.

There are several previous translations of the book into English, but all of them leave something to be desired in method, or accuracy, or both. The first translation, and several subsequent English versions, were based on the first edition of 1827, rather than the revised and definitive edition of 1840. Some of them have been extensively and badly cut, or use pseudo-archaic jargon for the dialogue – falling into the very trap that the original was the first to avoid.

The most recent version is that of Archibald Colquhoun, published by J. M. Dent, 1951. Even this contains a surprising number of mistakes of interpretation. It is also sometimes too literal, with extensive passages in the historic present – a device which never sounds right in modern English.

The text I have used for the present translation is the edition of Professors M. Barbi and F. Ghisalberti, which forms volume I of the collected works of Manzoni published by the Casa del Manzoni in 1942. The work has not been shortened or cut in any way.

My thanks are due to Professor C. C. Secchi of the Centro Nazionale di Studi Manzoniani in Milan, for much generous help and advice, and especially for reading the biographical part of this introduction in draft; to Dr L. Cagnolaro, Curator of the Museo Civico di Storia Naturale at Milan, for providing me

1. See page 64 of the present edition.

with a list of the correct Latin botanical names of the weeds in Renzo's vineyard;[2] and to my wife, who, besides secretarial help, has read the entire English text to me aloud and has made many valuable suggestions for its improvement.

BRUCE PENMAN

2. See pages 621–2 of the present edition.

Bibliography

THE Cambridge Modern History, Volume IV, gives an excellent general picture of the historical background to *The Betrothed*. Chapters II, IV, XXII and XXIII are especially helpful; also index references to the Mantuan Succession.

La Monaca di Monza, by Mario Mazzucchelli, Milan, 1961, is an interesting biography of the historical figure upon whom the character of Gertrude in *The Betrothed* is closely based. It is especially valuable for its copious quotations from the original documents of her trial. *The Nun of Monza*, an English translation by E. Gendel, was published in 1963 by Hamish Hamilton and has since been reprinted by Penguin Books.

Manzoni and his Times, by Archibald Colquhoun, J. M. Dent, 1954, is the best full-length study of its subject in English.

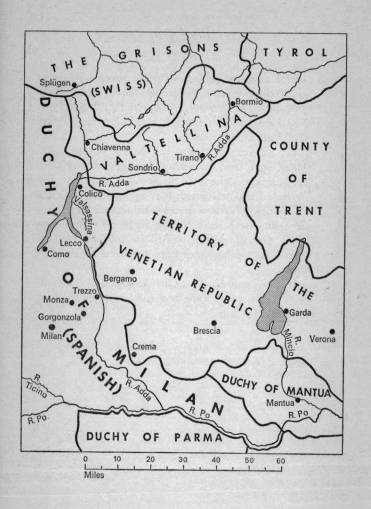

GEOGRAPHICAL NOTES

(SEE MAP ON OPPOSITE PAGE)

The Area around Lecco

Lucia's village is about a mile due east of Lecco, away from the lake.

Don Rodrigo's mansion is three miles north of Lecco, also well back from the lake.

Pescarenico is just south of Lecco, on the east shore of the lake.

The castle of the Unnamed is further south, and two or three miles back from the lake. It stands exactly on the frontier between Milanese and Venetian territory, where the boundary curves away from the lakeside towards the north-east.

Renzo's Escape Route from Milan to the District of Bergamo

After Renzo's escape from the police in Milan, he followed a zig-zag route through the villages to Gorgonzola and on to the point on the River Adda, just north of Trezzo, where he crossed over into the safety of Venetian territory. The village where his cousin Bortolo lived was nine or ten miles further on. This is roughly the same distance as the city of Bergamo itself, but evidently not in quite the same direction.

The Imperial Army's March on Mantua

The boundary between the Grisons (or Graubünden) and the Valtellina corresponds to the modern frontier between Italy and Switzerland.

The Grisons were a league of Swiss cities, allied to but not yet part of the main Swiss Confederation. At the time of the attack on Mantua, Imperial forces were allowed free passage through the Grisons, and the Valtellina was under the effective control of the Empire's Spanish allies. The Imperial army could therefore cross those two territories without difficulty.

Having entered the Duchy of Milan at Colico, the Imperial troops turned south along the lakeside, and then along the Valsassina to Lecco. After crossing the Lecco bridge, they went on down the west shore of the southern part of the lake, and along the line of the lower Adda to its confluence with the Po. They then followed the Po down to the Duchy of Mantua.

This route kept the troops clear of Venetian territory, gave them well-defined natural features to follow all the way, and avoided any close approach to the city of Milan.   B.P.

●●

Foreword

'*History may truly be defined as a famous War against Time;
for she doth take from him the Years that he had made
Prisoner, or rather utterly slain, and doth call them back into
Life, and pass them in Review, and set them again in Order of
Battle. But those braw Champions, that in such Lists doth reap
the Harvests of Palms and of Laurels, may carry off in their
Nief only the most pompous and grandiloquent of their Spoils,
embalming in their Inks the Enterprises of Princes and Powers
and such qualified Personages, and embroidering with the most
delicate Needle of Wit the Threads of Gold and of Silk, that
form a perpetual Tapestry of glorious Actions. But it is not
lawful for my Infirmity of Genius to raise itself to such Arguments, and periculous Sublimities, with turning again amid the
Labyrinths of Politic Devices, and the resounding of warlike
Trumpets; yet having had news of some memorable Facts,
though they did befall mechanical Folk, and of but small
Account, I do now gird up my loins to leave some Memorial of
them to Posterity, by making of all that did chance a sincere
and genuine Account, or Tale. Wherein ye shall see in a narrow
Theatre sorrowful Tragedies of many Horrors, and Scenes of
Magniloquent Wickedness, with Interludes of virtuous Enterprises and angelic Goodness, opposed to those devilish Operations. And truly, if a Man consider that these Climes of ours
doth lie under the Protection of His Catholic Majesty our Royal
Lord, a Sun that doth never set, and that over them doth shine
with reflected Light, as a Moon never declining, the Hero of
noble Lineage who pro Tempore doth stand in his stead, and
the most generous Senators as fixed Stars, and the other most
venerable Magistrates as errant Planets that everywhere shed-
deth their Lights, and thus portrayeth the Likeness of a most
noble Heaven, no other causatory Reason can I find to see it
transformed into a very Hell of tenebrous Actions, Wicked-*

nesses and Cruelties, which rash Men do daily multiply, save it be the Arts and dark Deeds of the Devil, seeing that human Malice by itself could never suffice to resist so great a Band of Heroes, who with Eyes of Argus and Arms of Briareus, goeth trafficking through the public Emoluments. Wherefore by describing this Tale which came to pass in the green days of my own Youth, notwithstanding that most of the Persons that therein playeth a Part hath vanished from this worldly Theatre, by making themselves Tributaries to the Fates, yet for certain worthy Respects, I will pass over their names in silence (that is the Families of which they were sprung), and likewise with the places of the Story, only indicating the Topography generaliter. Nor shall any man say that this be an Imperfection in the Tale, or a Deformity in this my unlicked Cub, unless indeed such Critic be a man who hath no Part in Philosophy; for those who are versed in that Discipline shall soon see that nothing be lacking to the Substance of the Narrative. For verily, seeing that it be a most evident Fact, and denied of no Man, but that Names are the purest of all pure Accidents . . .'

. . . but when I have laboured through the heroic task of transcribing this ancient story from its defaced and faded manuscript – when I have brought it to the light of day, to use the common phrase – who will labour through the task of reading it?

This doubt stole into my mind as I was wrestling with the job of deciphering a large blot which came after the word 'Accidents'; I laid down my pen, and began to think seriously about what ought to be done. 'It's true enough', I said to myself, leafing through the manuscript, 'that the shower of conceits and tropes does not fall so heavily as this throughout the whole work. In his seventeenth-century way the worthy author clearly wanted to begin with a major display of his talents; but further on, in the main part of his narrative, his style follows a much simpler and more natural course, often for many pages at a time. But what a crude, graceless, faulty style it is even then! All those lapses into northern dialect, alternating with correct expressions used in the wrong sense; that arbitrary grammar, those disjointed sentences, those flowers of Spanish eloquence scattered here and there . . . But worst of all is what happens in the most horrifying or pitiful parts of the story, and at every opportunity to excite the reader's wonder or give him cause to think. Such occasions do indeed call for a little eloquence, but it should be discreet, subtle and in good taste. This author, however, never fails to celebrate them with his own kind of eloquence, as exemplified in his prologue.

'And then he shows a remarkable ability to combine the most opposite qualities, and finds a way of sounding both gross and affected on the same page, in the same sentence, with the same word.

'It's nothing but turgid declamation built up out of heavy-footed solecisms; and running through it all is that fatuous stylistic ambition which is so characteristic of the writings of the time in Italy.

'This is really not the kind of thing to set before modern readers, who see through that sort of exaggerated stuff, and do not like it. It's as well that the thought came to me before I had gone any further with this wretched job. I'll wash my hands of it here and now.'

But just as I was closing the papers up to put them away, it began to grieve me that such a good story should remain unknown for ever – for I really believe, whatever the reader may think about it, that it is a good story; an excellent one, in fact.

'Why not take the sequence of facts contained in this manuscript', I thought, 'and merely alter the language?' There were no logical objections to this idea, and I decided to follow it. And that is the origin of this present work, explained with a simplicity to match the importance of the book itself.

But certain of the facts mentioned by our author, and some of the customs he describes, seem so strange and improbable, to say the least, that before putting our faith in them we wanted to hear other witnesses; and so we began to search among the memoirs of the period, to satisfy ourselves whether that was really the way things happened in those days. But our inquiries soon dispelled all those doubts; we found ourselves constantly running into things of the same kind, or even stranger. What seemed most decisive of all was that we found mention of certain persons whose names we had never previously encountered except in the pages of our manuscript, and whose existence we had begun to doubt. We proposed to quote some of these other sources from time to time, to obtain the reader's credence for things so strange that he might be tempted to withhold it from them.

We have rejected the language of our author as intolerable; but what have we substituted for it? That is the all-important question.

Anyone who, without invitation, takes it upon himself to redo another man's work, makes himself liable to render a strict account of his own version, and indeed to some extent contracts a firm obligation to do so. This is a rule based on custom and right, and we do not wish in any way to claim exemption from it. On the contrary, by way of conforming voluntarily with the practice, we had originally proposed to provide a minute analysis at this point of the method of writing we have followed. With this object we constantly tried, all the time we were at work on the book, to imagine every possible criticism, whether essential or otherwise, that might later be levelled against it, meaning to rebut them all in anticipation. Nor was this so difficult a task in itself; for, to tell the truth, not a single criticism ever came into our mind that was not accompanied by a triumphant retort – the sort of retort that may not resolve the question, but makes it appear under a different light.

And often we were able to set two criticisms by the ears, so that each defeated the other; or we would establish and demonstrate by a careful examination and comparison of them both that though very different at first sight they were really both of the same kind, both springing from inattention to the facts and the principles on which judgement should have been based, so that we were able to pair them off (doubtless to their great surprise) and send them packing together. No author would ever have proved as clearly as ourselves that he had done his job well . . . But, then as we reached the point of bringing together all those objections and answers and putting them in some sort of order, we found to our horror that they added up to a whole book.

So we abandoned the idea, for two reasons which the reader will certainly approve: first, that a book written to justify another book (let alone the style of another book) might well seem a somewhat ridiculous undertaking, and secondly that one book at a time is quite enough, and may in fact be too much.

technical geog. descr.
(note active verbs).

Chapter 1

ONE arm of Lake Como turns off to the south between two unbroken chains of mountains, which cut it up into a series of bays and inlets as the hills advance into the water and retreat again, until it quite suddenly grows much narrower and takes on the appearance and the motion of a river between a headland on one side and a wide stretch of shore on the other. The bridge which connects the two banks at that point seems to make the change of state still clearer to the eye, marking the spot where the lake comes to an end and the Adda comes into being once more – though further on it again takes the name of a lake, as the banks separate, allowing the water to spread out and lose its speed among more bays and fresh inlets.

The stretch of shore we mentioned is formed by the silt from three considerable streams, and is backed by two adjoining mountains, one known as St Martin's Mount, and the other by the Lombard-sounding name of Resegone because of the many small peaks that make up its skyline, which do in fact give it the look of a saw. This is enough of a distinctive sign to make the Resegone easy to pick out from the long and vast chains of other mountains, less well known by name and less strange in shape, in which it lies, even if the observer has never seen it before – provided that he sees it from an angle which shows its full length, as for example looking northward from the walls of Milan.

The slope up from the water's edge is gentle and unbroken for quite a long way: but then it breaks up into mounds and gullies, terraces and steeper tracts, according to the geological structure of the two hills and the erosion of the waters. Along the extreme fringe of the slope, the terrain is deeply cut up by watercourses, and consists mostly of gravel and pebbles; but the rest of the area is all fields and vineyards with townships, estates and hamlets here and there. There are also some woods, which extend upwards into the mountains. Lecco is the largest of the townships, and gives its name to the territory; it lies not far from the bridge on the shore of the lake. In fact it lies partly in the lake, when the water level rises above normal. It is a sizeable town today, and on the way to becoming a city.

At the time of the events we are about to relate, Lecco was already a place of some importance, and was also a fortress. For that reason it had the honour of accommodating a garrison commander, and the advantage of providing lodging for a permanent force of Spanish soldiers, who gave lessons in modest deportment to the girls and women of the area, and who tickled the backs of the odd husband or father with a stick from time to time. They also never failed, at the end of summer, to spread out across the vineyards and thin out the grapes, so as to lighten the labours of the peasants at harvest-time.

Roads and tracks, some steep and some gently sloping, ran then, as they do today, from township to township, from mountain to shore, from knoll to knoll. They often sink into the earth, buried between high walls, so that if the traveller raises his eyes he can see nothing but a small patch of sky, and perhaps a distant peak. At other times the tracks run across high open terraces; and then the eye can wander over landscapes of varying extent, but always superbly beautiful and always with something new about them, as the different viewpoints take in now more and now less of the vast surrounding countryside, and as its various features appear and vanish, come into prominence and fade away, each in its turn. Now one small portion of the great varied mirror of the waters catches the eye, now another, and now a larger expanse. Here we see a lake cut off at the end by mountains, or rather lost in a cluster, a maze of foothills, but gradually widening out in another direction among peaks which spread out in sequence before the eye, and then appear again upside down in the water, with the villages that stand on their lower slopes. There we see a stretch of river, that widens out into a lake and narrows into a river again, which winds away from the observer in a bright serpentine course between mountains which accompany it into the distance, dwindling with it until they too are almost lost in the horizon.

And the place from which you look out at those varied scenes itself offers the most beautiful sights on every hand. The mountain on whose lower slopes you walk unfolds its precipices and peaks around and above you, high, clear and changing in form with every step you take. What seemed a single ridge opens out and takes the form of a complex of ridges; a feature which you saw but now as part of the hillside now appears on the skyline as a separate peak. The gentle domestic beauty of the slopes pleasantly moderates the wildness of the landscape, and brings out the magnificence of its other parts.

Along one of those tracks, returning home from a walk, on the evening of the 7 November 1628, came Don Abbondio, the curé of one of the villages mentioned above. But the name of the place, and the surname of the priest, are not to be found in our manuscript, either now or later. He was peacefully recit-ing his office. From time to time, between one psalm and another, he would shut up his breviary, keeping the forefinger of his right hand tucked into it as a bookmarker, and then clasping both hands together behind his back, while he looked down at the ground and kicked to the side of the track any pebbles that obstructed the way. Then he raised his head and directed his gaze idly around until it fell on a part of the hillside where the light of the sun, which had already set behind the mountains opposite, penetrated through the gaps in the ridge and picked out certain projecting rocks with wide, uneven patches of purple. Then he reopened his breviary and recited another passage, which took him to a bend in the track, where it was his habit to raise his eyes from the book, and look straight ahead, as he did on this occasion.

After the bend the track ran straight for a matter of sixty yards or so, and then split into two paths, like the arms of a capital Y. The right-hand path went uphill toward the curé's house, while the other one went down to a stream in the valley; on that side the wall was no more than waist-high. The inner walls of the two converging paths did not meet in a sharp angle, but ended in a wayside shrine. On it were painted long, snaky shapes with pointed ends, that were meant by the artist and understood by the local inhabitants to be flames. Alternating

with the flames were other indescribable shapes which repre-
sented souls in purgatory. Both souls and flames were painted in
brick-red on a greyish background, which had flaked off here
and there.

As the curé came round the bend, and looked straight ahead
towards the shrine, as was his custom, he saw something he did
not expect or want to see at all. Two men were there, facing
each other at the junction of the two paths. One sat astride the
low wall, with one foot dangling over its outer surface, and the
other resting on the solid ground of the track. His companion
was standing slouched against the other wall, with his arms
crossed over his chest. Their clothes, attitudes and what the
curé could see of their faces at that distance left no doubt
about what they were. Each of them wore a green hairnet,
which hung down on his left shoulder, ending in a large tassel,
while a huge quiff emerged from it in front to hang over his
forehead. Each had long, pointed moustaches, a polished leather
belt bearing two pistols, a small powder-horn hanging down on
his chest like a pendant, a dagger the hilt of which stuck out of
its special pocket in his wide and well-padded breeches, and a
heavy sword with a great polished glittering guard composed of
a network of narrow strips of bronze arranged in a sort of
monogram. The first glance showed that they were members of
the species known as bravoes.

This species is now totally extinct; but at that time it was in a
most flourishing condition in Lombardy, where it had been
established for many years. For the benefit of readers who do
not know about it, here are some authentic passages from
documents of the time, which will give an adequate idea of its
main characteristics, of the efforts made to exterminate it and of
its resistant and luxuriant vitality.

As early as 8 April 1583 the most illustrious and excellent
Lord Don Carlos of Aragon, Prince of Castelvetrano, Duke of
Terranuova, Marquis of Avola, Count of Burgeto, Grand
Admiral, and Grand Constable of Sicily, Governor of Milan
and Captain-General of His Most Catholic Majesty in Italy,
'being fully informed of the intolerable affliction in which this
City of Milan has lived and still lives on account of bravoes and

vagabonds', published an edict against them. *'We decree and pronounce'* – he went on – *'all men to be affected by this edict, and to be rightly esteemed as bravoes and vagabonds ... who, whether they be foreigners or local residents, have no lawful occupation, or if they have such, are not employed therein ... but devote themselves, either with or without payment, to the service of some noble or gentleman, or officer or merchant ... to give him support and help, or rather, it may be supposed, to lay snares for other men.'*

The edict formally instructs all such persons to quit the country within six days, prescribes the galleys for those who fail to comply, and gives all officers of justice the most strangely arbitrary and loosely defined powers to enforce those orders.

But on 12 April the following year, the same noble lord remarked that *'the city is still full of the aforesaid bravoes, who have returned to their former way of life, without changing their habits or decreasing in number'*. So he put out another edict, of a still more forceful and memorable kind, which, among other things, decrees the following:

'Every person, whether by origin of this city, or a foreigner, who shall be certified by two witnesses as being regarded as or commonly held to be a bravo, or as going by the name of a bravo, even though it cannot be shown that he has committed any crime whatever ... merely because of that reputation of being a bravo, without other evidence, may be by the aforesaid judges or by any one of them subjected to flogging and torture, by way of interrogation ... and even though he may not confess any crime whatever, yet shall he be sent to the galleys, for a period of three years as aforesaid, because of his mere name and reputation of a bravo, as heretofore.'

All this, and much more which we omit, because *'His Excellency is resolved that his will shall be obeyed by all men.'*

Such words, coming from so great a lord, so bold and confident in their tone, and accompanied by such specific orders, can only inspire us with the wish to believe that their very utterance in those resounding terms may have been enough to make the bravoes vanish for ever. But the testimony of an equally authoritative nobleman, with an equally splendid list of names, compels us to take the opposite view. This was the most illustrious and excellent Lord Juan Fernandez de Velasco, Constable of Castille, Great Chamberlain of His Majesty, Duke of the city of Frias, Count of Haro and Castelnovo, Lord of the House of Velasco and of the House of the Seven Infantes of Lara, Governor of the State of Milan, etc.

On 5 June 1593 he too was fully informed about *'The damage and the disasters caused by ... bravoes and vagabonds, and the most evil effects which such men have, both in the harming of the commonwealth, and the cheating of justice.'* He again informed them that they must quit the country within six days, repeating very much the same measures taken and the same penalties threatened by his predecessor.

On 23 May 1589, *'having learned, with great grief of heart, that from day to day in this city and state the number of such men'* – i.e., bravoes and vagabonds – *'does still increase, nor can anything be heard regarding them either by day or by night save wounds given with malice aforethought, murders and robberies and other kinds of crime, which they undertake the more readily, as they trust in the help of their lords and protectors'*, he prescribes the same medicine again, though increasing the dose, as is customary with obstinate diseases. *'Let all men'*, he concludes, *'take care not to contravene the present proclamation in any respect whatever; for if any man should do so, he will experience not the clemency of His Excellency, but the full rigour of his wrath ... seeing that he is resolved that this shall be the final and peremptory warning.'*

But this was not the opinion of the most illustrious and excellent Lord Don Pietro Enriquez de Acevedo, Count of Fuentes, Captain and Governor of the State of Milan; and in fact he had very good reason for not sharing it.

On 5 December 1600, *'being fully informed of the misery in which this city and state do live by reason of the great number of bravoes that abound therein ... and being fully resolved utterly to root out that most pernicious seed'*, Don Pietro published a fresh proclamation against them, which was also full of the severest comminations, *'in the firm resolve that they be in every respect carried out, with all rigour, and without any hope of remission'.*

And yet we can only think that His Excellency did not tackle the problem with all the enthusiasm of which he showed himself capable when it was a matter of organizing intrigues, and stirring up hatreds against his great enemy Henry IV; since history teaches us how successfully he brought Savoy into the field against the King (whereby the Duke of Savoy lost several cities), and how he induced the Duke of Biron to conspire against the King (whereby the Duke of Biron lost his head). But as regards the most pernicious seed of bravoes, there is no doubt that it was still germinating on 22 September 1612. *calumniatur*

For on that date the most illustrious and excellent Lord Don Juan of Mendoza, Marquis of Hynojosa, Gentleman of etc., Governor of etc., took serious steps to root them out. With that object he sent the customary proclamation to the viceregal printers, Pandolfo and Marco Tullio Malatesti, with improvements and additions, so that it might be printed to the final confusion and destruction of the bravoes.

And yet on 24 December 1618 they were still there to receive similar but even harder blows at the hands of the most illustrious and excellent Lord Don Gomez Suarez de Figueroa, Duke of Feria, etc. Governor, etc.

And even those blows cannot have been mortal; for the most illustrious and excellent Lord Don Gonzalo Fernandez of Cordova, under whose rule Don Abbondio's walk took place, found himself compelled to republish the usual proclamation against the bravoes, with further improvements, on 5 October 1627 – one year, one month and two days before that memorable event.

Nor was that the last such edict; but there is no point in our listing the later ones, since they fall outside the period of our story. We shall merely mention one dated the 13 February 1632, in which the most illustrious and excellent Lord the Duke of Feria (now governor for the second time) informs us that *'the most scoundrelly actions are committed by those who are known as bravoes'*. This is enough to make it certain that bravoes still existed at the time of which we are speaking.

It was only too obvious that the two bravoes we mentioned earlier were waiting for someone; but the thing that Don Abbondio liked least of all was being forced to realize by certain unmistakable signs that they were waiting for him. For as he appeared they looked at each other, raising their heads as they did so in a movement which clearly went with the words 'Here he is!' Then the man astride the wall swung his leg over on the track and got up, the other man parted company with the wall against which he had been leaning, and both of them began to walk towards the priest.

Don Abbondio still kept his breviary open in front of him, as if he were reading, but kept peeping over the top of it to see what they were doing. When he saw them coming straight towards him, a dozen unpleasant thoughts struck him at once. First he wondered whether there was a side-turning anywhere between himself and the bravoes, either to the right or the left; but he remembered clearly that no such paths existed. He rapidly searched his mind to see if he had fallen into the sin of offending men of power, or men of vengeance; but even at this moment of distress he could draw a little comfort from the witness of a perfectly clear conscience. And yet the bravoes drew nearer, looking straight at him as they did so. He put the first two fingers of his left hand under his collar, as if to adjust it; and he ran them round his neck, as he turned his head and looked behind him out of the corner of his eye, as far into the distance as he could, twisting his lips at the same time, to see if anyone was coming along from that direction. But there was no one there. He looked over the side wall into the fields, and there was no one there either. He directed a more cautious glance straight ahead, but there was nobody there except the bravoes.

What was he to do? It was too late to turn back, and to run for it would be to invite pursuit, or worse.

Not being able to avoid the danger, he hurried to meet it, for he found the moments of uncertainty so distressing that his main wish was to shorten them as much as possible. He quickened his step, recited a verse or two in a more audible voice, composed his face into as calm and carefree an expression as he

32

could manage and made every effort to prepare a smile. When he found himself face to face with the two worthy fellows, he silently thought: 'Well, this is it!' and came to a halt.

'Your Reverence!' said one of them, staring him straight in the eyes.

'What can I do for you?' replied Don Abbondio immediately, looking up from the book, which remained open in his hands, as if on a lectern.

'And so you have it in mind,' said the bravo in the threatening manner of a man who has caught a subordinate in the act of committing a blackguardly crime, 'you have it in mind to marry Renzo Tramaglino and Lucia Mondella tomorrow!'

'Well!' said Don Abbondio in a trembling voice, 'well, you see ... you gentlemen are men of the world, and realize how these things go. It's nothing to do with the poor curé; these people make their own muddled arrangements, and then ... why, they come to us just as they might go to a bank to draw money ... we are ... just the servants of the community.'

'Very well,' said the bravo, speaking into the priest's ear, quietly, but in a tone of impressive command, 'that wedding is not to take place. Not tomorrow, and not any other time either.'

'But, gentlemen,' replied Don Abbondio, in the soft and winning voice we use to persuade the impatient, 'be so kind as to put yourselves in my position. If the thing depended on me, it would be another matter ... well, you can see for yourselves that I don't stand to make anything out of it.'

'Come, now,' interrupted the bravo, 'if these things had to be settled by talk, you'd make rings round us. We don't know all these things, and don't want to know them. A warning's a warning ... and I'm sure you understand us.'

'But you gentlemen are too fair-minded, too reasonable ...'

'But, but ...!' interrupted the other member of the pair, who had not spoken before. 'But that wedding is not going to take place, or ...' – a loud oath followed. 'And the man who performs it won't regret it, because he won't have time to, and ...' – another oath followed.

'Less of it now!' said the first of these gifted speakers. 'His Reverence is a man who understands the world we live in, and we're decent fellows who don't want to hurt him, provided he shows a bit of sense. Your Reverence, the most noble lord Don Rodrigo, whom we serve, sends you his very best regards.'

The effect of that name on Don Abbondio's mind was like a flash of lightning in the middle of a storm at night, which illuminates one's surroundings confusedly for a moment, and makes them more terrifying than before. He bowed deeply as if by instinct.

'If you gentlemen could make some suggestion as to how...?'

'Suggestions!' interrupted the bravo again, with an oafish yet terrifying laugh. 'We wouldn't like to make suggestions to your Reverence, who's a learned man and knows Latin. It's up to you, sir. But above all don't let a word pass your lips about this warning, which we've given you for your own good. Otherwise...' – and here he made a curious, significant noise in his throat – '... why, otherwise it'd be just the same as if you'd married them after all. But come, sir, what answer shall we take back to the noble lord Don Rodrigo from you?'

'All my respect...'

'Be more definite, sir!'

'... and always his obedient servant!'

As Don Abbondio said those words, he himself hardly knew whether he was making a promise, or uttering a polite formula. But the bravoes took it, or pretended to take it, in the more serious sense.

'Just as well, sir – and good night to you!' said one of them, as he turned to go off with his companion.

But though a few moments earlier Don Abbondio would have given his eye-teeth to be rid of them, he now felt a desire to prolong the talk and continue the negotiation.

'But, gentlemen...!' he called after them, shutting up the book with both hands.

But they were not prepared to give him any further audience, and went off in the direction from which he had come, singing an unpleasant song which we will not record here. Poor Don Abbondio stood open-mouthed for a moment, in a half-dazed condition; then he took the path which led to his house, finding some difficulty in putting one foot in front of the other, for his legs seemed to have gone suddenly numb.

We can give the reader a better picture of his mental state, if we begin with a description of his character, and of the times in which he happened to live.

As the reader will have noticed already, Don Abbondio did not come into the world provided with the heart of a lion. But from his earliest years he had had to learn that the worst of all conditions at that period was the state of an animal which had neither claws nor teeth, and yet had no inclination to be devoured. For the forces of the law gave no protection to the tranquil, inoffensive type of man, who had no other means of inspiring fear in anyone else. We do not mean that there was any lack of laws with penalties directed against private acts of violence. There was a glut of such laws in point of fact. The various crimes were listed and described and detailed in the most minute and long-winded manner. The penalties were of insane severity; and, as if that were not enough, they were almost invariably subject to augmentation at the whim of the magistrate himself, or of any one of a hundred subordinate officials. The legal procedures involved were designed solely to free the judge from any factor which might have been an obstacle to a verdict of guilty. The passages we have quoted from the proclamations against the bravoes provide a small but faithful sample.

But in spite of all this – indeed largely because of it – those proclamations, repeated in ever stronger terms by each successive government, only serve to provide a pompous demonstration of the impotence of their authors. If they had any immediate effect, it lay principally in the addition of many new harassments to those which the pacific and the weak already suffered from their tormentors, and an increase in the violence and the cunning shown by the guilty; for their impunity was an organized institution, and had roots which the proclamations did not touch, or at least could not shift. There were places of asylum; there were privileges attached to certain social classes, which were sometimes recognized by the forces of the law, sometimes tolerated in indignant silence, and sometimes disputed with empty words of protest. Meanwhile the favoured classes upheld and defended those privileges with deeds showing the activity which comes from personal interest, and the jealous concern associated with the point of honour.

Their impunity was threatened and insulted, but not destroyed, by the proclamations. With every additional threat and insult, they might naturally be expected to employ fresh efforts and new inventions to keep that impunity in being. And this did in fact happen. With the appearance of each proclamation designed to repress men of violence, those concerned searched among their practical resources for the most suitable fresh methods of continuing to do what the edicts prohibited.

What the proclamations could do was to put stumbling-blocks in the way of simple folk, who had no special power of their own nor protection from others, and harass them at every step they took. For the proclamations were framed with the object of keeping everybody under control, in order to prevent or punish every sort of crime; and so they subjected every action of the private citizen to the arbitrary will of all kinds of officials.

But anyone who took steps before committing a crime to provide himself with a refuge in a monastery, or in a palace, where the police would never dare to set foot; anyone who, without other precautions, wore a livery that ensured him the support of the pride and interests of a powerful family, or of a whole class, had a free hand to do what he liked, and to laugh at all the stir created by the edicts.

Of the men who were deputed to see to the enforcement of the proclamations, some belonged by birth to the privileged classes, and others were in a state of feudal subjection to them. Both groups had imbibed the principles of the privileged, by early training, by self-interest, by force of habit, or by imitation, and would have thought many times before setting out to offend them for the sake of a bit of paper stuck up on a street corner.

And the men charged with the physical execution of the orders might have been as bold as heroes, as obedient as monks, and as ready for self-sacrifice as martyrs, and they would still have been unable to perform their task; for they were inferior in numbers to those whom they should have forced into submission, and ran a considerable risk of being deserted by the officials who in abstract theory had imposed the task on them. But, apart from that, they were generally among the basest and most ruffianly men of their time. Their work was despised even by those who might be in terror of it, and their name was an insult. And so they were naturally disinclined to risk their lives or to throw them away in a desperate venture; preferring to sell their inactivity, or even connivance, to men of importance, and to reserve the exercise of their hated authority and of the powers they really possessed for the sort of job where there was no danger – in other words, for the oppression and harassment of peaceful and defenceless men.

A man who wishes to hurt others, or who is constantly afraid of being hurt by them, naturally looks for allies and companions. That period accordingly saw a very marked development of the natural tendency for men wherever possible to keep themselves grouped together into associations, or to form new ones; and also the tendency for everyone to further the authority of the association to which he belonged to the greatest possible extent. The clergy were alert to maintain and extend their immunities, and similarly the nobles with their privileges and the military with their exemptions. The merchants and artisans were enrolled in guilds and fraternities; the lawyers and even the physicians had their own associations. Every one of these little oligarchies wielded its own special and particular powers; in each of them the individual found a personal advantage in being able to use the combined strength of many colleagues on his own behalf, in proportion to his own authority and skill. The more honest among them employed this advantage only for purposes of defence; but the cunning and the lawless made unscrupulous use of it to carry out crimes for which their personal resources would have been insufficient, and to ensure themselves immunity from the consequences.

But the actual powers of those different associations varied greatly. A wealthy and violent noble, for example, and especially one living in the country, with his troops of bravoes round him, and a local population of peasants compelled by family tradition, self-interest or brute force to regard themselves as his subjects, or indeed as a militia at his orders – a man in that position wielded a power which virtually no combination of interests in his territory could resist.

Poor Abbondio was not noble, nor rich, and still less was he courageous; and so, almost before reaching years of discretion, he came to see his situation in the society of the day as that of an earthenware jar compelled to travel in the company of many iron pots. He had consequently been quite willing to obey his parents when they wanted him to enter the priesthood. To tell the truth, he had not thought very deeply about the duties or the noble objects of the ministry to which he dedicated himself. To win the means of living with some degree of comfort, and to join the ranks of a revered and powerful class, seemed to him two more than sufficient motives for such a course.

But no class can protect an individual, or ensure his safety, beyond a certain point – it cannot free him from the necessity of constructing a personal system of his own. Don Abbondio was always absorbed in thinking out how to ensure himself a quiet life, and was not interested in advantages of the sort which can only be obtained by hard application or by taking a few risks. His personal system consisted primarily in avoiding conflict whenever he could, and in giving way whenever conflict became unavoidable.

His policy was one of unarmed neutrality in all the wars that broke out around him, such as the conflicts which were then so frequent between clergy and lay authorities, between military and civilians, between noble and noble – right down to quarrels between two peasants, arising from a hasty word, and settled with fists or knives.

If Don Abbondio could not help taking sides, he always sided with the stronger of the two contendants – very circumspectly, however, and making every effort to show the weaker party that he had no real feelings of enmity towards him.

'Why couldn't you have been stronger than the other fellow?' he seemed to say. 'Then I could have been on your side.'

He kept away from bullies when he could; he pretended not to notice passing, capricious acts of arrogance, and greeted those

38

that arose from a serious and deliberate intention with total submission. With his low bows and his air of respectful cheerfulness, he could induce even the most forbidding and contemptuous of men to give him a smile when they met in the street. In this way poor Don Abbondio had reached the age of sixty without ever getting into serious trouble.

But that did not mean that he had no bile in his composition; and the continual trials of his patience, the frequent admissions that the other man was right, the many bitter pills he swallowed in silence would have stirred it up to the point of damaging his health, if he had not had the means of venting it from time to time. But luckily there were people in the world, and not too far away, that he knew to be incapable of harming him. With these he could occasionally work off his bottled-up bad temper, and satisfy the need that he too felt of being unreasonable sometimes, and sometimes shouting people down.

He was highly censorious of men who did not follow the same system as himself, whenever censoriousness could be indulged without even the most distant shadow of danger. Anyone who was beaten up had been imprudent, to say the least; anyone who was murdered turned out always to have been a trouble-maker. Whenever someone stood up for his rights against a man of power and got a crack on the head for his pains, Don Abbondio could always show that the poor fellow had been in the wrong – and that was not too difficult, since right and wrong are seldom divided by so precise a line that either side can ever have a monopoly of one of them.

But above all he used to declaim against those of his colleagues who took the risk of supporting the weak and oppressed against a powerful bully. That, he used to say, was going out and looking for trouble; it was deliberately setting oneself an impossible task; worse still, he would add severely, it was an interference in the things of this world, which lessened the dignity of a priest's holy calling. The more such priests were known to be free from feelings of resentment in personal matters, the more vehemently Don Abbondio would denounce them – though never before an audience of more than one or two people. And he had a favourite observation, with which he would always bring discussions of such matters to a fitting end.

'A decent man', he would say, 'who minds his own business, and keeps himself to himself, never runs into these ugly situations.'

My couple of dozen readers can easily imagine what the poor man felt when he himself ran into the situation we have just described. The terror inspired by those hideous faces and ugly words, the threats of a great lord known never to threaten in vain, the sudden overthrow of a system of peaceful existence which had cost him so many years of study and patience, a predicament from which he could see no way out – all these troubled thoughts buzzed tumultuously together in Don Abbondio's bowed head as he walked along.

If Renzo were only the sort of boy you could fob off with a firm 'No!' – he thought. – But he'll want to know why, and what can I say to him then, for Heaven's sake? He's another one who flies off the handle if he doesn't get his own way. Gentle as a lamb if he's treated properly, but if you cross him ... Oh dear! And then he's hopelessly in love with that Lucia of his, in such a state ... great children they are who fall in love because they've nothing better to do, and then want to get married, without a thought for the trouble it'll make for a poor decent man ... Heaven help me! To think of those two ugly brutes having to lie in wait for me and attack me like that! What's it to do with me after all? Am I the one that wants to get married? Why couldn't they have simply gone off themselves and talked to him ... ? But there now; it's always the way with me. The right answer comes into my head as soon as the occasion for it has gone by. If only I'd thought of suggesting to them that they might as well deliver their own message ...

But at this point it struck him that to regret his failure to counsel and cooperate with the forces of evil was not a very good thing in itself. So now he turned his wrath against the nobleman who had shattered his peace in that way.

He knew Don Rodrigo only by sight and by reputation, and had never had anything to do with him, beyond bowing his head and sweeping the ground with his hat on the few occasions when he had met him on the road. More than once he had had to defend the gentleman's reputation against people who had cursed him for some misdeed, raising their eyes to heaven, sighing and speaking in whispers. The priest had maintained a dozen times that Don Rodrigo was a perfectly respectable member of the nobility. But now he found himself mentally applying to him the very same harsh words which he had always interrupted with a cry of 'For shame!' when he heard them uttered by others.

Lost in these tumultuous thoughts, he reached his house, which was at the end of the village, and hastened to unlock the door with the key which he had been holding ready in his hand as he walked along. He pushed the door open, went in and locked it carefully behind him. Longing for the comfort of a trusted companion, he began to call 'Perpetua! Perpetua!' as he walked towards the dining-room where he knew she would be laying the table for his supper.

Perpetua, as the reader will have guessed, was Don Abbondio's housekeeper – a devoted and faithful servant, who knew when to obey and when to command, as it might be necessary; how to put up with the tantrums and odd fancies of her master, and also on occasion how to make him put up with her own, which were becoming rapidly more frequent. For she had passed the Tridentine age of forty without ever getting married; because she had refused all the offers that had been made to her, as she used to say herself, or because she had never been able to find anyone who would look at her twice, if you believed her friends among the women in the village.

'Coming!' she replied, setting a bottle of Don Abbondio's favourite wine on the table in its usual place. Then she began to move slowly towards the door; but Don Abbondio reached it before she did, and came into the room with so halting a gait, so gloomy a look in his eye, and so strange an expression on his face, that it did not need Perpetua's expert eye to see straight away that something really extraordinary must have happened.

'Mercy on us! What's wrong, your Reverence?'

'Oh, nothing, nothing,' said Don Abbondio, breathing heavily, and fell into his armchair.

'Nothing, sir? Do you think you can pull the wool over my eyes, with a look like that on your face? Something pretty bad must have happened.'

'Why, for Heaven's sake! When I say nothing, either I mean nothing, or I mean something I can't talk about.'

'Can't talk about, even to me? Why, then, who's to look after your health? Who's to give a word of advice . . . ?'

'Oh, do be quiet, Perpetua, and stop laying that table. Just give me a glass of my wine.'

'And you're still trying to tell me there's nothing wrong!' said Perpetua, filling the glass, but keeping it in her hand as if unwilling to give it to him except as a reward for the confidence that was taking so long to emerge.

'Come on, let me have it!' said Don Abbondio, taking the glass from her with unsteady hand and swallowing it quickly, as if it were a medicine.

'Well, then!' said Perpetua. 'Do you want me to be forced to go and ask every Tom, Dick and Harry what's happened to my own master?' She was standing in front of him with hands on hips and elbows pulled forward, glaring at him as if she wanted to tear the secret out of his heart.

'For the love of Heaven! This is no time for your chattering and cackling! It's a matter of . . . of staying alive.'

'*What!*'

'Of staying alive, I said.'

'You know very well, sir, that whenever you've told me something fairly and squarely in confidence, I've always respected it, and . . .'

'Well done, Perpetua! and when was that, pray?'

Perpetua realized that she was on the wrong foot here, and changed her tone at once.

'You know I've always been fond of you, sir,' she said with a touching note of emotion in her voice. 'If I want to know what's going on, it's out of concern for your welfare, it's because I want to be able to help you, give you a bit of advice, cheer you up a little . . .'

In point of fact Don Abbondio was just as anxious to unload his unhappy secret as Perpetua was to know it. His resistance grew weaker as her assaults were pressed closer home. He made her promise several times that she would never breathe a word about it, and finally, with many pauses and many groans, he told her the whole wretched story.

When he came to the terrible name of the author of his instructions, Perpetua had to take a fresh and more solemn oath of silence; and as he pronounced the name he threw himself back in his chair with a great sigh, raising both hands in a gesture at once of command and supplication, and saying 'Not a word now, for Heaven's sake!'

'So he's up to his old tricks again!' cried Perpetua. 'What a blackguard the man is, to be sure! What a bully! He hasn't the fear of God in him at all!'

'Will you be quiet, Perpetua? Or do you want to ruin me altogether?'

'Why, we're all alone here and no one can hear us. But what's my poor master going to do then?'

'Just listen to her!' said Don Abbondio in angry tones. 'What invaluable advice she gives me! "What're you going to do?" she says, "What're you going to do?" – as if she were in trouble and I were going to help her to get out of it.'

'Really, sir! I could give you my humble opinion, for what it's worth; but then again . . .'

'But then again, let's hear what it is.'

'Well, everyone says that our Archbishop's a saintly man, and a strong man, who's not afraid of anyone in the world, and when he gets a chance of backing up a poor priest against one of these tyrants, and putting him in his place, he's delighted. What I'd say is this, and I do say it now – you ought to write the Archbishop a proper letter, and tell him all about it, and . . .'

'Will you be quiet, Perpetua? *Will* you be quiet? What sort of advice is that to give a poor man in my position? If I get a bullet in the back, Heaven forbid! will the Archbishop be able to undo the effects of that?'

'Why, sir, people don't really dish out bullets like sweets at a party. These dogs don't bite every time they bark, and it would be a pity if they did. And I've always noticed that it's those who show their teeth a bit, and make people take notice of them, who're respected in this world; and it's just because you won't stick up for yourself that we're reduced to the point where anyone can come along, begging your pardon, and . . .'

'Be quiet, Perpetua!'

'Yes, sir, I'll be quiet; but for all that you can't expect anything else, when people see that someone's always ready in any argument to bend over and drop his . . .'

'Stop it, Perpetua! This isn't the time for that sort of . . .'

'Very well, sir; you'll think about it in the night. But meanwhile don't start off by doing yourself an injury. Don't ruin your health, and try to eat something.'

'I'll think about it tonight, sure enough!' grumbled Don Abbondio. 'There's not much risk that I'll forget about it.'

He stood up, and went on: 'I won't have anything to eat; nothing at all. It's not food I want just now, you can be sure of that. I realize as well as you do that I've got some thinking to do. But there it is! These things have to happen to me.'

'Drink another drop of this, sir, anyway,' said Perpetua, refilling his glass. 'You know it always makes you feel better in your stomach.'

'It'll take more than that to make me feel better this time. More than that . . .'

With these last words, he picked up the light, still grumbling: 'A fine thing to happen to a decent man like me!' and 'What'll come of it tomorrow?' and other such lamentations, he crossed the room, to go upstairs to his own quarters. When he reached the door, he turned towards Perpetua, and put his finger on his lips.

'Remember now!' he said. 'For the love of Heaven! Not a word!' And he vanished from her view.

Chapter 2

Ironic of

THE Prince of Condé is said to have slept soundly the night
before the battle of Rocroi: but in the first place he was very
tired; and in the second place he had already made all the
necessary dispositions, and determined what needed to be done
in the morning. But Don Abbondio knew nothing yet except
that the following day would be a day of battle, and much of his
night was spent in painful deliberation. To ignore the villainous
message, disregard the threats, and perform the wedding ceremony, was a possibility which he did not even wish to consider.
As for telling Renzo what had happened, and making a joint
effort with him to find a solution ... Heaven forbid! 'Not a
word about all this,' one of the bravoes had said, 'or else ...'
and then had followed that growling noise which still rang in
Don Abbondio's ears. Far from proposing to infringe such a
commandment, he regretted having mentioned the matter even
to Perpetua. Should he run away? But where could he go? And
later on what difficulties would follow, what laborious explanations! Every time the poor man rejected a possible course of
action, he turned over in bed. From every point of view the best
plan – or the least disastrous – seemed to be to gain time by
putting Renzo off from day to day. And now he came to think
of it, a few days' delay would take them into a period when
weddings were not allowed. If I can keep the lad at bay for that
short time, he thought, I shall have another two months' breathing space; and a lot can happen in two months. He began to
devise excuses for delay; and though they all seemed rather
feeble, he comforted himself with the thought that his authority
would lend them the necessary weight. And his many years of
experience would give him every advantage over an ignorant
boy. After all, he said to himself, Renzo's mind is on his sweet-
heart, but mine is on my own skin; so I have more at stake,
apart from having more brains. My dear boy, if you get

45

scorched, I'm sorry, but I won't pull your chestnuts out of the fire. Having got so far towards a decision, he was at last able to close his eyes – but what broken sleep followed! What terrible dreams of the bravoes, Don Rodrigo, Renzo, narrow paths, cliffs, flight, pursuit, shouting, bullets . . .

Waking up on the morning after a misfortune, to face its consequences, is a bitter moment. As the mind regains consciousness, it dwells on the habitual ideas of earlier, more peaceful days. Suddenly the thought of the new situation thrusts itself rudely forward, all the more vividly unwelcome in that second of contrast. Don Abbondio felt this moment of distress to the full, and then quickly began to go over the plans he had formed the night before, confirming his decisions and improving the details. Next he got up and waited for the young man to arrive, with mingled fear and impatience.

Lorenzo, or Renzo as everyone called him, did not keep Don Abbondio waiting long. As soon as he felt he could decently do so, he walked round to the curé's house, with the happy eagerness of a man of twenty on the day of his wedding to the girl he loves. He had been left alone in the world in his early teens, and he followed the trade of silk-spinner, which was in a sense the hereditary trade of his family. In earlier years it had been a fairly lucrative calling, and though it had fallen off a skilful worker could still make an honest living out of it. The amount of work available dwindled from day to day; but there was also a steady fall in the number of workers who were lured away to neighbouring states by promises, privileges and high wages, so that there was still a fair amount to do for those who remained behind. Renzo also had a small plot of land under cultivation – when there was no spinning to do, he worked on it himself – so that, for a man in his position, he could be called comfortably off. And though the year had been a bad one, even worse than the last couple, and a time of real shortage had begun, the young man had been saving up ever since he set his heart on Lucia, and had enough put by to be in no danger of going hungry. He now presented himself to Don Abbondio dressed in his best clothes, with feathers of different colours in his hat, the decorated handle of his dagger sticking out of its special trouser pocket, and with that air of festivity combined with bravado assumed by even the quietest of men at such times. Don Abbondio's hesitant and mysterious greeting was in marked contrast to the cheerful and resolute manner of the young man.

'Well, sir,' he said, 'I've come to ask you what time it would suit you to see us in church.'

'Yes, yes . . . What day do you mean?'

'What day, sir? D'you not remember we arranged it for today?'

'Today?' said Don Abbondio, as if this was the first he had heard of it. 'Today? I'm sorry, but I can't do it today.'

'You can't, sir? What's happened then?'

'In the first place . . . I don't feel well, you see.'

'Why, I'm sorry to hear that; but surely it's a very quick job, and not much trouble.'

'And then, you see, and then . . .'

'And then what, sir?'

'And then there are complications.'

'What's complicated about it then?'

'You need to be in the Church yourself to realize how many difficulties crop up in these cases, or what responsibilities a priest has to shoulder. I'm too kind-hearted, that's the trouble. I think of nothing but removing obstacles, smoothing the way, arranging things to suit other people; and so I neglect my duty, and reprimands come my way – reprimands or worse.'

'For God's sake, your Reverence, don't torture me like this! Tell me straight out what's gone wrong.'

'Well . . . do you realize just how many formalities are involved in arranging a properly conducted wedding?'

'I think I should do, sir,' said Renzo, beginning to get angry. 'You've been ramming them down my throat enough for the past few days. But isn't everything straightened out now? Hasn't everything been done that needed to be done?'

'It may seem so to you; but, forgive me for saying so, it's all my fault for neglecting my duty so as not to hurt other people. And now . . . no, I won't say that; but I know what I'm talking about. We poor curés are between the hammer and the anvil; on the one hand there's yourself, impatient of course, and I feel

47

for you, poor lad; and on the other my superiors, who ... well, I can't go into that. And here am I in the middle of it all.'

'But tell me what this other formality is, that you say we've got to attend to, and we'll do it at once.'

'Do you know what the effective impediments are?'

'What would I know about impediments?'

> ' "*Error, conditio, votum, cognatio, crimen,*
> ' "*Cultus disparitas, vis, ordo, ligamen, honestas,*
> ' "*Si sis affinis ...*" '

began Don Abbondio, counting the points on his fingers.

'Are you making fun of me, your Reverence?' interrupted the young man. 'What good do you think your Latin is going to do me?'

'Well, if you don't understand these things, you must be patient, and leave it to those that do.'

'But, good God, sir ... !'

'Listen, my dear fellow, don't lose your temper – I'm ready to do whatever depends on me personally. For my part, I want to see you happy; I'm fond of you, you know. Dear me! When I think how well off you were before! Everything you wanted ... And now you've got this idea of marriage in your head ...'

'Whatever are you saying, sir?' cried Renzo, his face full of angry stupefaction.

'I'm saying "Be patient", that's what I'm saying. I want to see you happy.'

'And so ...'

'And so, my dear boy, I'm not to blame: I didn't make the law. And before we perform a marriage ceremony, we priests have to make inquiry after inquiry, to make sure there are no impediments.'

'But listen, sir – you must tell me what this impediment is that's suddenly cropped up.'

'Be patient, Renzo. You can't expect these things to be worked out for you in two seconds. There may be nothing at all, and that's what I hope; but these inquiries still have to be made. The words of the rule are clear, very clear :– '*Antequam matrimonium denunciet ...*'

'I've told you I don't want your Latin, sir.'

'But you want me to explain . . .'

'Haven't you done all these inquiries already?'

'Not quite all of them, not as I should have – that's what I'm telling you.'

'Why didn't you do them at the right time then? Why did you tell me that everything was ready? Why wait until . . .'

'Ah, Renzo! Now you're reproaching me with my kindness of heart. I made everything as easy as I could, so as to be able to do what you wanted more quickly. And now I've had a . . . No, I can't tell you about it, but it's serious.'

'What d'you expect me to do, then?'

'Just be patient, Renzo, for a few days. My dear boy, a few days don't last for ever : be patient.'

'How long for?'

'I've done it!' thought Don Abbondio to himself. 'Well,' he went on, with a more sycophantic air than ever, 'in a fortnight I'll see what I can do . . . I'll do my best.'

'A fortnight, sir ! This is really something I didn't expect. We did everything you asked us to do; we fixed the day; the day's arrived; and now you tell me we've got to wait another fourteen days ! Fourteen . . .' he went on, in a louder and more angry voice, raising one arm and shaking his fist. Who knows what unsuitable expression would have followed the number, if Don Abbondio had not seized his other hand and interrupted him, with anxious and timid affection? 'Come, come !' he said, 'don't lose your temper, for Heaven's sake. I'll try, I'll see what I can do, in a week . . .'

'And what am I to say to Lucia?'

'That I've made a mistake.'

'And what about the things other people will say?'

'Tell everybody, by all means, that Don Abbondio has made a mistake, out of too much haste, too much kindness of heart – let me take all the blame. I can't say more than that. Just a week . . .'

'And then, there won't be any more difficulties?'

'I assure you . . .'

'Very well then. I will be patient, for one week. But please understand that after the week has gone I won't accept any more of this rigmarole. Meanwhile, sir, I respectfully take my leave.' And off he went, giving Don Abbondio less of a bow than usual, and looking at him in a way which had more expressiveness than reverence about it.

Once outside he began to walk reluctantly towards Lucia's house – a thing he had never done reluctantly before. Furious as he was, he began to turn his recent conversation over very carefully in his mind. The more he thought, the odder it seemed. Don Abbondio's chilly and embarrassed way of greeting him; his halting yet impatient manner of speech; the way those pale grey eyes dodged about all the time while he was talking, as if they were afraid to meet the words that came out of his mouth; his treatment of Renzo's marriage as a new idea, when it had already been arranged in such detail; and, above all, his constant hints at some important new development, without any clear indication what it was – all this made Renzo suspect that the explanation of the mystery was something quite different from what Don Abbondio wanted him to believe. For a moment he was on the point of going back and cross-examining the priest more closely, to get a clear statement out of him. But then he looked up and saw Perpetua walking along in front of him; she was just turning off into a small kitchen garden which stood a short way from the house. He called out her name as she was opening the garden gate, then he quickened his pace and caught her just as she was going in. In the hope that she would tell him something more definite, he struck up a conversation with her.

'Good morning, Perpetua. I'd been hoping this would be a merry day for all of us.'

'I know, you poor lad. Well, God's will be done.'

'Will you tell me something, Perpetua? Don Abbondio, bless him, gave me a garbled story I couldn't understand at all. Why can't he marry us today – or why doesn't he want to?'

'Oh, Renzo! D'you think I know all my master's secrets?'

'Secrets, eh? I knew there was something behind it,' said Renzo to himself. Hoping to learn more, he went on 'Listen,

Perpetua, we've always been good friends. Tell me what you know; help a poor boy who's alone in the world.'

'It's a sad thing to be born poor, dear lad.'

'That's true enough,' said Renzo, his suspicions growing stronger and stronger; and then trying to get to the heart of the matter – 'it's true, all right; but is it for the priests to illtreat the poor?'

'Listen, Renzo, I can't say anything because ... because there's nothing I know; but I can assure you of one thing, my master doesn't want to wrong anyone, neither you nor anyone else. It's not his fault.'

'Whose fault is it then?' asked Renzo, as casually as he could; but his heart missed a beat, and he strained his ears for her reply.

'I tell you, Renzo, I don't know anything about it ... but I must say something in defence of my master, because I hate to hear of anyone thinking he'd try to hurt anybody. Poor man! If he goes wrong, it's out of too much kindness of heart. And there are such blackguards in the world, such arrogant brutes ... men with no fear of God at all.'

Blackguards? Arrogant brutes? thought Renzo. That doesn't sound like Don Abbondio's superiors. 'Come on,' he said, hiding his growing disquiet with some difficulty, 'come on, tell me who it is.'

'Ah! you want to make me talk, but I can't talk, because I don't know anything. Not knowing comes to the same thing as promising not to tell. You could put me on the rack, and you'd never get anything out of me. Good-bye; I must go now; we're both wasting our time.' She hurried into the kitchen garden, and shut the gate. Renzo returned her farewell, and made his way back towards the house, treading very softly, so that she would not realize which way he was going. But as soon as he was out of earshot he lengthened his stride, and in a moment he was back at Don Abbondio's door. He went in, and marched right into the room where he had left the priest. Don Abbondio was still sitting there, and Renzo strode up to him with fists clenched and eyes blazing.

'Eh! What's the meaning of this?' said Don Abbondio.

51

'Who is the arrogant brute who doesn't want me to marry Lucia?' said Renzo in a voice which showed that he meant to have a proper answer.

'What's that? What? What?' stammered the poor man, taken aback. His face suddenly went white and soft, like a rag coming out of the washtub. Then, still muttering, he jumped out of his armchair and made a dash for the door. But Renzo must have been expecting this move; he was on the alert, and got there before the priest. He turned the key, and put it in his pocket.

'Well, sir, will you talk now? Everyone knows my business except for me, and now I mean to know it too. What's his name?'

'Renzo! Renzo! Be careful! Think of the welfare of your immortal soul!'

'All I can think about is that I want that name, now, at once.' Perhaps unconsciously, his hand went to the handle of his dagger, which stuck out of his pocket.

'Mercy on us!' exclaimed Don Abbondio weakly.

'I want it now.'

'But who told you . . . ?'

'I won't have any more humbug. Tell me now, straight out, at once.'

'Do you want me to be killed?'

'I want to know what I have a right to know.'

'But if I tell you, I'm a dead man. Haven't I a right to value my own life?'

'If you do value it, you'd better talk.'

These words came out with such violence, and Renzo's expression grew so threatening, that Don Abbondio had to give up all thought of resistance.

'You must promise, you must swear, not to tell anyone about this,' he said, 'never to say anything . . .'

'I'll promise you one thing – I shall do something I'll be sorry for if you don't tell me who it is at once.'

At this new threat, Don Abbondio's features contorted and his eyes flickered like a dentist's patient with the forceps in his mouth; finally he got out the word 'Don . . .'

'Don ...?' said Renzo after him, as if encouraging the sufferer to spit out the rest. He bent forward, one ear turned towards the priest's mouth, arms held stiffly back, fists clenched.

'Don Rodrigo!' gabbled the victim, tumbling the four syllables out quickly, and slurring the consonants – partly out of genuine agitation, and partly because he was devoting the few mental resources he still had available to a search for some sort of compromise between the two terrors that possessed him, trying to call back and cancel the words in the very moment in which he was compelled to let them pass his lips.

'The swine!' shouted Renzo. 'What happened? What did he do? What did he say to make you ...'

'What happened, eh?' said Don Abbondio, with something like indignation in his voice, for he felt that he had just made a sacrifice which put Renzo in his debt. 'What happened indeed! I wish it had happened to you instead of to me, when it's nothing to do with me at all; it might have got some of the silly ideas out of your head.' And he painted a terrible picture of his ugly encounter with the bravoes. As he spoke, he became more and more aware of a great rage hidden somewhere within him, which had previously been masked by fear. Noticing at the same time that Renzo, caught between anger and confusion, was standing motionless, with bowed head, the priest went gleefully on to say: 'What a hero you've been! What a good turn you've done me! What a trick to play on a decent man, and your parish priest at that! In his own house, a sacred place! A fine thing! Making me say something which will be a disaster for me and a disaster for you – something I was keeping from you out of prudence, for your own good ... Now that you know, what happens next? I'd like to see what you'd do. Heavens above! it isn't a joking matter. It's not a question of right or wrong, it's a question of power ... just now, when I gave you a piece of good advice, you flew off the handle at once. I was using my judgement for my own benefit and for yours too; but what's the use? ... Well, you might unlock the door at least, and give me my key.'

'Perhaps I've done wrong,' said Renzo, in a voice which held no harshness towards Don Abbondio, though it had an undertone of fury towards the man he now knew to be his enemy, 'perhaps I've done wrong; but be honest, sir, and put yourself in my place . . .'

While saying these words, he got the key out of his pocket and went to open the door. Don Abbondio followed him, and came up beside him while he was turning the key in the lock. With a serious and anxious expression, he raised his right hand with three fingers outstretched to the level of the young man's eyes, as if to give him what help he could, and said 'At least swear that you won't . . .'

'I may have done wrong; forgive me,' said Renzo, throwing open the door and preparing to leave.

Don Abbondio seized his arm, in a trembling grasp. 'Promise me . . .' he said.

'I may have done wrong,' repeated Renzo, freeing himself, and he strode rapidly away, cutting short the argument, which otherwise could have gone on for hundreds of years, since each of the parties merely repeated what he had said before – just like a literary or philosophical controversy.

'Perpetua! Perpetua!!' shouted Don Abbondio, after unsuccessfully trying to call Renzo back. But there was no answer from Perpetua; the priest felt that the world was falling about his ears.

It has quite often happened to people in much higher positions than Don Abbondio to find themselves in such a ticklish and unpleasant situation, and such uncertainty which course they should follow, that the best answer seems to be to take to bed with a high fever. Don Abbondio did not have to rack his brains to find this solution; it came to him unbidden. The terror he had felt the day before, the restless agony of the night, the terror of the interview just concluded, the anxious fears about the future, all took their toll. Dazed and panting, he fell back into his armchair. He began to feel a shuddering in his bones, gazed at his nails with a sigh, and shouted for Perpetua every few minutes in a trembling, angry voice. Finally she came in, with a big cabbage under her arm, as bold as brass, as if nothing had happened. We will spare the reader his groans, her sympathy, his accusations, her defence, the cries of 'It must have been you!' and 'I never said a word!', and in general all the confused details of their conversation. It is enough to say that Don Abbondio told Perpetua to bolt the door, and not to open it again on any account; if anyone knocked, she was to put her head out of the window and say that the curé had gone to bed with a high fever. He went slowly upstairs, pausing on every third step to say: 'I'm done for this time.' Then he really went to bed, where we will leave him.

Meanwhile Renzo walked with angry speed towards his house, uncertain what he should do, but itching to do something strange and terrible. Bullies, oppressors and all men who do violence to the rights of others are guilty not only of their own crimes, but also of the corruption they bring into the hearts of their victims. Renzo was by nature a peaceful young man with a horror of bloodshed, a straightforward young man, with a hatred of the underhand. But at that moment his heart and mind were full of fantastic plans for a treacherous murder. At first he wanted to go straight to Don Rodrigo's house and seize him by the throat – but then he remembered that the place was like a fortress, with a garrison of bravoes within, and bravo guards without; that only well-known friends or servants of Don Rodrigo could enter freely without being looked over from head to foot; that an unknown artisan would never be able to get in without a close examination – and that he himself was probably all too well known there. Next he had visions of taking his musket, lying behind a hedge, waiting for the unlikely event of Don Rodrigo passing that way alone. Sinking himself in his new role with ferocious enthusiasm, he imagined himself hearing a footstep, his enemy's footstep; he softly raised his head, recognized the infamous tyrant, levelled his musket, took aim, fired, saw him fall and die, cursed his soul, and sped away towards the frontier and the safety of exile. And what would happen to Lucia then? As soon as her face appeared among these dismal visions, the better thoughts which normally occupied Renzo's mind flocked home again, his last memories of his parents, thoughts of God, of the Madonna and of the saints all came back to him. He recalled the happiness he had often felt in the knowledge that he had never committed a crime, and of the

55

horror he had often felt at the news of a murder. He awoke from his bloody dream with terror, remorse and a sort of joy that it had gone no further than imagination. But the thought of Lucia brought so many other ideas with it! . . . So many hopes, so many promises; a future so warmly desired, and regarded as so certain; and the day they had longed for above all others! How could he tell her? What words could he find? And then what was he to do? How could he make her his own against the will of that powerful and evil man? Together with these thoughts, a shadow, too formless to be called a suspicion, passed painfully across his mind. This arrogant intervention by Don Rodrigo could only be attributed to a brutal passion for Lucia. The idea that she might have given him the slightest provocation or encouragement hardly entered his thoughts. But had she known about it? Could Don Rodrigo have come to feel that disgraceful passion for her without her being aware of it? He surely must have made some sort of approach to her, before going to these extremes . . . and Lucia had not said a word to Renzo, whom she had promised to marry!

Sunk in these thoughts, he went past his own home in the middle of the village and walked on to the far end, where Lucia's cottage stood, a little apart from the others. It was separated from the road by a small courtyard, and surrounded by a low wall. Renzo walked into the courtyard and heard a buzz of women's voices, in continual ebb and flow, that came from an upper window. Friends and neighbours, paying their respects to the bride, he thought, and jibbed at appearing in that throng, with his terrible news burning in his heart, and showing in his face. A little girl who was in the courtyard ran up to him, shouting 'The bridegroom! here's the bridegroom!'

'Shhh! Bettina – be quiet!' said Renzo. 'Listen to me! Go upstairs and get Lucia on one side, and whisper in her ear – don't let anyone hear, or notice, mind. Tell her I must speak to her, that I'm waiting downstairs, and that she's to come at once.' The child ran upstairs, happy and proud to be the bearer of a secret message.

At that very moment Lucia's mother had finished dressing her in all her finery, and she came out to her friends. Each of them wanted Lucia all to herself; they tried to force her to let them see her properly; and she was warding them off with all the somewhat brusque modesty of a peasant girl, shielding her face with one arm, or ducking it down against her bosom. The long dark line of her eyebrows was gathered in a frown, but her lips opened in a smile at the same time. Her dark young hair was divided in front by the narrow white line of her parting; at the back of her head it was twisted up into a series of concentric rings, secured by long silver pins arranged in a pattern like the rays of a halo – a fashion still followed by peasant girls in the territory of Milan. She wore a necklace of alternate garnets and filigree gold beads; a smart bodice of flowered brocade, and sleeves laced with coloured ribbons; a short skirt of rough silk with many small, fine pleats; scarlet stockings; and embroidered slippers, also of silk. But besides the special ornaments that she had put on for her wedding morning, Lucia had one which she wore every day – a modest beauty, which was thrown into relief and enhanced by the various emotions which appeared in her face – a great happiness, qualified by a faint air of confusion, and that calm melancholy which appears from time to time on the face of a bride, not detracting from her beauty, but giving it a special character. Little Bettina dived into the throng, pushed her way through to Lucia, neatly caught her attention, and whispered her message.

'I'll be back in a minute,' said Lucia to her friends, and ran downstairs. She noticed Renzo's uneasy bearing, and an unfamiliar expression on his face, which gave her a foretaste of terror.

'What is it?' she said.

'Oh Lucia!' said Renzo. 'It's all up with our plans for today; and God knows when we can be man and wife.'

'*What?*' said Lucia in bewilderment. Renzo gave her a short account of the morning's events. She listened in agony, and when she heard the name of Don Rodrigo, 'Oh!' she gasped, blushing and trembling, 'Who would have thought it would have gone as far as that?'

'So you did know about it?' said Renzo.

'I did,' she said sadly, 'but I never thought . . .'

'What did you know?'

'Don't ask me now; don't make me cry. I must call my mother at once, and send all the other women away. We must be alone to talk about this.'

As she went, Renzo whispered: 'You never said a word to me.'

'Oh Renzo!' said Lucia, looking back at him for a moment, without stopping. He understood very well what she meant by saying his name in that tone, at that moment: 'Can you think that I stayed silent from any but the best and purest of motives?'

Meanwhile Agnese, the bride's mother, who was anxious and puzzled about Bettina's whispered message and Lucia's sudden disappearance, was on her way downstairs to see what had happened. Lucia left her with Renzo, and went back to the women. Putting on the best face and the best voice she could, she said: 'The priest has been taken ill, and nothing can be done today.' Then she bade them all a quick farewell, and went out again. The women filed out of the house, and spread the news through the village. Two or three of them went round to the curé's house to ask if he were really ill.

'He's got a high fever,' replied Perpetua from the window. This sad news was carried back to the other women, and cut short the conjectures which were already thronging into their brains, and finding expression in various pithy and mysterious remarks.

Chapter 3

WHEN Lucia came downstairs Renzo was miserably telling his story and Agnese was miserably taking it in. Both of them turned towards Lucia, who knew more of the matter than they did, looking for an explanation, which could only be a painful one. Corresponding to the two different kinds of love they felt for her, their faces showed, amid all their grief, two different kinds of anger with her for having kept a secret from them – and a secret of such a kind. Though impatient to hear her daughter's story, Agnese could not help scolding her. 'Fancy not telling your own mother about a thing like that!' she said.

'Now I'll tell you the whole story,' said Lucia, wiping her eyes on her apron.

'Yes – tell us! tell us!' cried her mother and her lover together.

'Holy Mother of God!' exclaimed Lucia, 'who would have thought it would ever have come to this?' and she went on, in a voice broken by sobs, to tell them how, a few days earlier, on the way back from the spinning mill, she had been walking behind the other girls, and Don Rodrigo had gone by with another gentleman. Don Rodrigo had tried to get her to stop and talk to them; and what he'd said hadn't been at all nice, Lucia continued. But she hadn't given in; she'd quickened her step and caught up with her friends. Meanwhile she had heard the other gentleman laugh very loudly, and Don Rodrigo had said 'Let's have a bet then!' The following day there they both were again at the same place; but Lucia was walking in the middle of a group of other girls this time, and keeping her head down; and the second gentleman had sniggered and Don Rodrigo and said: 'We'll see, we'll see.'

'Heaven be thanked,' said Lucia, 'that was the last day of the spinning. So I went straight and told . . .'

'Who was it you told?' broke in Agnese, waiting, with some impatience, and a little indignation, to hear the name of the confidant who had been preferred to her.

'I told Father Cristoforo at confession, mother,' said Lucia, with a gentle note of apology in her voice. 'I told him all about it, last time we went to the church by the monastery. You remember, I kept finding little jobs to do that morning, and spun them out until some other people went by who were going there too, so we could go with them, because after that trouble I was so afraid to go out in the road . . .'

At the honoured name of Father Cristoforo, her mother's indignant expression softened. 'You were right to tell him,' she said. 'But why not tell your mother too?'

Lucia had two good reasons: first, she didn't want to alarm or upset her mother over something she couldn't help to put right; and secondly she didn't want there to be any chance of lots of people repeating a story she wanted buried without trace – especially as she'd hoped that getting married would put an end to this detestable persecution before it went any further. But she only mentioned the first of these two reasons.

'And, Renzo,' she said, turning to him, with the special voice we use to persuade a friend that he has been unjust, 'do you really think I should have told you about it? I only wish you didn't know about it now !'

'And what did Father Cristoforo have to say?' asked Agnese.

'He told me to do what I could to speed up the wedding, and meanwhile to stay indoors; to pray to God; and to hope that the man would forget about me if he didn't see me. And that was the time I did something I hated,' she went on, turning to Renzo again, but not looking him in the face, and blushing furiously, 'that was when I had to come to you like a brazen girl, and ask you to try to speed things up, and marry me before the time we'd arranged. I don't know what you can have thought of me. But I did it for the best, and on good advice – and I was sure it would be all right – and the last thing I expected this morning was . . .' – here her words were cut short by a violent fit of weeping.

'The damned swine ! The blackguard !' shouted Renzo, strid-

60

ing up and down the room, and grasping the handle of his dagger every so often.

'Oh, what a mess, good heavens; what a mess!' exclaimed Agnese. The young man stopped suddenly in front of the weeping girl. He looked at her with sad and angry tenderness, and said: 'I'll see he never does a thing like this again.'

'No, Renzo, no! – not that, for the love of Heaven!' cried Lucia. 'God is the God of the poor as well as the rich; but how can you expect him to help us if we sin against him?'

'No, no, not that!' repeated Agnese.

'Renzo,' said Lucia, with an air of hope, and calmer determination, 'You have a trade, and I know how to work. Let's go away, so far away that Don Rodrigo will never hear of us again.'

'Oh, Lucia! What would happen afterwards? We're not man and wife yet. We'd still need a certificate from our own priest, saying we were free to marry – and can you see Don Abbondio giving it to us? A coward like him? Oh, if only we were really married . . . !'

Lucia began to cry again, and all three of them stood in a gloomy silence, which contrasted dismally with the festive splendour of their clothes.

'Listen, children, and take my advice,' said Agnese a few moments later. 'I've been in this world longer than you, and I know something about it. We mustn't lose our heads – things aren't always as bad as they seem. Poor folk like us see our troubles as more tangled than they really are, because we haven't got the key to them; but then sometimes the advice of a man who knows his books, just a couple of words from him . . . I know what I'm talking about. Take my advice, Renzo, go to Lecco, find Dr Quibbler,[1] and tell him about it – but don't call him that, for heaven's sake, it's only a nickname. You'll have to ask for Dr . . . oh, dear, I've forgotten his real name, everyone calls him that. Anyway, look for a tall, thin lawyer, with a bald head, a red nose and a strawberry mark on his cheek.'

'I know him by sight,' said Renzo.

'Good – well, he's a wonderful man! I've known several

1. 'Azzecca-Garbugli' – an adroit weaver of tangles.

people who were caught by the feet like a wasp in honey, and didn't know which wall to bang their heads against next – well, after an hour alone with old Quibbler (mind you don't call him that!) I've actually seen them laughing about the very same thing! Take those four capons I was going to kill (poor things) for the party on Sunday, and give them to the Doctor; because it would never do to go and see one of these legal gentlemen empty-handed. Tell him the whole story, and see if he doesn't come out with something, right off, that you or I would never think of in a hundred years.'

Renzo was delighted with this idea; Lucia liked it too, and Agnese, proud of having thought of it, went to the hen-house and picked out the four unfortunate fowls one after the other, their eight legs gathered into a bundle like the stalks of a bunch of flowers, lashed them tightly together with a string, and handed them to Renzo. After an exchange of encouraging words, he left by way of the back garden, so that he would not have a crowd of children running after him with cries of 'Look at the bridegroom!' He made his way across country by small field paths, trembling with anger, thinking about the disaster that had struck him, and going over the things he was going to say to Dr Quibbler. I leave it to the reader to imagine what sort of journey the poor capons had, trussed up and held upside down by the feet in the hands of a man who was in the throes of several different passions, and suited his gestures to the thoughts that thronged tumultuously through his brain. He stretched out his arm in anger, threw up his hand in despair, shook his fist in threat, and everything he did jolted them cruelly, and made their dangling heads bounce up and down, while they tried to peck at one another, as happens too often among companions in misfortune.

He reached the outskirts of the town, asked the way to the lawyer's house, followed the instructions he was given, and found himself at the door. When he went in, he was overcome by the embarrassment which poor, uneducated people feel as they approach the presence of a gentleman who is also a scholar. He forgot all the speeches he had prepared in advance; but then his eye fell on the capons, and he felt better. He went into the kitchen, and asked the maid-servant if he could see the master. She looked at the capons, and, as she was used to presents of that sort, she grabbed them at once, though Renzo tried to hold them back, because he wanted the Doctor himself to see them and realize that he had brought something with him. The lawyer happened to come in just as the woman was saying 'Give them to me, and then you can go in.' Renzo bowed deeply, the doctor greeted him affably, with the words 'Come in, my lad' and took him into his study. It was a huge room; three of its walls were occupied by portraits of the first twelve Roman emperors, and the fourth was taken up by a vast bookcase full of dusty old volumes. In the middle of the room was a table, covered with statements, pleas, applications and edicts. Three or four chairs stood round it, and one large armchair, with a high, square back, at the corners of which rose two carved wooden ornaments, like horns. The leather cover of the armchair was secured by heavy round-headed tacks; but some of them had been missing for a long time, so that the leather had come loose at the corners, and was flaking off at various points. The doctor was in his dressing-gown, which meant that he was wearing a tattered old robe, which had formerly served him many years earlier for the great occasions when he went to Milan to plead in cases of importance. He shut the door, and said encouragingly: 'Well, my boy, what's your problem?'

'I wanted to have a word with you, in confidence . . .'

'Well, here I am,' said the doctor. 'Tell me all about it.' And he sat down in his armchair.

Renzo stood very upright in front of the table, put one hand in the crown of his hat, and span it round with the other. 'There's one thing I wanted to ask you, sir, with your knowledge of the law . . .' he began.

'Just give me the facts,' interrupted the doctor.

'You must excuse me, sir; we're poor people who don't know how to talk properly. What I want to know is this . . .'

'You infernal people are all the same! Instead of giving me the facts, you start putting questions to me, because you've already made up your mind what to do.'

'I'm sorry, sir. I wanted to ask whether it's a crime if some-one threatens a priest, to stop him marrying people.'

'So that's it! I understand now,' thought the doctor, though he had not really understood at all. He put on a serious expression, but the seriousness was mixed with sympathy and concern. He pursed his lips, and made a curious sound that hinted at a view of the case which he went on to express in words: 'This is a bad business, my boy: a case covered by the law. It's a good thing you came to me. A clear case, covered by a whole series of proclamations, including . . . yes, including one issued last year by the present Governor. I'll show it to you now; you shall see it with your own eyes.'

He rose from his chair, and thrust his hands into the chaotic heap of papers, stirring them up from the bottom like grain in a measure.

'Where's it got to this time? I'll have it in a minute. We have to keep so many papers by us! But it must be there, because it's an important proclamation. Ah, yes; here it is!' He picked it up, and spread it out; he looked at the date, and put on an even more serious expression. 'The 15th of October 1627!' he exclaimed. 'Just as I thought; it's one of last year's. It's a recent proclamation; which makes it all the more disturbing. Can you read, my boy?'

'I can read a bit, sir,' said Renzo.

'Well, then, look over my shoulder, and you'll see for yourself.'

He lifted the sheet off the table, holding it open with both hands, and began to read – some passages in a rapid mutter, and others slowly, clearly and emphatically, according to their relative importance.

'*Whereas, by the proclamation published at the order of the Duke of Feria on the 14th day of December 1620 and confirmed by the most Illustrious and Excellent Lord the Lord Gonzalo Fernandez of Cordova,* and so on, and so on, *extraordinary and rigorous remedies were provided against the oppressive, coercive and tyrannical acts which some men have dared to commit against these most devoted servants of His Majesty,* nevertheless *the frequency of such abuses,* and so on, and so on, *has* grown to such a point, that it has compelled His Majesty, and so on. *Wherefore, on due advice of the Senate and of a Committee he has resolved that these presents be published.*

'*To speak first of the tyrannical acts: Experience has shown that many men, both in the cities and in the countryside* – hear that? – *of this realm do practice coercions and oppressions against weaker men in divers ways: as contracts concluded under duress for sale or hire* and so on and so on – where's it got to, now? Ah, here it is; listen to this – *forced marriages or preventions of marriage*. What about that?'

'That's it,' said Renzo.

'Yes, but listen; there's plenty more to it, and at the end come the penalties. *Forced witness or prevention of witness; forced change of habitation;* then some stuff about payment of debts, molestation, forced labour in mills, and so on which doesn't concern us. Ah, here we are! *Any priest who refuses to perform the duties of his office, or performs actions which lie outside his duty.* What about that?

'It could have been written with me in mind, sir.'

'That's true, isn't it? Now listen to this: *and all other such acts of violence, whether committed by feudal lords, nobles, men of middle station, men of low degree, or the common people*. No escape, you see. Everybody comes into this one; it's like the Last Judgement. Now for the penalties: *These and similar actions have long been prohibited, yet now sterner measures are required; wherefore His Excellency, by these presents, not derogating* and so on and so on, *does order and command that against all men who offend in any of the sorts herein mentioned the ordinary judges of this State shall proceed with monetary and bodily penalties, including condemnation to the galleys, and the penalty of death* – quite a striking little afterthought, that! – *at the discretion of His Excellency or of the Senate according to the nature of the case, the person, and the circumstances. Without remission and with full rigour,* and so on, and so on! They haven't forgotten much, have they? and here are the signatures: *Gonzalo Fernandez of Cordova;* then *Platonus;* and a note here, *Vidit Ferrer.* Nothing missing at all.'

While the Doctor was reading, Renzo ran his eye slowly along the words of the text, trying to extract their precise meaning, and taking special heed of those golden phrases which seemed to promise him help. The doctor was amazed to see that his new client's expression was one of interest rather than terror. This one must really be an old hand, he thought to himself.

'Why!' he said to Renzo a moment later, 'I see you've had your quiff cut off. That was very sensible of you; though it wasn't really necessary, if you were going to put yourself in my hands. It's a serious case all right, but you'll be surprised what I can do, when I put my mind to it.'

In explanation of this remark of the Doctor's, we must inform the reader, or perhaps only remind him, that at that time professional bravoes and criminals of all kinds used to wear a long quiff, which would be pulled down over the face, like a mask, in any encounter where one of them wanted to conceal his identity, or felt that the occasion called for prudence as well as force. The proclamations had plenty to say about this fashion.

'*It is the will of His Excellency* (the Marquis of Hynojosa) *that any man who wears his hair long enough to cover his whole forehead down to the eyebrows exclusively, or who wears it plaited, either behind or in front of his ears, shall be fined three hundred scudi, or three years in the galleys in default of payment for the first offence; and for the second offence shall suffer further monetary and bodily punishment over and above those just mentioned, at the discretion of His Excellency.*

'*Except that, if any man be bald, or have a wound or other mark, he may, for the sake of his personal appearance or health, grow his hair so long as may be necessary to cover such defects and no longer; but he must be careful not to exceed the strict requirements of necessity, or he will incur the same penalties as are laid down for other offenders.*

'*Barbers are also commanded, under pain of a fine of one hundred scudi, or three strokes of the lash, to be given in public, not to leave their clients any plaits, locks or tresses, nor in general any hair longer than is usual, either in front, at the sides, or behind the ears, but all are to be cut in the same manner, except for the bald, or those having other physical defects, as above.'*

Thus the quiff, or *ciuffo*, could almost be regarded as part of the armament of bravoes and bullies, or as a badge by which they could be recognized; which is why they were often called *'ciuffi'*. This figure of speech is still alive in the Milanese dialect, though the meaning has been softened a little. Every one of our readers in Milan will probably have heard the term in his childhood, and remember hearing his parents, or his teacher, or a family friend, or a servant, describe him as a *'ciuffo'* or a *'ciuffetto'*.

'To tell you the truth,' said Renzo, 'on a poor man's honour, I've never worn a quiff in my life.'

'Then I can't do anything for you,' said the Doctor, shaking his head, with a cunning impatient smile. 'If you don't trust me, there's nothing I can do. Listen, my boy, a man who lies to his lawyer is a fool – a big enough fool to tell the truth to the judge. It's your job to tell us the plain facts; it's our job to confuse the issue. If you want me to help you, you must tell me the whole story, from A to Z, as truthfully as you'd tell it to your confessor. You must tell me for whom you were acting; presumably a person of some standing, and in that case I shall go and see him, to pay my respects. I won't tell him, of course, that you told me you got your instructions from him – you can trust me for that. I shall say that I've come to beg his help for a poor young man who's been falsely accused. And with his help I shall make the necessary contacts to produce a happy ending to the story. You can see that he'll be saving himself by saving you ... Or if the whole thing was your own idea, why, I still won't refuse to act for you; I've got people out of worse scrapes than that ...

'So long as you haven't upset any person of consequence, d'you follow me, I'll guarantee to get you out of trouble; though it'll cost you something, d'you follow me. You'll have to tell me the name of the so-called offended party; and according to our friend's position, standing and character we'll see whether it's best to quieten him down with promises of patronage, or to find some way we can bring him up on a criminal charge, and give him something to think about like that. If you really know your way around the proclamations, d'you follow me, there's no such thing as guilty, and no such thing as innocent. As for the priest, if he's sensible he'll keep his mouth shut; and if he's one of these obstinate fellows, we know how to deal with them too. There's a way out of every scrape; but you've got to have the right man to find it for you – and your case is a bad one, d'you follow me, really bad. The proclamation is as clear as daylight; and if it's to be a straight fight between you and the law you're done for. I'm talking as your friend now; these pranks have to be paid for. If you want me to get you off, you'll have to find the money, and you'll have to tell me the facts; you'll have to trust a man who wishes you well, carry out instructions, do exactly what you're told.'

While the Doctor poured out this flood of words, Renzo watched him with wide-eyed, absorbed attention, like a bumpkin in a city square watching a mountebank who first stuffs pound after pound of waste into his mouth, and then goes on to pull miles and miles of ribbon out of it, till you'd think he'd never stop. But when he finally saw just what the doctor was driving at, and realized exactly how he had misjudged the situation, he severed the ribbon of misunderstanding as it issued from the lawyer's lips, saying: 'Oh, Doctor! what do you think I meant? It's just the opposite of what you suppose. I haven't threatened anybody. I don't do that sort of thing; you can ask anyone in my village, and they'll tell you I've never been in trouble with the law. The dirty trick I'm telling you about was played on me. I came to you to find out how to get my rights, and I'm very glad to have seen that proclamation.'

'To hell with it!' cried the Doctor, opening his eyes very wide. 'Are you trying to get me into trouble? But there it is – you're all the same. Will you never learn to tell a story so a man can understand it?'

'But, excuse me, sir, you didn't give me time to; but now I'll tell you just what happened. I was supposed to be getting married today' – here Renzo's voice broke – 'I was supposed to be getting married today, to a girl I've been courting since the summer. As I told you, today was the day we'd arranged with the curé, and everything was ready. Suddenly the curé began to bring out all sorts of excuses ... well, sir, I won't bother you with all the details, but I made him tell me the truth, which I was entitled to know, and he told me he'd been forbidden on pain of death to carry out the marriage. That arrogant brute Don Rodrigo ...'

'That's enough!' snapped the Doctor at once, scowling, wrinkling up his red nose, and twisting his mouth, 'that's quite enough. How dare you come and bother me with these empty rumours? You can use that sort of language with your own friends, who don't know any better; but don't come and talk like that to a respectable man, who's accustomed to weigh his words. And now go away – get out! You don't know what you're saying; I'm not getting involved with children, I'm not going to listen to this sort of thing, this idle chatter.'

'But, sir, I assure you ...'

'Be off with you, I say. What do you expect me to do with your assurances? The whole thing is nothing to do with me; I wash my hands of it.' And he began to rub his hands together, as if he were really washing them. 'Learn how to talk properly! Don't come and play that sort of trick on a respectable man!'

'But listen, sir, listen!' repeated Renzo; but it was no good – the Doctor went on shouting, and pushed him towards the exit with both hands. Having got Renzo as far as the door, he opened it, called his servant, and said 'Whatever this man brought, you're to give it back to him. I'll take nothing from him, nothing at all.'

In all the time she had been in that house, she had never heard an order like that before; but it was pronounced with such vigour, that she had no hesitation in carrying it out. She fetched the four unfortunate capons, and gave them back to Renzo with a glance of contemptuous pity, as if to say 'You must have put your foot in it properly.' Renzo did his best not to take them, but the Doctor was implacable; so the young man, more puzzled and indignant than ever, had to pick up his rejected offering and go back to the village, to tell the womenfolk about the brilliant result of his expedition.

While he was away, the two women had sadly changed out of their Sunday clothes, and begun to talk the whole thing over again, Lucia in tears, and her mother sighing heavily. When Agnese had finished talking about the wonderful results that were to be expected from the approach to the Doctor, Lucia said that they ought to try every possible source of help. Father Cristoforo, she went on, was not only a man of good counsel, but a man of action, when it came to helping the poor and oppressed.

'It'd be a fine thing to let him know what's happened,' she said.

'You're right,' replied Agnese, and they began to discuss how it could be done; for the journey to the monastery – a walk of perhaps two miles – was more than they felt they could face that day; and certainly no sensible person would have advised them to try it. But while they were discussing the pros and cons, they heard a gentle knock at the door, and a quiet but distinct murmur of *'Deo gratias'*. Guessing who it was, Lucia ran to the door. With a friendly little bow, in came a Capuchin lay brother who was collecting for the monastery. Over his shoulder was slung a sack, the mouth of which he held tightly twisted with both hands against his chest.

'Oh, brother Galdino!' exclaimed the two women.

'God be with you,' replied the lay brother. 'I'm collecting walnuts today.'

'Go and get the walnuts for the fathers,' said Agnese. Lucia stood up and went off to the other room; but she stopped for a moment on the way, and standing behind Brother Galdino, who had not moved from his first position, she put one finger to her lips, and begged her mother to keep their secret with a look which had in it tenderness, supplication, and a certain touch of authority.

Brother Galdino cast an inquisitive glance across the room at Agnese, and said: 'What happened about the wedding? Wasn't it to be today? As I came through the village, there seemed to be a bit of excitement, as if something unexpected had occurred. What did happen?'

'The curé was taken ill, and we had to put the wedding off,' said Agnese quickly. Without the lead from Lucia, her answer would probably have been quite different. 'How's the collection going?' she added, to change the subject.

'Badly, madam, badly. This is all I've got.' He swung the sack off his shoulder and tossed it up and down in both hands. 'That's the lot – and I've had to knock on ten doors even for that.'

'Well, Brother Galdino, we've had bad harvests, you know; and when bread itself is short people can't be too lavish with other things.'

'And what can you do to bring back better weather, madam? Generous alms-giving is the only thing. Have you heard about the miracle of the walnuts, that happened many years ago in one of our monasteries in the Romagna?'

'No, I haven't – please tell me about it.'

'Well, then: there was a holy father there, a real saint, and his name was Father Macario. One winter's day he was walking along a path through a field which belonged to one of our benefactors, who was also a very good man, and he saw him standing by a big walnut tree; and four of his men were just beginning to dig round the trunk with their mattocks and to expose the roots. "Whatever are you doing to that poor tree?" asked Father Macario. "Well, father, it hasn't given me any nuts for years now, and I'm going to cut it up for firewood." – "Let it be," said the good father; "I'll tell you this; it'll have more walnuts on it than leaves this year." Our benefactor knew very well what sort of man was telling him that, so he told his men to fill in again. Then he called after the good father, who'd walked on, and said: "Father Macario, the monastery shall have half the crop from that tree." The news of the prophecy spread far and wide, and everybody came hurrying to see the tree. And sure enough in spring it had flowers galore, and later on it had walnuts galore. Our good benefactor didn't have the pleasure of gathering them, because he was called away, before harvest-time, to receive the reward of his charity. But the miracle was all the greater for that, as I'll tell you in a minute. He'd left a son behind him, who was a very different kind of fellow. Now when the time came, one of the brothers went to ask him for

71

the half of the crop that was due to the monastery; but he made out he'd never heard anything about it, and he even said that he never knew that Capuchins could produce nuts before. And what do you think happened after that? One evening the silly fellow had invited one or two of his friends who were the same sort as himself, and as they sat boozing he was telling them the story of the walnut tree, and laughing at the good brothers. Those young louts wanted to go and see the great heap of nuts he had from that tree, and he took them up to the barn. Now listen to this: he opens the door, goes over to the corner where that great heap of walnuts had been piled up; 'Look at that,' he says, and looks himself, and what does he see? A heap of dry walnut leaves. Wasn't that a fine lesson? And the monastery didn't lose at all by it; it did better than ever, for after a wonder like that everyone gave us so many walnuts in the ordinary collection that in the end another of our benefactors had pity on the poor brother who was doing the collecting and gave the monastery a donkey to help carry the nuts. And they got so much oil out of them, that all the poor people came and took some, each according to his need; for we are like the sea, that takes in water on every side, and distributes it back again to all the rivers.'

At this point Lucia came back, with her apron so full of walnuts that she could hardly support their weight; she was straining to hold up the two corners of the apron, with her arms stretched to their full length. While Brother Galdino was getting his sack off his back again, lowering it to the floor, and opening its mouth to receive this abundant flood of alms, Agnese gave Lucia a look of astonished severity, reproaching her for her extravagance; but Lucia looked back at her in a way which meant: I've got good reasons. Brother Galdino was profuse in praise, good wishes, promises and thanks, and, swinging the sack back on to his shoulder, he made off. But Lucia called him back, and said: 'There's one thing I'd like you to do for me. Please tell Father Cristoforo that I very badly need to talk to him, and ask him if he'd be so kind as to come and see us poor women, just as soon as he can manage it, because unfortunately we can't go to the church.'

'Is there nothing else I can do for you . . . ? Very well; I'll see that Father Cristoforo gets your message within an hour.'

'Yes, please do. We're relying on you.'

'You can trust me.' And off he went, with a heavier load and a lighter heart than he had had when he came to them.

The fact that a poor peasant girl could send for Father Cristoforo with such confidence, and that the lay brother accepted her message without showing surprise or raising any difficulty, does not mean that the good father was an insignificant friar at everybody's beck and call. He was, in fact, a man of great authority, both within the monastery and outside it. But the condition of the Capuchins at that time was such that nothing was too low for them, and nothing too high. To serve the weak, and be served by the strong; to enter palace and hovel with the same humility and the same confidence; often to be, even in the same house, both a subject of jest and a person of authority, without whom no decision could be taken; to beg everywhere for alms, and to distribute them to all comers at the monastery – these things were all in the day's work for a Capuchin. As he went along the road, he might meet a prince who would reverently kiss the end of the cord which served him for a belt; equally he might encounter a gang of louts who would stage a scuffle among themselves, during which his beard would be splashed with mud. The word 'friar', in those days, was sometimes pronounced with the greatest respect, and sometimes with the bitterest contempt. The Capuchins were probably the most exposed of all the orders to these contrary feelings, and contrary fortunes; for they owned nothing, wore a dress more strikingly different from other men than the other orders, made a more open profession of humility, and in all these ways exposed themselves more openly to both the veneration and the vilification which such things attract from men of various dispositions and various opinions.

When Brother Galdino had gone, Agnese exclaimed:

'Fancy giving him all those nuts, in a year like this one!'

'Forgive me, mother,' said Lucia, 'but if we'd given him the usual amount, heaven knows how far he'd have had to go to fill

73

his sack, heaven knows when he'd have got back to the monastery; and with all the chattering he'd have done and listened to by then, heaven knows whether he'd have remembered our message.'

'You're right – and anyway it's all good charity, which always brings its reward,' said Agnese, who had her little defects, but was a good, kind woman all the same, and would cheerfully have gone to the stake for her child, who was her only pride and joy.

Meanwhile Renzo arrived. He came in with an indignant and mortified look on his face, and slammed the capons down on the table – which was the last unpleasant shock of a bad day for the birds.

'Fine advice you gave me!' he said to Agnese. 'A true-blue gentleman you sent me to see, a real friend to the poor!' And he told them the story of his encounter with the Doctor. Agnese was flabbergasted by the wretched outcome of her plan, but began to argue that the advice had been good in itself, and that Renzo must have made some mistake in carrying it out. But Lucia put a stop to this discussion by announcing that she hoped she'd found a better source of help. Renzo gave the new suggestion a warm welcome as the unfortunate and afflicted always will.

'But if the good father can't get us out of trouble', he said, 'I will, one way or another.'

The two women advised calm, patience and foresight.

'Father Cristoforo will be here tomorrow for sure,' said Lucia, 'and see if he doesn't find a way out of it which we poor folk would never think of at all.'

'I hope so too,' said Renzo, 'but anyway, I'll either get my rights myself, or make sure they're given to me. This is a world with justice in it after all.'

These gloomy discussions, together with all the coming and going mentioned earlier, had taken up the whole day, and it was beginning to get dark.

'Good night,' said Lucia sadly to Renzo, who could not make up his mind to go home.

'Good night,' said Renzo, more sadly still.

'One of the saints will help us,' said Lucia. 'We must be prudent, and resign ourselves to what's happened.'

Her mother added some more advice of the same kind, and the young man went off, with a storm raging in his heart, and saying the same strange words over and over to himself: 'This is a world with justice in it after all!'

For it is true enough that when a man is overcome by grief he no longer knows what he is saying.

Chapter 4

THE sun was not yet fully above the horizon when Father Cristoforo left the monastery of Pescarenico to climb up to the cottage where they were waiting for him. Pescarenico[1] is a little hamlet on the left bank of the Adda – we might almost say on the left shore of the lake – not far from the bridge. It is a small group of houses, mostly belonging to fishermen, with nets of various kinds hung here and there to dry. The monastery stood – and its shell still stands – a little apart, on the other side of the main road from Lecco to Bergamo, across which it faces the entrance to the hamlet. The sky was perfectly clear that morning, and as the sun rose behind the mountains its rays first struck the peaks opposite, and then the brightness travelled down the slopes, spreading rapidly out, and lit up the valley. An autumnal breeze blew through the mulberry trees, detaching the withered leaves, which fluttered a few yards before falling to earth. On both sides were vineyards, with vines still stretched between their supports; their leaves shone brightly, in various shades of red. Strips of freshly ploughed land showed up black and sharply defined among the whitish fields of stubble, which were glistening with dew. The scene was a cheerful one in itself, but every human figure that appeared in it saddened the eye and the heart. From time to time ragged and emaciated beggars came into view, some of whom had grown old in the trade, while others were now driven to it for the first time by necessity. They walked quietly past Father Cristoforo, with a respectful look; and though they could expect nothing from him, since a Capuchin never handled money, they gave him a grateful bow, thinking of the alms they had received, or hoped to receive, from the monastery. The workers in the fields presented an even sadder picture. Some were sowing; but they cast the seed thinly, sparingly and grudgingly, like a man taking a

1. See map on page 16, and notes on facing page. Translator's note.

risk with something he can ill afford to lose. Others were digging the earth, with obvious effort, turning the sods over painfully with their spades. A half-starved girl was tugging a desperately bony cow along on a rope, looking for pasture; the child scanned the ground in front of her, and bent quickly down from time to time to deprive the brute of some herb which hunger had taught her to recognize as food on which men too could live, and which she could take home for her family. With every step that he took, these sights further saddened the friar, who had set out with an unhappy presentiment that the story he was to hear was one of tragedy.

But why was he so concerned about Lucia? Why had he set off so promptly, at the first word from her, as if he had received a summons from his Provincial? And who was Father Cristoforo in the first place? We shall clearly have to answer all these questions.

Father Cristoforo of —, then, was a man in his late fifties. His shaven head – bare except for a circlet of hair round the scalp in the Capuchin manner – raised itself from time to time with a movement which betrayed a restless pride, but sank again at once into its habitual position of humility. The long white beard which covered his cheeks and his chin gave additional relief to the striking contours of the upper part of his face, marked by an abstinence, habitual for many years, which had added gravity to his features without making them less expressive. His eyes were deeply sunk, and were generally bent upon the ground; but sometimes they blazed with a sudden flame. They reminded you of a pair of high-spirited horses in the hands of a driver whose control they know very well they cannot break; but they still allow themselves an occasional buck, which they pay for at once with a good jab on the bit.

Father Cristoforo had not always been like that; nor had his name always been Cristoforo. He had been baptized Lodovico. His father was a rich merchant of — (all these dashes are due to the prudence of my anonymous author), who had found himself, towards the end of his life, very comfortably off, with only the one son to provide for, and had decided to retire from business and live the life of a gentleman.

In his new-found idleness he began to feel deeply ashamed of all the time he had spent doing something useful in this world. It became an obsession with him, and he studied every possible manner of making people forget that he had been in trade; he would have liked to forget it himself. But the shop, with its bales, its account books, and its yard measure, forced its way into his memories like the ghost of Banquo appearing to Macbeth, even at the most splendid dinners, even among the applause of parasites. And it is hard to imagine the trouble those poor wretches had to take to avoid any word which might seem to refer to the earlier status of their host. At the end of dinner one day, for example, at a moment of the purest and most genuine gaiety, when it was hard to say whether the host was happier at having paid for the meal or the guests at having eaten it, he began in a friendly, superior way to tease one of the company, who was one of the pleasantest gluttons you could wish to meet. Without a shadow of malice – with childlike simplicity, in fact – the guest replied to the chaff with the words: 'I'll turn a deaf ear to that; I'm a long-suffering sort of merchant.' He himself was horrified by the sound of the last word, as soon as it passed his lips. He looked uncertainly at his host's face, and saw it cloud over; both of them would have liked to unsay what had been said, but there was no chance of that. Every one of the other guests tried to think of a way to end this embarrassing situation and create a diversion; but while they were racking their brains their tongues were silent, and the sudden hush made the embarrassment all the more noticeable. Everyone tried to avoid the eyes of his fellow guests; everyone knew that all others' minds were full of a single thought, which all of them wanted to hide. There was no more enjoyment to be had that day; and the tactless guest – 'unlucky' is perhaps a fairer word – was not invited again. So Lodovico's father passed his last years in continual torment, always afraid of mockery. He never reflected that the act of selling has nothing more ludicrous about it than the act of buying, nor that the profession he now found so shameful was one which he had practised in public for many years without a single qualm. He gave his son the education of a nobleman of those days, as far as was permitted by law and custom; he provided him with teachers of knightly exercises and literature; and finally he died, leaving him a rich young man.

Lodovico had acquired the habits of a nobleman; and the flatterers among whom he had grown up had accustomed him to respectful treatment. But when he wanted to mingle on equal terms with the leading men of the city, he found that things were very different. He could see that if he wanted to live in their society, as he would have wished, he would have to take a fresh course of lessons in patience, submission, perpetual inferiority and the act of swallowing continual snubs. This agreed neither with his education nor his character. He indignantly absented himself from their company. But he was sorry to stay apart from them; he felt that they were really his natural companions and only wished that they would be more amenable. Fascinated and resentful at the same time, he was unable to live on familiar terms with them, yet wanted to keep up some sort of contact. He began to compete with them in ostentation and magnificence, paying in good cash for hatred, envy and ridicule. He had an honest yet vehement nature, which soon involved him in more serious struggles. He felt a spontaneous and genuine horror of bullying and foul play – all the more so when he saw the privileged position of those who indulged most constantly in these things. They were in fact the very men with whom he was already on the worst terms for the other reason. To quieten all these various passions at once – or perhaps to give them a run for their money – he eagerly took the side of the weak and oppressed, and prided himself on putting a spoke in a bully's wheel here, interfering in a dispute there, inviting a quarrel on another occasion; so that he gradually began to set himself up as a protector of the down-trodden and a righter of wrongs. This was an onerous task, and there is no need to inquire whether poor Lodovico had his share of bitter enemies, difficult duties and painful anxieties. In addition to his struggle against external foes he was much troubled by an internal conflict; for the execution of his more successful exploits (not to mention his failures) involved the use of tricks and acts of violence which his conscience could not subsequently

79

approve. He had to keep a good number of bravoes around him. Both for the sake of his own safety and to have the most effective aid for his plans, he had to recruit the most desperate characters among them – who were also the most wicked. He had to consort with blackguards, out of love of justice. He was often discouraged after some unsuccessful enterprise, or uneasy about some imminent danger, or tired of having to remain permanently on his guard, or disgusted by the company he had to keep, or worried about the future as both his good works and his desperate deeds made daily inroads into his fortune. More than once in fact the idea of going into a monastery had flitted through his mind; it was the commonest way of getting out of an impossible situation in those days. The idea might well have remained no more than a recurrent fancy for the rest of his life, but it was suddenly converted into a resolution by an incident more serious than anything which had happened to him before.

He was walking one day along one of the streets of his native city with two bravoes at his heels; by his side walked a man called Cristoforo, who had started as an assistant in the family shop, and, when it was closed down, had become steward of the household to Lodovico's father. He was a man of about fifty who had been devoted to Lodovico for many years, having known him since he was a baby. Partly in salary and partly in gifts Lodovico provided him with not only a livelihood but the means to keep and bring up a large family.

Lodovico saw a certain nobleman appear in the distance, an arrogant man and a professional bully, to whom he had never spoken in his life, but who nourished a cordial hatred for him, which he returned no less heartily. For one of the privileges this world offers us is the right to hate and be hated by those whom we have never met. The other man, with four bravoes behind him, came straight on with arrogant stride, head high and mouth fixed in an expression of disdainful pride. They were both walking within arm's length of the wall. But Lodovico (and this is the important point) had it on his right hand; and this, according to a custom of the time, meant that he did not have to leave the shelter of the wall and give way to any man in the world. This was a right – to misuse an ill-treated word – to which great importance was attached in those days. But the other man held that this right belonged to him as a nobleman, and that it was for Lodovico to step aside into the middle of the road – a view based upon another custom of the time. As often happens to this day, two contrary customs were both in force together without any ruling to say which ought to prevail; and this created the opening for a quarrel every time an obstinate man met another of the same stamp. So the two men drew closer and closer, keeping up against the wall like figures from an animated bas-relief. When they were face to face, the noble-man scowled imperiously, with head held high, looked Lodovico over, and said 'Make way!' in a tone suited to the words.

'Make way yourself,' said Lodovico. 'The right of way is mine.'

'The right of way is always mine with people of your sort.'

'It would be, if the arrogance of your sort made the rules for us.'

Both sets of bravoes had halted behind their masters, glaring at each other with hand on dagger, ready for battle. A crowd began to collect, keeping its distance, and waiting to see what would happen. The presence of spectators increased the two men's obsession with the point of honour.

'Out of my way, you cowardly huckster, or I shall have to give you a lesson in respect for your betters.'

'When you call me a coward, you lie.'

'When you call me a liar, you lie.' (This was the form of words sanctioned by custom.) 'And if you were of noble birth, as I am,' he went on, 'my sword would soon show which of us is lying.'

'You seem to have found an excellent excuse not to back up the insolence of your words with any kind of action.'

'Throw this swine in the gutter,' said the other, turning to his own supporters.

'We'll see about that!' said Lodovico, taking a quick pace back and putting his hand to his sword.

'You presumptuous fool!' cried his opponent drawing. 'When this blade has been stained with your ignoble blood, I shall break it across my knee.'

Then they flew at each other, and the retainers dashed forward to defend their masters. It was an unequal contest, both in numbers, and because Lodovico was trying primarily to defend himself and disarm his opponent, rather than to kill him, whereas the nobleman was bent on having blood at any price. Soon Lodovico had a stab wound from a bravo's dagger in his left arm, and a cut across one cheek. His principal enemy was charging in to finish him off, when Cristoforo, seeing the desperate plight of his master, came in with his dagger against the nobleman, who turned all his wrath against the steward, and ran him through with his sword. Nearly out of his mind at this sight, Lodovico thrust his sword into the belly of the murderer, who fell dying at almost the same instant as the unfortunate Cristoforo. The nobleman's retainers saw that it was all over, and took to their heels in a battered state; Lodovico's bravoes, who had also suffered a good deal of damage, saw there was nothing more for them to do and did not want to get caught up in the throng of people who were already hastening to the scene, so they made off in the opposite direction. Except for the two dismal companions stretched at his feet, Lodovico was left alone, in the middle of a crowd.

'What happened, then?' 'There's one down, anyway.' – 'Two, I think.' – 'Someone's let the daylight into his belly.' – 'Who's been killed?' – 'It's that swaggering fellow.' – 'Mother of God, what a massacre!' – 'He asked for it.' – 'It's a quick way of paying a lot of old debts.' – 'This one's done for too.' – 'What a blow that must have been!' – 'It looks like a serious business.'

'Look at that other poor devil!' – 'Mercy on us, what a sight!' 'Help him, somebody!' – 'He's dying, too.' – 'Just look at him, pouring with blood all over!' – 'Run for it, sir! Don't wait for them to come and arrest you!'

These last words emerged as the outstanding theme of the confused buzz of remarks coming from the crowd, and expressed the general view of its members – who, as it happened, were able to provide help as well as advice. All this had occurred near a Capuchin church, and, as everyone knows, such buildings were then places of refuge, out of bounds to the watch, and to the whole complex of men and institutions which was collectively known as the Law. Almost unconscious, the wounded killer was half led, half carried to the church, and the friars accepted him from the hands of the crowd, who vouched for him by saying – 'He's a decent man who's just done in an arrogant bully; it was in self-defence, and he didn't have any choice.'

Lodovico had never killed a man before. Though murder was so common in those days that everyone was used to the news of violent death and the sight of blood, the impression made on him by the spectacle of the man who had died for him, and the man who had died at his hands, was something novel and indescribable – a revelation of feelings he had never known before. To see his enemy fall to the ground, to see the change in his face, as it passed in a moment from fury and menace to the vanquished, solemn peace of death, was an experience which transformed the soul of the killer. When he was dragged into the monastery, he hardly knew where he was or what was happening; later he came to, and found himself in a bed in the infirmary in the hands of the brother surgeon – there was generally one in every Capuchin monastery. The monk was putting plasters and bandages on the two wounds he had received in the fight. One of the fathers, whose special duty it was to tend the dying, and who often had to perform this service in the streets, had been summoned at once to the scene of the clash. A few minutes later, he returned and went into the infirmary. He came up to Lodovico's bed, and said: 'Be comforted, my son; at least he made a good end. He charged me to beg your forgiveness, and to assure you that he had forgiven you.'

These words restored poor Lodovico to complete consciousness, and revived in keener and clearer form the confused feelings which had thronged into his mind: sorrow for his friend, horror and remorse at the blow he himself had struck, and at the same time an anguished compassion for the man he had killed.

'What about the other man?' he asked the friar anxiously.

'The other man was dead when I got there.'

Meanwhile the area around the monastery, and the roads

leading to it, were thronged with curious sightseers. Then the watch arrived, dispersed the crowds, and took up its position – some way from the monastery gate, but so placed that no one could get out without being seen. A brother of the dead man with two cousins and an elderly uncle also arrived, all armed from head to foot, with a large escort of bravoes. They prowled around the monastery, their expression and gestures showing a lowering hatred of the sightseers, who did not dare to utter the words 'it serves him right', though they could be read on every face.

As soon as Lodovico had had time to gather his thoughts, he called a brother confessor, and asked him to find Cristoforo's widow, to beg her to forgive him for being the cause – the unwilling cause – of the disaster, and to assure her that he would make her family his own responsibility. When he went on to reflect on his own affairs, the idea of becoming a monk, which had passed through his mind several times previously, sprang up again, much more urgent and serious than ever before. It struck him that God himself had pointed the way, and given him a sign of his will, by granting him refuge in a monastery at that particular time; and in a moment his mind was made up. He called the Father Superior, and told him of his decision. The answer was that he should beware of resolutions taken in haste, but that if he persisted in his intention he would not be refused. Then he sent for a lawyer, and dictated a deed of gift making over all his remaining property (which was still a considerable fortune) to Cristoforo's family: a substantial sum to the widow, as if he were giving her a marriage settlement, and the rest to the eight children that Cristoforo had left behind him.

Lodovico's decision was most welcome to his hosts, whom he had put in an awkward situation. To expel him from the monastery and expose him to the mercy of the law – in other words, to the revenge of his enemies – was a course which they could not even consider. That would have been to renounce their privileges, to discredit the monastery in the eyes of the public, to invite the censure of all the Capuchins in the world for having connived at the violation of rights common to all of them, and to draw down the wrath of all the ecclesiastical authorities who regarded themselves as the protectors of those rights. On the other hand, the family of the dead nobleman was a powerful one in its own right, and stronger still through its connections; and it had resolved upon revenge, and announced that anyone who got in the way would be treated as an enemy. We are not told that they felt a very profound sorrow at the death of their relative, nor even that a single tear was shed for him by any of the family; we merely learn that they all had a fervent desire to get his killer into their clutches, dead or alive. By putting on the habit of a Capuchin, Lodovico solved the whole problem. He was making amends, in a certain sense; he was imposing a form of penitence on himself; he was implicitly admitting that the blame was his; he was withdrawing from every kind of struggle. He was, in fact, in the position of an enemy who lays down his arms. If they liked, the relations of the dead man could believe that he had become a monk out of despair, or boast that he had done so in terror of their displeasure. And, anyway, to reduce a man to give away all his possessions, to shave his head, to walk barefoot, to sleep on a pallet and to beg his bread might seem a sufficient punishment, even to the most self-important offended party.

With tranquil humility the Father Superior paid a visit to the brother of the dead man; and after many protestations of respect for the illustrious family of the deceased, and of his wish to oblige them in anything that lay within his power, he spoke of Lodovico's repentance and of his monastic resolution. He neatly suggested that this was something which should satisfy the family, and then gently implied, with even more tactful skill, that this was what had to happen anyway. The brother had many furious things to say about this, and the Capuchin let him get them off his chest, merely saying from time to time: 'You have good reason for your grief.' The brother made it clear that his family would in any case make sure of obtaining some further satisfaction; and the Capuchin, whatever he thought of this, made no protest. Finally the nobleman imposed the condition that his brother's killer must leave the city at once. The Father Superior had already decided on this step, and replied that it would be done, leaving the man free to think, if it pleased him, that his threats had prevailed; and so the whole matter was cleared up. The family were happy to come out of the dispute with honour; the friars were happy to be able to preserve a man's life and their own privileges without making any enemies; the connoisseurs of points of chivalrous etiquette were pleased to see an affair terminated in so praiseworthy a fashion; the common people were happy to see a popular man out of trouble, and were impressed by his remarkable conversion; but the happiest man of all, even in the midst of his sorrow, was Lodovico himself, who was now beginning a life of expiation and service, which might not be able to undo the effects of his crime, but could at least make reparation for it, and blunt the intolerable sting of remorse. The thought that his resolution might be attributed to fear afflicted him for a moment, but he consoled himself quickly with the reflection that this unfair judgement could also be regarded as a punishment for his sin, and as a means of expiating it. And so he put on the habit at thirty years of age. According to custom he had to give up his old name and take a new one. He chose one which would serve as a continual reminder of the sin he had to expiate, and called himself Brother Cristoforo.

As soon as the ceremony of ordination was over, the Father Superior informed him that he must serve his novitiate at —, sixty miles away, and that he must leave the following day. The novice bowed deeply and asked a favour.

'Before I leave this city, father, where I have shed the blood of a man, before I turn my back on a family I have cruelly wronged, I beg you at least to allow me to make amends for the insult I have offered them, and to show my regret that I cannot make good the harm that I have done, by begging the forgiveness of the dead man's brother, in order to lift the burden of hatred for myself from his soul, if Heaven blesses my intention.'

The Father Superior considered that this was both good in itself and a further step towards a complete reconciliation between the family and the monastery. He went straight to the house of the offended nobleman and put Brother Cristoforo's request before him. On hearing so unusual a suggestion, he felt not only amazement but a fresh access of rage; yet there was a touch of satisfaction in it too. After a moment's thought, he replied 'Let him come tomorrow', and named an hour for the visit. The Father Superior returned to the novice and told him that his wish had been granted.

The nobleman reflected that the more solemn and conspicuous the amends were the more his credit would rise with the rest of the family, and also with the public. To use one of our elegant modern expressions, it would make a fine chapter in the family history. He quickly passed the word around all his relations that, if they would graciously be pleased to honour him with a visit – such was the language of the time – at noon on the following day, satisfaction would be made to the whole family. At noon the whole palace was thronged with nobles – men and women, old and young. Heavy capes, high-plumed hats, great dangling swords swirled and intermingled, starched and pleated ruffs moved in solemn deliberation, elaborately patterned gowns trailed an uneasy way through the crowd. The anterooms, the courtyard and the street were alive with servants, pages, bravoes and sightseers. The friar saw all these preparations, and guessed the reason for them. He felt a touch of dismay, but a moment later he said to himself : 'It is right that it should be so – I killed him in the open street in the presence of many of his enemies. That was the public scandal, and this is the reparation.' With lowered eyes, and with his spiritual father at his side, he entered the door of that house, crossed the courtyard, amid a crowd which looked him up and down with unceremonious curiosity, went up the stairs and through a second throng, this time of nobles, who fell back and made way for him, and finally, watched by hundreds of eyes, he reached the presence of the master of the house. With his closest relatives around him, the noble stood upright in the middle of the room, chin thrust forward, eyes looking obliquely down at the floor, the hilt of his sword clasped in his left hand, while his right clutched the lapel of his cloak against his chest.

A man's face and manner can sometimes provide such a direct impression of what is in his heart – such a tangible model of it in fact – that a large crowd of spectators will all come to the same conclusion about him. Brother Cristoforo's face and manner proclaimed unmistakably to the assembled company that he had neither become a monk, nor exposed himself to this humiliation, out of fear for any man; and this began to win them over. When he caught sight of the bereaved nobleman, he quickened his pace, knelt down at the man's feet, crossed his hands over his chest, bowed his shaven head, and said 'I am the killer of your brother. God knows I would gladly restore his life to him at the cost of my own; but all I can do is to offer you an ineffective and belated request for forgiveness. I beseech you, for the love of God, to grant it to me.'

Every eye was fixed on the novice and the man to whom he spoke; every ear tensely awaited the reply. When Brother Cristoforo had finished, the whole room was filled with a murmur of compassionate respect. The nobleman, whose stance was meant to suggest strained condescension and suppressed wrath, was shaken by his words. He bent over the kneeling figure. 'Stand up,' he said in a trembling voice. 'It was a crime . . . a sad thing . . . but then seeing the habit you now wear . . . and not only the habit, but you yourself, and what you have done today . . . stand up, father . . . my brother . . . I can't deny it, he was a gentleman . . . a man of impetuous nature, quick temper. But everything that happens is the will of God. There's no more to say . . . But, father, it's not right for you to stay in that position.' And he took him by the arm, and raised him to his feet. Standing with bowed head, Brother Cristoforo replied: 'So now I can hope that you have forgiven me in your heart! And whose pardon may I not hope to receive, when I have yours? . . . If only I could hear the word "forgiveness" from your own lips!'

'Forgiveness?' said the nobleman. 'There's no need of that now, surely? But since it is your wish – why, yes, I forgive you, from my heart. I forgive you, and so do we all . . .'

'So do we all!' cried the others, with one accord. The friar's face shone with an expression of grateful happiness, through which they could still read a humble and profound awareness of a sin which could not be wiped out by the forgiveness of man. Overcome by the sight, and carried away by the general emotion, the nobleman threw his arms around him and they exchanged the kiss of peace.

Cries of 'Well done! That's right! Well done!' rang out from all over the room. Everybody came forward, and gathered around the friar. Servants entered with great trays of refreshments. The nobleman made his way up to Brother Cristoforo again – he was showing signs of wishing to leave – and said: 'Father, please take something. Give me this proof of your friendship.' And he was going to serve him first of all the company; but the friar stepped back in an attitude of amicable resistance, and said: 'These things are not for me; but never let it be said that I refused your gift. I am about to set out on a journey; pray be so kind as to send for a loaf of bread, so that I can say that I have enjoyed your charity, eaten your bread and had a token of your forgiveness.'

Deeply moved, the nobleman gave the necessary order. A footman in full livery at once brought in a loaf on a silver tray, and presented it to the friar. He accepted it with thanks, and put it in his scrip. Then he took his leave; he embraced the master of the house once more, and all the guests who were standing near enough to be able to monopolize him for a moment exchanged embraces with him as well, so that he had some difficulty in getting away. He also had quite a struggle in the anterooms, to escape from the servants, and even the bravoes, who kissed the hem of his garment, the ends of the rope that served him as a belt, and his hood. Finally he found himself in the street, and started off in something of a triumphal procession, with a crowd of the common people around him, towards one of the city gates, from which he set out on the long walk to the place where he was to serve his novitiate.

The dead man's brother, and the rest of the family, had expected to savour the dismal pleasures of satisfied pride that day, instead of which they found themselves full of the serene happiness that comes from forgiveness and good will. The assembled company stayed together for some time in an unusually friendly and cheerful atmosphere. The talk was of a kind for which none of them had been prepared in advance.

The obtaining of satisfaction, the punishment of arrogance, the outcome of desperate deeds were replaced as topics of conversation by the praises of the new friar, of reconciliation and of meekness. One noble, who would normally have recounted for the fiftieth time how his father, Count Muzio, had put that notorious braggart the Marquis Stanislao in his place on a certain famous occasion, found himself talking about the admirable patience and penitence shown by one Brother Simone, who had died many years before. When his guests left, the master of the house, still deeply moved, went over the whole thing again in his mind, marvelling at what he had heard, and what he himself had said. 'The devil take that friar!' he muttered between his teeth (for we must report his exact words), 'the devil take that friar! If he'd stayed there on his knees a second longer damned if I wouldn't have found myself apologizing to him, for his murder of my brother!'

The chronicle expressly records that from that day forward the nobleman became a little less hasty and a little more gentle in his ways.

Father Cristoforo strode on feeling an inward peace he had never known since that terrible day, to the expiation of which the rest of his life must be dedicated. Complete silence was prescribed for novices; but he kept the rule without noticing it, so absorbed was he in the thought of the labours, the privations and the humiliations he would undergo to pay off his debt. At dinner time he stopped at a benefactor's house, and ate some of the bread of forgiveness with a sort of voluptuous pleasure. But he set a piece of it aside, and put it back in his scrip, to keep as a perpetual reminder.

We do not propose to record the detail of his monastic life; we will merely say that his two official duties were those of preaching and of tending the dying, which he carried out willingly and conscientiously, but that he never missed a chance of performing two other duties, which he had set himself – the composing of quarrels and the protection of the oppressed. Unknown to Father Cristoforo an old habit had, to some extent, found its way back into his heart, together with a small remnant of his old combative spirit, which neither humiliation nor fasting had wholly been able to extinguish. His language was generally humble and measured; but in any question of injury to justice or truth, the man would suddenly be animated by all his original fiery vigour, which, reinforced and subtly modified by the solemn emphasis he had learned in the pulpit, gave a singular character to his speech. Not only his face, but his whole manner, showed evidence of a long struggle between a passionate, touchy nature and a strong will, in which the will generally prevailed, remained permanently on guard, and drew its guidance from the highest motives and most lofty inspiration. A friend and brother monk who knew him well once compared him to one of those words, too crudely expressive in their natural state, which respectable men will sometimes use at times of overpowering passion in a mutilated form, with the change of one or two letters, and which retain something of their primitive force even when travestied in this manner.

If Father Cristoforo had received an appeal for help from some poor girl he had never met, who was in the same trouble as Lucia, he would have answered her call at once. He did so the more readily for Lucia, because he knew and admired her sweet and innocent nature, and because he was already deeply concerned about the danger in which she stood, and filled with holy indignation at the ignoble persecution she was suffering. Besides this he had given her advice – the advice to say nothing and hush the matter up, as the lesser of two evils – and now he was afraid that his counsels had produced some ill effect. So he felt not only the anxiety of Christian love, which was part of his nature, but that special self-questioning anguish which often troubles good men.

But we have taken so long over telling the good father's story that he has reached the cottage and is standing at the door; the women have stood up, dropping the handle of the creaking spinning-wheel which they were turning, and said with one voice: 'Oh, Father Cristoforo! Bless you for coming!'

Chapter 5

FATHER CRISTOFORO stood for a moment upright in the doorway. His first glance at the women showed him that his presentiment was not unfounded. He tilted his head back and his beard forward, and spoke in the special tone of voice that expects an unhappy answer. 'Why have you called me, my children?' he said. Lucia burst into tears. Her mother began to apologize for having presumed to trouble him, but the friar advanced into the room, sat down on a three-legged stool, and cut these formalities short. 'Calm yourself, my poor daughter,' he said to Lucia; 'And you,' he went on, turning to Agnese, 'you tell me what's happened.' While the good lady told her sad story to the best of her ability, the friar went pale with anger. He raised his eyes to heaven, he stamped impatiently, and when the story was over he covered his face with his hands and exclaimed, 'How long, dear Lord, how long must this ... ?' But without finishing his sentence, he turned back to them and said : 'Poor women ! God has visited you. Poor Lucia !'

'You won't desert us, will you, father?' sobbed Lucia.

'Desert you?' he replied. 'How could I ever ask God for anything for myself again if I deserted you in this state, when he has entrusted you to my care? Do not lose heart. He will help you; he sees everything; he knows how to make use even of a worthless fellow like myself to bring confusion to a ... Come now, we must consider what can be done.'

With these words he set his left elbow on his knee, leant his forehead against his left hand, and grasped beard and chin in the other hand as if to hold all the powers of his mind firmly together. But the most careful consideration did nothing but bring out more clearly the urgent and complex nature of the problem, and the scarcity, uncertainty and danger of the possible solutions. – Should I try and put a little shame into Don Abbondio, and make him realize how far he is falling short of his duty? But shame and duty mean nothing to him when he's frightened. Should I try to frighten him myself? But what have I got to frighten him with that'll impress him more than the prospect of a shot in the back? Should I report the whole thing to the Cardinal Archbishop, and invoke his authority? It's a slow process, and what would happen in the meantime? And what would happen afterwards – would it really make much difference to that man, even if the poor innocent girl were married? Who knows what lengths he'll go to? And how can I oppose him? Oh! thought the poor friar, if only I could get the support of the friars in my own monastery, or our brothers in Milan! But this is a special case; they'd all desert me. Don Rodrigo poses as a friend to the monastery; he makes out that he's a supporter of the Capuchins. Why, his bravoes have come to us for asylum more than once. I'd be on my own this time. I'd get a reputation for being an impatient, intriguing, trouble-making fellow. I might even make things worse for the poor girl by trying to do something for her, at the wrong time.

Having weighed the pros and cons of every possible course, he decided it would be best to confront Don Rodrigo himself, and try to make him give up his despicable intentions, by supplication or by invoking the terrors of the world to come – and the terrors of this world too, if possible. At the very worst, he thought, I'll get a clearer idea just how determined he is in this dirty plan of his, and find out more about what he means to do. It'll help me to see what to do next.

While the friar was turning all this over in his mind, Renzo appeared in the doorway – for various reasons, which are not hard to guess, he could not keep away from the house. But when he saw Father Cristoforo deep in thought, and the women signalling to him not to disturb the good friar, he stopped just outside the door in silence. When Father Cristoforo lifted his head to tell the women what he had decided, he caught sight of Renzo, and greeted him in a manner which expressed a long-standing affection, with the added warmth that comes from compassion.

'Have they told you about it then, father?' said Renzo, his voice breaking a little.

'They have, alas, and that's why I am here.'

'What do you think about that swine?'

'What do you expect me to say? He's not here to listen to my words; what's the use of saying what I think of him? One thing I will say though, Renzo, and I say it to you; trust in God, and God will not abandon you.'

'May his blessing light on your words!' exclaimed the young man. 'You're not one of the sort that always think the poor are in the wrong. But what about the curé? What about the lawyer who's so fond of lost causes?'

'Don't keep on turning things over in your mind which can only distress you for nothing. I'm just a poor friar; but I'll say again to you what I've just said to the women. I may not be able to do much; but I'll do what I can for you, and I'll never desert you.'

'Oh, you're different from the friends of this world! A big-mouthed lot they are! You wouldn't believe what they were ready to do for me, when things were going well! They were ready to die for me; to back me up against the devil himself. If I'd an enemy, I'd only to say his name, and he'd soon have breathed his last. And now, you should just see how they're all finding excuses . . .'

At this moment he looked up and saw a very disapproving look on Father Cristoforo's face, which made him realize he had said the wrong thing. Then he got into rather a tangle trying to put it right. 'What I meant was – I don't mean anything like . . . you see, what I meant was . . .'

'What did you mean? I can see you've been doing your best to spoil what I was going to do for you, even before I've begun! Just as well you've been disillusioned so quickly. So you've been trying to find friends to help you – and I can imagine what sort of friends too! They couldn't have done anything for you, even if they'd wanted to. And at the same time you've been doing your best to lose the only Friend who can and will help you. Don't you know that God is the friend of all those in trouble who put their trust in him? Don't you know that the weak gain nothing by showing their teeth? Or if they do . . .' – here he seized Renzo's arm in a powerful grasp; his expression, without

94

losing any of its authority, took on an air of solemn contrition; he lowered his eyes, and spoke in a slow voice, with a subterranean quality – 'if they do gain by it, they pay a most terrible price for the gain. Renzo! Will you put your trust in me? No, not in me, wretched little creature, insignificant little friar that I am – will you put your trust in God?'

'Yes,' said Renzo, 'I will. God is our only refuge.'

Lucia sighed deeply, as if a great burden had been lifted from her back, and Agnese said: 'Well done, Renzo!'

'Listen, my children,' said the friar. 'I will go and talk to the man today. If God touches his heart, and gives power to my words, well and good; if not, he will help us to find some other way. While I'm away, stay quietly indoors, don't gossip, and don't attract attention. You'll see me again this evening, or tomorrow morning at the latest.'

He cut short their thanks and their blessings, and left them. First he went to the monastery, where he arrived in time to take his part in singing sext. Then he dined and set out at once for the den of the beast he had resolved to try and tame.

Don Rodrigo's mansion[1] stood in isolation like a watch-tower, on top of one of the small peaks which add height and variety to the view along that side of the lake. Besides this hint our anonymous author (who would have been better advised to tell us the name of the place right out) indicates that it was about three miles from the village where Renzo and Lucia lived, but higher up and about four miles from the monastery. At the foot of the peak, looking out to the south over the lake, was a small group of hovels where Don Rodrigo's peasants lived – the little capital of his little kingdom. No one who walked through the hamlet could fail to form a clear idea of the nature and the customs of the place. Wherever a door had been left open, so that you could see into the ground-floor rooms, muskets, blunderbusses, mattocks, rakes, straw hats and hairnets were hanging higgledy-piggledy on the walls. The people you met were big, powerful, surly fellows, with great quiffs thrown back over their heads and secured with a hairnet; or old men who had lost

1. See map on page 16, and notes on facing page. Translator's note.

95

their fangs, but looked ready to gnash their gums on the slightest provocation; or women with rough masculine faces, whose burly arms could be used in support of a scolding tongue when necessary. Even the children playing in the road had something arrogant and challenging about their looks and their movements.

The friar crossed the village, climbed up a winding path and came out on to a small open space in front of the mansion. The main doors were shut, which meant that the master was at dinner, and did not wish to be disturbed. The windows overlooking the road were small and few in number. The shutters that covered them had rotted over the years, and were hanging from their hinges. But the windows were all protected by heavy iron bars, and those on the ground floor were so high from the ground that a man standing on a companion's shoulders could hardly have reached them. Everything was very silent, and a passer-by might have thought the house was empty, but for four figures – two alive and two dead – which were symmetrically grouped outside it and indicated that it was occupied. Two huge vultures, with outstretched wings and dangling skulls were nailed to the great doors, one on each side, one featherless and eaten away by the passage of time, the other newly dead and fully feathered; and two bravoes, sprawling on benches to right and left of the doors, were on guard, waiting to be called to dine on the remains of their master's dinner. Father Cristoforo halted and stood there in the attitude of a man prepared to wait, but one of the bravoes got up and said: 'Come in, father, come in. We don't keep Capuchins waiting in this place. We're good friends of the monastery. I've been there myself, when the air outside wasn't too healthy, and if you people hadn't opened the door then, things wouldn't have gone well for me.' He banged the door a couple of times with the knocker. The sound was immediately answered by the baying of mastiffs and the yapping of smaller dogs. Presently an old servant appeared, muttering between his teeth; but when he saw the friar, he bowed deeply, cuffed and scolded the dogs into silence, took. him into a narrow courtyard, and shut the door. Then he led the way into a big room, where he stopped and looked at him with respectful amazement, and said: 'Aren't you Father Cristoforo ... Father Cristoforo of Pescarenico?'

'I am.'

'And you've come here?'

'You can see I have, surely, my good fellow.'

'You must have come to do good ... Doing good,' he muttered, as he set himself in motion again, 'doing good ... After all, that's something you can do anywhere ... anywhere at all.'

Passing through several more large, dark rooms, they finally reached the door of the banqueting hall, where they heard a loud, confused clatter of knives and forks, plates and glasses, and, louder still, the sound of discordant voices, apparently trying to shout each other down. The friar wanted to withdraw, and stood for a moment outside the door arguing with the servant, urging him to take him to some secluded corner where he could wait until the meal was over. But then the door opened. A certain Count Attilio – he was Don Rodrigo's cousin, and we have already spoken of him, without mentioning his name – happened to be sitting opposite the door. He noticed a shaven head and a long robe, and saw the good father's modest attempt to retire.

'No! no!' he cried. 'Don't run away from us, reverend father! Come in, come in!'

Don Rodrigo could not guess the exact object of this visit; but some confused presentiment made him feel that he could have done without it. But since Attilio, the thoughtless idiot, had shouted out like that, Don Rodrigo could hardly draw back.

'Yes, come in, come in, father,' he said.

The friar advanced, bowed low to the master of the house, and raised both hands in response to the greetings of the guests.

When an honest man meets a villain, most of us (not all, perhaps) like to picture him to ourselves standing with head held high, chest thrown out, a confident look in his eye, and a fluent command of his subject. In practice, however, many different circumstances must be present, some of which seldom arise in combination, before the honest man can take up this attitude. So we must not be surprised if Father Cristoforo, despite the support of a good conscience, a firm conviction of the justice of the cause he had come to sustain and a feeling of mixed horror and compassion towards Don Rodrigo, showed a touch of submissive respect when he found himself in the nobleman's presence. For Don Rodrigo sat there at the head of his table, in his own house, in his own kingdom, surrounded by friends, by deference, by the trappings of power, with an expression on his face well calculated to make anyone think twice before addressing even a humble supplication to him – let alone advice, admonition or reproof. On his right sat Count Attilio, his cousin, and, we need hardly add, his fellow-rake and fellow-bully, who had come from Milan to spend a few days in the country with him. On his left, round the corner of the table, sat the mayor,[2] whose face expressed profound respect, qualified by a certain air of self-assurance and pedantry. This was the magistrate whose job it was, in theory, to grant justice to Renzo Tramaglino and keep Don Rodrigo within the bounds of duty, as mentioned before. Opposite the mayor, in an attitude of the purest, the most abject respect, sat our old friend Dr Quibbler, in a black cloak, his nose even ruddier than usual. Opposite the two cousins sat two less distinguished guests, of whom we are only told that they did little but eat heartily, nod their heads, smile, and praise the wisdom of every remark made by one of their fellow-guests, provided no other fellow-guest disagreed with it.

'Give the father a seat,' said Don Rodrigo. A servant brought a chair, and Father Cristoforo sat down, apologizing for having come at an inconvenient time. 'I would very much like a private word with you, when you can spare the time, to discuss a matter of importance,' he added in a quieter voice, speaking close to Don Rodrigo's ear.

'Very well, we'll have a talk then,' said Don Rodrigo, 'but first of all – a drink for the good father!'

Father Cristoforo did his best to refuse, but Don Rodrigo, raising his voice above the general din, which had started up

2. This official's functions included control of the police. – Translator's note.

again, cried: 'No, by Heaven, you shall not do me this wrong. Never let it be said that a Capuchin has left this house without tasting a wine drawn from my cellar, nor that an impertinent creditor has ever left it without tasting a cudgel cut from my woods.' These words raised a general laugh, and led to a brief pause in the argument which was being so hotly debated by the company. A servant brought in a decanter on a salver, and a tall glass shaped like a chalice, and presented them to the friar. Not wishing to refuse so pressing an invitation from a man whose good will he needed so badly, the friar at once poured out some wine, and slowly began to sip it.

Count Attilio reopened the conversation. 'The authority of Tasso doesn't help your case at all, your worship,' he shouted at the mayor. 'In fact it's against you. That learned writer, that truly great man, knew every detail of the rules of chivalry, and when he describes the embassy of Argante, he tells us how the Saracen envoy asked the permission of the pious Godfrey before throwing down the challenge to the Christian knights.'

'But that's a detail, an insignificant detail,' shouted the mayor, no less loudly. 'It's a mere poetic ornament, because the bearer of a message is sacred in his own right, by the laws of the nations, or *jus gentium*. Without going so deeply into the matter, it's obvious from the proverb which says "messengers must never be blamed" – and proverbs, sir, are the garnered wisdom of mankind. And since the envoy said nothing in his own name, but merely presented the challenge in written form . . .'

'But can't you see that the envoy in the present case was a reckless idiot, who hadn't the least idea . . .'

'Gentlemen, gentlemen, kindly allow me to make a suggestion,' broke in Don Rodrigo, who did not want the thing to go too far. 'We'll ask Father Cristoforo to arbitrate, and we'll accept his decision.'

'Yes, yes – a brilliant idea!' said Count Attilio, to whom it seemed a very happy stroke to make a Capuchin judge a point of chivalry. But the mayor, who cared far more deeply about such things, preserved a strained silence, while his expression seemed to say: What a stupid, childish trick!

'From the little I heard just now,' said Father Cristoforo, 'I gather that the subject is not one I can be expected to understand.'

'You holy fathers always produce these modest excuses,' said Don Rodrigo, 'but I'm not going to let you off. Come, sir! We know very well that you weren't born in a hood, and that you're a man of experience in the world. Now then: listen to the questions.'

'The facts are these . . .' began Count Attilio, at the top of his voice.

'Let me tell the story, Attilio; I'm neutral, you know. Here it is then. A Spanish nobleman sends a challenge to a Milanese nobleman; the messenger finds the challenged man is not at home and hands the letter to his brother, who reads the challenge, and gives the messenger a couple of blows with a stick by way of answer. Now the question is . . .'

'The beating was well deserved and well applied,' shouted Count Attilio. 'It was a real inspiration.'

'A real inspiration of the devil,' said the mayor. 'To strike the sacred person of an envoy! Reverend father, tell us if that was worthy of a gentleman.'

'Yes, sir, it was worthy of a gentleman,' shouted the count, 'and let *me* tell you so, because I ought to know what befits a gentleman and what doesn't. If it had been a matter of fists, now that would be quite different; but a cudgel doesn't dirty your hands. What I don't understand is why a couple of weals on a ruffian's back should upset you so much.'

'Who mentioned backs or weals, my dear count? You put the most ridiculous things into my mouth – things which would never even cross my mind. I'm talking about characters, not about backs. Above all, I'm talking about the laws of nations. Now just tell me this, if you'll be so kind. When the *fetiales* were sent out by the Romans to carry challenges to other nations, did they ask permission before explaining their errand? And can you tell us a single author who mentions that a *fetialis* was ever beaten?'

'What have these ancient Roman officials to do with us? The Romans carried on as best they could, no doubt; but they were a long way behind ourselves. According to the laws of the only true chivalry, which is the chivalry of today, I say and maintain that a messenger who dares to put a challenge in the hand of a gentleman, without having first asked his permission, is a presumptuous fool, worthy not of sacred respect, but of a damned good thrashing.'

'Let's hear your answer to a bit of logical argument.'

'To hell with your logical argument!'

'No, but listen, listen ... To strike an unarmed man is a treacherous act; *atqui* the messenger *de quo* was unarmed; *ergo* ...'

'Steady on, your worship!'

'What do you mean, steady on?'

'I mean steady on. Whatever are you saying? Wounding a man with a sword from behind is a treacherous act, or giving him a shot in the back with a musket – though even there, in certain cases ... but let's stick to the subject of discussion. I admit that this may indeed be generally called a treacherous act – but not giving a ruffian a couple of knocks with a stick! The next thing will be that we'll have to give him fair warning – 'See! I am about to cudgel you!' – as we might tell a gentleman to put his hand to his sword. As for you, my dear Doctor, instead of simpering at me like that to show me you agree, why don't you back me up with a specimen of your eloquence, and help me to persuade this gentleman?'

'I, for my part,' said the Doctor, a little confused, 'I'm enjoying this erudite discussion; and I'm grateful to the happy chance that has provided the occasion for so brilliant a clash of wits. But it is not for me to give judgement; our noble host has already appointed an arbitrator, the reverend father here.'

'True enough,' said Don Rodrigo, 'but how do you expect the judge to give his verdict, when the litigants won't stop talking?'

'I'll be quiet,' said Count Attilio. The mayor tightened his lips, and raised his hand in a gesture of resignation.

'Thank Heaven for that! It's your turn to speak now, father,' said Don Rodrigo with a faintly mocking seriousness of manner.

'I've already made my excuses – I don't understand these things,' said Father Cristoforo, giving his glass back to a servant.

'Your excuses are inadequate,' said the two cousins. 'We insist on having your verdict.'

'In that case,' said the friar, 'my humble opinion would be that there should be no challenges, no messengers and no beatings.'

The guests looked at each other in amazement.

'That's absurd!' said Count Attilio. 'Forgive me for saying so, father, but that's absurd! Anyone can see that you don't know the world.'

'Who – Father Cristoforo?' said Don Rodrigo. 'Why make me repeat something we all know? He knows the world as well as you do, my dear cousin. Isn't that right, father? You served a full apprenticeship in worldly matters, didn't you?'

Instead of answering this affectionate question, the friar addressed a silent reminder to himself: These blows are falling on your back; remember that you did not come here for yourself, and that anything which affects only yourself is of no account.

'It may be so,' said Count Attilio; 'but Father ... what's the good father's name?'

'Father Cristoforo,' said several voices.

'But Father Cristoforo, most reverend Father Cristoforo, with principles like that, you'll turn the whole world upside down. No challenges! No beatings! it would be the end of the point of honour, the beginning of impunity for every ruffian in the land! It's a good thing that it can never happen.'

'Come on, Doctor,' said Don Rodrigo, still anxious to shift the discussion as far away from the two original contenders as possible, 'come on, Doctor, it's your turn to say something. You can make out a case for any man – let's see what sort of case you can make out for Father Cristoforo's opinion on this occasion.'

'To tell you the truth,' said the doctor, waving his fork in the air and turning towards the friar, 'I can't understand how Father Cristoforo, who combines the character of a perfect man of religion with that of a man of the world, can have failed to realize that, while his observation would have been sound, excellent and weighty if he had uttered it from the pulpit, it is, with all due respect, quite valueless as a contribution to a discussion on points of chivalry. The good father undoubtedly knows better than I do that everything is good in its own place and time; and I believe that on this occasion he has made use of a subterfuge to save himself from the embarrassment of having to give a proper verdict.'

What could anyone conceivably reply to an argument drawn from a wisdom which is ages old, and yet ever fresh and new? No answer was possible; and the friar made none.

But Don Rodrigo, to be rid of this discussion once and for all, decided to initiate a new one. 'By the way,' he said, 'I hear there's talk of a compromise at Milan.'

As the reader knows, there was a dispute that year over the succession to the duchy of Mantua. Vincenzo Gonzaga had died without leaving any legitimate issue, and the Duke of Nevers, his nearest relative, had taken possession of the territory. Louis XIII of France (or rather Cardinal Richelieu), backed the Duke of Nevers, who was his loyal supporter and a naturalized Frenchman. For precisely the same reasons, Philip IV of Spain (or rather Count d'Olivares, generally known as the Count–Duke) wanted the duke out of Mantua, and had mounted an attack against him. Again, the duchy of Mantua was a fief of the Holy Roman Empire; and so both the parties were trying the effect of intrigues, demands and threats on the Emperor Ferdinand II, the French endeavouring to make him proceed with the investiture of the new duke, while the Spaniards tried to induce him to withhold recognition, and perhaps even to help them to expel the duke from Mantua.

'I am not unwilling to believe', said Count Attilio, 'that compromise is possible. I have certain information . . .'

'Don't you believe it, my dear count,' broke in the mayor. 'Even living in an out-of-the-way spot like this, I have my way of knowing these things, because the commander of the Spanish garrison is kind enough to treat me as a friend, and he's very well informed, because his father is a member of the Count–Duke's household . . .'

'Let me tell you that in Milan I have occasion to speak every day with people of a very different stamp; and I have it on excellent authority that the Pope, in his great desire for peace, has put forward certain proposals . . .'

'Naturally, naturally; that always happens; his Holiness is doing his duty; a pope should always promote peace between Christian princes; but the Count-Duke has his own policy, and so . . . and so . . .'

' "And so, and so," indeed! Do you, my dear sir, know what the Emperor has in mind at this moment? Do you suppose that Mantua is the only place in the world? There are many other things to be taken in consideration. Do you know, for example, to what extent the Emperor can trust that Prince Valdistano or Vallistai, or whatever his name is?'

'The correct pronunciation in German is Vagliensteino,'[3] said the mayor, interrupting again. 'I've heard it several times from the Spanish garrison commander. But you needn't worry about that because . . .'

'Do you think I need your lessons, sir?' cried the count, but Don Rodrigo caught his eye in a way which clearly meant – as a favour to me, don't contradict him. So the count said no more, and the mayor, like a ship that has got clear of a sandbank, swept ahead on his eloquent course, with full sails.

'I'm not worried about Vagliensteino; the Count–Duke keeps an eye on everything everywhere; and if Vagliensteino wants to try anything on, he'll soon put him straight again by fair means or foul. He's got his eye on everything, as I just said, and he's got a long arm, and if he's got this idea in his head, which he has, and quite rightly too, like the great statesman he is, that he won't let the Duke of Nivers take root in Mantua, why, you'll find that the Duke of Nivers won't be able to, and Cardinal Riciliù will look like a fool. I'm sorry for the Cardinal, really I am, wanting to try his strength against a man like Count-Duke Olivares. I'd like to come back in two hundred years time and

3. 'Vagliensteino' – the mayor substitutes a Spanish mispronunciation of 'Wallenstein' for the Italian one used by the count. In his next speech, he makes further mistakes with the names 'Nevers' and 'Richelieu'. – Translator's note.

see what posterity says about his presumptuous ideas. Envy and ill will aren't enough, in this sort of thing; you need brains as well; and there's only one set of brains like the Count–Duke's in the world. The Count–Duke, gentlemen,' went on the mayor, still sailing with a fair wind, but beginning to feel a little surprised himself at the total absence of obstructions, 'the Count–Duke is an old fox – be it said with all due respect -- who can shake anybody off his trail; if he seems to break away to the right, you can be sure that he'll double back to the left; so that no one can ever claim to know his plans. Even the people who carry the plans out, even those who write his despatches, don't understand them at all. And I can say that I know what I'm talking about, because that worthy gentleman the garrison commander is kind enough to take me into his confidence . . . The Count–Duke himself, now, is just the opposite; he knows exactly what the people in every other court have got up their sleeve; and all those other politicians (there're some fine specimens among them too, you can't deny it!) can hardly form a plan, before the Count–Duke knows all about it, with that brilliant brain of his, and his secret channels of information, his spider's web all over the world. And poor Cardinal Riciliù scratches away here, sniffs there, sweats, puts all he's got into the job, and what's the use? When he manages to dig a mine, he finds that the counter-mine has been prepared in advance by the Count–Duke . . .'

Heaven knows when the mayor would ever have reached port. But Don Rodrigo, seeing the grimaces which his cousin was making, turned to a servant, as if by a sudden inspiration, and told him to bring a certain special bottle. 'My dear mayor,' he said, 'and gentlemen all! Pray silence for a toast to the Count–Duke – and you shall tell me whether the wine is worthy of the man.' The mayor replied with a little bow, in which an element of personal acknowledgement could be detected; for he regarded anything said or done in honour of the Count-Duke as partly directed towards himself.

'Long live Don Gasparo Guzman, Count of Olivares, Duke of San Lucar, Great Private of King Philip the Great, our lord and master!' he exclaimed, raising his glass.

'Private', we should perhaps explain, was the term in general use at that time to signify the favourite of a prince.

'Long live the Count–Duke!' replied everyone.

'Give the good father a glass of wine!' said Don Rodrigo.

'Forgive me,' replied the friar, 'but I have already broken my rule once, and I must not . . .'

'What!' said Don Rodrigo. 'This is a toast to the Count–Duke! Do you want us to think that you are of the Navarrese party?'

'Navarrese' was a mocking name for the French, in reference to the Princes of Navarre, who had reigned over them since the days of Henry IV.

After such an injunction, there was no choice but to drink. All the company broke out into exclamations, in praise of the wine; except for the Doctor, who sat there with head held high, eyes fixed, and lips pursed, expressing by his attitude far more than he could have put into words.

'What do you think of that, eh, Doctor?' said Don Rodrigo.

Having taken his nose out of the glass – a nose of a brighter red than the wine itself – the Doctor replied as follows, weighing heavily on every syllable:

'I say, pronounce and declare that this wine is a true Olivares among wines. *Censui et in eam ivi sententiam*, that such a nectar is not to be found anywhere else in the twenty-two kingdoms of our sovereign lord, God bless him. I hold and maintain that the dinners of the most noble Don Rodrigo surpass the feasts of Heliogabalus, and that famine is exiled and banished in perpetuity from this palace, which is the seat and reign of magnificence.'

'Well said! Well pronounced!' cried the guests with one voice. But the word 'famine', which the Doctor had unthinkingly uttered, at once made them think of that gloomy subject, and they all began to talk about it. They all held the same views this time, in the essential points at least; but the noise was probably greater than it would have been if they had disagreed. Everyone was talking at once.

'There's no famine at all really,' said one. 'It's profiteers, cornering the market . . .'

'And bakers,' said another, 'hiding their stocks of grain. Hanging is the only thing for them.'

'Exactly – they must be hanged, without mercy.'

'After proper trial though!' shouted the mayor.

'Trials, indeed!' shouted Count Attilio, even louder. 'Summary justice, that's what's wanted. Take three or four – five or six, maybe – of those who are generally known to be the richest and dirtiest dogs, and hang them!'

'We must make examples! otherwise nothing gets done.'

'Hang the swine! – and then ample stocks of grain will appear everywhere.'

Anyone who has ever been to a fair, and found himself in a position to enjoy the symphony produced by a troupe of strolling musicians tuning their instruments between two acts, each of them making the loudest noise he can so as to be able to hear his own notes above the din made by the others, can easily imagine the harmonious sound produced by the expressing of all those opinions – if that is the right word. Meanwhile the glasses were refilled and filled again with that remarkable wine, and its praises, as was right and proper, mingled with the legal and economic pronouncements; so that the words which rang out most sonorously and frequently were 'nectar' and 'hangings'.

Meanwhile Don Rodrigo glanced once or twice at the only silent guest. He saw him sitting very still, with no sign of haste or impatience, doing nothing to remind anyone that he was waiting, but with an air that suggested that he would not go before he had a hearing. Don Rodrigo would have been glad to send him to the devil and avoid the coming interview; but it was not his policy to dismiss a Capuchin without listening to what he had to say. Since the annoyance could not be avoided, he decided to face it at once, and get it over. He stood up from table, and so did all the rosy-faced company, without any pause in their noisy chatter. Don Rodrigo bowed to his guests, and walked gravely over to the friar, who had stood up at the same time as the others.

'I am at your disposal,' he said to Father Cristoforo, and led him into another room.

Chapter 6

'In what way can I be of assistance to you?' said Don Rodrigo, taking up his stance in the middle of the room. His words were as we have just reported them; but his way of uttering them plainly said: remember to whom you are speaking, consider what you are saying, and be brief.

Now there was no swifter nor surer way of putting fresh heart into Father Cristoforo than to treat him in a high-handed manner. He had been in a state of uncertainty, searching for words, and running the beads of the rosary at his belt through his fingers, as if he hoped to find a suggestion for his opening remarks concealed in one of them; but Don Rodrigo's manner had such an effect on him that he felt more words coming to his lips than he needed. But he remembered how important it was not to damage his own interests, or, more vital still, the interests of others, and he revised and softened the phrases which thronged into his mind. With cautious humility, he said:

'I have come to suggest an act of justice, to implore an act of charity. Certain men of evil life have made use of your honour's name to terrorize a poor curé, to prevent him from doing his duty and to deprive a pair of innocent people of their rights. With one word you can confound those wicked men, restore power to the forces of righteousness and raise up those who have been so cruelly cast down. You can do it, I repeat, and the influence of conscience, of honour . . .'

'You may speak to me about my conscience, when I present myself to you for confession. As for my honour, I would have you know that I am its sole guardian. If anyone tries to argue with me about the way I guard my honour, in my eyes he is making a presumptuous attack on me.'

Father Cristoforo could see from these words that Don Rodrigo would take everything he said in the worst possible sense, and try to turn the conversation into a quarrel, to prevent him from getting to grips with the real problem. So the friar summoned up fresh stocks of patience, and resolved to swallow whatever insults the other might choose to utter. He quickly answered in a submissive tone:

'If I have said anything that displeases you, it was certainly contrary to my intention. Pray correct me, and reprove me, if I show myself unable to speak in a suitable manner; but I beg you to hear me out. For the love of Heaven, and of the God before whose presence we must all one day appear –' (as he said these words, he took the little wooden death's-head on his rosary between his fingers, and held it up before the eyes of his scowling listener) – 'do not be obstinate in the denial of an act of justice which is so easy to perform, and so clearly due to those poor folk. Remember that God has them always in his sight, and that their cries and their groans are heard on high. Innocence is a mighty thing in his . . .'

'Father Cristoforo!' said Don Rodrigo abruptly, 'I have the greatest respect for the habit you wear; but if anything could make me forget that respect, it would be to see the habit on the back of a man who dared to enter this house as a spy.'

This last word brought a flush to the friar's face, but he went on with the air of a man swallowing a very bitter medicine:

'You know that I do not deserve the name of spy. You know in your heart that there is nothing cowardly or contemptible about the errand on which I have come. Listen to my words, sir; God forbid that the day should ever come when you repent of not having listened to them. Do not put your own glory – and what sort of glory can it be called, Don Rodrigo, even in the sight of men! – while in the sight of God . . . You, sir, have much power here below, but . . .'

'Are you aware', said Don Rodrigo, interrupting him angrily, but not without an inward shudder of fear, 'that any time the fancy takes me to hear a sermon, I am quite capable of finding my own way to church, like anyone else? But in my own house . . .! – Ah, I see it now!' he went on, with a forced, mocking smile. 'You want to give me more than my due. The services of a private chaplain – that is the privilege of a prince.'

'And the same God who expects princes to account for the

use they make of his Word, which he causes them to hear in their palaces, the same God in his great mercy sends you his servant, wretched and unworthy though he may be, on behalf of an innocent girl . . .'

'Well, Father Cristoforo,' said Don Rodrigo, moving towards the door, 'I have no idea what you are talking about, except that there seems to be some girl who means a great deal to you. You can go and inflict your confidences on anyone you like; but don't take the liberty of wasting any more of a gentleman's time with them.'

When Don Rodrigo moved toward the door, the friar stood in his way, very respectfully, raising his hands in supplication, and also in order to prevent his escape.

'It is true that the girl means a great deal to me,' he said, 'but I care just as much about you . . . two souls that mean more to me than my own life. Don Rodrigo! the only thing I can do for you is to pray for you; but I shall do it with all my heart. Do not reject my appeal; do not keep a poor innocent girl in anguish and terror. One word from you can put everything right.'

'Very well,' said Don Rodrigo, 'since you believe that I can do so much for this person; since this person means so much to you . . .'

'Yes . . .?' said Father Cristoforo anxiously; for Don Rodrigo's attitude and expression did not inspire confidence in the hope suggested by his words.

'Then advise her to come and place herself under my protection. She will lack nothing, and no one will dare to molest her, as sure as I am a knight.'

The friar had controlled his indignation up to this point with some difficulty, but now it burst out. All his good resolutions of calm and prudence went up in smoke. His old character found itself for once in complete accord with his new one. On occasions like this, Fra Cristoforo really had the strength of two men. 'Your protection!' he cried, stepping back a couple of paces. Poised boldly on his right foot, with his right hand on his hip, he raised the other hand with forefinger outstretched towards Don Rodrigo, and looked him straight in the eye, with a furious glare. 'Your protection indeed! It is just as well that you used those words, that you made that infamous proposal to me. You have filled the measure even to overflowing, and I no longer fear you.'

'What language is this, friar?'

'The right language to use to a man abandoned by God, who can no longer inspire fear. You speak of your protection. I knew before that the poor innocent was under the protection of God, but now you have made me feel the truth of it with such certainty that I no longer need to choose my words. Her name is Lucia – see with how high a head and how steady a gaze I pronounce it.'

'What! In my own house . . .'

'I pity this house; the curse of God is hanging over it. You will see if the justice of God can be overawed by a few bricks, or terrorized by a few hired thugs. You believe that God made a creature in his own image to give you the pleasure of tormenting her. You think that God will not defend her, and you despise his warning! You have judged yourself. The heart of Pharaoh was as hard as yours; but God knew the way to break it. Lucia is safe from you. I tell you so, poor friar as I am; and as for you yourself, you shall hear what I have to tell you. A day will come . . .'

Up to this point, Don Rodrigo had been suspended between rage and amazement, too stunned to speak. But now that the friar's words took on this prophetic note, a hint of mysterious terror was added to the anger that he felt.

He reached out and grabbed that threatening hand; and, raising his voice to drown the words of the prophet of doom, he shouted:

'Get away from me, you presumptuous peasant, and take that coward's uniform with you.'

The sheer clarity of these words brought immediate calm to Fra Cristoforo. Abuse and insult had been associated in his mind, so thoroughly and for such a long time with patient suffering and silent acceptance that this mode of address calmed his wrath and quenched his fires, and left him with nothing but a firm resolution to listen quietly to whatever Don Rodrigo might care to add. He gently withdrew his hand from the nobleman's clutch, lowered his head, and stayed motionless; just as, when the wind drops in the middle of a great storm, a tempest-tossed oak reverts to its natural shape, spreading out its branches to receive the hail which heaven sends.

'You behave like what you are,' Don Rodrigo went on, 'a yokel educated above his station. You can thank the robe that covers your rascally back for protecting you from the blows we usually give your sort, to teach them how to speak to their betters. You can leave on your own two feet this time; and we'll see what happens next.'

He pointed, with imperious contempt, towards a door facing the one by which they had come in. Father Cristoforo bowed his head and went out, leaving Don Rodrigo pacing fiercely up and down the field of battle.

The friar shut the door behind him, and looked round the room where he now stood. He saw a man creeping away along the wall very quietly, as if to avoid detection from the room where the interview had taken place. He recognized the old servant who had opened the front door to him. The old man had served that family for perhaps forty years, since before Don Rodrigo was born. His first master had been Don Rodrigo's father, a very different sort of man. On his death the new master had made a clean sweep of most of the servants, bringing in new faces; but he had kept on this particular retainer, partly because he was already an old man, and partly because, although his principles and habits were entirely different from those of Don Rodrigo, he had two compensating virtues – a high opinion of the dignity of the house, and a profound knowledge of ceremonial, of which he knew the oldest traditions and the minutest details better than anyone else. In his master's presence the poor old man would never have ventured even to hint at his disapproval of the things he saw happening all day long, much less to express it openly. Even with his fellow-servants, the most he would allow himself was an occasional exclamation, a rebuke muttered between his teeth. They used to laugh at him, and sometimes amused themselves by egging him on to say more than he intended, or to sing the praises of the old way of life in that house in earlier days. His criticisms never reached his master's ears except as part of an account of the merriment they had caused; and so Don Rodrigo treated them with mockery but without resentment. On days of festivity and hospitality the old man came into his own again as a serious and important personage.

Father Cristoforo looked at him in passing, bade him good day, and was walking on; but the old man came up to him with a mysterious air, put his finger to his lips, and then motioned him, with the same finger, towards a dark passage. When they were there, he said, 'Father, I heard everything, and I must talk to you.'

'Be quick about it then, my good fellow.'

'I can't talk here. It would be terrible if the master caught me . . . but I've many things to tell you. I'll try and come to the monastery tomorrow.'

'Is there some plot afoot?'

'There's something in the air, for certain; I'd noticed it earlier on. But now I'll keep a special watch, and with luck I'll find out all about it. Leave it to me. The things I have to hear and see! Flames of hell . . . what a house I serve! But I want to save my own soul.'

'The Lord bless you!' said the friar softly, laying his hand on the servant's head. Though older than the friar, he stood before him with bowed head, like a son.

'The Lord will reward you,' added Father Cristoforo. 'Be sure to come tomorrow.'

'I will,' said the servant. 'But now you must go at once, father. And for God's sake, never mention my name.'

He looked round, and went along the passage to another room, which opened into the courtyard. Seeing that the coast was clear, he called the good father, whose face conveyed a surer answer to the last appeal than any verbal protestation could have done. The servant pointed the way to the great door, and the friar went off without another word.

The man had listened at his master's door. Had he done well? And did Father Cristoforo do well to praise him for it? According to the commonest and most unquestioned rules of conduct, it was a most unseemly action. But could this particular case not be regarded as an exception? And can there be exceptions to the commonest and most unquestioned rules? These are important matters, which the reader can decide for himself, if he feels like it. We do not propose to sit in judgement; it is enough to for us to have facts to relate.

Once outside, Father Cristoforo turned his back on that house of ill omen, and began to breathe more freely. He hastened down the hillside, very red in the face, deeply stirred and confused, as anyone can imagine, both by what had been said to him and by what he had said himself. But the totally unexpected approach which the old servant had made to him cheered him greatly. He felt that Heaven had given him a visible sign of its favour. 'This is a thread,' he said to himself, 'a thread which Providence has put into my hand. In that very house! and without the idea of seeking it there having even crossed my mind!'

As he thought these things over, he raised his eyes toward the west, saw the sun very low in the sky, scarcely clearing the mountain top opposite, and realized there was very little time left before nightfall. Though his bones ached heavily within him after all the varied ill usage of the day, he quickened his pace. He wanted to make his report, dismal as it was, to the friends who trusted in him, and get back to the monastery before the gates were shut for the night. (This was one of the most definite and strictly enforced rules of the Capuchin order.)

Meanwhile in Lucia's cottage certain plans had been put forward and carefully considered, about which the reader should now be informed. After the departure of the friar, the three of them had spent some time in gloomy silence. Lucia was sadly preparing dinner; Renzo was trying to make up his mind to go home, away from the heartbroken sight she presented, but could not manage it. Agnese was to all appearance intent on her spinning-wheel; but she was really thinking out a plan. When it was ready, she broke the silence with these words:

'Listen, children! If you'll show you've got a stout heart and a quick hand; if you'll trust your mother, both of you' – the words 'mother' and 'both of you' made Lucia jump – 'I'll undertake to get you out of this trouble, better and quicker perhaps than Father Cristoforo, wonderful man as he is.'

Lucia stood still, and looked her with an expression that showed more amazement than belief in so splendid a promise. Renzo quickly said 'Stout heart? quick hand? Go on – tell us what we can do.'

'Well then; don't you agree', said Agnese, 'that if you two were married it would be quite a step forward? Wouldn't the rest be easier afterwards?'

'No doubt about that,' said Renzo. 'Once we're married . . . we'd have the world to choose from; and there's the territory of Bergamo, not far from here at all, where silk workers are welcomed with open arms. You know how many times my cousin Bortolo has said I ought to join him there and make my fortune, like he has. The only reason I've never gone is . . . well, because of Lucia here. If we were married we could all go together, and set up house there, and live in God's own peace, out of the clutches of that blackguard, away from the temptation to do anything silly. Isn't that true, now, Lucia?'

'It's true, right enough,' said Lucia, 'but how in the world . . .'

'It's the way I said just now,' replied her mother. 'With a stout heart and a quick hand, it'll be easy.'

'Easy?' said Renzo and Lucia together, thinking how strangely and painfully difficult the whole thing had become.

'Yes, easy, once you see how to do it,' replied Agnese. 'Listen carefully, and I'll try to explain. This is something I've heard from people who know what they're talking about, and in fact I've seen a case of it myself. If you want to have a wedding, you must have a priest, but he doesn't have to agree to it; it's enough for him to be there.'

'Whatever do you mean?' asked Renzo.

'Listen – I'll tell you then. You need two witnesses – quick-witted, willing lads. You go to the curé's house – and the thing is to catch him when he isn't expecting you, so that he can't get away. The man says "Your Reverence, this is my wife", and the woman says "Your Reverence, this is my husband." As long as

115

the curé hears the words, and the witnesses hear them too, it's a valid marriage, just as sacred as if the Pope had done it for you. Once the words have been said, the curé can scream and shout as much as he likes; it doesn't alter the fact that you're man and wife.'

'Can it really be true?' cried Lucia.

'Why,' said Agnese, 'do you think that I never learnt anything at all in the thirty years I spent in this world before either of you were born? It's the truth I'm telling you, and to prove it, one of my friends wanted to marry a man whose parents wouldn't agree to it, and it worked all right for her. The curé suspected what they had in mind, and was on his guard; but those two clever devils managed so well, that they caught him at the right moment, said their piece, and became man and wife; though the poor girl was sorry enough for what she had done only three days later.'

Agnese was quite right about it being possible, and also about it being dangerous if it went wrong. For the only people who tried this route to matrimony were those who had met with some obstacle or been denied passage by the ordinary one; and consequently the priests did their very best to avoid being caught up in any such forced cooperation. If a curé was surprised by one of those couples and their witnesses, he always struggled furiously to get out of it, like Proteus escaping from the hands of those who wanted to compel him to prophesy.

'If only it were true, Lucia!' said Renzo, with a pleading, expectant look.

'What do you mean, "If it were true"?' demanded Agnese. 'So you think I'm talking nonsense too! I do my best for you, and you won't even believe what I say. All right then – get out of your troubles by yourselves! I wash my hands of the whole thing.'

'No, no; don't do that,' said Renzo. 'I only said what I did because it sounded too good to be true. I'm in your hands; I look on you as if you were really my own mother.'

At these words Agnese recovered from her fit of pique, and forgot her vow to leave them to their fate, which was never a very serious one anyway.

'But why didn't Father Cristoforo think of this way out, then?' said Lucia, in her gentle, submissive way.

'He'll have thought of it, right enough,' said Agnese. 'But he wouldn't want to tell us about it.'

'Why not?' said Lucia and Renzo together.

'Because ... because ... if you must know, the clergy say that it isn't really right to do that.'

'How can it be wrong to do something, if it's right when it's done?' asked Renzo.'

'How should I know?' said Agnese. 'They make the rules to suit themselves; and we poor folk can't understand them all. There are so many things like that. Look, it's like giving someone a punch on the jaw. You shouldn't do it at all; but once you've done it, not even the Pope can undo it again.'

'If it isn't really right,' said Lucia, 'we'd better not do it.'

'Nonsense!' said Agnese. 'Do you think I'd give you a piece of advice that hadn't the fear of God in it? If it were against the wishes of your parents, now, so that you could marry some good-for-nothing fellow ... but as it is, I'm happy about it; and it's Renzo here you want to marry; and the man who's making the difficulties is that blackguard; and the curé ...'

'Anyone would understand why we'd had to do it,' said Renzo.

'We mustn't tell Father Cristoforo about this until after we've done it,' said Agnese. 'But once it's done and turned out all right, what do you suppose the good father will say to you? "Ah, my dear daughter, that was very wrong of you! You've let me down!" The clergy have to talk like that. But you can be quite sure that in his own heart he'll be very pleased about it.'

Though Lucia could not find any answer to this argument, she did not seem convinced. But Renzo was greatly heartened, and said, 'Well, if it's really true, the thing's as good as done.'

'Steady a moment now!' said Agnese. 'What about the witnesses? How are you going to find two of them with courage to do the job and enough sense to keep quiet about it in the meantime? And how are you going to get hold of the priest, who's locked himself up in his own house this last couple of days? And then you've got to get him to stay put – for though he's a heavy man, he'll be as nimble as a kitten when he sees the four of you arrive, and you won't see him for dust.'

'I've got it!' said Renzo, bringing his fist down on the table, and jingling the cutlery which lay there ready for dinner. And he told them his plan, which Agnese fully approved.

'It's a trick,' said Lucia. 'It's not ... straightforward. Up to now we've been honest about this; let's have faith, and go on in the same way. God will help us; Father Cristoforo said so. Let's listen to his advice.'

'Be guided by those who know more than you do,' said Agnese with a grave expression. 'What do you need more advice for? God's message is: "I help those who help themselves." We'll tell Father Cristoforo about it after it's done.'

'Lucia,' said Renzo, 'surely you won't let me down now? We've done everything we should have done, like good Christians. Isn't it true that we ought by rights to be man and wife already? The curé fixed the day for our wedding himself ... and whose fault is it if we've got to use a bit of cunning now? No, I know you won't let me down. I'll be back presently with some news for you.'

He bade farewell to Lucia with an imploring look, and to Agnese with a glance of complicity; and hurried away.

Tribulations sharpen the wits. In the straight and narrow path which his life had previously followed, Renzo had never had occasion to put much of an extra edge on his mental faculties. But on this occasion he had thought up a scheme which would have done credit to a lawyer. His plan took him straight to the cottage of his friend Tonio, who lived near by. He found him in his kitchen, with one knee on the fender; on the hot coals in front of him was a round pan, which he held by the rim with one hand, while he stirred its contents – a small grey buckwheat polenta – with a curved wooden spoon which he held in the other. Tonio's mother, brother and wife were sitting at the table, and three or four little boys were standing round their father, with their eyes fixed on the pan, waiting for him to dish up. But the scene lacked the gaiety which the sight of dinner normally imparts to a group of people who have earned it by their labours. The size of the polenta was proportionate to the quality of the harvest, not to the number and the enthusiasm of the assembled company. They were all staring at the communal dish with a grim look of rabid desire, every one of them obviously thinking of the amount of hunger that would still be with him after the meal. While Renzo exchanged greetings with the family, Tonio ladled the polenta on to the beechwood platter which was ready to receive it. The polenta looked like a very small moon surrounded by a large nimbus of vapour. Yet the women still said politely to Renzo, 'Will you do us the honour of joining us at table?' – words which the peasants of Lombardy, and of many other lands, will always say to anyone who finds them at dinner, even if he is a wealthy glutton and they are down to their last mouthful.

'Thank you,' said Renzo, 'but I only came to have a quick word with Tonio. Look, Tonio, we don't want to disturb the womenfolk, let's go and eat at the inn, and we can talk there.'

Tonio found this a surprising suggestion, but all the more welcome for that. Both the children (for children understand these things from a very early age) and the women were far from sorry to see the polenta relieved from one of the claims outstanding against it – the most formidable of those claims in fact. Tonio asked no questions, but went off with Renzo.

They reached the inn; they sat down in perfect solitude, for poverty had weaned all the customers of that haven of delight from the habit of going there; they ordered up the little that the place had to offer; they drank a glass of wine apiece; and then Renzo said mysteriously to Tonio: 'If you'll do a little thing for me, I'll do a big thing for you.'

'Just name it,' said Tonio, pouring out another glass. 'There's nothing I wouldn't do for you today.'

'Well, you owe the curé twenty-five lire rent for that field you hired from him last year.'

'Ah, Renzo, Renzo, you're spoiling my treat. Why bring that up, just when I was beginning to feel better?'

'The only reason I mentioned the debt', said Renzo, 'is that I've got it in mind to give you a chance of paying it.'

'Do you mean it?'

'I do. D'you like the idea?'

'Do I like it? I should think I do! If it was only so that I wouldn't have to see the reverend gentleman grimace and shake his head at me any more, every time he'd be meeting me in the road! With his "Don't forget now, Tonio!" – and his "Tonio, when are you coming to see me about that little matter?" It's got to the point where if he happens to look at me while he's preaching, I'm afraid he'll take twenty-five lire as the text of his sermon! To hell with his twenty-five lire! Besides he'd have to give me back my wife's gold necklace, and I'd soon turn that into good polenta. But . . .'

'There's no buts about it. If you'll give me a little bit of help, the money's in your pocket.'

'Go on – tell me what it is, then.'

'Not a word to anyone, mind!' said Renzo, putting a finger to his lips.

'No need to say that. You know me well enough.'

'His Reverence keeps on bringing up a lot of silly excuses for putting off my wedding, and I don't want to wait any longer. Now I'm told that it's quite certain that if my girl and I appear in front of him with two witnesses, and I say "This is my wife" and she says "This is my husband", we'll be as truly man and wife as if he'd married us in church. Do you follow me?'

'You want me to be a witness for you?'

'That's it.'

'And you'll pay off the twenty-five lire for me?'

'I will.'

'Done, then!'

'But we'll have to find a second witness.'

'I've found one already. My fool of a brother Gervaso will do whatever I tell him. You'll buy him a drink, of course?'

'And a meal,' said Renzo. 'We'll bring him here and have a party for the three of us . . . but can he do what's wanted?'

'I'll tell him what to do; you know I've got his share of brains as well as my own.'

'Tomorrow then.'

'Good.'

'Towards evening.'

'Better still.'

'And remember!' said Renzo, putting his finger to his lips again.

'Bah!' said Tonio, drooping his head towards his right shoulder, and raising his left hand, with a look on his face which said 'You're doing me wrong.'

'But what if your wife asks you a lot of questions, as she probably will . . .?'

'I'll tell her some lies then. I owe her a good few over the years; so many, in fact, that I don't think I'll ever catch up with her. I'll find some story that'll quieten her down.'

'We can have a longer talk about it tomorrow morning', said Renzo, 'and arrange all the details.'

They left the inn, and Tonio walked home, trying to think of a good story for his womenfolk, while Renzo went off to tell Agnese and Lucia what had been agreed.

In the meantime Agnese had tried hard to win her daughter over, but in vain. Lucia met every argument with one or other of her pair of logical alternatives: either the whole thing is wrong and we shouldn't do it, she said, or else it isn't wrong and why not tell Father Cristoforo about it?

Renzo came back glowing with triumph, and told them what he had done, ending with the words 'What d'you think of that?', in a tone of voice which conveyed: Haven't I played the part of a man? and Could there be a better answer? and Would you ever have thought of that for yourselves? and a dozen other similar messages.

Lucia gently shook her head, but the other two enthusiasts took no notice of her, as if she were a child, who could not be expected to understand the ins and outs of what was going on, but could be cajoled or compelled to do what was required of her later on.

'That's fine,' said Agnese, 'that's fine; but there's one thing you haven't thought of.'

'What's that, then?' said Renzo.

'You haven't thought about Perpetua. She'll let in Tonio and his brother all right, but not you two! She'll have orders to keep you away from his Reverence as if you were small boys and he were a pear-tree.'

'What shall we do, then?' said Renzo, slightly confused.

'Listen – I've thought of something. I'll come with you myself; there's something only I know that'll draw her like a magnet, and put such a spell on her that she won't even see you're there, and you can go straight in. I'll call her to me, and I'll touch the right string . . . you'll see.'

'Bless you for it!' cried Renzo. 'I've always said you were our best help in everything.'

'But all this is no good,' said Agnese, 'if we can't persuade Lucia here that it isn't a sin.'

Renzo added his eloquence to Agnese's, but Lucia would not budge an inch.

'I can't answer all these arguments of yours,' she said, 'but I can see that if it's your way we take, every yard of it's paved with tricks, lies and deceit. Oh Renzo! that's not the way we started out together. I want to be your wife' – she still couldn't say the word, or express the wish, without a blush – 'but I want it to be in an honest, God-fearing way, in front of the altar. Leave it to God to find the way. Don't you think he knows how to help us, better than we can help ourselves with all those lying tricks? And why keep Father Cristoforo in the dark about it?'

The argument was still going on, and showed no signs of being near its end, when a rapid clatter of sandalled feet, and a sound of flapping robes like the wind in a slackened sail, announced the arrival of Father Cristoforo. They all fell silent, and Agnese scarcely had time to whisper in Lucia's ear: 'Mind you don't tell him anything now!'

Chapter 7

FATHER Cristoforo's attitude as he reached the cottage was that of a good general who has lost an important engagement through no fault of his own, and now, saddened but not discouraged, deeply concerned but not dismayed, in haste rather than in flight, speeds to the places where his presence is needed; sending reinforcements to threatened positions, regrouping his scattered forces, and issuing fresh orders.

'Peace be with you!' he said as he came in. 'There's nothing to be hoped from that man; which is all the more reason to trust in God. I have already received something of a pledge of his help.'

None of the three had ever had very high hopes of Father Cristoforo's mission. For a man of power to withdraw from an act of oppression without being compelled to do so, as a voluntary response to an unarmed appeal, was not merely unusual, but unheard of. But the miserable certainty of failure was still a blow to all of them. The women lowered their heads; but anger prevailed over sorrow in Renzo's heart. Father Cristoforo's words found him already embittered by so many painful surprises, frustrated endeavours and shattered hopes, and still more deeply distressed, at that moment, by Lucia's non-cooperation.

'I'd like to know,' he cried, grinding his teeth and raising his voice as he had never done before in the presence of Father Cristoforo, 'I'd like to know what reasons that swine gave for saying that my bride wasn't to marry me.'

'Poor Renzo!' said the friar in a grave and compassionate voice, enjoining calm on the young man with a look of affectionate command, 'if a man of power had to give reasons every time he wanted to commit an injustice, the world would be a very different place.'

'You mean the swine said he didn't want to let us get married because he didn't want to?'

'He didn't even say that, my poor boy! It would be something if these people had to make an open admission of their iniquities.'

'But he must have said something, the blackguard, may he fry in hell! What did he say?'

'I heard what he said, but I cannot repeat it to you. The words of a powerful oppressor pierce the heart and fly away. He can rage at you for showing suspicion of him, and at the same moment make it clear that what you suspect is true; and he can insult you and claim that you have insulted him, mock you and demand satisfaction, threaten and complain at the same time. He can be both shameless and irreproachable. Do not ask me to repeat what he said. He never even mentioned this innocent girl's name, nor your name, Renzo; it was as if he had never heard of you; he made no claim; and yet . . . and yet . . . it was all too clear that nothing would move him. But trust in God! Do not lose heart, my poor daughters, nor you, Renzo. Believe me, I can put myself in your place, I can feel all that you feel in your heart. But be patient! Patience is a poor word, a bitter word for those who have no faith. But you, Renzo, can you not give God a day, or two days, or whatever time it pleases him to take, to make justice triumph? Time belongs to him, and he has promised us so large a portion of it. Leave things to Him, Renzo . . . and listen, my boy, listen, all of you! I've already got something in hand, only a thread, but a thread to help us out of this trouble. For the moment I can't tell you more than that. I will not come up here tomorrow; I must stay at the monastery all day to do something for you. Try to come and see me there, Renzo. If for any reason you cannot come yourself, send someone you can trust, some sensible lad, so that I can let you know what's happened. It's getting dark, and I must go back to the monastery. Have faith; be brave; farewell.'

He hurried out, and ran down the rough, winding path, jumping from rock to rock, to avoid being late back at the monastery, which would have earned him a reprimand, or, worse still, a penitence which might have prevented him from being ready to do whatever was needed for his three friends the following day.

'Did you hear what he said about . . . a thread or something that he's got which can help us?' said Lucia. 'We ought to trust the good father! He's a man who doesn't promise more than he'll do; in fact . . .'

'That's all very well!' Agnese interrupted. 'He should have spoken out clearly; or called me on one side, and told me what it is . . .'

'I've had enough of all this talk. Something needs to be done, and I'm going to do it,' said Renzo, interrupting in his turn. His voice, his expression and the way he strode up and down the room left no doubt about what he meant.

'Oh, Renzo!' cried Lucia.

'What are you saying?' cried Agnese.

'There's no need to say anything. I'll do it. He may have twenty devils in his heart, but he's a man of flesh and blood the same as me, when it comes down to it . . .'

'No, no, for the love of God . . .' began Lucia, but her voice was choked by sobs.

'You shouldn't say things like that, even for a joke,' said Agnese.

'A joke?' shouted Renzo, standing over Agnese as she sat in her chair, and glaring fiercely into her eyes. 'I'll show you if it's a joke!'

'Oh, Renzo!' said Lucia, getting the words out with difficulty between her sobs, 'I've never seen you like this before.'

'Don't talk like that, for the love of God!' said Agnese in a quick, low voice. 'Have you forgotten the number of thugs that man can call on? And if you brought it off – heaven forbid! – the strong arm of justice is always ready to punish the crimes of the poor.'

'Justice'll be done, and it'll be done by me! It's about time! I know it won't be easy. He looks after himself all right, the murdering swine; he knows what's what; but that doesn't matter. Determination and patience are what's needed. Sooner or later the time will come. Justice will be done by me; the countryside will be freed of a monster by me. Countless victims will bless my name ... and then a short, sharp dash for the frontier!'

The awful, final clarity of this last speech struck Lucia with such horror, that she was able to stop weeping and find her voice again. She lifted her tearful face from her hands, and said in heartbroken but resolute tones, 'So you don't care any more about having me for your wife! It was a God-fearing young fellow who had my promise; but a man who'd done that ... no, no, even if he were safe from the law and safe from revenge, not even if he were a royal prince ...'

'Very well then,' shouted Renzo, his face more contorted with fury than ever. 'So I shall never have you! But he won't have you either. I'll be living here on my own, and he'll be frying in ...'

'No, no, for mercy's sake, don't talk like that, don't glare at me like that; I can't look at you with that face!' cried Lucia, tears pouring from her eyes, beseeching him with hands joined as if in prayer; while Agnese called him by name again and again, running her fingers over his shoulders, arms and hands to calm him down. He stood motionless and thoughtful for a minute, gazing at Lucia's imploring face, then, suddenly, his countenance darkened, and he stepped back, raised one arm and pointed at her with his forefinger, shouting 'He wants to get her! Her! He must die!'

'And what harm have I done you, that you should want to make me die too?' said Lucia, falling on her knees before him.

'You!' he said, in a voice which expressed anger of a different kind, but still anger none the less. 'You! How can you say you love me? What proof have you ever given me? Haven't I begged, and begged, and begged you? and all you can say is no! no! no!'

'I'll say yes then,' said Lucia very quickly. 'I'll come with you to the curé's house tomorrow, or now if you like. Be like you were before, and I'll come.'

'Do you promise that?' said Renzo, whose voice and expression had suddenly grown much gentler.

'I do, I do.'

'Very well then; you've given me your word.'

'Oh, thank God! thank God for that!' exclaimed Agnese, doubly happy now.

Intermingled with Renzo's fury, had there been a thought of the advantage he might gain from Lucia's fears? Had he not used a little artifice to make them grow, so that he could gather their fruits? Our author protests ignorance on this point, and I personally doubt whether Renzo was clear about it himself. There is no doubt that he was genuinely furious with Don Rodrigo, nor that he ardently desired Lucia's consent to his plan; and when two strong emotions are clamouring together in a man's heart, it is often impossible for anyone, even the patient himself, to distinguish them, or to say with certainty which of the two predominates over the other.

'I've given you my word,' said Lucia, in a tone of timid and affectionate reproach, 'but earlier on you gave me your word not to make a scandal, and to follow Father Cristoforo's advice.'

'Oh Lucia! Why do you think I care so much about it? For whose sake? Are you going to go back on your promise now, and make me do something I shall be sorry for?'

'No, no,' said Lucia, her fears returning. 'I've given you my word, and I won't take it back. But you know yourself how you got that promise out of me. God forbid that . . .'

'Why say things that'll bring bad luck on us, Lucia? God knows very well that we aren't hurting anyone in the world.'

'Well then, promise me that this'll be the last time.'

'I swear it, on a poor man's honour.'

'But this time you must stick to it,' said Agnese.

Here our author admits his ignorance on another point. Was Lucia wholly unhappy that Renzo had forced her to agree to his plan? We too must leave the question in doubt.

Renzo wanted to stay on and arrange the details of what had to be done the following day; but it was dark now, and the women wished him good night, thinking that it would look better if he did not stay too late.

For all three of them, the night that followed was of the sort to be expected after a day of agitation and grief, with the prospect of a day to come for which an important and dangerous enterprise was planned. Renzo appeared again at an early hour the following morning, and arranged the details of the coming evening's vital operation with the women, or rather with Agnese. They took turns at thinking of difficulties and finding solutions to them, and trying to foresee what might go wrong. One after another, they repeatedly described the whole performance as if it were something that had already happened. Lucia listened; she did not approve in words anything that she could not approve in her heart, but she promised to do all that she could to help.

'Are you going down to the monastery to talk to Father Cristoforo, like he said yesterday evening?' said Agnese to Renzo.

'Not likely!' he replied. 'You know how sharp-eyed the holy father is. He'd see from the first glance at my face that there was something up; and once he started to question me I'd be in real trouble. Besides I ought to stay here and attend to everything. It'd be better if you sent someone else.'

'I'll send Menico then.'

'That's fine,' said Renzo, and he went off to attend to everything, as he had said.

Agnese walked round to a neighbouring house to find Menico, who was a boy of about twelve, and a bright lad too. Taking a line through various cousins and in-laws, he was a sort of nephew of hers. She asked his parents if she could borrow him for the day, 'To do a job for me,' she said. They agreed, and she took him into her kitchen, gave him some breakfast, and told him to go down to Pescarenico and find Father Cristoforo, who would send him back with a message later on. 'You know Father Cristoforo, Menico,' she said. 'That fine-looking old man with the white beard, the one they call the Saint.'

'Yes, I know,' said Menico, 'the one who always pats us boys on the head, and sometimes gives us little pictures of the saints.'

'That's the one, Menico. And if he asks you to wait a bit, don't wander off. Mind you don't go off with some of your friends down to the lake to watch them fishing, or to fool about with the nets that'll be hanging up to dry; or that other favourite trick of yours . . .'

It should be realized that Menico was particularly good at the game of ducks and drakes; and it is well known that all of us, old and young alike, enjoy showing off at things for which we have a special gift – though it doesn't always stop there.

'Why, Aunt Agnese, I'm not a kid now, you know.'

'That's right, my lad. You be sensible then, and when you come back with the answer . . . look, I've got two bright new pennies for you.'

'Let me have them now; it comes to the same thing.'

'No, no; you'd gamble them away. Run along now, and if you do a good job you may get even more.'

During the remaining part of that long morning, several curious things happened which gave considerable further cause for alarm to the two women, who had been uneasy enough before. A man came to the door to beg – but he did not look starved or ragged enough to be a real beggar, and had something ill-favoured and sinister about him. As he came in to the house, he glanced around him as if spying out the land. He took the piece of bread they offered him with ill-concealed indifference, and put it away. Then he delayed his departure, with a curious mixture of impudence and hesitation, and asked a lot of questions. Agnese answered them promptly, but always with the opposite of the truth. When he did leave, he pretended to have forgotten which was the front door, and went through the one leading to the stairs, up which he quickly glanced, as best he could. 'This way! this way!' Agnese shouted after him. 'Where are you going, good man?' He came back, and went out as directed, apologizing with an abject, affected humility which did not seem at home among the harsh features of his face.

Other strange figures continued to appear from time to time after he had gone. It would have been hard to say exactly what sort of men they were; but no one could have taken them for the honest travellers they were meant to resemble. One of them came in with the excuse that he wanted to ask the way. Others slowed their pace as they passed the cottage, and glanced furtively across the courtyard into the main room, as if they wanted to see something without attracting attention. Finally this unpleasant procession came to an end at about midday. Every few minutes Agnese got up, crossed the courtyard, leant over the gate, looked right and left, and came back saying 'No one there' – words that she was glad to pronounce, and Lucia was glad to hear, though neither of them could have said exactly why. But they were left with an uneasy feeling, which robbed both of them (but especially Lucia) of a large part of the stock of courage they had been saving up for the evening.

It is time that the reader had some more definite information about these mysterious visitors to the village. To put him fully in the picture, we must retrace our steps and go back to Don Rodrigo, whom we left yesterday alone in one of the great rooms of his palace after Father Cristoforo had gone.

Don Rodrigo, as we said before, was pacing with long strides across the great room where the portraits of his ancestors, for many generations back, hung on the walls. When he reached the wall at one side of the room and turned round, he came face to face with an old warrior, once the terror of his enemies and of his own soldiers alike, grim-faced, with short, bristly hair, moustaches twisted into points which stood out past his cheeks on either side, and chin thrust obliquely forward. The hero stood very upright, with greaves, cuisses, breastplate, vambraces and gauntlets all of iron. His right hand rested on his flank, and his left hand on the handle of his sword. Don Rodrigo looked steadily at him, and when he reached the wall where the picture hung, and turned round, he found himself face to face with another ancestor, a magistrate this time, once the terror of litigants and lawyers alike, sitting in a great chair covered with red velvet. He was clad in a vast black robe. Everything about him was black, except for a white collar, with two wide bands, and the sable[1] lining of his robe, which was well in evidence. (This was the distinctive dress of a senator, but only worn in winter; which is why we shall never see a portrait of a senator clad for the summer.) He was very lean and scowling, and in his hand

1. Despite the common use of the word 'sable' in English as a poetic synonym for 'black', sable fur is in fact brown in colour. – Translator's note.

was a plea; he seemed to be saying, 'We shall see . . . we shall see . . .' In another place was the picture of a great lady, once the terror of her maids; in yet another an abbot, once the terror of his monks. To sum up, every one of them had inspired terror in his lifetime, and still inspired it from the canvas. At the sight of all these reminders of past glory, Don Rodrigo was possessed by rage and shame, and could not find a moment's peace at the thought that a friar had dared to come and attack him with words like those used by Nathan to David. Various plans for revenge flashed into his mind and were rejected. He tried to think of a way of satisfying the requirements both of his fury and of what he called his honour. From time to time, strange to say, the words with which Father Cristoforo had begun to prophesy before him rang in his ears, a shudder ran through his body, and he almost abandoned the idea of obtaining either kind of satisfaction. In the end, feeling that he must do something, he called a servant and sent him to tell his guests that he was sorry to neglect them, but had been delayed by urgent business. The man came back to report that the gentlemen had gone, leaving messages of regard and respect.

'What about Count Attilio?' asked Don Rodrigo, still pacing up and down.

'He went with the other gentlemen, your honour.'

'Very well, I'm going out. I want an escort of six retainers at once. Also my cape, my sword and my hat, at once.'

The servant bowed in reply, and left the room. A moment later he came back carrying a richly decorated sword, which his master girded on, a cape, which he flung around his shoulders, and a feathered hat, which he put on his head, ramming it fiercely down over his brows with a blow of his hand. (This was known to be a sign of dirty weather.) At the palace door he found six villainous figures waiting for him, all fully armed. They formed into line, bowed, and fell in behind him as he walked on. With an even more bullying, arrogant and scowling air than usual, he set out for a walk towards Lecco. All the peasants and artisans who saw him coming backed away against the wall; they bared their heads and bowed deeply, but he ignored their salutes. Men whom these humble folk regarded as their natural masters also bowed as inferiors before Don Rodrigo; for there was no one in those parts who could begin to compete with him in name, wealth or number of followers – or in the determination to use all these things to maintain his superiority over all other men. He acknowledged the greetings of this second class with stately condescension. He did not happen to meet the Spanish garrison commander on that particular day; but when he did, they exchanged bows of identical depth – two potentates who had nothing in common, but paid due respect to each other's rank out of regard for the decencies.

To get himself into a better mood, and also to replace the image of Father Cristoforo, which was still uppermost in his mind, by images of a totally different sort, Don Rodrigo called at a house where there were generally plenty of visitors, and where he was received with the pleasant bustle of respectful cordiality which we reserve for men who inspire unusual affection or unusual fear. It was already evening when he went back to his palace. Count Attilio had just returned, and supper was served. Don Rodrigo was deep in thought, and said little.

'You know that bet of ours, cousin Rodrigo – when are you going to pay up?' said Count Attilio, with an air of cunning mockery, as soon as the servants had cleared the table and left them alone.

'St Martin's day is not yet past.'

'You might as well pay up now all the same, because all the saints' days in the calendar will go by before you . . .'

'That remains to be seen.'

'You're a good politician, cousin Rodrigo; but I know what's happened, and I'm so sure of winning the bet, that I'm ready to make another.'

'Let's hear it.'

'I'll bet that Father . . . Father What's-his-name – that friar anyway – has converted you.'

'What do you think you're talking about?'

'Conversion, cousin Rodrigo, conversion, I say. And I'm very pleased about it. It'll be a splendid sight to see you all conscience-stricken, with downcast eyes! And what a glorious thing for the holy father! How his bosom must have swelled with pride as he went back home! Such fish are not caught every day, nor in every man's net. You can be sure he'll use you as an edifying example, and even when his holy work takes him far from here, he'll still have something to say about you. I can hear him now.' (He adopted the nasal voice and exaggerated gestures of a bad preacher.) ' "Dearly beloved, in a part of the world which, for good and sufficient reason, I shall not name, there lived – nay, there still lives – a nobleman of disorderly life, who loved good-looking women better than good-living men; and this nobleman, ever ready to fill the cup of inquity to the brim, once set his eye on . . ." '

'That's enough, that's enough,' interrupted Don Rodrigo, half-amused and half-annoyed. 'Would you like to double the bet?'

'Good God! You must have converted the friar!'

'Don't talk to me about the friar. As for the bet, St Martin will decide it for us.'

The count's curiosity was aroused, and he asked many questions; but Don Rodrigo contrived to elude them all. He repeatedly said that St Martin's day must decide. He did not want to reveal plans which he had not yet set in motion, nor even completely formulated, to the other side in the dispute.

When he woke up the following morning, Don Rodrigo was himself again. No trace remained of the fears inspired by the words *A day will come*. Those fears had passed away with the dreams of the night, leaving behind nothing but a furious rage, embittered still further by the thought of his shameful temporary weakness. More recent memories had helped to restore him to his normal state of mind – the bowing and scraping and the warm welcome he had received during the triumphant excursion, also the mockery of his cousin.

As soon as he was dressed, he sent for Griso. 'There's really something up this time,' said the messenger to himself; for the man who went by the name of Griso was none other than the head bravo, to whom the most dangerous and iniquitous tasks were always given – the man in whom the master had absolute trust; the man who belonged to him body and soul, both out of gratitude and out of self-interest. Long before, he had murdered a man in full daylight in the open street, and had gone to implore the protection of Don Rodrigo, who had clad him in his livery and thus put him out of the reach of the law. The murderer won impunity from the consequences of his first crime by undertaking to commit any further crimes that might be required of him. For Don Rodrigo the acquisition was one of considerable value, for Griso, besides being much the most valiant of his followers, was also a living proof of the extent to which his master had been able to defy the law; so that Don Rodrigo's power was increased both in public estimation and in fact.

'Griso!' said Don Rodrigo, 'this is a job that'll really show what you are worth. The girl Lucia has got to be here in this palace, by tomorrow morning.'

'No one will ever be able to say Griso failed to carry out his noble master's orders.'

'Take as many men as you need, make what plans and give what orders you like, so long as you get the results. But be very careful not to hurt her.'

'We'll have to give her a bit of a fright, sir, to keep her quiet. Otherwise we can't do it.'

'A fright ... yes ... I see that. But she's not to be hurt; and above all, she must be treated with the greatest respect. Do you understand?'

'Well, sir, if you ask me to pick a flower and bring it to your Honour, I can't manage without touching it. But we won't do anything at all that's not strictly necessary.'

'You'd better not. Now then ... how will you set about it?'

'I was just thinking about that, sir. It's a good thing that the cottage is on the outskirts of the village. We need a place to assemble, and we're in luck again there, because not far off there's that lonely, deserted place, that house in the fields ... but of course you wouldn't know about it, sir; it's a house that had a fire a few years back, and they didn't have the money to rebuild it, and it's empty now. The witches go there sometimes; but today's not Saturday, and I don't give a damn for them. These peasants now are so superstitious that they wouldn't go

134

near the place any night of the week for any money; so we can go there and stay as long as we like, and be sure that no one will interfere.'

'Good – and then what?'

Griso put forward various plans, and Don Rodrigo examined them carefully, until they had agreed on ways to carry the enterprise through to its conclusion without leaving anything to show who its authors were; to lay a false trail to divert suspicion elsewhere; to force poor Agnese to keep her mouth shut; to terrify Renzo into forgetting his grief and giving up the thought of recourse to the law or even of complaint; and all the other minor villainies necessary to the success of the principal one. We shall not report the details of these plans, because, as the reader will see, they are not necessary to the narrative; and in any case, we do not in the least want to trouble him further with the dialogue of those two disgusting blackguards. But we must mention that, just as Griso was going away to get on with the job, Don Rodrigo called him back and said: 'Listen – if that presumptuous yokel falls into your clutches of his own accord tonight, it wouldn't be a bad idea to give him a good taste of your cudgel in advance. That'll make it all the easier for him to follow the advice he'll be receiving tomorrow about keeping his mouth shut. But don't go out of your way to look for him, and risk spoiling the most important part of the operation. Do you understand?'

'Leave it to me, your Honour,' said Griso, bowing with an air of swaggering obsequiousness; and he went away. The morning was devoted to reconnaissance. The supposed beggar who had forced his way so roughly into the poor little house was none other than Griso himself, who had come to memorize the layout of the rooms. The supposed travellers were his villainous subordinates, for whom a more superficial knowledge of the surroundings was enough. They had disappeared when they had finished their examination, to avoid arousing too much suspicion.

When they were back at the palace, Griso made his report and gave final form to his plan. He allotted each man his role, and issued detailed instructions. The old servant, whom we mentioned earlier, had his eyes and ears open, and could hardly fail to notice, from all these preparations, that something important was afoot. He listened constantly, he asked a few questions, he picked up half a sentence here and half a sentence there, he put his own interpretation on a mysterious phrase, he worked out the meaning of an obscure errand; and finally he had a clear picture of what was planned for that night. By then, however, it was already late in the day, and a small vanguard of bravoes had already gone off to conceal themselves in the ruined house. The poor old man knew very well what a risk he was running, and also realized that his help might be too late, but he was as good as his word. Saying that he needed some fresh air, he left the palace, and hurried off toward the monastery, to give Father Cristoforo the information he had promised him.

Soon afterwards the bravoes moved off – one at a time, to avoid giving the appearance of a gang. Griso followed them, and everything was then in position, except for a litter, which was to be carried down to the ruined house later in the evening. When this had been done, and the whole company was assembled there, Griso sent three of them to the village inn – one to wait outside, watch the street, and see when the local people were all home for the night; and the other two to sit inside, drinking and gambling like ordinary customers, and keep their eyes and ears open for any information that might turn up. Griso, with the bulk of his force, remained in hiding for the moment.

The poor old servant was still trotting along, the three scouts were just approaching the inn, and the sun was setting, when Renzo went to make his report to the women.

'Tonio and Gervaso are waiting for me outside,' he said. 'I'm going to the inn with them, and we'll have a bite to eat. When the bell rings for Ave Maria, we'll come and fetch you. You'll be brave now, won't you Lucia? Everything's going to depend on just the one moment.'

Lucia sighed, and said 'Brave . . . yes, I'll be brave!' but her voice belied the words.

When Renzo and his two friends reached the inn, they found the first bravo already there on sentry duty. He took up half the width of the entrance, leaning his back against a doorpost with his arms crossed on his chest, glancing constantly to left and right with an alternate flashing of the whites and the pupils of his hawk-like eyes. A flat cap of red velvet sat crookedly on his head, and covered half of his quiff, which was divided over his scowling forehead into two strands, that were carried round under his ears and ended in two pigtails, held in position by a comb at the back of his neck. A big cudgel hung from one hand. There was no outward sign of weapons, in the strict sense, about him; but the look of his face would have suggested to anyone – even a child – that he probably had as many concealed about his person as he could find room for. When Renzo, who had arrived before his friends, was about to enter the inn, the man stared him straight in the eye, with insolent assurance. Having a ticklish affair on his hands already, Renzo was above all anxious to avoid trouble; so he pretended not to notice anything, and did not even ask the man to make way for him, but squeezed sideways, close against the other doorpost, through the gap left by that strange caryatid. His two friends had to perform the same manoeuvre to get inside. When they were in, they saw two other men, whose voices they had heard from outside. These were the bravoes, who were sitting at one corner of the table playing the game of *mora*, both shouting at the same time (which, to be fair, is part of the game) and helping themselves in turn from a large bottle which stood on the table between them. They also stared at the newcomers. One of the two especially sat there with his hand still raised and three thick fingers splayed out in the air, and his mouth not yet shut from a great shout of 'six!' which he had just uttered, and looked Renzo over from head to foot; next he glanced first at his neighbour, and then at the man in the doorway, who replied with a nod. Alarmed and uncertain, Renzo looked at his two guests, as if hoping to find an explanation of those signals in their faces; but there was nothing to be read there except the signs of a healthy appetite. The host caught Renzo's eye, as if expecting him to order; Renzo beckoned him into a neighbouring room, and ordered supper.

'Who are those strangers?' he inquired finally, in a low voice, when the host returned, with a coarse tablecloth under his arm, and a bottle of wine in his hand.

'I don't know them,' answered the host, spreading the cloth.

'What, none of them at all?'

'You must know,' replied the host smoothing the cloth with both hands, 'that the first rule of our trade is never to inquire into other people's business. Even our women aren't inquisitive. We'd be in a fine mess otherwise, with all the people we get coming and going. It's just like a busy sea-port; though now I'm talking of years when the harvest's all right. But let's look on the bright side; those times are bound to come back sooner or later. All that matters to us is that our customers should be good citizens – it's no concern of ours who they may be or may not be. And now I'll bring you a plate of meat balls the like of which you never tasted before.'

'How can you tell . . .?' began Renzo; but the host had already moved off towards the kitchen, and did not turn back to answer him. While he was taking the pan of meat balls off the stove, the bravo who had looked Renzo up and down quietly came up to the host and softly said,

'Who are those people?'

'Good folk who live here in the village,' answered the host, ladling the meat balls into the dish.

'Yes, yes, but what are their names? Who are they?' insisted the bravo, in a low but rather discourteous voice.

'One is called Renzo,' replied the host, also speaking quietly; 'he's a good, orderly sort of lad, a silk-spinner, with a sound knowledge of his trade. The next one is a peasant called Tonio; a good, cheerful companion. I wish he had a great deal of money, for he'd spend it all here if he had. The last one is a simple fellow, but a good eater, when someone else is paying for him. Excuse me . . .' he sidestepped away between his questioner and the stove, and took the dish to its rightful destination.

'How can you tell,' said Renzo when the host returned, pursuing his former question, 'how can you tell that your customers are good citizens, if you've never seen them before?'

'By their actions, my dear fellow; all men are known by their actions. A man who drinks his wine without criticizing it, pays his bill without argument, and doesn't quarrel with the other customers; a man who, if he happens to have to stick a knife into somebody, goes and waits for him a good long way off from the inn, so that the unfortunate host doesn't get involved in it – that's what I call a good citizen. But of course it's better still if you know people personally, the way we four know each other. But why the devil are you asking all these questions, when you're just getting married and ought to be thinking about something quite different, and when you've got the finest meat balls in the world in front of you?'

He went back to the kitchen.

Our author remarks that the different style of the host's replies to those various questions reveal him to have been a man whose words professed great friendship for all good citizens, but whose actions showed more willingness to please those who had the reputation or outward appearance of knaves. A most extraordinary character, we must agree.

The supper was not a very cheerful meal. Renzo's two guests would have liked nothing better than to enjoy it to the full without a care in the world; but Renzo himself was preoccupied by matters well known to the reader, and also annoyed and somewhat alarmed by the odd behaviour of the three strangers, so that he was impatient to get out of the place. Because of the strangers, Renzo and his friends spoke softly, and their conversation was fitful and half-hearted.

'What luck for us', exclaimed Gervaso unexpectedly, 'that Renzo wants to get married and needs us to . . .' Renzo scowled at him. 'Shut up, will you, you fool!' said Tonio, jabbing him in the ribs with his elbow.

Their conversation grew more and more languid as the meal approached its end. Renzo ate and drank less than his two witnesses, whom he plied with wine, though only in moderation, hoping to infuse a little dash into them without making them too silly. The table was cleared, the bill was paid by the smallest eater, and then the three of them again had to run the gauntlet of those villainous looks, which were directed especially toward

Renzo, as they had been when he came in. Having walked a few yards away from the inn, Renzo turned round and saw that the two strangers whom he had left sitting inside had now followed him out. He stopped for a moment, with his two companions, as if to say: 'Let's see what those fellows want from me.' But when they saw that they had been observed, they halted too, whispered something to each other, and went back inside. If Renzo had been near enough to hear what they were saying, it would have struck him as very odd.

'It'd be a fine honour for us, not to speak of the extra reward we'd get,' one of the two blackguards was saying, 'if when we got back to the palace we could tell how we'd dusted his jacket properly for him – and just the three of us what's more, without Signor Griso being here to tell us what to do.'

'A fine honour we'd get for ruining the main operation!' said his companion. 'Look! He's noticed something; he's stopping and staring at us. What a pity it's not a bit later! Let's go back inside, and not make him suspicious. Why, there are people coming this way from all sides. Let's wait till they've all gone to roost.'

It was, in fact, that time of evening when a final stir and bustle takes possession of a village for a few minutes before the deep peace of night sets in. Women were coming in from the fields, some carrying a baby on their shoulders, others leading an older child by the hand, and listening to him as he repeated the evening prayer. The men were coming home too, with spades and mattocks on their shoulders. Doors were opened, and through them fires could be seen sparkling here and there – cooking fires, for the villagers' scanty suppers. Greetings were exchanged in the street, and remarks about the poverty of the crops and the wretchedness of the harvest. Louder than their words were the measured, sonorous notes of the bell that announced the end of day.

When Renzo saw that the two intruders had vanished, he continued on his way through the gathering shadows, from time to time whispering some final reminder to one or other of the two brothers. It was already night when they reached Lucia's cottage.

> 'Between the acting of a dreadful thing
> And the first motion, all the interim is
> Like a phantasma or a hideous dream.'

to quote a barbarian who was not devoid of genius. Lucia had been in the throes of just such a dream for many hours now; and Agnese, even Agnese, who had devised the plan, was very thoughtful, and could find words to encourage her daughter only with difficulty. But at the moment of waking from the dream, which is the moment when the main action is set in motion, everything is changed. The terrors and the courage which previously contended for the conspirator's being are replaced by new terrors and a different courage. The enterprise presents itself in a totally new light. The things which appeared most terrifying before may suddenly seem quite easy; an obstacle to which he had hardly given a thought may suddenly loom gigantic in his path. His imagination recoils in horror; his limbs refuse to obey him; his heart fails to keep its most confident promises.

When she heard Renzo's soft knock at the door, Lucia was overwhelmed with such terror that she resolved momentarily to suffer any fate, to part from her man for ever, rather than go on with their plan. But when she saw him, and heard him say: 'Here I am; let's go then'; when the whole party was evidently ready to move off, without hesitation, as if on a fixed and irrevocable course; then Lucia had neither the time nor the strength to raise any difficulties. As if dragged along, she took Agnese's arm with one trembling hand, and Renzo's with the other, and set out with the adventurous company.

Out of the cottage they went and into the shadows, very quietly, with measured tread, and took side roads, away from the village. The shortest way would have been straight across it; that was the route which led direct to Don Abbondio's house. But they went the other way to avoid being seen. They took various little paths which led between the villagers' back gardens and the open fields, and when they were near the curé's house they split up. Renzo and Lucia hid round the corner of the building; Agnese hid near them, but closer to the door, so that she could come up quickly to take charge of Perpetua and keep her out of mischief; and Tonio, with the idiot Gervaso (who could do nothing by himself, yet without whom nothing could be done), walked boldly up to the door and knocked.

'Who's there, at a time like this?' cried Perpetua, as she opened the window. 'Nobody's ill, that I know of; has there been an accident?'

'It's me,' said Tonio, 'me and my brother, to speak to his Reverence.'

'Is this a time for God-fearing people to be abroad?' said Perpetua roughly. 'Are you out of your minds? Come back tomorrow.'

'Listen, Perpetua, I might come back and I might not. I've had a little windfall, and I was thinking of paying up that small debt you may have heard of. I've brought twenty-five fine new lire with me. But if it can't be managed tonight, never mind: I've a very good idea what I can do with the money, and I'll be back when I've saved a bit up again.'

'Wait a bit then, Tonio. I'll be back in a moment. But what made you come so late?'

'Why, I only got the money just now, like I said; and if I took it home and slept on it, I don't know how I'd feel about it in the morning. But if you don't want me here so late, why, I don't know what to say. I'm here now, but if you don't want me, I'll go.'

'No, no, wait a minute. I'll be back at once.'

Perpetua shut the window. Agnese moved away from Renzo and Lucia, whispering 'Be brave, now, Lucia; it's only a moment, like having a tooth out.' She went up to the two brothers in front of the door, and began chatting to them, so that Perpetua would think she had been passing that way by chance and that Tonio had stopped her for something.

Chapter 8

'CARNEADES! who was he now?' Don Abbondio was murmuring to himself, as he sat in his big armchair, in an upstairs room, with a book in front of him, when Perpetua came in with her message. 'Carneades! I'm sure I've seen or heard that name somewhere. He must have been a learned man, one of the great scholars of antiquity; one of those ancient names; but who was he?' – such was the distance the poor fellow was from foreseeing the storm which was gathering over his head!

The reader must realize that Don Abbondio liked to read a little every evening. A neighbouring priest, who had a small library, lent him one book after another, generally giving him the first volume that came to hand. Don Abbondio was passing the period of convalescence from the attack of fever caused by his recent fright – though he had recovered from the fever, at least, more completely than he chose to admit – in the perusal of a panegyric on San Carlo Borromeo, which had been pronounced in an exaggerated style and welcomed with excessive admiration in Milan Cathedral a couple of years before. In it the saint was compared with Archimedes for his love of study; and that reference gave Don Abbondio no trouble, for Archimedes did so many strange things, and got himself so much talked about, that little erudition is needed to know something about him. But the next comparison introduced by the orator was a comparison with Carneades, and on that shoal Don Abbondio ran aground. At that very moment in came Perpetua to announce Tonio's visit.

'At a time of night like this?' said Don Abbondio, naturally enough.

'What do you expect? These people have no sense. But if you don't take the opportunity . . .'

'You're right there, Perpetua. If I don't take this opportunity,

when will I ever have another? Bring him in ... but listen!
Are you quite sure it really is Tonio?'

'Sure, indeed!' said Perpetua, and went downstairs. She
opened the door and said, 'Well, where are you?' Tonio came
forward, and so did Agnese, who called Perpetua by name.

'Good evening, Agnese,' said Perpetua, 'and where might
you be coming from at this hour of the night?'

'From ...' said Agnese, naming a near-by village. 'And as a
matter of fact, Perpetua, it was on your account that I stayed
there a bit later than I'd meant to.'

'Whatever do you mean?' asked Perpetua. Turning to the
brothers, she said, 'Go on in; I'll be with you in a minute.'

'Well,' said Agnese, 'I met a stupid woman there, one of
those who don't know anything but have to be talking all the
time, and, you'll never believe it, but she maintained that the
reason you never married Beppe Suolavecchia or Anselmo Lun-
ghigna was that they wouldn't have you. I kept telling her that
it was all the other way round, that you'd turned them down,
both of them, one after the other ...'

'Why, that's just what happened. Oh, what a liar! What a
wicked liar! Who was it?'

'Ah, don't ask me that, now, Perpetua. I hate to cause
trouble.'

'No, no, no – tell me, you must tell me. Oh, the liars there are
in the world!'

'Very well, then – but you can't think how upset I was not to
know the whole story. Then I could have put her in her place
properly.'

'It's truly wicked the things people make up,' cried Perpetua,
'As far as Beppe's concerned, everyone knows, for it was quite
obvious ... Tonio, push the door to, and go on up; I'll be there
in a couple of minutes.'

'I will,' said Tonio from inside, and Perpetua went on with
her impassioned narrative.

Opposite Don Abbondio's door was a narrow track, which
led away between two small cottages, and then turned off across
the fields. Agnese moved off in that direction, as if in search of
a quiet place where they could talk more freely, and Perpetua

followed her. When they were round the corner, out of sight of the curé's front door, Agnese coughed loudly. This was the signal; Renzo heard it, and squeezed Lucia's arm encouragingly. They crept forward on tiptoe, close to the wall, very quietly; they reached the door, and pushed it open very gently. Bent double in their caution, they went silently into the hall, where the two brothers were waiting for them. Renzo softly pushed the door to again, and all four of them went upstairs, making less noise than one ordinary visitor. When they were on the landing, the brothers approached the door of the curé's room, which was next to the staircase. Renzo and Lucia flattened themselves against the wall.

'*Deo gratias,*' said Tonio loudly.

'Is that you, Tonio? Come on in!' said Don Abbondio's voice.

Tonio opened the door just enough to allow the passage of himself and his brother, one at a time. A ray of light fell suddenly across the floor of the darkening landing, making Lucia jump, as if she had been discovered. Tonio shut the door behind himself and his brother; Renzo and his bride remained outside in the shadows, holding their breath and listening intently. The loudest noise to be heard was the beating of poor Lucia's heart.

Don Abbondio was still sitting in his old chair, wrapped up in an old cassock, with an old bonnet on his head framing his face in the feeble light of a small lamp. He had two thick strands of hair emerging from the bonnet, a pair of thick eyebrows, a thick moustache, and a thick tuft of beard on his chin. All these whitish whiskers, scattered over his brown, wrinkled face, had the look of snow-covered bushes growing out of a moonlit rock.

'Ugh! ugh!' he said, by way of greeting, as he took off his spectacles and tucked them into the book he was reading.

'Your Reverence'll be thinking that I've come rather late,' said Tonio, with a bow. Gervaso bowed clumsily in his turn.

'It's late, all right, in more ways than one. And didn't you know I was ill?'

'Oh, I'm sorry.'

'You must have heard, surely. I'm not well, and I don't know when I shall be back to my duties . . . But why did you bring that . . . that lad with you?'

'Why, just for company, your Reverence.'

'All right; let's have a look at the money then.'

'It's twenty-five fine new lire, the kind that have St Ambrose riding his horse on them,' said Tonio, bringing out a screw of paper from his pocket.

'Let's have a look,' repeated Don Abbondio. He took the paper, put his spectacles on again, opened it up and took out the coins, counted them, turned them over, turned them over again, and found them perfect.

'Now, your Reverence, will you please give me back my wife's necklace again?'

'That's right enough,' said Don Abbondio. He went to a cupboard, took a key from his pocket, and looked round defensively, as if to keep the spectators at a distance; then he opened up one section of the cupboard, and quickly blocked the aperture with his body. He inserted first his head, to see where the necklace was, and then his hand, to take it out. He relocked the cupboard, and gave the necklace to Tonio, saying, 'Is that all right?'

'Now,' said Tonio, 'I'd like something in black and white, if your Reverence would be so kind.'

'Black and white!' said Don Abbondio. 'There's not much you people don't know nowadays. What a suspicious world this has become! Don't you trust me?'

'Trust you, your Reverence! Of course I do. But as you've got my name written down already in your great black book, as one of your debtors . . . since you've had the trouble of writing it down once before . . . and there's many a slip . . .'

'Yes, yes, all right, then,' Don Abbondio interrupted him. Still muttering, he opened one of the drawers of his writing-table, took out pen, paper and ink, and began to write, saying each word aloud as he formed its letters. Meanwhile Tonio made a little sign to Gervaso, and both of them planted themselves in front of the desk, blocking Don Abbondio's view of the door. As if for lack of anything better to do, they began noisily shuffling their feet, to let the couple outside know it was time for them to come in, and also to mask the sound of their steps. Don Abbondio was immersed in the task of writing, and had eyes and ears for nothing else. Hearing the stir made by those two pairs of feet, Renzo took Lucia's arm, squeezed it to encourage her, and walked in, pulling the trembling girl behind him, as she could not put one foot in front of the other by herself. They went in on tip-toe, very quietly, holding their breath, and hid behind the two brothers. Meanwhile Don Abbondio finished what he was writing, and reread it carefully, without raising his eyes from the paper. He folded the sheet in four, saying 'I hope you're content now.' Then he took off his glasses with one hand while he held out the receipt to Tonio with the other, raising his eyes as he did so. As Tonio put his hand out to take it, he stepped to the right, at the same time motioning Gervaso to step to the left. Between them appeared Renzo and Lucia, as if revealed by the parting of the curtains in a theatre. Through Don Abbondio's mind passed a confused image, a clear picture, horror, bewilderment, rage, reflection, and a practical resolution – all in the time it took Renzo to utter the words: 'Your Reverence, in the presence of these witnesses, this is my wife.' His lips were still moving when Don Abbondio dropped the receipt, seized the lamp with his left hand and held it up, grabbed the table-cloth and tugged it violently towards him with the other hand, hurling books, paper, pen, ink and sand-box to the floor, sprang up, dodged between writing-table and chair and rushed at Lucia. The poor girl's gentle voice, trembling with emotion, had hardly got out the words: 'And this is . . .' when Don Abbondio roughly threw the tablecloth over her head, to stop her completing the formula. Then he dropped the lamp, freeing both hands for the task of gagging her, and indeed half-smothered her. Meanwhile he screamed for Perpetua with the full force of his lungs.

'Perpetua! Perpetua!' he cried. 'Help! We're betrayed! Help!'

The lamp lay on the floor, its dying wick shedding a faint and flickering light on Lucia, who was completely dismayed, and did not even try to disentangle herself. She stood there like a clay figure over which the sculptor has thrown a damp cloth. Then the light went right out, and Don Abbondio left the poor girl and groped his way towards the door which led to an inner room. He found the handle, got inside and locked the door behind him, still shouting: 'Perpetua! Help! We're betrayed! Get them out! Out of the house! Get them out!'

Confusion reigned supreme in the first room. Renzo was trying to stop the curé, making swimming motions with his arms, as if playing blind man's buff. Finally he found the inner door, and banged on it, shouting 'Open up, sir! Stop shouting and open up!' Lucia was calling weakly for Renzo, and saying: 'Let's go now, for heaven's sake, let's go!' Tonio was crawling about on all fours, sweeping the floor with his hands in an attempt to recover his receipt. Demented with fear, Gervaso was screaming and hopping about in search of the door which led to the stairs and to safety.

Amid all this commotion, we must pause for a moment to make one comment. On the one hand Renzo, creating a disturbance at night in another man's house, which he had entered by fraud, keeping the householder besieged in one of his own rooms, had all the look of a persecutor; yet he was really the persecuted party. On the other hand, Don Abbondio had been surprised, put to flight and terrorized, while he was peacefully minding his own business; he seemed to be the victim, yet he was in fact the oppressor. It is often like that in this world – at least, it used often to be like that in the seventeenth century.

Seeing that his besiegers showed no sign of withdrawing, the curé opened a window which looked out over the church square, and began to cry 'Help! Help!' It was a beautiful moonlit night. The shadow of the church lay black and sharp-edged across the grassy, shining surface of the square, and beyond it lay the long, pointed shadow of the bell-tower. Everything was almost as clear as by daylight. But whichever way Don Abbondio looked, there was no sign of life at all. Against the side wall of the church, however, opposite the curé's house, was a small building, a mere hovel, where the sexton slept. Don Abbondio's wild cries woke him up, and he quickly jumped out of bed, drew aside the piece of cloth which served as a curtain to his little window, and blearily put out his head.

'What's up?' he shouted.

'Help! Help!' cried the priest. 'Come quickly, Ambrogio! There's someone in my house.'

'I'm coming,' said Ambrogio. His face vanished from the window, and the rough curtain fell back into position. Though he was half asleep, and more than half terrified, he very soon thought of a way of providing all the help he had been asked for, and more, without getting himself involved in whatever devilry was afoot. He grabbed his breeches, which were on the bed, tucked them under his arm as if carrying his best hat, and leaped down the rickety wooden steps. He ran straight to the bell-tower, seized the rope of the larger of the two bells, and rang an alarm.

Clang! Clang! Clang! Men sat up in bed; the boys in the hay-lofts heard the sound and jumped up. 'What is it? What is it? The alarm bell! Is it a fire? Or robbers? Or bandits?' Women advised or implored their husbands to stay where they were and let others answer the call. Some men got up and looked out of the window. The cowards got back into bed as if in response to their wives' appeals. Those who were most curious or most courageous went downstairs, got out their pitchforks and muskets, and ran out to find the source of the noise; others watched them.

But before any of them were ready for action – before they were fully awake, in fact – the noise reached the ears of various other people not far away, who had not yet gone to bed, and were still fully dressed and awake: the bravoes in one place, and Agnese and Perpetua in another. First we must give a brief account of what the bravoes had been doing since we last saw them, with the main party in the ruined house and the advance party in the tavern. When the doors of all the houses were shut and the street was deserted, the three in the inn left hurriedly, as if they had suddenly realized how late it was, saying they must go straight home. They walked right through the village, to make sure that everyone was indoors; and in fact they met no one, and heard not the slightest noise. They also walked softly past the poor little house where Lucia lived, which was the quietest of all, since there was no one at home. Then they went straight to the ruined house, and reported to Griso. He at once put on a great ugly hat, threw a waterproof cape covered with sea-shells over his shoulders, and picked up a pilgrim's staff. 'Let's do this job like true bravoes,' he said. 'Be very quiet, and pay attention to your orders.' Griso led the way, the others followed, and in a couple of minutes they were at the cottage, which they approached from the opposite direction to that taken by our friends, when their little band set out on its own expedition. Griso halted his men a short way back, and went on alone to spy out the land. As there was no sign of life out of doors, he called up two of his villains, and told them to climb over the courtyard wall and hide in the corner, behind a leafy fig-tree which he had noticed the previous morning. Then he knocked softly at the outer gate, intending to pose as a pilgrim who had lost his way and was looking for a night's shelter. No one answered; he knocked again, a little louder; still no sound. So he called up another of his ruffians and sent him over the wall like the others, with orders to disconnect the latch, so that it would be easy to get in and out. All this was done very carefully, and with complete success. Griso fetched the rest of the gang, led them into the courtyard, and hid them in the same place as the first two. He pushed the outer gate to, posted two sentries just inside it, and went straight on to the front door. He knocked on it, and waited a little – as well he might. He very quietly unfastened this door too. No one challenged him from inside; nothing could be heard. The whole thing seemed to be turning out very well, and he decided to go on. He softly called up the men from behind the fig-tree, and led them into the downstairs room where, the morning before, he had treacherously begged that piece of bread. He got out flint and steel, tinder and slow matches, and lit a small lamp that he had with him. Then he went into the backroom to make sure that it was empty; and so it proved. He came back, and went to the door leading to the stairs. He looked up them, and listened; not a sound, no sign of life. He posted two sentries on the ground floor, and went on up with Grignapoco, a bravo from Bergamo, who, according to the plan, was to undertake whatever threatening, cajoling, and issuing of orders might be necessary – to do all the talking, in fact – so that Agnese might think, from his accent, that the gang came from those parts. With Grignapoco at his side, and the others behind him, Griso went very softly up, silently cursing every creaking stair, and every noisy movement made by his followers. At last he reached the top. This is it, he said to himself. He gently pushed the door of the first room; it yielded, leaving a crack to which he put one eye, but could see nothing in the dark. He put an ear to it, in case anyone might be snoring, breathing heavily, or stirring in there; not a sound. He decided to go on. He raised his lamp in front of his eyes, so that he could see without being seen; he pushed the door right open, and saw a bed, which he quickly approached. But the bed was empty, tidily made up, with the bedclothes turned back over the pillow. He shrugged his shoulders, turned to his companions, and signalled to them that he was going into the other bedroom and that they should follow him quietly. He went in, and followed the same procedure again, with the same result.

'What the devil can this mean?' he said. 'Has some treacherous swine been spying on us?' They all began to look round in a less cautious manner, groping in every corner, turning everything upside down. While this was going on, the two men who were guarding the outer gate heard a noise of scurrying little feet, rapidly approaching. Thinking that, whoever it might be, he would go straight by, they kept quiet, though remaining on the alert. But the hurrying feet stopped at the gate. It was Menico, who had run all the way with a message from Father Cristoforo, telling the two women for God's sake to leave their house at once and take refuge in the monastery, because ... well, we know the reason already. The boy took hold of the handle of the latch, to knock on the gate with it, and it swung loose in his hand, since the nails that held the latch to the wood had been pulled out. 'What can have happened?' thought Menico, timidly pushing the gate. It swung open. Menico stepped inside, very frightened, and both his arms were seized in the same moment, while two threatening voices, from left and right, whispered simultaneously 'Keep quiet, or I'll kill you!'

In spite of this warning, Menico uttered a yell. One ruffian put a hand over his mouth, while the other pulled out a great knife, to frighten him. The boy shook like a leaf, and made no further attempt to call out. But a different sound suddenly reached their ears – the first loud, isolated stroke of the bell, followed by the rapid series of similar strokes that made up the alarm.

A bad conscience makes a timid heart, according to the Milanese proverb. Each of the two blackguards seemed to hear his Christian name, surname and nickname spelled out in the ringing of that bell. They let go of Menico, withdrawing their hands with a start. Their jaws dropped, their fingers slackened; they gaped at each other, and dashed towards the house, where the bulk of their companions were. Menico fled down the road towards the bell-tower, where, he thought, there must be someone who could help him.

The other ruffians who were searching the house were equally affected by the sound of that terrible bell. Confused and dismayed, they jostled each other as each one of them scrambled to find the shortest way to the door. These were all men of tried quality, used to bold action; but they could not stand firm against an indeterminate danger, which gave no sign of its coming before it was on them. Griso had to use all his authority to hold them together, and prevent the retreat turning into a rout. Just as a swineherd's dog dashes here and there to round up stragglers, grabbing one by the ear to pull it back into line, pushing another with his muzzle, barking at a third which is just about to break ranks; so the man in the pilgrim's cloak seized one who had already reached the door and pulled him back, used his staff to thrust back two more who were making off in the same direction, shouted at the others who were running around without knowing where they were going, and finally shoved them all together in the middle of the courtyard.

'Quick, now!' he cried. 'Pistols drawn; knives at the ready; form up properly and then we can go. That's the way to do it. No one'll touch us if we keep together, you fools! But if we split up, the peasants will knock us off one by one. You ought to be ashamed of yourselves! Now follow me, and keep together.' After this short speech, he put himself at the head of his troop, and led the way out. The cottage, as we mentioned before, was at the end of the village; Griso took the road that led out into the country, and his men followed him in good order.

Here we must leave them, and return to Agnese and Perpetua, whom we left talking in the lane by the curé's house. Agnese had done her best to lure Perpetua as far away as possible; and the thing had gone very well up to a certain point. But suddenly the servant remembered that the door had been left open, and insisted on going back. There was little Agnese could do; to avoid arousing suspicion, she had to turn round and follow her back, though she tried to delay her, every time that she noticed her warming to her tale of matchmaking that had come to nothing. She let Perpetua see that she was listening very carefully, and from time to time she showed interest, or started her off again, by saying 'Why, now I understand', or 'Of course, that's clear enough', or 'And then what did he say? and what did you tell him?' But meanwhile Agnese was carrying on a separate conversation with herself: 'Will they have done it and got out by now, or are they still inside there? What fools we were, all three of us, not to have agreed on a signal to let me know when it was all over! We must have been mad! But it's too late now; all I can do is to hang on to Perpetua as long as I can. It won't cost me more than a little wasted time anyway.'

With a brief halt here, and a little spurt there, they had returned to a point not far from Don Abbondio's house, though it was still out of sight round the corner. Perpetua had reached an important point in her story, so that she let herself be halted again, without resistance and in fact without noticing what had happened. Suddenly, echoing from on high, ringing through the empty stillness of the air, through the vast silence of the night, came that first tremendous yell from Don Abbondio: 'Help! Help!'

'Mercy on us! What was that?' said Perpetua, preparing to run.

'What is it? What is it?' said Agnese, holding her by the skirt.

'Mercy on us! Can't you hear?' said Perpetua, disengaging herself.

'What is it? What is it?' said Agnese again, grabbing her by the arm.

'Blast the woman!' cried Perpetua, pushing Agnese away to free herself, and breaking into a run. Just then another cry was heard – a shorter, sharper, more distant sound. It was Menico's voice.

'Mercy on us!' exclaimed Agnese in her turn, and she dashed off behind Perpetua. But they had scarcely got up speed when the bell began to ring: one, two, three, four, five, six, seven . . . its strokes would have served as a spur to the two women, if they had needed one. Perpetua reached the house a second before Agnese. Just as she was going to open the door, it was flung open from inside, and Tonio, Gervaso, Renzo and Lucia appeared on the threshold. They had found the stairs in the end, had hurried down them, and were now making all the speed they could to get away from the sound of that terrible bell, and into safety.

'What's happened? What's happened?' panted Perpetua; but the brothers just pushed her out of the way and ran for it.

'You! What on earth are you doing here?' she said to Renzo and Lucia, when she had made out who they were. But they too made off without answering. Perpetua decided not to waste any more time on questions, but to hurry to the place where she was most needed. She quickly went into the hall, and hastened towards the stairs, as best she could in the dark.

The betrothed couple – still betrothed, alas! – then found themselves face to face with Agnese, who arrived quite out of breath. 'There you are then!' she said, getting the words out with difficulty. 'How did it go? What's the bell for? And didn't I hear . . .?'

'We must get back home at once,' said Renzo, 'before the whole village turns out.' They set off; but just then Menico ran up. He recognized them and made them stop. Trembling all over, he hoarsely said; 'Not that way! Turn back! Turn back! Come this way, to the monastery.'

'Menico, was it you who . . .?' began Agnese.

'What's the rest of the news?' said Renzo. Quite bewildered, Lucia trembled and said nothing.

'There's something hellish going on at the cottage,' said Menico, panting. 'I saw them myself; they wanted to kill me . . . Father Cristoforo said that, and said you were to come at once too, Renzo . . . I saw them myself. Thank God I found you all together! I'll tell you the rest when we've got safely away.'

Renzo, who was the most self-possessed of the little band, reflected that they must make a move one way or the other, before a crowd collected, and concluded that it would be best to follow the course that Menico had suggested – or rather commanded, with the authority of terror. When they had gone a little way, and were out of danger, it would be easy to get a clearer explanation out of the lad.

'Lead on, Menico,' he said. 'Let's follow him,' he added, turning to the women. They all turned round, and made their way quickly towards the church. They crossed the church square, where by the mercy of heaven there was still no one to be seen, found their way along a narrow lane between the church and the curé's house, dodged through the first gap that they saw in the hedge, and made off into the fields.

They had not gone more than fifty yards, when a crowd began to collect on the church square, and rapidly grew to a considerable size. Its members looked inquiringly at each other; every one of them had a question on his lips, to which nobody knew the answer. The first to arrive went straight to the church door; but it was locked. They ran on to the bell-tower; and one of them put his mouth to a little window, a sort of grating, and shouted 'What the devil's happening?'

Ambrogio knew the voice, and let go of the rope. The buzz of conversation from outside gave him the comforting assurance that plenty of people had arrived. 'I'll just open the door,' he called out. He quickly put on the garments he had been carrying under his arm, went through to the main door of the church, and opened it.

'What's all this disturbance for, then?' – 'What is it?' 'Where is it?' – 'Who is it?'

'What do you mean, "Who is it?"' said Ambrogio, holding

155

on to the edge of the door with one hand, and holding up his breeches, which he had put on with such perilous speed, with the other, 'Don't you know, then? There's someone got into his Reverence's house! Show what you're made of, lads – go and help him.'

They all turned and looked at the curé's house, and then thronged towards it. They looked up at the windows and listened; all was quiet. Some ran round to his front door; it was locked, and apparently undamaged. They looked up at the front windows, which were all shut. Not a sound could be heard.

'Who's that inside there? Answer us!' – 'Your Reverence! Your Reverence!'

Don Abbondio had shut his window as soon as he was sure that the invaders had really gone. He was now having a whispered discussion with Perpetua, who had deserted him in his time of trouble; but when he heard all those voices calling him he had to go back to the window. Seeing the number of helpers who had answered his call, he regretted having raised the alarm.

'What happened?' – What did they do to you, sir?' – 'Who was it?' – 'Where are they?' – Fifty voices were shouting at him at once.

'They've gone – thank you very much – now please go home.'

'But who was it?' – 'Where did they go?' 'What happened?'

'They were bad people – the sort of people who wander round at night – but they've run away. Go home now, my children; there's no one here now. I'll tell you the rest of it some other time. Many, many thanks for all your kindness.'

His head vanished, and the window was shut. There was some grumbling among the crowd, some mockery, and some swearing. Some people shrugged their shoulders, and were just going away, when a messenger appeared who was so out of breath that he could hardly get a word out. He lived almost opposite Lucia's cottage; the noise made by the bravoes had brought him to his window, and he had seen them milling about in the courtyard while Griso was trying to get them back into order. When he had got his breath back, he shouted: 'What are you doing here, friends? This isn't where the trouble is at all; it's down the other end, at Agnese Mondella's house. There's a band of armed men there; they'd got inside, and seemed to be trying to kill a pilgrim. God knows what's happening!'

'What's that?' – 'What's that?' – 'What's that?' – a tumultuous discussion broke out. 'Let's go, then.' – 'Let's see, first.' – 'How many of them are there?' – 'How many are there of us?' – 'Who are they, anyway?' – 'The headman! Where's the headman?'

'I'm here,' replied the headman's voice, from the middle of the crowd. 'But you people must help me, and do what I say. Quick now! Where's the sexton? Ring the alarm, Ambrogio! And quick again! I need someone to run down to Lecco and get help. All gather round me now.'

Some gathered round; others squeezed away through the crowd and made off. The confusion was tremendous. Then another messenger arrived, who had seen the bravoes' hurried retreat. 'Come on, lads,' he cried. 'It's a gang of thieves or bandits who've kidnapped a pilgrim. They're heading away from the village now. Come on, follow them!'

At this news the crowd moved off in a mass, without waiting for their captain's orders, and poured down the street. As the army moved forward, one or other of those in the front rank slowed his pace from time to time, and let the others overtake him, so that he was lost in the main body. The people at the back pushed valiantly on. Finally the whole confused swarm reached their destination. The traces of invasion were recent and obvious – the gate flung open, with its disconnected latch – but the invaders had vanished. They went into the courtyard, and up to the front door, which had also been tampered with and was wide open. 'Agnese! Lucia!' they shouted. 'Where's the pilgrim?' – 'Stefano must have imagined the pilgrim.' – 'No, no; Carlandrea saw him too.' – 'Where are you, pilgrim?' 'Agnese! Lucia!' – No reply. – 'They've been kidnapped! They've been kidnapped!'

One or two voices were raised in favour of following the kidnappers, saying that it was a disgraceful thing, and would bring shame on the village, if any crook could just calmly come and carry off their women, like a kite snatching chicks from a deserted farmyard. There was another and even more tumultuous discussion, in the middle of which someone (it was never established exactly who) let fall the statement that Agnese and Lucia had escaped and were safe in someone else's house. The word passed quickly round, and was generally believed. No more was heard about pursuing the enemy, the meeting gradually broke up, and everyone went home.

There was a whispering and a clatter, a knocking and an opening of doors; a flashing and a disappearing of lamps; questions from women at windows and answers from men in the street below. When the street was empty and deserted again, the talk began afresh indoors, and finally died away in yawns, though it started up again in the morning. Nothing else actually happened, except that, on that very same morning, the headman was in the middle of his field, his chin resting on his hand, his elbow resting on the handle of his spade, which was halfway embedded in the soil, and his foot resting on the cross-bar, deep in speculation about the mysteries of the previous night, and the double problem of what action his duty demanded and what action his interest would permit, when two men appeared before him. They were of valiant bearing, and as long-haired as the earliest monarchs of the Franks. They were strikingly like the two men who had accosted Don Abbondio five days before, and may even have been the very same. In an even more unceremonious manner they warned the headman not to make any statement to the mayor about what had happened, not to tell him the truth if he asked about it, not to gossip about it nor to encourage the gossip of the villagers, if he valued his chances of dying in bed.

Our fugitives went on in silence at a good speed for some time, one or other of them turning round from time to time to see if they were being followed, in great distress from the fatigue of their flight, the anxiety and suspense through which they had passed, the bitterness of failure, and the confused apprehension of their new, obscure danger. Even more nerve-racking was the continual ringing of the bell, which was soon muted and deadened by distance, but somehow seemed all the more dismal and sinister as a result. Finally the ringing came to an end. At that moment the fugitives were in a field far from the nearest house, and as they could hear no sign of life around them, they slackened their pace. Agnese was the first to get her breath back and break the silence, asking Renzo how the main enterprise had gone, and Menico what he meant by something hellish going on at her house. Renzo told his sad story in a few words, and all three of them turned to Menico, who gave them a more exact account of his message from Father Cristoforo, and told them about the things he had seen and the dangers he had run, which confirmed that message all too well. They understood more from Menico's words than he himself was able to tell them, and they shuddered at what they understood. All three of them halted, and looked at each other in horror; and then all three reached out and put a hand on the boy's head or shoulders, to show their affection for him, their gratitude for the role of guardian angel which he had played, and their sympathy for the distress he had suffered and the perils through which he had passed for their sake; and in a sense to beg his pardon for all those things.

'Now go home, Menico, so that your mother won't be worried about you any more,' said Agnese. She suddenly remembered the two pennies she had promised him, and took four out of her pocket. 'That's all I can give you now,' she said. 'Pray God we shall meet again soon, and then . . .' Renzo gave him a new lira, and urged him never to mention Father Cristoforo's message to anyone. Lucia patted his shoulder again, and bade him farewell in a broken voice; and Menico's own voice was unsteady as he said good-bye and turned away. The other three went sadly on their way, the women in front, and Renzo guarding the rear. Lucia held tightly to her mother's arm. In her gentle, deft way, she was careful not to accept the help Renzo offered her in the difficult parts of that cross-country journey. Amid all her other distress she was secretly ashamed of having already spent so much time alone with him, on such a familiar footing, during the time when she had thought that a few more minutes would see them man and wife. Now that that hope had been so painfully destroyed, she was sorry that she had gone so far. Though she had many other reasons to tremble, she trembled also from shame – not the shame which arises from the dismal consciousness of sin, but the shame that hardly knows its cause, like the fear of a child in the dark, who does not know of what he is afraid.

'What about the cottage?' said Agnese suddenly. But though this was an important question, no one replied, because no one could find a useful answer. They walked on in silence, until finally they came out on the little square in front of the church by the monastery.

Renzo went up to the church door, and gave it a push. The door began to swing open, and the moonlight that penetrated through the crack lit up the pale face and silvery beard of Father Cristoforo, who was standing there waiting for them. He looked round to make sure they were all there, and, with a murmur of 'Thanks be to God', motioned them to come inside. Next to him stood another Capuchin – the lay brother who served as sexton. With much argument and many prayers, Father Cristoforo had induced the sexton to stay up with him, to leave the door unlocked, and to keep guard over it, so that those poor folk could find refuge from the threats that hung over them. It had taken all the good father's authority, and all his reputation as a saint, to persuade the sexton to agree to that inconvenient, dangerous and irregular concession. Once they were all inside, Father Cristoforo gently pushed the door to again. This was too much for the sexton, who called him on one side, and whispered: 'Really, father, really! At night ... in a church ... with women ... closed doors ... the rules of the order ... my dear father!' He shook his head.

'Good heavens!' thought Father Cristoforo, while the sexton was stammering out those words, 'if it was a matter of a common murderer, with retribution at his heels, Brother Fazio wouldn't mind at all, but when it's a poor innocent girl, escaping from the jaws of the wolf ...'

'*Omnia munda mundis*,'[1] he said in the end, suddenly turning to Brother Fazio, and forgetting that he could not understand Latin. But it was just as well. If he had started putting

1. 'To the pure all things are pure.'

160

forward logical arguments, Brother Fazio would easily have found other logical arguments to oppose to them; and heaven knows when it would have finished or what would have come of it. But when the sexton heard those words, pregnant with mysterious significance, and pronounced with the greatest resolution, he felt that they must contain an adequate answer to all his doubts. His face cleared, and he said: 'Very well! you know more about it than I do.'

'You must trust me then,' said Father Cristoforo. In the uncertain light of the lamp that burnt before the altar, he went up to the refugees, who were waiting for him in great suspense, and said 'My children! Give thanks to the Lord, who has saved you from a great danger. At this very moment, perhaps . . . !'

He went on to explain the brief message he had entrusted to Menico in more detail. He had no idea that they knew more about it than he did, supposing that Menico had found them undisturbed at home, before the ruffians got there. No one put him right on this point; not even Lucia, though she felt a secret remorse at so blatant a deception of so fine a man. But this was a night of intrigue and subterfuge.

'After all that,' continued Father Cristoforo, 'you can see very well, my children, that this part of the world is no longer safe for you. It is your home; you were born here; you have done no harm to anyone; but such is the will of God. It is a trial that he has sent you, my children. Endure it with patience, with trust and without hatred, and be sure that a time will come when you will see that what is happening now was all for the best. I have been thinking about finding you a place of refuge for the immediate future. Soon, I hope, you will be able to return safely to your own homes; in any case, God will provide for you and do what is best for you. I for my part will try not to be unworthy of the grace he has shown me, in choosing me to be his servant in the care of you, his poor, beloved, afflicted people. Now you,' he said, turning to the two women, 'can stay for a while at —. There you will be sufficiently far away from danger, and, at the same time, not too far away from home. Go to our monastery there and ask for the Father Superior. Give him this letter; he will be another Father Cristoforo to you. And you, my dear

Renzo, for the moment you must go somewhere where you will be safe from the consequences of the anger of others, and of your own anger too. Take this letter to Father Bonaventura da Lodi, at our monastery by the East Gate in Milan. He will be a father to you, will give you guidance, will find you work, until you can return to your peaceful life here again. Now you must all go down to the shore of the lake, near the mouth of the Bione.' (This is a stream not far from Pescarenico.) 'There you will see a boat tied up. Call out: "Ship ahoy!" They'll call back "Who for?" and you must say: "St Francis." They'll take you on board, and carry you across to the other side of the lake. There you will find a cart which will take you straight to —.'

If anyone wonders how Father Cristoforo could get all the transport he needed, both by land and by water, at such short notice, he shows his ignorance of the powers of a Capuchin who was regarded as a saint.

Arrangements still had to be made for the guarding of the fugitives' houses. The good father accepted the keys, and undertook to deliver them to the people named by Renzo and Agnese. The poor woman sighed deeply as she took her key out of her pocket, remembering that the door was open, the place had been ransacked, and it was doubtful how much was still there to be guarded.

'Before you go,' said Father Cristoforo, 'let us all say a prayer to God: that he may be with you in this journey, and for always; and above all that he may give you strength, and put it into your hearts to desire that which is his will.' He knelt down in the middle of the church; and so did the others. After they had prayed in silence for a few moments, the good father uttered these words in a low but clear voice, 'We pray to thee also for the poor wretch who has brought us to this pass. We should be unworthy of thy mercy, if we did not heartily beg it for him also, knowing how sorely he needs it. In all our tribulation we have this comfort, that we are travelling the road that thou hast chosen for us; we can offer thee our sufferings, and they become a blessing. But that man! He is thine enemy. Unhappy creature! He is in strife with thee. Have pity on him, O

Lord; touch his heart, return him to thy friendship, and grant him all the good things that we wish for ourselves.'

He rose quickly to his feet, and said 'Come, my children; there is no time to lose. God protect you, and may his angels go with you; now you must be on your way.' As they moved off, stirred in a way which does not find expression in words but is plain to see without them, the good father added, with a catch in his voice, 'My heart tells me that we shall meet again soon.'

Certainly the heart always has something to say about the future to those who will listen to it. But what does the heart really know? At best, only a little about what has happened in the past.

Without waiting for a reply, Father Cristoforo went off towards the vestry. The travellers went out of the church, and Brother Fazio shut the door behind them. He too had a catch in his voice as he bade them farewell. They went very quietly down to the agreed place on the lakeside. The boat was there, the passwords were duly exchanged, and they went on board. The boatman pushed off with one oar; then he picked up the other and sculled out across the lake towards the opposite shore. There was not a breath of wind. The water was calm and smooth, and would have seemed quite motionless but for the trembling and wavering reflection of the moon, which rode high in the heavens above them. All that could be heard was the slow lapping of the sluggish waves against the pebbled beach, the more distant gurgling of the waters passing between the piers of the bridge, and the measured beat of the oars, which cut into the blue surface of the lake, suddenly emerged with dripping blades, and dipped into the water again. The bow cut through the swell, which joined up again behind the stern into a rippling wake, further and further out from the shore. The silent passengers turned their heads back to look at the mountains, and the moonlit countryside, varied here and there by great patches of shadow. Villages, houses and cottages were plain to see. Don Rodrigo's palace, with its squat tower, standing high above the little houses crowded together on the lower slopes of the promontory, looked like a savage villain standing wide awake and upright in the shadows amid a group of sleeping figures, plotting a crime. Lucia saw it and shuddered; then she ran her eye down the slope to her own little village, looked intently at its outskirts, and made out her own cottage. She could even see the dense foliage of the fig-tree that rose above the courtyard wall, and the window of her own room. She was sitting at the bottom of the boat, and now she laid her arm along the gunwale, and laid her forehead on her arm, as if to sleep, and wept quietly.

Farewell, you mountains which rise straight out of the water and up to the sky; you jagged, uneven peaks, which we who have grown up with you know so well, and carry impressed in our minds like the faces of our own family. Farewell, you streams, the murmur of whose voices we can tell apart like the voices of our closest friends. White houses spread glimmering across the slope, like flocks of grazing sheep, farewell! With what a melancholy tread any man must leave you who has grown up in your midst! Even those who leave you of their own free will, to seek their fortune, find that the dreams of wealth lose their glitter at that moment. They are amazed that they could ever have taken the decision to go, and would turn back at once, were it not for the thought of returning later with their pockets full of money. As they advance into the plain, their eyes turn away listless and weary from its vast uniformity; the air they breathe seems heavy and dead. Sad and preoccupied, they go on into the bustling towns. The houses huddled against each other, the streets that lead only into other streets, have a suffocating effect. They stand in front of buildings admired by foreigners, and think, with uneasy longing, of the little plot of land near their own village, the cottage on which they have so long had their eye, and which they intend to buy when they make their prosperous return to their beloved mountains.

What then must be the feelings of those who have never had a passing thought or a fugitive wish that went outside the boundaries of their mountain home, who have made the hills the background for all their future plans, and yet are torn far away from them by a perverse fate; who, swept away from their most cherished habits, frustrated in their dearest hopes, have to leave the hills, to go and seek out unknown people whom they have never felt any desire to meet, without even being able to guess at a possible time for their return!

'Farewell, my mother's house, where I used to sit, with a secret in my heart, listening to the ordinary sound of ordinary people's feet, and learning to distinguish the sound of one particular tread, which I awaited with a mysterious terror. Farewell that other house, to which I am still a stranger, and at which I have so often glanced out of the corner of the eye in passing, with a blush; in which my heart thought to find a tranquil, lasting home with my husband. Farewell, little church, where my soul so often recovered its peace, singing the praises of the Lord; where a certain rite was prepared for me, and promised to me; where the secret desire of the heart was to be solemnly blessed, and love was to become a holy duty; farewell! He who gave you so much joy is everywhere; and he never disturbs the happiness of his children, except to prepare for them a surer and greater happiness.'

These thoughts, or thoughts very much like them, passed through Lucia's mind, and similar thoughts occupied her two companions, as the boat carried them nearer and nearer to the right bank of the Adda.

Chapter 9

PRESENTLY the boat grounded; Lucia felt the shock, secretly wiped away her tears, and raised her head, as if waking up. Renzo went ashore first, and gave a hand to Agnese, who got out and gave a hand in her turn to Lucia; then all three of them sadly thanked the boatman.

'There's no need to thank me,' he said. 'We're here to help each other.' He withdrew his hand, with a horrified gesture, as if invited to take part in a robbery, when Renzo tried to slip into it a few of the small coins he had in his pocket. (He had taken the money with him that evening with the intention of rewarding Don Abbondio generously for a certain involuntary service.) The cart was waiting for them; the driver greeted his three passengers, helped them up, gave his horse the word to go on, and a cut of the whip; and they were on their way.

Our author gives no details of that nocturnal journey, and does not name the place to which Father Cristoforo had directed the two women. In fact he specifically says that he does not want to name it. The reasons for his reticence will appear as the story continues. Lucia's adventures during her stay there were entangled in a shadowy intrigue involving a person belonging to a family which was apparently very powerful at the time when our author was writing. To explain that person's strange behaviour in this particular episode he was forced to include a brief account of her early life; and in it the family appears in a light which the reader of these pages will judge for himself. But the information which the poor fellow hoped to withhold from us out of caution has been established beyond any doubt by certain further researches which we have completed.

A Milanese historian[1] who has occasion to mention the same

1. Josephus Ripamontius, *Historiae patriae*, Fifth Decade, Book VI, Chapter III, pp. 358 ff.

person also avoids naming both her and the place; but he does say in one passage that it was an ancient and noble town, a city in all but name; in another that it was situated on the Lambro; and in a third that it was the seat of an arch-priest.

Putting these facts together, we conclude that it can only have been Monza. In the vast treasure-house of scholarly inference, there may well be some specimens of greater subtlety than this one, but I doubt if there are any of more certainty. On a basis of well-founded conjecture, we could also add the name of the family; but, although it has been extinct for some time, we think it better to pass over it in silence, since we do not wish to risk wronging even the dead, and we prefer to leave future scholars some subjects for research.

So it was to Monza that the three travellers came, soon after sunrise. The driver took them to an inn; and as it was a place where he had often been, and he knew the inn-keeper well, he asked for a room for them, and took them up to it. They thanked him, and Renzo again tried to pay something for benefits received. But the driver, like the boatman, had a different reward in mind, of a less immediate but more abundant sort. He too withdrew his hand, and fled away to look after his beast.

After an evening such as we have described, and a night such as the reader can imagine – full of mournful reflections, in constant fear of some unpleasant encounter, exposed to an autumnal, not to say wintry breeze, and to the continual jolting of a most uncomfortable vehicle, which rudely awakened any of the passengers who began to nod off to sleep – it seemed like heaven to the three of them to be sitting on a stationary bench in a room of any description. They ate a meal, but its size was proportionate to the poverty of the times, the small sum of money they could afford in view of the uncertain future, and their lack of appetite. All three thought of the banquet they had planned two days earlier, and all of them sighed deeply.

Renzo wanted to stay there at least for the rest of the day, to see the women safely lodged, and give them what help he could in the time; but Father Cristoforo had advised them to send him on his way at once. So they told Renzo what the good father had said, and added various other reasons: that people would talk; that the more they put off the parting the more painful it would be; that he could come back before long to give them his news, and to hear theirs; and so on until he made up his mind to go. They made what plans they could to meet again as soon as possible. Lucia wept openly; Renzo held back his tears only with difficulty. Wringing Agnese's hand very tightly, he choked out the word 'Good-bye!' and left.

The women would have been in great difficulty but for the good carter, whose instructions were to take them to the Capuchin monastery, and give them any other help they might need. So they set out with him; the monastery, as everyone knows, was only a short way from the town. When they reached the door, he rang the bell, and asked for the Father Superior, who came at once and took the letter from him, as he stood on the threshold.

'Father Cristoforo, eh!' he said, recognizing the writing. His voice and expression showed clearly that he was speaking of a great friend. Father Cristoforo must have recommended the women very warmly, and described their plight very feelingly; for the Father Superior made movements of surprise and indignation as he read on; and when he raised his eyes from the paper, he fixed them on the two women with a look of compassion and interest. He finished the letter, and stood deep in thought for a moment; then he said: 'Only the Signora can help. If the Signora will take the responsibility . . .'

He took Agnese to one side, on the square in front of the monastery, and asked her some searching questions, to which she returned satisfactory answers. Then they walked back to where Lucia was standing, and he said: 'Well, ladies, I'll do my best for you; and I hope I shall be able to find you a very safe and honourable place of refuge, until it pleases the Lord to make better provision for you. Will you come with me?'

The two women nodded respectfully; and he went on: 'Good – I'll take you straight to the Signora's convent. But please walk a little way behind me. People always enjoy a bit of ill-natured gossip, and heaven knows what they'd say if they

168

saw the Father Superior walk down the street with a pretty girl
. . . in female company, I should have said.'

He walked on in front. Lucia blushed; the carter smiled at
Agnese, who could not help smiling back. The three of them
moved off, when the good father was well on his way, and they
walked about ten yards behind him. Then the women asked the
carter a question they had not ventured to put to the Father
Superior – who was the Signora?

'The Signora is a nun,' he replied; 'but she's not a nun like
the others. It's not that she's the abbess, nor yet the prioress; in
fact they say she's one of the youngest nuns there. But she can
trace her descent right back to Adam and Eve; and her ancestors long ago came from Spain, and had great authority
there. So they call her the Signora, to show that she's a great
lady. Everyone here calls her by that name, because they say
there's never been anyone like her in that convent; and her
family, down in Milan, still count for a lot – they're the sort of
people who always come best out of an argument. And that's
even more true in Monza, because her father, though he doesn't
live here, is the most powerful man in the place. And so she's
got the upper hand in the convent; and people outside have a
great respect for her too. When she takes anything on, she sees it
through to the end; so if this good father manages to put you in
her care, and she accepts you, you can be sure you'll be as safe
with her as if you were clinging to the altar.'

Soon they were approaching the town gate, which at that
time was flanked by an ancient, half-ruined old tower and part
of a tumble-down old castle – one or two of my readers may
remember a time when it was still there. The Father Superior
stopped and looked round to see if the others were coming;
then he strode through the gate and went straight to the convent. He stopped again when he reached its door, and waited
for the little band to catch up with him. He asked the carter to
return to the monastery a couple of hours later and take back a
message to Pescarenico. The carter promised to do so, and said
good-bye to the women, who loaded him with thanks and with
messages for Father Cristoforo. The Father Superior took
Agnese and Lucia into the outer courtyard of the convent, left

them in the portress's lodge, and went on alone to plead their case. A little later he came back, looking very pleased, and told them to follow him – none too soon for Lucia and Agnese, who had been much embarrassed by the remorseless questioning of the portress. As they crossed a second courtyard, he gave them some advice on their behaviour with the Signora.

'She's well disposed towards you,' he said, 'and she can do you any amount of good. Be modest and respectful, answer her frankly when she asks you a question, and leave the rest of the talking to me.'

They entered a ground-floor room which led into the parlour; before going in, the good father pointed to the door and whispered, 'She's in here', as if to remind them of his advice. Lucia had never been in a convent before, and when she went into the parlour, she looked all round in search of the Signora, meaning to curtsy to her. When she found there was no one in sight, she was very puzzled. Then she saw the good father and Agnese go towards a corner of the room, and, looking over there, she saw a curiously shaped window, covered by two heavy, close-barred gratings, with a hand's-breadth interval between them, beyond which stood a nun. She looked about twenty-five years old, and the first impression was one of beauty – a flawed beauty, however, which had lost its bloom and was almost ready to fall into decay. The black veil which was stretched across the top of her head fell on either side of her face, clear of her cheeks; under the veil a band of the whitest linen covered half her forehead, which was equally white in its different way. A second, pleated band framed her face, ending under her chin in a wimple, which hung down a little over her chest, covering the top of her black dress. That snowy forehead often wrinkled in an apparently painful spasm, and then her black eyebrows twitched rapidly together. Her eyes were very black. Sometimes they stared intently into your face, with arrogant inquiry; sometimes their gaze was rapidly lowered, as if in search of somewhere to hide. There were moments when an acute observer might have detected in them an appeal for affection, understanding and compassion; others when he might think he saw in them the instantaneous revelation of an inveterate, suppressed hatred, something strangely threatening and ferocious. Sometimes her eyes remained motionless, staring at nothing: one observer might have thought her possessed by a proud and slothful indifference, while another might suspect the affliction of a hidden sorrow, a preoccupation of long standing which had more power over her mind than the objects around her. The descending line of her pallid cheek followed a delicate and graceful curve, but its full beauty had begun to waste away. The colour of her lips was the palest pink; and yet they stood out against the pallor of her skin. Their motions, like those of her eyes, were abrupt and lively, full of expression and mystery. Her figure was tall and shapely; but the effect was lost in a certain carelessness of posture, or spoilt by her movements, which were hasty, uneven and much too full of determination for a woman – let alone for a nun. Even in her dress, there was something here and there that showed too much or too little regard for her appearance; which suggested a somewhat unusual nun. Her waist was laced in with a care which could not be called unworldly, and a curl of black hair emerged from the band over one temple. This showed forgetfulness or disregard of the rule which said that a nun's hair must always be kept short, from the day when it was cut off in the solemn ceremony of taking the veil.

These things made no impression on the two women, who knew little of the difference between one nun and another; and the Father Superior, who had seen her a number of times before, was already accustomed, like many others, to something strange in her appearance and manner.

At that moment she was standing behind the grating, as we mentioned before, with one hand languidly resting on the iron, and her white fingers entwined between the bars. She looked very fixedly at Lucia, who came hesitatingly forward.

'Reverend Mother – illustrious benefactress,' said the Father Superior, with bowed head, and hand on heart, 'this is the unfortunate girl; and I thank you for allowing me to hope that you will afford her your most effective protection . . . and this is her mother.'

Lucia and Agnese curtsied deeply, and the Signora made a

gesture which meant 'That's enough!' Then she turned to the good father, and said, 'I am most happy to be able to do something for our good friends the Capuchin Fathers. But first of all', she went on, 'tell me about her case in a little more detail, so that I can have a better idea what we can do for her.'

Lucia blushed, and lowered her head.

'Well, you see, Reverend Mother,' began Agnese, but the Father Superior silenced her with a look and said, 'This young woman has been recommended to my care by one of my brothers in the order. She has had to make a secret departure from her village to escape from terrible dangers. For some time she will be in need of a refuge where she can live without fear of recognition, and where no one will dare to molest her, even if . . .'

'What sort of dangers?' interrupted the Signora. 'Please don't talk in riddles, my dear father! You know we nuns like to hear a story in all its detail.'

'These', replied the Father Superior, 'are dangers regarding which no more than a hint should ever reach the chaste ears of the Reverend Mother.'

'Yes, yes – of course,' said the Signora quickly, reddening a little. Was this a blush of modesty? Anyone who saw the quick look of anger which accompanied her change of colour might well have had his doubts, especially if he compared it with the blush which from time to time spread across the cheeks of Lucia.

'It is sufficient to say this,' the Father Superior continued, 'that a certain arrogant nobleman – for not all those who have power in this world use the gifts of God to his glory and to the benefit of their neighbour, as you do, madam – a certain arrogant nobleman, I repeat, began by persecuting this poor creature with unworthy flatteries, and then, seeing that they had no effect, found it in his heart to persecute her openly, with brute force, so that the poor girl has had to flee from her own home.'

'Come here, young woman,' said the Signora to Lucia, beckoning with her finger. 'I know that the Father Superior is the soul of truthfulness; but no one can be better informed about this matter than yourself. It is for you to say whether this nobleman was a hateful persecutor to you, or not.'

As far as coming nearer was concerned, Lucia obeyed at once; but answering the question was another matter. Any inquiry on this subject, even from an equal, would have disturbed her considerably; coming from a great lady, who put it forward with a certain air of malicious doubt, it left her without the courage to reply.

'Signora ... Reverend Mother ...' she stammered, and seemed to have nothing further to add. Then Agnese, knowing that she was, after Lucia, the best informed person on that matter, felt that it was for her to come to her daughter's help.

'Most illustrious lady,' she said, 'I can bear witness that my daughter hated that nobleman the way the devil hates holy water; though she wasn't the devil, in this case, he was; but you'll excuse me if I put things badly, because we're just ordinary folk. The fact is that this poor girl was engaged to a young man of our own sort, a God-fearing young fellow, and well up in his trade; and if the curé had been a bit more of what I call a man – there, I know that I'm talking about one of the clergy, but after all Father Cristoforo, this good father's friend, is one of the clergy too, and he's a man full of goodness and charity, and if he were here, he could bear witness that ...'

'You are very quick to give your opinion without being asked for it,' the Signora interrupted, with a gesture of angry pride, which made her look almost ugly. 'Be quiet! I know very well that parents are never short of an answer to give in the name of their children.'

Very mortified, Agnese gave Lucia a look which meant, 'See the trouble I get into because you are so easily embarrassed!' The good father also signalled to the young woman, catching her eye and making an encouraging movement with his head, that now was the time for her to find her tongue and say something to help her mother out of difficulty.

'Reverend lady,' said Lucia, 'what my mother has just told you is the purest truth. The young man who was courting me ...', here she went very red, 'I chose him for my husband of my own free will. You must forgive me if I speak too boldly, but it's because I can't let you think badly of my mother. As for that nobleman – may God forgive him! – I'd rather die than fall

173

into his clutches. And if you will do this act of charity and give us a safe place to stay in, since we're reduced to begging for shelter and giving good people a lot of trouble, well, God's will be done, but you can be sure of one thing, Signora, that no one will ever say a more heartfelt prayer than the one we poor women'll say for you.'

'I believe what you say,' replied the Signora in a softer voice. 'But I would like you to tell me about it without anyone else being there. – Not that any other clarification or any other reasons are needed before we agree to the Father Superior's charitable wishes,' she added, turning to him with studied courtesy. 'In fact,' she went on, 'I already considered the matter, and this is what I think would be best for the moment. The portress's youngest daughter got married a few days ago. These women can have her old room, and can take over the little jobs that she used to do. As a matter of fact, father,' – she beckoned him closer to the grating and went on in a whisper, 'in view of the bad harvest, we weren't going to replace the other girl. But I'll talk to the abbess about it. A word from me . . . a charitable wish of the Father Superior . . . we can safely consider it as done.'

The good father began to express his thanks, but she cut him short.

'There's no need for too much ceremonious gratitude,' she said. 'If the case arose, if I needed it, I'd call on the Capuchin fathers for help too. And in any case,' she went on, with a smile that had something bitter and ironical about it, 'in any case, are we not brothers and sisters?' She called a lay sister (one of two who had been assigned to her personal service by a very unusual concession), and told her to inform the abbess about the transaction, and to make the necessary arrangements with the portress and with Agnese. Then she dismissed Agnese, said goodbye to the Father Superior, and kept Lucia with her. The good father accompanied Agnese as far as the door, giving her some further instructions, and went off to write his report to his friend Cristoforo. 'A scatter-brained woman, the Signora!' he said to himself as he walked along, 'a very strange woman indeed! But if you know how to approach her, you can get her to do anything you like. My friend Cristoforo certainly won't have expected such quick and excellent service as this from me. What a man he is! There's no help for it; he's always taking on some new obligation – but he does it from the best motives. It's a bit of luck for him this time that he turned to a friend who was able to bring the matter to a happy conclusion straight away, without a lot of fuss and ceremony, without making heavy weather of it. He'll be pleased, good fellow that he is, and he'll realize that we in this monastery are good for something too.'

In the presence of a mature Capuchin father, the Signora had watched her actions and her speech; but now that she was left alone with an inexperienced country girl, she no longer exercised the same self-control. Her remarks gradually took such an extraordinary turn, that instead of reporting them here, we feel that it will be better to give a brief account of the earlier history of that unhappy woman – enough at least to explain the air of oddity and mystery which we have already noted, and to clarify the motives of her conduct at a later stage.

She was the youngest daughter of Prince —, a leading nobleman of Milan, who could count himself among the richest men in the city. But the high opinion he had of his title made him regard his resources as barely sufficient – actually inadequate, in fact – to support its dignity. His one thought was to preserve the family fortune at least at its present level, and to ensure that it would never be split up, as far as lay in his power. We are not told exactly how many children he had, but only that all the younger ones were destined to the religious life, so that his wealth could pass intact to the eldest son, whose fate it was to carry on the family name – in other words, to beget children, and then torture them and himself in the same way that his father had done. The poor Signora was still hidden from view in her mother's womb when her future status was irrevocably fixed. It only remained to decide whether she would be a monk or a nun; and for this decision her consent was not necessary, but only her presence. When she was born, her father the prince wanted to give her a name which would carry immediate suggestion of the cloistered life, and which had been borne by a saint of noble birth; so he called her Gertrude. Dolls dressed as nuns were the first toys that she received; then she was given little images of female saints, always nuns again. These presents were always accompanied by urgent instructions to look after them well, as precious possessions, and by the affirmative question: 'Pretty, aren't they?'

When the prince, the princess or their eldest boy – the only one of their sons to be brought up at home – wanted to tell her how well she looked, the only words they seemed able to find to express the idea were: 'You look a proper little abbess!' But no one ever said to her in so many words: 'You've got to be a nun.' The idea was implied or touched on in passing in every conversation about her future. Sometimes little Gertrude might allow herself some arrogant or imperious action – her character was inclined that way. 'That's no way to behave for a little girl of your age,' they would say to her. 'Wait till you're an abbess; then you'll be able to tell people what to do, and have your own way in everything.' Sometimes again the prince would correct her for being too free and easy in her manner – a fault to which she was equally inclined. 'Now then!' he would say. 'That's not the behaviour for a girl like you. If you want people to respect you as they should later on, you must learn to respect yourself now. Remember that you will always have to hold the first place in everything at the nunnery. Noble blood goes with you wherever you go.'

All these remarks helped to implant in the little girl's brain the idea that she was already destined to be a nun; but her father's words made more impression than all the rest put together. The prince's normal manner was one of austere command; but when he spoke about the future status of his children, every line of his face and every word he uttered showed an inexorable resolution, a touchy concern for his own authority, which conveyed the impression of ineluctable necessity.

At the age of six Gertrude was installed in the convent where we have just seen her, for her education, and also to direct her mind towards the vocation chosen for her. The selection of the place was deliberate. As the good carter mentioned earlier, the Signora's father was the most powerful man in Monza. Putting this casual fragment of evidence together with the other indications that our anonymous author lets fall from time to time, we might also conclude that he was the feudal lord of the town. There is in any case no doubt that he enjoyed very high authority in Monza, and so the thought occurred to him that there, more than anywhere else, his daughter would be treated with the special distinction and the subtle favour that might allure her towards the idea of choosing that nunnery as her permanent home. Nor was his trust misplaced: for the abbess and certain other scheming nuns, who ruled the roost, as the saying is, were delighted to be offered this living pledge of his protection – a protection so useful in every emergency, so honourable at any time. They accepted the proposal with expressions of gratitude which, though strongly worded, did not exaggerate their real feelings in the least; and they did their very best to further the hopes which he let them see he entertained of installing Gertrude there permanently – hopes which coincided most happily with their own.

As soon as Gertrude entered the convent, she was generally known as 'the Signorina', instead of being called by her own name. She was given a special place at table and in the dormitory, and her conduct was held up to the others as an example. She received countless sweets, and endless caresses, tinged with that somewhat respectful familiarity which so flatters children when it comes from those who are known to treat other children with a habitual air of superiority. Not that all the nuns were in a conspiracy to lure the poor child into the snare. Many of them were simple souls, far from any thought of intrigue, who would have been revolted at the idea of anyone sacrificing a daughter to his own selfish interests. But all of them were much taken up in their individual occupations, and some of them never really noticed all those manoeuvrings, others did not realize how much harm there was in them, others refrained from passing judgement on them, and others again said nothing, to avoid a useless scandal. One or two of them remembered how similar arts had led them to do what they later regretted, felt sorry for the poor little innocent and relieved their feelings by lavishing tender and melancholy endearments on her; but Gertrude was far from suspecting that they had any secret reason for this behaviour, and the plot went forward. It might, indeed, have gone on as smoothly as that to the end, if Gertrude had been the only girl in the convent. But among her fellow-pupils were several who knew that they were intended for marriage.

Little Gertrude had been brought up to believe in her own superiority, and painted a magnificent picture of her future glory as abbess, as reigning princess of the convent. She wanted above all to be a subject of envy to the others, and it was with amazement and anger that she saw that some of them did not feel anything of the sort towards her. To the visions that were summoned up by the idea of the rule of a nunnery – majestic visions indeed, but cold and circumscribed – they opposed the varied and sparkling images of weddings, dinners, receptions, routs (as they were called in those days), holidays in the country, fashionable clothes and splendid coaches. These images produced the same sort of commotion, the same stir, in Gertrude's brain which we might see in a great basket of freshly picked flowers, if we set it down in front of a beehive. Her parents and her teachers had cultivated and nourished her natural vanity, to give her a taste for the cloister. But once that vanity was stimulated by other ideas, of a far more closely related kind, her imagination pounced on them with a much more lively and spontaneous enthusiasm. So she kept up with her new companions, and gave reign to her new feelings, by announcing that in the last resort no one could put the habit on her back without her consent; that she could get married, live in a palace and enjoy the pleasures of this world just as well as they could, better in fact; that she could do all this if she so desired; that she probably *would* desire; and finally that she *did* so desire. By now it was true that she did.

The idea that her consent was necessary had previously been tucked away unobtrusively in a corner of her brain, but now it began to develop, and its full importance became clear to her. She continually summoned up that idea, so that she could enjoy her visions of a pleasant future with more confidence. But a second thought always followed the first – that she would have to deny her consent to the prince her father, who regarded it, or appeared to regard it, as already given. At this thought, Gertrude was far from feeling the confidence which she expressed in her words. She compared herself with her fellow-pupils, who had no doubts on the matter at all, and began feeling towards them the painful envy which she had earlier expected to inspire. Envy turned to hatred, and sometimes hatred led to bad temper, rudeness, and biting remarks. At other times her feelings softened towards her companions, because her inclinations and her hopes were the same as theirs; and then a brief period of apparent intimate friendship would follow. Sometimes she felt the need of some real benefit at the present time, and she made the most of the favour with which she was treated, letting her companions feel the full weight of her superiority; at other times she could not stand the loneliness of fear and unfulfilled longing any more, and meekly sought out her companions as if to implore them to give her kindness, advice and courage. It was during this period of deplorable petty strife with the others, and with herself, that she passed out of childhood and entered that critical stage when a mysterious new power seems to enter the soul, which nourishes, beautifies and invigorates every inclination and every idea, often transforming them or turning them aside into an unexpected channel.

The most vivid features of Gertrude's dreams of the future had previously been external splendour and pomp; but now a soft, affectionate feeling, which at first merely suffused those dreams with a light mist of emotion, began to spread over and dominate all her imaginings. In the most private recess of her mind she had made a splendid retreat for herself, where she took refuge from her real surroundings, and entertained a strange company of imaginary guests, based partly on confused memories of her early childhood, partly on the little she could see of the outside world and partly on what she had learnt from the talk of her companions. There were long conversations in which she spoke to those guests, and answered for them; in which she gave orders, and received homage of every kind. From time to time thoughts of religion would visit her and disturb those brilliant and exhausting celebrations. But religion, in the form in which it had been taught to the poor girl and received by her, did not forbid pride at all; it sanctified pride and put it forward as a means of winning earthly happiness. Having lost its true essence in this way, it had ceased to be a real religion, and become an empty ghost, like the others that surrounded her. There were intervals when this ghost took the first place in her thoughts, and loomed gigantic before her eyes. Then poor Gertrude would be overcome by confused terrors, and oppressed by confused ideas of duty, until she imagined that her repugnance towards the cloistered life, and her resistance to the subtle influence of her elders in the matter of her choice of a future, constituted a sin, which she would resolve to expiate by voluntarily taking the veil.

The law was that no young woman could be accepted as a nun before she had been interviewed by an ecclesiastic, known as the vicar of the nuns, or by another cleric acting as his deputy, to ensure that she was going into the convent of her own free choice. This examination could only take place a full year after she had expressed her wish to do so to the said vicar, with a written application. The nuns who had accepted the lamentable task of inducing Gertrude to bind herself to a life-long obligation, with the least possible knowledge of what she was doing, seized one of the moments we have just described to get her to write out and sign the application in question. To persuade her more easily, they were careful to tell her again and again that this was a mere formality, which could have no effect – and this was the truth – unless it was supported by later declarations, which would depend on her own choice. For all that, the application had not reached its destination before Gertrude began to repent having signed it. Then she repented of her repentance, passing days and months in a ceaseless alternation of contrary feelings. For a long time she concealed the steps she had taken from her companions, sometimes out of fear that they would oppose her good resolution, sometimes out of reluctance to let them know of her folly.

But finally the need to express her feelings, and to obtain advice and encouragement, was too strong for her. There was another law which laid it down that a potential nun must spend at least a month outside the convent where she had been educated before the final interview that was to test her vocation.

Twelve months had already passed since Gertrude had signed her application, and she was informed that very soon she would have to leave the convent and return to her family home, where she would have to remain for the prescribed month, and take the necessary steps to complete the business which she had undeniably set in motion. The prince and the rest of the family now took the whole thing for granted, as if it had already happened. But the young woman had other ideas. She was not thinking about completing the remaining steps, but about the best way of withdrawing the step she had already taken. In these desperate straits she decided to confide in one of her fellow-pupils – the boldest of them and the one most ready to give resolute advice. She suggested that Gertrude should inform her father of her new decision by letter, since she did not feel capable of throwing the words 'I won't do it!' boldly in his face. Since advice in this world is seldom free, she made Gertrude pay for it with a good deal of teasing about her faint-heartedness. Four or five friends helped to concoct the letter, which was privately copied out and delivered by a well-devised secret route. Gertrude was left anxiously waiting for an answer which never arrived – though a few days later the abbess sent for her, and, with an air of mystery, distaste and pity, began to hint that her father was very angry, and that Gertrude must have committed some serious fault. She managed, however, to imply that if the girl behaved well from then on, there was hope that the whole thing would be forgotten. The girl understood, and did not venture to ask any details.

Finally the day arrived which had been the subject of so much fear and so much longing. Gertrude knew that she was on the way to a battle; and yet to escape from the nunnery, to leave behind the walls where she had been enclosed for eight years, to drive freely through the open country in a coach, to see the city again, and her own house, were things which filled her with tumultuous happiness. As regards the battle the poor child had taken the advice of her friends, had decided on a course of action, and had worked out a detailed plan, as we might put it today.

'They may try to force me into it,' she said to herself. 'In that case I shall stand firm. I shall be humble and respectful, but I won't give in. It's only a matter of not saying 'yes' this time, and I won't say it. Or perhaps they'll try and do it by gentle persuasion; and I shall be more gently persuasive than they are – I'll weep, I'll utter prayers, I'll make them sorry for me. After all, all I'm asking is not to be made a sacrifice.'

But as so often happens after this sort of careful forecasting, neither of her two alternatives actually happened. The days went by, without her father or anyone else talking to her about her application, or her change of mind, and without any course of action whatever being urged upon her, either with caresses or with threats. Her parents' behaviour to her was unsmiling, gloomy and harsh, but they never told her why. All that could be gathered was that they regarded her as a criminal – as an unworthy child. A mysterious anathema seemed to hang over her, separating her from the rest of the family, to whose company she was admitted only as much as was necessary to let her feel the full weight of its disapproval. It was rarely, and only at certain fixed times, that she was allowed into the presence of her parents and her eldest brother. The three of them seemed to be on the best and most trusting of terms, and this made Gertrude's isolation all the more noticeable and all the more painful. No one spoke to her; and when she risked a timid remark on some matter of small consequence it was either ignored, or answered only with an indifferent, contemptuous or cruel glance.

But if she could no longer stand this hateful and humiliating discrimination, and continued to speak, trying to reestablish herself as a member of the family, or if she sought for some sign of affection, there would be an immediate hint, indirect but unmistakable, at the matter of her choice of a future, with a covert implication that this was the way to regain the affection of her family. Then Gertrude, who did not want to buy that affection at so high a price, had to draw back, to reject the first signs of the kindness she had so longed for, and send herself back into the outer darkness, with a certain unavoidable suggestion that it was her own fault.

This experience of reality made a painful contrast with the

delightful visions that had occupied Gertrude's mind for so long, and still occupied it in secret. She had hoped that her father's magnificent palace, with its throngs of guests, would afford her at least a taste of the real pleasure that lay behind her imaginings; but she was utterly disappointed. She was as closely and effectively shut up as she had been in the nunnery. Walks and drives were never so much as mentioned. There was even a private chapel which led from the palace into a neighbouring church, which removed the one remaining excuse for going out of doors. The company was gloomier, scantier and less varied than it had been in the nunnery. If visitors came, Gertrude was sent up to an attic, where she had to sit with certain old serving women; and she had to eat up there when there were guests for dinner. The servants in general followed the example and the intentions of their master in the way they treated her and spoke to her. Gertrude's natural inclination was to be friendly to servants, without being too familiar. At this particular time she would have been glad if they had shown her any sign of human affection, even as if between equals; in fact she stooped to begging for it, only to be left humiliated and sadder than ever when she found herself treated in return with obvious indifference, thinly veiled by a show of formal respect. But she could not help noticing that one of the pages, very different from the rest of them, showed a respect and a sympathy for her that had something special about them. This boy's bearing and manner, in fact, were the nearest thing Gertrude had ever seen to the order of things on which her imagination had dwelt for so long – the nearest to the bearing and manner of the inhabitants of her dreams.

A gradual change was noticed in the poor girl's demeanour – a strange tranquillity accompanied by a new inquietude; a behaviour as of someone who has found something which means a great deal to him, which he would like to look at all the time, but does not want anyone else to see. She was watched more closely than ever, amid speculation about the reason for all this; and one morning she was caught by one of the serving women as she furtively folded up a sheet of paper, on which she would have been better advised not to write anything. After a brief tug of war the letter passed into the maid's hands, and from hers into those of the prince.

Gertrude's terror as she heard his footsteps approach can neither be described nor imagined. He was the father she knew so well; he was very angry; and she felt herself to be guilty. When she saw him appear, scowling, letter in hand, she would not have minded being a hundred feet underground, let alone in a convent. His words were few, but terrible. Her immediate punishment was to be no more than imprisonment in the room where she stood, under the guard of the woman who had made the discovery; but this was evidently only a beginning, a temporary precaution. Implicit in his words, looming almost visibly in the air, was some further obscure punishment, all the more terrible for being undefined.

The page was dismissed, naturally enough, and he too was threatened with terrible consequences if he ever dared, at any time, to breathe a hint of what had happened. While telling him this, the prince twice struck him hard across the face, so that the adventure might be linked in the lout's mind with a memory that should remove any temptation to boast about it. It was not difficult to find a pretext to justify the dismissal of a page; and as far as Gertrude was concerned they said that she was indisposed.

So she was left with her terror, her shame, her remorse, her fears for the future, and with no other companion except a woman she hated for being the witness of her offence and cause of her misfortune. In her turn the woman hated Gertrude, through whom she found herself reduced to the monotonous existence of a jailer for an indefinite period, and condemned for ever to be the holder of a dangerous secret.

The first confused tumult of Gertrude's different emotions gradually quietened down; and the devils seemed for a moment to have been cast out; but then they came back one at a time. Each in turn entered her mind, grew to enormous size, and settled down to torment her at more leisure with more clearly defined horrors. Whatever could the mysterious punishment be, with which she was threatened? Many, various and strange were the images that thronged into Gertrude's heated and inexperienced brain. But the most probable seemed to be that she would have to go back to the convent at Monza, not in her previous glory as the Signorina, but as a sort of criminal, and be shut up for heaven knows how long, in heaven knows what conditions! This was a picture full of painful features for her; but worst of all was the apprehension of shame. Every sentence, every word, every comma of that wretched letter passed again and again before her mind's eye; she imagined the phrases being studied and weighed by her father – so unexpected a reader and so different for the one for whom she was writing – and thought how they might have been seen also by her mother or her brother, or heaven knows who else; and compared with that aspect of the affair the others hardly seemed to matter. The image of the boy who had been the original cause of the whole scandal also often came to trouble the unfortunate prisoner; and the reader can imagine what a strange figure his phantom cut among the others who were so different from it in their cold, unsmiling, threatening way. But Gertrude found that she could not separate his image from the others, nor return for a moment to those pleasanter memories without her mind immediately passing to the present distress that was their result; and so she began to think of him less and less frequently, to keep those memories at arm's length, and finally to banish them altogether. And she no longer let her mind dwell long and fondly on the happy, brilliant imaginary world of a few weeks before; it contrasted too violently with her present circumstances and with any probable view of her future. There was now only one fortress, apart from castles in the air, where Gertrude could imagine herself finding a peaceful and honourable refuge, and that was the convent – provided she took the decision to return there permanently. There could be no doubt that that decision would put everything right, pay every debt, and produce an immediate transformation of her position.

All the passions that had thronged her mind for so long cried out against this course of action. But times had changed. Viewed from the abyss into which Gertrude had fallen, and in comparison with the fate which at times seemed to hang over her head, the condition of a privileged nun, applauded, deferred to and obeyed by her fellows, had a real magnetic force. From time to time two factors of very different kinds helped to undermine her resistance. Sometimes it was remorse for her lapse, combined with an illusory feeling of religious devotion; at other times it was pride – a pride outraged and embittered by the behaviour of her jailer. This woman revenged herself on Gertrude – not without provocation, it must be admitted – now by terrifying her with the mysterious threatened punishment and now by shaming her with references to her lapse. Sometimes again she would put on a show of kindness, adopting an air of compassionate protection that was even more odious than her insults. To vanish out of her clutches, and reappear later clad in a dignity far out of reach of both her anger and her pity, was Gertrude's constant wish, and at moments such as those just described, it became such an overwhelming and clamorous desire, that anything which might help to satisfy it became highly attractive.

One morning, after four or five long days of imprisonment, Gertrude was exasperated beyond bearing by one of her guardian's fits of bad temper. She threw herself down in the corner of the room, and lay for some time with her face hidden in her hands, weeping tears of rage. She felt an overpowering need to see other faces, to hear other voices, to be treated differently. She thought of her father, and of the rest of the family; and her mind recoiled from them in horror. But then it occurred to her that it lay within her power to regain their friendship; and the thought gave her an unexpected happiness. A sensation of upheaval followed, with an extreme feeling of remorse for her lapse and an extreme desire to expiate it. It was not that her heart was now permanently set on the course of action required of her, but merely that she embraced it for the moment with more fervour than ever before. She rose to her feet, went to a writing-table, took that fatal pen in hand once more and wrote her father a letter full of enthusiasm and contrition, of affliction and hope, imploring his forgiveness, and showing herself utterly willing to fall in with all his wishes in return for it.

Chapter 10

THERE are certain moments when the human heart, especially in youth, is so disposed that only the faintest pressure is needed to persuade it to undertake any action than has something of virtue and self-sacrifice about it; just as a newly opened flower nods softly on its stem, ready to grant its fragrance to the first air that breathes upon it. Those moments should be treated with admiration and the tenderest respect by the rest of us; but cunning and self-interest carefully spy them out and catch them on the wing, binding in chains the will which they have taken off its guard.

When the prince read Gertrude's letter, it was as if the door separating him from his ancient, unchanging purpose had opened a crack. He at once sent for Gertrude. As he waited for her to come, he prepared himself to strike the iron while it was hot. She came in, and, without venturing to look her father in the eyes, she threw herself on her knees before him, only just able to whisper the words 'Forgive me!' He motioned her to rise to her feet; but his voice was far from encouraging as he replied that it was not enough to desire forgiveness nor to plead for it, which were things which came all too naturally and easily to those who had been detected in transgression and feared punishment for it – that forgiveness had to be earned. Submissive and trembling, Gertrude asked what she must do. The prince (for we cannot find it in our hearts to refer to him by the title of 'father' at this moment) did not answer her question directly, but spoke at great length about her offence. His words had the same effect on the poor girl's heart as the passing of a rough hand across an open wound. He went on to say that any intention he might once have had of establishing her in the society of the secular world must now come up against an insuperable obstacle, placed there by herself; for an honourable nobleman like himself could not possibly offer the hand of a daughter who had behaved in such a manner to any respectable gentleman. Poor Gertrude was utterly crushed by this; and the prince went on to say, gradually softening both his voice and his words, that every offence had its remedy and could find forgiveness; that hers was one for which the remedy was particularly obvious; and that she ought to regard this unfortunate incident as a warning that the life of secular society was too full of dangers for her.

'Oh, yes!' cried Gertrude, shaken by fear, weakened by shame and touched at that instant by a momentary feeling of tenderness.

'So you see that yourself!' said the prince quickly. 'Very well, then; we won't say any more about the past – that's all forgotten. You've taken the only honourable and respectable road which was still open to you – but since you've taken it so willingly and cheerfully, it is now for me to ensure that it's made as pleasant as possible for you, in every way, and that you get the full advantage and all the credit for it. I will give the matter all my attention.'

He rang a little bell that stood on his desk, and a servant came in. 'Ask the princess and the young prince to come here at once,' said the nobleman; and then, turning to Gertrude, he added: 'I want to let them share my happiness at once. I want everyone to start treating you with due respect immediately. You have seen, to some extent, what it is like to have a severe father; but from now on you will have a very loving one.'

Gertrude was stunned by these words. That cry of 'Oh, yes!' which had escaped from her lips – however could it have taken on so much significance? She tried to think of a way of withdrawing it, or at least limiting its sense; but her father's conviction seemed so absolute, his happiness so delicately poised and his kindness so conditional, that Gertrude dared not say a word that might upset him in the smallest degree.

A few minutes later her mother and brother came in. When they saw Gertrude, they stared at her with amazement and doubt. But the prince put on a happy and loving expression, clearly setting them an example to follow. 'See,' he said, 'our lost lamb has come back to us! and let that be the last word anyone ever says that might bring back unhappy memories! See the family's pride and joy! Gertrude does not need any more advice. The course that we wanted her to take, for her own good, is the very one that she has spontaneously chosen. She has made up her mind, she has shown me clearly that she has made up her mind' – here Gertrude raised her eyes to her father's face, with a terrified, beseeching look, as if to implore him to stop, but he went cheerfully on – 'her mind to take the veil.'

'Good girl! Well done!' cried mother and son together, and they kissed Gertrude, one after the other. She received their embraces with tears, which were regarded as tears of relief. Then the prince described at length all the things he would do to make his daughter's life a happy and honourable one. He spoke of the distinctions she would enjoy in the convent, and in the town of Monza. As the representative of the family, her position would be that of a princess; as soon as she reached a fitting age, she would be made abbess; in the meantime she would be a subordinate only in name. The princess and the young prince renewed their congratulations and their applause every moment, but Gertrude seemed to be in a dream.

'Well, we must fix a day to go to Monza and ask for the abbess's agreement,' said the prince. 'How pleased she will be! I can tell you, the whole convent will know how to value the honour that Gertrude is doing them. But . . . Why not go today? Gertrude would probably like some fresh air.'

'Yes – let's go today!' said the princess.

'I'll go and order the carriage,' said the young prince.

'But . . . but . . .' whispered Gertrude softly.

'Just a minute, then,' said the prince. 'We'll leave it to her to decide. Perhaps she doesn't feel up to it today, and so she'd rather wait until tomorrow. You say, Gertrude – would you like to go today or tomorrow?'

'Tomorrow,' said Gertrude brokenly, feeling that it was something done if she could gain a little time.

'Tomorrow, then,' said the prince solemnly. 'Gertrude has decided that we shall go tomorrow. Meanwhile I will go and see the vicar of the nuns, to fix a day for the examination.'

No sooner said than done. He left the room, and really did go himself to see the priest, which was a remarkable piece of condescension on his part. The interview was arranged for two days later.

For the rest of that day, Gertrude did not have a moment's peace. She would have liked to let her spirit rest for a time after so much tumult, to leave her thoughts to clear a little, to go over in her own mind what she had done and what remained for her to do, to think out what she really wanted, and to slow up, at least for a moment, the wheels of the machine she was caught up in, which seemed to turn with such dizzying speed once they had been set in motion; but it could not be done. There was an uninterrupted, interlocking series of things to be done. As soon as the prince had gone, she was whisked off to her mother's boudoir, where her mother's maid did her hair and dressed her smartly, under the princess's personal supervision. The maid was still at work when dinner was announced. Gertrude went down between rows of bowing servants, who expressed their happiness at the improvement in her health. In the dining-room she found a group of close relations, who had been hastily invited in her honour, and to congratulate her on the double blessing of her recovery from sickness and her announcement of her vocation.

'Little bride' was the title given at that time to young women who were about to take the veil, and Gertrude was saluted with that name by everyone when she came in. The little bride had as much as she could to acknowledge all the compliments which rained upon her from every side. She knew very well that every answer she made must appear as an acceptance and a confirmation of what had been said; but how could she reply in any other way?

Soon after dinner it was time for the evening drive, and Gertrude went in the same carriage as her mother, together with two uncles who had been at the dinner. The carriage went round the town on its usual route, and came out on to the Marina, a street which then ran across the area of the present public gardens, and was the place where the fine society of Monza came in their carriages to recuperate from the fatigues of the day. Gertrude's two uncles spoke a good deal to her, as was expected of them on such a day. One of them seemed to have an unrivalled knowledge of every face, every carriage, and every livery that went by; every moment he had something to say about the gentleman in one coach or the lady in another. Suddenly he turned to Gertrude and said, 'Ah, you cunning little thing! You've no time for all this nonsense; you know what you're about! You leave us poor worldly folk stuck in the mire; you take yourself off to lead a holy life, and in the end you drive away to heaven in a coach-and-six!'

It was quite late when they returned, and the servants hurried out with torches to tell them that many visitors were waiting for them. The news had got around, and friends and relations were flocking to do their duty. They went into the drawing-room. The little bride was the idol of the gathering, its plaything and its victim. Everyone wanted to monopolize her; some of them made her promise to send them sweets, some promised to visit her; one spoke of Mother This who was a relation, another of Mother That who was a friend; some praised the climate of Monza, others spoke with relish of the prominent position she would occupy there. Others again, who had not yet been able to make their way through the throng that pressed around Gertrude, were anxiously looking out for a chance to approach her, feeling an uneasy guilt until they had done their duty. In the end, however, the company began to thin out. The guests all left without a backward glance of pity, and Gertrude was left alone with her parents and her brother.

'At last,' said the prince, 'at last I have had the satisfaction of seeing my daughter treated in a truly befitting manner. We must also admit that she has behaved very well indeed, and has proved that she will have no difficulty in taking a leading position, and upholding the dignity of the family.'

They had a hasty supper, and went to bed soon afterwards, to be ready for an early start the following morning.

Gertrude was depressed and irritated; at the same time her head had been a little turned by all those compliments. She remembered all she had suffered from the woman who had acted as her jailer, and, seeing how ready her father now was to please her in everything – with one exception – she decided to use the credit in which she now stood to gratify at least one of the passions which tormented her. She showed great unwillingness to have the woman with her any more, saying that she could not stand her manner.

'What!' said the prince. 'Has that woman been disrespectful to you? Tomorrow yes, tomorrow I'll put her in her place properly. Leave it to me; she won't be left in any doubt about who you are, and what she is. In any case a daughter who deserves my love must not have anyone about her whose company is distasteful to her.'

He immediately called another woman and appointed her to serve Gertrude. Turning over and savouring the reparation that had been granted to her, Gertrude was astonished to find that so feeble a sense of satisfaction could follow so fierce a desire for revenge. The thought that occupied her mind completely, whether she liked it or not, was the thought of the long way she had travelled that day along the road that led to the nunnery, so that to withdraw from it now would require far more strength and resolution than had been needed a few days before – when even that smaller amount of resolution had been more than she could raise.

The woman who now joined her in her room was an old retainer. She had been the governess of Gertrude's eldest brother. She had taken charge of him almost as soon as he was out of the cradle, and looked after him up to the age of adolescence. All her happiness, all her hopes, all her triumphs were centred on him. She was as pleased about the decision that had just been taken as if her own ship had come home. Gertrude's final treat that day was to swallow the old woman's congratulations, praises and advice, and to hear all about certain of her aunts and great-aunts who had been very happy after taking the veil, because, belonging to that noble family, they had always enjoyed the highest honours, and had always been able to keep one foot in the outer world, and get things done from the convent parlour which the greatest ladies could never achieve from their salons. She spoke to her about the visits she would receive. Some day, no doubt, the young prince would come to see her with his bride, who would certainly be a very great lady indeed; and then not only the nunnery, but the whole of Monza, would be in great commotion. The old woman talked while she was undressing Gertrude, she talked as Gertrude went to bed, and she was still talking when Gertrude went to sleep. Youth and exhaustion had proved stronger than all her worries. Her sleep was restless and troubled, full of painful dreams, but the first thing that woke her was the shrill voice of the old woman, coming to wake her to get ready for the trip to Monza.

'Come, my lady; come, little bride! The sun's up, and it'll take us at least an hour to get you dressed and get your hair done. The princess is getting dressed; and they woke her up four hours earlier than usual. The young prince has already been down to the stables, and up again; and he's ready to start whenever we are. He's as quick as a flash, the little devil, but there! he's always been like that from a baby, and I should know, for I've carried him in my arms. But once he's ready, it doesn't do to keep him waiting, because, though he's the best-hearted boy in the world, he does get impatient and make a fuss. Poor lad! you can't help being sorry for him, because it's his nature to be like that; and this time, after all, he's got a right to be, because he is putting himself out for you. It's dangerous to go near him at times like this! He's no respect for anyone but the prince himself. But then one day he's going to be the prince himself, though let's hope it'll be as long as possible . . . But hurry up, Signorina. Why do you look at me in that dazed way? You ought to be up and about by this time of day!'

At the thought of her brother and his impatience, all the other worries that had flocked into Gertrude's mind as she awoke scattered like sparrows at the coming of the hawk. She did as she was told, she dressed quickly, she sat still while they did her hair, and soon she was down in the great room where her parents and her brother were waiting for her. An armchair was offered to her, and a cup of chocolate was brought for her, which at that time had the same significance as the conferring of the *toga virilis* on an ancient Roman.

When the servants came to say that the carriage was ready, the prince took his daughter on one side, and said: 'Listen, Gertrude – you acquitted yourself honourably yesterday, but today you must surpass yourself. Today you have to make a formal appearance in the convent – and the town – where you are destined to take the first place. They are waiting for you ...' (for of course the prince had written to the abbess the day before) '... and all eyes will be upon you. Dignity, easy, natural dignity is the thing ... The abbess will ask you what you want – that's a pure formality. You could reply that you want to be admitted to take the veil in the convent where you have been educated so lovingly, where you have received so many marks of special attention – which is the purest truth, after all. Just say those few words quite naturally – we don't want them to be able to hint that you had to be taught a speech because you can't speak for yourself. The good nuns don't know anything about what's happened; that's a secret which must remain buried in the family. So don't look penitent and uncertain, and make them suspicious. Let them see what blood runs in your veins – scrupulous manners and modest bearing, yes; but remember that no one will be above you, in the place where you are going, except your own family.'

Without waiting for an answer, the prince left the room. Gertrude, the princess, and the young prince followed him; they went down staircase after staircase, and got into the coach. The troubles and the tediousness of worldly society, and the happy blessedness of the cloistered life, especially for girls of the very highest birth, were the main subjects of conversation during the journey. As they approached Monza, the prince again went over the instructions he had given his daughter, repeating the words of her reply to the abbess several times. As they entered the town, Gertrude felt her heart sink; but then her thoughts were diverted for a moment by some gentlemen, who stopped the carriage to deliver themselves of some compliment or other. Then the carriage went on again towards the convent at a walking pace, through a staring crowd, which quickly gathered from all sides. When the coach stopped outside those well-known walls, in front of those well-known gates, Gertrude felt her heart sink more than ever. She walked in between two rows of spectators, who were held back by the servants.

The poor girl had to think constantly about the figure she presented, because of those watching eyes; but the eyes that had a more oppressive effect on her than all the others put together were her father's. She could not help glancing at them every moment, for all the terror that they inspired in her. Those eyes controlled her movements and her expression, as if by invisible strings.

They crossed the first courtyard, and went on into a second one, where the entrance to the inner cloister could be seen. The door was wide open and the space was filled with nuns. In the first row was the abbess, surrounded by the older sisters; behind them a mass of other nuns, some standing on tiptoe; and last of all were the lay sisters, standing on benches. Here and there little eyes could be seen sparkling, little faces peeping out among the habits. These were the quickest-witted and the boldest of the pupils; pushing and squeezing their way among the nuns, they managed to make themselves gaps, through which they too could see something. Acclamations poured from the throng; many arms waved in a sign of welcome and delight.

They reached the door, and Gertrude found herself face to face with the abbess. When the first greetings were over, she asked Gertrude, in a tone of solemn happiness, what she wanted in that place, where no one would deny her anything.

'I have come here . . .' began Gertrude – but at the moment of uttering the words which were to decide her future almost irrevocably, she hesitated for a moment, and stood with her eyes fixed on the throng before her. She caught sight of one of her old companions, whom we have met before. She was looking at Gertrude with an air of compassion, and of irony too, and seemed to be saying 'How are the mighty fallen!' That glimpse gave fresh life to all Gertrude's earlier feelings, and also restored some of her scanty earlier courage. She tried to think of an answer – any answer but the one which had been put into her mouth. But then she raised her eyes to look at her father, as if to try her strength, and she saw so dark a foreboding in his face, so threatening an impatience, that she went quickly on, with panic resolution, as if taking to her heels from some terrible disaster, and said: 'I am here to ask to be admitted to take the veil in this convent, where I have been so lovingly educated.'

The abbess replied at once that she was very sorry on this occasion that the rules did not permit her to give an immediate answer. That answer must be put to the general vote of all the sisters in the convent, and must be approved in advance by her superiors. But Gertrude, she said, must know the feelings they had for her in the convent, and could therefore guess what the reply would be, with complete certainty. There was anyway nothing in the rules that forbade the abbess and the sisters from showing how much happiness her request had given them. At this a confused murmur of congratulation and applause was heard. Great trays of sweets were quickly brought in, and presented first of all to the little bride, and then to her family. While some of the nuns gathered round Gertrude, each in turn trying to monopolize her, and others complimented her mother and brother, the abbess sent a message to the prince, asking him to come to the parlour, where she would be waiting to speak to him through the grille. She had two of the older nuns with her, and when she saw him come in she said, 'Your Highness . . . to comply with the rules . . . to carry out an essential formality, though of course in a case like this . . . I must still say this to you . . . Every time a girl asks to be admitted to take the veil . . . the Mother Superior . . . myself in this case, unworthy as I am . . . she has to warn the parents . . . that if by any chance they forced their daughter to take the veil . . . they would incur the penalty of excommunication . . . Forgive me . . .'

'Well said . . . well said indeed, Reverend Mother. I admire the scrupulous way in which you carry out your duties. So true . . . so true . . . But you can hardly have any doubts . . .'

'My dear prince! I said what I did because it was my unavoidable duty to do so . . . otherwise . . .'

'Of course, Reverend Mother, of course . . .'

Having exchanged these few words, the two speakers bowed and took leave of each other, as if they were both reluctant to prolong the *tête-a-tête*. They went off to rejoin their respective companies, one outside the cloistral barrier, and one within.

'Come along now,' said the prince. 'It won't be long before Gertrude can have as much as she wants of the good sisters' company; and the rest of us have given them enough trouble for today.' He bowed, the family prepared to move, there was a final exchange of compliments, and off they went.

Gertrude was not very talkative on the way home. She was horrified at the further step she had taken, ashamed of her cowardice, and angry with the others and with herself. She gloomily reckoned up the remaining times when she would have a chance to say no, and promised herself, in a weak and confused way, that on this occasion, or that, or the other, she would be cleverer or braver than last time. But these thoughts did nothing to banish her terror of her father's frown. In fact, when she glanced at him out of the corner of her eye and assured herself that there was no sign of anger in his face – indeed he appeared to be very pleased with her – it seemed for an instant that the clouds had really rolled away, and she felt a momentary glow of happiness.

As soon as they were back at home, she had to change her dress and smarten herself up again; then came dinner, one or two visits, the evening drive, the reception and supper. When supper was nearly over, the prince raised a new question – the selection of a godmother. That was the title given to the lady who, at the invitation of the parents of a girl destined for the cloister, became her escort and her guardian during the interval between her request for admission and her final entry into the convent. The interval was spent in visits to churches, public buildings, social gatherings, country houses and religious shrines – all the most notable features of the town and its surroundings, in fact – so that a girl could see just what she was rejecting before she took that irrevocable oath.

'It's time we thought of a godmother,' said the prince. 'The vicar of the nuns will be here tomorrow, for the formality . . . the examination . . . and directly after that Gertrude's name will be put forward in chapter for acceptance by the good sisters.'

As he said these words, he turned towards the princess, who

thought he wanted her to make a suggestion, and began 'What about . . .' – but the prince interrupted her, saying 'No, no, madam; the godmother ought first of all to be acceptable to the little bride. It is true that the general custom gives the choice to the parents; but Gertrude has such perfect judgement, such good sense, that she fully deserves to have an exception made for her.'

Then turning to Gertrude with the air of a man announcing an extraordinary favour, he went on: 'All the ladies who were at our reception this evening have the qualities of a godmother for a daughter of our house, and I do not think there is one who would not be honoured if she were selected. Gertrude, you shall choose whichever lady you prefer!'

Gertrude knew very well that to make this choice was to commit herself still further. But the offer had been made with such pomp that a refusal, no matter how humble in manner, must appear insulting, or at least capricious and affected. So she took this further step along the road; and she named the lady whom she had found most agreeable that evening – in other words the lady who had showered the most endearments on her, who had praised her warmly, who had treated her in the familiar, affectionate, obliging manner which imitates the ways of an old friendship at the very first stage of an acquaintance.

'A very good idea!' said the prince, who had hoped and expected that she would make that particular choice. Whether by chance or design, what had happened was very like the conjuror's trick of flicking rapidly through a pack of cards under your nose, inviting you to think of one of them, and then guessing which it is – the point being that he handles the pack so that only one card catches your eye. That lady had spent so much time with Gertrude that evening, and had so impressed herself on her mind, that the poor girl would have had to make a special effort of the imagination to think of anyone else . . . There was a reason for all this friendly interest. For a long time back, the lady had had her eye on Gertrude's brother, as a husband for her own daughter, and so she looked on the affairs of the prince's family almost as if they were her own, and it was quite natural that she should take an interest in dear Gertrude, just as much as any of her closest relations.

When Gertrude woke up next day, the thought of the priest who was coming to examine her was uppermost in her mind. While she was considering whether she could make use of this decisive occasion to turn back from the road that led to the nunnery, and how she should set about it, the prince sent for her.

'Well, now, Gertrude,' he said, 'you've done extraordinarily well so far; now it's a matter of crowning your efforts. Everything that has been done up to now has been done with your agreement. If, in the past few weeks, you had felt any doubts, any small regrets or girlish fancies, it would have been your duty to bring them to light; but at the stage where we are now it's too late for any childishness of that sort. The worthy man who is coming to see you today will ask you dozens of questions about your vocation. Are you becoming a nun of your own free will? ... and why? ... and how? ... and if? ... and whether? If you hesitate in your answers, he'll keep you at it for heaven knows how long. That would be embarrassing and painful for you; and it could lead to a more serious misfortune. After all the public attention the thing has had, if you were to display the slightest uncertainty, it would put my honour at stake; it would suggest that I had taken a passing fancy of yours for a firm resolution, that I had precipitated matters, that I'd ... heaven knows what. In that case I would have to choose between two very painful alternatives. I could let the world form a shabby opinion of my conduct, which would be absolutely inconsistent with the duty I owe to myself. Or I could reveal the real motive of your decision . . .' – but here he noticed that Gertrude had gone scarlet, that her eyes were swelling, and that her face was crumpling together like the petals of a flower in the heavy closeness that precedes a storm. So he did not finish that sentence, but began again, very smoothly: 'Come, Gertrude, everything depends on you, on your good sense. I know you have plenty of that, and that you're not a girl to spoil a fine job right at the end; but it is my duty to consider every possibility. We'll say no more about it. We'll leave it that you will answer the worthy man's questions with perfect frankness, and in a manner which will not sow any doubts in his mind. That's the way for you to get it over as quickly as possible.'

He went on to suggest specific answers to some of the most probable questions, and then reverted to the familiar subject of the joys and delights that were being prepared for Gertrude in the nunnery. He kept her on that topic until a servant came to announce the vicar. The prince rapidly refreshed her memory on the most important points, and left her alone with the priest, as laid down in the rules.

The worthy man had to some extent already formed the opinion that Gertrude had a great vocation for the cloister, for the prince had told him so, when he went to arrange the visit. It is true that the good priest, who knew that mistrustfulness was one of the most necessary qualities in his calling, held the principle that one should be very slow to believe such protestations, and should be on one's guard against preconceptions. But it is very rare that the positive and self-assured words of a man in authority, in any sphere, fail to tinge the minds of his hearers with something of their own colour.

After the first exchange of compliments, he said: 'Signorina, I have come to play the Devil's part. I have come to put in doubt all the things that you have set down as certainties in your application. I have come to set all the difficulties before your eyes, and to assure myself that you have given due consideration to them. Permit me to put some questions to you.'

'Of course,' said Gertrude.

Then the good priest began to interrogate her, in the form prescribed by the rules. 'Do you feel a free and spontaneous resolution in your heart to become a nun? Have no threats or promises been used with you? Has any sort of authority been employed to induce you to take this step? Speak frankly, speak sincerely; for you are speaking to a man whose duty it is to discover your true will, and to prevent the use of force of any kind against you.'

The true answer to these questions flashed into Gertrude's mind with terrible clarity. To give that answer, she would have to provide an explanation, to say that she had been threatened, to tell the full story of ... The poor wretch recoiled in horror from that idea, and quickly tried to think of another reply. But she could find only one that could free her promptly and surely from her torment; and that was the reply furthest removed from the truth.

'I am taking the veil,' she said, hiding her agitation, 'I am taking the veil of my own inclination, freely.'

'How long ago did that thought come to you?' asked the good priest.

'It has always been in my mind,' said Gertrude. Now that the first step was taken, she found she could bear false witness against herself more boldly.

'But what is the principal motive that leads you to become a nun?'

The good father had no idea how barbed a question he had asked. Gertrude made a mighty effort of will to prevent the feelings it roused from showing in her face.

'My motive', she said, 'is to serve God, and to flee from the dangers of this world.'

'Nothing in the way of a disappointment then? Nor ... forgive me ... a caprice? Sometimes a temporary cause produces an effect on us which seems as if it must last for ever; later on the cause vanishes, our mind changes, and then ...'

'No, no,' said Gertrude hastily. 'The cause is the one I have already given you.'

More from a conscientious desire to carry out his duty to the full than from any conviction that it was really necessary, the priest persisted with his questions; but Gertrude had now made up her mind to deceive him. Apart from the revulsion that she felt at the thought of revealing her past weakness to that grave and honest cleric, who seemed so far from suspecting her of anything of the sort, she reflected that, though he could prevent her from becoming a nun, that was all he could do for her, and he had no further powers of protection. Once he had gone, she would be left alone with her father. And whatever she might then suffer in her parents' house, the priest would never even hear about it; or if he did, however good his intentions might be, what could he do but feel sorry for her, with that calm and temperate compassion that we extend, as if out of courtesy, to those who have themselves been the cause or furnished the pretext for the ill-treatment they suffer?

The examiner ran out of questions before the poor wretch ran out of lies. Her answers were perfectly consistent, and he had no reason to doubt their sincerity; so in the end he changed his tune, and began to congratulate her and almost to apologize for having taken so long over the performance of his duty. He added the few words he thought appropriate to confirm her in her good intentions, and took his leave.

As he went out, he ran into the prince – who, it seemed, happened to be passing that way – and gave him the good news about the admirable frame of mind he had found in Gertrude. Up to that moment the prince had been in a painful state of anxiety; but now he breathed again. Forgetting his accustomed gravity of demeanour, he almost ran to find Gertrude, and load her with praises, endearments, and promises, showing a happy cordiality and a tenderness which were in fact very largely sincere – so strange and confused a piece of work is the human heart.

We do not propose to follow Gertrude in her continued round of spectacles and amusements, nor will we provide a detailed or a chronological account of her feelings during all that time. Such a story of suffering and of changes of heart would be too monotonous, and too much like what has gone before. The beauty of the places she visited, the variety of the things she saw, the pleasure she felt in driving this way and that in the open air, all helped to blacken the idea of the place where, in the end, she must dismount from her coach for the last time, and for ever. Crueller still was the impression made on her by the receptions and parties. Whenever she saw the face of a bride – a bride in the obvious and normal sense of that word – she felt an intolerable, gnawing envy. And the sight of a man's face sometimes made her feel that to be called a bride must be the highest happiness in the world. The pomp of the palaces, the splendour of their furnishings, the bustle and the cheerful clamour of the feasts, sometimes caused her such an intoxication, such an ardent desire, for a life of enjoyment, that she swore to herself that she would go back on her word, and endure any consequences, rather than return to the cold and deathly shadows of the cloister. But all those resolutions faded on calmer consideration of the difficulties, or died as soon as her glance fell on her father's face. Sometimes again the thought that she must soon abandon those pleasures for ever imparted a painful bitterness even to the brief taste of them that she was allowed – just as a feverish patient looks angrily at the spoonful of water which the doctor reluctantly allows him, and almost thrusts it away.

Meanwhile the vicar of the nuns had lodged the necessary statement, and permission was granted for the convent to hold the chapter to decide on Gertrude's admission. The chapter was held; the two thirds majority of secretly cast votes demanded by the rules was obtained, as was to be expected; and Gertrude was accepted. Tired of her long drawn-out torment, she herself then asked to be admitted into the convent as soon as possible. No one showed any sign of wanting to curb her impatience. So she had her wish. She was conducted in state to the nunnery, and put on the habit. The twelve months she served as a novice were full of regrets and repentance. Then came the moment of taking the final vows – the moment when she had either to say no (a refusal more extraordinary, more unexpected and more scandalous than it would have been at any earlier stage), or to say yes once again, as she had said it so many times before. She said yes, and was a nun for ever.

One of the strangest faculties of the Christian religion, and one of the hardest to understand, is her power of giving direction and consolation to everyone who has recourse to her, in no matter what circumstances, at no matter what time. If there is a remedy for what is past, she prescribes it, and gives us the vision and the strength to carry it out, whatever the cost. If there is no remedy, she shows us how to make a literal reality of the proverbial expression 'to make a virtue of necessity'. She teaches us to continue wisely in the course we entered upon out of frivolity. She chastens our heart to accept gladly that which is imposed on us by tyranny, she gives a reckless but irrevocable choice all the sanctity, all the wisdom, all the – let us say it – all the joyful happiness of a true vocation. She is like a great road, which a man may find after wandering in the most tangled labyrinth, amid the most dangerous precipices, and once he has taken one stride along it, he can walk on safely and gladly, and be sure of a happy end to his journey.

In this way Gertrude might have found holy contentment as a nun, however she had happened to become one. But the poor wretch struggled under the yoke, which made her feel its weight and its jolting all the more. The main occupations of her mind were an incessant regret for her lost freedom, a loathing for her present condition, and a painful dwelling on desires destined never to be satisfied. She ruminated over the bitter events of the past, went over all the circumstances which had led to her being where she was. Time and again her thoughts unavailingly disavowed the words that her tongue had uttered. She accused herself of cowardice, and the others of tyranny and bad faith; she tortured herself unmercifully. She worshipped her own beauty, and wept over it; she mourned for her own youth, condemned to perish in a slow martyrdom. At times she envied any woman – any woman at all, whatever the conditions of her life or the state of her conscience – who could enjoy the fruits of her youth and beauty freely in the world.

The sight of those nuns who had helped to lure her into the convent was loathsome to her. She remembered the arts they had used, the strategems they had devised, and repaid them with rudeness, bad temper and even with open reproaches for what they had done. The nuns generally had to swallow her insults and say nothing. The prince had been willing enough to tyrannize over Gertrude as much as was necessary to force her into the nunnery; but, now that he had achieved his object, he would by no means have been equally ready to admit that anyone outside the family could be right in a dispute with his daughter. Any complaint from them might have lost the convent his powerful protection, or might even convert their protector into an enemy. One might think that Gertrude should have felt a certain warmth towards the other sisters, who had not taken part in the intrigues; who had not sought her as a companion, but gave her their love now that she was one;

whose pious, cheerful busy appearance showed her that it was possible not merely to exist in a nunnery, but to be happy there. But they inspired her with loathing too, for a different reason. Their holy contentment seemed to her like a reproach for her restlessness and bad temper. She did not miss any opportunity of ridiculing them behind their backs as bigots, or of accusing them of hypocrisy. She might have been less hostile to them if she had known or guessed that the few black balls found in the box at the time of her election had been cast by them.

Sometimes she seemed to find a certain consolation in the giving of orders, in the homage of the other nuns, in the complimentary visits she received from people outside, in the achievement of her will in certain matters, in the granting of her protection, in being called the Signora. But what pitiful consolations these were! Finding her heart so little satisfied, she would gladly have added to them, and mingled with them, the consolations of religion. But the consolations of religion only come to those who cast aside the others: just as a shipwrecked sailor cannot grasp the plank which may take him safely to shore until he unclasps his fingers from the seaweed to which he is clinging in instinctive, frenzied desperation.

Soon after taking her final vows, Gertrude was put in charge of the pupils in the convent. It can be imagined how they fared under her discipline. The friends in whom she had confided had all left; but she still kept all the passions of that time alive in her heart; and the pupils, in one way or another, had to bear the full weight of them. When she reflected that many of them were destined to live in that world from which she had been excluded for ever, she felt a bitter envy for the poor girls, almost a desire for revenge. She kept them down, she ill-treated them, she made them pay in advance for the pleasures they would one day enjoy. Anyone who had seen her at such a time, and heard the tone of contemptuous authority with which she scolded them for every little escapade, would have thought she was a woman who carried spiritual discipline to a harsh and indiscreet extreme. At other times her horror of the cloistered life, with its regulations and its discipline, led her to excesses of a totally opposite character. Then she would not only tolerate the clamorous high spirits of her pupils – she would egg them on. She would take part in some wild game, and make it wilder than ever; she entered into their talk, and spurred them on to go further than they had intended to go. If one of them mentioned the gossipy manner of the abbess, their mistress would do a long imitation, which turned into a scene of comedy. She would ape the expression of one of the sisters, or the walk of another. Then she would laugh uproariously; but her mirth left her no happier than before. She continued in this way of life for several years, having neither occasion nor opportunity to do anything more. But then her bad fairy put an opportunity in her way.

Among the distinctions and privileges granted to her, as compensation for the fact that she could not yet be an abbess, was the right to have her own private quarters. Neighbouring that side of the nunnery stood the house of a young man who was a professional blackguard – one of the many in those days who, with the aid of their bravoes and their alliances with other blackguards, could often laugh at the forces of law and order. Our manuscript calls him Egidio, without mentioning his family. One of his windows overlooked a small courtyard which formed part of Gertrude's quarters. Noticing her once or twice as she passed through the courtyard, or strolled idly round it, he found the difficulty and the wickedness of the enterprise an attraction rather than a deterrent, and plucked up his courage to speak to her. The poor wretch answered him.

It was certainly not an unmixed happiness she felt in those first few moments, but it was a keen happiness none the less. The melancholy emptiness of her heart was now occupied by a vivid, continuous interest, one might almost say a powerful fresh vitality. But her new-found happiness can only be compared to the restorative drink which the ingenious cruelty of the ancients used to prepare for the condemned criminal, to give him strength to survive longer under torture.

There were signs at the time of a great change in all her habits. She suddenly became steadier and calmer, abstained from mockery and complaint, and seemed quite affectionate and affable. The good sisters congratulated each other on this turn for the better. They were far from guessing the real motive, or realizing that these new virtues were only hypocritical disguises for the old blemishes. But this outer covering, this coat of whitewash, if we may use the expression, did not last long – not, at least as a continuous or unvarying feature. Presently her usual fits of temper, her customary caprices reappeared; the bitter complaints, and the mockery against the monastic prison were heard again, sometimes expressed in language seldom heard in that place, or even from those lips. But every such outburst was followed by repentance and a great effort to ensure, by kind and flattering words, that the indiscretion was forgotten. The sisters endured these ups and downs with all the patience they could, attributing them to the Signora's touchy and extravagant character.

For some time, no one seemed to attach any more importance to it than that. But one day the Signora had words with a lay sister over some triviality, and scolded her with unreasonable harshness and at excessive length. The lay sister put up with it, and bit her lips in silence, for a considerable time, but finally lost her patience, and blurted out that she *knew something, and would tell all when the time came*. From that moment on, the Signora never knew a moment's peace. Not long after, a morning came when the lay sister did not appear to carry out her usual duties. They looked in her cell, and there was no sign of her; they shouted her name, and there was no reply. They searched here and there, round and round, up and down; no trace of her anywhere. Heaven knows what they would have thought, but for the fact that a hole in the wall of the kitchen garden was discovered in the course of the search, and that gave everyone the idea that she must have made off by that route. Extensive inquiries were made in Monza and the surrounding country, and especially at Meda, where the lay sister's family lived. Letters asking for news of her were sent off to various destinations. But nothing was ever heard of her again.

(Instead of all these far-flung inquiries, a little actual digging nearer at home might have told them more.)

Everyone was very surprised, because no one thought her capable of behaving like that. After much discussion they concluded she must have gone very far away. One of the sisters dropped the remark 'She must have gone to Holland'; this was at once taken up, and for some time it was generally held, both in the nunnery and outside, that she had actually taken refuge there. But the Signora does not appear to have shared this view. Not that she made a show of her disbelief, or produced any special reasons for disagreeing with the general opinion – if she had any, they were the most carefully hidden special reasons the world has ever known. In fact there was no subject of conversation that she was less anxious to revive, no problem that she was less curious to see solved.

But the less she spoke of it, the more she thought about it. Many times a day the woman's image thrust itself unexpectedly into her mind, and planted itself there, and would not go away. Many times she wished she could see the woman in front of her as a living reality, instead of having her always in her thoughts, and being accompanied day and night by that terrible, unsubstantial, unfeeling form. Many times she wished she could really hear the woman's voice, whatever it might threaten, rather than to have the imaginary whispering of that same voice always present in her inner ear, repeating certain words with a pertinacity, a tireless insistence, that no living person could ever match.

About a year had gone by after that event when Lucia was introduced to the Signora, and had with her the conversation of which we were speaking when we broke off our main narrative. The Signora asked Lucia question after question about Don Rodrigo's persecution of her, going into certain details with a freedom which Lucia, quite rightly, found very strange. It had never occurred to the girl that a nun's curiosity could be aroused by a subject like this. No less strange were the opinions which the Signora expressed, or failed to conceal, in the course of her interrogation. She almost seemed to be laughing at the great horror which Lucia had always had of the nobleman, or asking if he were a monster, to inspire so much fear. One might almost have thought that she would have regarded the girl's reluctance as silly and unreasonable, if it had not been caused by her preference for Renzo. And she went on to ask questions about Renzo too, which made Lucia blush in amazement. Then the

208

Signora realized that her tongue had had too much freedom in expressing the whimsies of her brain, and tried to correct what she had said, or put a better interpretation on it; but it was too late to prevent Lucia being left with a feeling of distasteful amazement and a sort of confused fear.

As soon as the girl had a chance to speak privately with her mother, she told her all about it. With her wider experience, Agnese was able to sweep aside all those doubts with a few words, and solved the whole mystery.

'You mustn't be too surprised at all this, Lucia,' she said. 'When you've known the world as long as I have, you'll see that there's nothing to be amazed at in it at all. It's the gentry, you see – it takes some of them one way, and some of them another, some more, and some less; but they're all a bit touched. You just have to let them say what they like, particularly when you want something from them; pretend you're listening to them seriously, as if they were talking sense. Did you hear how she went for me earlier on, as if I'd said something terrible? I didn't take any notice of it; they're all like that ... And anyway, heaven be thanked, it does look as if the Signora likes you and really is going to give us her protection. But if you get out of this, Lucia, and if you ever have to have dealings with the gentry again, you'll find yourself listening to even more nonsense than this time.'

Various influences were at work on the Signora – a desire to help the Father Superior; the pleasure of granting protection; the thought of the credit to be gained by so holy a use of her power to protect; a certain attraction towards Lucia; a certain feeling of happiness at being able to do good to an innocent creature, to give succour and consolation to the oppressed : so that she really did want to take the two poor fugitives under her wing. At her request, and in consideration of her special position, they were lodged in the portress's quarters, just outside the inner cloister, and treated as if they were in the service of the nunnery.

Mother and daughter congratulated each other on having been able to find a safe and honourable place of refuge so quickly. They would have preferred their presence to remain unknown, but that was not easy in a nunnery – especially as there was a man outside who was all too anxious to have news of one of them, with the anger of frustration and disappointment in his heart now, as well as the original passions of lust and pride. And now we must leave the women in their place of safe retreat and return to that man's palace at the time when he was waiting for news of the infamous expedition on which he had sent his men.

Chapter 11

A PACK of hounds that have lost their hare, and come unhappily back toward their master with heads held low and tails between their legs, present the same picture as Don Rodrigo's bravoes on that night of confusion, as they made their way back to the palace. Their master was walking up and down in the shadows of an unused attic room on the top floor, which looked out over the level space in front of the palace. From time to time he halted and listened, or looked out through the gaps in the worm-eaten shutters. He was very impatient, and a little worried too; not only because of possible failure, but because of possible consequences. For this was the grossest and most dangerous piece of villainy our hero had ever put in hand. But he reassured himself by the thought of the precautions that had been taken to suppress all evidence, if not all suspicion, that might connect him with the enterprise. As for suspicion, he thought, I can snap my fingers at that. I'd like to see anyone raise the enthusiasm to climb up here to see if there's a girl in the place! That bumpkin can come if he likes; we'll look after him when he gets here. The friar is also welcome to pay us a visit. The old woman? She can go to Bergamo.[1] The forces of the law? I needn't worry about them. The mayor wasn't born yesterday, and he's no fool. Milan? Who is there at Milan that cares about these people? Who'd listen to them? Who knows they exist? They're like a sort of lost tribe; they haven't even got a master. They belong to no one. There's nothing to fear ... Attilio will have a shock in the morning! He'll see whether I'm a man of words or a man of deeds ... and then – if by any chance there were any trouble, like ... like some enemy who wants to take advantage of the occasion ... then Attilio ought to be able to advise me; the honour of the whole family is involved.

1. See page 150 – Translator's note.

But the thought on which he dwelt most of all, because it contained both comfort for his fears and nourishment for his main passion, was the thought of the flattery and the promises he would use to win over Lucia. 'She'll be so terrified,' he said to himself, 'so terrified to find herself alone here, among those grisly countenances, that ... well, I've got the most reassuring face in these parts, damn it! – she'll have to turn to me, and implore my help ... and once she starts imploring ...'

In the middle of these edifying reflections, he heard a trampling of feet, and went to the window. He opened it a little, and looked round the corner. There they were – but where was the litter? Damnation! he thought, where is it? Six, seven, eight – they're all there, including Griso; but no litter. Devil take it! Griso will have some explaining to do.

They entered the palace, and Griso leant his staff in the corner of one of the ground floor rooms, took off his pilgrim's hat and cloak, and went upstairs to provide Don Rodrigo with that explanation which it was his duty to present as commander of his master's forces – a title which no one envied him at that moment. Don Rodrigo was waiting for him at the head of the stairs, and saw him approach with the awkward, clumsy bearing of a disappointed bully.

'Well!' he said, or rather shouted, 'what is the meaning of this, Captain Swaggerer, Captain Leave-it-to-me?'

'It's a hard thing,' replied Griso, halting with one foot on the first step of the flight, 'it's a very hard thing to have to listen to a lot of harsh words, when a man has worked faithfully, and tried to do his duty, and risked his skin into the bargain.'

'Well, what happened, then?' said Don Rodrigo. 'Tell me all about it.' He led the way to his room; Griso followed him, and quickly reported the plans he had made, the way he had carried them out, all he had seen and failed to see, all he had heard and feared, and how he had tried to retrieve the situation. His narrative had about it the same mixture of order and confusion, of doubt and dismay, which inevitably prevailed at that moment among his ideas.

'It's not your fault – you behaved very well,' said Don Rodrigo finally. 'You did all that could be done. But ... to think that there might be a spy under this roof! If there is one, and if we find out who he is – which we will do, if there is one – I'll take care of him for you. I promise you, Griso, that he'll get his Christmas box all right.'

'I was thinking just the same,' said Griso. 'If it's true, if we do find that there's a swine like that among us, your honour ought to give him to me to deal with. A fellow who thought it was funny to give me a night like the one I've just had! It'd be for me to pay him out. But you know, sir, there were several things that gave me the idea that there was something quite different going on all the time, some plot we don't know about. I'll find out all about it tomorrow.'

'You weren't recognized, at least?'

Griso said that he hoped not, and the end of the conversation was that Don Rodrigo ordered him to do three things the following day, all of which he might very well have thought of for himself. He was to send two men early in the morning, to deliver a warning to the headman, which we already know about; two others were to be sent to the deserted house, to patrol around it, to keep away any idle yokels that might come along, and to make sure that no one saw the litter until the following night, when it could be fetched away, since no suspicious movements must be made in the meantime; and Griso was to send some of his more resourceful and intelligent men into the village, and go there himself, to mix with the people and try to find out what had gone wrong the night before. Then Don Rodrigo went off to bed, allowing Griso to do the same. He dismissed him with words of praise, which were obviously intended to compensate him for the hasty abuse with which he had been greeted.

Sleep well, poor Griso! You must need the rest. Busy all day, working half the night, not to mention the risk of falling into the hands of the villagers, or of having yet another price put on your head, for *abduction of a virtuous woman* – and then to get a reception like that! But there's human gratitude for you! At least you have been able to see, in the present instance, that though justice may not follow our actions immediately, it often does follow them sooner or later, even in this world. Sleep well tonight; it may be that the day will come when you will provide us with another, even more striking, proof of the same thing.

Next morning Griso was already up and about his business, when Don Rodrigo came down and began to look for Count Attilio. When the count saw his cousin appear, he put on a mocking expression and attitude, and cried 'Happy St Martin's Day!'

'I don't know what to say to you,' replied Don Rodrigo, coming up to him. 'I'll pay the bet, of course; that's the least of my worries. I didn't tell you anything about this before, because I must admit, I thought I'd be giving you a surprise this morning. But now . . . well, I'd better tell you all about it.'

'Believe me,' said the count, having heard the whole story, 'the friar had a finger in the pie somewhere.' He spoke more seriously than might have been expected from such a light-headed fellow. 'That friar', he went on, 'may act like a simpleton and talk a lot of nonsense, but it seems to me that he knows what he's about, and that he's a mischief-maker. And you didn't trust me – you never told me what lying nonsense he inflicted on you when he came to see you the other day.'

Don Rodrigo repeated his conversation with the friar.

'Do you mean to tell me you put up with all that?' exclaimed Count Attilio. 'You let him walk out untouched just as he walked in?'

'Do you expect me to bring all the Capuchins in Italy about my ears?'

'I don't think,' said the count, 'that I would have been able to remember, at a moment like that, that there were any other Capuchins in the world except that presumptuous villain. But surely, even if you want to play it safely, there are ways of obtaining satisfaction even from a Capuchin? Double your loving-kindness to the body as a whole, at the right time, and you'll find that you can give a hearty thrashing to one of its members with complete impunity. Very well; he's got away without the punishment that would have suited him best of all; but from now on I'm going to take him under my protection, and I look forward to teaching him the right way to address people like us.'

'Don't make things worse, will you?'

'Trust me, for once. I will give you the help you expect from a relation and a friend.'

'What are you thinking of doing?'

'I'm not sure yet; but I'll certainly take care of that friar. I'll think of something . . . But of course, our noble uncle the Privy Councillor is the man to do this for me. The dear old count! Dear old uncle! How I laugh every time I have a chance to get him to do a job for me – a politician of that calibre! I'll be in Milan in a couple of days, and then in one way or another the friar will be taken care of.'

Meanwhile breakfast was served; though so serious a discussion could not be interrupted by a meal. Count Attilio spoke his mind freely. He took the attitude demanded by his friendship for Don Rodrigo and by the honour of the name they shared – according to his ideas of friendship and honour– but he could not help smiling from time to time behind his great moustache at the sorry outcome of his cousin's plan. But Don Rodrigo, being personally involved, and having hoped to achieve a master-stroke in complete silence and seen it end in noisy failure, was vexed by deeper passions and distracted by more unwelcome thoughts.

'A fine story those villains will make of it,' he said. 'It'll be all round the countryside. But what does that matter to me? . . . I can snap my fingers at the forces of the law. There are no proofs, and if there were I'd snap my fingers just the same. By the way, I arranged for the headman to be warned this morning that he'd better not report the incident. So nothing will come of it; but that sort of chatter does annoy me, if it goes on too long. And it's all wrong that I should have been fooled in that barbarous way.'

'You were very wise,' said Count Attilio. 'That mayor of yours . . . he may be obstinate, empty-headed, and a tremendous bore, but he's also a good fellow, a man who knows where his duty lies. When you have to deal with a man like that, you have to be careful not to embarrass him. If a blackguardly headman makes a report, the mayor, with the best will in the world, can't help . . .'

'But you spoil everything for me', Don Rodrigo broke in with

215

a touch of anger, 'by your habit of contradicting the mayor and interrupting him, and making fun of him too, when you get the chance . . . What the devil does it matter that a mayor is a stupid animal, an obstinate mule, and so on, if he's a good fellow at the same time?'

'Do you know, my dear cousin,' said Count Attilio, looking at him in surprise, 'I'm beginning to think you must be just the least bit frightened? Taking the mayor seriously . . .'

'But you said yourself just now that we've got to take him into account!'

'Yes, I did say that; and when we're up against something serious, I'll show you that I can play the part of a man. Do you know what I'm going to do for you? I'm man enough to go straight out and make a personal call on the mayor! How pleased he'll be at such an honour! And I'm man enough to let him talk to me for half an hour about the Count-Duke, and about our noble Spanish garrison commander; and to agree with everything he says, even if it's some of his worst drivel. I'll put in a word or two about our uncle the Privy Councillor; and you know what effect that'll have on the worthy fellow! After all he needs our protection more than you need his favour. I'll do my good deed, and go and see him, and leave him better disposed towards you than ever before.'

After some other words in the same vein, Count Attilio went out hunting; and Don Rodrigo waited anxiously for Griso to come back. He finally returned at dinner time, and made his report.

The confused events of that night had made so much noise, and the disappearance of three people from a small village was such a striking event, that many questions were bound to be asked, urgently and persistently, both by those who were genuinely concerned over what had happened, and by those who were merely curious. Also there were too many people who knew part of the story for there to be any possibility that they would all get together and agree to suppress all the facts.

Perpetua could not open the front door without being besieged by people who wanted to know who had given her master such a fright the night before. Going over the circumstances in her mind, and putting two and two together, she finally realized what a fool Agnese had made of her, and was so furious at her treachery that she really needed to speak her mind about it to somebody. Not that she went complaining to all and sundry about the exact manner in which she had been fooled; she kept very quiet about that. But the trick they had tried to play on her poor master was something she could not pass over in silence; especially seeing that the people who had tried to play it were that decent young man, that virtuous widow, and that little plaster saint Lucia. With emphatic instructions and with heartfelt appeals Don Abbondio tried to make her keep quiet; and she replied that there was no need to tell her anything so obvious and so natural. None the less the poor woman found it no easier to keep a secret of that importance locked up in her heart than an old barrel, with perished hoops, finds it to hold a very new wine, which ferments and gurgles and bubbles, and, if it does not blow out the bung, works round it and comes out in the form of froth, and makes its way between stave and stave, and oozes out here and there, so that you can taste it and get a very good idea what wine it is.

Gervaso could hardly believe that for once he really knew more about something than other people. He thought it was a very fine thing to have been so thoroughly well frightened, and felt that the fact of having a hand in something with the smell of illegality about it had made him a man like other men. He was dying to boast about it. Tonio was seriously concerned about possible inquiries and court cases and the explanations he might have to give. He shook his fist under Gervaso's nose as he ordered him not to breathe a word to anyone; but there was no way of keeping him permanently gagged. Besides, Tonio himself had been out of his house at an unusual time of night, and had come home in the end at an unusual pace and with an unusual look about him, and, moreover, had been in an agitated state of mind which predisposed him towards telling the truth. He had not been able to conceal the facts from his wife, who had a tongue.

The one who talked the least was Menico. When he told his

parents about the events and the objects of his mission, they were so horrified to hear that a son of theirs had taken part in the thwarting of one of Don Rodrigo's designs, that they hardly let the boy finish speaking. They immediately warned him with the most fearful threats never even to hint at what had happened. The following morning they still did not feel that they had done enough for safety, and decided to keep him locked up indoors all that day, and the next couple of days as well. But what was the use? They themselves got talking to the people in the village; they did not mean to show that they knew more than anyone else, but when the conversation touched on the mysterious flight of our three poor friends, and how, why, and where they had gone Menico's parents mentioned, as if it were generally known, that they had gone to Pescarenico. So this fact also became common knowledge.

With all these scraps of information, sewn together in the usual manner, and with the extra fringe that always gets added in the sewing, the materials were there for a story definite and clear enough to satisfy the most penetrating intellect. But the invasion of the bravoes was too serious and also too noisy an event to be left out of the account; and as no one had any exact information about it, it ruined the consistency of the narrative. People murmured the name of Don Rodrigo; everyone was agreed that he must have had something to do with it, but otherwise all was obscurity and various conjecture. There was a lot of talk about the two bravoes who had appeared in the street as darkness fell the previous evening, and the other bravo who had stood in the doorway of the inn. But what light could be shed on the question by those isolated facts? When asked who had been at the inn on the previous evening, the host, so he said, could not even remember whether he had had any company or not. He added that an inn is like a busy seaport.

But it was the pilgrim who did most to confuse and misdirect the villagers' thoughts – the pilgrim whom Stefano and Carlandrea had seen, whom the bandits had tried to murder, and who had finally gone off with them, or been carried away by them. What had he been doing in the village? Was he a spirit from Purgatory, who had been sent to help the women, or a spirit from Hell – the damned soul of a criminal impostor who had once posed as a pilgrim, and now walked at night in the company of those who still followed his ancient trade? Or was he a real, living pilgrim, whom they had tried to kill to stop him shouting and waking the village? Or could it be – for the strangest suspicions enter men's minds – that he was in fact one of the bandits, disguised as a pilgrim? So many suggestions were put forward, that even Griso's experience and sagacity would have been insufficient to the task of establishing who he was, if Griso had had to work out this part of the story from what was being said. But, as we know, the aspect of the episode which was most obscure for the villagers was the very one that was clearest to him. He used it as a key with which to interpret the other information which he gathered himself, or picked up through the other spies working under him, and was able to put together quite a connected narrative for Don Rodrigo.

He went straight to Don Rodrigo's room, and told him about the trick that the two poor lovers had tried to play on the priest. That explained why the cottage had been empty, and why the alarm bell had been sounded, without any need to suppose that Don Rodrigo's palace contained a traitor – to use the word employed by those two pillars of rectitude. Griso told his master about the lovers' flight, and that also could easily be explained by their terror at being detected by the priest, or by their hearing about the irruption of the bravoes during the confusion which followed its discovery, when the whole village was in turmoil. In conclusion he said that they had fled to Pescarenico. That was all he had to report.

Don Rodrigo was pleased at the news that no one had betrayed him, and that no incriminating evidence had been left behind; but it was a poor sort of pleasure, and lasted only a moment.

'So they got away!' he shouted. 'And they got away together at that! That swine of a friar! Damn the friar!' The words emerged from his throat in a sort of rattle, and were further distorted as they passed between his teeth, which were furiously biting his forefinger; his face was as ugly as his passions.

'That friar will pay for this! Griso! I'll never hold my head up again, unless ... I must know, they must be found to-day ... I must know where they are by this evening. I'll have no peace ... Go to Pescarenico at once, search for them, find them ... We must know. You'll get four *scudi* at once, and my protection for the rest of your life. But I must know by this evening ... That swine of a friar !'

So Griso set out again; and he did in fact manage to provide his worthy master with the required information that very same evening. This is how it came about.

One of the greatest comforts of this life is friendship; and one of the comforts of friendship is that of having someone we can trust with a secret. But friendship does not pair us off into couples, as marriage does; each of us generally has more than one friend to his name, and so a chain is formed, of which no man can see the end. When we allow ourselves the comfort of depositing a secret in the bosom of a friend, we inspire him with the wish to enjoy the same comfort himself. It is true that we always ask him not to tell anyone else; and this is a condition which, if taken literally, would break the series of comforting confidences at once. But the general practice is to regard the obligation as one which prevents a man from passing the secret on, *except to an equally trusted friend and on the same condition of silence*. From trusted friend to trusted friend, the secret travels and travels along that unending chain, until it reaches the ears of the very man or men from whom the first speaker meant to keep it for ever. It would generally take quite a long time to get there, if each of us only had two friends – one to confide the secret to us, and another to whom we can pass it on. But there are some privileged men who have hundreds of friends, and once a secret reaches one of them, its subsequent journeys are so rapid and multitudinous that no one can keep track of them.

Our author could not make out exactly how many mouths had passed on the secret that Griso was under orders to un-earth. But it is certain that the worthy fellow who had escorted Lucia and Agnese to Monza got back to Pescarenico with his cart about an hour before sunset. Just before he reached his home, he met a trusted friend, to whom he told the story of his good deed, and the rest of the tale, in the greatest confidence. It is also certain that two hours later Griso was in a position to speed back to the palace and report to Don Rodrigo that Lucia and her mother had taken refuge in a convent in Monza, and that Renzo had gone on to Milan.

Don Rodrigo felt a villainous pleasure at hearing of the lovers' separation, and also felt hopes of achieving his villainous object reviving a little within him. He spent a great part of the night thinking about ways and means, and got up early, with two plans in his head, one fully worked out, and the other still no more than half-formed. The first was to send Griso straight off to Monza, to get some more definite news of Lucia, and see what more could be done. So he sent for his faithful servant, handed him his four *scudi* and praised him again for the masterly skill he had shown in earning them, and gave him his new instructions.

'Well, sir, . . .' said Griso, hesitantly.

'Well? Haven't I made myself clear?'

'Oh, yes, sir; but I was wondering if you couldn't send someone else.'

'*What?*'

'My honoured lord, I'm ready to risk my skin for my master any time; it's no more than my duty. But I know that you don't like endangering your servants' lives unnecessarily.'

'Well, then?'

'Your Honour knows that I've a price on my head, and one or two rewards out for me . . . Here I'm under your protection; we're all together; the mayor is a friend of the family. The police respect me, and I, for my part – it's not a thing I'd boast about, but it helps towards a quiet life – I treat them as friends. In Milan everybody knows your honour's livery . . . but in Monza they all know me. And do you realize, sir, without boasting, anyone who handed me over to the law, or just my head, wouldn't do at all badly out of it? A hundred *scudi*, paid on the nail, and the right to have two ordinary bandits let out of prison.'

'Devil take it!' said Don Rodrigo. 'You're beginning to look like a cowardly dog, that's just about got the courage to snap at people's ankles as they pass the door, looking back over his shoulder to see if anyone's coming out to back him up, but hasn't the guts to go twenty yards down the street!'

'I did think, sir, that I'd shown I could do better than that.'

'Very well then!'

'Very well then, sir,' said Griso more boldly, on his mettle now. 'Please forget what I said. Brave as a lion – quick as a flash – ready to go. That's Griso for you!'

'I never said you were to go alone. You can take a couple of the best men we've got – Sfregiato and Tiradritto,[2] say. And pull yourself together, and be like the Griso I used to know. Devil take it! Three men with faces like yours, minding their own business – anyone ought to be glad to let you pass. The police at Monza must be pretty tired of life, if they risk it against a hundred *scudi* in such a dangerous game. And then I don't believe that my name is so unknown in those parts that it counts for nothing to be my servant.'

Having brought a blush to Griso's cheek, he went on to give him fuller and more detailed instructions. Griso picked up his two companions, and set off, with a bold and cheerful smile on his face, but inwardly cursing Monza, and women, and the prices on good men's heads, and the whims of their masters. He walked like a wolf that ventures out, urged on by hunger, belly tucked up and ribs sticking out, and comes down from its mountain home, where there is only snow to eat, and advances suspiciously into the plain; it stops every minute, with one paw raised and its mangy tail waving,

'Lifting its nose to snuff the faithless wind.'

If that wind brings with it a smell of man or of steel, the wolf pricks up its pointed ears and looks around, its reddened eyes glistening with blood-lust and, at the same time, with the fear of pursuit.

(If anyone wants to know the origin of the beautiful line just quoted, it comes from a remarkable unpublished work about the Lombards in the Crusades, which will be coming out before long and will make a name for itself. I have borrowed it because

2. 'Scarface' and 'Stop-at-Nothing'.

it suited me, and I mention the source, because I do not care to strut in borrowed plumes. I hope no one will think that this is just a cunning way of letting people know that the author[3] of that remarkable work and I are like brothers, and that I can rummage in his manuscripts to my heart's content.)

The other thing that Don Rodrigo had in mind was to ensure that Renzo should not be able to come back with Lucia later on; nor indeed return to the village at all. He considered spreading rumours that Renzo's life would be in danger and that traps would be set for him if he came back, hoping that Renzo would hear of this through some friend and be discouraged from coming home. But then the thought struck him that it would be a safer method if he could have him officially exiled from the state. He realized that his ends would be better served by recourse to the law than by the use of force. It might be possible to make something of Renzo's intrusion into the curé's house; to represent it as a violent aggression, or an act of sedition, and so to persuade the mayor that he ought to issue a warrant of arrest against Renzo. But then Don Rodrigo reflected that it would hardly be fitting for him to dirty his hands with that sort of thing himself. Without racking his brains any more, he decided to take Dr Quibbler into his confidence as far as it might be necessary in order to make him see what was required.

There are so many proclamations, he said to himself. And the Doctor's no fool. He'll find something that fits the case, some legal quibble with which to entangle that oaf; otherwise I'll have to find a new name for him.

But (see how things sometimes turn out in this world!) while his thoughts were on the Doctor as the person most able to help him, another man was already eagerly doing so; and this was the last man anyone would have thought of, namely Renzo himself. In fact he was setting about it in a surer and swifter way then the Doctor could have devised.

More than once I have seen a nice, bright little boy – somewhat too bright, to tell the truth, but showing every sign of intending to turn out a good citizen – doing his best, as

3. The line comes from a poem by Tommaso Grossi, one of Manzoni's friends. – Translator's note.

evening falls, to round up his little herd of guinea-pigs, which have been running free all day in the garden. He would like to get them all trotting into the pen together; but that's hopeless. One breaks away to the right, and while the small swineherd runs after him to chase him back with the others, another one – or two, or three – dash off to the left – or all over the place. After a little impatience he adapts himself to their methods, and begins by pushing inside those who happen to be nearest to the pen, and then goes to fetch the others, singly, or two or three at a time, as best he can. We have to play much the same game with our characters. We managed to get Lucia under cover, and ran off after Don Rodrigo; and now we must drop him and catch up with Renzo, who is right out of sight.

After the unhappy farewell which we described earlier on, Renzo set out from Monza towards Milan, in a state of mind which can easily be imagined. To leave his house, to abandon his trade and, worst of all, to separate from Lucia; to set out on a journey with no idea where he would next be able to lay his head; and all because of that blackguard! When he let his mind rest on any of these things, he was overwhelmed with rage and with the desire for revenge, but then he would remember the prayer which Father Cristoforo had said in the church at Pescarenico, and how he had joined in it himself, and he would pull himself together again. His anger returned once more; but then he would see a crucifix by the wayside, and take off his hat and stop a moment to say another prayer. In the course of his journey, he must have murdered Don Rodrigo in his thoughts and brought him to life again at least twenty times. The road was a sunken one with high banks; it was muddy, boulder-strewn, and cut up by deep ruts, which turned into rivulets whenever it rained. At certain low-lying points the road became a lake, which would have been easier to cross in a boat. In such places a steep little path with steps would lead up the bank, showing where other travellers had found a way round through the fields. As Renzo climbed up one of those paths to a higher level, he caught sight of the vast mass of the cathedral standing up alone out of the plain, as if it had been built not in a city but in the middle of a desert. He stood quite still, forgetting all his troubles, and gazed at the prospect, distant as it was, of that eighth wonder of the world, which he had so often heard of ever since he was a child. But after a few moments he turned round and saw a jagged range of mountains on the horizon, among which he recognized his own Resegone standing tall and clear. Deeply moved, he stood and gazed sadly at it for a minute, and then sadly turned and went on his way. Presently he began to see a campanile here, a dome there, and towers and roofs. He rejoined the main road, and went on for some distance; and when he realized that he was on the outskirts of the city, he approached another traveller, gave him his most elegant bow, and said: 'Excuse me, sir . . .'

'What can I do for you, young man?'

'Could you tell me the shortest way to the Capuchin monastery where Father Bonaventura lives?'

The other traveller was a wealthy man who lived some way out of the city. He had been to Milan that morning on business, but had achieved nothing and was returning in great haste. He wanted to be back home as soon as possible, and would have preferred not to be held up in this manner. But he gave no sign of impatience, and replied very civilly:

'My dear boy, there's more than one monastery in Milan. You'll have to tell me more clearly which one you want.'

Renzo took Father Cristoforo's letter out of his pocket, and showed it to the gentleman, who saw the words 'East Gate' and gave it back to him, saying:

'You're in luck, young man; the monastery you want is quite near here. Take this path on the left here; it's a short cut. In a couple of minutes you'll come to the corner of a long, low building, which is the lazaretto. Follow the ditch that runs round it, and you'll come out by the East Gate. Go through the gate, and walk on for another three or four hundred yards. Then you'll see a small square with some fine elm trees; that's where the monastery is. You can't go wrong. God bless you, young man.'

The last words were accompanied by a graceful wave of the hand, and he went his way.

Renzo was amazed and edified by the polite way in which

these city people spoke to country folk; he did not realize that it was a special day, a day on which long capes made way for short jackets. He followed his instructions, and soon reached the East Gate. – But here we must warn the reader against imagining the East Gate as he knows it today. When Renzo arrived there, the road outside took a straight line only as far as the other end of the lazaretto; thereafter it followed a narrow, winding course between two hedges. The gate itself was flanked by two great pillars, and there was a roof over it to protect it from the weather. At one side was a little house for the excisemen. The bastions formed an irregular descending line on each side, and the ground was rough and uneven with rubbish and broken earthenware scattered at random. The street which then confronted those who passed through the East Gate was rather like the one we now see when we go through the Porta Tosa. An open drain ran down the middle of the road to a point just short of the gate, dividing it into two narrow, winding ways, thick with dust or deep in mud according to the time of year. The drain ran into a larger sewer at the point where there was – and still is – an alley known as the Via di Borghetto.

A column stood there, with a cross on top of it, called the Cross of St Denis. To the left and right were kitchen gardens marked off by hedges, and little houses at intervals, mostly inhabited by washerwomen.

Renzo walked through the gate and on. None of the excisemen took any notice of him. This surprised him; for there were one or two people in his village who could boast of having been to Milan, and he had heard a good deal from them about the questioning and searching to which people arriving from the country were subjected. The street was empty, and if he had not been able to hear a distant murmur like the sound of a large crowd in movement, he might have thought that he was entering a deserted city. He walked on, not knowing what to think, and saw long white lines of something soft and light on the ground, as if it were snow. But it could hardly be snow, which does not lie in lines like that, nor fall so early in the year, as a rule. He bent over one of the drifts, looked at it carefully, and touched it. It was flour. They must be well off for food in Milan, he thought, if they misuse the bounty of God in this manner. And then they say there's famine everywhere! That's to keep us poor country folk quiet.

A few more paces took him to the side of the column, and at its foot he saw something stranger yet. On the steps of the plinth were scattered some things which could hardly be stones, and if you had seen them on a baker's stall, you would not have hesitated a moment before calling them loaves. But Renzo dared not believe the evidence of his own eyes at once. After all, it wasn't exactly the place you'd expect to find bread. Let's see what this means, he said to himself. He went up to the column, bent down, and picked one up. It really was a loaf, a round loaf of the whitest bread, such as Renzo seldom ate except on feast days.

'It really is bread!' he said, speaking out loud in his amazement. 'Do they throw it around like that in these parts, in a year like this? Can't they even be bothered to pick it up when it falls? Is this the Land of Cockaigne?'

He had walked ten miles in the fresh morning air, and the sight of that bread aroused his hunger as well as his wonder. Should I take it? – he thought. Well, they've left it here where the dogs can get at it; so there can't be much harm in a man helping himself. Anyway, if the baker turns up, I'll pay him for what I take. – He transferred the loaf in his hand to his pocket, picked up a second loaf and stuck it in the other pocket, and finally took a third loaf and began to eat it. Then he walked on, more puzzled than ever, and wondering what all this could mean. He had only gone a few steps, when he suddenly saw some people coming from the centre of the city; he looked carefully at the first to approach. It was a man and a woman, with a boy a couple of yards behind them. All three were carrying loads which seemed too heavy for them, and they all looked very strange. Their clothes, or rather rags, were covered with flour; and there were streaks of flour on their faces, which were contorted and fiery red. They were bent double by the weight of their load; but apart from that there was something painful about their gait, as if their very bones ached from a thrashing.

The man's burden was a great sack of flour, which his shoulders could barely support. It had holes here and there, and flour dribbled out of them every time he stumbled or lost his balance. Much more unpleasant was the spectacle presented by the woman. Her arms were curved under the enormous mass of her belly, and seemed scarcely able to hold it up; it looked like a great earthenware jar with two handles. Below that belly came a pair of legs, naked to above the knee, and staggering unsteadily forward. Renzo looked again, and saw that the main mass was formed by the woman's skirt, which she was holding up by the hem, with as much flour packed inside it as it would hold, and a little more; so that some of it blew away in the breeze at almost every step she took.

The boy had a basket full of loaves on his head, which he was holding with both hands. But his legs were not so long as his parents', and he gradually got left behind. From time to time he would lengthen his stride to catch up, and then the basket would sway and one or two loaves would fall to the ground.

'Why don't you throw them all away, good-for-nothing that you are?' said his mother, snarling at him.

'I'm not throwing them away; they keep on falling out by themselves. What am I to do?' replied the boy.

'It's just as well for you that I've got my hands full,' said the woman. Her hands twitched as she spoke, as if she were giving the poor lad a good shaking; and the movement sent more flour flying than would have been enough to make two more loaves like the ones the boy had just dropped.

'Oh, never mind!' said the man. 'We'll come back for them; or someone else'll pick them up. We've had a hard time for long enough; now that there's plenty to eat again, let's enjoy it without quarrelling amongst ourselves.'

Just then some more people came in through the gate. One of them went up to the woman and said: 'Where do we go for bread?'

'Further on, further on!' said the woman, and when they had walked on ten paces or so she muttered: 'These damned peasants! They'll come and clear out every bakery in the city, and every shop, so that there'll be nothing left for us.'

'There'll be something for everyone,' said the man. 'What a misery you are! There's plenty of food, plenty!'

From these and various other things which he heard and saw, Renzo began to realize that he had arrived at a city in revolt, and that this was a day of victory; in other words, that everyone was taking what he liked, in proportion to his hunger and his strength, and paying for it with blows. Though we like to show our poor young hero from the mountains in the most favourable light, historical accuracy compels us to admit that his first reaction was one of pleasure. He had so little reason to be pleased with the ordinary course of events, that he found himself inclined to approve of anything that would change it. And besides he was in no way a man who rose above the general intellectual level of his age, and therefore he too held the common opinion – which might almost be called a common passion – according to which the shortage of bread was the fault of the hoarders of grain and the bakers. He was ready to see justice in any method of making them loose their hold on the food which they (according to that opinion) were cruelly denying to the needs of a famished nation. But he fully intended to keep out of the disturbance, and was relieved to think that he was on his way to seek out a Capuchin, who would find him shelter and be a father to him. Thinking these thoughts, and glancing from time to time at the conquerors, fresh from their victory, who were going past laden with booty, he covered the short distance that separated him from the monastery.

A fine palace, with a lofty colonnade, now stands on the spot; but in Renzo's day the space was taken up by a little square, which in fact was still there just a few years ago. On the far side stood the monastery and the church of the Capuchins, behind a row of four tall elm trees. We congratulate those of our readers who cannot remember seeing the place while it looked like that; in fact we envy them, for they must be very young, and cannot have had time to commit many follies. Renzo went straight to the monastery door, hid the half-eaten loaf under his jacket, got out the letter and held it ready in his hand, and rang the bell. A panel opened with a grating across it, and the face of the brother porter appeared. He asked who Renzo was.

'I'm from the country, and I've brought Father Bonaventura an urgent letter from Father Cristoforo.'

'Let me have it,' said the porter, putting his hand up to the grating.

'No, no,' said Renzo; 'I've got to give it to him personally.'

'He's not in the monastery.'

'Please let me in, then, and I'll wait for him.'

'Take my advice, and go and wait in the church,' said the friar. 'Then you can do some good while you're waiting. We're not letting anyone into the monastery at present.' He shut the panel.

Renzo was left standing there, with the letter in his hand. He took a few steps towards the church, intending to follow the porter's advice; but then he decided to have another look at the disturbances. He traversed the square, and stood at the side of the road, with his arms crossed, looking over to the left, towards the centre of the city, where the murmur of the crowd was loudest and most concentrated. The trouble-centre began to attract the listener.

'Let's see what's going on,' he said to himself. He got out what was left of his loaf, and nibbled it as he began to walk towards the noise. While he is on the way, we will give the briefest possible account of the causes and the beginning of the disturbance.

Chapter 12

THIS was the second year of bad harvests. The year before, stocks of food left over from earlier harvests had filled the gaps to a certain extent. The population had got through to the autumn of 1628 – the year of which we are now speaking – without being either overfed or starved, but it was left with absolutely nothing in hand. Then the longed-for harvest turned out to be even more wretched than the one before; partly because the weather was worse, not only in the territory of Milan but for a considerable distance around it, but also through the fault of mankind. The damage and waste caused by the war – that magnificent war which we have already mentioned – were such that in the part of the state nearest the fighting many more farms than usual remained uncultivated, having been deserted by peasants who were compelled to go out and beg their bread instead of growing it by the sweat of their brow for themselves and for their fellow men. 'More than usual', I said, because other causes also contributed to the abandonment of farms. The unbearable level of taxation, levied with incredible greed and incredible folly; the habitual behaviour of the troops quartered in the villages, which even in peacetime was indistinguishable from that of enemy invaders, according to the melancholy testimony of contemporary documents; and various other factors which need not be mentioned here had been slowly helping to produce that tragic result throughout the territory of Milan. The particular circumstances which we are about to describe were like a sudden turn for the worse in a chronic illness. And that miserable harvest was not yet fully gathered in, when requisitions for the army, together with the wholesale waste that always accompanies them, made such a hole in it that the shortage of grain began to be felt immediately. With the shortage came its painful, salutary, inevitable consequence, a rise in prices.

But when prices rise more than a certain amount, they always produce a certain effect – or at least they always have done up to the present day. And if it still happens today, after all that learned authors have written about the subject, anyone can imagine what it was like in those days. This effect is a common conviction that it is not in fact the shortage of goods that has caused the high prices. People forget that they have feared and predicted the shortage, and suddenly begin to believe that there is really plenty of grain, and that the trouble is that it is being kept off the market. Though there are no earthly or heavenly grounds for that belief, it gives food to people's anger and to their hopes. Real or imaginary hoarders of grain, landowners who did not sell their entire crop within twenty-four hours, bakers who bought grain and held it in stock – everyone in fact who possessed or was thought to possess grain was blamed for the shortage and for the high prices, and made the target of universal complaint and of the hatred of rich and poor alike. The storehouses and granaries were known to be full, overflowing, bursting with grain; their location was known too, and the number of sacks they contained, which was impossibly large.

People talked with certainty about the vast quantities of grain that were being secretly exported to other territories. (In those territories, no doubt, people were shouting with equal certainty and with equal fury that their grain was being sent to Milan.)

There are certain official measures which the multitude always regards (or always has regarded up to the present day), as fair, simple and ideally calculated to bring out the grain that has been secreted – or walled up, or buried, to use the language then in fashion – and to bring back times of plenty. The magistrates were implored to take those measures at once; and they did take certain steps. They fixed maximum prices for a number of foodstuffs, they decreed penalties for anyone who refused to sell at those prices, and passed one or two other regulations of that kind. But all the official measures in the world, however vigorous they may be, cannot lessen a man's need for food, nor produce crops out of season. The measures actually taken on this occasion were certainly not calculated to attract imports from other areas where there might conceivably be a surplus.

And so the trouble continued and grew worse. The multitude attributed this result to the small number and the half-heartedness of the measures taken, and screamed for more full-blooded and decisive action. And unfortunately the multitude got just the man it was looking for.

The Governor of Milan, Don Gonzalo Fernandez of Cordova, was away commanding the troops at the siege of Casale, in Montferrat, and the Grand Chancellor Antonio Ferrer – another Spaniard – was acting as his deputy. Ferrer saw, as anyone could see, that it is highly desirable that there should be a fair price for bread. He also thought – and this was where he went wrong – that an order from him could do the trick. He fixed the price of bread at the level that would have been right with corn at thirty-three *lire* per measure. But it was really being sold at up to eighty. Ferrer was behaving like a lady of a certain age, who thinks she can regain her youth by altering the date on her birth certificate.

Orders much less stupid and unjust than these had often remained a dead letter through the sheer resistance of natural forces. But the crowd itself saw to the execution of this order. It had seen its dreams given the force of law, and would not allow them to be turned into a mockery. People hastened to the bakeries to demand bread at the official price; and they demanded it with that air of threatening resolution which comes from the combination of passionate conviction, physical strength and legal rights.

There is no need to ask what the bakers thought about it. They were mixing, kneading, putting dough into the ovens and taking bread out of them all day long, without ever pausing for breath; for the people had a confused feeling that there was something unnatural about the situation, and so they besieged the bakers all the time, wanting to take advantage of this utopia while it was still there. The bakers were sweating and toiling twice as hard as usual, and making a dead loss on every loaf; anyone can imagine their feelings. But on the one hand they had the magistrates threatening them with prison, and on the other hand the multitude, which wanted service. If a baker was a moment late in responding, the mob would begin to shove, and to grumble, in that loud and fearsome voice that mobs have, and to threaten one of those acts of popular justice which are among the worst acts of justice the world ever sees. There was no salvation for the bakers; they had to go on mixing, kneading, baking and selling. But to keep them going on those lines the most fearsome threats and the most pressing orders were not enough. They also had to have the physical means to carry them out; and if the thing had gone on just a little longer the means would have been lacking.

The bakers made it clear to the magistrates how iniquitous and intolerable a burden had been placed on their shoulders; they swore that they would rather throw their shovels in the fire and emigrate than go on like that; and meanwhile they carried on as best they could, hoping that sooner or later the Grand Chancellor would see reason. But Ferrer was what would now be called a man of character. He replied that the bakers had done very well indeed in the past, and would do very well indeed again as soon as times of plenty returned; that the matter would be considered and they might possibly receive some sort of compensation; and that in the meantime they must carry on as best they could. Was he truly convinced by his own arguments, or did he realize the impossibility of enforcing his edict, but prefer to leave the odium of revoking it to someone else? Who can now enter into the mental processes of Antonio Ferrer? In any case, he stood firm on his decision. Finally the decurions – a body of municipal magistrates drawn from the nobility, which survived until 1796 – decided to act. They wrote a letter to the Governor, describing the state of affairs, and asking him to find a way out of the impasse.

Don Gonzalo was up to his eyes in military problems. The reader can guess what he did, which was to nominate a commission with authority to fix a workable price for bread, at a level which would make life bearable for all parties. The commission held a meeting (or rather a *junta*, to use the half-Spanish jargon of the secretariat in those days), and after much bowing, complimenting, prefacing, lamenting, postponing, kite-flying and shilly-shallying, they were all impelled to a decision by a necessity of which all were aware. Knowing that they were doing something pregnant with consequences, but convinced that there was nothing else to do, they decided to put up the price of bread. The bakers breathed again, but the people went mad with fury.

The evening before Renzo reached Milan, the city's streets and squares had been swarming with men. Possessed by a common anger and dominated by a common thought, all of them, whether they knew each other or not, began to form into groups. They joined forces without any prearrangement, almost without being aware that they were doing so, like drops of water coming together as they run down the same slope. Every speech that was made increased the conviction and the passion both of the listeners and the speaker.

Amid all those enthusiasts, there were some cooler heads, who were very pleased to see the muddy water stirred up, and did their best to stir it up still further. They put forward arguments and stories of a kind that the cunning can always invent and the hot-headed will always believe. They had no intention of letting the troubled waters settle again without doing a little fishing in them.

Thousands of men went to bed with a vague feeling that something must be done, and that something would be done.

Before dawn, there were again a number of groups of people to be seen in the streets. Boys, women and men, the old, the workers, the destitute, all assembled together at random. In one place there would be a whispering of many voices; in another there would be a single speaker with an applauding audience. When asked a question by his neighbour on one side, a man would repeat it to his neighbour on the other; a second man would pass on all the exclamations that reached his ears in the same way. Complaints, threats and cries of astonishment could be heard on every side; but the total number of different words that made up the vocabulary of all that talk was very small.

To convert words into deeds, all that was needed was a chance, a push, an initial movement of any kind; and it was not long before one occurred. Soon after daybreak the delivery boys always came out of the bakeries, each with a great basket of loaves on his back, to be taken round to the houses of regular customers. The first appearance of one of those unfortunate lads in a place where a crowd had gathered had an effect like a fire-cracker falling into a keg of gunpowder.

'And they say there's no bread!' shouted a hundred voices.

'There's bread enough for our tyrants, who wallow in plenty, and want to starve us to death!' cried one man. He went up and slapped his hand on to the rim of the lad's basket, gave it a shake, and said 'Let's see what you've got in there!'

The poor boy went scarlet, and then white; he trembled, and wanted to say: 'Let me go!', but the words died on his lips. He dropped his arms, and tried to free himself from the shoulder-straps.

'Let's have the basket, then!' shouted someone meanwhile. Many hands seized it at once. In a moment it was on the ground, the canvas cover flew through the air, and a warm fragrance began to spread around.

'We're human beings too; we need bread as much as anyone else,' said the first speaker. He pulled a round loaf out of the basket, raised it on high for all to see, and sank his teeth into it. Many hands grabbed at the basket, and the loaves took wing; it was empty in a moment. Those who got nothing were angry at the sight of the gains won by the others, and encouraged by the easiness of the enterprise. They moved off in groups to look for other baskets; and all that they found were quickly emptied of their contents. There was no need to manhandle the delivery boys. Those who were so unlucky as to be on their rounds at the time soon saw what an unpleasant turn things were taking, put down their burdens willingly enough, and ran for it. But even so those who got nothing were by far the greater part. Even the winners were dissatisfied with the size of their haul; and mingled among both those classes were those who were aiming at a more thoroughgoing revolt.

'The bakery! Let's go to the bakery!' was the cry.

In the street called the Corsia de' Servi, there is still today a bakery which bears the same name that it did then. In Tuscan it would be called the 'Forno delle Grucce'; but in the Milanese dialect its name is made up of such strange, uncouth and bar-barous sounds that our alphabet has no symbols to represent them.[1] The crowd hurried off in that direction. The shop people were questioning the delivery boy, who had returned without his basket, looking very frightened and tousled. He was stammering out an account of his lamentable adventure, when they heard a sound of trampling and howling. It grew louder and nearer, and then the forerunners of the revolt came into sight.

In great confusion and haste one of the bakers sped off to ask for the help of the captain of police, while the others quickly closed the shop and barred the doors. The crowd gathered outside, and began to shout: 'Bread! Bread! Open up! Open up!' A few minutes later the captain of police arrived, with an escort of halberdiers.

'Out of the way, lads; go home; make way for the captain of police!' shouted the officer and his men. The crowd was not yet really dense, and it made a little room for them to pass. They managed to make their way through to the shop and took up their position, together though not in any precise military formation, in front of the door.

'Listen, good people!' said the captain, from that vantage-point, in sermonizing tones. 'What are you doing here? Go home! Go home! Have you no fear of God? No respect for our sovereign lord the King? We don't want to do you any harm; but you must go home! Be good lads! Gathering together in a great mob like that ... what do you think you're up to? Nothing good, I'll be bound, nothing good for body or soul. Go home! Go home!'

But even those who could see the speaker's face and hear his words – even if they had wanted to obey him – how could they do what he said? They were being pushed and trampled by the people just behind them, who in turn were being pushed by others, wave on wave, back to the edge of the crowd, which was still growing. The captain began to find himself short of breath.

1. 'The Bakery of the Crutches' – the Milanese equivalent contains a word ending with the sound we write in English as 'sh'. Final 'sh' never occurs in Tuscan, the dialect in which Manzoni is writing, and the alphabet, as used for Tuscan, or standard Italian, affords no way of transliterating it. – Translator's note.

'Push them back a bit and let me breathe,' he said to the halberdiers, 'but don't hurt anybody. We'll see if we can get into the shop. Knock at the door. And make these people stand back.'

'Back! Back!' cried the halberdiers, pushing forward all together against the front row of the crowd, and shoving them back with the handles of their halberds. The front row howled and drew back as best they could, pushing their shoulders against the chests, their elbows against the stomachs, and their heels against the toes of the people behind them. The result was a crowding and jostling which those in the middle would have given something to avoid. Meanwhile a small open space did appear in front of the door. The captain knocked, and knocked again, shouting for the people inside to open up. They looked out of the windows, saw who it was, and ran down to open the door. The captain went in and called the halberdiers after him. They squeezed in one after the other, the last couple of them holding back the crowd with their halberds. When they were all inside, they quickly put the chain on the door and barred it again. The captain ran upstairs and put his head out of the window. What an ants' nest met his gaze!

'Listen, good people!' he shouted. Many faces turned up towards him. 'Good people, listen! Go home! A free pardon for everyone who goes home straight away!'

'Bread! Bread!' – 'Open up! Open up!' were the phrases easiest to make out in the horrible clamour the crowd gave him for his answer.

'Be reasonable, good people! Think what you are about! It's not too late yet. Be off with you; go home! You'll get your bread all right, but this is not the way to set about it ... What are you doing down there? What's happening to the door? Shame on you! I can see what you're up to. Be sensible! Think what you're doing. It's a serious offence ... I'm going to come down. Drop those iron bars! Down with those hands! It's a disgraceful thing for you Milanese to do, who are so famous for your good nature. You've always been such good lads ... Bastards!'

The sudden change in his style was caused by a stone which

left the hand of one of the good lads, flew through the air, and struck the captain in the forehead, on the left-hand bump of the metaphysical cavity.

'Bastards! Bastards!' he continued to shout as he jumped back quickly and shut the window. But though he shouted with the full strength of his lungs his praise and his oaths alike had been carried away and dispersed in the tempestuous clamour that rose up from below. When he had said that he could see what they were up to, he had been watching a lot of heavy work going on with big stones and iron bars – the first implements they had been able to find in the streets – around the door, which they were trying to break down, and the windows, from which they were trying to wrench the protective gratings. The work was already well advanced.

Meanwhile both the shop-keepers and their apprentices were standing upstairs at the windows, armed with stones – probably cobbles which they had torn up from an inner courtyard. They howled and made threatening gestures at the mob below, to drive them away. They also held out the stones, and made as if to hurl them down into the crowd. Seeing that this had no effect, they really did begin to throw their stones. None of them missed its mark, for the crowd was so thick now that – as they say in those parts – you could drop a grain of millet and it would never reach the ground.

Cries of 'Swine! Blackguards! Is this the bread you give to the poor?' came up from below, mingled with screams of pain. A number of people were hurt; two boys were actually killed. Rage gave new strength to the multitude. The door was broken in, the bars over the windows were torn down, and the human flood poured in at every gap. Seeing the ugly turn things were taking, the people indoors took refuge in the attic. The captain, the halberdiers and one or two of the shop people stayed there, stranded in the corners. Some of the others got out of the sky-lights and climbed up over the roofs like cats.

When the conquerors saw the booty before them, they forgot their plans for revenge. They dashed to the shelves and quickly emptied them of bread. Others made for the till, broke the lock, seized the boxes, and helped themselves by the handful. They filled their pockets, and went away loaded with coin, meaning to come back later for some stolen bread, if any were left. Then the mob invaded the store-rooms. They seized the sacks, dragging them around, and turning them upside down. One man grabbed a sack between his knees, unfastened its mouth, and poured out part of the contents to reduce it to a manageable load; others cried 'Wait! Wait!' and bent down with apron, neck-cloth or hat held out to receive this bounty from heaven. Another ran to a bin and took a lump of dough, which soon began to dribble out of his grasp and fall all over the place. Another, who had won himself a sieve, held it high in the air as he bore it off. Newcomers replaced those who left. Men, women and children were pushing and howling at each other, while a fine white powder settled over everything, lifting and resettling with every movement, veiling and misting over the whole scene. Outside two long processions, travelling in opposite directions, continually got in each other's way and jostled one another – one lot going home with its booty, the other trying to get in and secure a share of the spoils.

While that particular establishment was being turned upside down, none of the other bakeries in the city was safe or quiet. But none of them was mobbed by a crowd large enough to have its own way. In some cases the bakers had recruited extra hands to guard their premises. Others saw themselves outnumbered and came to terms with the mob when it began to collect at their doors, giving bread away to its members on condition that they went home. And they did go away in fact, not so much because they were satisfied as because the halberdiers and the police, while keeping clear for the most part of the terrifying situation at the Forno delle Grucce, showed their faces boldly enough at other points, turning out in sufficient numbers to intimidate ruffians whose numbers did not constitute a mob. But this meant that the position went from bad to worse at that first unhappy bakery. For everyone who felt the itch to carry out some memorable exploit preferred to go to the place where his friends had the upper hand, and impunity was more or less guaranteed.

This was the stage things had reached when Renzo, who had

now finished munching his bread, made his way through the East Gate quarter of the city. Though he did not know it, he was heading for the very centre of the storm. He walked on, now moving briskly, and now held up by the crowd, but always watching and listening in the hope of gathering a clearer idea of what was going on from the continual buzz of conversation. This is roughly what he heard in the course of his walk:

'Now the truth's out!' shouted one man. 'The wicked deceit of those blackguards who said there was no bread, no flour and no grain! Now the truth's clear for all to see, and they won't be able to pull the wool over our eyes again. Long live the time of plenty!'

'I'll tell you one thing,' said another, 'all this is no good at all. It's quite useless; in fact things will get worse again afterwards, if they don't really make an example of somebody. We'll get cheap bread now all right; but it'll be poisoned, and we poor folk'll die off like flies. They say there are too many of us. They said that in the junta; and I happen to know it's true, because I heard it myself with these ears, from my kids' godmother, who's a friend of a relation of a scullion in the household of one of those noble gentlemen.'

Another man was holding a ragged neckcloth to his tousled, bleeding scalp, foaming at the mouth, as he uttered words which we cannot repeat here; though some of the bystanders echoed them, as if to console him.

'Please be so kind as to make way, gentlemen; let a poor father come past, who is carrying food for a family of five children.' These words came from a man who was staggering under the weight of a huge sack of flour; and everyone did their best to move aside and make way for him.

'For my part,' said another to his companion, speaking almost in a whisper, 'I'm getting out of here. I'm a man of the world and I know how these things go. By tomorrow or the day after, all these idiots who're making such a noise now will be back in their homes, shivering with fear. I've noticed certain faces in the crowd, certain gentlemen going around in the mob, apparently doing nothing in particular; but they were making a careful note of who was there and who wasn't. When it's all over, there'll be a settling of accounts, and those who've asked for trouble will get it.'

'The man who protects the bakers,' shouted a sonorous voice, which caught Renzo's attention, 'is the commissioner of provisions.'

'They're all rogues,' said the man standing next to him.

'Yes, but he's the biggest rogue of all,' said the first speaker.

The official of whom they were speaking was appointed every year by the Governor from a short list of six nobles, drawn up by the council of decurions. He became president both of the council of decurions itself and also of the tribunal for provisions, which consisted of twelve more nobles, and had various functions, the most important being the control of the year's supply of food. Whoever occupied a post of that description was bound to be regarded as the root of all evil in times of general ignorance and general hardship – unless he had adopted the policy followed by Ferrer. That would have been beyond his powers, even if it had crossed his mind.

'What swine!' cried another. 'Could they do worse if they tried? Now they're saying that the Grand Chancellor is in his second childhood; they want to destroy his authority and run everything themselves. It'd be a fine thing to build them a big hen-coop and put them inside to feed on vetches and tares, the way they want us to live.'

'Talk about bread!' said another, trying to run, despite the throng, 'Nice pound loaves of granite! Stones this big, coming down like hail! And you could get your ribs crushed, just in the crowd. I can't wait to be back in my own house.'

It is hard to say whether these remarks did more to inform Renzo or to confuse him, but he continued on his way, despite the shouting and the pushing of the crowd, until he reached the famous bakery. The crowd was much thinner now, and the ugly picture of recent damage was clear to see. The walls had been stripped of plaster and dented by stones and bricks, the windows were off their hinges, the door was demolished.

'This is an ugly sight,' said Renzo to himself. 'If they treat all the bakeries like this, where are they going to make their bread? In the wells?'

Every so often someone came out of the shop carrying part of a cupboard or a breadbin or a sifting-machine, or the pole from a kneading trough, or a bench, a basket or an account-book – anything in fact which belonged to that unfortunate bakery. They shouted: 'Make way! Make way!' and forced their way through the crowd. They all went off in the same direction, and you could see they were all going to a pre-arranged destination.

What's this again, then? thought Renzo. He noticed a man make up a bundle of broken planks and splintered wood, swing it on to his shoulder and walk off in the same direction as the others. Renzo decided to follow him. The man went along the road which passes the north side of the cathedral, and is now called after the steps that used to be there, but were removed a short time ago. Keen as he was to find out what was happening, the young hillman could not help stopping when the great edifice appeared before him, and looking up at it with open mouth. Then he quickened his pace, to catch up with the man he had chosen as his guide. He turned the corner and glanced up at the façade of the cathedral, which was still to a large extent in a rough and unfinished state at that time, and went on again, still following the other man, who was heading for the centre of the square. The crowd got thicker as he went on, but it made way for the man with the load. He cut his way through the mass of people, and Renzo, still in his wake, arrived with him at the centre of the mob. There was an open space there, and in the middle of it a heap of hot ashes, which was all that was left of the equipment mentioned before. All round there was a clapping of hands and a stamping of feet, a mixed roar of triumph and of cursing.

The man threw his bundle on to the ashes; another man stirred them with the charred remnant of a baker's shovel. Smoke rose up and thickened; the flames came to life again, and the shouting grew loud again to match.

'Long live the times of plenty! Death to those who starve the people! Down with famine! To hell with the commission for provisions! To hell with the junta! Long live this plenteous supply of bread!'

The destruction of sifting machines and breadbins, the wreck-

243

ing of bakeries and the mobbing of bakers are not really the best methods of ensuring long life to a plenteous supply of bread. But that is one of those philosophical subtleties which a crowd can never grasp. Even without being a philosopher, however, a man will sometimes grasp it straightaway, while the whole matter is still new to him and he can see it with fresh eyes. It is later, when he has talked and heard others talk about it, that it becomes impossible for him to understand. The thought had struck Renzo at the very beginning, as we have seen, and it kept coming back to him now. But he kept it to himself; for when he looked at all the people around him he could not imagine any of them saying: 'Dear brother, if I go wrong, pray correct me, and I will be duly grateful.'

The fire had died down again, and no one appeared to be bringing any more fuel for it. The crowd was beginning to get bored, when someone was heard to say that a bakery was being attacked at the Cordusio – a small square, or rather crossroads, quite near at hand. In such cases the rumour often produces the event. As the word spread among the mob, an impulse to go and see spread with it. 'I'm going; are you?' 'I'm coming; let's go!' were phrases heard on every side. The crowd broke up and formed into a procession. Renzo held back, only moving when he was carried along by the human torrent. Meanwhile he was carefully considering whether he should leave the noisy throng and go back to the monastery to try to find Father Bonaventura, or go and have a look at this new development. Curiosity again proved the stronger influence. But he resolved not to force his way into the thick of the mob, where he would run the risk of bruised ribs, or worse, but to keep his distance and watch. He soon found he had a little more room around him, and taking his second loaf out of his pocket, he bit into it, and marched off in the rear of the clamorous army.

The mob had already left the great square and got into the short and narrow street known as the Old Fishmarket, and made their way through a crooked archway into Merchants' Square. As they passed before the recess which divides the colonnade of the building then known as Doctors' College, very few of them failed to glance up at the great statue that towered there, portraying the gloomy, the arrogant – no words of mine can do justice to it – the scowling face of King Philip II. Even from the marble he imposed a mysterious respect, with his arm held out as if to say: 'I'll come and see to you in a minute, you miserable rabble!'

That statue is not there today, and the explanation is a strange one. About one hundred and sixty years after the events we are describing, they gave His Majesty a new head, put a dagger in his hand instead of a sceptre, and rechristened him Marcus Brutus. The statue remained there in its renovated form for a year or so. But one morning some people who were no friends of Marcus Brutus, and in fact must have had a secret grudge against him, put a rope round the statue, pulled it over, and subjected it to all kinds of indignities. They mutilated it and reduced it to a formless torso; they pulled it through the streets, their eyes starting from their heads and their tongues lolling from their mouths; and when they were completely exhausted, they dumped it somewhere – I cannot say where. How surprised Andrea Biffi, the sculptor, would have been if he had known all this while he was carving the statue!

From Merchants' Square the rabble passed through another archway into the Via dei Fustagnai and rolled on into the Cordusio. As the rioters entered the little square, each of them looked first at the bakery which was the subject of the rumour. But instead of the crowd of friends they hoped to find already at work on the building, they saw only a small group, standing hesitantly some way back from the shop. The doors were shut, and armed men, who seemed ready to defend themselves, stood at the windows. At this sight, some were amazed, some swore, and some laughed. Some turned round, to tell those who were still approaching what had happened. Some halted; others wanted to retreat; yet others cried; 'Push on!' There was shoving from behind and holding back in the foremost ranks; something like a river reaching a dam. There was hesitation, and a confused murmur of argument and consultation. Then there came a fiendish cry from the middle of the crowd: 'It's only a couple of yards to the commissioner's house. Come and give him what he deserves! Come and smash up his house!'

The mob reacted as if it were being reminded of a decision already taken, rather than invited to take a new one. 'The commissioner! Down with the commissioner!' was now the only cry to be heard. The crowd moved off, all together, towards the street where the house so unhappily singled out was situated.

Chapter 13

THE unfortunate commissioner was having a dyspeptic and troubled siesta after a dinner at which both appetite and fresh bread had been lacking. He was waiting very anxiously to hear what the end of the day's disturbances would be; but he was far from suspecting that it would fall so catastrophically on his own head. A good citizen ran on ahead of the mob to warn him what was coming. The commissioner's servants had been attracted to the door by the noise, and were standing there looking fearfully along the street towards the approaching uproar. While they listened to the messenger, the vanguard of the mob came into sight. They quickly took the message in to their master. He decided on flight, and was thinking how to get away, when a second messenger arrived to say that it was already too late. The servants hardly had time to shut the door, which they rapidly bolted and barred. Then they ran to shut the windows, as people do when the sky goes very black and a hailstorm is expected from one moment to another.

The howling outside grew louder and louder. In the court-yard it seemed to be coming down from the sky, like the sound of thunder; and every room and hollow space in the building resounded with it. Amid the vast, confused clamour could be heard the loud, rapid impact of heavy stones against the door.

'The commissioner! The tyrant! The starver of the people! We'll have him, dead or alive!'

The wretched man wandered from room to room, pale, breathless, slapping one trembling hand against the palm of the other, imploring God to show him mercy and his servants to stand firm and help to get him out of the house. But how could it be done, and where could he go? He went up to the attic and looked anxiously out of one of the little windows into the street, which was full of furious faces. He heard many voices calling for his death, and withdrew, more bewildered than ever, to look for the safest and most secluded hiding-place in the house. He cowered there, and listened feverishly for some sign of reduction in the volume of that ill-omened uproar. But then he heard the clamour grow louder and fiercer than ever, while the battering on the door redoubled. Overcome by the thumping of his own heart, he put his fingers in his ears. Then, as if out of his mind, he gritted his teeth, screwed up his face, and stretched out his arms in front of him, pushing, pushing, with the actions of a man trying to hold a door shut . . . But we cannot be sure exactly what he did next; for he was alone, and history can only guess at the details. Fortunately she has had plenty of practice . . .

This time Renzo was in the thick of it. He had not been carried there by the movement of the crowd, but had thrust his way into the centre of things deliberately. He had felt a thrill of revulsion at the first cry for blood. As regards breaking into the house and ransacking it, he could hardly have said whether that was right or wrong in the circumstances; but the idea of murder inspired him with an immediate feeling of unmixed horror. Passionate natures are all too ready to accept the passionate assertions of a crowd, and Renzo was utterly convinced that the commissioner was the main cause of the famine and the enemy of the people. And yet . . . and yet . . . as the crowd moved off towards the commissioner's house, Renzo happened to overhear someone saying that he would do anything to save the unfortunate man, and at once decided to do what he could to help. With that object he had pushed his way through the throng almost up to the door, which was suffering many different kinds of assault at once.

Some people were banging away with large stones at the nails which held the lock in position, hoping to work it loose. Others were using heavy poles, hammers and chisels in a more regular attack. Others again were using broken knives, pieces of stone, iron nails, sticks or their bare fingers if they had nothing else, scraping and picking at the wall, trying to loosen the bricks and make a breach. Those who could do nothing to help encouraged the others with loud cries; but at the same time they kept thronging in towards the wall and getting in the way of the workers, who were already getting in each other's way as they vied with one another in their uncoordinated enthusiasm. This is a thing we often see in good works – that the most ardent participants become a hindrance to the others – but mercifully it sometimes happens in bad works too.

As soon as the magistrates heard what was happening, they at once sent for help to the commander of the fortress, which was then known as the Castello di Porta Giovia; and he did send some troops. But by the time the message had been delivered, the orders given, the soldiers formed up and given the word to move off and marched to their destination, the house was already surrounded by a vast mob. The detachment halted on the edge of the crowd, at quite a distance from the door. The officer in charge did not know what to do next. Immediately in front of him was nothing but a rabble of spectators, of all ages and both sexes. When they were told to move on, or to make way, their only response was a long, ugly, rumbling sound; not one of them budged an inch. To open fire on this mass of people seemed to the officer to be not only inhumane, but also highly dangerous; for it would have hurt only the least vicious elements in the crowd, and roused its more violent members to a frenzy. Besides he had no instructions to use fire-arms. To open a way through that outer throng, pushing them back on either side as his men went in, and to go forward to attack the aggressive elements in the centre, would be the best plan; but how could he bring it off? As the soldiers moved in, would they be able to keep together, in proper formation? . . . If, instead of breaking up the crowd, they were themselves split up in the middle of the throng, they would be at the mercy of the rioters, after having roused them to wrath.

Rightly or wrongly the hesitation of the officer and the immobility of the troops were attributed to fear. The people nearest them merely stared them in the face, as much as to say: we don't give a damn for you. Those who were a little further into the crowd defied them with grimaces and derisive shouts. Further in still, few members of the mob either knew or cared that they were there. The men who were demolishing the wall went on with their work, without any other concern than its speedy completion, and the spectators continued to urge them on with shouts of encouragement.

Among the spectators was one – a debauched looking old man – who was a spectacle in himself. With his deep-set, bloodshot eyes stretched as wide open as they would go, with the wrinkles of his face distorted into a smirk of fiendish pleasure, with hands held high above his unreverend white locks, he was brandishing a hammer, a rope and four large nails. When the commissioner had been killed, he said, these things would be used to hang his body up on the front door of his own house.

'For shame!' cried Renzo. He was horrified by the old man's words, and by the faces of many bystanders who seemed to approve them; but at the same time he was encouraged by others he saw who looked as deeply shocked as himself, though they were keeping quiet about it. 'For shame! Do we want to do the hangman out of a job? Do we want to kill a fellow-Christian? How can we expect God to send us bread, if we do terrible things like that? It's thunderbolts, not bread, that he'd be sending us!'

'You swine! You traitor to your country!' cried a bystander who had managed to hear this praiseworthy speech among the general din, turning a face contorted with devilish passion towards Renzo. 'Look at him! He's one of the commissioner's servants, disguised as a peasant; he's a spy! Kill him! Kill him!'

Many more voices took up the cry: 'What is it?' – 'Where is he?' – 'Who is it?' – 'It's one of the commissioner's servants!' – 'It's a spy!' – 'It's the commissioner himself, trying to escape disguised as a peasant!' 'Where?' – 'Where?' 'Kill him!' – 'Kill him!'

Renzo kept quiet and tried to look as small as possible. He would gladly have vanished altogether. One or two of his neighbours gathered round him protectively, and shouted other slogans as loudly as they could to confuse and drown the voices of those who were crying for blood. But what really saved him was a great cry of 'Make way! Make way!' which suddenly rang out close at hand. 'Make way! Here it comes! This is what we want! Make way!'

What could it be? – It was a long ladder, which some men were bringing up, with the intention of leaning it against the wall and getting in at an upper window. Once in position, it would have made the task easy enough; but getting it there fortunately proved very difficult. It was carried by a man at each end and others on either side; they were pushed, jostled, and separated from each other by the crowd, so that their advance was slow and irregular. One man had his head between two rungs, and the supports on his shoulders; he was weighed down and shaken from side to side as if beneath a yoke, and was roaring with pain. Another was pushed right away from the ladder by a movement of the crowd. The end he had dropped cracked against the backs, arms and ribs of the bystanders, whose comments can be imagined. Others hoisted the free end up again on to their shoulders, crying: 'All's well now! Come on! Let's go!' The fateful object staggered and wound its way forward. It arrived just in time to distract and disorganize Renzo's enemies. He took advantage of the local confusion which was now superimposed on the general one, and made off. He covered the first few yards bent almost double, as unobtrusively as possible, and then made free use of his elbows to get away from a spot which was clearly unhealthy for him. He decided to get right out of the mob as soon as he could, and really go back to the monastery this time to find Father Bonaventura, or wait for him if necessary.

But suddenly a strange ripple of excitement seemed to pass through the crowd from a point on its outskirts. A name was heard, passing from mouth to mouth across the throng: 'Ferrer! Ferrer!'. Amazement, joy, anger, affection, repugnance seemed to vie for expression wherever the name was heard. Some shouted it loud and clear; others tried to shout it down; affirmations were mingled with denials, and blessings with curses.

'Ferrer is here!' 'No, he's not; it's not true!' – 'Yes, he is here; long live Ferrer! He's the one who brought down the price of bread.' – 'Nonsense!' – 'He *is* here! He's come in his

251

carriage!' – 'What does it matter? What's it got to do with him? We don't want anyone to tell us what to do.' – 'It's Ferrer! Long live Ferrer, the friend of the poor! He's come to take the commissioner off to prison' – 'No, no! we'll see justice done ourselves! Away with him!' 'Yes! Yes! We want Ferrer! Let him take the commissioner to prison!'

Everyone stood on tiptoe and turned to look in the direction where the unexpected visitor was said to be. With everyone on tiptoe no one could see any more than he would have seen if everyone had kept his weight on his heels; but the fact is that they all got up on their toes.

Antonio Ferrer, the Grand Chancellor, had in fact arrived at the edge of the crowd, on the side furthest from the soldiers. His conscience had probably been troubling him with the thought that his own folly and obstinacy had been the cause, or anyway the occasion, of the revolt, and now he had come to try to quell it, or at least to prevent the most terrible and irreparable of its consequences. He had come to make good use of the fund of goodwill that he had acquired by doubtful means.

In popular uprisings there are always a certain number of men, inspired by hot-blooded passions, fanatical convictions, evil designs, or a devilish love of disorder for its own sake, who do everything they can to make things take the worst possible turn. They put forward or support the most merciless projects, and fan the flames every time they begin to subside. Nothing ever goes too far for them; they would like to see rioting continue without bounds and without an end. But to counterbalance them, there are always a certain number of other men, equally ardent and determined, who are doing all they can in the opposite direction, inspired by friendship or fellow-feeling for the people threatened by the mob, or by a reverent and spontaneous horror of bloodshed and evil deeds. God bless them for it!

In each of the two groups we have just mentioned, the conformity of the individual members' wishes provides an instant coordination of their actions, even if there has been no previous agreement about what should be done. The bulk of the mob – what we may term its raw material – is made up of a fortuitous conglomeration of human beings, who range from one end of the scale to the other without any clear-cut divisions. A little hot-headed; a little cunning; a little too fond of their own special brand of justice, and inclined to hanker after flagrant examples of it; quick to ferocious violence and quick to feelings of pity; quick to both loathing and to adoration, whenever a convincing occasion for either sentiment offers itself; greedy at all times to hear and to believe something outrageous; always looking for a reason to shout, to applaud someone or to howl for his blood. 'Long live Peter!' and 'Death to Paul!' are the phrases that come most readily to their lips. If you can persuade them that a man does not deserve to be hanged, only a few more words will be needed to convince them that he ought to be carried shoulder high in triumph. They will play the part of actors, spectators, tools or obstacles, according to the way the wind blows. They will also be quite ready to keep silent, when they can hear no more slogans to repeat; to stop rioting, when the agitators cease their work; to break up, when a sufficient number of voices unites in saying 'Let's call it a day', without anyone saying the opposite; and finally to go home, asking each other what it was all about.

But since the main power of the mob resides in that central mass, each of the two active extremes uses every trick to win it over and gain control of it. One might think that two rival and hostile souls were fighting to enter into possession of that great ugly body and set it in motion. They vie with each other in spreading rumours calculated to rouse the passions and direct the actions of the mob in ways that will favour their own respective ends; in reporting news that will rekindle or extinguish the wrath of the crowd, and revive its hopes or its fears; in finding the key slogan which, once taken up and shouted loudly by the greater number, will simultaneously create, express and confirm a majority vote in favour of one party or the other.

So much by way of prelude to the fact that a struggle was going on between the two parties for control of the mob assembled in front of the commissioner's house, and that the appearance of Antonio Ferrer at once gave a great advantage to the more humane section, which had been clearly the weaker force before. Indeed, if his intervention had been only a little later, they would have had no power to defend their cause, and indeed no cause to defend. Ferrer was popular with the mob because of the prices he had fixed at a rate so favourable to the consumer, and because of his heroic stand against every argument to the contrary. Those who were already favourably disposed to him were still more captivated by the confident courage of the old man, who had brought no guards with him, no official pomp, as he came out to face a stormy and furious multitude. And then the story that he had come to take the commissioner to prison had a remarkable effect. Popular fury against the unfortunate official would have raged higher than ever, if anyone had bluntly opposed it, without offering any concessions; but this sop to Cerberus quietened it a little, so that it gave way to feelings of an opposite character in the hearts of many of the crowd.

The party that favoured peace felt a new surge of vitality, and set about helping Ferrer in every possible way. Those who were nearest to him applauded and led the public applause, at the same time doing their best to induce the crowd to make way for his carriage. Those further away cheered loudly, and repeated and passed on every word that Ferrer uttered, or that they thought he should have uttered, shouting down those who were obstinate in their wish for blood, and turning the latest mood of the fickle crowd against them. 'Who's this who doesn't want us to shout "Long live Ferrer!" So you don't want bread to be cheap, eh? These swine who don't want justice to be done in a Christian way! Some of the noisiest of them are trying to make a diversion so that the commissioner can escape. To prison with the commissioner! Long live Ferrer! Make way for Ferrer!'

More and more people echoed these views, and the morale of the opposite party declined in proportion. In the end those who were for peace went over from words to deeds against those who were still battering at the wall, pushing them away from it and wrenching the tools out of their grasp. They fumed and threatened, and tried to get back to work again; but the cause of those who thirsted for blood was already lost. The words that dominated the tumult were 'prison', 'justice', and 'Ferrer'.

After a certain amount of argument the demolition workers were repulsed. The other party took control of the door, both to protect it from further attack, and to prepare the way for Ferrer to go in. One of them called out to the people in the house – there were plenty of holes to speak through – and told them that rescue was at hand, and that the commissioner must be ready to leave at a moment's notice, 'to go to prison – prison, I said. Do you understand?'

'Is that the same Ferrer who helps them to make the proclamations?' said Renzo to one of his new neighbours. He was thinking of the words *'Vidit Ferrer'* which Doctor Quibbler had bawled in his ear while pointing them out to him at the bottom of one particular proclamation.

'That's right – the Grand Chancellor.'

'Is he a good man?'

'Is he a good man, indeed! He's the man who brought down the price of bread; and the others wouldn't have it; and now he's come to take the commissioner away to prison, because of the unjust things he's done.'

There is no need to say that Renzo was all for Ferrer at once. He wanted to go right up and see him; it was not an easy matter, but he shoved and used his elbows like a true hillman, and managed to push his way into the front rank, right next to the carriage.

The carriage had already made its way a certain distance into the crowd, and had halted there – one of the frequent stops that are inevitable in such a journey. Old Ferrer looked out of the windows, first on one side, and then on the other, with a humble, smiling, affectionate expression, which he had previously always saved for the moments when he found himself in the presence of His Majesty King Philip IV; but he was compelled to put it on for this occasion as well. He spoke to the crowd too; but the clamour and the buzzing of many voices, the cheering addressed to Ferrer himself, were such that very few people could hear anything at all of what he said, and even they could not hear much. So he did what he could with gestures, putting the tips of his fingers to his lips, and then separating them to blow kisses with both hands to right and left in thanks for the goodwill of the people. Then he put his hands right out of the window and waved them gently to ask the crowd to make way, or gracefully motioned for a little silence. When the uproar did quieten a little, those nearest to him heard and repeated his words: 'Bread ... yes ... plenty ... yes ... I have come to see justice done ... make way for me a little, if you please ...'

Overcome and almost suffocated by the discord of so many voices and by the sight of so many serried, staring faces, he withdrew from the window for a moment, blew out his cheeks, sighed deeply, and muttered to himself: *'Por mi vida, que de gente!'*[1]

'Long live Ferrer! Don't be afraid, sir! We know you're a good man. Bread! Bread!'

'That's right – bread, bread,' said Ferrer. 'Bread and plenty – I give you my word' – and he laid his hand on his heart.

'Make way now,' he went on a moment later. 'I have come to take him to prison, and see he gets the just punishment that he deserves.' Under his breath he added the words *'Si es culpable.'*[2] Then, leaning forward toward the coachman, he said: *'Adelante, Pedro, si puedes.'*[3]

The coachman also smiled with graceful affection at the mob, as if he had been a gentleman of rank. With indescribable elegance he swung the whip very slowly to left and right, to ask the bystanders who were in the way to move back a little and make way for the coach. 'If you please,' he said, echoing his master's words, 'if you please, gentlemen, let us have just a little room, just a little; just enough to let us get through.'

Meanwhile the more active men of good will set about getting him the room that he had requested so politely. Some of them got in front of the horses and moved people to one side, with flattering words, or by laying their hands on people's chests and giving them the gentlest of pushes. 'Over there, please, gentlemen; a little room, if you please.' Others were performing the same operation on the flanks of the carriage, so that it could get

1. 'Good God, what a lot of people!' (In Spanish)
2. 'If he is guilty.' (In Spanish)
3. 'Go on, Pedro, if you can.' (In Spanish)

by without crushing toes or bloodying noses; for that would not only have been painful for their owners, but would have imperilled Antonio Ferrer's popularity.

Renzo gazed for a few moments at that venerable old face, which was marked by strain, and heavy with fatigue, but alive with concern for others, and shining with the hope of rescuing a man from the terrors of death. The young man put aside all thought of leaving the throng, and resolved to help Ferrer, and to stay with him until he had achieved his object. So he promptly joined the others in making way for the coach, working as hard as any of them. Soon the necessary space opened up. 'Come on, then!' cried several men to the coachman, moving aside or pushing on ahead to make more room for him. '*Adelante, presto, con juicio,*'[4] said Ferrer, and the carriage began to move. Amid all the salutations that Ferrer showered on the public in general, he reserved certain special gestures of gratitude, certain smiles of complicity, for the individuals who were visibly exerting themselves on his behalf. Several of those smiles came Renzo's way – and he certainly deserved them, for he was working harder for the Grand Chancellor that day than any of his confidential servants could have done. The young hillman was charmed by his courtesy, and almost felt that he was now a personal friend of the great man.

Once the carriage began to move, it kept on moving, slowly enough, but with only momentary halts. The whole distance it had to cover probably did not amount to more than a musket-shot; but if you went by the time it took, it might seem quite a long journey, even for someone who had not Ferrer's irreproachable reasons for haste. The crowd swirled round the carriage, in front, behind and on either side, like great waves around a ship advancing through the middle of a tempest. But no tempest could have matched that shrill, discordant, deafening uproar.

Ferrer looked out first on one side and then on the other. As he posed and waved, he tried to make out what people in the crowd were saying, so that he could respond appropriately. He

4. 'Go on; be quick, but be careful.' (In Spanish)

wanted to exchange a few words with his band of supporters; but it was a difficult matter – perhaps the most difficult that had come his way in all his years as Grand Chancellor. But from time to time the odd word, or even the odd phrase, would be repeatedly called out by a group of men as he went by, and he would pick it out clearly, like the louder noise of a big rocket amid the immense, crackling din of a firework display. Now trying to find a truly satisfactory answer to those cries from the crowd, now merely giving a reply which he knew would be acceptable, or which seemed appropriate to the demands of the moment, Ferrer had something to say at every step.

'Yes, yes, gentlemen . . . Bread, bread and plenty . . . I will take him to prison myself; he shall be punished . . . *si es culpable*[5] . . . Yes, yes; I will give the necessary orders . . . bread shall be cheap again. *Asi es*[6] – that's it, I meant to say. Our sovereign lord the King does not want faithful subjects like yourselves to suffer from hunger . . . *Guardaos*![7] Mind you don't get hurt, gentlemen. *Pedro, adelante con juicio.*[8] Plenty, plenty for everybody. Let us have a little more room, if you please. Bread! yes, bread! Prison! yes, prison! – What was that?' he finished abruptly, as a man thrust the top half of his body through the window and howled some words of advice, entreaty or applause. But the man did not even have time to take in Ferrer's question before being pulled back again by a bystander who noticed that he was about to fall under the wheels. Amid repartee and cheering, and also the odd ripple of opposition, which made itself felt here and there but was quickly suppressed, Ferrer finally arrived at the commissioner's door, thanks mainly to his well-intentioned helpers.

The others, who had reached the door earlier, with equally good motives, as we mentioned before, had been trying very hard to clear, and keep cleared, a space in front of it. They begged, exhorted and threatened; they pushed and pushed again, making a little ground here and there, with that extra

5. 'If he is guilty.' (In Spanish)
6. 'That's it.' (In Spanish)
7. 'Look out!' (In Spanish)
8. 'Pedro, go on carefully.' (In Spanish)

vigour that comes from the knowledge that one's goal is in sight. Finally they managed to split the mob into two parts, and to push both of them so that a little opening appeared between the door and the coach, which had now halted just in front of it. Between clearing the way and acting as escort, Renzo reached the door at the same time as the carriage, and was able to take his place in one of the two lines of men of good-will who were flanking the carriage and holding back the two surging divisions of the mob. And as he lent his powerful shoulders to the task of restraining one section of the crowd, he found himself in an excellent position to see what was happening.

Ferrer sighed with relief when he saw that open space, and the front door still shut – though 'shut' must be taken in the limited sense of 'not open'. The hinges were almost out of the door-posts. The two leaves of the door were splintered, dented, and wrenched apart in the centre. You could look through the gap and see a piece of stretched and twisted chain, almost torn from its moorings, which just about held them together. One worthy citizen had put his mouth to the gap, and was shouting to the people inside to open up; another quickly flung open the carriage door. The old man put out his head, rose from his seat, grasped his helper's arm with his right hand, and got down on to the footboard. On either side the crowd was standing on tip-toe. Hundreds of faces turned towards him; hundreds of beards pointed in his direction. General curiosity and universal attention brought about a momentary complete silence. Ferrer stood for a moment on the footboard, looked round him, bowed formally to the crowd, as if from a pulpit, laid his left hand on his heart, and shouted 'Bread! Bread and justice!' Bold, erect and dignified in his long robes, he stepped down on to the pavement amid frenzied cheering.

Meanwhile the people inside had undone the door – or rather finished undoing it. They removed the chain, together with its damaged staples, and widened the gap between the leaves just enough to admit the welcome guest. 'Quick! quick!' he said. 'Open up properly, so that I can get in; and you gentlemen out there, be good fellows and hold the crowd back. Don't let them get through to me, for heaven's sake. Try to keep a little space open for a minute, until I come back ... And you gentlemen inside! Just a moment now!' he went on, turning back towards them. 'Steady with that door, and let me in! Oh, my ribs! Mind my ribs! You can shut the door now ... no, not yet; mind my gown! My gown, I said!' His gown would in fact have been caught between the leaves of the door, if he had not adroitly twitched at the train which vanished like the tail of a snake taking refuge in a hole.

The two halves of the door were brought together again; they even managed to bolt them, after a fashion. Outside, the men who had assumed the functions of a bodyguard made full use of shoulders, arms and lung-power to keep a little space free. They also put up a silent prayer that Ferrer would be quick.

Ferrer himself was urging the servants to be quick, as they gathered round him in the inner porch, gasping with relief and crying: 'Oh, Your Excellency! God bless Your Excellency!'

'Be quick, then, be quick!' said Ferrer. 'Where's that blessed commissioner?'

The poor man was coming down the stairs, half dragged and half carried by other servants, his face as white as a sheet. When he saw his rescuer, he uttered a deep sigh of relief. His heart beat again; a little strength returned to his legs, and a little colour to his cheeks. He made all the haste he could towards Ferrer, saying: 'I am in the hands of God and the hands of Your Excellency. But how are we to get out of here? There are people who want my blood all round the house.'

'*Venga usted conmigo*,[9] and don't be afraid. I've got my carriage just outside; but be quick! be quick!' He took the commissioner by the hand, and led him towards the door, saying all he could to encourage him; but inwardly he was thinking: '*Aqui esta el busilis; Dios nos valga!*'[10]

The door opened. Ferrer went out first, followed by the commissioner, hunched, clinging as if glued to the protective robes of the Grand Chancellor, like a child holding on to its mother's skirts. The men who had kept a space clear in front of the door now raised their arms and waved their hats, making a

9. 'Come with me!' (In Spanish)
10. 'This is the difficult part. God be our aid!' (In Spanish)

sort of screen to protect the commissioner from the danger of being sighted by the mob. The poor man got into the carriage before Ferrer, and cowered in a corner. Ferrer followed him, and the door closed behind them. The crowd dimly saw, heard or guessed what had happened, and sent up a great roar of mingled applause and cursing.

The next stage might well have seemed the most difficult and dangerous. But public opinion had come down definitely enough on the side of allowing the commissioner to be taken to prison; and while Ferrer was inside the house, a number of the men who had made it possible for him to reach it in the first place were busy opening up and keeping open a kind of corridor through the crowd for his retreat. The carriage was therefore able to pass through the mob this second time at a better pace, and with fewer stops. As it went forward, the two sections of the crowd, which had been held apart to let it through, came together again and mingled in its wake.

As soon as Ferrer had taken his seat, he had leant over to warn the commissioner to keep down out of sight, for the love of heaven; but there was no need for this reminder. Ferrer, on the other hand, had to show himself, so that the attention of the crowd should be directed and concentrated on him. He repeated the performance he had given on the way to the commissioner's house, addressing his changeable audience with a speech which lasted throughout the journey. Nothing more continuous in delivery, nor more unconnected in content, can ever have been heard. He did however intersperse an occasional word in Spanish, which he whispered rapidly into the ear of his invisible companion.

'That's right, gentlemen. Bread and justice! He's going to prison, in the castle, in my custody. Thank you, gentlemen, thank you! No, no; he won't get away. *Por ablandarlos*.[11] Quite right . . . quite right. There will be an inquiry; we shall see. Thank you, thank you – I feel the same regard for all you gentlemen. Yes, the punishment must be most severe. *Esto lo digo por su bien*.[12] A fair price, a just price, and the starvers of

11. 'To put them in better humour.' (In Spanish)
12. 'I say this for your good.' (In Spanish)

the people must be punished. Make way, if you please. Yes –
you're right. I am an honest fellow, and the friend of the
people. He must be punished. You're right again – he is a
villain, he is a blackguard. *Perdone, usted.*[13] Yes he's in for a
rough time, all right ... *si es culpable.*[14] Yes, yes, I'll see the
bakers do their duty in future. Long live the King, and the
good people of Milan, his most faithful subjects! Yes, he certainly is in trouble! *Animo; estamos ya quasi fuera.'*[15]

They had in fact got through the worst of the crowd, and
were nearly clear of it altogether. Just as Ferrer was beginning
to rest his vocal cords, he saw that largely ineffective force, the
detachment of Spanish soldiers. They had not been completely
useless right at the end, in point of fact. With the support and
guidance of one or two citizens in the crowd, they had helped to
persuade a few people to go home quietly, and were able to
keep the way open for the last stages of Ferrer's retreat. When
the carriage reached them, they lined its route and presented
arms to the Grand Chancellor. He made a final salute to right
and left. Then the officer in charge came up to greet him, and
was met with a wave of the hand and the words: *'Beso a usted
las manos',*[16] which he correctly interpreted as meaning: 'A
fine lot of help you've given me!' He saluted again and
shrugged his shoulders. It would have been a perfect opportunity for the Grand Chancellor to trot out the tag *'Cedant
arma togae'.*[17] But Ferrer had no time to think of quotations;
and in any case it would have been lost on the officer, who did
not know Latin.

As Pedro passed between those two rows of Spanish soldiers,
and those respectfully raised muskets, his ancient courage returned at once. He recovered completely from his dazed condition, and remembered who he was, and whom he drove. Shouting 'Out of the way! Out of the way!' without ceremony, to a

13. 'Forgive me, sir.' (In Spanish)
14. 'If he is guilty.' (In Spanish)
15. 'Take heart; we are nearly out of the wood.' [There are some oddities in Manzoni's Spanish.]
16. 'I kiss your hands.' (In Spanish)
17. 'Let arms give way to civil robes.' (In Latin)

crowd which had now thinned out enough to be safely addressed in that manner, he whipped the horses on towards the castle.

'*Levantese, levantese; estamos ya fuera*,'[18] said Ferrer to the commissioner. Reassured by the silence, the rapid movement of the carriage and by Ferrer's words, the poor man bestirred himself, lifted his weight off his haunches, and got up. When he had recovered a little, he began to shower unending thanks on his rescuer. Ferrer sympathized with him over the dangers he had run, and rejoiced with him over his present safety, but suddenly broke off. 'Good God!' he cried, striking his bald head with his hand, '*que dirà de esto sua excelencia*,[19] who is already in such a state over that infernal Casale, which refuses to surrender? *Que dirà el conde duque*,[20] who takes umbrage every time a dog barks louder than usual? *Que dirà el rey nuestro señor*,[21] who can hardly help hearing something about an uproar like this? Can we even be sure that it is finished? *Dios lo sabe* . . .'[22]

'Well,' said the commissioner, 'as far as I am concerned, I decline to have anything more to do with it. I resign all interest in the matter. I shall hand over my office to Your Excellency, and go and live in a cave in the mountains as a hermit, far, far away from these savage brutes.'

'You will have to do whatever suits the requirements of *el servicio de su magestad*,'[23] replied the Grand Chancellor gravely.

'His Majesty will not want me to die,' replied the commissioner. 'A cave shall be my home . . . a cave far away from these people.'

Our author does not tell us what became of the poor fellow's resolution. We can follow him as far as the castle, but then we lose sight of him.

18. 'Get up; we are out of it now.' (In Spanish)
19. 'What will His Excellency say?' (In Spanish)
20. 'What will the Count-Duke say?' (In Spanish)
21. 'What will our sovereign lord the King say?' (In Spanish)
22. 'God knows.' (In Spanish)
23. 'The service of His Majesty.' (In Spanish)

Chapter 14

THE crowd left behind began to break up, dispersing in different directions, along various roads. Some went home to get on with their own affairs; others moved off to find an open space and fill their lungs with fresh air, after so many hours in a crowded throng; others again went off in search of friends with whom to discuss the great events of the day. There was a similar exodus at the other end of the street, and the mob thinned out enough for the detachment of Spanish soldiers to be able to move forward without resistance and station themselves before the commissioner's house. The last dregs of the mob were still concentrated at that point – a villainous band, who were most unhappy to see so tame and incomplete a result emerge from so promising an affair. Some of them were grumbling, some were cursing, some were discussing whether some substantial enterprise might not yet be set in motion. As if by way of experiment, they were banging and pushing at the unfortunate front door, which had been bolted together again as securely as possible.

When the soldiers arrived, they all moved away in the opposite direction, some going straight off, while others were very slow and reluctant about it. The battlefield was left to the Spaniards, who occupied it and took up positions from which they could guard the house and the street. But all the neighbouring roads were full of groups of people. Wherever two or three men came to a halt together, four, five and then twenty others would join them. Here a group would shed a few members; there another would roll forward as a single unit. It was like the clouds which sometimes remain scattered across the sky after a storm, travelling across the blue background, so that we look up at them and say: 'It hasn't really cleared up yet.'

The reader can imagine the bedlam that passed for discussion in those groups. Some gave exaggerated descriptions of what they had seen; others of what they themselves had done. Some expressed their pleasure that the thing had ended so well, praising Ferrer, and prophesying serious trouble for the commissioner; others sniggered and said: 'Don't worry; he'll be all right. Dog doesn't eat dog.' Yet others complained, in angrier tones, that the thing had been handled all wrong, that they had been cheated, and that it was all nonsense to make so much noise about it and then let themselves be hoodwinked like that.

Meanwhile the sun had gone down, and a greyness spread over everything. Tired after a long day and bored with gossiping in the dark, many people went off home. Renzo had helped to make way for the carriage, as long as his help had been needed; and he had passed between the two rows of soldiers in its wake, as if in a triumph. He was glad to see it trot away in safety, unimpeded. He moved off along the road with the crowd for a short way, but turned off at the first corner, for a breath of air. He walked on a short distance, and then, though still deeply stirred by the confusion of strange emotions and strange sights that he had so recently experienced, he began to feel a great need of food and sleep. He looked up at the houses he passed on either side, hoping to see an inn-sign, for it was now too late to go back to the Capuchin monastery.

Walking along in this way with his head in the air, he came across a group of men, and stopped to listen to them. They were discussing what might be expected to happen the following day, and what their plans should be. After a minute Renzo could not help stating his own views. He felt that, after all he had done, he could put forward a proposal himself without presumption.

The things he had seen that day had convinced him that, from that time on, all you needed to get any idea put into practice was that it should appeal strongly to the crowd in the streets.

'Gentlemen!' he cried by way of introduction, 'shall I give you my humble opinion? My humble opinion is this – that there's plenty of dirty work in other things besides the matter of bread. Now we've seen today that if you speak up you get your rights. We ought to go on in the same way, until all our other wrongs have been righted, and everyone in the world behaves a bit more like Christians should. Isn't it true, gentlemen, that we've got a pack of tyrants on our backs, who turn the ten commandments upside down, and seek out peaceful folk, who've never troubled their heads about them, and do them every sort of harm, and then always manage to make out they're in the right? In fact, when they've done something worse than usual, don't they hold their heads higher than ever before, as if the world owed them something for it? There must be people like that in Milan too.'

'All too many of them!' said a voice from the crowd.

'I thought so,' said Renzo. 'We hear stories about it even in my village . . . and, after all, it stands to reason. Say one of those gentlemen I'm talking about spends half his time in the country, and half in Milan. If he behaves like a swine there, I don't suppose he'll be an angel here. And tell me now, have you ever seen one of them looking out through the bars of a prison window? And the worst of it is – and I know what I'm talking about – that the proclamations are there, in black and white, to give them the punishment they deserve; and I'm not talking about those silly proclamations either, but ones that are well drawn up, and we wouldn't want to alter them at all. They name all sorts of dirty tricks as clear as you could wish, just like they happen, and fix the right punishment for each of them. And they say, how it's to be the same for everybody, be he of the common people or of low degree, and all that. Now suppose you go to the lawyers – scribes and pharisees, *I* call them – and ask them to get you your rights, according to what it says in the proclamation. Do you think they'd listen to you? – like the Pope would listen to a blasphemer! It's enough to drive an honest fellow mad.

'It's clear enough that the King, and the people at the top, want the criminals punished; but nothing happens, because they're all in league with each other. What we've got to do is to break that league. We must go and see Ferrer tomorrow morning, for he's an honest man, a real gentleman; and we could all see today how pleased he was to be among us poor folk, how he tried to hear whatever people said to him, and to say something pleasant in reply. We must go to Ferrer, and tell him what's going on. For my part, I've got some things to tell him, all right, for I've seen a proclamation myself, with these very eyes, that had a great coat of arms at the top, and it had been drawn up by three powerful men, who all had their names in black and white at the bottom of the sheet, and one of those names was Ferrer, for I saw it myself. Well, then, that proclamation was about cases just like mine; and I spoke to a lawyer about it, and asked him to get justice done for me, as those three gentlemen wanted it to be done, and Ferrer was one of them like I said; and that lawyer, who'd shown me the proclamation himself, which is the funniest part of the whole story, went on as if I must have been mad to think of such a thing. I'm sure if that nice-looking old man hears all this – for he can't know everything himself, especially if it happens in the country – when he hears about it, he won't like to think of things like that happening, and he'll know what to do to put a stop to it. And after all, if those gentlemen draw up the proclamations, they must want them to be obeyed; for it's not respectful, it's making a mockery of their names, if people don't take any notice of the proclamations. And if those swine don't want to give in, and go on behaving like that, we're here to help Ferrer, like we did today. I don't mean that he's got to go round in his carriage catching them all himself, those blackguards, those bullies, those tyrants; for he'd need a carriage the size of Noah's Ark. But he's got to give his orders, to the right people, and not just in Milan, but everywhere, and make people do what it says in the proclamations, and really take them to court, the people who do those dirty tricks; and where it says prison it's got to really mean prison, and where it says ten years in the galleys, it's really got to mean that. And the mayors have got to be told to enforce it properly, or else they've got to be sacked, and better men put in their place; and like I said, we're here to help with that. And the lawyers have got to be made to listen to us poor folk, and stick up for our rights. Am I right, gentlemen, or not?'

From the very beginning of Renzo's speech, his heartfelt manner had made many of the group interrupt their own conversation and turn towards him. Later on everyone was listening to him. A confused round of applause, and cries of 'Well said!' – 'Of course!' – 'He's right!' – 'It's all too true!' were the crowd's reply when he finished. But there were also some critics present.

'Yes, yes,' said one, 'to listen to these hill-folk, you'd think every one of them was a lawyer'; and he walked away.

'Every ragged fellow wants to say his piece,' muttered another, 'and with this asking for other things we shall end up without the cheap bread we set out to get in the first place.'

But Renzo heard only the complimentary remarks, and found both his hands being warmly shaken by his admirers.

'Let's meet again tomorrow' – 'Where?' – 'In the Cathedral Square.' – 'Very well!' – 'Good!' – 'And something must be done!' – 'Something will be done!'

'Which of you kind gentlemen will tell me the way to an inn, where I can get a bite to eat, and a bed to suit my pocket?' said Renzo.

'I can help you, my lad,' said a man who had listened carefully to Renzo's speech, but had not said anything himself so far. 'I know just the inn for you, and I'll introduce you to the host, who's a friend of mine and a very good fellow.'

'Is it near by?' asked Renzo.

'Not very far,' replied the other.

The meeting broke up. Renzo shook hands with a series of other strangers, and then went off with the first stranger, thanking him for his courtesy.

'There's no need for thanks,' replied his guide. 'One hand washes the other, and both of them wash the face. And aren't we all bidden to help our neighbour?'

As they walked along, he asked Renzo a series of questions, by way of conversation.

'Don't think I'm being inquisitive,' he said, 'but I can't help noticing that you're very tired. Where have you come from?'

'All the long way from Lecco!' said Renzo.

'From Lecco? So that's where you live, is it?'

'Yes, Lecco . . . at least, that part of the country.'

'Poor young fellow! And as far as I could gather from what

you were saying, you've been having a bad time with them up there.'

'Why, sir! I had to talk a bit carefully, because I didn't want to blurt all my private affairs out in front of the crowd, but ... well, it'll all come out one day, and then ... But here's an inn-sign, and, upon my word, I don't feel like going any further.'

'No, no, come on with me, to the place I was telling you about,' said the other. 'This one wouldn't do for you at all.'

'I expect you're right,' said Renzo. 'I'm not a young lord who has to have cotton sheets on his bed. All I want is a bit of grub and a straw mattress; and all I care about is finding them quickly. Ah, here's a bit of luck!'

He turned off into a shabby entrance, which had a signboard showing the full moon hanging over it.

'Very well, then; I'll take you in here, as you fancy the place so much,' said Renzo's unknown companion, and turned in after him.

'There's no need for you to give yourself any more trouble,' said Renzo. 'But, if you'd care to have a drink with me,' he added, 'you'd be very welcome.'

'I accept your invitation, with many thanks,' said the man, and led the way, since he seemed to know the place better than Renzo, through a courtyard, towards the kitchen door. He undid the latch, opened the door and went inside, followed by Renzo. Two small lamps, hanging from poles attached to the beams of the ceiling, gave a dim light. A considerable number of people were sitting on two benches, one each side of a long, narrow table, which stretched almost from wall to wall. For all their easy attitude, their hands were not idle; for here and there along the table were squares of cloth, with plates standing on them; here and there cards were being turned over, and dice thrown, while bottles and glasses could be seen everywhere. The flash of *berlinghe*, *reali*, and *parpagliole* might also be noted; and if those coins could speak, they would probably have said: 'This morning we were in the till of a bakery, or in the pocket of one of the spectators during the riot, who was so concerned about public affairs that he forgot to keep an eye on his private concerns.'

There was a great deal of noise. A single waiter was dashing to and fro, as he provided for the needs of this combined dining and gambling table. The host was sitting under the chimney-hood on a small bench, apparently absorbed in the task of drawing pictures with the tongs in the ash on the hearth, rubbing them out, and drawing them again, though in reality he was taking very careful note of all that went on around him. He heard the latch click, and walked over to greet the new arrivals. When he saw Renzo's guide, he said to himself 'To hell with the fellow! He always comes here and gets in the way just when I least want to see him.' Then he glanced at Renzo himself, and thought 'Well, I've never seen you before; but if you come here in such company, you must be either a fox or a goose, and I'll know which it is when you've said a couple of words.' But none of these thoughts found expression in his face, which did not change at all. It was a round, shining face, with a thick fringe of reddish beard, and light-coloured, unmoving eyes.

'What would the gentlemen like to order?' he said.

'First of all, a good bottle of honest wine,' said Renzo, 'and then a bite to eat.'

He sat down with a bump on one of the benches, near the head of the table, and let out a long, sonorous 'Ah!' – as if to say: it's good to sit down, after a long, busy day on one's feet. But then he suddenly remembered the last time he had sat on a bench at a table like that, with Lucia and Agnese beside him, and he uttered a sigh. He shook his head, as if to rid himself of that thought; and then the host came up with the wine. Renzo at once poured a drink for his companion – who was now sitting opposite him – and said 'This'll lay the dust.' Then he filled the other glass, and drained it at one gulp.

'What can you let me have to eat, then?' he asked the host.

'There's some stew; will that suit you?'

'Yes, that's fine. Stew, then.'

'Very good, sir,' said the host to Renzo. Then he turned to the waiter and said: 'Look after this stranger.' He was just going back to the fireplace, when he turned back towards Renzo. 'But . . . I've no bread today,' he said.

'As for bread,' said Renzo, without lowering his voice, and

smiling broadly, 'Heaven will provide – in fact Heaven has provided!' And he pulled out the third and last of the three loaves he had picked up by the Cross of St Denis, and brandished it in the air, calling out 'Bread from Heaven!'

At the sound of his voice, many faces turned his way. Seeing that trophy held on high, one man called out: 'Long live cheap bread!'

'Cheap, indeed!' said Renzo. 'Long live free bread!'

'Better still!'

'But I wouldn't like you gentlemen to think badly of me,' added Renzo quickly. 'I didn't pinch it. I found it lying on the ground; and if I could find the baker I'd gladly pay him for it.'

'Good for you!' roared the boon companions, guffawing louder than ever. It did not occur to a single one of them that Renzo meant what he said.

'They think I'm joking, but it's true for all that,' said Renzo to his guide. He turned the loaf over in his hand, and said: 'See what's happened to it; it's squashed as flat as a pancake. What a crowd that was! If anyone had been there whose bones weren't very strong, he'd have been in trouble.'

As soon as Renzo had swallowed three or four mouthfuls of the bread, he washed them down with a second glass of wine, saying: 'I can't get these crusts down by themselves. I've never had such a dry throat! We certainly shouted a lot!'

'Get a bed ready for this worthy young fellow,' said his companion. 'He's planning to spend the night here.'

'Do you want to sleep here, then?' asked the host, coming up to the table.

'Yes, please,' said Renzo. 'I'm not fussy about the bed, as long as it has freshly washed sheets; for I'm a poor lad, but used to cleanliness.'

'We'll see to that all right,' said the host.

He went to the desk which stood in a corner of the kitchen, and came back with an ink-stand and a piece of paper in one hand, and a pen in the other.

'Why, what's that for?' cried Renzo, swallowing a mouthful of the stew which the waiter had just put before him. He smiled a puzzled smile, and went on: 'Are these the freshly washed sheets we were talking about?'

The host did not answer, but set the ink-stand and the paper on the table, and leaned his left forearm and right elbow on its surface. He lifted his pen in the air, raised his face towards Renzo, and said: 'Now kindly tell me your Christian name, surname, and place of origin.'

'*What?*' said Renzo. 'What's all that to do with wanting a bed?'

'I'm only doing my duty,' said the host, whose eyes were resting on the guide's face. 'We have to render a report on all the people who stay the night with us. "*Christian name, surname, place of origin, nature of business in Milan, whether carrying arms, probable duration of stay*" – I'm quoting the words of the proclamation to you.'

Before replying, Renzo emptied another glass of wine – that was his third, and from now on I am afraid we shall lose count. Then he said:

'Ha! ha! So you've got a proclamation, have you? Well, I happen to be a lawyer myself, and I know how much notice people take of those proclamations.'

'I'm not joking,' said the host, still looking towards Renzo's silent companion. He went back to the desk, and took out a big sheet of paper – an actual copy of the proclamation in question – and spread it out under Renzo's nose.

The young man filled his glass again and lifted it to his lips with one hand, while he stretched out the other towards the proclamation, pointing with one finger.

'There it is!' he cried, setting the glass down again empty, 'there's that fine work of art! I'm very glad to see it. I know that coat of arms, and I know the meaning of that fellow with the outlandish face and the rope round his neck.'

(In those days the arms of the Governor always appeared at the head of every proclamation; and those signed by Don Gonzalo Fernandez de Cordova showed a Moorish king, chained by the neck.)

'That face', went on Renzo, 'means "Let those command who can, and let those obey who want to . . ." Now if that face had sent my lord Don . . . never mind his name . . . a certain gentleman to the galleys, like it says in another work of art very like this one; or if the face had arranged things so that a decent young man could marry a decent girl who had a mind to marry him: then I wouldn't mind telling the face my name, and giving it a nice big kiss into the bargain. Now I might have very good reasons to keep quiet about my name. And suppose a certain blackguard, with a pack of other blackguards he could call upon – for if it was only the one, I'd know what to do,' said Renzo, with a significant gesture – 'if a man like that wanted to know where I am, to play some dirty trick on me, I wonder if that face would come and help me! And so I've got to state my business, have I! It seems a very strange thing to me. I might have come to Milan to confess myself perhaps; but I'd make my confession to a Capuchin father, and not to an inn-keeper.'

The host said nothing, and continued to look at the guide, who gave no indication what he thought of all this. Renzo, we regret to say, swallowed another glass of wine, and went on: 'I'll give you a real knock-down argument now, my dear host. If the proclamations that say what's right, in favour of good citizens, don't count for anything, the ones that say what's wrong ought to count for even less. So take all this nonsense away, and let's have another bottle instead, for this one seems to be a leaker.' As he said this, he tapped it lightly with his knuckles, and said: 'Listen, host, see how falsely it rings.'

Once again, Renzo had gradually attracted the attention of the bystanders, and once again they applauded him.

'What shall I do?' said the inn-keeper, looking towards the guide, who might be unknown to Renzo, but was certainly not unknown to him.

'It's all nonsense,' cried several of the boon companions sitting at the table, 'the young fellow's quite right. These are just ways of robbing, entangling and persecuting people like us. And it's a brand-new law; we never heard of it before.'

Meanwhile the guide gave the host a look of reproof, for having consulted him so openly, and said: 'Give him his head for a while, and don't make a scene.'

'I've done my duty,' said the host out loud, and added under his breath: 'I've got my back to the wall now.' He picked up paper, pen, ink-stand, and proclamation, and gave the empty bottle to the waiter.

'Bring another bottle of the same then,' said Renzo, 'for I can see it's an honest wine, and I'll find somewhere to put it, the same as I did the other one, without asking about its Christian name and surname, and where it comes from, and what its business is, and if it means to stay a long time.'

'Same again then,' said the host to the waiter, giving him the bottle; and then he went back to his seat under the chimney-hood. 'You're a goose, all right!' he thought, as he started a fresh picture in the ashes. 'And you've fallen into the right hands, no doubt of that! Idiot! If you want to cut your own throat, go ahead; but you won't find the host of the Full Moon paying for your follies.'

Renzo thanked his companion, and all the other men who had taken his side. 'My dear, good friends!' he said. 'I can see now that it's true that all decent people stick together, and help each other.'

Then he held up his right hand over the table, and took up his preaching attitude again. 'It's a strange thing', he cried, 'that all our masters, who rule the world, want to bring paper, pen and ink into everything! Pens, pens, pens! Those gentlemen must have them on the brain!'

'Well, my worthy young friend from the country – do you want to know the reason?' cried one of the gamblers, with a smile – he happened to be winning at the time.

'Let's hear it then,' said Renzo.

'Why, you see,' said the man, 'those gentlemen are the ones who eat all the geese, and they have so many quills to get rid of, that they have to do something with them.'

Everybody laughed, except the gambler who happened to be losing.

'Why,' said Renzo, 'the fellow must be a poet. So there are poets here too! But then I suppose you find them everywhere. I'm a bit of a poet myself, come to that, and sometimes I make some pretty odd remarks ... but only when things are going well.'

To understand this nonsense of poor Renzo's, the reader

must realize that the common people of Milan, and still more those who live in the surrounding country, do not use the word 'poet' as the gentry do, to mean a consecrated genius, dwelling on Parnassus, a pupil of the Muses. For them, it means a hare-brained, eccentric fellow, whose actions and words are governed, not by reason, but by an odd, penetrating low cunning. For those meddling common people have the nerve to illtreat our language, and give words a meaning poles apart from the real one! What, I ask you, is the connection between being hare-brained and being a poet?

'But now I'll tell you the real reason,' added Renzo. 'It's because the pen stays in their hands; and so the words they say fly away and disappear, while if a poor man says anything, they're listening carefully, and they catch it in mid-air with their pen, and stick his words down on paper to be used later on. And then they've another trick – when they want to muddle a poor working lad, who's never studied, but has a bit of . . . of . . . of . . . I know what I'm trying to say, now' – and, to make himself clear, he prodded and battered his forehead with the tip of one finger – 'if they see that he's beginning to work out what they're up to, why, the next thing is that they start using Latin words, and make him lose the thread, and muddle his ideas. That sort of thing has got to stop! Today, now, everything was done in good Italian, without any nonsense about paper, pen and ink; and tomorrow, if people know how to behave, even better things will be done – without hurting a hair of anyone's head though, and all by the way of justice.'

In the meantime some of the boon companions had gone back to their gambling, while others were getting on with their dinners; many were talking loudly; some had left, and new-comers had taken their places; the host kept a watchful eye on all of them; but none of this concerns our story. Renzo's unknown guide was anxious to leave; he did not seem to have any business there, but did not want to go until he had had a few further words of private conversation with Renzo. He turned towards him and reintroduced the subject of bread. After one or two remarks of the kind which everyone had been making for some time past, he came out with a suggestion of his own.

'Well!' he said, 'if I were in charge, I know what I'd do to set things to rights.'

'What would you do, then?' asked Renzo, his eyes small and bright with the drink he had taken, and his mouth twisted in the effort of attention.

'Why, I'd make sure there was bread for everybody, for rich and poor alike.'

'That's the idea!' said Renzo.

'And this is the way I'd do it. A fair price that anyone could afford; and then give out the bread according to the number of mouths there are to eat it; for there're some greedy swine who'd want to hog the lot – they'd just dive in and help themselves, and then there wouldn't be enough for the poor folk. So the bread must be divided up properly. This is the way it would be done. Every family would have a card, saying how many mouths there were to feed, to take with you when you went to the baker. This is what it would say on my card, for example: Ambrogio Fusella; sword-maker by trade; wife and four children, all of an age to be eating bread (for that's the important point); entitled to so much bread, against payment of so much money. All fair and square; so much bread for so many mouths to feed. Now you, for example, you'd have a card for ... what did you say your name was?

'Lorenzo Tramaglino,' said the young man, so taken with the idea, that he never noticed it was based on pen, ink and paper, nor that the first thing it involved was the recording of everybody's name.

'Good!' said the other. 'But have you got a wife and children?'

'I ought to have, by rights ... at least, no, not children; there hasn't been time ... but I ought to have a wife, if there were justice in the world.'

'Ah, so you're on your own! Then I'm sorry, but you get a smaller amount of bread.'

'That's fair too ... but before long ... if it turns out as I hope ... with the help of God ... but never mind all that; suppose that I had a wife?'

'Then your card would be changed, and you'd be given more

bread. As I said just now, so much bread for so many mouths to feed,' said the other man, getting up.

'That's the way it ought to be,' cried Renzo; and then he went on at the top of his voice, and banging his fist on the table: 'and why don't they make a law like that?'

'Why, what do you expect me to say? But I'll have to leave you now, for I've been keeping my wife and children waiting long enough.'

'Another drop – just one more little drop!' cried Renzo. He filled the other's glass again quickly, jumped to his feet, grabbed him by the doublet, and tried to pull him down on the bench again.

'Just another little drop,' he said. 'Don't insult me by refusing.' But his friend wrenched himself free, bade him goodnight despite his muddled entreaties and reproaches, and went out. Renzo went on haranguing him until he was well out into the street; then he fell back heavily on to the bench. He stared at the glass he had just refilled; and as the waiter went past, Renzo held up one hand to stop him, as if he had something important to say. Then he pointed to the glass and spoke as follows, slowly and solemnly, bringing his words out very clearly,

'I poured it out for that gentleman, in the friendliest way; you can see how full it is. But he wouldn't drink it. People have the strangest ideas sometimes. I'm not to blame, for I've given this proof of my friendly feeling. But now the thing is done, we mustn't waste the wine.' He picked the glass up and emptied it at a single gulp.

'I know just what you mean,' said the waiter, moving away.

'Aha! So you know just what I mean!' said Renzo. 'It must be true then. When a man says what's right and fair . . .'

Nothing but the very high regard in which we hold the truth could make us continue with this faithful account of an episode so little to the credit of such an important character – we might almost say the leading actor in our story. But the same impartial love of truth also compels us to add that it was the first time anything of the sort had happened to Renzo. In fact it was largely his inexperience of dissipation which made this first experiment so disastrous for him. He had begun by gulping down a few glasses of wine, one after another, quite contrary to his usual habit, partly because his throat was so dry, and partly out of a feeling of excitement which made him unwilling to do anything by halves. The wine had gone straight to his head, though the same amount would have had no effect on a more experienced drinker, beyond quenching his thirst.

Our anonymous author makes a comment on this, which we will record for what it is worth. Temperate and honest habits, he says, have this advantage, that the more firmly rooted they are in a man, the more readily he will be aware of the slightest divagation from them; so that he will remember what has happened for a long time, and even his folly will be a lesson to him.

However that may be, once the first fumes of wine had reached Renzo's brain, drink continued to pour in at Renzo's mouth, and words out of it, at the same intemperate speed. By now he had got into a very unstable condition. He felt a great desire to talk, and there were plenty of listeners around, or at least men whom he could regard as listeners. For a certain length of time, the words had come into his mind as he needed them, and had arranged themselves in quite reasonable order. But then the business of finishing sentences gradually became alarmingly difficult. Thoughts came into his mind in a clear, definite form, but misted over or melted away a moment later. Words were slow to come to him; and when they did come they were the wrong ones. In these difficulties, one of those false instincts which so often lead to ruin took hold of him and he turned to the bottle for help. But what help he hoped to find there is more than we can say.

We will report only a few of the many words he uttered during that unhappy evening; the greater part of what he said must be omitted as unsuitable. It is not merely that most of his remarks did not have any sense; they did not even appear to have any, which is a minimum requirement for a printed book.

'My dear host!' he began, following the inn-keeper with his eyes as he went round the table, or sat by the hearth; sometimes indeed staring in the wrong direction and addressing him in his absence, always finding difficulty in making himself heard amid the clamour of the other guests. 'My dear, good host! I can't get over that trick of yours . . . Christian name, surname and business, indeed! With a decent lad like me! You shouldn't have done it. What satisfaction, what pleasure, what sense can there be in getting a poor working lad down on paper like that? Don't you agree, gentlemen? Inn-keepers ought to be on the side of poor working lads! Listen, host, I want to give you a comparison . . . just to keep the argument straight . . . now you're all laughing at me . . . well, I may have had a couple of drinks, but I can still keep an argument straight just the same. Tell me, host, who keeps you in business anyway? Isn't it the poor working lads? Aren't I right? Do those fine gentlemen with their proclamations ever come in here for a drink?'

'Why, they're water-drinkers, every man of them!' said one of Renzo's neighbours.

'All they think about is staying sober, so that they can tell the right lies at the right time,' said another.

'Aha!' shouted Renzo. 'The poet has spoken again . . . so all you fellows can follow my argument. Well then, host, tell me this – what about Ferrer, who's the best of the lot – has he ever come here and drunk anyone's health? Has he ever spent a brass farthing in this inn? And as for that murderous swine Don . . . no, I won't say it – I'm still too sober, and that's the whole trouble. Ferrer and Father Cr . . . a certain holy father I know . . . are two decent men, but there are very few decent men about. The old ones are worse than the young, and the young ones . . . why, they're even worse than the old. But I'm glad there was no bloodshed; that's a rotten business, and ought to be left to the hangman . . . Bread, yes, of course; we've got to have bread. I was at the wrong end of a lot of shoving today, but I gave as good as I got. *"Make way!"* – *"Plenty for everybody!"* – *"Long live His Excellency!"* – that's the stuff! And yet, you know, I heard even Ferrer gabble something in Latin . . . *siés baraòs trapelorum* . . . What a rotten habit that is! *"Long live justice! Long live bread!"* – that's what we want to hear. I wish they'd been there, all those decent fellows I met today, when that damned bell began to ring – ding ding ding

ding. Then we wouldn't have had to run away. Then I'd like to see what his holy Reverence . . . but I won't say his name.'

Struck by his own words, he lowered his head and sat for a while sunk in thought. Then he sighed deeply, and raised his head again, with eyes wet and shining, and with so ridiculous an air of melting sorrow that it was just as well that the objects of his thoughts could not see him. But the ruffians who had been listening to Renzo's passionate and muddled eloquence with such amusement were even more entertained by his grief. His neighbours drew the attention of those who were sitting farther away, and everyone turned to look at him, so that he became the butt of the whole company.

It must not be thought that at that particular time all of them were in full possession of their senses – such senses, that is, as they normally enjoyed. But none of them had departed from the path of reason as far as poor Renzo; who was, moreover, a country bumpkin. One after another they began to mock him with coarse and foolish questions, with ironic displays of ceremonious respect. Now he showed signs of taking offence; now he treated what was said as a joke; now he started talking about something quite different, without paying any heed to all the voices around him; now raising questions and now answering them; all by fits and starts, and all at cross purposes. But amid all his confusion, he fortunately never lost his instinctive reluctance to mention names. He did not pronounce even the name which must have been most deeply embedded in his mind. Indeed we should be very sorry if that name, which we too love and respect, had been profaned by those brutal lips, or bandied about by those evil tongues.

Chapter 15

THINKING that the game had been going on long enough, the inn-keeper came up to Renzo, politely asked the others to leave him alone, and began to shake him by the arm, trying to persuade him to go to bed. But Renzo kept on getting back on to the subject of Christian names, and surnames, and occupations, and proclamations, and honest working lads. Finally, however, the words 'bed' and 'sleep' forced themselves into his head by dint of sheer repetition. They gave him a clear idea how much he needed those two things, and produced a kind of lucid interval. The small amount of sense that came back to him was enough to make him realize that a great deal more had gone – rather as the last survivor of a group of candles illuminates the burnt-out stumps around it. Renzo plucked up courage, spread out his hands on the table, and pressed his finger-tips hard against its surface; swaying and sighing, he made two attempts to get on to his feet; the third time he succeeded, with some help from the host, who steered him out between the table and the bench. Still supporting Renzo with one hand, he picked up a lamp with the other, and half led, half dragged him to the door at the foot of the stairs. When they got there, there was such a chorus of loud farewells from the other guests that Renzo swung quickly round, and if the host had not promptly grabbed his arm, he would have gone head over heels. Having turned, he waved his free arm in a series of complicated salutations, as if drawing in the air one of those trick knots that appear to have no beginning and no end.

'Let's go to bed then! Bed! Bed!' said the inn-keeper, dragging him along. He got him through the door, and pulled him up the stairs with more difficulty yet, and finally got him into the room where he was to sleep. Renzo cheered up at the sight of the bed that was waiting for him, and looked very lovingly at the host. His eyes were small and bright – shining more brilliantly than ever, in fact, except that they went into periodic eclipse, like the light of a fire-fly. He was trying hard to keep his balance. Presently he reached out his hand towards the inn-keeper's face, meaning to pinch his cheek, as a gesture of friendship and gratitude; but he could not manage it.

'You're a good fellow, host!' he contrived to say, however, 'I can see now that you're a very good fellow. It's a fine thing to do, to give a bed to a poor working lad; but you didn't look like a good fellow, when you gave me all that stuff about Christian name and surname. It's a good thing I've got my head screwed on properly . . .'

The host had not supposed that Renzo was still capable of such connected thought. Knowing from long experience that men in that sort of condition are unusually subject to sudden changes of mind, he decided to take advantage of the lucid interval, and make one more attempt.

'My dear lad,' he said, adopting a soft and gentle voice and manner, 'I didn't do it to annoy you, or to poke my nose into your business. What can I do? It's the law, you know. We inn-keepers have to obey the law, or we're the first to get into trouble. It's best to do what they want you to do; and what does it amount to, after all? Only saying two or three words! Not for the people who make the laws, but to do me a personal favour. Come on, now; there's no one else here. Let's do what we have to do; tell me your name, and . . . and . . . and then you can go to sleep with a good conscience.'

'Why, you swine!' cried Renzo. 'You traitor! Are you starting up that dirty trick of Christian name, surname and business again?'

'Be quiet, you fool, and go to bed,' said the inn-keeper.

But Renzo went on, even louder: 'I see it all now; you're in the plot yourself. Just wait a minute, and I'll fix you up properly!' And he turned towards the stairs and shouted louder than ever: 'Friends! Friends! The inn-keeper is in the plot!'

'I only said that for a joke!' shouted the inn-keeper straight into Renzo's ear, pushing him towards the bed. 'A joke, I say! Can't you understand that it was meant to be a joke?'

'A joke, eh?' said Renzo. 'Now you're talking! If you said it for a joke ... why, it's a joke ...' He fell face down on the bed.

'Come on now; get undressed, be quick!' said the host. In addition to the advice, he gave him some help, which he certainly needed. When Renzo had got out of his doublet (which took some doing), the inn-keeper quickly went through the pockets, to see if there was any money there. He found some; and it occurred to him that his guest would probably have to settle accounts with others besides himself, the following morning, and that the cash would probably finish up in hands from which an inn-keeper would never be able to get it back. So he decided to see whether he could bring this other matter to a satisfactory conclusion.

'I believe you're an honest lad, and a good citizen?' he began.

'Yes, yes ... honest lad ... good citizen ...' replied Renzo, his fingers struggling with the buttons of the clothes which he had not yet managed to take off.

'That's fine,' said the host. 'Then why not settle up this little bit of a bill you owe me? I've got to go out early tomorrow to attend to some business.'

'That's right enough,' said Renzo. 'I may be a cunning devil, but I'm perfectly honest. But what about the money? I can't go looking for money at this time of night!'

'The money's here,' said the host. With practised skill and endless patience, he managed to settle the bill with Renzo and get the money that was due to him.

'Give me a hand now, and help me to get the rest of my clothes off,' said Renzo. 'You're right about one thing – I do need some sleep.'

The host did as he was asked, and put a blanket over him as well, before bidding him an ungracious good night. Renzo was already snoring. Then the host felt the force of that odd fascination which sometimes makes us gaze at the object of our wrath as if it were an object of love – the common factor being perhaps the wish to know thoroughly that which affects us powerfully – so he paused a moment to contemplate his infuriating guest, holding up the lamp and shading it with his hand so that the rays fell on Renzo's face; rather in the attitude in which

283

artists depict Psyche, as she furtively examines the sleeping form of her unknown spouse.

'You idiot!' he thought, as he looked at the poor unconscious wretch. 'You've really been asking for it! Tomorrow you'll be able to say whether you like the taste of your medicine or not. Damned yokels! Wandering round the world, not knowing left hand from right, and making trouble for themselves and for everyone else.'

Then he took the light away from Renzo's face, left the room, and locked the door. He called his wife to him on the landing, and told her to leave the children with the serving-maid, and go down to the tavern and take over his duties.

'I've got to go out,' he said, 'thanks to an infernal fellow from God knows where, who's turned up here God knows how, as a bit of bad luck for me.' And he told her the whole lamentable story.

'Keep an eye on everything,' he concluded, 'and above all be careful; this is a bad day. We've got a collection of light-headed rogues down there, and light-tongued too, what with the drink they've taken and the way they are naturally. They're saying all sorts of things. It only needs some reckless idiot to . . .'

'Oh, that's all right; I'm not a child, and I know what to do as well as you do. I'd say that so far it doesn't amount to . . .'

'Very well, then; but see they all pay up. And when they start talking about the commissioner and the Governor and Ferrer and the decurions and the nobles and Spain and France and all that nonsense, you pretend not to hear; for if you contradict them, there'll be trouble at once, and if you agree we may have trouble later on. Besides, as you know, the very ones who say the most outrageous things are sometimes . . . well, never mind that now. If you hear anything of that sort, just turn your head away, and say "Coming sir!", as if someone had called you from the other end of the room. I'll be back as soon as I can.'

He went down with her into the tavern, and looked round to see if there had been any noteworthy developments. Then he took his hat and cloak from the peg, picked up a cudgel which stood in the corner, gave his wife a last meaning look to remind

284

her of her instructions, and went out. But while he was getting ready to go he had already taken up the thread of his silent address to Renzo again, and he continued to develop the theme as he went down the street.

'Pig-headed hillman!' he thought. (For all Renzo's efforts not to give away any information about himself, his words, his accent, his appearance and his behaviour all showed that he came from the mountains.) 'With my knowledge of the world, and my common sense, I just about get to the end of a day like this without any trouble; and then you have to come along at the last minute and put your foot in it. Are there no other inns in Milan that you could have gone to instead of mine? If at least you'd arrived on your own . . . then I could have turned a blind eye for tonight and made you listen to reason in the morning. But that wasn't good enough for you. You had to come in company – and in the company of a police spy at that.'

At every step the inn-keeper met solitary walkers, or couples, or groups of people who whispered to each other as they went. At this stage of his soliloquy he saw a squad of soldiers. He stood aside to let them pass, watched them out of the corner of his eye, and went on again: 'There go the wages of folly! What an idiot the man must be! He sees a few people going around stirring up a bit of a riot, and he gets it into his head that the whole world is going to be changed overnight. With nothing to go on but that bright idea, you've ruined yourself, and had a good shot at ruining me too – which isn't fair. I did everything I could to save your bacon, and, like a fool, you did nothing in return except just about turn my tavern upside down. Now it's up to you to get out of the mess you've made; I'm going to look after myself. As if I'd want to know your name out of idle curiosity! What do I care whether you're called Tom, Dick or Harry? As if I enjoyed all this paperwork myself! But you people aren't the only ones who want things arranged to suit them . . . I know that there are proclamations that aren't enforced, as well as you do. We don't need hillmen to come and tell us things like that! But what you don't realize is that the proclamations against inn-keepers *are* enforced . . . You want to travel the world, and say your piece, and you don't even realize that if a man wants to go his own way and get round the laws, the first thing he's got to do is to express the utmost respect for them. And suppose some poor devil of an inn-keeper agrees with you, and doesn't record the names of his guests – would a fellow like you know what happens to him?

' "*A fine shall be imposed on any such hosts, inn-keepers or other citizens as specified above of* 300 *scudi.*" Three hundred *scudi*, they'd have off me; and what a noble use they'd find for the money ! "*To be applied in the proportion of two thirds to the expenses of the Court and one third to the accuser or the informant.*" A nice treat for the little fellow ! "*In cases of inability to pay the fine, the penalty shall be five years in the galleys or any other more severe penalty financial or bodily as may be determined at the discretion of His Excellency.*" Thank you very much indeed !'

At this point, the host reached the door of the Palace of Justice, which, like all the other public offices, was full of activity. The whole place was busy with the issuing of orders designed to keep things under control the following day : to damp the ardour of those who wanted more riots, and deprive them of excuses to start anything; and to reinforce the authority of those accustomed to exercise it. Further troops were despatched to the commissioner's house, and the entrances to the street where it stood were blocked with carts and barricaded with beams. All the bakers were ordered to work non-stop. Messengers were sent out to the neighbouring villages, to tell them to send grain into the city. Members of the nobility were posted to all the bakeries, with instructions to get there early in the morning, to supervise the distribution of bread, and keep the rowdier elements in the crowd under control with their natural authority, and with fair words.

But to make assurance double sure, and to back up good advice with a little intimidation, they were also thinking how they could get their hands on some individual agitator, and make an example of him. This was primarily the business of the captain of police. Anyone can imagine what his feelings were about the riots and the rioters, with that plaster on one of the bumps of his metaphysical cavity. His agents had been on the prowl from the beginning of the troubles; and the man who called himself Ambrogio Fusella was in fact a police spy in disguise, as the host had remarked. He had been sent out specifically to look out for someone taking an active part who would be easy to recognize, to take mental note of him, and keep him under observation, so that he could be arrested later on, in the middle of the night, or the following day. Having heard half a dozen words of Renzo's speech to the crowd, he began to have high hopes of him; for he could see that Renzo was just the kind of simple-minded criminal that he needed. When he discovered that Renzo did not know his way around Milan at all, he tried to bring off the master-stroke of leading him straight to the prison, with the pretence that it was the safest inn in the city. But that plan went wrong, as we have seen. However, he took with him Renzo's Christian name, surname and place of origin, and a lot of other useful information of a more conjectural nature; so that when the inn-keeper arrived at the Palace of Justice to tell them about Renzo, they already knew more about the young man than he did.

He went to the office he usually visited, and made a statement to the effect that a stranger had come to stay at his inn and had refused to give his name.

'You have done your duty in reporting the matter,' said a criminal notary, laying down his pen. 'But we already know about it.'

'Fancy discovering a well-kept secret like that!' said the inn-keeper to himself. 'The man must be a genius!'

'We also know your worthy friend's name,' added the official.

'How the hell did you manage that?' thought the host, genuinely impressed this time.

'But you haven't made a clean breast of the whole story,' said the other, with a serious air.

'Why, what else do you expect me to say?'

'We know very well that the criminal brought a quantity of stolen bread into your inn – bread acquired by robbery with violence, breaking and entering, and seditious conduct.'

'I saw a man come in with a loaf in his pocket; and I neither knew nor cared where he had got it from. I'll tell you this, as true as if I was on my death-bed – I never saw him with more than that one single loaf.'

'Yes, yes ... you people are never short of excuses and defences. To hear you talk, you're all good citizens. How can you prove that the bread was honestly come by?'

'Why should I have to prove anything? I don't come into this; I'm just the host.'

'Anyway you cannot deny that this associate of yours had the temerity to utter insulting words on the subject of the proclamations, and to display a wrongful and improper attitude to the arms of His Excellency the Governor.'

'Forgive me, your Honour, but how can he be my associate when I've never seen him before? With all respect, I think it must have been the devil that sent him to my inn in the first place ... and after all, your Honour, if I'd known him I wouldn't have needed to ask him for his name.'

'But the most terrible things were said in your tavern, and in your presence too – reckless words, seditious utterances, rebellious complaints, screaming and shouting ...'

'How does your Honour expect me to take note of all the nonsense talked by a pack of loud-mouthed fellows who all speak at once? I have to look after my own affairs, for I'm a poor man. Besides, your Honour knows very well that men who are free with their tongues are often free with their fists as well, especially when they're in a group.'

'I see. So you just let them do and say what they like. We'll see if they've got over their fancies tomorrow ... What do you think is happening in Milan?'

'I don't think anything, your Honour.'

'It seems to me you think the mob has got permanent control of the city.'

'What an idea!'

'You'll see ... you'll see tomorrow.'

'I know what's what, sir. When this is over, the King will still be King – and the man who's asked for trouble and got it will still have a sore back, or worse, and naturally that's not what a poor fellow with a family wants at all. You gentlemen in authority have the power to take action, and it's up to you to take it.'

'Have you still got a lot of people in your tavern?'

'Yes, quite a few.'

'And what is your associate doing now? Is he still creating a disturbance, rousing the mob, preparing fresh riots for tomorrow?'

'The *stranger*, sir – for I think that's the word you meant to use – the *stranger* has gone to bed.'

'So there are still a lot of people in your place . . . well, mind you don't let him escape!'

'So I'm to be a policeman myself now, am I?' thought the host; but he said nothing out loud.

'Go home now; and be careful,' said the official.

'I'm always careful, your Honour. Have I ever been in trouble with the law in all my life?'

'Well, don't think that the law has lost its power.'

'Good God, sir, I don't think anything. I just mind my own business, which is running an inn.'

'We've heard all this before. You never have anything else to say.'

'Why should I have anything else to say? The truth is always the same.'

'Very well then. For the present, we'll content ourselves with the statement you've just made. If necessary later on, you must give us more detailed information in response to any further questions you may be asked.'

'What information? I don't know anything else; it's all I can do to look after my own affairs.'

'Mind you don't let him get away.'

'Well, sir, I hope his Honour the captain of police will hear that I lost no time in coming here to do my duty. And now I respectfully beg to take my leave.'

At daybreak, Renzo had been snoring for about seven hours, and was still sleeping sweetly, poor lad, when he was rudely awakened. Rough hands grabbed both his arms and shook them, and there was a shout of 'Lorenzo Tramaglino' from the foot of the bed. He regained consciousness, got his arms free, opened his eyes with some difficulty, and saw two armed men standing on either side of his bed, and a figure in black standing at its foot. What with the surprise, and being half asleep, and the after-effects of the wine we have heard so much about, he lay there for a moment as if in a trance. Thinking that this must be a dream, and an unpleasant one at that, he shook his head as if to wake himself up properly.

'Do you hear what I say, Lorenzo Tramaglino?' said the man in the black cape, who was none other than the notary we met the night before. 'Come on then; get up and come with us.'

'Lorenzo Tramaglino!' said Renzo. 'What's all this about? What do you want with me? Who told you my name?'

'Less talk, and get on with it!' said one of the men at his bedside, grabbing him by the arm again.

'What's all this rough stuff for?' cried Renzo, freeing himself. 'Host! Come here, host!'

'Shall we drag him off in his shirt-tails?' said the same man, turning towards the notary.

'Did you hear what he said?' the official asked Renzo. 'That's what we'll do, if you don't get up at once and come with us.'

'What for?' said Renzo.

'You'll hear the reason from the captain of police.'

'But I'm a good citizen, and I've done nothing wrong. I'm amazed at . . .'

'So much the better, then. You'll be able to clear the whole thing up in a couple of words, and then you can go about your business.'

'Let me go now then,' said Renzo. 'I've nothing to say to the police.'

'Let's make an end of this!' said one of the two armed men.

'Shall we drag him out now?' asked the other.

'Lorenzo Tramaglino!' said the notary.

'How do you know my name, your Honour?'

'Do your duty!' said the official to the two men, who seized Renzo to drag him out of bed.

'Get your hands off me! I'm a good citizen . . . and I can dress myself, thank you.'

'Then dress yourself, at once!' said the official.

'Very well,' said Renzo. He began to gather up his clothes

which were strewn over the bed like wreckage on the beach after a storm. Then he started putting them on, continuing at the same time:

'But I won't go to the captain of police. I've nothing to say to him. Since I'm being exposed to this undeserved insult, I want to be taken to Ferrer. I know him, and I know he's a good fellow; and besides, he owes me something.'

'Very well, my lad; you'll be taken to Ferrer,' said the notary. At any other time he would have had a hearty laugh at a request like that, but this was not the time for laughter. On his way to the inn, he had noticed a certain activity in the streets – it was hard to say whether it was the fag-end of yesterday's riot, not yet fully burnt out, or the beginning of a new one. People seemed to be appearing from nowhere, gathering into swarms, going around in gangs, or forming stationary groups. He gave no sign of special attention – or at least he tried not to do so – but all the while he was listening carefully; and it seemed to him now that the noise was growing louder. For this reason, he wanted to be quick; but he also wanted Renzo to go with him of his own free will. If there were a struggle, the tables might easily be turned on him and his party when they got out into the street. So he glanced at the armed police in a way which conveyed to them that they must be patient, and not infuriate the young man; and he himself did his best to persuade Renzo to accompany them with fair words.

The young man put his clothes on very slowly, searching his memory for details of the events of the previous evening. He realized in a general way that proclamations and Christian names and surnames must be at the bottom of it – but how the devil had the fellow got his name, after all? And what the devil had happened during the night, so that the police had the courage to come confidently and seize one of the excellent lads who had enjoyed so much influence and consideration the day before? Early as it was, a good many of the other excellent lads were clearly up and about, to judge by the mounting clamour in the streets. He looked carefully at the notary's face, and saw unmistakable signs of the anxiety that the man was trying so hard to hide.

Renzo decided to test his theory of what lay behind all this, and see how the land lay; to gain a little time, and perhaps make a break for it later.

'I see what started all this,' he said. 'It's that business of Christian names and surnames. Well, I was a bit drunk last night. These inn-keepers sometimes give you a wine that's stronger than you think; and once it's inside you, why, it's the wine that does the talking. But if that's the only thing, I'm ready to do whatever you say. And you seem to know my name already. Who gave it to you?'

'That's right, my boy!' said the notary, all affability now. 'I can see you're a sensible fellow. Believe me – and I ought to know, in my job – you've got more brains than a lot of people. That's the way to get off quickly, without any further trouble. With your very proper attitude, you'll be clear of the whole thing in a couple of minutes, and allowed to go free again. Unfortunately I'm under orders, and I can't let you go here and now, as I'd like to. You just be as quick as you can, and come along. There's nothing to be frightened of. They'll see what sort of fellow you are, and I'll put in a word too ... You can leave it to me ... But do hurry up, my dear boy.'

'I see ... So you can't let me go yourself,' said Renzo. He went on getting dressed, motioning the armed men away every time their hands moved towards him to make him hurry up.

'Shall we be passing the Cathedral Square?' he asked.

'We'll go any way you like; the shortest would be the best, so that you can be free again as quickly as possible,' said the notary, grieved to the heart not to be able to take Renzo up at once on his mysterious question, which sounded a most fruitful starting-point for investigation.

'What vile luck!' he thought. 'For once I've got someone on my hands who actually seems to want to talk; and if I had time, I could have a friendly, informal, theoretical sort of discussion with him, which would end in his confessing everything I wanted him to, without even being tortured. He's a man you could interrogate fully on the way to prison, without his so much as noticing it – and I have to meet him at a hopeless moment like this. Well, it can't be helped,' he decided, cocking his ear and turning his head to listen. 'There's nothing to be done about it. Today could easily be even worse than yesterday.'

This last reflection was prompted by a truly extraordinary noise in the street. He could not resist the temptation of opening the shutters to see what was going on. A group of citizens had been told to break up by a military patrol; they had replied with insults in the first place, and were now finally dispersing, grumbling loudly as they did so. But what struck the notary as the worst sign of all was that the soldiers were being remarkably polite to them. He closed the shutters, and hesitated for a moment whether to finish the job himself, or to leave Renzo there in charge of the two men and hurry off himself to tell the captain of police what had happened.

'But then he'll only call me a cowardly good-for-nothing,' he thought, 'and tell me I should have obeyed my instructions. We're in at the deep end, and we've got to swim for it. Why do we have to be in such an infernal hurry? Why did I ever take up this damned profession?'

Renzo had got up now, and the two henchmen stood on either side of him. The notary signed to them not to be too rough with him, and said: 'Be a good lad; come along with us, and be quick.'

Renzo had been using his eyes, ears, and wits. He was completely dressed now, except for his doublet, which he was holding in one hand, while he went through the pockets with the other.

'Listen!' he said, looking meaningly at the notary. 'There was some money in here, and a letter. Where are they, sir?'

'You'll get everything back, everything, as soon as these few formalities have been completed,' said the official. 'Come on, come on!'

'No, no,' said Renzo, shaking his head. 'That's not good enough. I want my things now, sir. I don't mind accounting for my actions, but I want my property.'

'Very well, then; just to show that I trust you,' said the notary with a sigh, taking the confiscated effects out of his pocket and handing them over to Renzo. 'And now be quick,' he added.

Renzo put the things away in their rightful place, muttering: 'Good God! You've had so much to do with thieves that you've picked up their habits.'

The armed police could hardly control themselves at this; but the notary restrained them with a look. Inwardly he was thinking: 'Once I get you inside, my boy, you'll pay for that – you'll pay for it with interest!'

While Renzo was putting on his doublet and getting his hat, the notary signed to one of the men to take the lead going down the stairs; then to Renzo to follow him and to the other man to follow Renzo. He himself came last of all. They reached the kitchen, and just as Renzo was saying; 'I wonder where that damned inn-keeper has got to,' the notary signed to the armed police again. One grabbed Renzo's right hand and the other his left, and in a flash they had secured him on both sides with two instruments which at that time were known, with hypocritical euphemism, as 'wristlets'. (We are sorry to have to trouble the reader with details which are undoubtedly beneath the dignity of history, but the story would not be clear without them.) A cord slightly longer than the circumference of an average wrist was fitted at both ends with short wooden pegs. The cord was passed round the prisoner's wrist, with its ends tucked between the second and third fingers of the escort, who grasped the pegs in his fist. The cord could be tightened at will by twisting the pegs, and could be used not merely to prevent the prisoner's escape, but also to torture him if he resisted. With this object, the cord was knotted from end to end . . .

Renzo struggled and cried 'What a dirty trick! What a way to treat a respectable citizen!' But the notary who had fair words to cover every shabby action, quickly said: 'You must be patient; they are only doing their duty. It's just a formality, you know; we're not allowed to treat people the way we'd like to. If we didn't carry out our orders, we'd be in big trouble ourselves; much worse than you, in fact.'

As he was speaking, the two men gave the pegs a twist. Renzo steadied himself, like a spirited horse that feels the curb-chain tighten, and said 'Well, I'll have to put up with it, then.'

'Good lad!' said the notary. 'That's the way to get the whole thing over quickly. It's a nuisance for you; I can see that myself. But if you're reasonable, you'll be out of it in a couple of minutes. And since I can see you're a sensible lad, and I want to help you, I'll tell you something else, for your own good. Take my advice, for I've had a lot of experience in these things. Don't look right or left; walk straight along, and try not to attract attention. Then no one will bother about you; no one will notice what's going on, and there won't be any harm done to your reputation. You'll be free within an hour; they're so busy in the office that they'll be in a hurry to get your case over, and I'll put in a word as well. Then you can go about your business, and no one will even know that you've been in the hands of the police. And listen, you two,' he went on, turning to the escort with a severe expression, 'mind you don't hurt him, because he's under my protection. You have to do your duty, of course; but remember that he is a good citizen, and a well-behaved young man, who's going to be set at liberty very soon, and that he's naturally concerned about his reputation. Try to walk in such a way that no one will notice us; as if you were three ordinary citizens taking a walk. Is that understood?' he concluded, in an imperious voice, and with a threatening scowl.

Then he turned to Renzo, and his frown vanished and his face broke into a smile, as if to say: '*We* are good friends, aren't we?'

'Be careful now,' he whispered. 'Do what I say; no disturbance, no noise; have faith in those who are trying to help you. And now let's go.'

Then the party moved off. But Renzo did not believe a single word of all this friendly talk. He did not believe that the notary had more affection for him than for his escort, nor that he cared about his prisoner's reputation, nor that he really wanted to help him. He saw quite clearly that the notary was afraid there would be a chance for Renzo to escape as they went along the street, and was putting forward all those high-minded suggestions to prevent him from noticing or making use of the opportunity when it came. So all those exhortations had no other effect but to strengthen his determination to do just the opposite.

But anyone who concluded that the notary was an unpractised or inexpert twister would be quite wrong. He was a twister of the highest calibre, according to our historian, who seems to have been one of his friends; but at that particular time he was in a confused state. In a calmer moment he would have been the first to laugh at anyone who tried to get a man to do something suspect in itself by wheedling and persuasion, with the miserable trick of pretending to give him a piece of disinterested, friendly advice. But men who are troubled and perplexed, and see how easily another man could get them out of difficulty, generally go on far too long with anxious, repeated requests for help, accompanied by pretexts of every kind; and twisters are no exception, when they are troubled and perplexed. That is why they so often cut an extremely poor figure on such occasions. It is not that they lose the masterly powers of invention, the brilliant strokes of cunning, with which they are accustomed to triumph, which have become second nature to them, and which, when used at the right time and carried out with the inner calm and peace of mind they require, achieve their object precisely and without arousing suspicion – and which indeed earn universal applause at a later stage, when the job is successfully completed and people see how it was done. The poor fellows do not forget those tricks, when they find themselves in an emergency, but they use them hastily, recklessly, and without either skill or grace. And when people see them struggling and floundering like that, they make a most pitiable and ridiculous spectacle. Even if the man they want to overreach is far less intelligent than they are, he is sure to realize what they are up to, and to see all the more clearly because of their efforts to hoodwink him. For this reason, we cannot sufficiently impress on professional twisters the importance of always keeping a cool head – or, better still, of always negotiating from strength.

As soon as they were out in the street, Renzo began to look right and left, to lean from side to side, and to keep his eyes and ears open. But there was nothing you could call a crowd in sight; quite a few passers-by had something rebellious in their expressions, but they were all going about their business, and there were no signs of real rebellion to be seen.

'Careful, now careful!' whispered the notary from behind. 'Remember your reputation, my boy!'

But when Renzo saw a group of three red-faced men approaching, and heard them talking about bakeries, about hidden stocks of grain, and about justice, he began to wink at them, and to cough in that special way which has nothing to do with having a cold. The men took a close look at the little party, and stopped. Others, who were following them, stopped too; and yet others, who had already passed by, heard the buzz of conversation and turned back to join the throng.

'Look out, my boy; be careful. This is a bad thing for you. Don't harm your own interests; remember your reputation and your honour!' whispered the notary again. But Renzo started to behave even worse. His escorts exchanged a glance, and decided (for we all makes mistakes sometimes) that it would be best to give the wristlets a twist.

'Ow! Ow! Ow!' shouted the victim. People flocked around him, and people came running from both ends of the street. The little party was hemmed in.

'He's a really dirty fellow!' whispered the notary over his shoulder to those who were standing behind him. 'He's a thief, caught in the act. Make way, please; make way for the law.'

But Renzo saw that his time had come, saw his escorts' faces whiten, or turn pale at least, and thought: 'I must do it now, or I'm finished.'

'Friends!' he cried. 'Friends and brothers! They're taking me to prison because I shouted for bread and justice yesterday! I haven't done anything at all! I'm a good citizen. Help me! Don't desert me, brothers!'

There was a sympathetic murmur, followed by more definite expressions of support. The plain-clothes men ordered the nearest members of the crowd to move on, and to make way; but the order became a request, and the request a plea. The crowd thronged closer and pushed harder. The escorts saw that no good would come of this; they released the wristlets, with no further thought of anything but melting away into the crowd and making an unobtrusive departure. The notary was most anxious to do the same, but his black cloak made him conspicuous. Pallid and dismayed, doing his best to shrink to half his normal size, the poor man twisted and turned, and tried to sidle out of the crowd. But every time he raised his eyes from the ground, he saw many angry pairs of eyes glaring at him. He did everything he could to look like a stranger to the whole affair, who had happened to be passing that way and had got caught up in the crowd by chance, like a fly in amber. When he found himself face to face with a man who was glaring at him with an even more hostile scowl than the others, he managed to raise a smile, and feebly asked 'What's all this about, do you know?'

'You dirty vulture!' was the answer. 'Dirty vulture!' cried many other voices, all around. Then the jostling began; speeded by other people's elbows more than by his own legs, the notary was soon able to achieve his heart's desire of getting out of that rabble.

Chapter 16

'RUN for it, lad!' – 'There's a monastery over there!' – 'No, no; over here; run for the church!' – 'That way!' – 'No, this way!' called many voices. As far as running for it was concerned, Renzo did not need any advice. From the first moment that he had seen a glimmer of hope that he might escape from the notary's clutches, he had been thinking what to do next, and had decided that if he got away he would keep on going until he was safely beyond the city boundaries, and the boundaries of the duchy as well. 'Somehow or other they've found out my name and got it down in their infernal books,' he said to himself, 'Christian name, surname and the lot; and that means they can come and pick me up whenever they want to. But I won't take asylum in a church unless I've really got a policeman breathing down my neck; for if I've still got a chance of being a bird in the air I won't make myself a bird in a cage.'

So he had resolved to take refuge in the territory of Bergamo, in the village where his cousin Bortolo had settled, who had several times invited Renzo to join him there, as the reader may remember. The difficulty was to find out how to get there. Renzo was now in a completely unknown quarter of a city he only knew very slightly. He did not even know which of the city gates he should make for as a first step; and if he had known the gate, he still would have had no idea which street led to it. He was on the point of asking one of his liberators the way; but by now he had had time to think things over and form certain opinions about that obliging sword-maker with the family of four children, which made him rightly reluctant to announce his plans to so large a gathering, that might easily contain another friend of the same type. So he decided to get away from the scene of his rescue as fast as he could, and ask the way later on, in some place where no one would have any idea who he was, or why he wanted to know.

'Thank you, brothers; God bless you all!' he said, and moved off through the crowd, which made way for him at once. He gathered himself as if for a spring, and was gone, running down an alley, up a narrow street, and on again, without any idea where he was going. When he thought he had put enough distance behind him, he slowed up, to avoid arousing suspicion, and began to look around to try and select the right person to ask the way – someone whose face inspired confidence. But this too had its complications. The question was suspect in itself; but there was no time to lose, for the police must have started to look for the escaped prisoner as soon as they were clear of the little bit of difficulty they had encountered. The news of his flight might already have caught up with him. In this dilemma Renzo did not find a face he liked the look of until he had made snap judgements on nine or ten others.

There was a fat man standing in the doorway of his shop, with feet well apart, hands behind his back, and stomach thrust forward; with jaw stuck out and pendulous double chin. For lack of anything else to do, he was alternately hoisting his quivering bulk forward on to his toes, and letting his weight fall back on to his heels. He looked like an inquisitive, gossiping fellow, who would have asked a lot of questions instead of answering them.

Then came a figure with glazed eyes and projecting lower lip who was clearly not the man to tell a stranger the way, since he hardly seemed to know his own.

Then a youth who looked bright enough, but sly, too, as if he might easily have taken a crazy pleasure in misdirecting a poor visitor from the country.

A man who is in trouble already finds a further complication in almost everything he sees. But finally Renzo saw a man walking very rapidly towards him, and thought that anyone who was in so much of a hurry would probably give him a quick answer, without any unnecessary talk. He was talking to himself, too, which made Renzo think that he must be an open-hearted sort of person. Renzo went up to the man, and said:

'Excuse me, sir, but would you tell me the way to Bergamo?'

'Bergamo? East Gate.'

'Thanks very much; and how do I get to the East Gate?'

'That road to the left takes you to the Cathedral Square, and then ...'

'Thank you, sir; I know the way from there. God bless you.' He hurried off in the direction indicated. The man looked after Renzo for a moment, considering the way he walked in conjunction with the questions he had asked, and said to himself: 'Either he's cut someone's throat, or someone's after him with the same idea.'

Renzo reached the Cathedral Square, and went across it, passing a heap of charcoal and ashes in which he recognized the remains of the fire he had seen burning so brightly the day before. He passed close by the cathedral steps, saw the Bakery of the Crutches again, half dismantled and guarded by soldiers, and went straight on down the streets up which he had come with the mob. He reached the Capuchin monastery, and glanced at the doors of the church that stood in the little square. 'Well,' he said to himself with a sigh, 'that friar yesterday gave me a very sound piece of advice when he told me to go and wait in the church, where I could do some good while I was waiting.'

He stopped for a moment and looked carefully at the gate through which he had to pass; and even from that distance he could see it was heavily guarded. His imagination was a little overheated, as was natural enough in the circumstances, and he felt a certain unwillingness to go on. A place of asylum was so conveniently at hand, where he could rely on a welcome, thanks to Father Cristoforo's letter, and he was strongly tempted to make use of it. But he quickly took heart again, thinking:

'Didn't I say I'd be a bird in the air and not a bird in a cage for as long as I could? Who's going to recognize me? Those two policemen can't very well have cut themselves up into twenty policemen, to go and guard all the gates of the city against me.'

He turned round to see if by any chance they were coming up behind him; but there was no sign of them, nor of anyone else who seemed to be in the least interested in him. So he went on, forcing his legs to move slowly – they wanted to run, but this was a time for walking – and whistling a quiet little tune as he made his unhurried way towards the gate.

There was group of excisemen right in his way, with some Spanish soldiers to back them up; but their interest was concentrated on the world beyond the city wall, and on the task of preventing the entry of the trouble-makers who always hasten to the scene of an uprising, like vultures to the scene of a battle. And so Renzo strolled through, not looking up, but maintaining an indifferent air and a gait halfway between that of a traveller and that of a man going for a walk, without anything being said to him; though his own heart beat very loudly. He saw a lane leading off to the right, and turned down it, to get away from the main road. He walked on for some distance before even looking back over his shoulder.

He went on and on, past farms and through villages without even asking what they were called. He knew he was getting away from Milan, and hoped he was making progress towards Bergamo; and that was enough for the moment. From time to time he looked back over his shoulder, or glanced down at his wrists and rubbed them; for they were still a little painful, and marked all round with the pink lines left by the wristlets. As can readily be imagined, his head was buzzing with self-reproach, apprehension, anger and tenderer thoughts. It was not easy to recall and fit together the events and the conversations of the evening before, nor to make sense of the obscurer parts of the distressing story. How, above all, had they been able to get his name? His suspicions naturally fell on the sword-maker, for he clearly remembered revealing it to him. And now he came to think about the way the man had got it out of him, and his general manner, and his habit of introducing subjects of conversation which always ended in a question, Renzo's suspicions were transformed into near certainty. But he did remember in a confused way that he had gone on talking a lot after the sword-maker's departure, though he had no idea with whom. He tried hard to remember what he had been talking about, but memory could only reply that she had not been among those present. Poor Renzo's head began to swim. He was like a man who has signed a number of blank sheets of paper, and entrusted them to a friend for whom he has the highest possible regard; he then discovers that his friend is a swindler, and wants to get a clear picture how he stands; but how can he get a clear picture of a total chaos?

Renzo also had great difficulty in forming any idea of the future which could give him any pleasure. Apart from castles in the air, every prospect was black.

But the worst difficulty of all, he soon discovered, was that of finding his way. He walked on at random, so to speak, for a certain distance, but realized that this would not do. He felt a certain reluctance to utter the name of Bergamo, as if there were something suspect or improper about the word itself; but there was no help for it. He made up his mind to speak to the first traveller whose face he liked, as he had in Milan. Presently he did so.

'You're going the wrong way,' said the man he selected. He thought for a few moments, and then gave Renzo to understand, partly with words and partly with gestures, that he must go around another way and get back to the main road. Renzo thanked him, and pretended to follow his advice. He did in fact set off in the direction indicated; his intention was to get back to the neighbourhood of the main road, to take a course parallel with it and not let it out of his sight again, but to be careful not to set foot on its surface. This plan was easy to form, but difficult to carry out. He took a zigzag route, occasionally plucking up courage to ask the way again; sometimes following his instructions exactly, sometimes changing them a little to suit his own ideas or his private intentions; and sometimes simply following the line of the road along which he happened to be walking.

When he had walked twelve miles, he was still only six miles away from Milan; and as for Bergamo, he would have been glad to be sure that he was not further away from it than he had been when he set out. He began to realize that this would not do either, and tried to think of another method. It occurred to him that he might be able to trick someone into giving him the name of a village near the frontier, which could be reached by side roads; then he could ask for directions without leaving behind him a trail of people who had been asked the way to Bergamo, the name of which now seemed so contaminated by the ideas of flight, exile and criminality.

While he was considering how to obtain all the information he needed, without arousing suspicion, he noticed a bush hanging over the door of a lonely cottage, some way outside a hamlet. He had been feeling hungrier and hungrier for some time, and he thought he would kill two birds with one stone. He went in, and found no one there but an old woman, with a spindle in her hand and a distaff at her side. He asked for a bite to eat, and she suggested cream cheese and a glass of good wine. He accepted the cheese, but declined the wine with thanks, feeling a positive hatred for it after the shabby trick it had played him the night before. He sat down, and asked her to be quick. She had the food on the table in a moment, and at once began to bombard her guest with questions, both about himself and about the extraordinary events in Milan; for word of them had already reached this remote spot. Renzo not only managed to defend himself from all her questions, in the most natural way, but also extracted some benefit from this new difficulty. When the old woman asked him where he was going, he took advantage of her curiosity for his own ends.

'I've got to visit a number of places,' he said, 'and if I can fit it in, I'd like to spend a bit of time in that village . . . quite a big one, it is, on the road to Bergamo . . . near the frontier, but this side of it . . . what's its name, now?' (He was thinking to himself: surely there must be a village that answers that description.)

'You must mean Gorgonzola,'[1] said the old woman.

'Gorgonzola!' said Renzo, trying to fix it in his memory. 'Is it far from here?' he went on.

'I can't say, exactly; maybe ten miles, maybe twelve. I wish one of my boys was here; they'd be able to tell you.'

'And do you know if I can get there by going along these fine side-roads you have here? For there's a terrible amount of dust on the main road. It's such a long time since we last had rain.'

1. See map on page 16 and notes on facing page. – Translator's note.

'I think so; but you'd better ask again at the first village you come to down that road to the right over there.' And she gave him the name of the village.

'Thank you,' said Renzo. He stood up and pocketed a piece of bread— it was very different in quality from the loaf he had found by the Cross of St Denis the day before, but it was all that remained from his scanty meal. Then he paid his bill, went out, and took the road to the right.

To cut a long story short, he went on from village to village, asking the way to Gorgonzola, and got there about an hour before nightfall. He had already decided to make another brief halt at Gorgonzola, and have a rather more substantial meal there. His body would also have been glad of a few hours in bed, but he had no intention of obliging it in that matter; he would rather have driven it along the road until it dropped. He decided that he would make inquiries at the inn and find out how far away the Adda was, adroitly get some information about a side-road that led to it, and go on in that direction as soon as he had finished his meal. Having been born and bred by the lake which is, so to speak, the second source of the Adda, he had often heard that one section of its course formed the boundary between the territories of Milan and those of Venice. Where that section began or ended, he had no idea; but at that particular moment the important thing was to get across it, wherever it might be. If it could not be done that day, he was determined to push on as far as time permitted and his legs would carry him, and pass the night in a field, in a wilderness or wherever heaven might decree – so long as it was not in an inn.

He walked on a few yards down the street, saw an inn-sign, and entered the building. When the host came, Renzo asked him for a bite to eat and a quarter-bottle of wine; for his extreme, fanatical hatred of alcohol had not survived the last few miles and the last few hours of his journey.

'I'd like to have it quickly, if I may,' he added, 'for I've got to go straight on afterwards.' He said this not only because it was true, but also for fear the host would think he wanted to stay the night; and then, thought Renzo, he'll come and ask me my

Christian name, surname, place of origin, and business all over again. To hell with that!

The host said that it wouldn't be long, and Renzo sat down at the end of the table nearest the door – the place chosen by the humblest guests.

Some of the idler inhabitants of the village were already in the room. They had finished discussing and commenting on the news of the important events which had taken place in Milan the day before, and they were most anxious to find out something about the events of the day which was now ending. For the first lot of news had been better calculated to arouse curiosity than to satisfy it. There had been an uprising, neither wholly suppressed nor completely successful; nightfall had interrupted it rather than brought it to an end. It was an unfinished story – the end of an act rather than the end of a play. One of the local party left his companions and came over to Renzo, and inquired whether he had come from Milan.

'Who, me?' said Renzo. He was slightly taken aback, and wanted to give himself time to think of an answer.

'Yes, you, if you don't mind me asking.'

Renzo shook his head, pursed his lips, made a curious, inarticulate sound, and then replied: 'From what I've heard, Milan's no place to visit just now, unless you really have to.'

'Is the disturbance still going on today then?' asked the questioner, with even more insistence.

'You'd have to be there to know for sure,' said Renzo.

'But haven't you come from Milan yourself?'

'I've come from Liscate,' replied Renzo briefly, having used the previous exchange to think out his reply. What he said was true, strictly speaking, because he had come through Liscate, and had learnt its name from a traveller who had mentioned Liscate as the last village he would pass on the way to Gorgonzola.

'Oh!' said the man, as if to imply, you'd have done better to come from Milan, but it can't be helped now. 'But didn't they know anything at Liscate about what was going on in Milan?'

'It's quite likely that someone there knew something about

306

it,' said the young hillman, 'but I didn't hear anything about it myself.'

He put a certain finality into the way he uttered these last words. The questioner returned to his seat, and a moment later the inn-keeper came up with the food.

'How far is it to the Adda?' asked Renzo, with a mumbling voice and a sleepy manner which we have seen him use before.

'To cross over, do you mean?' said the host.

'Why, yes . . . to the Adda . . .'

'Do you want to use the Cassano bridge, or the Canonica ferry?'

'Anywhere . . . I'm just asking out of curiosity.'

'You see, those are the two places where good citizens cross over – people who can give a proper account of themselves.'

'Well, how far is it?'

'You can reckon that it'll be about six miles to either the bridge or the ferry.'

'Six miles! I didn't know it was as much as that,' said Renzo. 'Just suppose,' he added, with an air of indifference carried almost to the point of affectation, 'just suppose someone wanted to take a short cut, are there any other ways he could get across?'

'There are ways, sure enough,' said the host, staring at him with eyes full of sly curiosity.

That was enough to destroy Renzo's desire to ask the other question that he had got ready. He pulled the plate towards him, looked at the quarter-bottle which the inn-keeper had placed beside it, and said 'Is the wine all right?'

'It's perfect,' said the host. 'You can ask anyone in the village or the countryside round about, who know what's what, and they'll tell you.' He returned to his other guests.

'Damn all these hosts!' said Renzo to himself. 'The more I see of them the less I like them.' But that did not prevent him from eating heartily, though he listened hard at the same time, as unobtrusively as possible, to see how the land lay, and find out what people thought in Gorgonzola about the great events in which he himself had played no small part. In particular, he was trying to see if there was a decent fellow among all those loud-mouthed talkers, a man whom a poor lad like himself could ask the way, without any fear of being tormented with questions about his own affairs.

'Well!' said one of them. 'It looks as if the Milanese are really serious about it this time. We'll know more about it by tomorrow at the latest.'

'I'm sorry I didn't go to Milan this morning,' said another.

'If you go tomorrow, I'll come with you,' said a third man, and two more said the same after him.

'What I'd like to know,' said the first speaker, 'is whether those fine fellows in Milan ever think about the poor people in the country, or if they're just trying to get the laws altered to suit themselves. You know what they're like, don't you? Conceited city folk, who want everything for themselves. The rest of us might as well not exist at all.'

'But we've got mouths too; mouths that need to be filled, and mouths to state our case,' said another, whose voice was quieter, just as his views were more extreme. 'And once the thing is under way . . .' He evidently thought it better not to finish the sentence.

'There's plenty of hidden stocks of corn in other places besides Milan,' began another man, with a dark and shifty air; but just then they heard the sound of a horse approaching. They all ran to the door, recognized the new arrival, and went out to greet him. He was a merchant from Milan, whose business took him to Bergamo several times a year, and who generally stopped the night at that inn. As the company who met there every evening changed very little, he knew them all. They crowded round him; one man held his bridle, and another his stirrup. 'Welcome to you, sir, welcome!' they cried.

'Delighted to find you gentlemen here.'

'Have you had a good journey?'

'Very good, thank you; and how are you all?'

'Well, thank you. What's the news from Milan?'

'Aha! So it's news you want!' said the merchant, dismounting and handing his horse over to a servant. 'But I'll be bound you know more about it than I do,' he went on, entering the inn with his companions.

'We know nothing, nothing at all,' said several of them, hand on heart.

'Really?' said the merchant. 'Well, you've got some fine news to come – ugly news, I ought to call it, to tell the truth. Host? Is the room I generally have free tonight? Good. Then I'll have a glass of wine, and my usual bite to eat, at once, please. I want to get to bed early tonight, and start early tomorrow, so that I can reach Bergamo by dinner-time. And so you people,' he went on, sitting down at the other end of the table, far away from the silent and attentive figure of Renzo, 'you people here haven't heard about all the devilry that was going on yesterday?'

'We know about yesterday.'

'Just as I thought,' said the merchant. 'You do know the news. And so you should, sitting here all day, picking the brains of everyone who goes by.'

'But what about today? What happened today?'

'Today? Haven't you had any recent news?'

'No; no one's been by at all.'

'Just wait while I lay the dust, and then I'll tell you about it. All about it.' He filled his glass, and picked it up in one hand; with the first two fingers of the other he twisted up his moustache and stroked his beard. Then he drank, and continued: 'Well, my friends, today was very nearly as bad a day as yesterday, or even worse. I can hardly believe I'm here, peacefully talking to you all; at one time I'd given up all thought of travelling today, and decided to stay and guard my shop.'

'What the hell was going on?' asked one of the listeners.

'Hell is the right word. I'll tell you all about it.' He cut up the meat which had appeared in front of him and began to eat, going on with his story at the same time. The others stood listening with mouths agape, some on one side of the table and some on the other. Renzo sat in his place, unobtrusively listening harder than any of the others, and very slowly eating the last few mouthfuls of his meal.

'Well then; this morning the blackguards who were responsible for that terrible business yesterday turned up again at the places where they'd agreed to meet – for the whole thing was planned; there's no doubt about that. They gathered together at those various points, then, and set off to repeat their clever trick of roaming round from street to street, shouting their heads off to get other people to join them. You know how it is when someone's sweeping out a dirty room, if you'll pardon my mentioning it – the further the broom goes, the bigger the heap of muck in front of it becomes. When they felt they'd got enough people together, they set off for the house of the commissioner of provisions; as if the outrages to which they exposed the poor fellow yesterday were not enough! A gentleman like that! What swine they must be! And what filthy accusations they were making against him! All absolute lies; he's a most worthy, conscientious gentleman – and I should know, for I'm like a member of his household, and supply all the cloth for his servants' liveries. So there they were, approaching his Honour's house; you'd hardly credit what faces they had on them, the scum. Why, they went right past my shop, and they had faces that . . . well, the Jews you see in pictures of the *Via Crucis* were nothing to them. And the filth that was coming out of those ugly mouths! It was enough to make you stop your ears, except that it wasn't the moment to do anything that might attract their attention. There was no doubt about it; they were going to sack that house properly. But then, you see . . .' He raised his left hand with a flourish, spread out the fingers, and put the thumb to his nose in a significant gesture.

'But then what?' chorused almost all his listeners.

'But then they found the road blocked with carts and barred with heavy wooden beams. Behind the barricade was a row of Spanish soldiers, nicely drawn up with their arquebuses at the ready, all prepared to give them the reception they deserved. And when they saw what was waiting for them . . . well, what would you have done?'

'Gone back.'

'That's what they did, too. But listen to the next bit and see if it wasn't Satan himself that was prompting them. They were in that little square, the Cordusio, where there's a bakery which I believe they'd been thinking of attacking yesterday; and what do you think was going on in that bakery today? Bread was being distributed to regular customers, and there were noblemen of the highest character there, to superintend everything and see it was all properly done. But those scum, who must have had the devil in them, not to mention agitators egging them on, charged in like a lot of madmen. Everyone of them was helping himself, and in a couple of seconds everything was upside down; noblemen, bakers, regular customers, loaves, till, benches, dressers, cupboards, sacks, sieves, bran, flour, dough, all in one glorious mess.'

'What about the Spanish soldiers?'

'They had the commissioner's house to look after; even a Spanish soldier can't be in two places at once. It was all over in a couple of minutes, I tell you. Help yourself, everybody! was the cry, and everything of the slightest use or value was gone in a flash. Then someone had the same bright idea as yesterday, of taking the rest of the stuff out into the Cathedral Square and making a bonfire of it. And the swine were just beginning to drag the things out, when one of them, the biggest swine of all, had a still brighter idea, which you'll never guess.'

'What was that?'

'To make the heap inside the shop, set fire to it, and let the shop go up in flames with the rubbish. No sooner said than done . . .'

'They did burn the shop, then?'

'Wait a moment. A good citizen who lived near by had a heaven-sent inspiration. He ran upstairs and found a crucifix, which he stuck in a window-frame. Then he found two holy candles by one of the beds up there and stood them on the window-sill, one on each side of the crucifix. Everyone looked up. Now in Milan, you've got to admit it, there are still a lot of people who know what the fear of God means; and they all pulled themselves together at once. Most of them did, that's to say; for there were some devilish fellows there who would have set fire to the gates of heaven if there was a chance of stealing something afterwards. But it wasn't long before they saw that the majority was against them; and then they had to shut up. Then who do you think suddenly appeared? All the *monsignori* from the cathedral, a real procession, in full canonicals, with crosses in their hands. Monsignor Mazenta, the archpriest, was preaching at them from one side, and Monsignor Settala, the penetentiary, from the other. And then the other reverend gentlemen were haranguing them too. "Come, good people! What are you trying to do? What sort of example do you think you are setting your children? Go home, good people, go home! Haven't you heard that bread's cheap again now, cheaper than before? Why, go and look then, for the announcement's plain for you to see, stuck up at all the street corners!" '

'And was that true?'

'Why, dammit, do you think all those reverend gentlemen would come out in their long robes to tell you a lie?'

'What did the crowd do, then?'

'They trickled away, and went off to the street corners to see for themselves. For those who could read, there was the new price in black and white. What do you think it was? One *soldo* for an eight-ounce loaf!'

'That sounds like a bargain, all right!'

'A wonderful bargain, as long as it lasts ... Do you know how much flour has been wasted in the last two days? Enough to feed the whole duchy for two months!'

'And what have they done for the rest of us, who don't live in Milan?'

'What they've done for Milan will all have to be paid for by the city itself. I don't know what to say to you people. Out here, it'll be ... well, according to the will of Heaven. Anyway, the fighting is over. And I haven't told you everything, by the way. The best bit is still to come.'

'What's that, then?'

'A lot of the trouble-makers were arrested, some last night and some this morning. Very soon, it was common knowledge that the ringleaders were going to be hanged. As soon as that piece of news got around, everyone went home by the shortest possible route, so as not to run the risk of being one of them. When I left Milan, it was as quiet as a monastery.'

'Are they really going to hang them?'

'They certainly are, and there won't be any delay about it either.'

'What will the crowd do then?' asked the same voice.

'The crowd will go and watch!' said the merchant. 'They wanted to see one of their fellow men die in public so badly that their first idea, the swine, was to have the commissioner as the star of the show. Now, instead of the commissioner, four black-guards will be served up to them with all the trimmings. There'll be Capuchins there with them, and the other holy fathers who help you get ready for the next world; and after all they are people who deserve it. It's really providential; it's a thing which had to be done. These fellows were already getting into the habit of going into shops and helping themselves with-out putting their hands in their pockets. If you let that sort of thing go on, it won't stop at bread; it'll be wine next, and then one thing after another. Can you imagine them giving up such a convenient practice of their own free will? And I can tell you from my own point of view that it wasn't a very pleasant thought for a good citizen who happens to own a shop.'

'That's true enough!' said one of the listeners.

'True enough!' said all the others together.

'And another thing,' said the merchant, wiping his beard with his napkin, 'it had all been arranged in advance, you know. It was a conspiracy.'

'A conspiracy?'

'Yes, that's right. These are all things organized by the French, by that Cardinal in Paris – you know the one I mean, with the Turkish-sounding name – who doesn't let a day go by without scheming something against the King of Spain. But Milan is the place where he tries hardest, because he's cunning enough to see that it's the centre of His Majesty's power.'

'Yes, of course.'

'If anyone wants proof of that, here it is. The people who made most of the trouble were all strangers; Milan was full of faces no one had ever seen before. But I almost forgot; I can tell you about one case which I have on very good authority. The police caught one of these fellows in an inn . . .'

Renzo had not missed a syllable of this speech, and at the mention of the word 'inn' he jumped convulsively, before he had time to stop himself, and a very chilly feeling came over him. No one noticed him however, and the speaker went on, without breaking the thread of his narrative:

'Nobody seems to know where he came from, who sent him, nor what sort of fellow he was; but it's certain that he was one of the ringleaders. He was there in the thick of it yesterday, raising hell for all he was worth. And not content with that, he got on his hind legs and put forward the suggestion that they should murder all the gentry, if you please. The swine! Who'd keep the poor folk on their feet, I'd like to know, if all the gentry were killed off? The police spotted him all right, and got their hands on him. They found a whole bundle of letters that he was carrying too; and just as they were taking him off to gaol a whole lot of his friends, who were prowling around the inn, came along and rescued him, the blackguard.'

'What happened to him after that?'

'Nobody knows. Maybe he got clear away, and maybe he's still lying low somewhere in Milan. These people don't have any homes of their own, but they can find shelter – somewhere to hole up – wherever they go. But that can only last as long as the devil is willing and able to help them. They all get caught in the end, very often just when they least expect it. When the fruit's ripe, it's bound to fall . . . But luckily there's no doubt that the police managed to hang on to that bundle of letters, which contains details of the whole conspiracy. They say a lot of people are implicated. Well, it serves them right; they turned half Milan upside down, and would have done even worse, if they'd had the chance. These fellows say that the bakers are all crooks. Of course they are, and I hope to see them hang for it; but let's do it all legally. There are hidden stocks of grain – we all know that. But it's the job of the authorities to employ competent agents, and bring those stocks out into the open, and send the hoarders to the same gallows as the bakers. And if the authorities don't do anything it's up to the city to apply formally for the necessary action to be taken; and, if nothing happens the first time, to do it again; for that's the way to get what you want. The only thing they shouldn't do is to introduce a wicked custom like this business of going into shops and outfitters and helping yourself.'

The little food that Renzo had eaten seemed to have turned to something very unwholesome inside him. He could not wait to get out of the inn, and out of the village as well. More than a dozen times he had thought, I'll go now. But the fear of doing anything suspicious had grown so strong that it dominated all his thoughts, and kept him glued to the bench where he sat. In his perplexity the thought came to him that sooner or later this windbag would stop talking about him and his affairs, and he decided to make a move as soon as the conversation turned to another subject.

'That's it,' said one of the company. 'I knew very well how these things always turn out, and how wrong it is for good citizens to get mixed up in riots; and that's why I didn't give in to my feelings of curiosity, and stayed at home today.'

'You didn't see me going off to Milan today either, did you?' said another.

'Well, if I'd happened to be there for some quite different reason,' said a third, 'I'd have left my business unfinished, whatever it might be, and come straight home. I've got a wife and children to consider, and, to tell you the truth, that sort of thing doesn't appeal to me anyway.'

Just then the inn-keeper, who had been listening with the others, went down to the other end of the table to see how the stranger was getting on. Renzo seized the opportunity, beckoned the host to him, and asked him for the bill. He paid it without checking the details, though he was getting into very low water. Without another word he went straight to the door, stepped out into the night, and set off with Providence to be his guide, in the opposite direction to the way he had come.

Chapter 17

A SINGLE strong desire is often enough to leave a man no peace. If he is seized by two contrary desires at the same time, the effect can easily be imagined. As we know, Renzo had had two such desires together in his heart for many hours – the desire to make haste, and the desire to remain unnoticed. The merchant's untimely remarks had greatly intensified both of them. So his adventure had really created a sensation! The police must want to get hold of him at any price; heaven alone knew how many agents might already be on his track, what orders might have been sent out for searches to be made for him in the villages, at the inns, and on the roads! But then he reflected that there were only two policemen who knew him by sight, and that his name was fortunately not written on his forehead. On the other hand, he remembered various stories he had heard about fugitives who had been detected and recaptured through odd coincidences – recognized by their way of walking, or their suspicious manner, or some other unforeseen indication. All these thoughts alarmed him greatly.

Although the clocks were striking the hour of sunset as he left Gorgonzola, and gathering darkness made those dangers less and less acute, he was still reluctant to stay on the main road, and resolved to get on to the first byway that seemed to lead in the right direction. At first he met a few travellers, but his imagination was so full of ugly apprehensions that he could not bring himself to stop any of them and ask the way.

'That fellow said six miles,' he thought. 'If I go out of my way a little, perhaps it'll be eight or ten; but my legs have carried me so far today that they can do a little bit more. I'm certainly not headed for Milan, so I must be on the way to the Adda. If I keep going I'll reach it sooner or later. It's a river you can hear from a great way off, and once I get close to it, I won't need to ask the way. If I can find a boat, I'll cross over straight

316

away; otherwise I'll wait till the morning in a field, or perched up a tree like a sparrow. Better up a tree than in prison.'

He soon saw a small road which turned off to the left, and went down it. It was now late enough for him to feel less nervous about asking the way, but not a soul was to be seen. So he walked on wherever the road might take him, thinking many thoughts.

'So I'm a hell-raiser! I'm planning to murder all the gentry! I've a whole bundle of letters in my pocket! I've a gang of fellow-conspirators to back me up! Once I'm safely on the other side of the Adda – and it can't be too soon for me – I'd give something to meet that merchant again. I'd just stop him, and invite him to have a comfortable little talk with me, and explain to me where he gets all his information from. You might as well know, my dear sir, I'd say, that what really happened was such-and-such, and so-and-so; and that all the hell-raising I've done was to give Ferrer the same sort of help I'd have given him if he'd been my own brother. You might as well know that those blackguards you call my friends wanted to lynch me at one stage, because I said a couple of words on the decent Christian side; and that while you were busy guarding your shop I was getting my ribs bruised in the defence of your famous commissioner of provisions, though I'd never even seen him before. It'll be some time before I go out of my way to help any of the gentry again ... though it's a thing that should be done, for our religion's sake, since they are our neighbours as much as anyone else. And that great bundle of letters with all the conspirators' names in it, which you know for certain is in the hands of the police – would you like to bet that I can't produce it in front of your eyes here and now, without any help from the devil? Would it interest you to see that bundle of letters? Here it is ... What, just a single letter? ... yes, sir, just a single letter; and if you want to know the details, this letter was written by a holy father, who could give you a lesson or two any time you'd care to listen to him; a holy father whose little finger, without in any way detracting from your merits, sir, is worth more than your whole body. And the letter's addressed, as you can see, to another holy father, who's also a man that ...

But now you can see what sort of desperadoes I have for friends. So be a bit more careful what you say next time; and remember your duty to your neighbour.'

But after a little all thoughts of this sort left Renzo's mind, and the poor wanderer's attention was completely taken up by his present surroundings. He was no longer so much troubled by the fear of being immediately tracked down or detected, which had tormented him during the daylight section of his journey; but there were plenty of things to make the present section even worse for him. There were the darkness, the solitude, the increasing painfulness of tired muscles. There was a quiet, steady, penetrating breeze, most unwelcome to a man who was still wearing clothes suitable for a quick wedding and a short, triumphant walk home. But what made everything worse was having to grope his way at random through the uncertain darkness in search of a place of rest and safety.

Whenever he happened to pass through a village, he walked very slowly, and looked round carefully to see if there were any doors still open; but there never seemed to be any sign of life, beyond a glimmer of light just visible through a shutter. On stretches of road where there were no houses, he halted every so often, and listened to see whether he could hear the welcome voice of the Adda. But the only sound to be heard was the howling of dogs from some isolated farm – a sound which was borne through the air in mingled notes of sorrow and menace. When he approached one of those farms, the howling would change to a rapid, angry barking; and when he passed in front of the door he could hear the brute, almost see it in fact, with its nose to the crack of the door, barking louder than ever. That cured him of any wish to knock and ask for shelter. Even without the dogs, he might not have made up his mind to do so.

'What would they say?' he thought. ' "Who's there?" – "What do you want at this time of night?" – "How did you get here?" – "What's your name?" – "Why don't you go to an inn?" That's the very best I could expect, if I knocked at one of these doors. I might wake up some nervous fellow, who'd shout "Stop thief!" for good measure. I'd need to have something

318

definite to tell them straight away in answer to their questions – and what is there for me to say? If anyone hears a noise at night, he naturally thinks of thieves, rogues and treachery. You never expect a good citizen to be on the road at night, unless it's some nobleman in his carriage.'

He decided to treat knocking people up as a last resort, and went on, hoping to find the river that night, even if he could not cross it until the morning, since the last thing he wanted was to have to look for it by daylight.

He trudged on, and reached a point where all sign of cultivation died out in a waste land, with ferns and broom growing here and there. This seemed an indication, if not a proof, that the river should be near at hand, and he pushed on along a path which led across the heath. When he had gone a little way, he stopped and listened, but could hear nothing. He felt the misery of fatigue all the more keenly in those wild surroundings, where not a mulberry-tree nor a vine was to be seen, nor any of the other signs of human activity which had provided him with a sort of company up to that point. But he kept on, and when certain grisly ideas and images, which he had absorbed from stories heard in childhood, came back into his mind, he drove them away, or at least reduced their effect, by reciting the prayers for the dead as he walked along.

Soon he found himself passing among thickets of higher growth, composed of sloe, scrub oak and buckthorn. He went on, quickening his pace out of impatience rather than enthusiasm as he saw full-grown trees beginning to appear among the scrub. Still keeping on the same path, he quickly realized that he was entering a wood. He felt a certain revulsion against the idea of going on; but he overcame it and continued reluctantly on his way. The farther he went into the wood, the stronger his revulsion grew, and the more horror he felt of all he saw. The trees in the distance took on strange, distorted, monstrous shapes. Shifting shadows, cast on the moonlit stretches of the path by the gently waving upper branches of the trees, disturbed him greatly. Even the rustling sound of the dry leaves crushed or pushed aside by his feet had an oddly unpleasant quality about it. His legs were itching with the desire to break into a run, and yet at the same time they felt scarcely strong enough to carry his weight. The night-wind was blowing harder and more bitingly now against his forehead and cheeks. He could feel it finding its way between his clothes and his shrinking flesh, penetrating more and more deeply into his tired and aching bones, extinguishing the last flicker of energy in his limbs. The moment came when the indefinite disgust and terror that he had been fighting for some time seemed to overwhelm him. He was on the point of losing his head completely; but he was more afraid of giving way to his own fear than of anything else. He called up his reserves of courage, and forced his heart to steady itself. In full control of himself for the moment, he halted and stood a while in thought.

He decided to get out of the wood at once, by the same way that he had come in; to go straight back to the last village he had passed, back to the company of mankind; and to find shelter there, even if it were the shelter of an inn. But as he stood still there in the silence of the night, which was undisturbed now by the movement of his feet among the leaves, he began to hear a sound ... a murmur ... a murmur of running water. He listened more intently, and there was no doubt of it.

'It's the Adda!' he cried. It was like greeting an old friend, a brother, a rescuer. His tiredness vanished almost completely, and his pulse beat strongly. He could feel the blood coursing warm and free through all his veins. His confidence in his plans returned, and the uncertainty and the dangers of his situation lost most of their terrors. Without a qualm, he went on deeper into the wood, following that friendly sound.

In a few moments he had crossed the flat land which still separated him from the river, and was standing on the edge of a high bank, thickly overgrown with bushes, through which he could see the glint of running water far below. Then he raised his eyes, and saw the vast plain, dotted with villages, on the far side of the stream; and beyond that the hills, on one of which he could see a great whitish blur, which must be a city, must surely be Bergamo itself. He climbed a short way down the bank, and parted the undergrowth with his hands, pushing the branches wider apart with his forearms. He looked down to see if there was any sign of a boat moving in the stream, and listened for the sound of oars; but there was nothing in sight, and nothing to be heard. If it had been a less formidable river, Renzo would have gone straight on down and tried to wade across; but he knew he could not take liberties of that sort with the Adda.

Calm and collected now, he began to consider what he should do next. He thought of climbing up a tree and staying there until dawn; but that might well be another six hours, which would be more than enough, with the wind that was blowing, the frost on the ground, and the clothes he was wearing, to freeze him stiff. To pace up and down for that length of time would not have been an effective way of keeping warm under that clear, chilly sky, and would also have been asking too much of a pair of legs that had already done more than their duty ... Then he remembered a hut he had seen, in one of the last fields he had crossed before walking on to the heath. (It was one of those thatched huts, built out of logs and wattle and plastered with mud, which the peasants of the territory of Milan use at harvest time to store their crops and to provide shelter for the men who guard them at night. The huts remain empty for the rest of the year.) He immediately decided to make it his home for the night, and went back along the path, through the wood and the scrub-land and across the heath. Then he turned off towards the hut.

It had a worm-eaten door, half off its hinges, which had been pushed to, but was not secured by lock or chain. Renzo opened it and went inside. A sort of wicker-work hurdle had been hung up like a hammock, with supports of twisted wattle; but Renzo did not bother to climb up into it. He saw a small heap of straw on the ground, and decided that this would be just as good a place for a very pleasant little sleep.

But before he lay down on the bed that heaven had sent him, he knelt down on the straw and gave thanks for that mercy, and for all the other help Providence had given him during that terrible day. Then he said his usual prayers, and begged his Maker's pardon for not having said them the day before – for having gone to bed like a brute beast or worse, to use Renzo's own expression.

'That's what earned me the kind of awakening I had this morning!' he added to himself, putting his hands on the straw, and stretching out from the kneeling to the lying position. Then he pulled all the straw which lay around him over his body, making a sort of blanket, as best he could, to lessen the effects of the cold, which was still noticeable enough even inside the hut. So he snuggled down, with every intention of having a really good sleep – which he had certainly paid for, in advance, and several times over.

But as soon as he shut his eyes, something started up in his memory, or perhaps his imagination – it is hard to say which. There was a coming and going of human figures in so constant and dense a throng that they banished all thought of sleep. The merchant, the notary, the policemen, the sword-maker, the inn-keeper, Ferrer, the commissioner, the boon-companions in the inn; the whole crowd he had seen in the streets; then Don Abbondio, and finally Don Rodrigo. These were all people to whom Renzo would have had something to say, if he had met them again.

There were just three faces in the throng that were unaccompanied by bitter memories and suspicions, faces worthy of love in every respect. Two of the three appeared to him with special vividness; and though they were very unlike each other they were closely linked in the young man's heart. One had long black hair, the other a white beard ... But even the pleasure that he felt in fixing his thoughts on them was far from un-mixed, far from restful. When he thought of Father Cristoforo, he felt even more ashamed than before of his various escapades – his disgusting intemperance, and his neglect of the good friar's fatherly advice. And as for what he felt when the image of Lucia swam before his eyes, we will not attempt to describe it. The reader knows the circumstances, and he can use his own imagination. And poor Agnese; how could he have forgotten her? Dear Agnese, who had chosen him in the first place; who had long considered him and her only daughter as a single object of affection; who had used the language and shown the feelings of a mother towards him even before he began to call her by that name, and had given proof of a truly maternal concern for him in her actions. But this too was a grief to him, and not the least of his griefs, that her good intentions and her tender affection for him had led to the poor woman being driven out of her house, to a wandering, homeless existence, with a very uncertain future; and that the very things which she had expected to ensure the repose and happiness of her declining years were causing her the utmost sorrow and turmoil.

What a night poor Renzo had! And it should have been the fifth night of his marriage. What a room! And what a bridal bed! And what a terrible day lay behind him! And who knew what lay in store for the morrow, and the following days?

'It'll be as God wills,' thought Renzo, in answer to the most distressing of these thoughts; 'it'll be as God wills. He knows what He's doing, and He won't forget us. May it all go towards the debt I owe for the payment of my sins! Lucia is so good that He cannot want her to go on suffering for long.'

Busy with these thoughts, he gave up all hope of getting to sleep. The cold tightened its grip on him, making his body shiver and his teeth chatter every few minutes, as he lay longing for the dawn to come, and counting the hours as they went slowly by. He was really able to count them, for every half hour the strokes of a clock – probably the one at Trezzo[1] – rang out through the vast silence. The first time those unexpected notes reached Renzo's ears, he had no idea where they came from, and they gave him the mysterious, solemn feeling that he had received a warning in an unknown voice, from an unseen source.

Finally the bell sounded the hour at which Renzo had decided to get up – about one hour before sunrise. Half frozen with the cold, he rose to his feet, and then knelt down and said his morning prayers, with somewhat more fervour than usual. He got up again and stretched himself this way and that, and gave his shoulders and hips a shake, to regain control of what seemed to be a strangely independent set of limbs. He blew into

1. See map on page 16 and notes on facing page. – Translator's note.

one hand and then into the other, and rubbed them together; and then he opened the hut door. The first thing he did was to look round for signs of life, but there was no one in sight; so he looked round again for the path he had taken the night before, found it at once, and set off along it.

The sky showed every prospect of a fine day. On one side the moon, though pale now and lustreless, still stood out clearly against the grey-blue sky, which was already taking on shades of yellow and pink over towards the east. A few long, irregular streaks of blue-black cloud lay further over towards the horizon; the lowest of them were fringed underneath with a band of fire which grew brighter and sharper every moment. To the south again, a tangle of feathery, soft-looking clouds was beginning to light up with a thousand indeterminate colours. It was a typical Lombard sky, so nobly fair in fair weather, so magnificent, so peaceful. If Renzo had been at leisure, he would certainly have gazed at the heavens and admired the sunrise, so different from daybreak as he had often seen it among the mountains. But he was thinking about his journey, and strode out briskly, both to warm himself and to reach the river quickly. He crossed the fields and the heath, and went through the scrub-land and the wood, looking freely round him and smiling ruefully at the memory of fright the place had given him a few hours before.

Standing on the top of the bank, he looked down through the undergrowth, and saw a small fishing boat come slowly upstream, keeping close to the shore. He climbed quickly down, straight through the blackthorn scrub, and called out softly to the fisherman. He meant to give the impression of asking a trivial favour, but unconsciously adopted something of an imploring manner as he waved the man in to the shore. The fisherman glanced along the bank, looked long and carefully over the waters upstream, turned and gazed over the waters downstream, and finally steered towards Renzo and ran the craft ashore. Renzo had been standing on the very edge of the water, almost in it, in fact. He grabbed the bow of the boat, vaulted on board, and said: 'Please take me over the other side; I'll pay you, of course.'

The fisherman had guessed what he wanted, and was already

turning in that direction. Renzo noticed another oar lying in the bottom of the boat, and bent down to pick it up.

'Steady there, now!' said the owner; but then he noticed how skilfully the young man was handling the oar as he prepared to make use of it, and added: 'Aha! You know the trade, I see!'

'I do know something about it,' replied Renzo; and he began to row with a vigour and dexterity that showed he was no mere amateur. Without interrupting his efforts, he kept glancing distastefully at the bank behind, and impatiently at the bank in front, irritated to find that it was impossible to go straight across. The current was too strong for them to take the shortest way, and the boat had to take a diagonal route, cutting across the stream but also carried down by it.

In any serious scrape, it often happens that difficulties present themselves wholesale in the early stages, and later on continue to crop up in retail quantities. Now that Renzo had virtually crossed the Adda, he began to worry about the question whether it really did constitute the frontier at that point, thinking that even with that obstacle behind him there might be more to come. So he called over to the fisherman, nodded towards the whitish patch on the hill which he had noticed the night before, and said: 'Is that place Bergamo?'

'That is the city of Bergamo,' said the fisherman.

'And does the shore over there come under Bergamo too?'

'It comes under St Mark.'[2]

'Why, long live St Mark, then!' cried Renzo. The fisherman made no reply.

Finally they reached the other bank, and Renzo jumped out. He thanked God silently and then thanked the boatman out-loud. He put his hand in his pocket, and pulled out a *berlinga*, which was quite a sum of money to part with in the circumstances, and held it out to the good fellow, who looked over towards the Milanese shore, glanced up and down the river, took the money, and put it away. Then he pursed his lips, put his finger to them with a significant glance and said 'I wish you a good journey,' as he turned away.

2. The patron saint of Venice, which then controlled Bergamo. – Translator's note.

As the reader may be rather surprised by the promptitude, discretion and courtesy shown by the fisherman to a complete stranger, perhaps we should mention that he had often been asked to perform the same service for smugglers and bandits, and was quite used to it. His interest was not so much in the small and uncertain profit that he derived from it, as in the desire not to make enemies among people of that sort. He would always oblige in this way, if he was sure that there were no excisemen, policemen or military patrols watching him. He had no more affection for the first set of people than for the second; his object was to give satisfaction to both sides, with the impartiality which is commonly achieved by those who have to deal with one class of fellow-creatures, and account for their actions to another.

Renzo stood on the bank for a few moments, looking across at the other side of the river. How his feet had itched, an hour earlier, to leave that shore!

'Well, I've got clear away from all that!' was his first thought. 'It's good to see the last of a country with a curse on it like that one!' was the next – his farewell to the land of his birth. But the third thing to come into his mind was the memory of those he had left behind in that territory. He crossed his arms over his chest and sighed deeply; and then he looked down at the stream flowing past his feet, and thought 'Every drop of that water has passed under the bridge!' (In his village the word 'bridge' always meant the bridge at Lecco.) 'What a swine of a world it is! But no more of that; God's will be done.'

He turned his back on that melancholy sight and set off, taking the whitish patch on the hillside for his guide until he met someone who could tell him the right way to his destination. It was a pleasure to see with what an easy manner he addressed his fellow-travellers now, and how frankly he mentioned the name of the village where his cousin lived.

He still had nine miles to go, according to the first man he consulted. It was not a pleasant journey. Apart from the distress that Renzo carried with him in his own heart, painful sights continually caught his eye, which made it clear that he would find the same conditions of famine here as he had left behind him in his own land. All along the road, and still more in the villages and hamlets, there were people begging who were clearly not beggars by profession. Their destitution showed more in their faces than in their dress; there were peasants, hillmen, artisans, whole families, in a constant, low chorus of appeals, complaints and whimpering. Renzo not only felt compassion for them, and sorrow at their plight, but also began to worry about his own prospects.

'Shall I ever get anything worth while to do myself?' he thought. 'Is there plenty of work here, like there used to be in years gone by? – Never mind about that: Bortolo liked me well enough, and he's a good fellow, who's put plenty of money in his pocket, and has asked me to go to him time and again. He won't let me down. And after all, Providence has helped me up to now, and will help me again.'

Renzo had been hungry for some time, and was growing hungrier with every mile he walked. When he thought about it, he felt that he could manage to keep going for the two or three miles that still lay before him, without too much difficulty. But then he thought, on the other hand, that it would be a pity to present himself before his cousin in the guise of a beggar, and have no better first words of greeting for him than 'Give me some food!' He extracted all his capital from his pocket, laid it out on the palm of his hand, and totalled it up. It was not a sum that demanded much in the way of mathematics, but there was quite enough to pay for a modest meal. So he went into an inn for a little refreshment, and in fact he still had a few coins left after he had paid his bill.

As he came out, he saw two women sitting, or rather half-lying on the ground, so near to the door of the inn that he almost tripped over them. One of them was elderly; the other, still young, held a baby in her arms, which had sucked first one breast and then the other without success, and was weeping bitterly. All three were as pale as death. Standing beside them was a man, whose face and limbs still showed traces of great former strength, broken now and almost annihilated by long privation. Seeing a man walk past with bold step and refreshed appearance, all three held out their hands. They said nothing, for what could words add to their mute entreaty?

'Heaven sends you this today!' said Renzo, putting his hand in his pocket. He took out the few coins that remained in it, pressed them into the nearest hand, and walked on.

He was greatly comforted both by the meal and by the good deed (for we are made up of body and soul), and his spirits rose. The act of getting rid of his last few coins had given him more fresh confidence in the future than he could have derived from finding ten times the same sum.

For if Providence had set apart, as a reserve for the sustenance of those poor creatures perishing by the wayside, the last few pence of a foreigner, a fugitive, a man who also did not know how he would be able to support himself – why, then, how could Providence abandon the man who had given those pence away, the man whom it had filled with so lively, effective and resolute a sense of its own quality? Some such thought passed through the young man's mind, though he expressed it to himself with even less clarity than I have done. He devoted the rest of the journey to thoughts of his own affairs, and the clouds began to roll away. The famine could not go on for ever, for every year brings its own harvest with it; and meanwhile Renzo had his cousin Bortolo and his own talents to keep him going. He also had a little money at home, which he could send for at once. In this way he could at least carry on day by day until the times of plenty returned.

And once the times of plenty return, thought Renzo, letting his imagination spread its wings, there'll be work and to spare. The bosses will be fighting among themselves to take on Milanese craftsmen, who are the ones that know the trade the best. Then the Milanese craftsmen will find out what they're worth. Anyone who wants the best workers will have to pay for them. I'll be able to earn more than enough for one person, and be able to save a little, and then I'll get a letter written to the women and tell them to come ... but after all, why wait as long as that? Wouldn't we have got through the winter together somehow in Lecco, with the little bit we've got put on one side? We'll get through the winter here in just the same way. And you can always find a priest wherever you go. Lucia and her mother, bless them, can come here at once, and we'll set up house together. It'll be a fine thing when the three of us can come out for a drive along this very road; we'll take a cart down to the Adda one afternoon and have a picnic there, right on the bank. I'll show the two of them where I stood on the other side looking around for a boat, where I climbed down that thorny bit of bank, and where the fisherman picked me up.

He reached his cousin's village. As he arrived – in fact just before he came to the first houses – he noticed a very tall building, with several rows of long windows, which could only be a spinning-mill. He went straight in, and, speaking loudly above the splash of water and the hum of wheels, he asked if there were anyone there of the name of Bortolo Castagneri.

'Signor Bortolo? Yes, there he is.'

' "*Signor* Bortolo?" That sounds good!' thought Renzo. He saw his cousin, and ran up to him. Bortolo turned and recognised Renzo, who said 'Well, here I am!' There was a cry of surprise, and then Bortolo held out his arms to him and the cousins embraced each other warmly. After the first greetings were over, Bortolo took Renzo into a smaller room, away from curious eyes and out of the sound of the machinery, and said: 'Well, I'm very pleased to see you; but you're a funny lad all the same. I asked you to come here so many times, and you never would; and now you've arrived at rather an awkward moment.'

'As a matter of fact, I hadn't much choice,' said Renzo, and he went on to tell his cousin, briefly but feelingly, the whole lamentable story.

'That's a different matter altogether,' said Bortolo. 'Poor Renzo! Well, you've counted on me, and I won't let you down. To tell you the truth, no one's looking for extra hands at the moment; it's more a matter of trying to keep on the ones you've got, to hold your business together. But the boss here thinks a lot of me, and he's not at all badly off. And I can honestly say that he owes a lot of it to me. He provides the capital, and I provide my skill, such as it is. I'm the foreman, you know, and to tell you the truth I'm the general factotum as well ... Poor Lucia Mondella! I remember her as if it were yesterday. What a good girl she was! In church she was always the best behaved of the lot, and when you passed her cottage you could hear ... why, I can see that cottage now, just outside the village; there was a fine fig tree there with its branches spreading over the wall...'

'Ah, don't let's talk about it now,' said Renzo.

'I was only going to say, whenever you went by that cottage, you could hear her spinning-wheel turning and turning and turning ... Don Rodrigo was a bit that way inclined even in my day, but now he seems to be carrying on like a proper swine, from what you tell me. Heaven'll give him so much rope, and then ... Well, as I was saying, people are a bit short of food here too. By the way, how long is it since you had a meal?'

'I had something just now, on the way here.'

'And how are you off for money?'

Renzo shook his head sadly.

'It doesn't matter,' said Bortolo. 'I've got some. Don't worry about making use of it; for if God wills it won't be long before things change, and you'll pay me back and have plenty over for yourself.'

'I've got a little money at home, and I'll send for that.'

'Good. Meanwhile you can rely on me. God has been kind to me so that I can be kind to others; and it would be a funny thing if I didn't start with my relations and friends.'

'I knew I was right to trust in Heaven!' cried Renzo, affectionately grasping his good cousin's hand.

'So there must have been quite a disturbance in Milan,' said Bortolo. 'I think the people down there must be a bit touched. Of course, we'd heard something about it, even here; but I'd like you to tell me the details ... Well, we've plenty to talk about! It's different here, as you can see. A bit less noise and a bit more sense. The city has bought two thousand loads of corn from a trader down in Venice. It comes from Turkey, as a matter of fact; but when it's a question of eating or going hungry you can't be too particular about details. Then what do you think happened? The authorities at Verona and Brescia closed the roads, and said "We won't let any corn through here!" But the citizens of Bergamo are no fools. They sent a lawyer called Lorenzo Torre to Venice, and he really is a lawyer too! He left at once and hurried down to see the Doge. "Whatever are those gentlemen in Verona and Brescia thinking of?" he said, and ... and ... Oh, it was a wonderful speech, a speech worth putting in a printed book, so people say. It's worth something to have a good talker on your side. The next thing was an order that the corn must go through; and the authorities in those two towns not only had to let it go, but to provide an escort as well. So now the corn's on the way. And they didn't forget the country districts, either. Giovanbattista Biava, who's the representative of Bergamo in Venice, and is another of these clever fellows, got it into the heads of the senators that people were hungry in the country too, and the senate released four thousand bushels of millet. It all helps to make more bread. And if the bread does run out, we'll be able to afford something a bit better instead; heaven has been generous to me, as I said before. Now I'll take you in to see the boss. I've told him about you lots of times, and he'll give you a good reception. He's a fine, old-fashioned citizen of Bergamo, a generous-hearted fellow. Of course, he wasn't expecting you at this particular moment, but once he's heard your story ... and then he puts a proper value on good workmen; he realizes that famines come and go, but business goes on for ever. But first of all, I must warn you about one thing. Do you know the name the people here have for us folk who come from the territory of Milan?'

'No, what is it?'

'They call us cloth-heads.'

'That's not very pleasant.'

'Well, there it is. Anyone who was born in the Duchy of Milan and wants to live here has to put up with it. Calling a Milanese 'cloth-head', for these people, is just like calling a nobleman 'your Honour'.

'It sounds to me as if they say it to those of us who'll let them say it.'

'My dear Renzo, if you can't make up your mind to lump it and like it, you might as well give up the idea of living here.

You'd have to have your knife in your hand all the time otherwise. And even suppose you kill the first three or four fellows you fight, sooner or later one will come along and kill you. There's not much point in appearing before the judgement seat of heaven with three or four murders on your head!'

'But what about a Milanese who has something up here?' asked Renzo, tapping his forehead with the same gesture that he had used in the tavern of the Full Moon. 'Someone who knows his job really well, I mean?'

'It doesn't make any difference. He's a cloth-head too. Do you know what the boss says about me, when he's talking to his friends? "As far as my business is concerned," he says, "that cloth-head has been a blessing sent from heaven." And then again he'll say: "If it wasn't for that cloth-head, I'd really be in trouble." It's just habit, you see.'

'Well, it's a stupid habit then. When you think what we know about the trade – and after all we introduced it into Bergamo and we keep it going here – how can it be that they haven't stopped calling us that by now?'

'They haven't, anyway – not yet. Maybe they will one day. The boys who're growing up now may be different, but there's no hope as far as the men of our age are concerned. They've got this bad habit, and they'll never be rid of it. What does it matter, after all? You can't compare it with the treatment you had from our beloved fellow-countrymen in Milan – let alone all the other things that they were planning to do to you.'

'That's true enough. As long as there's nothing else of the same sort . . .'

'No, once you've got that one thing into your head, everything else will be all right. Come along and see the boss, and don't be down-hearted.'

In fact everything went off very well, exactly as Bortolo had said it would; so that there is no point in going into the details. And this was really providential; for we shall see very shortly how much use the money and the property he had left at home were going to be to Renzo.

Chapter 18

On that very same day, which was the 13th of November, a special messenger reached his worship the mayor of Lecco, and handed him a despatch from the captain of police, containing instructions to make all possible and appropriate inquiries to discover whether a certain young man named Lorenzo Tramaglino, a silk-spinner by trade, who had escaped from the forces of the *aforesaid most noble lord captain*,[1] had yet returned, *whether openly or in secret*, to his village, the exact situation of which was *unknown for the present, but was certainly in the territory of Lecco, and if in fact he was found to have returned to that place*, his worship the mayor was to make every effort, *with all possible diligence*, to seize his person: then he was to be placed under suitable restraint, viz. with good heavy manacles, seeing how unsatisfactory wristlets had proved in the present case, and was to be escorted to the gaol, and kept there under heavy guard, to be handed over later to the forces that would be despatched to collect him. And whether he could be found or not, '*you shall proceed to the house of the said Laurentius Tramalinus, and there with all due diligence seize whatever may be found that has a bearing on the matter in hand, and assemble evidence of his evil character, wicked conduct, and of his accomplices; and you shall also fully and diligently report all that is said or done, all that is found or left undiscovered, all that is seized or left untouched.*'

His worship the mayor began by making as sure as he could that Renzo had not, in fact returned to his village. Then the headman was summoned, and ordered to lead the mayor, who was accompanied by a large escort of police and by a notary, to the house in question. The house was locked up, and if anyone had the keys he kept quiet about it. So they broke in, and used

1. The phrases in italics on this page are in flowery official Latin in the original. – Translator's note.

all due diligence – the diligence generally used in a city taken by storm.

The story of the operation was all over the district in no time. It came to Father Cristoforo's ears, and he was astonished no less than grieved by the news. He asked everyone if they knew of any possible explanation for this unexpected development, but got only vague conjectures in reply. So he wrote off at once to Father Bonaventura, hoping to get some more definite information from him.

Meanwhile Renzo's relations and friends were summoned and asked to state all that they knew about his *evil character*. To bear the name of Tramaglino became a misfortune, a disgrace, a crime. The village was turned upside down. Gradually word got around that Renzo had escaped from the hands of the police right in the middle of Milan, and had then vanished. Some said that Renzo had done something really serious, but no one knew what – there were dozens of different versions. The worse the stories were, the less they were believed in the village, where Renzo was known to be a decent young fellow. Most people had the same idea, which was freely whispered around – namely, that the whole thing was a put-up job, instigated by Don Rodrigo to ruin his poor young rival . . . For inductive reasoning, unsupported by proper knowledge of the facts, can sometimes lead us to do grave injustice even to the blackest-hearted villains.

But we ourselves, who are in full possession of the facts, can state that Don Rodrigo had had no part in Renzo's misfortune, but that he was none the less just as pleased as if it had been all his own work, and that he exulted over it to his intimates – especially Count Attilio. The count would have been back in Milan by now, if he had kept to his original plan; but when he heard about the riots, and the scum of the earth roaming the streets of the city, apparently taking up an attitude quite different from their proper one of bending over to be kicked, he thought it would be better to stay in the country until things had quietened down. Indeed he had insulted so many people in his time, that he had some reason to fear that one or other of those who in the past had been too weak to do anything in

334

return might now take courage from the changed circumstances, and think that the right moment had come to avenge himself and his fellows. But the delay was not a long one. The arrival from Milan of the order detailing the action to be taken against Renzo was in itself an indication that things were back to normal, and definite news to the same effect arrived almost at once. Count Attilio set off immediately, urging his cousin to persist in his enterprise and go on to victory; and at the same time promising that he, for his part, would get on with arranging for the removal of the friar. For this purpose the accident which had so fortunately befallen Don Rodrigo's wretched rival would be extraordinarily useful.

As soon as Attilio had gone, Griso appeared, having got back safely from Monza, and reported to his master all the news that he had been able to gather. Lucia had taken refuge in such and such a convent, under the protection of such and such a noble lady, and was being kept permanently out of sight as if she were a nun herself. She never set foot outside the convent, and when she went to a service she sat behind a window with a grating over it. This, said Griso, annoyed a lot of people, who had heard some vague account of her adventures, had gathered that she was beautiful, and therefore wanted to have a look at her.

This report caused the devil to enter Don Rodrigo's heart, or rather instilled fresh wickedness into the devil that had long made it his home. All the circumstances that had favoured his plans had been so much extra fuel to his passion; that is to say, to the mixture of vanity, ill-temper and capricious lust which went by the name of passion with him. First of all Renzo had been removed from the scene – exiled and outlawed, so that anything done against him could be considered legitimate, and even his fiancée might to some extent be regarded as fair game. Secondly the only man in the world who was willing and able to take his side, and to create a stir about the matter which might attract the attention of far-off and influential circles – that furious Capuchin friar – would also soon probably be in no position to work any mischief. But now a new obstacle had arisen, which not merely outweighed those advantages, but annihilated them. Even if there had been no princely Signora in

335

the case, the convent at Monza would have been too hard a nut for Don Rodrigo's teeth to crack. His imagination hovered round that fortress, but could find no way of conquering it, either by force or by trickery.

He very nearly gave up the whole idea. He was on the point of making up his mind to go off to Milan, with a small detour so that he would not even have to pass through Monza. In Milan, he thought, I'll see all my friends and have a good time; more cheerful thoughts will soon chase away this single thought which has become nothing but a torment ... My friends, eh? ... I mustn't be in too much of a hurry there. Their company might be a fresh embarrassment rather than a comforting distraction. Attilio will never have kept his mouth shut; they'll all be waiting for me, wanting news of my high-land beauty, and I must have some answer for them. I wanted something; I tried to get it; and what was the outcome? I took something on – not a very creditable business, perhaps, but then a man can't always regulate his fancies, his whims – the import-ant thing is to be able to satisfy them – and what did I achieve? Defeat at the hands of a yokel and a friar!

I can imagine my friends talking about it, Don Rodrigo con-tinued to himself. 'The next thing that happened', they'll say, 'was that, without the poor half-wit having to do anything about it himself, the yokel was removed by a piece of pure luck, and the friar was removed through the good offices of an intelligent friend. And even then the poor half-wit wasn't cap-able of taking advantage of the situation! He chose that mo-ment to admit defeat, and retire with his tail between his legs.'

Why, he thought, I'd have to choose between hiding myself from all decent society, and having my sword in my hand every other minute. And then what about coming back here to this estate, in this district – what about staying here, for the matter of that? Apart from the fact that everything here would remind me of my passion for that girl all the time, I'd have the mark of failure on my forehead. And people would begin to hate me more and fear me less at the same time. I'd be reading an expression on every villain's face, even as he made his bow to

336

me, that said 'You've had a bitter pill to swallow, and I'm not sorry about it.'

Our manuscript remarks here that the road of iniquity is indeed wide, but that does not mean that it is a comfortable road to travel; it has its stumbling blocks and its difficult stretches; it is a painful road and a tiring one, although it goes downhill.

Now Don Rodrigo did not want to leave that road, nor to go back along it, nor to stand still; and he could not go forward along it by himself. A possible method of advance did occur to him; which was to ask the help of a certain person whose hands seemed able to reach out into places that were impenetrable even to the eyes of his fellow men – a man or devil who often seemed to regard the extraordinary difficulty of an enterprise as a sufficient reason for undertaking it. But this course also had its disadvantages and its dangers, which were all the more serious because they could not be calculated in advance. For no one could be sure how far or where he would go, once he set out in that man's company. He was a powerful helper, undoubtedly, but he was also a domineering and dangerous leader.

These thoughts kept Don Rodrigo uncertainly poised between two highly unpalatable decisions for several days. Meanwhile a letter arrived from Count Attilio, saying that the plot was now well under way. The lightning was quickly followed by the thunder; in other words, news arrived one morning that Father Cristoforo had left the monastery at Pescarenico. The thought of this quick success, and the memory of Attilio's letter, which imparted much encouragement and threatened much mockery, made Don Rodrigo incline more and more towards taking the plunge. What finally decided him was the unexpected news that Agnese had returned to her home in the village; which meant one obstacle the fewer between Lucia and the outer world. But we must explain these two events, beginning with the second one.

The two poor women had hardly settled down in their refuge, when the news of the troubles in Milan spread through Monza, and consequently into the nunnery. The general news of the main event was followed by an unending series of detailed items, which were exaggerated and modified as they passed from one person to another. The portress, whose quarters gave her a chance to hear what was said both in the street and inside the convent, gathered news from both sides and passed it on to her guests. 'They've put a lot of people in prison – some say two, some six, some eight, some four, some seven – and they're going to hang them, half of them in front of the Bakery of the Crutches, and the other half at the end of the road where the commissioner's house is ... And listen to this! One of them got away, and he comes from Lecco, or somewhere near there. I haven't got his name yet, but someone'll tell me; and then we can see if it's anyone you know.'

Hearing this, and remembering that Renzo had just arrived in Milan on the fatal day, the two women began to worry a little – especially Lucia. But imagine what she felt when the portress came back and said: 'That fellow who ran away to escape the gallows was from your district. He was a silk-spinner, by the name of Tramaglino. Have you ever heard of him?'

Lucia was sitting embroidering something; the work fell out of her hand, she went pale, her face changed completely, and the portress would certainly have noticed if she had been standing near her. But she was at the door, standing and talking to Agnese, who was also upset, though less so than Lucia, so that she was able to master her feelings. By way of reply she told the portress that in a small place like that everyone knows everyone else, and so she did know him. She added that she could not think how anything of the kind could have happened, since he was a very steady young fellow. Then she asked if he had got right away, and, if so, where he had gone.

'They all say he's got away, but no one knows where to. Maybe they'll catch him again, maybe he's reached safety. But if they get him back into their clutches, your steady young fellow ...'

At this point the portress was fortunately called away, leaving Agnese and her daughter in a state that can be imagined. For several days the poor woman and her sorrowing daughter remained in the same state of uncertainty, silently going over the portress's terrible words in their minds, or discussing them in whispers when they had an opportunity; and going over and over the questions how and why such an appalling thing could have happened and what its consequences might be.

Finally, on Thursday, a man came to the convent and asked for Agnese. He was a fishmonger from Pescarenico, who regularly went down to Milan to sell his wares. Father Cristoforo had asked him to stop at the convent as he passed through Monza, and give Agnese and Lucia a message. The good father sent them his best wishes, and what information he had about Renzo's misfortune, and urged them to have patience and trust in God. He told them that they could rely on their poor friar not to forget them, and to be always on the watch for an opportunity to help them; and that meanwhile he would send what news he could every week by the same hand or by some other means. The messenger had no fresh news about Renzo, no definite information, except the story of the official visit to his house, and the general search for him in the neighbourhood – but he did say that the search had been a failure, and that it was quite certain that Renzo had got safely away to Bergamo. This certainty was of course a great comfort to Lucia. From then on, her tears flowed more gently and easily, and she derived more consolation from her private talks with her mother, while her prayers began to contain an element of thanksgiving.

Gertrude often called her aside into a private parlour, and sometimes kept her there for a long time, taking pleasure in the poor girl's ingenuous sweetness of character, and also in having grateful blessings called down on her own head. She even told Lucia part of her own story – the more creditable part. She explained what misery she had had to suffer on the way to the place in which she was now so miserable; and Lucia's first suspicious astonishment at the Signora's ways began to change into compassion. The story seemed to her to explain quite adequately the oddities in her benefactress's manner – especially in the light of her mother's theory that all the gentry were a bit touched.

Lucia would have liked to return confidence for confidence; but she never even thought of telling Gertrude about her most recent cause for concern, her newest misfortune – that is, of

339

saying what she knew about the fugitive silk-spinner. For she did not want to give wider currency to so painful and scandalous a tale. To the best of her ability, she also evaded Gertrude's curious questions about the period that had led up to her engagement. But this time mere prudence was not the reason for her silence. That part of her story seemed to the poor innocent girl to be a thornier subject, a more difficult tale to tell, than anything she had heard or expected to hear from the Signora. Gertrude's story was one of tyranny, deceit and suffering, which were ugly and dismal things enough, but still things you could talk about. But running through her own story was a theme, a feeling, a word, which she felt she could never utter when speaking of herself, a word for which she could find no substitute that did not sound immodest in her own ears – the word 'love'.

Once or twice Gertrude almost took umbrage at Lucia's defensiveness – but the girl's affection and respect for the Signora, her gratitude and her trust were clear for all to see. Lucia's delicate, easily disturbed modesty occasionally irritated Gertrude even more for a somewhat different reason; but these feelings were dispelled by the sweetness of another thought that came to her every time she looked at Lucia: 'This is someone I can really help.' And that thought was a true one, for Lucia, besides owing her place of refuge to Gertrude, was greatly comforted by these conversations, and by the Signora's demonstrations of affection. She found another comfort in keeping her hands always busy, and often asked for more to do. Even when she went to the parlour, she always took some work with her, to keep her fingers moving. But painful thoughts will creep in through every gap! As she sat continually sewing and sewing, which was an unusual occupation for her, her thoughts kept wandering off to her familiar spinning-wheel, and then from the spinning-wheel to many other things . . .

The following Thursday a messenger appeared again – I am not sure whether it was the fishmonger or someone else – with more greetings from Father Cristoforo, and confirmation that Renzo had really escaped. There was no more definite news about his original misfortune. Father Cristoforo had hoped to hear something from his colleague in Milan, to whom he had recommended Renzo; but Father Bonaventura had written back to say that he had never received the letter nor seen its bearer. Someone from the country, he said, had come to see him while he was out, but had gone away and not come back.

On the third Thursday, no one came at all. For the poor women this meant not only the loss of the comforting message they had so hoped and longed for, but a new source of worry, a new ground for countless unpleasant conjectures – for almost any little thing will produce this effect on people who are already in difficulty and distress. Even before this, Agnese had been thinking of paying her cottage a brief visit, and the non-appearance of the expected messenger helped her to make up her mind. Lucia would rather have remained under her mother's wing; but her reluctance to be left was overcome by her impatience for news, and by the feeling of security inspired by that strong and holy place of refuge. So it was decided between the two of them that the following day Agnese would go and wait by the road-side for the fishmonger, who would have to pass that way on his return journey from Milan, and would ask him if he could give her a lift back into the hill-country on his cart.

When she saw the man, she asked him whether he had any message for her from Father Cristoforo; but he had been out fishing the whole day before his departure from home, and had had no communication from the good father. Agnese did not have to ask twice for her lift. She ran in and said good-bye to the Signora and to Lucia, not without a tear, promised to send them some news straight away and to be back soon, and drove off.

Nothing special happened on the way. They spent part of the night at an inn, as was usual on that journey, they left before dawn, and reached Pescarenico early in the morning. Agnese got down at the square by the monastery, and sped her helper on his way with many thanks and blessings. Now that she was there she decided to see the good father, who had done so much for her, before she went home. She rang the bell, and the door was opened by Brother Galdino, whom we have met before, when he was collecting nuts.

'Why, my dear madam, what brings you here today?'

'I've come to see Father Cristoforo.'

'Father Cristoforo? He's not here.'

'Oh ... Will it be long before he comes back?'

'What do you mean?' said the friar, raising his shoulders and withdrawing his shaven head into the shadow of his hood.

'Well ... where's he gone, then?'

'He's gone to Rimini.'

'Where was that, again?'

'Rimini.'

'Where's that then?'

'We-ell!' said the friar, sawing his outstretched hand up and down in the air, to indicate a vast distance.

'Heaven help us! Why did he go off so suddenly, like that?'

'Because the Provincial decided to send him there.'

'Why ever should he do that? Father Cristoforo was doing so much good here! Heavens above!'

'If our superiors had to explain the orders they give us, what would become of our discipline and our vows of obedience, madam?'

'Yes, I know, but this'll be the ruin of me.'

'You know what it probably is? Probably they wanted a good preacher at Rimini; we've got good preachers everywhere, of course, but sometimes a particular man is needed for a particular post. The Provincial down there wrote to our Provincial up here, and said "I want a man with this quality and that quality and so on"; and then our Provincial probably said: "Why, that means Father Cristoforo!" It must have been something like that; you can see for yourself.'

'God have pity on us! And when did he leave?'

'The day before yesterday.'

'Just as I thought! I knew I should have come here a couple of days ago! But don't you know when he might be back again? Just roughly, I mean?'

'Why, madam, no one can say except the Provincial – if he knows himself. Once one of our preaching fathers has taken wing, it's very hard to say where he'll finish up. They're in demand everywhere, you know; and we've got monasteries all over the world. Now suppose that when Father Cristoforo gets to Rimini, he makes a great stir with his Lenten sermons – for he doesn't always just preach whatever comes into his head, the way he does here, with only fishermen and peasants to hear him. In the pulpit of a city church he'll bring out his great written sermons, which are the finest thing you'd ever hear. Then word'll spread of the great preacher that's arisen in those parts, and perhaps he'll be sent for to go to ... to go to ... why, it might be to go anywhere. And then they'll have to let him go; for we friars live off the charity of the whole world, and so it's only fair that we should serve the whole world too.'

'Heavens above!' cried Agnese again, almost weeping, 'what am I going to do without that man? He was like a real father to us folk! It'll be the ruin of us!'

'Listen, madam; Father Cristoforo was a very fine man, as you say, but there are others like him in this place, you know. Men full of charity, full of the gifts of God, men who know enough to treat the gentry and the poor folk on the same footing. Won't you speak to Father Atanasio, now; or Father Girolamo; or Father Zaccaria? He's a worthy man, is Father Zaccaria; and you needn't be like some ignorant folk, who take heed of the fact that he doesn't look very grand, and has a cracked voice, and a miserable little bit of a beard. He may not be much of a preacher, for we're all sent here to do different things, but he's just the man to give you good advice, you know.'

'For heaven's sake!' exclaimed Agnese, with that mixture of gratitude and impatience with which we greet a display of good will which is not very helpful to us, 'what does it matter to me whether the other fathers are fine fellows or not, when I've lost that poor man who knew all about our affairs, and had made all his plans to help us?'

'Why, then you must have patience.'

'I know that,' said Agnese, 'and I'm sorry to have troubled you.'

'It's no trouble, madam, and I'm only sorry for your misfortune. And if you do decide to consult one of the good fathers here, the monastery will still be there when you come back.

343

And by the way, I shall be seeing you again soon, when the time comes for the collection of olive oil.'

'Good-bye, then,' said Agnese, and went off towards her village, as miserable, confused and disconcerted as a blind man who has lost his stick.

Since we are a little better informed than Fra Galdino, we are in a position to say what had really happened. When Attilio reached Milan, he kept his promise to Don Rodrigo, and went straight to see their common uncle, the member of the Privy Council. (This was a committee of thirteen members, drawn from the military and legal professions, who advised the Governor, and might also assume his functions temporarily in the event of his death or sudden replacement.) Attilio's uncle was a lawyer, and one of the senior members of the Council. He had a certain standing among his fellow-members; but where he really excelled was in making his position felt and respected wherever he went. Ambiguous utterances, significant silences, non-committal remarks, a way of closing his eyes which meant 'I can't comment on that', a way of flattering hopes without involving himself in a promise, a certain menacing formality : such were some of the means he used towards that end, and all of them met with fair success. When he uttered the words 'There's nothing I can do in this case', which might well be perfectly true, he would say them in such a way that no one would believe him, and his words would increase the general opinion of his power, and thus also increase his power in reality – just as we sometimes see boxes in a pharmacy, with certain words written on them in Arabic; they have nothing inside them, but they help to maintain the reputation of the shop.

The old count's reputation had been advancing steadily, by very slow stages, for a long time. More recently it had taken a sudden giant's stride forward, thanks to a most unusual opportunity. He had been sent to Madrid on a special mission to the Court, and his reception there had been of a kind which could be worthily described only by himself. We need only say that the Count–Duke had treated him with the most extraordinary condescension and admitted him to his fullest confidence; so much so that he had once asked him, in the hearing of half the court, how he liked Madrid, and had remarked to him on another occasion, privately, as they stood looking out of a window, that the cathedral of Milan was the largest in His Majesty's domains.

Having paid his respects to his uncle, and transmitted those of Don Rodrigo to him, Attilio put on a serious expression, which he knew very well how to adopt on occasion.

'I feel it my duty, sir,' he began, 'to warn you of a certain matter – though I would not wish to break any confidences of my cousin Rodrigo. It's an affair which could take a serious turn, without your help, and have consequences which . . .'

'He's been up to his usual games, I suppose.'

'To be fair, I must say that the fault is not on his side. But he's very angry about it; and as I said, sir, there's no one but yourself who is really in a position . . .'

'That remains to be seen.'

'There's a Capuchin friar in the district who's got a grudge against Rodrigo; and the thing has reached the point that . . .'

'How many times have I told you, both of you, to let those friars stew in their own juice? God knows they give enough trouble to those of us who have to . . . whose job it is to . . .' He puffed out his cheeks. 'But you people who are in a position to keep clear of them . . .'

'Well, sir, in the present case I must in fairness say that Rodrigo would have kept clear of this friar, if he could. But the friar's got a grudge against him, and has started provoking him in every possible way.'

'But what the devil has this friar of yours to do with my nephew?'

'Well, he's a tiresome, restless fellow; well known for it locally in fact. He makes it his business to be at loggerheads with anyone of noble blood. And then there's a peasant girl down there that he's taken under his wing, or under his direction – I don't know how to put it exactly, but he seems to have a feeling of charity towards her which is . . . well, I won't say there's anything wrong about it, but it makes him very jealous and suspicious and touchy about her.'

'I know what you mean,' said his uncle. The old count's face had originally been designed by nature as the portrait of a dunce; various later hands had painted over that image and inserted the features of a politician, and now it was illuminated by a flash of sly cunning, which made a most memorable picture.

'Now for some time past', continued Attilio, 'the friar has got it into his head that Rodrigo has some sort of designs on this girl ...'

'Got it into his head, has he? Got it into his head, eh? I know your cousin Don Rodrigo as well as you do, and it'll take more than your testimony, sir, to clear him in a case of that sort.'

'My dear uncle, I'm quite ready to believe that Rodrigo may have had a joke of some sort with the young woman, when he met her in the road. He's still young, and he's not a Capuchin, after all. But that's all nonsense, and I wouldn't bother you with it, sir; the serious part of the thing is that this friar has started talking about Rodrigo as if he were a common blackguard. He's trying to rouse the whole countryside against him.'

'What about the other friars?'

'They're keeping out of it, because they know he's a reckless fellow; and also they've the utmost respect for Rodrigo. But that friar is very highly regarded by the peasants, because he poses as a saint, and ...'

'I hardly think he can be aware that Rodrigo is my nephew.'

'Oh, but he does know it, sir, and that makes him behave worse than ever.'

'What did you say? What was that?'

'The point is – and this is what he says himself – that he takes a special pleasure in crossing Rodrigo because he has a natural protector of great authority like yourself. He says that he can afford to laugh at the politicians and the great ones of the earth, and that the cord of St Francis can hold the power of the sword in check, and ...'

'What a presumptuous brute of a friar! What's his name?'

'Friar Cristoforo of —,' said Attilio. His uncle took a memorandum book out of one of the drawers of his desk, puffed out his cheeks a couple of times, and wrote down that unhappy name. Meanwhile Attilio went on:

'He's always been like that; we know his whole story. He was a man of the people, that got a little money in his pocket and started trying to keep up with the nobles of his district. Then he was furious because some of them wouldn't have it, and he murdered one of them. Finally he took the habit to avoid the gallows.'

'What a delightful fellow! Splendid! We'll see about him, all right!' said the old count, continuing to puff.

'And now', continued Attilio, 'he's more furious than ever, because of the failure of one of his schemes, which was very close to his heart. This will show you the sort of fellow he is, sir. He wanted to marry off this protégée of his; perhaps to save her from the perils of this world, if you see what I mean, or perhaps for some other reason, he was very anxious to see her married. And he'd found a man for her – another protégé of his, whom you may know by name, sir; in fact I'd venture to say you must have heard of him, because I'm quite sure the Privy Council must have been busy with the affairs of this worthy fellow.'

'Who is he, then?'

'A silk-spinner of the name of Lorenzo Tramaglino, the man who . . .'

'Lorenzo Tramaglino!' exclaimed the old count. 'Splendid! The holy father is to be congratulated! Why, yes, now . . . that's right . . . he did have a letter for . . . pity they didn't . . . But never mind all that. But how is it that I never heard anything about all this from your cousin Don Rodrigo? Why has he let things go so far without turning for advice and help to his old uncle, who is able and willing to provide them?'

'I'd better tell you the whole truth about that too,' said Attilio. 'On the one hand, he knew that you, sir, are a very busy man, with countless intricate affairs in your head . . .' (Here the old count puffed again, and put his hand to his head as if to indicate the difficulty he had in keeping everything inside it.) '. . . and he didn't feel he should add to your worries. And then – since I'm telling the whole truth – as far as I can gather

347

he's so furious, so beside himself, so exasperated by the friar's insults, that he's thinking more of taking the law into his own hands, of obtaining summary satisfaction, than of trying to get justice in a regular and proper way with the help of his wise and powerful uncle. I tried to calm him down; but I could see the thing was taking an ugly turn, and I felt it was my duty to report the whole story to you, sir, as the head of our family and the main pillar of our house.'

'You'd have done better still to have told me all this earlier on.'

'You're right, sir, but I kept hoping it would clear up by itself: hoping that the friar would return to his senses, or perhaps leave that particular monastery, as often happens with these friars, who are here one day and gone the next. Then it would all have been over by now. But as it is . . .'

'As it is, I'll have to put things right.'

'That's just what I thought myself, sir. My uncle, I was saying to myself, with his authority and his quick wit, will know how to prevent a scandal and save Rodrigo's honour – which is his own honour too, after all. That friar's always talking about the great powers of the cord of St Francis; but to make proper use of them a man doesn't need to have the cord round his own waist. You must have plenty of strings in your hand that I don't know about; but I do know that the Provincial has a very great regard for you, as is only natural, and if it should strike you that the best thing would be a change of air for the friar, a couple of words . . .'

'Leave the thinking to me, sir; I'm used to it,' said his uncle, somewhat roughly.

'That's true enough!' exclaimed Attilio, with a little shake of his head, and a little smile of compassion for his own folly. 'I'm hardly the one to offer advice to a man like yourself! But it's the great love I have for the honour of the family that made me speak out like that . . . and then again, I'm afraid I may have been guilty of another mistake,' he continued sadly, 'I may have wronged Rodrigo by damaging your opinion of him. I'd never forgive myself if I'd made you think that Rodrigo is in any way lacking in the complete confidence, the submissive respect which he rightly owes to you. Believe me, sir, that this is a case where . . .'

'There's no need for all this talk about your wronging Rodrigo, or Rodrigo wronging you. You'll always be the best of friends – until one or other of you begins to get some sense into his head. You're a couple of reckless young idiots, always up to your tricks, always expecting me to get you out of trouble, you . . . you'll make me say something silly in a minute. The two of you are more nuisance than all these affairs of state . . .' – the reader can imagine what a puff accompanied these words – 'all these affairs of state I have to deal with!'

With yet more apologies, promises of amendment, and compliments, Attilio took his leave and went away, accompanied by the words 'And try to be more sensible in future!' – which was the old count's usual form of farewell to his nephews.

Chapter 19

As you pass by an ill-cultivated piece of land, you may sometimes see a weed – a fine growth of flowering dock, say – and
you may wonder whether the seed from which it sprang was a
product of the same field, or was blown there by the wind, or
carried there by a bird; but you will never know the answer. In
the same way we cannot tell whether it was from the natural
resources of his own brain, or from a seed planted there
by Attilio, that the old count raised the idea of making use of
the Provincial to solve this knotty problem in the best possible
way.

It was certainly no accident that Attilio had uttered those
words. Though he had to reckon with the possibility that so
openly expressed a suggestion would offend the old man's
touchy pride and so arouse his opposition, Attilio had still
thought it best at least to give him an inkling of the possibility
of this line of action, at least a sort of push in the direction he
wished him to take. But in any case the action was so much in
keeping with the old count's natural inclinations, so clearly
indicated by the circumstances, that we would be prepared to
bet that he would have thought of it himself anyway. What
mattered to him was that his nephew, a man of the same name
as himself, should not have the worst of any struggle which
took place – as this one unfortunately must – before the public
eye. That was essential for the maintenance of his reputation as
a man of power, which was so very dear to him. Any satisfaction which his nephew might be able to obtain on his own
would be a cure worse than the disease, a seed-bed of future
troubles. He must put a stop to anything of that sort by no
matter what means, and without any loss of time. He could
order Rodrigo to leave his estates immediately; but Rodrigo
would not obey him; and even if he did so that would be a
retreat, a yielding of ground by the family to the friars.

350

Injunctions, legal actions and the other terrors of the law had no effect against an opponent in that walk of life. The clergy – both ordained priests and lay brothers – were completely outside the jurisdiction of the state, and that applied not only to the persons concerned, but also to the buildings where they lived; as the reader must know, even if he is unlucky enough not to have read any other history besides that contained in the present work. The only possible step that could be taken against an adversary of that kind was to try to have him removed from the scene. The key to this was the Provincial, who had the power to order the friar to stay or to go as he pleased.

The Provincial and the old count had known each other for a very long time. They met infrequently, but always with a show of the warmest friendship, and with exaggerated assurances that each could rely on the other for any service in his power. A man who has many people under him is often easier to deal with than any one of them could be. Each of them only sees his own interest, only feels his own passions, only cares about his own affairs; whereas the man at the top can see a dozen different interrelations, a dozen possible consequences, all in a flash, together with a dozen varying interests, a dozen things to avoid, a dozen things to preserve. For this very reason, he can be manipulated in a dozen different ways.

Having considered everything very carefully, the old count invited the Provincial to dinner one day, and arranged for him to meet a set of fellow-guests who had been selected with extraordinary care and delicacy. There were one or two of the count's relations – men who bore the highest titles, men whose family names were high titles in themselves, and whose manner alone, with their innate self-assurance, their lordly air of contempt, their way of speaking in the most familiar way of the loftiest matters, was enough to impose initially and continually renew, without any conscious effort, the ideas of their superiority and of their power. Then there were certain dependants of the host, linked to the family by hereditary feudal obligations, and to its head by a lifetime of humble service. They began to say 'Yes' as the soup was served, and they went on saying it with their tongues, their eyes, their ears, with their whole heads, their whole bodies and their whole souls, until by the time the fruit arrived you might well have forgotten the sound of the word 'No'.

The guests had not been long at table when the old count introduced the subject of Madrid. There are many roads that lead to Rome, as the saying goes, but all roads led to Madrid for him. He spoke of the court, of the Count–Duke and of the ministers, of the Governor's family; of the bull-fight, of which he could give an excellent description, since he had watched it from a very good seat. He spoke of the Escurial, and here again he could give an account of all its details, since one of the Count–Duke's dependants had shown him round every corner of it. For some time the company, like the audience of a play, gave him all their attention. Then separate conversations sprang up; but he continued to speak on the same fascinating subject, privately now, to the Provincial, who was sitting next to him and let him go on and on with his story.

But the time came when the Provincial gave a little twist to the conversation, steering it away from Madrid, through a series of other courts, past a series of other dignitaries, until he reached Cardinal Barberini, who was the brother of the reigning Pope, Urban VIII, and was also one of his own Order, a Capuchin ... The old count had to let his guest do the talking for a while, and listen to him, and remember that there were after all other people in the world than those who shed lustre on his own name.

When they rose from table, he invited the Provincial to come with him into another room.

Then two powers faced each other, two grey heads, two memories full of long experience. The noble lord offered a chair to the most reverend father, sat down himself, and began to speak :

'In view of our old friendship, I felt I ought to have a word with your Reverence about a matter of common interest, which we ought to be able to clear up between the two of us without recourse to other channels which could so easily ... So I'll tell you quite honestly and frankly what the question is, and I'm sure we can reach agreement in a couple of minutes. Now tell me – isn't there a certain Father Cristoforo of — at your monastery in Pescarenico?'

The Provincial nodded.

'Now tell me something, quite frankly, your Reverence ... this man ... this Father Cristoforo ... I don't know him personally myself, mind you – though I do know quite a number of Capuchin fathers – admirable men, zealous, prudent and humble. I've been a friend of your order since I was a boy ... But in every large family, there's always someone ... someone different ... This Father Cristoforo, now; I know from certain reports that he's a man ... a man who's a bit given to wrangling, who hasn't quite got all the prudence, the restraint that ... I'm sure he must have given your Reverence cause for concern more than once in the past.'

So that's it! A piece of jobbery! thought the Provincial. But it's my own fault. I knew quite well that that fellow Cristoforo was a man who should be kept on the move from one pulpit to another, and never left as much as six months in any one place – especially in country monasteries.

'Oh!' he said aloud. 'I'm sorry to hear that my lord has such an opinion of Father Cristoforo. To the best of my knowledge, he's a friar of exemplary conduct in the cloister, and much respected in the world outside as well.'

'Yes, yes; I quite understand. Your Reverence has to ... But I do think, as a sincere friend, that I should mention one thing, which your Reverence really ought to know ... in fact, even if you know about it already, I think I should still be justified in drawing your attention to certain possible consequences; I only say "possible", mind you, nothing more than that. This Father Cristoforo, now, is known to have extended his protection to a man from those parts ... a man your Reverence will have heard of – the man who so scandalously escaped out of the hands of the police on that terrible St Martin's Day, after committing ... committing ... in a word, Lorenzo Tramaglino!'

Oh dear! – thought the Provincial. 'That', he added aloud, 'is something I had not heard. But my lord is very well aware that one part of our mission consists precisely in searching out lost sheep and bringing them back to ...'

'Yes, yes; of course. But extending protection to lost sheep of that particular kind! These are awkward questions, delicate matters...' Here, instead of blowing out his cheeks and puffing, he pursed his lips and drew in the same quantity of air which he normally expelled in a puff. Then he went on: 'I thought it would be as well to say a couple of words to your Reverence about these events, because if ever His Excellency ... Some steps or other might be taken at Rome ... I don't know these things myself, of course ... and then something might come back to you from there...'

'I am deeply indebted to my lord for telling me this. But I am sure that if we go into the matter, we shall find that Father Cristoforo has had nothing to do with the man you mention, apart from trying to make him see the error of his ways. I know Father Cristoforo.'

'I'm sure you know more than I do about his character before he took the habit, and about the exploits of his youth.'

'But the glory of the habit is this, my lord, that a man who may have made himself notorious in secular life becomes another man when he puts it on. And ever since Father Cristoforo has worn the habit...'

'There's nothing I'd like to believe more – and I say that sincerely. I'd like to believe it. But there's a proverb that sometimes turns out to be true – "The habit does not make the monk." '

The proverb did not fit the case exactly; but the old count had hurriedly brought it out to replace another one which was on the tip of his tongue – something about wolves in sheep's clothing.

'I have examples in this case,' he went on, 'and I have proofs.'

'If you have definite knowledge that this friar has done something wrong (as anyone may fall into error), I would be most grateful for information about it. Though unworthy, I am his superior. It is my task to correct, to find the remedy.'

'Yes ... well, I'll tell you. Apart from this unpleasant business of his openly extending his protection to the man I mentioned, there's another distasteful matter, which could ... But

I'm sure we can settle both things at the same time. The point is that the same Father Cristoforo has got himself at loggerheads with my nephew, Don Rodrigo.'

'Oh dear! I'm sorry to hear that, very sorry indeed.'

'My nephew is young, spirited, conscious of his rank, unused to provocation...'

'It is certainly my duty to investigate the matter thoroughly. As I have already remarked to my lord, whose fair-mindedness, I know, is equal to his knowledge of the world, we are all flesh and blood, all subject to error ... and that is true of both sides in every question. If Father Cristoforo has failed in his duty ...'

'Your Reverence ... as I was saying just now, these are things to be settled here and now, between the two of us, and then forgotten. They're the sort of things that you can make worse by stirring them up. You know what happens. These disputes, these wrangles, often start from the merest triviality; but then they go on, and on, and on ... If you try to get to the bottom of them, either you never reach the end of it, or else a dozen new thorny questions arise as well. Better to nip it in the bud, most reverend father ... yes, yes, nip it in the bud! My nephew's a young man; and the friar, from what I hear, still has all the spirit, all the ... the inclinations of a young man. So it's up to us, who unfortunately aren't quite so young – "unfortunately" 's the word for it, isn't it, most reverend father?'

If there had been a spectator in the room at this moment, he would have felt as if he were watching a grand opera, in the middle of which a back-drop was prematurely hoisted, revealing one of the cast talking normally to a colleague, quite oblivious of the public. As the old count uttered the word 'unfortunately', his face, his gestures and his voice all became completely natural.

There was nothing contrived about it; it was perfectly true that he was sorry to be as old as he was. Not that he hankered after the amusements, the gaiety, the charm of youth – those wretched, stupid frivolities! The cause of his regret was something far more solid and important than that. He hoped to obtain a certain high appointment, when it fell vacant, and he was afraid that he was running out of time ... If he got it, the

355

world could rest assured that he would not mind being old any more, would not want anything else, and would die happy; as everyone who wants something very badly is sure he will do, once he gets his desire.

But we must let the old count finish his speech. 'It's up to us', he continued, 'to show a little sense on behalf of the young, and put things to rights when they have committed some blunder. Luckily there's still time. The thing hasn't made any stir so far; it's still a case for *principiis obsta*[1] – for taking the torch away from the thatch. Sometimes a man who is no good in one place, or causes some trouble there, turns out to be a great success somewhere else. Your Reverence will easily find the right niche for this friar. And we mustn't forget that other matter, which might well cause suspicion to fall on him in circles where ... where they might want him to be moved away from here. Now if you placed him somewhere a fair distance away, two birds could be killed with one stone. Everything would come right of itself; or rather nothing would ever have gone wrong...'

This conclusion was the one that the Provincial had been expecting from the beginning of the old count's speech. Yes, of course, he had been thinking, I can see what you're after. It's the usual story. You people take a dislike to some unfortunate friar, or one of you does; or perhaps he arouses your suspicion somehow; and then straight away, without seeing whether he's right or wrong, his superior is expected to send him packing!

When the old count finished, with a long puff that had the value of a full stop, the Provincial said: 'I understand very well what you mean; but before I take the steps you...'

'It's not really taking any steps at all, your Reverence. It's something quite ordinary, quite natural. But if it isn't done, and done soon, I foresee a whole mass of troubles, a whole saga of disasters. It only needs someone to do something silly – not my nephew, I don't think it'll be him; that's what I'm there for – but at the stage the thing has reached, if we don't nip it in the bud, at once, with a firm, precise hand, then it can't be stopped, it can't remain a secret, and then it won't be only my nephew ... it's like stirring up a wasps' nest, most reverend father.

1. 'Prevent it at the beginning' – a Latin proverb. – Translator's note.

356

You know how it is; we are a family with connections that are . . .'

'Not to be overlooked,' said the Provincial.

'You know what I mean; they're all people with rather special blood in their veins, people who in this world . . . count for something. The point of honour comes into it too; it becomes a matter that involves the whole family, and then . . . even the most peaceful of men . . . it would be a most heart-breaking thing for me to have to . . . to find myself in a position where . . . I've always had such an affection for the Capuchin fathers. Now you fathers, to go on doing the good work you have always done, greatly to the edification of the public . . . you need to have peace, to avoid strife, to keep on good terms with those who . . . and then, another thing, you all have relatives in the secular world, and these affairs that involve the point of honour, if they go on for more than a very short time, they start growing and branching out; they draw in . . . practically everybody. I happen to be in a certain position, where I have to think of appearances . . . His Excellency . . . my worthy colleagues . . . the whole thing would take on a collective aspect . . . especially in view of that other matter . . . you know how these things can develop.'

'Well now,' said the Provincial, 'Father Cristoforo is one of our preachers, and I had been thinking, even before this . . . I've been asked for . . . but at this moment, in these circumstances, it might look like a punishment – a punishment without any proper investigation . . .'

'Not a punishment, no, no, not a punishment at all – a far-sighted provision, an adjustment to suit the common convenience, to prevent the disastrous results of . . . but I think you understand me.'

'Between my lord and myself, the matter will continue to be seen in those terms; I understand perfectly. But if the facts are as they were reported to you, I cannot think that the affair has remained unnoticed in the district. There are agitators and trouble-makers everywhere nowadays; or at best men whose ill-natured curiosity leads them to be delighted at the sight of a struggle between the gentry and the clergy. They sniff around, they put interpretations on the things they find, they gossip. Everyone has to think of appearances to some extent, and I, as a superior (though unworthy), have a positive duty in that respect ... the honour of the habit is not a personal matter for me. It is something with which I have been entrusted ... your nephew, my lord, if he is really as angry as you say, might take Father Cristoforo's transfer as a satisfaction offered to himself, and ... not exactly boast or triumph about it, but ...'

'Do you think there's any risk of that, most reverend father? My nephew is a nobleman who in the world at large enjoys a consideration ... the consideration properly due to his rank; but in front of me he's like a schoolboy, and he'll do just what I tell him – neither more nor less. In fact, I'll go further; he needn't know about it at all. We don't have to account to anyone for what we say to one another! These are things arranged between ourselves, as old friends, and between ourselves they should remain. There's no cause for concern here. I ought to know how to keep my mouth shut by now,' he added, with a puff. 'And as for gossip,' he went on, 'what can people say? A friar going off to preach in another district ... it's such a commonplace event! And anyway, people like ourselves who know ... who can foresee ... on whose shoulders so much ... we shouldn't bother too much about gossip and gossipers!'

'It's worth forestalling them, though, and it would be as well if your nephew did something to show ... some sort of public demonstration of friendship ... not for us personally, but for the honour of the habit ...'

'Yes, yes, of course; you're absolutely right ... but it's really hardly necessary, for I know that the Capuchin fathers always get the cordial welcome they deserve from my nephew. He does it by natural inclination, for it runs in the family; and then he knows he's acting in conformity with my wishes too. But anyway, in this case ... you're quite right ... something extra is called for ... leave it to me, most reverend father ... I'll tell him what to do ... or rather I'll have to put the thought in his mind tactfully, so that he doesn't realize what has passed between us. I don't want to go putting a plaster on a place where there isn't a cut. As for the main thing that we've agreed about,

358

the sooner it can be done the better. And if the niche you find for him is a good long way from here ... to make quite sure...'

'I have in fact just been asked for a preacher for Rimini, and it's quite possible that I would have thought of Father Cristoforo anyway...'

'Just the thing, just the thing! And when do you think...?'

'Since it has to be done, it shall be done quickly.'

'Yes, quickly, quickly, most reverend father. Better today than tomorrow. And if I can do anything,' he went on, rising to his feet, 'myself or my family, for our worthy Capuchin fathers...'

'The kindness of your family is already known to us from long experience,' said the Provincial, also rising, and walking to the door behind his conqueror.

'We have put out a spark,' said the count, stopping for a moment, 'a spark which could have blown up into a disastrous fire, most reverend father. A couple of words between two old friends can solve a big problem sometimes.'

When he reached the door, he threw it open, and positively insisted that the Provincial should go through it before him. They went back into the other room and rejoined the rest of the company.

The old count put much study, great skill and many fine words into the conduct of these affairs; but the results were proportionate to the effort. The conversation we have just reported was enough to make Father Cristoforo travel from Pescarenico to Rimini on foot, which is a good long walk.

One evening a Capuchin from Milan arrived at Pescarenico with an envelope for the Father Superior. It contained an *obedience*[2] for Father Cristoforo, bidding him go to Rimini, where he was to preach during Lent. The covering letter to the Father Superior instructed him to convey to the friar that he must not concern himself any more with any affairs that he might have in hand in the district he was leaving, nor must he keep up any correspondence with the people there. The friar who brought

2. The word used for an instruction in certain religious Orders. – Translator's note.

the message was to be his travelling companion. The Father Superior said nothing that evening. In the morning he sent for Father Cristoforo, and showed him the *obedience*. He then introduced him to the friar who was to go with him, and told him to fetch his scrip, his staff, his cloak and his girdle, and set out at once.

The reader can imagine what a blow this was for Father Cristoforo. The faces of Renzo, Lucia and Agnese at once swam before his eyes, and he silently exclaimed within himself. 'Dear God, what will those poor folk do when I am gone?' But then he raised his eyes to Heaven, and rebuked himself for little faith, for presumption in thinking that he could ever be indispensable. He crossed his hands over his breast, in token of submission, and bowed his head before the Father Superior, who took him on one side and gave him that other instruction; his words were words of advice, but the tone was one of command. Father Cristoforo went to his cell and picked up his scrip. He packed his breviary, his book of Lenten sermons and the bread of forgiveness[3] into it, and girded his habit tightly about him with his leather belt. He said farewell to those of his fellow friars who were in the monastery at the time, asked the blessing of the Father Superior, and set off with his companion along the road he had been ordered to take.

We mentioned earlier that Don Rodrigo, more determined than ever to carry his brilliant enterprise through to the finish, had decided to seek the assistance of a terrifying helper. We cannot give this man's name, nor that of his family, nor his title; we cannot even offer a guess at any of these things. This is all the stranger because the man is mentioned in several books – printed books that is – of that period. There is no doubt that the references are to the same person, from the complete identity of the facts described. But we find everywhere a determination to avoid giving his name, as if it might burn the writer's pen, or even his fingers. When Francesco Rivola has to speak of this man, in his life of Cardinal Borromeo, he calls him 'a certain lord, no less powerful in wealth than noble in birth', and tells us no more. Giuseppe Ripamonti mentions him at greater

3. See pages 88 and 89. – Translator's note.

length, in the fifth book of the fifth decade of his *Storia Patria*, but always calls him 'a certain person', 'the former', 'the latter', 'this man', or 'that personage'.

'I will report' – he says in his elegant Latin, which we must translate as best we can – 'the case of a certain person who, being one of the first among the great ones of the city, set up his residence on a country estate, situated on the frontier; and there, establishing his position by the number of his crimes, he held as of no account the judgements of the courts, the judges themselves and magistracies in general, and even the very Crown. He led a life of total independence. He harboured exiles, and had indeed been an exile himself, though later he returned home as if nothing had happened.'

We propose to borrow one or two other passages from Ripamonti, which may serve to confirm or elucidate the narrative of our anonymous author; to whom we now return.

To do whatever the laws forbade, or any other power opposed; to be judge and master in the affairs of others, in which he had no interest but the love of command; to be feared by everybody; to oppress those who were used to oppressing others – such had always been that man's principal passions. From his boyhood the sight and the rumour of so much arrogant violence and aggressive rivalry, the spectacle of so many petty tyrants, had filled him with mixed feelings of anger and of impatient envy. As a young man, living in the city, he never missed an opportunity – he was more likely to create one – of encountering the most famous members of the swaggering persuasion, and of clashing with them, in order to try his strength against theirs, and to make them either treat him with due respect, or seek his friendship. He had more money and more followers than most of them, and was probably more daring and more determined than any. He reduced many of them to withdrawing from all rivalry with him, and did many of them various injuries. Many of them also became his friends; not on a footing of equality, but friends of the only kind he valued – subordinate companions, who admitted his superiority and always played second fiddle to him. But as it turned out, he too became a sort of agent or tool for his associates; for they also asked for the help of this powerful ally in their enterprises, and he could not refuse his assistance without damaging his reputation and failing to fulfil his chosen role. In the end he committed so many offences, some on his own account and some for the sake of other people, that his name, his relations, his friends and his own audacious courage were all insufficient to withstand the many powerful private hatreds and the official decrees that threatened him. He had to give way and go into exile. A striking passage of Ripamonti seems to refer to this episode: 'Once he received the order to quit the country; see what secrecy and timid circumspection he used! He crossed the city on horseback, with a pack of hounds, to the sound of hunting horns; and when he passed the Governor's palace, he left a series of insolent messages for His Excellency with the guard.'

While he was away, he did not cease to correspond with those friends of his, nor give up his dealings with them. And they remained united to him (to translate Ripamonti literally) 'in a secret league of atrocious counsels and wicked deeds.' It seems to have been at this time that he initiated certain new and infamous dealings with various high personages, about which the historian just quoted speaks with mysterious brevity. 'Certain foreign princes also made use of his services for some assassinations of importance, and often sent him reinforcements of men from afar off to serve under his orders.'

He remained abroad for a period whose exact length is not known. Then perhaps the sentence of exile was lifted through the influence of some powerful intercession, or perhaps the man's audacity served as his only passport – in any case he decided to return home. And return he did; though not to Milan itself, but to a castle[4] on the frontier with Bergamo, which at that time, as everyone knows, was Venetian territory. 'That house', to quote Ripamonti again, 'was a veritable hotbed of murderous plans. There were servants who had prices on their heads, and whose task was to cut off the heads of others; neither cooks nor scullions were exempt from the duty of murder; the very boys had bloody hands.' Besides this happy band of immediate retainers, he had a further train of similar followers,

4. See map on page 16 and notes on facing page. – Translator's note.

according to Ripamonti, who were dispersed and quartered out at various points of the two states on the borders of which he lived, ever ready to carry out his orders.

All the local tyrants for a considerable distance around had been compelled at one time or another to make their choice between the friendship and the enmity of this tyrant in chief. But the first few who had tried to resist him had come out of it so badly that no one else felt inclined to make the same experiment again. Even by minding their own business, and keeping themselves to themselves, they found it impossible to stay clear of him. A messenger would arrive to say that such and such an enterprise must be abandoned, that such and such a debtor must not be harassed any more, or something of the sort; and then they had to reply either yes or no.

When one party to a dispute decided, with feudal submissiveness, to refer the matter to him, the other party was faced with the difficult choice of either accepting his judgement or opting to become his enemy – which was like opting for galloping consumption, as they used to say. Often men who were in the wrong came to him for a declaration that they were in the right. Often too men who were in the right came to him in order to stake a prior claim to that formidable advocacy, and thus deny it to their enemies. In either case they became especially dependent on him.

Occasionally the weak would come to him, after suffering oppression at the hands of some bully; and he would take the side of the weak, and force the bully to leave them alone, or to make reparation for the wrong he had done, or to apologize. If the bully resisted, he would drive him out of the district where he had played the tyrant, or exact a more summary and terrible penalty. In cases such as these, blessings might be called down on that abhorred and dreaded name for a time. For in those days there was no other public or private agency from which a man could expect any such act of ... not of justice exactly, but any remedy or compensation at all. But more often – as a general rule, in fact – his power was exercised on behalf of evil intentions, atrocious revenges, or tyrannical caprice.

Yet the various uses of his power all produced the same effect.

They filled men's minds with a powerful impression of what he was ready to plan and achieve in total disregard of both right and wrong – those twin opponents which place so many obstacles in the way of men's wishes, and so often make them abandon their enterprises. The fame of ordinary tyrants was generally limited to the small stretch of country where each of them held the upper hand. Every district had its own, and one petty despot was so like the next that there was no reason for people to concern themselves about any others besides the one on their own doorstep. But the fame of this man had already spread all over the territory of Milan. His life was already a subject of popular fable; his name had become associated with the idea of something strange, irresistible and legendary. There were suspicions everywhere about the activities of his allies and his hired assassins, which also helped to ensure that no one would ever forget about him in a hurry. It could only be a question of suspicions, for no one would openly confess to being a dependent of such a man. But any petty tyrant might easily be one of his allies, any thug might be one of his retainers. The very uncertainty of the matter made his influence seem vaster, more mysterious and more terrible. Every time strange bravoes, of exceptionally forbidding aspect, appeared in a district, every time some atrocious crime was committed, the authorship of which could not be immediately discovered or promptly guessed, it was always the same name that was put forward or muttered around – though the extraordinary circumspection (to use no harsher term) of our authorities compels us to call him 'the Unnamed'.

From his lair to Don Rodrigo's palace was no more than seven miles. Long before, when Don Rodrigo had inherited his present estate and his present despotic powers, he had had to admit that, if he were to live so near to such a formidable neighbour and still be a tyrant in his own right, he must be prepared either to wage war on the Unnamed, or come to terms with him. So he made him an offer of friendship, which was accepted – on the usual terms of course. Since then Don Rodrigo had been of service to him more than once – the manuscript gives no further details. On each occasion he had received in return an assurance of reciprocal aid whenever he might need it.

But Don Rodrigo was very careful to keep this friendship secret, or at least to conceal the closeness of the relationship and its true character. Don Rodrigo wanted to be a tyrant, of course; but not a completely barbarous one. For him despotism was a means, not an end in itself. He wanted to go on being free to live in the city, and enjoy the comforts, amusements and honours of civilized life. He consequently had to observe certain restraints, to consider the feelings of his family, to cultivate the friendship of high officials; to keep one hand on the scales of justice, so that he could incline them towards his own side if necessary, or whisk them out of sight; or even, in certain special circumstances, bang them down on the head of someone who was easier to get at in that way than by the use of private armed force. Now intimacy with a man like the Unnamed, and still more a definite alliance with such an avowed enemy of public order, would not have helped Don Rodrigo at all with those other interests of his. Least of all would it have helped him with his noble uncle.

To the extent that it was impossible to hide his friendship with the Unnamed, it could be passed off as an indispensable relationship with a man whose enmity would be too dangerous, and thus be excused as unavoidable. For if those who have the duty to protect us cannot or will not do so, they will end up by agreeing that we may take steps to protect ourselves up to a point. If they do not openly agree, they will close an eye to what is going on.

One morning Don Rodrigo rode out as if to go hunting, but with a small escort of bravoes on foot. Griso was at his side, and four other men walking behind. They took the road that led to the castle of the Unnamed.

Chapter 20

THE castle of the Unnamed towered above a narrow, dismal valley. It was situated on top of a peak, which stood a short distance away from a rough mountain ridge, but was joined to it – or perhaps we should say separated from it – by a wilderness of great rocks and precipices, a maze of chasms and cliffs, which spread out on both flanks of the castle as well. Access was only possible from the side towards the valley, where the slope, though steep, was uniform and continuous. There was pasture towards the top, and fields with cottages scattered here and there lower down. At the bottom of the valley lay a water-course, strewn with large pebbles, through which ran the stream – an ugly torrent in winter, a rivulet in summer – that then marked the boundary between the two states. The ridge on the far side, which formed the other wall of the valley, also had a little cultivation on its lower slopes; but the rest of it consisted of boulders and splintered stone, and steep declivities without either roads or vegetation, except for an occasional bush growing in the clefts and along the upper contours of the ridge.

From his lofty castle the ferocious noble, like an eagle looking out from its blood-sodden eyrie, dominated the whole area round him, wherever the foot of man could rest. He could see no one higher than himself, in any sense. When he looked around, the whole enclave was laid out before him – the slopes, the valley bottom, the roads that had been driven through the wilderness. The road that climbed the slope up to his terrible lair, with many zigzags and hairpin bends, was displayed like a winding ribbon before the eyes of anyone looking down from the castle. The Unnamed could sit at his ease, looking down from window or loophole, and count every step taken by a visitor toiling up that hillside, and could take any one of a hundred chances of putting a bullet through him. Even if he had been attacked by a large force, he and the garrison of bravoes he kept with him could have stretched a good few of them lifeless on the road, or sent them rolling down to the bottom of the slope, before any of their number reached the summit. But in any case, far from daring to climb that hillside, no one ever ventured to set foot in the valley, even to pass straight through it, unless he was on good terms with the lord of the castle. If a policeman showed his face there, he would have been treated like a spy caught in the camp of his enemies. Stories were still told about the tragic ends which had overtaken the last policemen who had made the attempt; but they were already ancient history, and none of the younger men who lived in the valley could remember ever having seen anyone of that sort there, alive or dead.

Such is our anonymous author's description of the place. He still mentions no name; in fact he is so careful not to give us a hint that might help us to discover it, that he says nothing about the details of Don Rodrigo's journey, but takes him straight into the middle of the valley, to the foot of the peak, at the beginning of that tortuous upward path. At that point there was a tavern – a tavern which might almost as well have been called a guard-house. Over the door hung an old sign, which was painted on both sides with the picture of a brightly shining sun. But common parlance, which sometimes accepts names as it hears them and sometimes remakes them to suit itself, never called it by any other name than 'The Ill-Starred Night'. At the sound of approaching horses' hoofs, an ugly, loutish boy, armed to the teeth, appeared on the threshold. He glanced at the newcomers, and went in to report to three ruffians who were gambling with a pack of very dirty, bent old playing-cards. The one who seemed to be their leader got up and went to the door. Recognizing one of the master's friends, he greeted him with great respect. Don Rodrigo returned his salute with much grace, and asked if his master was at home. The villainous corporal of the guard replied that he thought so, and Don Rodrigo dismounted, tossing his bridle to Tiradritto, one of his train of bravoes. Then he unslung his musket, and handed it to Montanarolo, with an air of ridding himself of an unnecessary burden before tackling the steep climb; but the real reason was

367

that he knew very well that no one was allowed to travel that road with a firearm. Then he took a few *berlinghe* out of his pocket, and gave them to Tanabuso, saying, 'You men stay here and wait for me; you can have a drink with these good fellows while I am away.' Finally he pulled out a few gold *scudi* and gave them to the corporal, half for himself and half for his men.

Then he began to walk up the path, accompanied by Griso, who had also left his musket behind. Meanwhile the other three bravoes who have already been mentioned, together with Squinternotto who was the fourth (what beautiful names they had, for our author to record them for us with such care!)[1] stayed behind with the three men of the guard and that boy with the mark of the gallows on him, to gamble, drink, and boast to each other about their past exploits.

Another of the Unnamed's bravoes, who was going up to the castle, caught up with Don Rodrigo a little later. He looked at the visitor carefully, recognized him, and accompanied him for the rest of the way, thus sparing him the trouble of stating his name and business to the other men he might meet, who would probably not know him. Don Rodrigo reached the castle and was let in – though Griso had to wait at the door – and then conducted through a labyrinth of dark corridors, through various great rooms, where the walls were covered with muskets, sabres and halberds, and there were always a couple of bravoes on guard. Finally, after a short wait, he was admitted into the master's room.

The Unnamed came forward to welcome him, and returned his salute, watching Don Rodrigo's face and also keeping an eye on his hands. This was an old habit of his, almost an involuntary reaction, whenever anyone came to see him, even one of his oldest and best-tried friends. He was a tall, dark-skinned man, bald except for a fringe of white hair. His face was deeply furrowed, and at a first glance you might have credited him with more than his sixty years; but his manner, his movements,

1. 'Squinternotto' means 'Slasher'. All the bravoes are known by names, or rather nicknames, suitable for such desperate characters. – Translator's note.

the harsh strength of his features and the sinister but intense light that shone in his eyes all indicated physical and mental powers that would have been remarkable in a young man.

Don Rodrigo explained that he had come for advice and help; having become involved in a difficult enterprise, from which his honour would not allow him to withdraw, he had remembered that he had previously received certain undertakings from a man whose promises never went beyond his powers, and were always redeemed. He went on to tell the tale of his villainy, and the tangle into which it had led him. The Unnamed had in fact heard part of the story already, though only in a confused version. He listened to Don Rodrigo intently, because he had a general interest in these matters, and also because this one involved a name that he knew well and hated bitterly – the name of Father Cristoforo, that declared enemy of all tyrants, who opposed them both with words and (where possible) with deeds.

Don Rodrigo knew his man well enough to dwell on the difficulties of the enterprise. Monza was so far away, the convent walls so high, the Signora's protection so powerful. The Unnamed abruptly intervened, as if some devil in his heart had given him an order, to say that he had decided to undertake the task. He made a note of poor Lucia's name, and dismissed Don Rodrigo, saying: 'It will not be long before you hear from me what you are to do.'

If our readers still remember that wretched fellow Egidio, who lived next door to the convent where poor Lucia had taken refuge, they must now be told that he was one of the closest and most intimate partners in crime that the Unnamed possessed. That, in fact, was why the old man had taken up the challenge in so prompt and resolute a fashion. But as soon as he was left alone, he began to feel ... not exactly repentant, but angry with himself for accepting it. For some time now he had been feeling not remorse but a sort of disquiet at the thought of his own past crimes. The numerous offences which had piled up in his memory, if not on his conscience, seemed to come to life again whenever he committed a new one. They came before his

369

mind's eye in too large and too ugly a throng; it was like a steady increase in the weight of an already uncomfortable burden. At the time of his first crimes he had felt a certain repugnance, which he had later overcome and almost completely banished from his mind, but now the feeling was beginning to come back. In those early days the thought of a long future, a future of indefinite length, and the consciousness of great vigour and vitality, had filled his heart with happy confidence; but now thoughts of the future were the very thing that poisoned his memories of the past.

'Old age! Death! And what then?' Strange to say, although in times of immediate danger, in face of an enemy, the image of death always breathed new spirit into him and filled him with angry courage, the same image appearing to him in the silence of the night, in the safety of his own castle, afflicted him with sudden dismay. For this time it was not death at the hands of a mortal like himself that threatened him; not a death that could be driven off by better weapons or a quicker hand. It was a death that came all alone, from within; it might still be far away, but every moment brought it a stride nearer. Even as the mind painfully thrust the thought of it away, the reality came closer. In earlier times the constant examples, the non-stop spectacle of violence, revenge and murder had filled him with a ferocious competitive spirit, and had also served as a sort of counterweight to conscience. But now a confused yet terrifying idea revisited his mind every so often – the idea that the individual is responsible for his own judgement, and that rightness cannot be established by examples. The fact that he had outdistanced the ordinary crowd of evil-doers and left them far behind sometimes gave him a horrifying feeling of loneliness.

That God of whom he had often heard – he had never troubled for many years either to acknowledge or to deny him, having been concerned only to live as if he did not exist; and yet now he had moments of inexplicable depression, of causeless terror, during which he seemed to hear a Voice within his own heart crying: 'AND YET I AM!' In those early, hot-blooded days he had seen nothing but an object of hatred in the law he heard proclaimed in God's name (for he had at least heard it).

But now, when the memory of that law suddenly came back to him, he found himself thinking of it, much against his will, as something destined to be fulfilled.

Far from confiding in anyone about this new source of disquiet, he covered it up as thoroughly as possible, masking it with an outward show of even more outrageous ferocity than before. He also sought to conceal it from himself, to suppress it altogether, by the same method. Since he could not forget or cancel those early days, when he had often committed the most atrocious crimes without any remorse, without any thought save that of success, he began to look back at them with envy, and did everything he could to make them return, to retain or recover his old proud, ready, implacable will, and convince himself that he was still the man he had been.

In the present instance he had given his promise to Don Rodrigo without a moment's delay, in order to leave himself no room for hesitation. But as soon as Don Rodrigo had left, the Unnamed felt the resolution he had summoned up to make that promise ebbing away, to be gradually replaced by other thoughts, which tempted him to break his word, and might have led him to lose face before a friend, an accomplice of secondary rank. To cut short this painful internal conflict, he sent for Nibbio,[2] who was one of the most skilful and daring of his assistants in crime, and also the one whom he normally used as a messenger in his dealings with Egidio. With a determined air the Unnamed ordered him to take horse at once, ride straight to Monza, tell Egidio about the task he had undertaken and ask for his help in carrying it out.

The villainous envoy returned sooner than his master expected, with Egidio's reply. The job, he said, presented no great difficulty or danger; if the Unnamed would send him a carriage with two or three bravoes, all well disguised, he would take responsibility for everything else, and would direct the operation himself. As soon as he received this message, the Unnamed, whatever his inner feelings might be, issued his instructions at once. Nibbio himself was to make all the arrangements

2. 'Nibbio' means 'kite', in the sense of a bird of prey. – Translator's note.

371

requested by Egidio, to take two other bravoes (whom his master named) and set off on this expedition immediately.

If Egidio had been compelled to rely on his ordinary resources to perform this repulsive service, he certainly could not have given so definite a promise at such short notice. But right within the walls of the place of refuge where everything seemed an obstacle, the young reprobate had resources known to him alone. The very thing which would have been the principal difficulty to another man became a ready instrument in his hands. We have already mentioned how on one occasion the unhappy Signora gave ear to his words; and the reader may have gathered that that occasion was not the only one – was in fact only the first step along a path of iniquity and bloodshed. The same voice to which she had listened those first few times had acquired fresh power over her – one might almost say fresh authority – as a result of the crime that had been committed; and now it demanded the sacrifice of the innocent girl who had been entrusted to her care.

The proposal made Gertrude's blood run cold. If she had lost Lucia through no fault of her own, through some unforeseen accident, she would have felt it as a grave misfortune, a bitter stroke of Providence. But now she was ordered to deprive herself of Lucia's company by a deed of atrocious treachery, to convert what had been an act of expiation into a new subject of remorse. The poor wretch tried every possible method of getting out of the abominable task – every method, that is to say, but the only certain one, which was open before her to take at any time. Crime is a rigid, unbending master, against whom no one can be strong except by total rebellion. Gertrude would not make up her mind to this – and so she did what she was told.

Soon the appointed day had arrived, and the appointed hour was approaching. Gertrude called Lucia into her private parlour, and treated her with even more outward kindness than usual, to which Lucia responded with happy acceptance and growing affection – like a lamb that feels no fear as the shepherd strokes her quivering body and urges her gently forward; she turns her head and licks his hand, not realizing that outside the stall stands the butcher to whom the shepherd has just sold her.

'I need someone to do something very important for me,' said Gertrude, 'and you're the only one who can do it. I've got plenty of people under my orders here, but no one I can really trust. There's a very urgent matter – I'll tell you all about it later on – which I must discuss with the Father Superior of the Capuchin monastery – the father who brought you to me in the first place, my poor Lucia. But it's most important that nobody knows that the message comes from me. You're the only person who can do this for me secretly.'

Lucia was terrified by this request. In her usual submissive manner, but without concealing her surprise, she at once tried to get out of it by mentioning various points which the Signora must surely understand, must surely have thought of for herself. Could she really go out like that without her mother, without any escort at all, in fact, along a lonely road, in a district which she did not know? But Gertrude had learned the devil's lessons in his own school. She showed the utmost surprise, and displeasure too, at finding this resistance to her wishes in the very person on whom she had been chiefly relying: and she poured such scorn on Lucia's excuses! A few hundred yards, in daylight, along a road which Lucia had travelled a few days before! Such a simple journey that Lucia couldn't misunderstand her directions, even if she hadn't been there before! It was not long before Lucia yielded to the reproaches of the Signora and those of her own heart, and breathed the words; 'Very well, then; what do you want me to do?'

'Go to the Capuchin monastery . . .' and here she described the route again. 'Then ask for the Father Superior, and tell him, privately, that I'd like him to come and see me at once, but that I don't want him to tell anyone that I sent for him.'

'But what am I to say to the portress? She's never seen me go out before, and she's sure to ask me where I'm going.'

'Try to slip out without her seeing you; and if she does, tell her you're going to a particular church, where you've promised to say a prayer.'

The idea of telling a lie presented the poor girl with a new

373

difficulty. But the Signora seemed so distressed by her objections, and made it seem so unkind to place considerations of scruple above considerations of gratitude, that Lucia, dazed rather than convinced, and more upset than ever, gave in in the end and said, 'Very well, then – I'll go! God have mercy on me!' And she set out.

Standing behind the grating, Gertrude watched with fixed and glassy eyes until the girl reached the doorway. Then she called out: 'Listen, Lucia!' as if carried away by an irresistible impulse.

Lucia turned, and came back towards the grating. But another thought – the one which normally predominated in Gertrude's heart – had already re-established its hold over the unhappy woman. So she pretended to think that the directions already given to Lucia were not sufficient, and explained the way that she had to go all over again. Finally she allowed her to depart, saying, 'Do everything just as I've told you, and come straight back!' Lucia set out.

She got out of the door without being noticed, and walked down the street, close to the wall, with downcast eyes. With the aid of the Signora's directions and her own memory, she found her way to the city gate and went out through it. With arms close to her sides, and trembling a little, she made her way along the main road until she reached the turning that led to the monastery, which she recognized at once. The side road was (and still is) a sunken track, like a river bed, between two high banks crowned with bushes, which almost make a tunnel of it. When Lucia turned down this road, and saw how deserted it was, she felt more frightened than ever, and quickened her pace. A moment later she was heartened by the sight of a travelling coach standing in the road, next to which stood two passengers looking this way and that as if uncertain of their route. As she walked on, she heard one of them say, 'There's a nice girl who'll tell us the way'; and as she came abreast of the carriage the same man turned and spoke to her pleasantly enough, though he did not look a very pleasant man, saying: 'Excuse me – could you tell us the way to Monza?'

'Why,' said Lucia, 'you're going away from it. This is the

374

way to Monza, over there' – and she turned, to point out the correct route with her finger. Then the other traveller (this was Nibbio) grabbed her round the waist and lifted her off the ground. Lucia twisted her head round in terror, and screamed, but the bravo hoisted her bodily into the coach. A man who was sitting on the backward-facing seat grabbed her and shoved her, struggling and screaming, on to the seat opposite. Another man put a cloth over her mouth and stifled her cries. Meanwhile Nibbio jumped quickly into the carriage, the door shut behind him, and they drove off at full speed. The other bravo, who had asked her that treacherous question, was left in the road. He looked round to see if anyone had heard Lucia's cries. No one was in sight; so he jumped for the top of the bank, grabbed one of the bushes that grew there, and vanished into the scrub. He was one of Egidio's hirelings, and had been waiting unobtrusively at his master's door to see when Lucia left the convent. He had taken a good look at her, so as to know her again, and had hurried off by a short cut to wait for her with the others.

Who could ever describe Lucia's anguish and panic, or express what passed through her mind? She opened her terrified eyes wider, in her anxiety to know more about the appalling situation into which she had fallen; but she shut them again at once in fear and disgust at the ugly faces around her. She twisted and turned but she was held tightly on all sides; she gathered all her strength and tugged away towards the door, but two muscular arms held her penned in the centre of the carriage, and four more great ugly hands held her down. Every time she opened her mouth to scream, the gag threatened to choke her. Meanwhile three devilish mouths kept repeating the same thing, putting as much humanity into their utterance as they could: 'Quiet, now; don't be frightened; we aren't going to hurt you.' After a few minutes of that anguished struggle, she did seem to grow quieter. Her arms relaxed, her head fell back; her eyes ceased to move, with the lids barely parted. The repulsive faces that surrounded her seemed to sway and run together in a monstrous confusion. The colour drained out of her cheeks and a cold sweat covered her limbs. She gave up the fight, and fainted.

375

'Come on, now; cheer up!' said Nibbio, and the other two thugs echoed his words; but Lucia, being completely unconscious, was spared the comfort of those horrible voices.

'To hell with it! She looks dead!' said one of them. 'And if she is . . .'

'Dead, indeed!' said the other. 'It's just one of those fainting fits that women have. I know very well that when I've had occasion to send anyone into the other world, whether it was a man or a woman, it needed a good deal more than this to do the trick.'

'Now then!' said Nibbio. 'You two just stick to the job in hand, and don't bother about anything else. Get the blunderbusses out of the locker, and keep them ready; there are always cut-throats lurking in this wood we're just coming to. But don't wave them about like that; lay them down behind you, out of sight. Can't you see that we've got a real ninny here, who'll faint for nothing at all? If she sees firearms, she might really die. When she comes to, take care not to frighten her again. Don't touch her unless I give you a sign; I can hold her by myself. And above all, keep your mouths shut; leave the talking to me.'

Meanwhile the carriage, still at the gallop, had travelled well into the wood.

Some time later poor Lucia began to wake up, as if from a deep and troubled sleep, and she opened her eyes. At first she had some difficulty in gathering her thoughts together and making out her horrifying surroundings. But finally she regained full awareness of her terrible situation. The first use she made of the little strength that had returned to her, was to struggle towards the door again, hoping to throw herself out. But she was pulled back, and had only a moment's glimpse of the wild and lonely country through which they were passing. She screamed again, but Nibbio held up the cloth in his great hand.

'Listen,' he said as gently as he could, 'it'll be better for you if you keep quiet. We don't want to hurt you, but if you try to make a noise, we've got to stop you.'

'Let me go! Who are you? Where are you taking me? Why have you kidnapped me? Let me go! Let me go!'

'I've told you not to be frightened. You're not a baby, and you must see that we don't want to hurt you. Couldn't we have killed you a dozen times over by now, if we'd meant any harm?'

'No! no! Let me go! I don't know who you are.'

'We know you, though.'

'Holy Mother of God! How do you know me? Let me go, for pity's sake. Who are you? Why have you kidnapped me?'

'Because we were ordered to.'

'Who could have given you an order like that? Who? Who?'

'Hush, now!' said Nibbio, with a stern look on his ugly face. 'We don't answer questions like that.'

Lucia tried once more to make a sudden dash for the door; but seeing that this was hopeless, she began to plead with them again. With head held low, tears streaming down her cheeks, and hands clasped together before her lips, 'Oh, for the love of God!' she cried, in a voice broken by sobs, 'for the love of the Blessed Virgin, let me go! What harm have I ever done you? I'm just a poor girl who hasn't done anything wrong at all! I forgive you for what you've done to me with all my heart; I'll pray for you. If you have a daughter, or a wife, or a mother, think what they would suffer if they were in the same state as I am. Remember that we must all die some time, and that one day you'll be hoping for God to show mercy to you. Let me go, put me down here. The Lord will help me to find my way.'

'We can't do that.'

'You can't? Dear heavens, why not? Where are you taking me? Why...?'

'We can't do it; it's no good ... Don't be frightened; we won't hurt you. Just be quiet, and no one will touch you at all.'

Anguished, agonized and terrified more than ever as she saw her words were having no effect, Lucia turned her thoughts to the Power that holds the hearts of men in its hand, and can soften even the hardest of them when it will. She huddled herself in the smallest possible space, in an angle of the carriage, crossed her arms over her breast, and prayed silently for a

377

while. Then she got out her rosary, and began to tell her beads, with more fervour and passion than ever before in her life. From time to time the hope came to her that the mercy she sought might have been granted, and she addressed new appeals to the men, but always without result. Then she fainted again, and again recovered consciousness, to suffer fresh anguish. But we cannot find the heart to describe her sufferings at any greater length. A painful sense of compassion bids us draw a veil over the rest of that journey, which lasted more than four hours, and after which there are yet more hours of misery to follow. Let us pass on to the castle where the poor girl was awaited.

She was awaited by the Unnamed with a disquiet and uncertainty which were most unusual for him. That man had brought many lives to an end in cold blood, and had never paid any attention to the sufferings all his exploits had caused, unless it were to savour in them the savage joys of revenge. Yet now, strange to say, the thought of laying hands on this unknown woman, this peasant girl, filled him with revulsion and something like terror. From a high window of his castle he had been looking out for some time towards a point far down the valley, when suddenly the carriage came into sight, and began to come closer – very slowly, because the first gallop had tired and dispirited the horses. Though at that distance it looked no bigger than one of the toy coaches that children play with, he recognized it at once, and felt his heart beat faster.

'Is she inside it?' he suddenly wondered; and then he thought: 'This girl's going to be a nuisance; I must be rid of her.'

He was just going to call one of his underlings, and send him down to meet the carriage and tell Nibbio he must turn back and take the girl straight to Don Rodrigo's palace. But another voice within him replied to this with a resounding 'No!' and that idea faded from his mind. But he was tormented by the need to issue orders of some kind, for it seemed intolerable to wait there and do nothing while that carriage crept closer step by step, like an act of treachery, like a ... a punishment. So he sent for a certain trusted old serving-woman.

This woman's father had been one of the castle guards; she had been born within its walls, and had spent her whole life there. Everything she had seen and heard, from the cradle on, had impressed her mind with grandiose and terrifying ideas of the power of her masters; and the main lesson she had learnt, both by precept and example, was that they must be obeyed in everything, because they could do you much good and also much harm.

The idea of duty is present like a seed in the hearts of all men; in hers it grew up together with feelings of deference, terror and servile greed, taking on their form and colour. When the Unnamed became the head of the family, and began to make such horrifying use of his power, she did at first experience a certain revulsion, though it was accompanied by a feeling of submission even deeper than before. As time went by she became accustomed to the things she saw and heard every day. The powerful and unbridled will of so great a lord as her master was in her eyes a sort of inexorable justice.

When she grew up, she married one of the family retainers. Soon afterwards he went out on a dangerous expedition and lost his life, leaving her a young widow in the castle. The speedy vengeance which her master took for his death gave her a fierce joy, and increased the pride she felt in living under such effective protection. From then on she hardly ever set foot outside the castle. All idea of other forms of human existence than the one around her gradually faded from her mind. She had no definite duties; but living in the midst of that host of cutthroats, she got odd jobs to do for one or other of them from time to time, much to her disgust. There might be ragged garments to darn, meals to prepare at short notice for men returning from an expedition, wounded men to nurse. The bravoes' orders, reproaches or thanks were seasoned with mockery and obscenities. They normally addressed her as 'old woman'; the epithets that some of them always added varied with the circumstances and disposition of the man concerned. Laziness and bad temper were two of her most marked characteristics, and when she was upset in either of them she would reply to the compliments of the bravoes with terms in which the devil would have recognized more of his own spirit than in the men's original words.

'Do you see that carriage down there?' said the Unnamed.

'Yes, I see it,' said the old woman, sticking out her pointed chin and staring with her sunken eyes until you might have thought she was trying to make them stand out of their sockets.

'Have a litter got ready at once, get into it, and get them to carry you down to the inn. And hurry up – you've got to get there before the carriage. God knows it's coming up slowly enough. Inside the carriage there'll be ... there should be a girl. If she's there, tell Nibbio my orders are that he's to put her in the litter, and he's to come straight up and report to me. You stay in the litter, with the ... the girl, and when you get back to the castle take her to your own room. If she asks you where you're taking her, or whose castle this is, mind you don't tell her ...'

'I should think not!' said the old woman.

'But mind you cheer her up,' said the Unnamed.

'Why, what am I to say to her?'

'What are you to say to her? Cheer her up, I said! You can't have reached the age you have without knowing how to cheer a girl up, when she needs it! Haven't you ever been in distress? Haven't you ever been afraid? Can't you remember the sort of thing that cheered you up at those times? Say the same sort of thing to her; or make something up, dammit! Be off with you!'

When she had gone, he stood at the window again for a while, staring at the carriage, which already looked much bigger than before. Then he gazed up at the sun, which at that moment was just vanishing behind the mountain; and then at the clouds just above it. Black a moment before, they had suddenly turned to flame. He withdrew from the window, closed it, and began to walk up and down, with the gait of a traveller in a hurry.

Chapter 21

THE old woman went off eagerly to obey her orders, and to issue other instructions with the authority of the name which assured prompt compliance from all in the castle, whoever pronounced it. For it never occurred to anyone that somebody might be rash enough to use that name without permission. She did reach the inn before the carriage arrived, and when she saw it drive up, she got out of the litter, signed to the coachman to stop, and went up to the door. Nibbio put his head out, and she whispered the master's instructions in his ear.

As the carriage stopped, Lucia shook herself, and woke up out of a sort of trance. Her blood ran cold again. She opened her mouth and eyes very wide, and watched to see what would happen. Nibbio had drawn back from the door, and the old woman, with her chin on the window-sill, was looking at Lucia.

'Come on, young lady,' she said. 'Come on, you poor little thing! Come with me, for I've orders to treat you well and cheer you up.'

At the sound of a woman's voice, poor Lucia felt a little comfort, a moment's return of courage; but then even darker terrors overtook her.

'Who are you?' she asked in a trembling voice, staring at the old woman with a dazed look in her eyes.

'Come on, then; come on, you poor little thing,' said the old woman again. Nibbio and the others drew their own conclusions about their master's intentions from the unwonted kindness of the old woman's words and voice. They also tried, as gently as possible, to induce Lucia to do what she was told. But she went on looking out of the window, and, though the wild and unknown countryside gave her little hope of rescue, and the confident bearing of her guards even less, she still opened her mouth to scream. But then she saw Nibbio scowl meaningly at the cloth in his hand, and she choked back her cry. Trembling and struggling, she was picked up and put into the litter. The old woman followed her inside while Nibbio told the other two bravoes to escort the litter, and quickly made his way up the slope, to report to his master in accordance with his orders.

'Who are you?' asked Lucia anxiously, looking at that ill-favoured, unfamiliar face. 'Why am I here with you? Where is this? Where are you taking me?'

'To see someone who wants to do you a kindness,' said the old woman. 'To see a fine ... Oh, it's a fine thing for people when he decides to do them a kindness. You're a lucky, lucky girl! Don't be frightened; and come on, smile now! For he's told me to cheer you up. You'll tell him I have, won't you? You'll tell him I have cheered you up?'

'But who is he? Why? What does he want with me? I don't belong to him! Tell me where I am! Oh, let me go! tell these men to let me go, to take me to a church! Listen, listen! You're a woman too – in the name of the Blessed Virgin Mary!'

The old woman had often repeated that sweet and holy name in her earliest years, but a very long time had gone by since it last passed her lips. As she heard it at this moment, a strange, faint, confused sensation came to the unhappy creature, like the memory of light to an old man blinded in early childhood.

Meanwhile the Unnamed stood at the great door of the castle, looking down the hill. The litter was coming up at a snail's pace, as the carriage had done before; in front of it, and leaving it further behind every moment, came Nibbio, running up the hill. When he arrived, his master beckoned to him, and led the way into one of the great rooms of the castle.

He halted and turned towards Nibbio. 'Well?' he said.

'All according to plan, sir,' said Nibbio, with a bow. 'The messenger was on time, the girl was on time; there wasn't anyone around at the place where we picked her up; she only screamed once, and nobody heard her. The coachman knew his job, and the horses were fine; we met no one. And yet ...'

'And yet what?'

'Well, sir, to tell you the truth, I'd just as soon you'd told me to put a bullet through her from behind, without all this business of having to listen to her and look at her face.'

'*What?* What was that? What do you mean?'

'You see, sir, it went on such a long time ... Somehow she made me feel sorry for her. Compassion, I suppose you'd call it.'

'Compassion? What do you know about compassion? What is compassion, anyway?'

'I never realized what it was before half so well as I have this time, sir. It seems to be something a bit like fear. If a man lets it get hold of him, he loses his manhood.'

'Let's hear what she did to inspire you with this remarkable feeling.'

'Oh, your Honour, it went on for such a long time! Weeping, begging for mercy, with those great eyes of hers; and going as pale as death, and sobbing, and begging for mercy again; and the things she said ...'

'I won't have her in the house,' thought the Unnamed. 'I was a fool to take this job on; but I've given my word. Well, once she's gone ...'

Then he raised his head and looked commandingly at Nibbio. 'Now then,' he said, 'forget about compassion, and all that. Get yourself a horse, and take one of the men with you – or two, if you like – and be off, as fast as you can, to Don Rodrigo's place – you know Don Rodrigo. Tell him to send someone – and he'd better be quick about it, because otherwise ...'

But at this point a second 'No!' even more imperious than the first, seemed to resound within him, forbidding him to finish his sentence.

'No!' he said resolutely, as if to express the command of that secret voice to himself. 'No; go to bed, Nibbio; and then tomorrow morning ... tomorrow morning you will carry out the instructions I shall give you then.'

'There's some special devil in league with that girl,' he thought, alone now, standing with his arms crossed and staring fixedly at the floor, where the rays of the moon, entering through a high window, made a patch of pale light, crisscrossed with the shadows of heavy iron bars, and cut up into smaller sections by the leading of the panes ... 'some special devil, or else there's a special angel to protect her ... To think of Nibbio talking about compassion! ... Tomorrow morning, early tomorrow morning, I'll have her out of here. She must go where her destiny leads her, and I shall never hear of her again; and what's more,' he went on, talking to himself in the same spirit in which we address a rebellious child, knowing that it will not do what it is told, 'I shall never think of her again either. That swine Don Rodrigo had better not come here pestering me with his thanks, because ... because I never want to hear her name again. I helped him because I promised I would, and I promised I would because ... that's where my destiny leads me. But I'll make him pay me for this service, and pay me properly ... let me see, what shall it be, now?'

He tried to think of some really horrifying job the performance of which he could exact from Don Rodrigo as a payment, or perhaps as a penalty, for this one. But his mind was struck again by the memory of that word 'compassion', coming so strangely from Nibbio. 'However did she manage to put that into his head?' he wondered, fascinated by the question. 'I must see her – no, damn it! – yes, I will see her!'

He went through various great rooms, found the entrance to a small staircase, and groped his way up to the old woman's room. Instead of knocking at the door, he gave it a kick.

'Who's there?'

'Open up!'

At the sound of that voice, the old woman scurried to the door. In a moment the bolt was creaking as it was drawn back, and the door was thrown open. The Unnamed stood in the doorway and looked round the room. By the light of a lamp burning on a small table, he saw Lucia huddled on the floor, in the angle furthest from the entrance.

'Who told you to fling her down in the corner like a bundle of rags, you old witch?' he said, with an angry scowl.

'You see, sir, it's her own choice, where she is,' said the old woman humbly. 'I tried everything to cheer her up, as she'll tell you herself, but it couldn't be done.'

'Stand up then!' said the Unnamed to Lucia, going up to her. But the noise he had made when demanding entry, the opening of the door, the apparition in the doorway, and the words he had uttered, all combined to instil new terrors into her terrified heart. She was now huddled more tightly than ever into the corner, with her face hidden in her hands, quite motionless except for a tremor that shook her from head to foot.

'Stand up, stand up! I don't want to do you any harm, and I'm in a position to do you some good,' said the nobleman. Finally he shouted the words 'Stand up!' loudly, in anger at seeing his order twice ignored.

Drawing fresh vigour from this new terror, the unfortunate girl got up on to her knees. She put her hands together, as if before the image of a saint, raised her eyes to the Unnamed's face and dropped them again at once, and said: 'Here I am: you can kill me now.'

'I've already told you that I don't want to do you any harm,' said the Unnamed, in a softer voice, looking intently at that sorrowful and terrified face.

'Cheer up, then; cheer up!' said the old woman. 'The master says himself that he doesn't mean you any harm.'

'Then why is he making me suffer all the pains of hell?' said Lucia in a voice trembling with fear, but also marked by the confidence that comes from despairing indignation. 'What have I ever done to him?'

'Have they ill-treated you? Tell me if they have!'

'Ill-treated, did you say? I've been treacherously kidnapped, dragged away by force! And why? Why did they kidnap me? Why am I here? What is this place? I'm only a poor girl; what have I ever done to you? In the name of God . . .'

'God, indeed!' interrupted the Unnamed. 'I'm always hearing about God. People who can't defend themselves, who haven't the strength to defend themselves, always bring God into it, as if they knew him personally. You bring in the name of God; and what claim do you suppose that gives you? Does it entitle you to make me . . .?' He left the sentence unfinished.

'Oh heavens!' "Claim", sir? What am I entitled to claim, poor wretch that I am, except your mercy? God will forgive so many things, for a single act of mercy! Let me go! For mercy's sake let me go! There's no profit in it for a man who has to die some day to torture a poor creature like this. You have the power to

385

give orders – tell them to let me go! They brought me here by force! Send me with this woman to —, where my mother is. Oh, blessed Virgin Mary, oh, my mother, for mercy's sake, my mother! Perhaps she's not very far from here – I saw my own mountains on the way ... Why do you want to make me suffer? Or get them to take me to a church. I'll pray for you, for the rest of my life. What does it cost you to say a couple of words? Oh, thank God! I can see the look of pity in your face! Say those words, say them! God will forgive so many things, for an act of mercy!'

'If only she were the daughter of one of those brutes who had me banished!' thought the Unnamed. 'Or of one of those swine who want to see me dead! Then I'd be glad enough to hear her screeching like this. But as it is ...'

'Don't turn a deaf ear to a good impulse, sir!' said Lucia fervently, animated by the sight of traces of uncertainty in her tyrant's expression and attitude. 'If you don't have mercy on me, the Lord will; he'll let me die, and that'll be the end of it for me – but not for you ... perhaps one day you too will ... but no, no; I'll always pray the Lord to preserve you from evil. What would it cost you to say a couple of words? If you could only feel what I'm suffering ...'

'Come, don't be afraid,' said the Unnamed, with a gentleness in his voice which made the old woman gasp. 'Have I done you any harm? Have I threatened you?'

'Oh, no, no! I can see that you're kind, that you feel pity for a poor girl ... If you liked, you could frighten me worse than all the others, you could have me killed. But you haven't – you've ... made me feel a little bit better. God reward you for it! But finish the work of mercy, sir – let me go, let me go!'

'Tomorrow morning ...'

'Oh, let me go now!'

'Tomorrow morning, I was saying, I'll see you again. Meanwhile don't be frightened. Get some sleep. And you must be hungry. I'll see they bring you something.'

'No, no; I nearly die when there's a knock on the door – it'll be the death of me. Take me to a church; God will reward you for every step you take on the way there.'

'I'll send a woman up with your food,' said the Unnamed. Once the words were out of his mouth, he was amazed to think that such an expedient could ever have come into his head, or that he should ever have felt the need of finding one, just for a little peasant girl's peace of mind.

'As for you,' he went on, turning to the old woman, 'you encourage her to eat something. And let her sleep in that bed. If she wants you in there with her, all right; if she doesn't, it won't do you any harm to sleep on the floor for one night. And cheer her up! Try to keep her happy – and don't let me hear any complaints about you from her!'

He walked quickly towards the door. Lucia jumped up and ran to hold him back, to renew her plea for mercy; but he was gone.

'God help me! Quick – shut the door!' said Lucia to the old woman. When she heard the leaves of the door come together and the bolt creak into position, she huddled back into her corner again.

'God help me!' she cried again, beginning to sob. 'Who'll lend an ear to my appeals now? Where am I? Tell me now, tell me for pity's sake, who is that gentleman who was here talking to me?'

'So you want me to tell you who he is? Listen to me, my girl. Because he's taken you under his wing, you're getting haughty, and you want to know everything, and get me into trouble. You'd better ask himself. If I did what you ask in this particular matter, it's not smooth words like he was saying to you that I'd be hearing ... I'm old now, an old woman,' she went on, muttering between her teeth. 'God's curse on these young girls, who look so sweet when they're laughing and when they're crying too, so that people always think they must be in the right.'

But as she heard Lucia continue to sob, she remembered the threatening words of her master. She bent over the girl's huddled form, and spoke in a gentler voice.

'Come on, now!' she said. 'I haven't said anything unkind to you. Let's have a little smile now; and don't ask me questions I can't answer. Apart from that, don't worry your head. If you only know how happy a lot of people would be to hear him talk to them the way he's been talking to you! Cheer up now, for in a minute there'll be something for you to eat, and I'm sure, from the way he spoke to you, that it'll be something nice. And then you'll go to bed; and I hope you manage to leave a little room for me too!' she ended, unable to keep a note of resentment out of her voice.

'I don't want to eat anything, and I don't want to sleep. Leave me alone. Don't come near me, but don't go out of the room.'

'I won't,' said the old woman, drawing away from her, and sitting down on a broken-down chair, from which she glared at the poor girl with mingled fear and rancour. Then she stared at her cot, biting her lips at the thought of being excluded from it for the night, and grumbling audibly about the cold. But the thought of Lucia's supper cheered her up, with the hope that there might be something there for her as well.

Lucia felt no cold and no hunger; half dazed, she now had only a confused consciousness of her own sufferings and fears, like a fever patient lost among his dreams. Then a knock on the door made her jump. She lifted her face up in terror and cried: 'Who's that? Who's that? No one's to come in!'

'Don't worry, now; it's something nice,' said the old woman. 'It's only Marta, bringing you your supper.'

'Shut the door! Shut it!' cried Lucia.

'I will, I will,' replied the old woman. She took a basket out of Marta's hands, and sent her away; she shut the door and came over to set the basket on a table in the middle of the room. Then she made several attempts to get Lucia to come and sample the good things that it contained. She used the words that were in her opinion best calculated to encourage the poor girl's appetite, breaking out into exclamations about the exquisite nature of the food. 'There are things here that ... well, when people like us have the luck to taste them, we aren't likely to forget them for a while! This is the wine the master drinks with his friends ... when someone special comes to see him, and they want to have a good time! My word!'

But seeing that all her wiles were ineffective, she went on:

388

'Well, it's your own choice. Now, when tomorrow comes, don't go saying that I didn't encourage you. I'll eat a bit myself; but I'll leave more than enough for you, when you come to your senses and make up your mind to do as you're told.'

The old woman began to eat greedily. When she had had enough, she went over to Lucia's corner, and again urged her to have something to eat, and then go to bed.

'No, no, I don't want anything,' the girl replied, in an exhausted, sleepy-sounding voice. Then, in more determined tones, she went on,

'What about the door? Is it shut? Is it shut properly?' She looked all round the room, got up, and walked suspiciously over towards the door.

The old woman hurried over ahead of her, stretched out her hand to the bolt and gave it a shake. 'Do you hear that?' she said. 'Can you see it's really shut? Are you happy now?'

'*Happy?*' said Lucia. '*Happy* in this place?' She settled back into her corner. 'Well, at least God knows that this is where I am!'

'Ah, come to bed now! What good d'you think you can do by cowering there in the corner like a dog? Why refuse to be comfortable while you can?'

'No, no; leave me alone!'

'Well, you must please yourself. Look, I'm leaving you the best place. I'm going to sleep right on the edge of the bed; I'm putting myself out for you. If you want to come to bed, you know what to do. And don't forget I asked you to lie down here several times.'

She got under the bedclothes, fully dressed, and everything was quiet.

Lucia sat motionless in the corner, all huddled together with her hands resting on her knees, and her face hidden in her hands. Neither fully awake nor fully asleep, she was visited by a rapid succession, a confused series of gloomy thoughts, vivid imaginings and grisly fears. At times consciousness returned almost completely, and she had a clear recollection of the hideous things she had seen and suffered that day; then she began a careful and painful examination of the terrifying,

389

obscure realities of her position. At other times her mind wandered off into dark regions, and struggled with the strange images called up by terror and uncertainty.

She sat there for a while in that agonized state; but finally weariness and exhaustion prevailed. Stretching out her aching limbs, she lay down, or rather collapsed into a lying position. Then followed a brief period of something more like real sleep. But suddenly she awoke, as if in response to a call from within her own being, and then felt a compulsive need to regain full alertness, and recover complete command of her senses: to know where she was, and why and how she had got there. She heard a noise, and listened intently. It was the slow, rattling snore of the old woman. She opened her eyes, and saw a weak glimmer that shone out and vanished, shone out and vanished ... it was the wick of the lamp, now on the point of going out, which put forth a fitful light and at once took it back again, like the sea lapping softly on a beach. That light, flickering away from the objects in the room before they could acquire definite shape or colour from it, offered the eye nothing but a series of spectral images. But soon the details most recently impressed on her memory returned to it, and enabled her to make sense of those confused visual impressions. It was an unhappy awakening to the realities of her prison; and all the memories of that terrible previous day, all her fears for the future, came flooding back together into her mind. The very calm which had followed all that agony, the very sleep (or rather loss of consciousness) into which she had fallen, filled her with new terrors. She was overcome by such anguish that she earnestly wished to die. And then she remembered that she could at least pray, and together with that thought a little hope returned to her. She took out her rosary again, and began to tell her beads. As the words of prayer passed between her trembling lips, an indefinite feeling of trust in Providence began to creep into her heart.

Suddenly another thought came into her mind – the idea that her prayers would be more likely to find acceptance and be answered if, at that desperate time, they were accompanied by a sacrifice of some kind. So she considered what it was that she held dearest in the whole world – or what she had formerly held dearest in the whole world, since at that moment her heart had no room for any emotion but terror, nor for any desire but the desire for freedom. With her mind on that dearest thing, she resolved to offer it up. She rose from the floor, knelt down, and clasped her hands together against her bosom, with the rosary still hanging from her fingers. She raised her face and looked up to heaven. 'Most Holy Virgin!' she said. 'I have turned to you so often, and you have consoled me so many times! You have suffered so many sorrows, and now dwell in such glory, and have worked so many miracles for the unfortunate and afflicted! Help me now! Save me from my present dangers, let me get back safely to my mother, O Mother of God, and I swear to you that I will remain a virgin all my life. I renounce my poor lover for ever, and will never belong to anyone but you.'

Having uttered those words, she lowered her head, and put the rosary round her neck, as a sign of consecration and at the same time as a protection – as the armour of the members of the militia in which she had just enlisted. She sat down on the floor again, and felt a degree of tranquillity, a greater trust in Providence. She remembered the words 'tomorrow morning' which the unknown lord had pronounced more than once, and seemed to find a promise of salvation in them.

Exhausted by so much turmoil, her nerves gradually relaxed as her thoughts grew calmer. With the name of her Protectress still on her lips, she finally fell into a sound and unbroken sleep, not long before dawn.

There was someone else in that castle who would have been delighted to do the same, but could not manage it. Having left Lucia – we might almost say escaped from her presence – and ordered her supper; having done his usual round of the strong points of the castle, with Lucia's face still before his eyes and her words still ringing in his ears, the Unnamed strode rapidly to his room, locked himself inside with desperate haste, as if barricading himself against a host of enemies, threw off his clothes with equal haste, and went to bed. But that face rose before his eyes again, clearer than ever, and seemed to say, 'No sleep for you tonight!'

'Why ever did I yield to that stupid, womanish curiosity of wanting to see her?' he wondered. 'That idiot Nibbio's perfectly right about one thing: you lose your manhood. It's true enough, you lose your manhood. And now it's come to me ... Am I not a man any longer then? ... What the devil has come over me? What's new about all this? I knew before today that women scream – and men too sometimes, when they can't do anything else. To hell with it! I've heard women make that wretched bleating noise often enough before.'

And at this point, without his having to search very far in his memory, various distinct recollections came to him of their own accord, of occasions when neither prayers nor tears had been enough to restrain him from carrying out his purpose. But those memories, far from giving him the strength he needed to carry out the present enterprise, far from banishing that unwelcome feeling of compassion, filled his heart with a sort of terror, a strange frenzy of repentance. In fact he found it quite a relief to go back to his earlier thoughts of Lucia – the very thoughts he had been trying to find fresh courage to suppress.

Well, she's alive, he said to himself, and she's here; it's not too late. I can tell her to go away – go away and be happy. I can see her face change as I say it ... I can ask her to forgive me – ask forgiveness of a woman? A man like myself? Never! ... And yet, if a couple of words, a couple of words like that could do me some good, could cure me of this hag-ridden feeling, why, I'd say them! I feel it in my bones that I'd say them! ... To what depths I've sunk! I'm not a man any longer – it's true, it's true!

To hell with it! he went on, rolling over on a bed that seemed strangely hard, under blankets that seemed strangely heavy. To hell with it! I've had nonsense like this pass through my mind and out again before. It'll pass this time too.

To help it to pass, he searched his mind for some important matter, some question of the sort that normally exercised his mind strongly, hoping to be able to concentrate all his attention on it. But nothing came to mind that was any use to him. Everything appeared to him in a new light. The things which had once stimulated his desires most vigorously now had nothing desirable about them. Passion, like a horse suddenly frightened by a shadow, refused to go any further.

When he thought of various other enterprises which he had set in motion but not yet completed, he could not raise any enthusiasm for finishing them off; he could not even raise any anger at the obstacles in the way – though anger would have been a welcome relief at that moment. He merely felt depressed and almost frightened at the thought of the steps he had already taken. Time to come stretched out before him empty of purpose, occupation and desire, full only of the prospect of intolerable memories, with every future hour similar to the one which was then crawling so heavily by. He held a mental parade of his villainous underlings, but could think of nothing which mattered that he could give any of them to do. In fact the idea of seeing them again, of being in their company, was burdensome in itself – a repulsive, uncomfortable notion.

When he tried to think of an occupation for the following day, a task he could perform, nothing came to mind but the possibility of freeing that wretched girl.

'Yes, I'll free her,' he said to himself. 'As soon as morning comes, I'll go straight to her and say: "You can go now! Go!" And I'll send an escort with her ... But what about my promise? What about Don Rodrigo? *And just who is Don Rodrigo, pray?*'

That last thought caught him out like an unexpected and embarrassing question from a superior. He at once began to search for an answer to the query just raised by himself – by that new self which seemed suddenly to have sprung up to a terrifying size, and to be sitting in judgement on his old self. Why had he decided so easily – almost before being asked – to take on the job of causing so much misery to a person he neither hated nor feared, to a poor unknown girl, just to oblige Don Rodrigo? Far from being able to find any reasons for what he had done which might seem to provide it with an adequate excuse, he hardly knew how to explain to himself how he had brought himself to do it at all. His willingness to take that action had been the fruit not of a deliberate decision, but rather the instantaneous response of a mind trained to follow long-standing, habitual ideas – the consequence of a thousand previous events.

Caught in the toils of self-examination, the unhappy man found that to explain a single action he must embark on a review of his whole life. He went back and back, from year to year, from job to job, from bloodshed to bloodshed, from villainy to villainy. Every detail of his actions appeared before his mind's eye; he knew them well, yet saw them as if for the first time, in isolation from the passions that had led him to will them and to carry them out. They came back to him in their full enormity – an enormity which the passions had previously concealed. Those crimes all belonged to the man who had committed them – in fact they *were* the man who had committed them. The horror of that thought, renewed by each successive remembered image, inseparable from each recollected event, drove him to despair. Suddenly he sat up and reached out towards the wall beside his bed. He seized a pistol, pulled it down and ... at the very moment when he was about to put an end to a life which had become unbearable, his heart was invaded by a new fear, a new disquiet which could almost be called posthumous; for he now cast his mind forwards into the future – that time which would ineluctably continue to flow on after his death. He thought with revulsion of his own disfigured corpse, motionless and defenceless against the vilest of living humanity; the astonishment and confusion in the castle the following day; everything upside down; himself powerless, voiceless, his body cast aside God knew where. He imagined what people would say in the house, in the neighbourhood, and far away. He imagined the joy of his enemies.

The darkness and the silence somehow made the idea of death even more melancholy and horrifying. He felt that he would not have hesitated like that in broad daylight, out in the open before a crowd. He could have thrown himself into a river, for example, and disappeared for ever. Sunk in these torturing reflections, he was cocking and uncocking the pistol with a convulsive twitch of the thumb, when another idea flashed into his mind.

'That other life which they told me about as a boy – which

394

they're always talking about, in fact, as if it were certain truth – perhaps it doesn't exist, perhaps it's all an invention of the priests. But if so, what am I doing? Why should I cut my life short? What does it matter what I've done, what does it matter? In that case it's crazy to think of putting an end to myself! On the other hand, if that future life *does* exist ... why then it's crazier than ever to think of death as the answer!'

This extra doubt, this additional peril, brought with them an even blacker and more oppressive despair, from which there was no escape, even in death. He dropped his weapon and tore his hair; his teeth chattered and his body trembled.

Suddenly certain words came back into his mind which he had heard more than once only a few hours before. 'God will forgive so many things, for an act of mercy!' But this time it was not with an accent of humble entreaty that they rang in his ears, but with a trumpet note of authority, which also brought with it a whisper of hope. It gave him a moment of relief. Calmer now, he lowered his hands from his temples, and fixed his inward gaze on the girl from whom he had heard those words. This time he saw her not as his prisoner, not as a suppliant, but as a gracious dispenser of consolation. He waited impatiently for day to break, so that he could hasten to her room and set her free, and hear from her mouth yet further words of comfort and of life. He imagined a scene in which he himself escorted her back to her mother ...

And then, he thought, what shall I do tomorrow, for the rest of the day? What shall I do the day after, and the day after that? What shall I do at night? It'll be night again in twelve hours. Nights are the worst of all, the very worst!

Returning to that painful study of the empty future, he searched vainly for a possible use for his time, a way of passing the days and the nights. At one time he thought of leaving the castle and going off to faraway lands, where no one would know him, even by name; but he realized that he would always be accompanied by his own hateful self. At other times he felt a baleful hope that he might recover his old fiery spirit and his ancient purpose, that all this might prove to be a passing aberration. Now he feared the dawn, which must show him to his men in such a lamentably altered state; now he longed for it, as if it might bring light to his heart as well as to his eyes. And then, just as the sky began to grow paler, a few minutes after Lucia had finally gone to sleep, a sound reached his ears, as he sat there motionless – a long-drawn, indefinite sound, that seemed to have something cheerful about it. He listened carefully, and realized it was bells, the distant ringing of bells for some far-off celebration. A moment later he heard the echo from the hills, which faintly repeated the harmony and then blended with it. Soon afterwards, he heard another set of bells, nearer this time, with the same happy notes; and then another.

'What's all this happiness for?' he wondered. 'What have they got to be so cheerful about?'

He sprang up from his comfortless bed, threw on a few clothes, quickly opened a window, and looked out. The mountains were partly veiled in mist; the sky was not so much covered in clouds as made up of a mass of grey vapour. But as the light grew steadily brighter, he could make out crowds of people moving along the road at the bottom of the valley, some emerging from the houses, but others coming from farther afield. They were all flocking in the same direction, to the right of the castle, towards the exit of the valley. They were all wearing their Sunday clothes, and walking very briskly.

'What the devil's up with them all?' thought the Unnamed. 'What is there to be so cheerful about in this damned place? Where are they all going, the scum?'

He called a trusted bravo, who slept in the next room, and asked him why all this movement was going on. The man knew no more than his master, but said he would go and find out at once. The Unnamed stayed where he was, with elbows on the window-sill, intent on the procession below. There were men, women and children, in groups, in pairs, and singly. One man would catch up with someone walking ahead, and would fall into step alongside him. Another would come out of his house and pair off with the first passer-by he saw; they would go on together like friends setting out on a pre-arranged journey. Their movements clearly showed a common haste and a common happiness. The ringing of those bells from near and far, in spiritual if not physical harmony, seemed to give a voice to their happy gestures, and to express the sense of the travellers' words, which were inaudible to the watcher in the castle. He stared and stared, his heart filled with a growing curiosity, and something more than mere curiosity, to know what it was that could give the same powerful happiness to so many different people.

Chapter 22

Soon afterwards the bravo came back to report. The day before, Cardinal Federigo Borromeo, the Archbishop of Milan, had arrived at —, and would be staying there for the whole of the day which had just begun. The news of his coming had spread through the villages the night before, and everyone wanted to see him. The bell-ringing was not so much to inform people of the occasion as to express the general happiness.

When the master of the castle was left alone again, he continued to stare down into the valley, more gloomily than ever.

'So it's all on account of one man!' he thought. 'They're all hurrying happily off to see just one man. And yet every one of those fellows down there must have his own devil to torture him ... But none of them has a devil like mine; none of them has just passed a night like I have. What is it about that man which makes them all so happy? He'll dish out a bit of money, no doubt, quite haphazard ... But they're certainly not all beggars looking for alms. Why, then it must be for a wave of his finger in front of their noses, a word from his mouth ... If he knew the word of consolation for me, now! And why shouldn't I go too? Why shouldn't I? I'll go, and I'll talk to him; I'll have a private talk to him ... What shall I say, though? I'll tell him that ... that ... Anyway, I'll hear what he's got to say for himself!'

Having made his decision in this rather confused manner, he quickly put on the rest of his clothes, including a jacket of military cut. He took up the pistol, which was still lying on the bed, and thrust it into his belt on one side, balanced by a second pistol on the other, which he took down from the wall. His dagger was stuck into the same belt, and finally he lifted down a carbine from the wall which was almost as famous as its master, and slung it from his shoulder. He picked up his hat, and went out. He made his way straight to the room where he had left Lucia. He stood his carbine in a corner outside the door, and knocked, calling out at the same time to let Lucia know who it was. The old woman got out of bed with a single jump, and scurried over to open the door. The Unnamed went in, looked round the room, and saw Lucia huddled motionless in the corner.

'Is she asleep, then?' he whispered to the old woman. 'Asleep on the floor? Are these the orders I gave you, you old wretch?'

'I did all I could,' she replied. 'But she refused to eat anything, she refused to come to bed . . .'

'Let her sleep in peace, then; mind you don't disturb her. And when she wakes up . . . Marta will have to stay in the next room, and you can send her to get anything the girl asks you for. When she wakes up, tell her that I . . . that the master has gone out for a short time, that he'll be back . . . and that he'll do whatever she asks him to do.'

The old woman was astounded by his words. 'Is the girl a princess, or something?' she thought. Her master went out, picked up his carbine, and sent Marta to take up her post in the next room. He sent the first bravo he met to act as sentry, and make sure that no one but Marta entered the room. Then he left the castle, and hurried down the slope.

Our manuscript does not tell us the distance from the castle to the village where the Archbishop was staying; but from the facts which we are now about to report it does not seem to have been more than a moderately long walk. This could not however be deduced from the mere fact that the inhabitants of the valley, and of the territory beyond it, went to see him; for contemporary memoirs speak of crowds of people assembling from a distance of twenty miles and more to see Federigo Borromeo.

The bravoes the Unnamed met on the slope halted respectfully as he went by. They stood there expectantly waiting to see what orders he had for them, and whether he wanted to take them with him on some expedition. They did not know what to make of his bearing, or of the way he scowled at them in reply to their bows.

The thing that amazed the passers-by, when he reached the

main road, was to see him without an escort. But they all made way for him, leaving him room enough to have accommodated an escort too, if he had had one; and they all respectfully raised their hats. When he reached the village, there was a big throng in the street; but his name passed quickly from mouth to mouth, and the crowd opened to let him through. He went up to a bystander and asked him where the Cardinal was. 'In the parish priest's house,' replied the man with a bow, and showed him where it was. The Unnamed walked on to the house, and went into a small courtyard, full of priests, who looked at him with astonished and suspicious attention. Before him he saw an open door, which led into a small sitting-room, also full of priests. He unslung his carbine and stood it in the corner of the courtyard. He went into the room, and there too met with dark looks, whispers, and the repetition of his name, followed by silence. He turned to one of the priests and asked him where the Cardinal was, saying that he wished to speak to him.

'I'm a stranger here,' replied the priest. He glanced around, and called out to the episcopal chaplain, who at that moment was standing in the corner of the parlour, whispering to a colleague: 'What? Is that the famous outlaw? Heaven forbid!'

But the chaplain's name rang out across the room in the general silence, and he had to answer the call. He went over, bowed to the Unnamed, and listened to his request. He looked up into the noble's face with uneasy curiosity, and looked down again quickly. He stood there silently for a moment, and finally said, or rather stammered:

'I'm not sure whether His Grace ... at the moment ... is able ... is in a position ... is free to ... well, anyway, I'll go and see.'

He went off uncomfortably with the message into the neighbouring room, where the Cardinal was.

At this point in our story, we cannot help pausing for a little; just as a traveller, tired and depressed after a long journey through a wild and arid landscape, will stop and spend a little time sitting on the grass by a fountain of living water, under the shade of a beautiful tree. Our story has now brought us into the presence of a man the mention of whose name, the memory of whose character, can never at any time fail to refresh the mind with the calm emotion of reverence, with a happy feeling of affection. How much more so at this particular moment, after so many scenes of sorrow, after contemplating such manifold and distasteful wickedness. We cannot possibly refrain from saying a few words about this man; anyone who does not care to listen to them, but wants to go on with the main story, can turn on to the next chapter.

Federigo Borromeo was born in 1564. He was one of those few men – rare in any age – who devote the resources of an exceptional intellect, of vast wealth and of a privileged position in society in an unbroken effort to seek out and practice the means of making the world a better place. His life is a stream which springs cleanly out of the rock, flows in a long course across varied country without ever growing stagnant or muddy, and finally flows on unsullied into the river. Born amid luxury and splendour, he paid due heed from his earliest childhood to those words of abnegation and humility, those maxims regarding the vanities of pleasure, the injustices of pride, and the nature of true dignity and true values, which are handed down from one generation to another (whether any notice is taken of them or not) in the most elementary religious instruction. Federigo Borromeo, as we were saying, did take heed of those words and those maxims; he took them seriously, tested them, and found that they were true. He realized that certain other words and maxims which contradicted them could consequently only be false, although they had been passed down from generation to generation with equal assurance, and often by the same lips. He decided to use those which were true as the standard for his own actions and thoughts. Convinced that this life is not meant to provide a treadmill for the majority and unending holidays for the few, but rather to furnish every one of us with a task to perform, of which an account must one day be rendered, he began at an early age to consider how to make his own life holy and useful.

In 1580 he declared his intention of dedicating himself to the ministry of the Church, and was ordained by his own cousin Carlo, who was generally regarded as a saint by a prevalent opinion which was of long standing even then. Soon afterwards he entered the college which Carlo had founded at Pavia, and which still bears the name of their family. While there, he applied himself assiduously to the tasks prescribed to him, and took on two extra ones of his own free will, which were to teach the doctrine of Christianity to the roughest and most derelict of the people, and to visit, serve, console and succour the sick. He made use of the authority which everyone in that place conceded him to induce his fellows to help him in works of that kind. In every good and meritorious activity, he exercised a sort of leadership by example – a leadership which his personal gifts would probably have won him, even if he had been of the lowliest birth.

But as for the other advantages which his family connections could have given him, far from demanding them, he did everything in his power to ensure that they did not come his way. He insisted on a diet which was not merely frugal, but parsimonious, and on clothes which were not merely simple, but austere; and all his behaviour, his whole way of life, was in keeping with his dress. He would never agree to changing his ways, though various relations cried out that he was lowering the dignity of the family.

He had further trouble with his own superiors, who tried, in furtive, unexpected ways, to introduce something more befitting his birth into his quarters, his dress, his surroundings – something which would distinguish him from the others, and make him appear as the outstanding figure in the establishment – we cannot say why. Perhaps they thought that this policy would in the long run gain them his good will; perhaps they were moved by the servile baseness which draws pride and pleasure from the glory of others. Perhaps they were of that prudent sort who are equally alarmed by virtues and vices, and always preach the doctrine that perfection lies in the golden mean; they fix the golden mean at the point which they themselves happen to have reached, and settle down there very comfortably. Far from yielding to those who attempted to deflect him from his path, he reproved them for it, though he was still hardly more than a boy.

His cousin Carlo Borromeo, now a cardinal, was his senior by twenty-six years. The Cardinal's grave and solemn bearing vividly expressed the idea of saintliness, and reminded the onlooker of the works of saintliness he had performed. If a further source of authority had been needed, it was there all the time in the obvious and spontaneous respect in which the Cardinal was held by all around him, whatever their rank. So it was not surprising that Federigo, in his boyhood and early youth, tried to model his behaviour and his thoughts on those of so eminent a superior. What is remarkable is that when the Cardinal died there were no signs that Federigo, still only twenty years old, was disorientated by the loss of his guide and mentor. The growing reputation of his intellectual powers, his learning and his piety, the support he would naturally receive from several influential cardinals to whom he was related, the credit of his family, the fact that he bore a name which his cousin Carlo had already enriched with the associations of sanctity and pre-eminence – in short, all the factors which would lead to preferment and all the factors that commonly do so – combined together to assure high office in the Church for Federigo.

But he was persuaded in his heart of a truth which no professed Christian can deny with his lips – namely, that no man can rightly claim superiority over his fellows, except in their service. So he feared the dignities that were offered to him and tried to avoid them. It was not that he wished to shun the opportunities of serving others, for few lives have ever been so devoted to that goal; but that he did not think himself either worthy or capable of such high and perilous service. In 1595, when Pope Clement VIII offered him the archbishopric of Milan, he was deeply perturbed, and refused without hesitation. Later he accepted office at the express command of the Pope.

Demonstrations of this sort are not all that difficult nor all that uncommon, as everyone knows. A hypocrite can imitate them without straining his ingenuity very far; and a cheap humorist can make fun of them with equal ease, whenever they occur. But does that mean that they can no longer be the natural expression of a wise and virtuous feeling? The touchstone of a man's words is his life; and the words that expressed that feeling may have passed the lips of every impostor and scoffer in the world without losing the beauty they have when spoken by a man whose previous and subsequent life are filled with unselfishness and sacrifice.

The new Archbishop showed a singular, sustained determination not to spend on himself any more of his wealth, his time, his thoughts and all that was his than was strictly necessary. He would often say – as all priests say – that the income of the Church is the patrimony of the poor. The practical meaning which he attached to these words can be seen from the following example. He ordered an estimate to be prepared of the total cost of his own personal expenditure and that of his servants. He was told that it came to six hundred *scudi*. ('*Scudo*' was the name then given to the gold coin which later, without any change in its weight or value, came to be known as a sequin.) He then ordered that the full corresponding sum should be transferred every year from his private account to that of his household. For he did not think it right that he, with his great wealth, should live on the patrimony of the poor.

Towards himself, he was a most frugal and precise administrator of his own resources. For he never threw away a garment until it was really worn out; though his passion for simplicity was accompanied by the most exquisite personal cleanliness, as various contemporary writers remark. These were indeed two most unusual habits in that age of dirty bodies and splendid clothes. To ensure that nothing should be lost of what was left over from his frugal table, he allotted the remnant to a hostel for the destitute, one of whose inmates came every day into his dining room, by his order, to collect what remained uneaten. Such concerns might give an impression of a narrow, mean, miserable sort of virtue, a mind enmeshed in petty detail and incapable of any noble project – were that splendid Ambrosian Library not still there to prove the contrary, which Federigo Borromeo conceived in a spirit of such brilliant splendour, and built up at such expense from its first foundations.

To furnish it with books and manuscripts, he not only

donated the private collection which he had built up himself at the cost of much time and money, but he sent out eight men, of the most expert and learned scholars he could find, to buy books for it throughout Italy, France, Spain, Germany, Flanders and Greece, in the Lebanon and at Jerusalem. In this way he got together about thirty thousand printed volumes and fourteen thousand manuscripts. To the library he attached a college of learned doctors. There were nine of them, salaried at his expense during his lifetime; but after his death it proved impossible to maintain so many out of ordinary funds, and the number was cut down to two. The task he set them was to cultivate various fields of study, such as theology, history, literature, research into the early history of the church, and oriental languages, each of them being under an obligation to produce published work on his subject. The archbishop added a school to which he gave the name of 'Trilingual', for the study of Greek, Latin and Italian; a college of pupils, who were to learn the various subjects and languages in order to teach them later on; a printing press for oriental languages (Hebrew, Chaldean, Arabic, Persian and Armenian); a picture gallery, a gallery for sculpture and a school for the three principal branches of draughtsmanship.

For those last few items, he could find ready-trained teachers. For the others ... we have already seen the trouble he had to obtain the relevant books and manuscripts, and there can be no doubt that the typefaces for those languages, which were much less studied then than now in Europe, must have been even harder to obtain; and men to teach them, hardest of all. It is enough to say that of his nine learned doctors he chose eight among the young students of the seminary. This shows what a judgement he had formed of the completed studies and the established reputations of the day in those fields – a judgement confirmed by posterity, which seems to have committed both to oblivion.

In the rules he set up for the use and administration of the library, we can detect an intention to ensure its permanent utility, which is not only a fine aim in itself, but shows a wisdom and kindness which in many respects go far beyond the common ideas and habits of the day. The librarian was instructed to maintain a correspondence with the most learned men in Europe, and obtain from them news of the state of every science, and advice of the best books that were published in every category, so that he could obtain copies of them; he was instructed to draw the attention of students to works which they did not know and which might be useful to them. The Archbishop laid it down that everyone, whether a citizen or a foreigner, should be allowed opportunity and time to use the library, according to his need. This may now strike everybody as the most natural thing in the world, and as inherent in the idea of founding a library. But then things were very different. In a history of the Ambrosian library, written with the elaborate elegance of the time by one Pierpaolo Bosca, who held the post of librarian there after the death of Federigo Borromeo, there is special mention of the strange fact that the books in this library, which had been built by a private citizen and almost entirely at his expense, were exposed to the view of the public and given out to anyone who asked for them; and that visitors were actually given somewhere to sit, and writing materials, so that they could make any notes they needed; whereas in every other famous public library of Italy, the books were not even on view, but shut up in cupboards, from which they could only be extracted by special favour of the librarians, when they happened to feel like giving someone a glimpse of them for a moment. The idea of giving rival scholars convenient conditions for study never crossed their minds. To give books to those libraries was in fact to take them right out of use. It was one of those systems of cultivation, of which there were many examples then, and still are today, which convert fertile land into desert.

There is no point in going into the effects which Federigo Borromeo's foundation had on the general state of culture. It would be easy enough to prove in a couple of lines, as things are commonly proved nowadays, that its effects were quite miraculous, or that it had no effects at all. We could search out and demonstrate, within certain limits, what they really were; but that would be most laborious, not very useful, and quite out of place here. But we can at least consider how generous, judicious, benevolent and persevering a lover of mankind and of human improvement the man must have been who conceived such an idea, who desired it so earnestly, and who carried it through to completion in the midst of general ignorance, general inertia and general antipathy to any form of studious effort – which means in the midst of cries of 'What's the use of it?' and 'Aren't there more urgent things to be done?' and 'What an extraordinary idea!' and 'This is really the limit!', and so on; cries which must have outnumbered the *scudi* he spent on the project, which came to one hundred and five thousand, mostly out of his own pocket.

It might be thought that, for such a man to be regarded as an outstandingly generous benefactor, we do not even need to know whether he spent further large sums on the immediate relief of the poor. There may even be some who think that expenditure of the kind just mentioned, or perhaps even expenditure in general, is the best and most effective form of charity. But Federigo regarded the giving of alms in the strict sense as a most important duty; and in this, as in everything else, his actions were in keeping with his principles. Throughout his life he poured out his wealth for the direct benefit of the poor. The famine which has already played a part in our story gave him occasion to show what special kindness and wisdom he could put into these acts of generosity, as we shall see later.

Out of the many examples of his liberality which his biographers have recorded, we shall mention a single instance here. He had heard that a certain nobleman was using undue pressure and underhand means to persuade his daughter to become a nun, although she wanted to get married. He sent for the father, and extracted from him an admission that the real reason for his persecution of his daughter was that he did not possess the sum of four thousand *scudi* which he regarded as necessary to marry his daughter honourably. Federigo himself gave her a dowry of four thousand *scudi*. Some people may think this act of generosity excessive, or ill-considered, or too great a concession to the views of an arrogant fool. They may think that four thousand *scudi* could have been better spent in any one of a dozen other ways. To this we have nothing to reply, except that we would like to see more examples of a virtue so free from influence by the reigning opinions of the day – for every period has its own – as this case of a man giving four thousand *scudi*, at that time, to keep a girl out of a nunnery.

The inexhaustible charity of Federigo Borromeo showed in everything else he did no less than in his giving. He was easily accessible to everybody, but it was towards those of so-called low degree that he felt he owed a special duty to show them a cheerful countenance and a friendly courtesy. The lower they were in the social scale the more strongly he felt this duty. This was another point over which he had trouble with the respectable advocates of *ne quid nimis*,[1] who would have liked to make him draw a line – their line – in everything he did. On one occasion, during a visit to a rough mountain village, Federigo was giving instruction to certain poor children; and as he was asking them questions and teaching them the truth he put his arms affectionately around them. At this one of his respectable companions warned him that he ought to be more careful about caressing those boys, because they were disgustingly dirty – as if the worthy man supposed that Federigo was too unobservant to notice the fact, or too stupid to think of a way of avoiding them. For there are times and circumstances where men who have achieved a high position suffer a strange misfortune – they find very few people who will ever tell them when they do wrong, but plenty of brave souls who will reprove them for doing right. But the good bishop replied, with some anger: 'They are souls in my care, who will probably never see my face again; and will you tell me not to embrace them?'

He was very rarely moved to anger, however, being admired for the gentleness of his ways, and for an imperturbable calmness of manner, which might have been attributed to an extraordinary equanimity of temperament, but was really a triumph of constant self-discipline over a lively and indeed fiery nature. If he sometimes appeared severe, or even hasty, it was with his subordinate priests, when he found them guilty of avarice, of negligence, or any other sins especially contrary to the spirit of their noble calling. In any matter which involved his own

1. 'Nothing too much.'

interests, or his temporal glory, he never gave any sign of joy, or resentment, or enthusiasm or agitation. His conduct was admirable if he did not feel any of those passions, and still more admirable if he did.

He attended many conclaves,[2] from which he brought away the reputation of never having aspired to that dignity the thought of which is so fascinating to the ambitious and so terrifying to the truly pious. In fact on one occasion, when a very influential colleague came to offer him the support of his 'faction' (an ugly word, but the one then in use), Federigo refused it in such terms that the other gave up the idea, and turned to another possible candidate. The same modesty, the same unwillingness to predominate, appear no less clearly in the common events of his life. Though he gave his full attention and all his efforts to the arts of planning and administration wherever he considered it to be his duty, he always avoided interfering in other people's affairs; in fact he made every effort not to become involved in them even on request. Such discretion and restraint, as we all know, are not common among men who are zealous for the good, as Federigo was.

If we were to allow ourselves the luxury of compiling a complete account of all his notable characteristics, the result would certainly be a strange mixture of apparently incompatible virtues – virtues which undoubtedly very seldom occur together. But we must record one other feature of that admirable life. Full as it was of activity – administrative duties, religious ceremonies, teaching, audiences, diocesan visitations, journeys and controversy – study still played a part in it, and a large enough part at that to have made the reputation of a professional scholar. And in fact Federigo Borromeo, among all his other claims to renown, did enjoy among his contemporaries the reputation of a very learned man.

We must however admit that among the opinions which he held with great conviction, and practised with long perseverance, were some which most people nowadays would regard as not merely wrong, but eccentric; even those of us who might be most anxious to find good in them. Anyone who wanted to

2. i.e., papal elections. – Translator's note.

defend him on those points could use the common and acceptable excuse that the mistakes were those of his time rather than his own personal errors. In certain cases, where a really careful examination of the relevant facts has been made, that excuse may have some validity – may even have a great deal of force – though it is often applied in so ill-considered and haphazard a manner that it means nothing at all. Since we do not wish to put forward an over-simplified answer to a complex question, nor to give too much space to a single episode in our story, we will not labour the point. It is enough for us to have hinted, in passing, that we do not wish to claim that this man, admirable as he was in so many respects, was admirable in everything. For we do not want to give the impression of having composed a funeral oration for him.

Without any offence to our readers, we may perhaps imagine that at this point one of them asks us whether a man of such intellect and such learning has not left any monuments of his scholarship to posterity? Monuments of his scholarship, indeed! He left about a hundred separate works behind him, some long and some short, some in Latin and some in Italian, some printed and some in manuscript. They are preserved in the library he founded – moral treatises, orations, historical dissertations, studies of antiquity both sacred and profane, studies of literature, the arts, and of other subjects.

'And how on earth has it happened,' the same reader may inquire, 'that all these works are forgotten, or at least so little known, so seldom sought after? With all that intellectual force, all that scholarship, all that practical experience of men and affairs, all that meditation, all that passion for the good and the beautiful, all that honesty of spirit, all those other qualities that go to make up a great writer, how is it that Federigo Borromeo, the author of a hundred works, has not left behind him a single book of the sort that are acknowledged as outstanding even by those who do not agree with them, and known by name even to those who have not read them? How is it that those works of his, by their sheer number if nothing else, have not won him literary fame among the members of the present generation?'

This is undoubtedly a reasonable question about a matter of interest. For the causes of this phenomenon could certainly be discovered by an adequate study of general principles; and, once discovered, they would help us to explain other similar phenomena. But it would be a long-winded business; and would you really enjoy it, or would you wrinkle up your nose at it? I think it would be better to take up the main thread of our story again, to abstain from further gossip about this man, and to see (with the help of our anonymous author) how he acquits himself in the world of action.

Chapter 23

It was not yet the hour for Cardinal Federigo Borromeo to go to the church and officiate at the service, and he was spending the time in study, as he always did when he had a few minutes to spare, when his chaplain came in, with an agitated expression.

'A strange visitor, Your Grace,' he said. 'A really extraordinary visitor, in fact.'

'Who is it?' asked the Cardinal.

'None other than my lord —!' said the chaplain, bringing out every syllable with significant emphasis, as he pronounced the name which we unfortunately cannot reveal to our readers. 'He's here, outside, in person – and he's asking for an interview with Your Grace, if you please!'

'My lord —!' said the Cardinal, with an animated look, closing his book and jumping up, 'Show him in! Show him in at once!'

'But . . .' said the chaplain, not moving, 'Your Grace must know who he is – the famous outlaw . . .'

'And isn't it a stroke of luck for a bishop, when a man like that takes a fancy to come and see him?'

'But . . .' said the chaplain obstinately, 'there are certain things which we can't normally talk about, because Your Grace says it's all nonsense; but when the situation actually arises, I feel it's my duty . . . Holy zeal makes many enemies, Your Grace, and we know that more than one villain has dared to boast that sooner or later he'd pay you out . . .'

'And what have they ever done?' interrupted the Cardinal.

'Your Grace, I'm trying to say that this man makes a business of organized crime; he's a desperado, who is in touch with the worst desperadoes in the country. It's quite possible that he's been sent here to . . .'

'Come now,' interrupted the Cardinal again, with a smile.

'It's a strange army where the soldiers encourage the general to be a coward!' Then his face took on a serious and thoughtful look, as he added, 'My sainted cousin would never have let himself get into an argument about whether he ought to receive such a man; he would have gone out to look for him. Bring him in at once; he's been waiting too long as it is.'

The chaplain went out, saying to himself: 'There's no help for it; these saints are an obstinate lot.'

He opened the door, and went back into the room where he had left the nobleman with the group of priests, who had drawn away to one side of the room, whispering and casting furtive glances at the Unnamed, as he stood alone in the opposite corner. The chaplain went over towards him, unobtrusively running an eye over him from head to foot, and thinking how easily a whole armoury of weapons could be hidden under that jacket; how really, before taking the man inside, he ought at least to suggest that he should ... but the words would not come out. He went up to the Unnamed, and said, 'His Grace is waiting for your lordship. Be so good as to come with me.' Then he led the visitor through that little gathering (which made way for them quickly enough), glancing from right to left with a look which said: 'What do you expect me to do? You know as well as I do that it's no use talking to His Grace!'

As soon as the Unnamed entered the room, Federigo went to meet him with a calm and friendly expression, and arms outstretched, as if to a welcome guest. Then he signalled to the chaplain to leave them together, which he did.

The two men stood there for a while, equally silent, though for very different reasons. The Unnamed had been driven there by the compelling force of a mysterious inner tempest, rather than led there by a reasoned decision; and it was the same force that made him stand there, tormented by two contrary passions – on the one hand, a powerful longing and a confused hope of finding relief from his internal torture, and on the other, wrath and shame at the idea of coming there like a penitent, an underling, a vulgar wretch, to admit himself in the wrong, and implore the help of a fellow man. He could find no words to utter, and hardly seemed to be looking for them. But when he

413

raised his eyes to that man's face, he felt himself more and more penetrated by powerful yet gentle feelings of veneration. They increased his sense of trust, calmed his wrath, and, though they did not make a frontal attack on his pride, they quelled it and so to speak imposed silence on it.

Federigo's appearance was in fact of a kind to inspire a conviction of his superiority simultaneously with an affection for his person. His bearing was naturally dignified and unaffectedly majestic, and the years had not bowed his back nor enfeebled his limbs. His eye was serious and yet lively, his forehead calm and thoughtful. His white hair, his pallor, all the marks of abstinence, meditation and laborious days, could not hide a sort of virginal bloom and vigour. Every feature of his face showed that he must at one time have been a handsome man in the strictest sense of the word; now the habits of serious and benevolent thought, the inner peace of a long and virtuous life, the love of mankind and the continuous joy of an ineffable hope had planted there that other beauty old men sometimes have, which struck the eye all the more when framed in the magnificent simplicity of the purple.

The Cardinal stood silent for a little, looking intently at the Unnamed with his penetrating gaze, which had had so much practice in reading the thoughts of men from their outward appearance. Beneath the noble's fierce and troubled look, he thought he could detect, in increasing measure, something which agreed with the hopes he had begun to entertain at the first news of this visit.

'Well!' he said briskly. 'This is a happy and precious occasion, and I am most grateful to you for taking your admirable decision to come and see me – though there is an element of reproof for me in it, of course.'

'Reproof!' exclaimed the visitor, amazed but at the same time softened by the Cardinal's words and manner, and also grateful to him for breaking the ice and getting a conversation under way.

'Yes, it is a reproof for me,' the Cardinal continued, 'in that I have let you take the first step, although there have been many times, over a long period, when I should have come to you.'

'Did you say that you should have come to me? Do you know who I am? Was my name given to you correctly?'

'And do you think that the pleasure I feel at seeing you, which I know you can read in my face, could have been inspired by the visit of a man of whom I had never heard? I feel that pleasure for you – for you, whom I should long ago have sought out; for you, whom I have so long loved, and on whom I have spent so many tears and so many prayers; for you who – heartily as I love all my children – are the one I would have most desired to welcome and embrace, if I had dared to hope that it might come to pass. But miracles are in the hand of God, and he makes good the feeble and sluggish efforts of his poor servants.'

The Unnamed was amazed at the Cardinal's passionate speech, at the words which formed so definite an answer to all that he had not yet said, nor even made up his mind to say at all. Deeply stirred, but dazed at the same time, he remained silent.

'Well?' continued Federigo, yet more affectionately. 'You have some good news for me; are you going to keep me waiting for it?'

'Good news? From me? When I've all hell raging in my heart, you expect to hear good news from me? Tell me, if you can, what sort of good news you think you might get from a fellow like me?'

'The news that God has touched your heart, and wants to make you his own,' replied the Cardinal evenly.

'God? God? If I could see him or hear him now! Where is this God of yours?'

'You ask me that? Yet who stands nearer to him at this moment than you do? Do you not feel him in your heart? Does he not oppress and agitate your spirit, never leaving you a moment's peace? And does he not at the same time allure you, giving you a foretaste of the hope of tranquillity and happiness – a happiness which will be complete and unbounded as soon as you acknowledge him, confess to him, implore his mercy?'

'Yes, yes! There is indeed something oppressing my heart, torturing my vitals. But where does God come into it? If your

God exists, if he is the God of whom we hear, what do you think he can do with me?'

Those words were uttered, with a note of desperation; but Federigo replied in calm, solemn, yet inspired tones: 'Do you ask what God can do with you – what it is his will that you should become? Why, a sign of his power and his goodness. He wants to gain from you a glory which he can gain from no one else. What glory is it for God that the whole world abhors your ways, that thousands of voices are raised to proclaim their detestation of your actions' – the Unnamed jumped at this, astounded to hear these words which no one had ever dared to address to him before, and more astounded still to note that his reaction was not one of anger, but almost one of relief – 'what glory is there for God in all that?' continued Federigo. 'Those voices are voices of ignoble fear, of narrow self-interest; perhaps they are also voices of justice, but what a facile, earthly sort of justice it is! Some, alas, may be voices of envy, aroused by the sight of the power you unhappily wield, or by the deplorable inner confidence you have so far displayed ... But when you yourself rise up to condemn your own life, and accuse yourself, that will be the day when God is glorified! And you ask what God can do with you! Poor wretch that I am, who am I to tell you what profit so great a Lord may find in you, and what use he may make of that ardent will, that unshakable resolution, when he has animated them and fired them with flames of love, hope and repentance? Poor wretch that you are, who are you to think that the deeds of wickedness which you have planned and carried out by yourself can outweigh the deeds of goodness which God may make you plan and carry out by his will? What can God do with you indeed! Is it nothing that he can forgive you, and save you, and fulfil in you the work of redemption? Are not such acts magnificent and worthy of him? Think now! If I – miserable little creature that I am, and so full of myself in spite of it – can be so deeply anxious for your salvation that, as God is my witness, I would cheerfully surrender in return the few remaining years of my life, then think what charity must be in him, who inspires me with this imperfect copy of it – imperfect indeed, but how deeply felt! How he must love you and wish you well, when he bids me love you and inspires me with the love for you which consumes me now!'

As these words left his lips, his face, his eyes, every movement of his body spoke the same language as his tongue. His listener's face had been strained and contorted; it changed first to a look of astonished and intent concentration, and finally took on a look of deeper but less painful emotion. His eyes, which had never shed a tear since his childhood, began to swell up; and when the Cardinal's speech was over, he covered his face with his hands, and broke into a passionate weeping, which was the final and the clearest possible response.

'Almighty God and Father of mercies!' exclaimed Federigo, raising eyes and hands towards heaven, 'Who am I, unfaithful steward and neglectful shepherd as I am, to deserve to be called by you to this feast of grace, to be made a witness of so happy a miracle!' As he spoke, he stretched out his hand to take that of the Unnamed.

'No, no!' cried the nobleman. 'Keep away from me – do not soil that innocent and virtuous hand! You do not know all that this hand of mine has done!'

But the Cardinal seized it with loving violence, saying: 'Do not prevent me from clasping that hand which is to right so many wrongs, which will perform such widespread good works, which will raise up so many of the afflicted, which will offer itself, unarmed, to so many enemies in peace and humility.'

'But this is too much!' sobbed the Unnamed. 'Leave me, Your Grace; my good lord Federigo, leave me! A great throng is waiting outside for you. All those good souls, those innocent people, who have come from far away so that they may see you at least once in their lives, and hear your voice; and you withhold your presence from them, while you talk to the unworthiest . . .'

'Never mind the nine and ninety sheep,' replied the Cardinal. 'They are safe on the mountainside; and I mean to stay here with the one that was lost. Those souls may well be happier at the moment than the sight of a poor shepherd like myself could make them. Perhaps God, who has granted you the miracle of his mercy, is filling their souls with a joy which they themselves do not yet understand. That crowd may be at one with us without knowing it; perhaps the Lord is instilling a mysterious, loving warmth into their hearts, inspiring their minds with a prayer which he is already granting for your sake, with a gratitude of which you are the still unknown cause.'

With these words he put his arms round the neck of the Unnamed, who at first tried to draw away, and resisted for a moment; but then he seemed to be overcome by that impulse of divine charity and threw his arms around the Cardinal, hiding his quivering, strangely altered face against his shoulder. His hot tears fell on the stainless purple of Federigo's robe, and the Cardinal's unsullied hands embraced the author of so much violence and treachery, clasping the jacket which had so often concealed the instruments of death.

The Unnamed freed himself from that embrace, put one hand over his eyes, and raised his face, saying: 'O truly great and truly merciful God! Now I know myself, now I understand what I am! My iniquities stand before my eyes, and I am revolted by myself – and yet ... and yet I feel a comfort, a joy ... yes, yes, a joy such as I have never known during all this repugnant life of mine!'

'That is a foretaste of joys to come,' replied Federigo, 'which God gives you to make you love his service, and to hearten you to enter resolutely into the new life in which you will have so much evil to undo, so many acts of reparation to perform, so many tears to shed.'

'God help me!' cried the nobleman. 'There are so many things I have done over which I can indeed shed tears, but for which I can make no other reparation now ... but at least there are other wicked enterprises which I have only recently set on foot, and which I can break off in the middle, if no more. There is one, in fact, which does offer me the chance to break it off, undo the wrong that has been done, and make full reparation.'

The Cardinal showed fresh interest at this, and the Unnamed told him briefly, but in terms of abhorrence even stronger than those we have used ourselves, about the outrageous treatment to which Lucia had been subjected, her terrors, her sufferings and the imploring appeals she had addressed to him; and how those appeals had filled him with a restless despair; and how she was still there in the castle.

'Then we must be quick!' exclaimed Federigo. drawing a deep breath of concern as he heard the pitiful story. 'God has been very good to you! This is a pledge of his forgiveness, that he has made it possible for you to be the instrument of salvation to the very person you were seeking to ruin. God bless you! ... but he has already blessed you! Do you know where this poor child's home is?'

The Unnamed mentioned the name of Lucia's village.

'Praised be God!' said the Cardinal. 'It is not far from here ... in fact probably ...' He went quickly over to the table, and rang a little bell. The chaplain bustled in anxiously at once. First of all he looked at the Unnamed, and saw his changed expression and his eyes red with weeping; then he looked at the Cardinal. Beneath the unshakable composure of Federigo Borromeo's face he could see a grave happiness, an almost impatient solicitude. He stood there for a moment with his mouth open, rapt in contemplation, until the Cardinal called him back to earth by asking him whether the parish priest of — was among the clergy assembled outside.

'Yes, Your Grace, he's there,' said the chaplain.

'Bring him in at once,' said Federigo, 'and bring in the priest of this parish as well.'

The chaplain went out into the room where all the other priests were gathered, and all eyes turned towards him. His mouth was still open, his face still full of the ecstatic contemplation of what he had seen. He raised his hands above his head and moved them gently from side to side as he said 'Friends! Friends! *Haec mutatio dexterae Excelsi!*'[1]

He stood there for a few moments without saying anything further. Then he reverted to a manner and a voice more befitting his mission, and added, 'The illustrious and most reverend Archbishop wishes to see the priest of this parish, and also the priest of —.'

The local curé came forward at once, and at the same time a

1. 'This change is from the hand of the Most High.'

strangled cry of '*Me?*', in tones of the utmost amazement, came from the middle of the crowd.

'Why, aren't you the curé of —?' said the chaplain.

'Yes, yes, I am; but . . .'

'Well, then, the illustrious and most reverend Archbishop wishes to see you.'

'Me?' said the same voice, in a tone that clearly meant: 'How do I come into it?' But this time the man himself came out of the crowd, together with the voice – Don Abbondio in person, with unwilling gait and astonished, disgruntled expression. The chaplain beckoned to him, with a gesture that meant: 'Come on! What are we waiting for?' He led the way for the two priests, and showed them in.

The Cardinal released the hand of the Unnamed, with whom he had meanwhile agreed what should be done. First of all he beckoned the local priest into a corner. He told him the story of Lucia as briefly as possible, and asked him whether he could find a trustworthy woman who would be prepared to go straight off to the castle with a litter to fetch Lucia – a good-hearted, intelligent woman, who would know how to conduct herself on such an unusual errand, and would be able to adopt the manner and use the words best calculated to hearten and tranquillize the poor girl – who after so much suffering and turmoil might well be thrown into yet deeper confusion by the very act of liberation itself. The curé thought for a moment, said he knew just the woman for the purpose, and went out. The Cardinal beckoned next to his chaplain, and told him to have the litter made ready at once, and instructions issued to the men who were to go with it, and to have two mules saddled. When the chaplain had gone out, Federigo turned to Don Abbondio.

The curé was already standing close to the Archbishop, in order to keep well away from the Unnamed. Glancing unobtrusively from one face to the other, and wondering what all this was about, Don Abbondio came closer still, bowed and said,

'I was told that Your Grace wished to see me; but I think it must have been a mistake.'

'Not at all,' said Federigo. 'I have good news for you to hear, and a most pleasant and delightful task for you to perform. You have been mourning for the loss of one of your flock, a girl named Lucia Mondella; now she has been found, near at hand, in the house of my dear friend here, and you and a good woman of this parish – the curé has gone to find her – are to go with him and fetch your poor daughter and bring her here.'

Don Abbondio did all he could to disguise the annoyance, fear and bitter distaste which he felt at this proposal, or rather command. He was not in time to dissimulate the grimace which had already distorted his features, but he hid it by bowing his head in token of obedience. And as soon as he raised his head, he bowed deeply again in the direction of the Unnamed, with a pitiful look which said, 'I am in your hands; have mercy on me; *parcere subjectis.*'[2]

The Cardinal asked him what relations Lucia had.

'She has only one close relative, living with her, and that is her mother,' said Don Abbondio.

'Is her mother at home now?'

'Yes, Your Grace, she is.'

'Well, then,' said the Cardinal, 'since the poor girl can't be sent straight home at once, it will be a great pleasure for her to see her mother as soon as possible. If the priest of this parish does not come back before I have to go to church, please ask him to find a cart or a saddle horse and send a reliable man to bring her here.'

'Or I could go, if Your Grace pleases,' said Don Abbondio.

'No, not you; I've already asked you to do something else.'

'I thought I might be able to prepare the mother for the shock. Poor woman, she's a very sensitive creature, and it really needs someone who knows her well – who knows how to handle her – to make sure the news doesn't do her more harm than good.'

'And that's just why I'm asking you to tell the curé to choose the right man to go and fetch her. You are much more urgently needed elsewhere,' said the Cardinal. He would have liked to go on and say: 'The poor girl has far more need of seeing a

2. 'Spare those who submit.'

face she knows, a person she trusts in that castle, after so many hours of cruel terror and appalling uncertainty about the future.' But he could not say that out loud in front of the Unnamed ... It seemed strange to the Cardinal that Don Abbondio had not grasped the point at once, or indeed thought of it for himself. The priest's alternative suggestion, and the insistence with which he put it forward, seemed so out of place that the Cardinal realized that there must be something behind it. He looked him in the face, and saw at once how terrified he was at the thought of travelling with that horrific companion, of entering that castle, even for a few minutes. He saw that he must do something to dispel those cowardly thoughts; but he did not want to take the curé on one side and whisper to him, with his new friend standing by. So he decided that the best course would be to go on with the very thing he would have done even without that extra motive, which was to say something further to the Unnamed, whose replies would doubtless make it finally clear to Don Abbondio that this was no longer a man of whom he should be afraid. So the Cardinal moved closer to the nobleman, and spoke to him with that air of spontaneous trust which can be inspired by a new and powerful affection no less than by an old and intimate friendship.

'You must not think', he said 'that I shall be satisfied with this single visit of yours today. You will come back, won't you, with this worthy priest?'

'Do you ask if I will come back?' replied the Unnamed. 'If you turn me from your door, I shall wait outside as obstinately as any beggar. I need to talk to you! I need to hear your voice and see your face! I need you!'

Federigo took his hand and clasped it tightly, saying: 'Then please stay and dine with us. I shall be waiting for you. But meanwhile I must go and pray, and give thanks with my people, and you must go to gather the first-fruits of the divine mercy.'

At this exchange, Don Abbondio looked rather like a timid boy, who sees a great ugly shaggy dog, with red eyes and a terrible name for biting and frightening people, being confidently patted by its master, who says it's a fine, gentle animal that wouldn't hurt anybody. The boy looks at the dog's owner, and neither contradicts nor agrees with him; he looks at the dog, without daring to go any nearer in case the fine, gentle animal should show its teeth at him, even as a friendly greeting. He does not like to slink away in case people notice; but he heartily wishes that he were safe at home.

As the Cardinal moved towards the door with the Unnamed, whom he was still holding by the hand, he was struck by the pathetic figure of the priest, who was left behind in a mortified and unhappy state, grimacing in spite of himself. Federigo thought that perhaps the trouble was that Don Abbondio felt neglected, and so to speak left in a corner; especially in comparison with the kind and loving treatment given to a man with many crimes on his head. So he turned towards the curé as he passed, paused for a moment, and said with an affectionate smile: 'Your Reverence is always with me in the house of the Lord; but here is someone who ... who ... *qui perierat et inventus est.*[3]

'I am overjoyed by what has happened,' said Don Abbondio, with a deep and reverent bow, addressed to both of them jointly.

The Archbishop went to the door and pushed it gently. Two servants, who were standing on either side of the door in the outer room, immediately flung its two leaves wide, and the astonishing couple appeared before the eager eyes of the clergy gathered there. The two faces displayed emotions which were equally profound, but very different in kind. A tender gratitude and a humble joy appeared on Federigo's venerable features, while on those of the Unnamed could be read a turmoil in which there was an element of comfort, a new sense of honest shame, and a compunction which did not conceal the vigour of that wild and fiery spirit. It was discovered afterwards that at that moment the words of Isaiah had come into the minds of several of those present,

'The wolf also shall dwell with the lamb; and the lion shall eat straw with the ox.'

Last of all came Don Abbondio, of whom no one took any notice.

3. 'Who was lost and is found.'

When they were in the middle of the outer room, the Cardinal's chamberlain entered from the other side, and came up to tell him that he had carried out the instructions he had received from the chaplain. The litter and the two mules were ready, and they were only waiting for the woman whom the parish priest had gone to fetch. The Cardinal told the chamberlain to make sure that the curé had a word with Don Abbondio as soon as he returned; after which everything was to be done in accordance with the instructions of Don Abbondio and the Unnamed.

The Cardinal grasped the Unnamed's hand again, in farewell this time, and said 'I shall be waiting for you.' He turned and said good-bye to Don Abbondio, and moved off towards the church. The clergy flocked behind him, forming something between a crowd and a procession. The two travelling companions were left together in the room.

The Unnamed's attention was turned inwards. Deep in thought, he was impatient for the moment to come when he could go and free his Lucia from her sorrows and open the door of her prison – for now he thought of her as his Lucia in a very different sense from that in which he might have used the words the night before. His face was full of a troubled concentration which could easily appear as something worse to the timid eye of Don Abbondio. He looked at the Unnamed out of the corner of his eye, and would have liked to start a friendly conversation with him.

'But then what am I to say to him?' he wondered. 'Shall I repeat that I'm overjoyed? But overjoyed about what? The fact that, having behaved like a devil incarnate up to now, he's decided to be a good citizen like anyone else? That doesn't make much of a compliment! But however I turn my congratulations round, they will inevitably come back to precisely that. And can it really be true that he has turned into a good citizen, just like that, in a flash? People so often put on an act in this world, and for so many different reasons! Haven't I been fooled myself, more than once? And now I've got to go with *him*! I've got to go to *that* castle! Oh, what a business! what a business! Who'd have thought this morning that anything like

424

this would happen! If I get back from this trip safe and sound, I shall have something to say to Madame Perpetua, who made me leave my parish and come to this place when it wasn't necessary at all. All the parish priests for miles around were flocking to see the Cardinal, she said, even those who lived further away than us; and I mustn't hold back in a thing like that; and so on and so on; until she got me launched into an adventure like this! Oh dear! Oh dear! ... But I must say something to this man.'

So he racked his brains for a suitable remark, and finally decided he could say: 'Well! I never thought I would have the good fortune to travel in such distinguished company!' He was just opening his mouth to utter these words, when in came the chamberlain, with the curé of the parish, who announced that the woman was now outside in the litter. Then he turned towards Don Abbondio, to receive the Cardinal's further instructions. Don Abbondio delivered the message as well as he could in the confusion of the moment. Then he went a little closer to the chamberlain, and said: 'Please give me a quiet beast to ride, anyway. To tell you the truth, I'm not much of a horseman.'

'It's quite all right,' said the chamberlain, with a slightly sneering smile. 'The mule you're getting belongs to the secretary, who's the scholarly type. She's quiet enough.'

'Good,' said Don Abbondio. But he put up a silent prayer that she would be quiet for him.

The Unnamed had begun to move as soon as he heard the chaplain's first words; but when he reached the door, he remembered Don Abbondio, who was left behind. He stopped and waited for him; and when the priest bustled up, with an apologetic air, the noble bowed to him and insisted that he should go out first, with a polite and modest gesture. This made the poor sufferer feel a little less queasy. But as soon as they were outside, he saw something else which took away that crumb of consolation – he saw the Unnamed go over to the corner and pick up his carbine, one hand grasping it by the barrel and the other by the sling; he flicked it quickly into place over his shoulder, as if practising arms-drill.

'Oh dear!' thought Don Abbondio. 'What does he want that thing for? Talk about hair shirts and scourges for the newly penitent! What happens if he gets another new idea into his head now? What a business! What an expedition!'

If the noble had had the slightest idea what sort of thoughts were passing through his companion's head, it is hard to say what he would have done to reassure him. But in fact the Unnamed was far from suspecting anything of the kind; and Don Abbondio was very careful not to say anything that might be taken as meaning 'I don't trust Your Lordship.'

When they reached the gate, there were the two mules ready and waiting. A groom offered one to the Unnamed, who jumped on its back at once.

Don Abbondio raised his foot towards the stirrup. 'She hasn't got any vices, has she?' he said to the chamberlain, lowering it to the ground again.

'If you'll just get up on her back, you'll find she's like a lamb.'

Clutching at the saddle, helped by the chamberlain, Don Abbondio managed to scramble up on to the beast.

The litter, carried by two mules, was a few yards in front. The driver shouted to his beasts, which began to move, and the whole party set off.

But first they had to pass in front of the church, which was crammed full of people, across a little square which was also full of people from the parish and from farther afield who had not been able to get into the building. The great news was already generally known; and when the group of travellers appeared, the sight of that man – so recently an object of terror and execration, and now an object of happy astonishment – caused a murmur of something like applause in the crowd. As people made way for them, there was also a certain amount of pushing at the back from others who wanted to get a closer view. First the litter went by, and then the Unnamed; as he passed the open door of the church, he took off his hat, and bowed the forehead whose frown had been so dreaded until it touched the mane of his mule, amid the murmur of many voices saying: 'God bless your Honour!'

Don Abbondio also lifted his hat, bowed and recommended

himself to Providence; but then he heard the solemn harmony of his colleagues' voices pealing out from the church, and he felt such sad tenderness, such melancholy, such envy, that he had difficulty in restraining his tears.

When they had got away from any sign of habitation, and were in the open country, following the windings of a road which was often completely deserted, the priest's thoughts took on a blacker hue. There was nothing in sight to inspire him with confidence, except the back of the driver of the litter, who was in the service of the Cardinal and therefore must be a good man, and who did not look like a weakling either. From time to time travellers appeared, often in groups, who were hurrying along the other way to see the Cardinal. This was a comfort to Don Abbondio – but only a passing one, for he was getting nearer and nearer all the time to that dreaded valley, where he would see no one but the retainers of his new friend – and what retainers they would be!

He wanted more than ever to have a talk to his new friend, both to find out more about him and to keep him in a good mood; but he saw that the Unnamed was sunk in thought, and changed his mind about speaking to him. This left him no alternative but to talk to himself – silently, that is. What follows is a part of what the poor man said to himself during that journey – a complete report would fill a book.

It's true enough that both great saints and great criminals have to have quicksilver in their veins, and that they're not content with being always in motion themselves, but want to have the whole world dancing to their tune; and the busiest men out of the lot of them have to come and bother me, though I never bother anyone myself, and drag me into their affairs, though I ask nothing more than to be left to live my life in peace! That crazy brute Don Rodrigo! He'd got all he needed to be the happiest man in the world, if he'd had a grain of sense. Rich ... young ... respected ... everyone paying court to him ... but he doesn't like being well off, so he has to go looking for trouble, trouble for himself and for every one else too. He could have lived the life of Michelaccio;[4] but no,

4. A fairly close equivalent to the life of Riley. – Translator's note.

nothing would do for him but this business of molesting women, which is the maddest, crookedest, craziest business in the world. He could go to heaven in a coach and six, and he chooses to go to the devil on a lame old nag ... And as for this one! – (Here he glanced at the Unnamed, as if afraid that he might be a thought-reader.) – This one, after turning the whole world upside down for so many years with his villainies, now wants to turn it upside down all over again with his conversion ... *if* it's genuine! And I'm to be the subject of the first test of its genuineness ... There's no help for it; if they're born with that restlessness in their veins, they have to go on making trouble to the end. Is it so very difficult to behave decently all through your life, like I've done? But that's not the idea at all – first you have to kill and murder and play the devil generally (God forgive me!) – and then cause more trouble and confusion with your repentance. With a bit of good will, repentance is a thing that can be attended to at home, unostentatiously, without all this inconvenience to everyone else. And His Most Illustrious Grace opens his arms to the man at once, with 'my dear friend', 'my very dear friend', and all the rest of it. He believes every word the man says, as if ... as if he'd seen him perform a miracle. He takes his decisions at once, straight in with both feet, 'you go off and do this!' and 'you go off and do that!' In my family we used to believe in the saying 'More haste, less speed.' ... And without any guarantee of good behaviour, His Grace puts a poor priest right into the man's power! That's what you might call playing pitch and toss with a man's life. A saintly bishop like His Grace ought to value his priests like the apple of his eye. I don't see why you can't have a little reflection, a little prudence, a little charity, and still be as saintly as you like. And supposing it's all a sham? Who knows what's in any man's heart? – let alone a man like that! And to think that I've got to go right into his castle with him! There may be some dirty work afoot. Heaven help me! it's better not to think about that ... And what's this complication about Lucia? Was there some sort of deal with Don Rodrigo? What terrible people there are in this world! But at least that would be something you could understand. But then how did she finish up in

428

this one's clutches? How should I know? His Grace keeps everything to himself. They tell me to trot all over the place, but they don't tell me what's going on. It's not that I'm curious about other people's affairs, but if a man has got to risk his skin, that gives him a right to know what it's all about. If it were really only a matter of fetching that poor girl, I wouldn't mind. But then why didn't he bring her with him when he came to see His Grace? If he's so converted as all that, if he's suddenly turned into a holy father, what need is there for me to come as well? Oh, what a chaotic muddle! Well, never mind; pray God that it is all true! It'll be a nasty business to look back on, but no matter. I shall be happy when it's over, for Lucia's sake, poor girl, as well as my own; she must have had a wonderful escape too. Heaven knows what she's suffered. I'm sorry for her, though she seems to have been born into this world to be the ruin of me. I wish I could really see into this man's heart, and know what he's thinking. How can you tell? Look at him: one moment like St Anthony in the desert, and the next like King Herod himself ... Oh dear, oh dear! Never mind, Providence is bound to help me, because I didn't get into this from any whim of my own.

It was true enough that the Unnamed's thoughts could be seen passing across his face, like clouds on a stormy day sweeping across the face of the sun, so that wild gleams of light alternate with moments of chilly gloom. His mind was still deeply affected by Federigo's gentle eloquence, so that he felt rejuvenated, or rather reborn into a new life, and his soul soared into the realm of pity, forgiveness and love – only to fall back again under the weight of his terrible past sins. He eagerly searched his memory for crimes which were not past all hope of reparation, for evil enterprises which could still be cut short. He considered which would be the most effective and the surest remedies to apply, how to cut through so many knots, and what to do with so many accomplices. It was enough to drive a man mad. This first task, though the easiest of the lot and now near to completion, filled him with impatience, and at the same time with anguish at the thought that the poor girl was suffering God knew what agony at that very moment, and that he himself, for all his eagerness to set her free, was still the gaoler who made her suffer.

When they came to a fork, the driver turned round for instructions; the Unnamed pointed out the right road to him, at the same time urging him with a gesture to make all the speed he could.

Then they entered the valley. You would have been sorry for Don Abbondio, if you could have seen him at that moment. The famous valley, of which he had heard so many horrible stories! And now he was there himself! Those notorious men, the very flower of the bravoes of Italy, men without fear or pity! And now he was seeing them in the flesh, meeting two or three of them at every bend in the road! They bowed respectfully enough to their master – but those bronzed faces! Those bristling moustaches! Those fierce eyes, in which Don Abbondio seemed to read the words, 'How about a really special reception for this priest?' He even reached the point of desperation where he found himself saying: 'I wish I'd married them after all! I couldn't have been worse off than I am now!'

Meanwhile they were travelling along a stony path, parallel with the stream. On the far side was a prospect of rugged, dark, uninhabited slopes; the near side was populated, but the company was such that the solitude of any desert would have been preferable. Dante was not worse off in the middle of the Malebolge.[5]

They passed the inn. Huge bravoes stood on the door step; they bowed to the nobleman, and looked curiously at his companion and at the litter. They did not know what to think. There had been something extraordinary about the way their master had gone off alone that morning, and his return now was equally strange. Were those prisoners with him? If so, how had he managed the operation single-handed? The litter did not belong to the castle; what was it doing there? Whose livery was the driver wearing? They stared and stared, but none of them moved, because their master restrained them with a look.

The party mounted the slope, and reached the top. The bravoes waiting by the door, and on the flat space in front of it,

5. Malebolge – the Eighth Circle of Dante's Inferno. – Translator's note.

drew back on either side to make way. The Unnamed signed to them not to move again. He spurred his way past the litter, and beckoned to the driver and to Don Abbondio to follow him. He led them through one courtyard and into another. He rode up to a small door, and waved back the bravo who ran up to hold his stirrup, saying 'You wait there – and don't let anyone in.' He dismounted, quickly tied his mule up to a grating, and went up to the litter. The woman inside had drawn back the curtain, and he softly said to her: 'Do what you can to make her happy as soon as possible; try to make her understand straight away that she is free, that she is with friends. God will reward you for what you do.' Then he signed to the driver to open the door of the litter, and went over to Don Abbondio.

There was a serenity in his face which the priest had not seen there before, nor ever expected to see there at all. All the joy of the good deed that was at last about to be completed shone clearly in his countenance, as he said to Don Abbondio, still in that low voice:

'Your Reverence, I will not ask your pardon for the trouble I have caused you, because what you are doing is for one who knows how to reward his servants, and for this poor child of his.'

Then he held Don Abbondio's bridle and stirrup while he dismounted.

The Unnamed's expression, his words, and this last gesture restored Don Abbondio to life. He let out a sigh, which had been wandering around inside him for the past hour, without ever being able to find the way out. He leaned towards the Unnamed, and whispered 'Really, sir, really!' Then he slithered off his mule as best he could. The Unnamed tethered her beside his own and told the driver to wait there for them. He took a key out of his pocket, opened the door and went in. He beckoned the priest and the woman to follow him, and led the way to the staircase. The three of them went up together in silence.

Chapter 24

LUCIA had begun to recover consciousness only a short time before, and had spent some of that time in the painful business of waking up completely, of separating the turbid visions of her dreams from the real images and memories of her true situation, which bore all too close a resemblance to a feverish nightmare. The old woman was by her side in a moment, and said, still with that note of forced humility in her voice:

'Ah! So you've been asleep? You could have had the bed; I told you that ever so many times last night.'

Receiving no answer, she went on, still in a tone of ill-tempered supplication,

'Do eat something now; be sensible! You do look cross! But you need to eat something. What'll become of me, if the master blames me, when he comes back?'

'No, no – I want to get out of here, to go back to my mother. Your master promised me I should. "Tomorrow morning," he said. Where is he?'

'He went out; but he said he would be back soon, and that then he'll do whatever you ask him to do.'

'Did he say that? Did he really say that? Then I want to go home to my mother, now, at once.'

Then she heard steps in the next room, followed by a knock at the door. The old servant hurried across the room. 'Who's there?' she called.

'Open up,' said that well-known voice, very quietly. The old woman undid the bolt, and the Unnamed pushed the two leaves of the door gently, so that a small crack opened. Next he called the old servant out, and sent in Don Abbondio with the good woman from the village. Then he shut the door, and took up his position just outside. He sent the old servant away to a distant part of the castle – he had already sent off the other woman who had been on guard in the next room.

The noise in the outer room, the moment of waiting that followed it, the first appearance of an unknown figure, all combined to throw Lucia into a fever of anxiety: for though her present situation was an intolerable one, any change in it still aroused renewed suspicion and fresh terrors in her heart. She looked at the newcomers, and saw a priest, and a woman, which cheered her a little; then she looked again more carefully. 'Can it be him? It can't!' she thought. But it was. She recognized Don Abbondio, and sat there with her eyes fixed, as if spellbound. The woman went across and bent over Lucia with a compassionate look, taking both her hands, as if to comfort her and to help her to rise to her feet at the same time. 'Poor girl!' she said. 'Poor child! Come with us!'

'Who are you?' demanded Lucia. But then, without waiting for an answer, she turned to Don Abbondio, who was standing two paces away, also with a compassionate look on his face. She stared at him again and cried,

'You? Can it really be you, your Reverence? Then where are we? Heaven help me, I've gone out of my mind!'

'No, no, don't think that,' replied Don Abbondio. 'It's really me. Take heart; don't be frightened. We have come to take you away. I really am your parish priest. I've come here on purpose to fetch you, on horseback . . .'

Lucia seemed to have regained full command of her faculties in a moment. She straightened up quickly, stared again at her two visitors, and said,

'Then it must be the Madonna that has sent you!'

'I think you're right!' said the woman.

'But can we go now, can we really go?' said Lucia, dropping her voice, with a timid and suspicious expression. 'What about all those men?' she went on, her lips tight and trembling with fear and horror. 'What about their master? That fearful man? Though it was he who gave me the promise . . .'

'He's here too, in person; he came here with us, on purpose to free you,' said Don Abbondio. 'He's waiting outside; we'd better not be too long. We ought not to keep a man like him waiting.'

Then the man of whom he was speaking pushed the door

open and showed his face. A little before Lucia had been anxious to see him – in fact, since she had had no hope in anyone else in the world, there had been no one else that she wanted to see. But now, after a few moments of seeing friendly faces and hearing friendly voices, she could not suppress a momentary revulsion at the sight of him. She quivered, held her breath, clasped the woman tightly in her arms, and hid her face against that comforting bosom.

The Unnamed had halted just inside the door, on catching sight of Lucia's face, at which he had been unable to look steadily even the night before. and which now was still more pale, distressed and exhausted by hours of misery and hunger. When he saw her instinctive movement of terror, he lowered his eyes, and remained for a moment silent and motionless. Then he spoke in reply to the reproach which the poor girl had not uttered,

'You are right, you are right!' he cried. 'Forgive me!'

'He's come to set you free; he's not like the same man any more; he's good now. Don't you hear him asking you to forgive him?' whispered the woman to Lucia.

'What more is there that he could say? Come on now, lift up your head. Don't be a baby; we must get away as soon as we can,' said Don Abbondio.

Lucia raised her eyes and saw the Unnamed's head bowed low, his eyes looking embarrassedly at the floor. A mixed feeling of comfort, gratitude and pity overcame her, and she said:

'Oh my dear lord! God reward you for the mercy you have shown towards me!'

'And may he reward you a hundredfold for the words you have just uttered, and for the good they have done me!'

With these words the Unnamed turned towards the door, and led the way out. In much better spirits now, Lucia came next, leaning on the woman's arm; and Don Abbondio brought up the rear. They went down the stairs to the door which opened into the courtyard. The Unnamed threw it open, and went out to the litter. With a gentle, almost shy consideration which was quite new to him, he opened its door and helped Lucia in, supporting her arm; and then he did the same for her

434

companion. Next he untied Don Abbondio's mule, and helped him up on to her back.

'Such kindness! Such condescension!' said the priest, getting up much more quickly than he had on the previous occasion.

The Unnamed himself mounted, and the party moved off. The nobleman's head was now held high again, and his look had recovered its old authority. The bravoes who saw him go by detected the signs of some deep thought, some abnormal preoccupation in his face; but that was all they understood, or could be expected to understand. Nothing was yet known in the castle about the great change that had overcome the man; and there was certainly no risk of anyone guessing it.

The woman had already drawn the curtains of the litter across; and now she affectionately took both Lucia's hands and started trying to comfort her, with words of tender sympathy and congratulation on her escape. Besides the fatigue caused by all that she had been through, the confused and obscure nature of what had happened prevented the poor girl from feeling the joy of her freedom to the full. Seeing this, the woman began to talk about whatever seemed most likely to disentangle and redirect the poor girl's thoughts. She told her the name of the village for which they were bound.

'Oh, good!' said Lucia, who knew that it was not far from her own. 'Holy Mother of God, how I thank you! My mother's near there! My mother!'

'We'll send someone to fetch her at once,' said the woman, who did not know that this had already been done.'

'Yes, please; God reward you for it . . . But who are you? How is it that you came here . . .?'

'Our parish priest sent me,' said the woman. 'It's this gentleman, you see; God touched his heart, bless him, and he came to our village to talk to the sainted Archbishop, who's visiting us; and he's repented of all his terrible sins, and wants to lead another life; and he told the Archbishop that he'd kidnapped a poor innocent girl – that's you, of course – as part of a plot with another man who's got no fear of God in him, though the curé didn't tell me who the other one was.'

Lucia raised her eyes to heaven.

'Perhaps you know who it is,' continued the woman; 'but never mind all that; anyway the Archbishop said that, as it was a girl, a woman ought to go too and keep her company, and he told our curé to get someone, and the curé was kind enough to think of me ...'

'Oh! God reward you for your charitable kindness!'

'Why, whatever do you mean, you poor girl? And then the curé told me to cheer you up, and encourage you, and help you to see that you have been saved by a miracle of the Lord ...'

'Yes, yes; a real miracle, through the intercession of the Madonna.'

'Well then, he said, be of good heart; and forgive the man who did you the wrong, and be happy that God has shown mercy on him too, and pray for him; for in that way you will not only acquire merit, but feel the good of it in your own heart.'

Lucia replied with a glance which said 'yes' as clearly as words could do, but with a gentle sweetness that no words could have expressed.

'Good girl!' said the woman. 'And then, you see, as your curé happened to be there too – for we've enough priests there today, from all around, to fill four churches by themselves – the Archbishop decided to send him along too, but he hasn't been much help. I'd heard before that he wasn't worth much, but this time I couldn't help noticing that he's a real wet hen.'

'And this man – the one who was so bad and is good now – who is he?'

'Why, don't you know?' said the woman, and told Lucia his name.

'Heaven help us!' cried Lucia.

That name! How many times had she heard it repeated with horror, in stories where its owner played the part of an ogre in a fairy tale! When she reflected that she had been in those grisly clutches and was now under the pious protection of the same hand; when she thought of that horrible experience and that unexpected deliverance; when she repeated to herself the name of the man whose face she had seen marked successively by tyrannical pride, overpowering compassion, and broken humiliation, she was quite overcome, and could only murmur the words, 'Heavens! What a mercy!' over and over again.

'It's truly a great mercy,' said the woman. 'It'll be a great relief to a power of people. To think of all the lives he's turned upside down! And now, as our curé says – and anyway you can see it for yourself, just to look at him – why, he's a saint! And you can see the results of the change already.'

If we said that the good woman was not extremely curious to know rather more of the details of the great adventure in which she herself was now playing a part, we should be straying from the truth. But it must be said, to her eternal credit, that she was so affected by feelings of compassionate respect towards Lucia and by thoughts of the importance and dignity of the mission entrusted to her, that it never even occurred to her to ask any tactless or unnecessary questions. Nothing passed her lips on that journey except words of comfort and of care for the poor girl's welfare.

'Heaven knows when you last had anything to eat!' she said.

'I can't remember ... it's quite a time,' said Lucia.

'Poor child! You need something to keep your strength up.'

'Yes,' said Lucia in a feeble voice.

'Thank goodness we shall be able to find something for you as soon as we reach my place. Don't worry, now; it's not far away.'

Lucia let herself fall weakly back against the cushions of the litter, as if half asleep, and the good woman left her in peace.

For Don Abbondio the return journey was certainly not such an agonizing business as the outward one had been; but it was no joy-ride. When he had got rid of his first deadly terror, he had for a while felt as if relieved of all his troubles; but soon afterward a dozen new worries sprang up in his heart; just as, when a big tree is uprooted, the ground remains bare for a certain time, but then becomes covered with weeds. Don Abbondio now had more attention to spare for his other difficulties, and whether he looked to the present or to the future there were plenty for him to torment himself with.

437

The physical discomforts of this mode of travel, to which he was not fully accustomed, were much more noticeable now than they had been on the outward journey; especially during the steep descent from the castle to the bottom of the valley. Urged on by impatient signs from the Unnamed, the driver kept the litter moving at a good rate, and the two saddle-mules kept close behind it, at the same speed. At certain particularly steep sections, poor Don Abbondio collapsed forwards on the mule's neck, as if someone had applied a lever to him from behind. To get straight again, he had to hold on tight to the saddle-bow. He did not dare to ask the Unnamed to go more slowly; and in any case he wanted to get away from that area as soon as possible.

Whenever the path ran along the verge of an embankment or the brow of a cliff, the mule, like all mules, seemed to take a perverse delight in walking on the very edge, so that Don Abbondio found himself looking straight down a steep drop, or rather, as he expressed it to himself, a precipice.

'So you're as bad as the rest of them,' he muttered inaudibly to his beast, 'always wanting to go and look for dangers, when here's so much room to walk in safety!' He pulled the rein on the other side, but it had no effect. In his usual way, he allowed himself, angry and frightened, to be carried along a course of others' choosing.

He found the bravoes less terrifying, now that he was more certain about the true state of mind of their master. But supposing that the news of the great conversion became generally known in the castle before the visitors were well away, who could say what the bravoes' reaction would be? 'Anything might happen!' he thought to himself. 'They might get it into their heads that I'd come here as a sort of missionary! Heaven help me! They'd make a martyr of me.'

Don Abbondio was not at all distressed now by the scowl worn by the Unnamed. 'To keep those other ugly faces away from us,' he thought, 'he has to look like that himself. It's understandable enough; but why should I have to be here in the middle of a lot of people like that at all?'

Anyway they reached the bottom of the slope, and finally

made their way out of the valley as well. The frown gradually vanished from the Unnamed's forehead. Don Abbondio's face too relaxed into a more natural expression. His head lifted itself from its cramped and sunken position between his shoulders, and he stretched his arms and legs and began to arch his back a little. He looked a different man now, as he began to breathe more deeply, and, with mind more at ease than it had been, started to consider other, more distant perils.

'What's that brute Don Rodrigo going to say about all this? To be left with his nose out of joint like this, hurt in his interests and his pride – he's not going to like it a bit. Just the sort of thing that brings out the worst in him. We'll have to see whether he bears me a grudge for having been present at this ... this ceremony. If he was ready to send those two fiendish bullies to threaten me on the public highway before, Heaven knows what he'll do now! He can't quarrel with His Grace who's a far more important man than he'll ever be; he'll have to keep himself in check there. Meanwhile his heart will be full of venom, and he'll want to work it off on somebody. How do these things always end? It's the man at the bottom of the ladder who gets the kicks: it's the poor man's rags that get ripped off, not the rich man's robes. Lucia, now, will be all right; His Grace will naturally look after her safety: the other poor unlucky fellow is a long way from here, and has had his punishment already; so who's the ragged man at the bottom of the ladder going to be, if not myself? After all this physical discomfort, all this distress of mind, and without getting any credit for it, it would really be too barbarous if I get the kicks for it as well ... What will His Grace be able to do in my defence, now that he's got me involved in a thing like this? Can he guarantee that that fiendish blackguard won't do something worse to me than he did last time?

'His Grace has got so many other things to think about! He takes a hand himself in so many different matters! And then how can he give his attention to all of them? Sometimes people like that leave things in worse confusion than they found them. People who want to do good often want to do it on the grand scale; and when they've enjoyed the satisfaction of their good deed, that's enough for them. They don't want to bother themselves with all the boring, detailed consequences. But those who prefer to do evil take more trouble over it, and watch the thing through to its finish, and never take a rest until it's over, because they've got an itch to do wrong that never leaves them alone ... And am I to say that I came here at the express command of His Grace, and not of my own free will? That would sound as if I were on the side of the forces of evil. Heavens above! Me, on the side of the forces of evil! Out of gratitude, I suppose, for all the pleasure they've given me! No, no; the best thing to do will be to tell Perpetua the whole story, exactly as it really happened, and leave it to her to spread it around. So long as His Grace doesn't take it into his head to make some sort of public show out of the thing, some pointless scene, in which I shall have to play a part! Well, as soon as we get back, I shall go straight to take my leave of His Grace as quickly as I can, if he's out of church by then; if not, I'll leave my apologies and go straight home. Lucia's in good hands, and doesn't need me any more; and after all I've been through I can surely claim the right to go and have a rest. And then ... but Heaven forbid that His Grace should take a fancy to hear the whole story from the beginning, so that I'll be called on to explain that business of the wedding! That would really be the last straw! And supposing His Grace's next visit is to my parish! Oh, dear ... well, what must be, must be. I'm not going to torture myself before I have to; I've got enough troubles already. To start with, I'll shut myself up in my own house. As long as His Grace is in these parts, even Don Rodrigo won't have the face to do anything silly. And afterwards ... what'll happen then? Oh dear, I can see that my declining years are doomed to be passed in misery!'

The travellers arrived before the end of the church service. They passed through the crowd, which was as deeply stirred by the sight of them as it had been the first time; and then the two riders turned off towards the rectory, which stood in a little square at the side of the big one, while the litter went straight on towards the home of Lucia's companion.

Don Abbondio carried out his plan. As soon as he had dis-

mounted, he took his leave of the Unnamed in the most grovel-
ling terms, and begged him to make his apologies to the Archbishop, as he had to go straight back to his parish on urgent
business. Then he went to look for his pony, as he called it – the
walking-stick he had left in a corner of the parlour – and set off.
The Unnamed waited for the Cardinal to return from church.

The good woman made Lucia sit down on the best chair in
her kitchen, and bustled round to get her something to keep her
strength up, refusing, in her cheerful country way, to accept the
thanks and apologies which Lucia offered her every so often.
She quickly made up the fire under a big cooking pot, in which
a fine capon was already stewing. Before long the pot was boiling again, and she poured some of the broth into a soup-plate,
which already had some pieces of bread in it, and presented it to
Lucia. Seeing the poor girl's spirits improve with every spoonful, she thanked Heaven out loud that this adventure had happened on a day when there was something in the pot.

'Everyone's trying to do something special today,' she said,
'except for the very poor people who can hardly get enough
vetch bread and millet polenta to keep alive; though they all
hope to get something today from a charitable and generous
lord like the Lord Archbishop. But we are not in that situation
ourselves, thank Heaven. My husband has his trade, and what
with that and the bit of land we own, we get on all right. So
don't be afraid to eat up while you're waiting; and soon the
capon will be ready to serve, and you'll be able to do better for
yourself then.' She went back to watch her cooking, and prepare to serve it up.

As her strength returned and her peace of mind came back,
Lucia began to set herself to rights, in accordance with her
habits and instincts of cleanliness and modesty. Her hair was
loose and ruffled; she tidied it and put it firmly back into
position. She adjusted the neckerchief over her bosom and
around her throat. Then her fingers brushed against the rosary
which she had put round her neck the night before; she glanced
down at it, and was immediately seized by a most violent agitation. The thought of the vow she had taken had been forgotten
up to that instant, swept away by the flood of intervening

events; but now it was suddenly there again, as clear and distinct as ever. Then all her fortitude, so recently recovered, vanished again at once. If her soul had not been disciplined by a life of innocence, trust, and resignation to the divine will, the panic she felt at that moment would have turned to utter despair. After a flurry of thoughts of the kind that do not come clad in words, she murmured 'Heaven help me, what have I done?'

But as soon as the words had passed her lips, she felt terrified at having uttered them. She remembered all the circumstances of her vow – the unbearable agony of her situation, the total absence of any hope of rescue, the fervour of her prayer, the full sincerity of the feeling that had led her to make the promise. Now that her prayer had been answered, she felt that to repent of the promise would be an act of sacrilegious ingratitude, of treachery towards God and the Madonna; that such a breach of faith would bring new and more terrible disasters down on her head, with no hope of escaping from them even by the power of prayer. So she hastily swallowed back the words that had expressed her momentary regret. She reverently lifted off the rosary from her neck, and, holding it in her trembling hand, she confirmed and renewed her vow, begging at the same time, in sorrowful supplication, to be given the strength to carry it out; to be allowed to avoid the thoughts and to be spared the hazards which might, if not shake her resolution, at least break her heart.

The fact that Renzo was so far away, and so little likely to return, had been a bitter affliction to her up to this time, but now she saw in it a special dispensation of Providence, which had evidently caused both things to happen with a single object. So she tried to see in one event a sort of consolation for the other ... Next came the thought that the same Providence, to complete its work, would know how to bring resignation into Renzo's heart as well, so that he would be able to forget ... But that conclusion, which it had cost her some trouble to reach, at once brought fresh consternation to her mind. Poor Lucia again felt her heart ready to repent of its decision, and again had recourse to prayer and to repetitions of her vow, engaging in a struggle from which she emerged as the weary and wounded conqueror of a felled but still living enemy.

Suddenly she heard a scuffling of feet and a sound of happy voices. It was her hostess's family coming back from church. A small boy and his two little sisters came jumping in. They stopped for a moment to glance curiously at Lucia, and then ran to their mother and gathered round her. One wanted to be told the name of the unknown guest, and all about her; one wanted to tell the story of the wonderful things they had seen; and their mother replied to everything with the words: 'Hush now, all of you!'

Then the master of the house came in, in less of a hurry, but with an air of affectionate concern on his face. He was a tailor, in case we did not mention the fact before – the tailor of the village, and of the area all round it – and a man who could read, and had in fact read all through, more than once, the *Lives of the Saints*, the *Guerrin Meschino*, and the *Reali di Francia*;[1] so that he passed, in that place, for a man of talent and learning. He modestly refused to accept any such praise, however, saying only that he had missed his vocation – if he'd really gone in for studying, now, instead of a lot of other people, who'd only wasted their time at it . . . ! With all this, he was one of the best people you could find anywhere.

He had been there when the priest had asked his wife to undertake her charitable mission; and he had not only given his approval, but would have encouraged her if she had needed it. And now that the service in the thronged church, with all its pomp, and above all the Cardinal's sermon, had fortified all his best feelings, he had come home with an expectant, anxious desire to know how the expedition had gone, and to see the poor innocent girl who had been rescued.

'Here she is!' said his wife, as he came in, pointing to Lucia, who blushed, stood up and began to stammer an apology. But he came up to her and interrupted her words with a most friendly greeting, saying: 'Welcome! Welcome to this house, to which you bring the blessing of Heaven! How glad I am to see you here! I was sure you would be all right, because the

1. Popular story-books, of small literary value. – Translator's note.

Lord does not leave his miracles half-finished; but I am delighted to see you here. Poor girl! Poor girl! But it's a great thing to have been the subject of a miracle!'

(It must not be thought that this man, because of his reading of the *Lives of the Saints*, was the only person to use the word 'miracle' of Lucia's adventure. In point of fact everyone throughout the village and far around spoke of it in those terms for as long as the memory of the story lasted. And, to tell the truth, the tale was soon so embroidered with additional material that you could hardly call it anything else.)

Then the man went quietly over to his wife, who was taking the pot off the hook, and said; 'How did it go?'

'Fine, fine; I'll tell you later.'

'Yes, of course; when you're ready.'

Having served up, the woman went over to Lucia, accompanied her to the table and gave her a seat. Then she cut off a wing from the capon and put it in front of her. She and her husband sat down, both of them encouraging their exhausted and shamefaced guest to eat something.

As the first mouthfuls went down, the tailor began to hold forth in very emphatic terms, amid interruptions from the children, who were also at the table, and who had certainly seen too many wonderful things themselves that day to be content with the role of audience for long. Their father described the solemn ceremonies in the church, and then switched to the subject of the miraculous conversion of the Unnamed. But the thing which had made most impression on him, the subject to which he returned most frequently, was the Cardinal's sermon.

'To see him there in front of the altar,' he said, 'a great lord like that, just like an ordinary priest...'

'And with that gold thing on his head too!' said one of the little girls.

'Be quiet. To think that a great lord like that, and a great scholar, who's read all the books in the world, so they say, which is something no one has ever done before, even in Milan ... to think that he can adapt himself to ordinary folk, and say those wonderful things in a way that everyone can understand.'

'Yes, I could understand too!' said another little chatterbox.

'Be quiet! ... What do you think you could understand anyway?'

'I understood that he was explaining the Gospel instead of his Reverence.'

'Be quiet! I don't mean only people with a bit of knowledge, who you'd expect to understand. Even the stupidest and most ignorant folk were following the whole thread of his argument. Now if you went and asked them to repeat the words he used, why, that's another matter and they wouldn't be able to give you a single one; but they've all got his meaning there inside them. And though he never mentioned that other nobleman, you could tell well enough that he had him in mind ... Well, you couldn't help but understand him, when you saw the tears in his eyes; and then everyone else began to weep too ...'

'That's true enough,' burst out the little boy. 'But why were they all crying like that, as if they were babies?'

'Be quiet! Though there are some hard-hearted folk in this village, as we know. And he explained how, even if there's a famine, we must thank the Lord, and be content. We must work hard, help each other, and be content ... Because the worst thing that can happen to you isn't suffering or being poor; the worst thing is doing what's wrong. And it's not just a lot of fine words, because we all know that he lives like a poor man himself, and takes the bread out of his own mouth to feed the hungry, and all the time he could live in luxury, if he wanted to, more than anyone. Now that's the sort of man that's good to listen to; not like so many others, who'll tell you: "Do what I say, not what I do" – and then he made it quite clear that it's not only the gentry, but all of us, if we have more than we need, have a duty to share it with those who are in want.'

Here he suddenly stopped, as if struck by a thought. He paused for a moment, and then made up a plateful of the good things on the table, and added a hunk of bread. He put a napkin under the plate and twisted up the four corners together and said to the elder of the two little girls: 'Get hold of this!' He put a small bottle of wine in her other hand, and said: 'Run round to Maria's house, the widow, you know, and give her this lot. Tell her that it's for her and the kids, to have a bit of a

445

party. But do it nicely, mind; don't make it look like charity. And don't say anything if you meet somebody on the way; and don't break the plate.'

Lucia's eyes were full of tears, and a warmth stole over her that did her heart good. Even before this, the words that she had heard around that table had brought her a peace that no speech made on purpose to comfort her could have provided. Her mind was uplifted by her host's words – by the description of the pomp and circumstance in the church, and of those feelings of pity and wonder among the people – and she was carried away by the enthusiasm of the narrator, so that her attention was distracted from the painful reflections that were centred on herself; and when they did return she felt that she had more strength to deal with them than before. The bitterness of the great sacrifice that she had made was still with her, but it was mixed with a certain feeling of solemn and austere joy.

Soon afterwards the local priest came in. The Cardinal had sent him, he said, to see how Lucia was, and to tell her that His Grace would like to see her that same day; His Grace also sent his thanks to the tailor and his wife.

Their emotion and confusion did not allow any of them to reply to such messages from so exalted a source.

'And hasn't your mother arrived yet?' said the curé to Lucia.

'My mother?' cried Lucia in amazement. The curé explained that he had sent a messenger to fetch her, on the Cardinal's orders; and Lucia put her apron over her face and burst into a passionate fit of weeping, which lasted until some time after the priest had left. But when the strong emotions aroused by the news began to give way to calmer reflection, the poor girl remembered that the consolation of reunion with her mother – so near at hand now, so beyond all hope only a few hours before – was something she had expressly mentioned in her prayers during those hours of terror, something that she had made a condition of her vow. '*Let me get back safely to my mother, O Mother of God!*' she had said, and the words now rang in her ears again. They gave yet more strength to her resolution to keep her promise, and made her repent afresh, and yet more

446

bitterly, of the despairing cry of 'What have I done?' which had passed her lips when she first remembered her vow.

Agnese was already quite close, as they were speaking of her. It is easy to imagine what the poor woman had felt when she received that unexpected invitation, accompanied by the news – necessarily incomplete and muddled – of a danger which was indeed in a sense already past, but was still horrifying; a terrible event, of which the messenger could give no details and no explanation, while she had no information on which to base an explanation of her own. She tore her hair; she cried 'Oh God! Oh Mother of God!' several times; and she asked the messenger various questions which he could not answer. Then she jumped into the cart and sped away, still uttering exclamations and asking fruitlessly for more details. But when she had gone a certain distance, she met Don Abbondio, who was walking along very slowly, with his stick tapping in front of him at every step. There was a cry of surprise from either side, and the priest halted in his tracks, while Agnese stopped the cart and got out. They stepped aside into a chestnut grove that stood near by, and Don Abbondio told her all that he had been able to learn from others, and all that he had been compelled to see for himself. The story was still far from clear; but at least Agnese was fully assured that Lucia was safe, and she breathed more freely.

Then Don Abbondio changed the subject, and tried to give her a long lecture on the right way to conduct herself with the Archbishop, if he wanted to talk to her and her daughter, as he probably would; with a special word about the importance of not mentioning the subject of Lucia's postponed wedding ... But Agnese saw at once that the dear man was concerned only with his own interests, and she cut him short without promising or agreeing to anything at all; for she had other things to think about. And so she drove on again.

Finally the cart reached the village, and stopped at the tailor's house. Lucia sprang up from her seat; Agnese jumped down from the cart and ran in, and in a moment they were in each other's arms. The tailor's wife, who was the only person in the house at the moment, made encouraging and soothing remarks, visibly sharing in their happiness, and then tactfully left them alone together, saying that she must go and get a bed ready for them; she had enough room to do that without any inconvenience, she said, but even if she hadn't, she and her husband would gladly have slept on the floor rather than send Lucia off to look for another lodging elsewhere.

After the first flurry of embraces and tears was over, Agnese wanted to hear all about her daughter's adventures, and Lucia breathlessly embarked on her narrative. But, as the reader is aware, it was a story which no one person yet knew in all its details. Even for Lucia herself, there were some obscure passages in it, some of them quite inexplicable – above all, the fatal coincidence that the ill-omened carriage had been there on the road just as she was passing on a most unusual errand. Mother and daughter both put forward various conjectures, none of which hit the mark, or indeed came anywhere near it.

As for the original author of the plot, neither of them could avoid the conclusion that it must be Don Rodrigo.

'The black-hearted, damned villain!' cried Agnese. 'But his day of reckoning will come! God will pay him as he has deserved, and then he'll know what it's like to suffer ...'

'No, no, mother, no!' interrupted Lucia. 'Don't wish him to suffer like that! Don't wish it for anybody! If only you knew what it's like! If only you'd felt it yourself! No, no! Let's pray God and the Madonna to help him; so that God will touch his heart, as He touched the heart of that other poor gentleman, who was worse than Don Rodrigo; and now he's a saint.'

Lucia went on with the story, though the renewal of such recent and cruel memories made her stop several times. More than once she said that she hadn't the heart to go on, and was barely able to take up the thread again, after many tears. But at one point a different feeling made her pause, and that was when she came to the vow she had made. She was afraid that her mother would say that she had been hasty and unwise; or that she would put forward some less rigid moral views of her own and try to force Lucia to accept them, as she had done over the question of the wedding; or that the poor woman would tell someone else about it, in confidence, if only to have the benefit

448

of another opinion, and so make it a matter of general knowledge – Lucia could feel her face going red at the very thought of it.

She also felt a sort of shame at the idea of discussing the question with her mother, an inexplicable reluctance to open the subject. All these factors together had the result of making her leave that important event out of her story, with the intention of telling Father Cristoforo about it before anyone else.

What a shock she had when she asked after the good father, and was told that he was not there any more; that he had been sent away to a far-off place with a strange name!

'How about Renzo, then?' said Agnese.

'He is safe, isn't he?' said Lucia, anxiously.

'Yes, he must be, everyone says so; they think he's got away to the territory of Bergamo, but no one knows the exact place, and so far he hasn't sent any news of himself. He can't have found a way of getting a message through yet.'

'Ah, if he's safe, thank God for that!' said Lucia, and tried to change the subject. At that moment there was an unexpected interruption – the arrival of the Archbishop.

When the Cardinal had come out of church, which is where we last saw him, he had heard from the Unnamed that Lucia had arrived safely. He had then taken the nobleman off to dine with him, seating him on his right hand, in a circle of priests, who could not help glancing continually at that face – tamed now, but not weak; humbled now, but not debased – and comparing it with the image of the Unnamed which had long been in their minds.

When they had dined, the Archbishop and the Unnamed went off together for another private talk, which lasted much longer than the first one had done. Then the Unnamed rode away to his castle, on the same mule which he had used in the morning, while the Cardinal called the local priest and asked to be taken to the house where Lucia was resting.

'Oh, Your Grace,' replied the curé, 'don't put yourself to so much trouble. I'll send for them to come here – the girl, her mother if she's arrived, and their host and hostess if Your Grace wants to see them – whatever Your Grace wishes.'

'I wish to go to them,' replied the Cardinal.

'Your most noble Grace really should not put himself out like that. Let me send for them; they'll be here in a moment,' insisted the uncomprehending curé. An excellent man in many ways, he had failed to grasp that the Cardinal wanted to make this visit as an act of homage to misfortune, innocence, hospitality and to his own ministry. But when his superior repeated his wish for a third time, the curé bowed and led the way.

When the two men were seen coming out into the street, all the people waiting there surged around them, and more came running up in the next few moments. Those who could get a place at the Cardinal's side walked there, and the others crowded along behind. The curé anxiously muttered: 'Back a little! Back now, please! Really! Really!' The Cardinal said, 'Let them do as they wish', and walked slowly on, now raising his hand to bless the crowd, now lowering it to pat the heads of the children who ran in front of him. And so they reached the house and went in, while the crowd remained close packed round the door.

In the middle of the throng was the tailor, who had followed on behind with the staring open-mouthed crowd, without knowing the Cardinal's destination. When he realized what that unexpected destination was, he struggled through the throng with a noisy vigour which can easily be imagined.

'Let me pass!' he shouted. 'I've a right to pass!' And so he went into his house.

Agnese and Lucia heard a murmur in the street, which grew steadily louder; and while they were wondering what it could possibly be they saw the door open, and there was a towering purple-clad figure, accompanied by the curé.

'Is this the girl?' said the Cardinal to the priest, who nodded.

The Cardinal walked over to Lucia, who was standing there with her mother, both of them dumb and motionless with awe and amazement. But the tone of Federigo Borromeo's voice, the expression on his face, his manner, and above all his words, soon brought them back to life.

'Poor girl!' he began. 'God has allowed you to be sorely tried; but he has also shown you clearly that his eyes have never left you, that he has never forgotten you. Now he has set you free; and in so doing he has made use of you for a great work, to show his almighty mercy to one man in particular, and to relieve many others of their troubles at the same time.'

At this point the mistress of the house came into the room. She had been upstairs when she heard the noise in the street, and had looked out of the window. When she saw who was coming into her house, she tidied herself up as well as she could and ran downstairs, just as her husband was coming in at the other door. Seeing that the conversation was already under way, they went and stood together in a corner of the room in respectful silence. The Cardinal greeted them politely, and went on talking to Lucia and her mother, speaking words of comfort to them, among which he mingled some questions, to see whether, from their answers, he could find an opportunity of helping those who had so greatly suffered.

'It would be a fine thing if all the priests were like Your Grace, and sided with the poor folk a bit more, and weren't so ready to drop them in the mire so as to get out of it themselves!' said Agnese, encouraged by the Cardinal's familiar and affectionate manner, and angry to think how Don Abbondio, who always sacrificed other people's interests to his own, had claimed the right to stop her getting her grievance off her chest and saying what she thought about it to his superiors, on the one occasion when she had a chance to do so.

'Say anything you want to say,' replied the Archbishop. 'Speak as freely as you like.'

'Well, what I want to say is this – if our curé had done his duty, things would have been very different.'

The Cardinal insisted on hearing more of the details; and Agnese began to feel somewhat embarrassed at having to tell a story in which she too had played a part she did not want everyone to know about – least of all anyone like the Cardinal. But she found a way of putting that right, with a small adjustment. She told him about the arrangements for the wedding, and about Don Abbondio's refusal to conduct the ceremony, and she did not omit his pretext that his superiors had raised objections to it (Oh, Agnese! Agnese!) – but then she jumped to an account of Don Rodrigo's attempted abduction of Lucia, and of how they had warning of it and were able to escape.

'We got away that time, all right,' she added in conclusion, 'but it wasn't long before we were right back in trouble again. Now if the curé had been honest with us, and told us the whole story, and had married those two poor children then and there, we could all have gone away at once, secretly, to some far-off place and no one need ever have known about it. But the chance was lost, and that was how things took the turn they did.'

'Your curé will have some explaining to do,' said the Archbishop.

'No, sir, no!' said Agnese at once. 'It wasn't for that that I told you the story at all; please don't scold him for it. What's done is done; and it wouldn't do any good. That's what the poor man is like; if it all happened over again, he'd do exactly the same thing.'

But Lucia was not happy at her mother's way of telling the story.

'We did wrong too,' she said. 'You could see that the thing didn't have God's blessing on it.'

'What wrong could you have done, my poor child?' said the Cardinal.

Agnese glared at her once or twice, as unobtrusively as she could, but the girl went on and told the story of the attempt to trick Don Abbondio into marrying them, and ended with the words:

'We did wrong, and God has punished us.'

'Then accept at his hands the sufferings you have undergone, and be of good heart,' said Federigo Borromeo. 'For who has a right to hope and to rejoice more than those who have suffered and will admit that it was their own fault?'

Then he asked where Lucia's young man was. The girl remained silent, with lowered head and cast-down eyes, while her mother explained that he was on the run. The Cardinal showed surprise and displeasure at this, and wanted to know exactly what had happened.

Agnese told him the whole story of Renzo's adventure, as far as she knew it.

'I've heard something about this young fellow,' said the Cardinal. 'But however does a man who'd get involved in that sort of thing come to be engaged to a girl like your daughter?'

'He was a good young man,' said Lucia, going red, but speaking very steadily.

'He was a quiet boy – too quiet, if anything,' said Agnese. 'You can ask anyone about that, even the curé himself. How can we tell what plots and intrigues have been going on in Milan? It doesn't take much to make a poor man look like a criminal.'

'That is true, alas!' said the Cardinal. 'I shall certainly look into the matter.'

He asked for the young man's name, and wrote it down in a notebook. He went on to say that he would visit their village within a few days, and that then Lucia would be able to come home without fear. Meanwhile he would find her a place of refuge where she could remain in safety, until everything had been arranged for the best.

Then he turned to the tailor and his wife, who came forward immediately. He repeated the thanks which he had already sent to them through the parish priest, and asked whether they would be prepared to give shelter, for those few extra days, to the guests that God had sent them.

'Yes, sir,' said the woman; her voice and face expressed a good deal more than the words of that curt reply, choked by embarrassment, would suggest. Her husband was deeply stirred at the thought of being asked a question by so great a visitor, and felt the need of rising to an occasion of such importance. So he tried desperately to find words that would express the solemnity of the moment. His forehead wrinkled, his eyes rolled in their sockets, his lips twitched. He drew the bow of his intellect to its fullest extent; he searched, he groped, he felt a tumult of half-conceived thoughts and half-finished phrases within him. But time was short; there were already signs that the Cardinal was about to accept his silence as tacit approval.

So the poor man opened his mouth and said,

'Delighted, I'm sure!'

He had not been able to think of anything better! The immediate humiliation he felt was bad enough; but even worse was the recurring, unwelcome memory of his words which ever after came back to spoil his recollected pleasure in the great honour he had received.

Countless times afterwards his mind went back to that scene, and he imagined himself in the same position again; and dozens of things would come into his head, as if in spite, any one of which would have been better than that feeble 'Delighted, I'm sure!'

As the old proverb says, 'Brilliant after-thoughts litter every roadside.'

The Cardinal left, saying, 'The blessing of the Lord rest upon this house!'

That evening he asked the parish priest how he could best recompense the tailor, who could not be a rich man, for a hospitality which could not be cheap, especially in a time of famine. As far as that year was concerned, said the priest, neither the tailor's professional earnings nor the return from certain small plots of land that he owned could put him in a position to be generous to outsiders; but he had been able to put something by in previous years, which made him one of the more prosperous men in the neighbourhood. He could afford to pay something extra without distress, and he was certainly willing enough to do so on this occasion. In any case, said the curé, there would be no way of making the tailor accept any reward.

'He has probably got debts that he has no means of paying,' said the Cardinal.

'Well, Your Grace, look at it like this. These people can only pay their debts with the surplus left over from the harvest. Last year there was nothing left over, and this year it wasn't even enough for their immediate needs.'

'Very well,' said Federigo Borromeo. 'I will take his debts over. I shall ask you to get the details from him, and to make the necessary payments on my behalf.'

'It will be quite a sum.'

'So much the better. But I am afraid you must have plenty of other people in even worse need, who have no debts because no one will give them credit.'

'Yes, Your Grace, I'm afraid we have. We do what we can, but how can we see to everything, in times like these?'

'Get the tailor to make clothes for them at my expense, and pay him at a good rate ... to tell you the truth, everything that's not spent on food this year gives me the feeling that it has been stolen from the hungry; but this is a special case.'

We cannot end the story of that day without a brief account of the manner in which the Unnamed spent its closing stages.

This time the news of his conversion reached the valley before he did. It spread rapidly from house to house, bringing with it amazement, anxiety, dismay, and murmurs of discontent. The first bravoes or servants – for it came to the same thing in his household – that the Unnamed met were summoned to follow him by a wave of his hand, which he repeated to the others whom he met further along the way. They all fell in behind him, with their usual terrified obedience, but in a most unusual uncertainty about what was to follow. With a steadily growing train behind him, he finally reached the castle. He beckoned to the men waiting around the door to follow with the others, rode into the first courtyard and took up his stand in the middle of it. Without dismounting, he let out the thunderous shout which was his normal rallying cry, and would always bring everyone within earshot running to him. In a moment everyone inside the building answered the call, and came to join those who were already gathered in the courtyard. All of them looked towards their master.

'Go and wait for me in the main hall,' he said, and sat high in the saddle as he watched their departure. Then he dismounted, took his mule to the stable himself, and went to the hall where they were waiting for him.

The general buzz of whispered conversation came to an abrupt stop as he entered. Everyone drew back to one end of the room, leaving ample space for him. There were about thirty of them.

The Unnamed raised his hand, as if to maintain that sudden

hush. He drew himself up to his full height, towering above the others, and said,

'Listen, all of you! No one is to speak unless I ask him a question. My lads! The road along which we have been travelling up to now leads to the depths of Hell! I am not reproaching you, for I have led the way along that road myself. I have been the worst of us all – but hear what I have to say. God in his mercy has summoned me to change my life, and I am going to change it – I have changed it already. May he summon all of you likewise! Know, therefore, and hold it for certain, that I have resolved to die rather than to do anything further against his holy law. I release all of you from the evil orders that I have given you – you understand me. I forbid you to carry them out. Hold this for certain too, that none of you, from now on, will ever be able to do wrong with my protection, or in my service. Anyone who wishes to stay with me on those terms will be treated by me as if he were my own son. If ever we lack bread in this house, I will cheerfully let the last of you eat the last crumb and go hungry to bed myself. Those who do not want to stay will receive the balance of their wages, and a farewell present, and they can go. But they must never set foot in this house again – unless they decide after all to change their ways and change their life, for in that case they will be welcomed with open arms.

'Think it over tonight. Tomorrow morning I shall call you before me, one by one, and hear your answers. And then I shall give you fresh orders. Now you may go, each to his own place, and may God, who has shown me such mercy, fill your hearts with good counsel.'

Here he finished, and all of them were silent. Whatever storms raged in those uncouth minds, there was no outward sign of them. These men were accustomed to accept the Unnamed's voice as the manifestation of a will which could not be gainsaid; and there were no traces of weakening about that voice, as it announced these changes in the objectives to which that will would in future be addressed. It never even occurred to any of them that it might be possible, now that he was converted, to take advantage of the fact and answer him back as if he were an ordinary man. They saw him as a saint, but as one of those saints whom we see depicted with head held high and sword in hand.

And fear was not the only feeling he inspired in his followers. Many of them – especially those born on his estates, who were a large part of the total number – felt for him the loyal love which a faithful retainer owes his lord. Every man there had the affection for him which springs from admiration. In his presence they felt the awe which even the most surly and insolent spirits experience when confronted by a superiority which they have already acknowledged. The words they had just heard from his mouth were indeed odious to their ears, but did not strike their minds as untrue or even as unfamiliar. If they had often mocked at those ideas, it was not because they did not believe in them, but because mockery was a sort of shield against the terror that would have seized them if they had thought seriously about the subject. And now that they could see the effect of that terror on a mind like that of their master, there was not one of them who was not affected by it himself, at least for a time.

It must also be added that those of them who had happened to have business outside the valley that morning, and had consequently been the first to hear the astonishing news, had also witnessed the joy and elation of the people and the sudden affection and respect for the Unnamed which had replaced their previous hatred and terror of him. Those who had witnessed these things had also spoken of them after their return to the castle. His followers had always looked up to him with awe, even when his power was based mainly on the strength of their own arms; now they saw in him the wonder and the idol of the multitude, so that he still towered above everyone else – not in the same way as before, but to no less an extent. He still stood apart from the common herd, was still their chief.

But they were bewildered to begin with, everyone uncertain of his neighbour and of himself. Some blazed with inner fury; some began to consider where they should go to seek protection and employment; some took a fresh look at themselves to see whether they could adapt to the idea of becoming good citizens;

457

some were sufficiently moved by the Unnamed's words to feel a certain inclination in that direction. Some took no decision except to promise whatever might be asked of them and to stay on for a while, eating the bread which was so generously offered to them and which was so scarce elsewhere; and thus to gain a little time. No one spoke. And when their master had finished, and raised that imperious hand again in sign of dismissal, they all filed submissively out like a flock of sheep.

Last of all, he followed them out, and stood in the middle of the courtyard, watching them in the twilight as they broke up and went off to their various posts. Then he went upstairs to fetch his lantern, and did a round of all the courtyards, passages, and halls, and inspected the guard on every gate. Having seen that all was quiet, he finally went off to his bedroom, for now he felt that he could sleep.

Though tangled problems requiring instant solutions had always been meat and drink to him, he had never before been confronted by so many at a single time; and yet he felt he could sleep. The remorse and regret that had woken him up the night before were far from being quietened – he could hear their voices louder, harsher and more outspoken than ever – and yet he felt that he could sleep. The whole system, the whole method of government that he had set up in his castle over the years, with such care, with so rare a combination of audacity and perseverance, had now been shaken to its foundations by himself, by a few words from his mouth; the utter submission of his men, their willingness to undertake any task in the world for him, their gangsterish fidelity, on which he had so long been accustomed to rely, had all been swept away by his own hand; the strings which had controlled his little kingdom were tangled and broken; he had filled his household with confusion and uncertainty; and yet he felt that he could sleep.

He went up to his room then, and stood beside the bed which he had found so hard and uninviting the night before. He knelt down and tried to pray ... From some deep and secret compartment of his brain emerged the prayers that he had been taught to say as a child, and he began to say them now. The words that had spent so long heaped up in that hidden store

458

now came jostling out in rapid succession. He felt an indescribable mixture of sensations. There was a certain sweetness in that return to a habit dating from the time of his innocence; a quickening of pain at the thought of the abyss which lay between that time and the present; a yearning for the day when works of expiation would win him a better conscience, a state as close as possible to the innocence he could never regain; a feeling of gratitude and of trust in that mercy which alone could lead him to that state, and which had already given him so many indications that such was its will.

Finally he stood up, got into bed and went straight to sleep.

Such was the end of that day, whose events were still so famous when our anonymous author was writing. And yet, if his work had been lost, we would know nothing about them – none of the details at least. For Ripamonti and Rivola, whom we have already quoted, merely say that that famous tyrant had a meeting with Federigo Borromeo, after which he underwent an astonishing and permanent change of heart. And how many people have read those two books? Even fewer than those who will read this one. And, if a determined and resourceful investigator went to that very valley now, who knows whether there would be any faint and confused tradition of the facts for him to discover? So many other things have happened since!

Chapter 25

In the village where she lived and throughout the territory of Lecco, people were talking on the following day of little else but Lucia, the Unnamed and the Archbishop – and of one other person, who generally liked people to talk about him, but would gladly have done without it on this occasion. This was my lord Don Rodrigo.

Of course people had been talking about his activities long before this time; but only in secret, disjointed conversations. Two men had to know each other very well before opening a discussion on such a subject. And people had never spoken about it with the full feeling that the matter deserved. For when it is dangerous to express indignation to the full most men do not merely conceal or understate their sense of outrage, but really feel less indignation than they would otherwise have done. But now no one was likely to feel shy about asking questions or stating opinions regarding a widely known story, in which the hand of Providence could clearly be seen – a story with two such remarkable heroes, one of whom united so vigorous a love of justice with so lofty an authority, while the other was a man in whom tyranny itself seemed to be humbled, and gangsterism itself to have laid down its arms and sued for peace. In comparison with those towering figures Don Rodrigo began to look rather small. Anyone could now see just what it meant to torture innocent people in the hope of making them surrender their honour, to persecute them with such shameless insistence, such atrocious violence, such abominable, underhand villainy.

A whole series of Don Rodrigo's earlier exploits were remembered, and people now said what they thought about them, each individual taking heart from the discovery that everyone else agreed with him. There was a general murmur and a general unrest – still at a discreet distance, however, because of all the bravoes Don Rodrigo had around him.

A good deal of the public hatred fell upon his friends and protégés. His worship the mayor, who had always been blind, deaf and dumb when it came to Don Rodrigo's activities, received his full share of it; though again only from a distance, because he too was effectively guarded – not by bravoes, but by the police. Dr Quibbler (whose only weapons were those of sophistry and intrigue) and other minor protégés received less consideration. They were greeted with pointing fingers and scowling looks; so that they felt it better to keep off the streets for some time.

Don Rodrigo was thunderstruck by the astonishing news, so utterly different from the message he had been expecting to hear from one day to another, from hour to hour in fact. He shut himself up in his palace for a couple of days, grinding his teeth, and with only his bravoes for company. On the third day he went off to Milan. If it had only been a matter of the popular murmur against him, he might have stayed on (since things had already gone so far) to face it out, and perhaps to single out one or two of the most daring spirits and make an example of them for the benefit of the others. The thing that shifted him was definite news that the Archbishop was about to visit that part of the state. Don Rodrigo's noble uncle, who knew nothing of the whole story except what he had been told by Attilio, would certainly have insisted that his nephew should take a leading part on any such occasion – that he should receive the most conspicuous public greetings from the Cardinal.

Anyone could see how that would turn out ... His uncle would not only have insisted on Don Rodrigo playing his part, but would have wanted a full and detailed report afterwards, because it would have been a significant opportunity to demonstrate the respect in which the family was held by one of the greatest authorities in the duchy. To escape from this embarrassing situation, Don Rodrigo rose before dawn one morning, and got into a carriage, with Griso and various other bravoes outside it, in front of it and behind. He left orders that the rest of the household should follow as soon as possible, and set off like a fugitive, after the manner of Catiline – if we may presume to dignify our characters with an occasional classical analogy – of Catiline fleeing from Rome, snarling and swearing to return before long in a very different guise and take his revenge.

Meanwhile the Cardinal continued his journey, visiting the parishes of the territory of Lecco at the rate of one a day. On the day when he was due to arrive at Lucia's village, many of the inhabitants went out early to meet him. At the entrance to the village, right next to Agnese's cottage, was a triumphal arch, with uprights of scaffolding and wooden poles across the centre, hung with straw and moss and decorated with green boughs of butchers' broom and holly, with their bright red berries. The west front of the church was hung with coloured cloths, and blankets and sheets dangled below every window, with streamers improvised from babies' swaddling bands. All the poor necessities of life that could make some show of being festive decorations had been called into service.

At about three in the afternoon, when the Cardinal was due to arrive, the villagers who were still in their houses – old men, women and children for the most part – also went out to meet him, some in orderly procession, some in a confused throng. At their head was Don Abbondio, a gloomy figure in the middle of all the rejoicing, because of the noise that deafened him and the surging crowd that made him feel giddy, as he kept on remarking – and also because of his secret terror that the women might say something about Lucia's wedding day, and he might have to render an account of his own conduct.

Then they caught sight of the Cardinal, or rather of the crowd amid which he was riding in his litter, with his suite around him. All that could be seen of his party was something borne high in the air, well above the heads of the people – the top of the cross carried by the chaplain, who was riding a mule. The people with Don Abbondio now surged forward to mingle with the other crowd.

'Not so fast!' cried the curé three or four times, and 'Keep in file!' and 'What are you thinking of?'

Then he turned back, very disgruntled, muttering the words

'What a muddle! What pandemonium!' over and over again. He went into the church, which was still empty, and waited there.

The Cardinal made his way forward, blessing the crowd with his hand, while they blessed him with their voices. His suite struggled to get him a little breathing space. As this was Lucia's village, the inhabitants wanted to do something special for the Archbishop; but this was not easy, because people always did the utmost they could in his honour wherever he went. At the very beginning of his time as Archbishop, during his first formal entry into the cathedral, the crowd had thronged in on him with such force that his life had been in danger. Certain noblemen who were near at hand had drawn their swords to frighten the mob into holding back. So disordered and violent was life in those days, that even demonstrations of good will towards a bishop in his own cathedral – and even attempts to moderate those demonstrations – could lead to something very close to murder. And the protection of the nobles' swords might not have been enough, if Clerici and Picozzi, the Master of Ceremonies and his assistant, who were two stout-hearted and stout-limbed young priests, had not lifted the Archbishop in their arms and carried him bodily from the cathedral door to the great altar. From then on, throughout the episcopal visitations that he had to make, his first entry into every church was seriously to be reckoned among the labours of his office, and sometimes among its dangers.

So he made his way into this church too, as best he could. He went up to the altar, and stood in prayer for a little, and then gave the people a short talk, as was his habit. He spoke of his love for them, of his care for their salvation, and of the way in which they should prepare for the ceremonies of the following day. Then he withdrew to the house of the parish priest, and asked him, in the course of conversation, what he knew about Renzo. Don Abbondio replied that he was a rather hasty young man, and inclined to be obstinate and quick-tempered. But when pressed with more detailed and precise questions, he could only reply that Renzo was a good citizen, and that he too, could not imagine how the young fellow could have got involved in all the deeds of darkness in Milan that had been attributed to him.

'And the girl then,' went on the Cardinal. 'Do you think it is safe, now, for her to come back and live in her own home?'

'For the moment', said Don Abbondio, 'she can come and stay here just as she pleases. For the moment, yes; but,' he added with a sigh, 'it wouldn't be any good in the long run, unless Your Grace were always here, or at least always near at hand.'

'The Lord is always near at hand,' said the Cardinal. 'But I will think of a safe place for her anyway.' And he gave orders that the litter should be sent off, with an escort, early the following day, to fetch the two women.

Don Abbondio went out very pleased that the Cardinal had spoken to him about Lucia and Renzo without asking for an explanation of his refusal to marry them. 'So he doesn't know about it!' thought the priest. 'Wonder of wonders, the mother must have kept her mouth shut! It's true that she'll be seeing him again; but I'll have another word with her first; I certainly will!' The poor man had no idea that Federigo Borromeo had kept off the subject for the moment only because he intended to go into it thoroughly at a more convenient time, and to hear what the priest had to say before passing judgement.

But the good prelate's concern to find a safe place for Lucia was no longer needed. After he had left her, various things had happened, of which we must now give an account.

During the few days they spent in the hospitable cottage of the tailor, the two women took up their normal way of life again, as far as they could. At the very beginning, Lucia had asked for some work to do, and settled down, as she had in the convent, sewing all day in a little room where no one could see her. Agnese went out some of the time, and some of the time she sat and worked with her daughter. Their talk was affectionate, and all the sadder for that – for both of them had made up their minds to the necessity of a separation. The lamb could hardly return to a fold so near the den of the wolf . . . But when and how would that separation ever end? The future was dark and confused – for one of them especially.

Agnese trotted out a series of cheerful suggestions. Renzo, after all, unless something had happened to him, must soon let Lucia have some news of himself. If he had found work and a place to live, if he were true to his promise – and there could be no doubt about that – why shouldn't they join him later on?

She spoke again and again of these hopes to her daughter. I cannot say whether Lucia was more oppressed by the pain of hearing Agnese's words, or by the embarrassment of answering them. She had never disclosed her great secret to anybody. Though distressed by the thought of employing a subterfuge with so good a mother – and not for the first time either – she was irresistibly constrained to silence by feelings of modesty and by the various fears which we mentioned before; and so she went on from one day to the next without saying anything. Her plans were very different from those of her mother; or, more accurately, she had no plans at all. She had abandoned herself to the care of Providence. So she tried to let the subject drop, or to turn the conversation aside to a different one. Or she would say, in general terms, that she had no other hope or desire left in this world except that of an early reunion with her mother. More often than not, her tears came at the right moment to interrupt their talk.

'Do you know why everything looks so black to you?' said Agnese. 'It's because you've had such a bad time that you can't imagine things taking a turn for the better. But you must leave everything to Heaven, and if . . . just you wait until a glimmer of hope appears, only a glimmer, and we'll see how you feel then!'

Lucia kissed her mother, and wept.

Meanwhile a great friendship had suddenly sprung up between the two women and their hosts – and where should friendship spring up, if not between the givers and the receivers of a kindness, if they are all good people? Agnese, in particular, was always chatting to her hostess. The tailor entertained them with stories and moral disquisitions, especially at dinner-time, when he always had something interesting to tell them about Bovo d'Antona or about the holy fathers in the desert.

Not far from that little village was the country residence of a distinguished couple, who were there at the time on holiday. Our anonymous author tells us that they were called Don Ferrante and Donna Prassede; but he withholds their surname, in his usual way.

Donna Prassede was an old lady with a great inclination towards doing good – certainly the worthiest of all occupations to which a man can devote himself, but still an occupation in which it is possible to take a wrong turning, like any other. To do good, we have to be able to recognize it; and we have to identify it, like everything else in this world, in the midst of our passions, by means of our powers of judgement, and with the help of our ideas, which are not always very firmly based. In the matter of ideas Donna Prassede followed the policy we are told we should follow with our friends – she had only a few, but she was very strongly attached to them. Among the few she had were unfortunately a number of shaky ones, to which she was if anything more attached than the others. So it sometimes happened that she took on a 'good cause' which was really nothing of the kind; or made use of means which could all too easily frustrate her ends. Sometimes she thought that certain methods were permissible when they were really quite the contrary, from a muddled idea that those who do more than their duty are thereby entitled to exceed their rights. Sometimes she would miss the realities of a given situation, or see in it other things which were not really there; and other similar mishaps often befell her. These are things that can happen to anyone, and do happen sometimes to the best of us; but they came Donna Prassede's way much too often – sometimes all of them at once.

When she heard about Lucia's strange adventure, and all the other things that people were saying about the girl at that time, Donna Prassede felt curious to see her. So she sent off a carriage, with an old admirer of hers, to fetch Lucia and her mother. The girl shrugged her shoulders, and asked the tailor, who brought her the message, to make some excuse so that she need not go. As long as such requests had come from ordinary folk who were trying to make the acquaintance of the miracle girl, the tailor had been glad to do this for her; but in the

466

present case he felt that refusal would almost amount to rebellion. He gave voice to all sorts of protests, exclamations and arguments. You couldn't do that sort of thing, he said; and it was an important family; and you mustn't say no to the gentry; and it could be the making of their fortunes; and Donna Prassede was a saint, apart from everything else. He said so much, in fact, that Lucia had to give in; all the more so because Agnese kept backing up the tailor's arguments by saying: 'That's right! That's right!'

When they were shown into the lady's presence, she greeted them warmly, with many congratulations on Lucia's escape. She asked them questions, and gave them advice – all with a certain air of innate superiority, which however was offset with so many expressions of humility, tempered with so much affectionate concern, tinged with such piety, that Agnese very soon began to feel less oppressed by the sensations of awe which had afflicted her to begin with in that noble presence, and before long Lucia felt the same relief. In fact both of them found a certain charm in the lady's manner. And, to cut a long story short, when Donna Prassede heard that the Cardinal had undertaken to find a place of safety for Lucia, she was moved by the desire to second his good resolution, and at the same time to anticipate it. So she expressed herself as willing to take Lucia into her own household, where, without being given any specific duties, she could help the other women as and when she pleased. And she said that she would see about informing the Cardinal of what had happened.

Apart from the obvious good that must result from such an action, Donna Prassede could see, and resolved to grasp, a chance to do good in another respect, which was even more important in her eyes – to redirect the thoughts of a disordered mind, and lead back into the paths of righteousness a fellow-creature who badly needed such guidance. From the very first time that she had heard about Lucia, she had been convinced that a girl who could promise her hand to a good-for-nothing, seditious gallows-bird like that must have some taint, some secret defect about her. Birds of a feather ... And when she saw Lucia she felt sure that she was right.

467

Not that she didn't look like a good girl at heart, as they say; but there was plenty of scope for criticism. Her way of keeping her little head bent forward, with her chin pressed against the hollow of her throat, her way of not answering you when you spoke to her, or answering very briefly, as if against her will ... all that could be taken as indicating modesty, but it certainly showed a good deal of obstinacy too. It was easy to guess that that little head was full of its own wilful ideas. And then that continual blushing, and those sighs that she always seemed to be holding back. And a pair of great eyes finally, which Donna Prassede didn't like the look of at all. She was quite sure – as sure as if she had heard it on good and sufficient authority – that all Lucia's misfortunes were a judgement on her for her friendship with that ne'er-do-well, and a sign from heaven that she ought to be separated from him for good. Such being the case, she decided to do all she could to help the good work.

For Donna Prassede, as she often explained both to others and to herself, put all her efforts into seconding the will of Heaven; but she often made the serious mistake of confusing her own whimsies with the divine intent.

She was careful not to give any outward indication of her second objective. One of her maxims was that, if you want to do good to people, the most important thing, in many cases, is not to tell them what you have in mind.

Mother and daughter looked at one another. Given the sad necessity of parting from each other, they both felt that the lady's offer should be accepted, if only because her estate was so near to their own village – which meant that, at the very worst, they would be in the same neighbourhood and able to see each other again when holiday time came round next year. They read the decision in each other's eyes, and both turned towards Donna Prassede to thank her in tones of grateful acceptance. She repeated her kind assurances and promises, and said that she would send them a letter for the Cardinal at once.

When Lucia and Agnese had left, she got Don Ferrante to draw up the letter for her – he was a literary man, as we shall see, and she made use of him as a secretary on important occasions, such as the present one. So Don Ferrante brought all his learning to bear; and when he handed the draft over to his spouse he warmly recommended the spelling to her special attention. For spelling was one of the many things he had studied, and also one of the few matters in which his word carried any weight in that house. Donna Prassede copied it out very carefully indeed, and sent the letter off to the tailor's house. This was two or three days before the Cardinal was to send the litter to fetch the two women home to their own village.

In due course they made the journey, and got out at Don Abbondio's house, where the Cardinal was. Orders had been given to let them straight in. The chaplain was the first person to see them, and he obeyed the instruction, delaying them only long enough for a quick word about the ceremony to observe with the Cardinal, and the correct titles to give him. He used to do this whenever he could manage it without the Cardinal finding out. It was a constant torment to the poor chaplain to see how badly organized these things were in Federigo Borromeo's household.

'It's all the blessed man's own fault,' he would say to other members of the suite, 'being too kind and too familiar with everybody.' And he would go on to tell them how he had more than once heard, with his own ears, people say things like 'Yes, sir,' and 'No, sir,' to His Grace.

At that moment the Cardinal was talking to Don Abbondio about parish matters, which meant that the curé did not have a chance to add his own word of advice to the two women, as he would have liked to do. As he came out, he passed them on their way in, and could only give them a look, which was meant to convey that he was pleased with their behaviour so far, and that they should be good people and continue to keep their mouths shut.

The Cardinal greeted them warmly, and they bowed to him; and then Agnese took the letter from her bosom and gave it to him, saying,

'This is from Donna Prassede, who says that she knows Your Grace very well – as of course all the nobility know each other. And if you'll read it, Your Grace, you'll see what it's about.'

'Good!' said Federigo, when he had finished reading, and had extracted the essence of meaning from the flowers of Don Ferrante's eloquence. He knew that household well enough to be sure that the intentions with which Lucia was invited there must be good, and that she would be safe from the violence and the wiles of her persecutor as long as she stayed there. What he thought about Donna Prassede and her ideas we cannot exactly say. She probably was not the person he would have chosen for the purpose; but, as we have said or implied before, it was not his habit to upset other people's arrangements in order to re-arrange matters better himself.

'Accept this separation, and the uncertainty of your present position with peaceful hearts,' he went on after a pause. 'Have faith that it will soon be over, and that the Lord will guide your affairs towards the end he seems to have planned for them. But be sure that, whatever his will may be, that will be the best for you.' He gave a few more words of loving counsel to Lucia, and a few more words of comfort to both of them; and then he blessed them and let them go.

As soon as they were outside, a swarm of friends crowded round them (for the whole population, we may say, was waiting for them), and accompanied them to their house, as if in triumph. All the women vied with each other in cries of con-gratulation, sympathy or inquiry; all of them were loud in their regrets when they heard that Lucia was leaving the next day. The men vied with one another in offers of service. Every one of them wanted to do guard duty outside the cottage that night. This prompted our anonymous author to coin a proverb.

'The best time to find plenty of willing helpers,' he says, 'is when you don't need them.'

All these greetings confused and bewildered Lucia – Agnese was not so easily put out of her stride – but they did Lucia more good than harm all the same, by distracting her to some extent from the thoughts and memories which came back to her all too readily, despite the bustle, at the sight of that door, those little rooms and all the cottage contained.

Then the bell rang to announce that the service was about to begin, and everyone moved off towards the church – another triumphal procession for the two women.

When the service was over, Don Abbondio hurried home to make sure that Perpetua had made the best possible arrangements for dinner. Then he was summoned by the Cardinal. He immediately answered the call of his mighty guest, who waited until he had come quite close, and then said 'Father Abbondio' – in a tone which indicated clearly enough that this was the beginning of a long and serious conversation – 'Father Abbondio – tell me about this poor girl and her bridegroom. Why did you not join them in marriage?'

'So they did spill the beans this morning, after all!' thought Don Abbondio.

'Your Grace must have heard about all the confusion that arose in that matter,' he stammered. 'It was such a muddle that even now it's hard to tell exactly what happened – as Your Grace can see from the fact that the girl is here, after so many extraordinary events that it seems like a miracle, while the young man, after another series of extraordinary events, has vanished, and no one knows where he is.'

'I am asking you', said the Cardinal, 'whether it is true that you, before any of those events had taken place, refused to marry this young couple, when requested to do so on the day arranged for the ceremony, and, if so, for what reason?'

'Well … if Your Most Illustrious Grace only knew … the threats … the terrible orders I've had not to talk about this …' and he stopped there without completing his sentence, in a way which respectfully suggested that it would be indiscreet to inquire further into the matter.

'Indeed!' said the Cardinal, with an unusual sternness in his voice and manner. 'Kindly remember that it is your bishop who is putting this question to you, as part of his duty, and so that you may clear yourself … the question why you did not perform a task which, in the ordinary course of events, it was your duty to perform.'

'Your Grace,' said Don Abbondio, shrinking visibly, 'I did not mean that … I just thought that, as these are complicated matters, that happened long ago, about which nothing can now

471

be done, there was no point in going into them again. But of course ... of course ... I know that Your Grace would never betray a poor priest like myself. Because you can see for yourself, Your Grace – you can't be everywhere all the time, and I shall be unprotected here when you go away ... But if you order me to tell you the whole story, I will.'

'Tell me the whole story. My dearest wish is to find you free from guilt.'

Then Don Abbondio began to tell the whole unhappy tale; but he left out the name of the principal actor, saying only 'a certain great lord'. Thus he paid prudence what little tribute he could in those difficult circumstances.

'And did you have no other reason?' asked the Cardinal, when Don Abbondio had finished.

'Perhaps I haven't made myself clear,' said the priest. 'They threatened me with death, if I married that couple!'

'And does that seem to you to be a sufficient reason to neglect a clearly defined duty?'

'I have always tried to carry out my duty, even to my own serious disadvantage. But when life itself is at stake ...'

'And when you offered your service to the Church, to take up that ministry which you now exercise,' said Federigo Borromeo, in yet sterner accents, 'did the Church guarantee your life? Did she tell you that the duties of the ministry had no difficulties attached to them, and no dangers? Did she say that duty ends where dangers begin? Or did she tell you the very opposite of all this? Were you not warned that you were sent forth as a lamb among wolves? Did you not know that there were violent men abroad, who might be displeased by the works that you would be called upon to perform? Did he whose doctrine and example we follow, in imitation of whom we call ourselves and let others call us shepherds – did he, when he came down to this world to play the shepherd's part, make it a condition that his life should be saved? And to save your life, or rather to prolong it for a little space upon this earth, at the cost of all charity, all duty, what need was there of holy oil, of the laying on of hands, of the special grace of the priesthood? This world is quite capable of inspiring such virtues and of teaching such doctrines ...

But what am I saying? Shame on such thoughts! The world itself rejects them! For this world has its own laws, which prescribe evil instead of good; it has its own gospel, which is a gospel of pride and hatred; and it will not accept a man's wish to save his life as an excuse for breaking its odious commandments. It will not tolerate that excuse; and it makes sure that its views are respected in this matter. What then of us, who are the children and the preachers of the divine promise? What would become of the Church, if your views were shared by all your brothers in the ministry? Where would the Church be now, if she had adopted those doctrines when she first appeared in the world?'

Don Abbondio hung his head. As he listened to the Cardinal's words, his soul was transported, like a chick in the talons of a hawk, to an unknown region, to a level whose air he had never breathed before. But he realized that he must make some reply.

'Your most noble Grace,' he said, with an air of forced submission, 'I can see I must be wrong. If a man's own life is to count for nothing, I don't know what to say. But when you have to deal with people like that – people who have power in their hands and who won't see reason – even if one wanted to be a hero, I don't know what would be gained by it. When you quarrel with a man like that noble I mentioned, there's no hope of victory, nor even of coming to terms.'

'But do you not know that to suffer for the sake of justice *is* victory, for us? If you do not know that, what do you preach? What instruction can you give? What *good news* do you proclaim to the poor? Who has ever suggested to you that you should meet force with force? You will never be asked if you have succeeded in compelling men of power to remain in the path of duty – that is neither within your mission nor within your means. But you will be asked, one day, whether you have at all times used the resources that were in your hand to perform the duties that were prescribed to you – even when men of power had the temerity to forbid you to do so.'

These saints have their oddities, like the rest of us – thought Don Abbondio. What it boils down to is that he cares more about the love that two young people have for each other than about the life of an unfortunate priest.

As far as the curé was concerned, he would have been delighted to let the conversation end there; but at every pause he could see the Cardinal remaining in the attitude of one expecting an answer – a confession, perhaps, or an apology; a reply of some kind, in any case.

'I can only repeat, Your Grace,' he said, 'that I must be wrong ... But courage isn't a thing that a man can give himself if he hasn't got it.'

'Then I could ask you why you ever took on a ministry which demands that you should struggle against the world and its passions. But I would rather ask you a different question. Since in this ministry, however you came to enter it, courage is necessary for the fulfilment of your duties, how have you failed to reflect that there is one who will infallibly give you courage when you ask him for it? Do you believe that all the millions of martyrs who died for our faith had natural courage, or that they had no natural concern for their lives? All those young people who were just beginning to taste the pleasure of life; all those old men who had grown used to complaining that their life was approaching its end; all those maidens, wives, mothers ...? Yet they all had courage, for courage was necessary, and they had faith. Knowing your weakness, and knowing your duties, did you never think to prepare yourself for the difficult times that might lie ahead – that did in fact lie ahead of you? Why! if through all your years of pastoral duty you have loved your flock – as you surely must have done – if you have devoted all your care and all your heart to them and found all your pleasure in them, your courage should not have failed you in the hour of need. For love casteth out fear. And so if you loved those who are entrusted to your spiritual care, those whom you call your children, and found that two of them were being threatened, together with yourself – then while the weakness of the flesh made you tremble for your safety, the spirit of charity must have made you tremble for them. You must have felt humiliated by that first fear, since it came from your own weakness; you must have implored Heaven to grant you the strength to conquer it and cast it out, as a temptation. But what of the holy and noble fear for the others, for your children? You must have listened to that fear; it must have given you no peace, it must have stirred you up and compelled you to think what could be done to overcome the peril which hung over their heads ... But what effect did those fears, that love, have on you? What did you do for your children? What thoughts passed through your mind?'

He fell silent, in the attitude of one expecting a reply.

Chapter 26

DON ABBONDIO had managed to find some answer to the less precise questions that had gone before, but this one left him speechless. And we too, to tell the truth, as we sit here with our manuscript before us, pen in hand, with only words to contend with and only the criticism of our readers to fear – even we in fact feel a certain reluctance to go on. For we find something strange in this long series, uttered with so little effort, of fine precepts and encouragements to fortitude and charity, to anxious care for others, and to unlimited sacrifice of self. But then we reflect that all these things were said by a man who subsequently put them into practice; and this gives us heart to continue.

'Have you nothing to say?' asked the Cardinal. 'But if you had done, for your part, that which charity and duty required, you would not lack for an answer now, no matter what the outcome had been. See for yourself what you have done! You have obeyed the forces of iniquity, without caring for the things which your duty prescribed. You have obeyed those forces most diligently. They appeared openly to you, to tell you what they required; but they wished to remain unknown to those who might have learnt of the coming danger and guarded against it. They did not want the matter bruited abroad; they wanted it kept secret, while they completed their plans of fraud and violence in their own good time. Neglect of duty and silence were what they demanded of you; you did neglect your duty, and you said nothing.

'And now I must ask you whether you did not go further than that. Is it true that you sought out wretched excuses for your refusal, to hide its true motives?'

He paused, again expecting an answer.

So they let that cat out of the bag, too! thought Don Abbondio. As he gave no sign of having anything to say, the Cardinal went on,

'If it is true that you told those poor folk a lie, to keep them in the ignorance and obscurity in which the powers of iniquity wanted them kept ... but now I see that I have no alternative but to believe it; to blush with you for your sins, and to hope that you will weep for them with me. See to what straits you have been led by your love of this transitory life – which but now you were producing as an excuse! It has led you to ... you are free to refute these words if they seem unjust to you; but, if not, take them as the medicine of salutary humiliation ... it has led you to deceive the weak, and to lie to your own children.'

So that's how it goes! – thought Don Abbondio. – Affectionate embraces for that devil incarnate – he meant the Unnamed – and for me, all this noisy reproach for a half-lie, told with the sole object of saving my skin. But people at the top of the tree are always in the right. It's my destiny to get kicks from everyone, even from saints.

'I've done wrong,' he said aloud. 'I can see that I've done wrong – but what ought I to have done, in a crisis like that?'

'Do you ask me that again? Have I not already answered you? And did you need that answer? You should have loved, my son; loved and prayed. Then you would have seen that the forces of iniquity have power to threaten and to wound, but no power to command. You would have joined together, according to the law of God, that which man wished to put asunder. You would have given those poor innocent folk the service they had a right to ask of you. God would have been the surety for the consequences, for you would have walked in his way. But you took another way, and the surety for the consequences – and what consequences they are! – must be yourself. But can you truly say that you had no human resources on which to call? Was there no way out, if you had really looked round for one, really thought about it, really searched? Now indeed you must know that those poor children of yours were ready – had they but been married – to find their own way out. They were prepared to flee from before the face of their tyrant, and had already chosen their place of refuge. But even if that had not

477

been so, did it never cross your mind that you had a bishop? And how could that bishop have the authority to reprove you for not doing your duty, as now, if he were not under an obligation to help you to carry it out? Why did you not think of informing your bishop of the obstacles that an infamous tyrant was placing in the way of your performance of your duties?'

Just what Perpetua said! thought Don Abbondio angrily. Through all this conversation, the thing that was most vividly present to his mind was the picture of those bravoes who had threatened him, and the reflection that Don Rodrigo was alive and well, and would come home again one day or another in all his power and pride, and also in a bad temper. The splendid presence of his guest, his noble appearance and his eloquent words inspired the curé with confusion and with a certain fear; but it was not a fear that mastered him completely, or prevented his mind from formulating objections, because the thought was in his mind that the Cardinal, at least, would never have recourse to bravoes, or swords or muskets.

'How did you fail to see,' went on the Archbishop, 'that, if no other refuge were open to receive those persecuted innocents, I was there, to welcome them and find a place of safety for them, if you had sent them to me – if you had sent those waifs to their bishop, as belonging to him of right, as a precious part of his charge – nay, not of his charge, but of his riches.

'And as for you,' he went on, 'I would have been deeply concerned for you; I would not have slept until I was sure that not a hair of your head would be touched. Do you think I had no means of securing your safety? However reckless that man might be, can you doubt that his daring would have been blunted by the knowledge that his schemes were known far from here – that they were known to me, and that I was on guard and resolute to use every means at my command to protect you? Did you not know that, just as men often promise more than they will perform, so they often threaten worse crimes than they are prepared to commit? Did you not know that the forces of iniquity rely not only on their own strength, but on the credulity and cowardice of others?'

Perpetua's views exactly! – thought Don Abbondio, without

reflecting that if his servant and Federigo Borromeo held this same opinion about the things that he could and should have done, the very fact of their agreement told heavily against him.

'But you,' said the Cardinal, 'could see nothing, and wished to see nothing, but your temporal danger. What wonder then that it seemed so terrible to you that you neglected all else because of it?'

'Yes, but I was the one who had to see those faces,' said Don Abbondio, the words escaping from him in a rush. 'I was the one who had to hear those words. Your Grace is very eloquent; but it's another thing to be in the shoes of a poor parish priest, and to go through it yourself.'

As soon as he had uttered those words, he bit his tongue, realizing that he had let himself be carried away by his feelings. – Now there'll be trouble! – he thought. But a moment later, when he timidly raised his eyes, he was astonished by the expression on the face of the Cardinal, whose thoughts he could neither predict nor understand. The look of authoritative, critical gravity was changing to one of serious, thoughtful compunction.

'It is but too true!' said Federigo. 'Such is our wretched and horrifying condition! We have rigorously to exact from others that which only God knows whether we could give ourselves. We have to judge, to correct, to reprove; and only God knows what we ourselves would do in the same situation, or what we have done in similar circumstances in the past. Yet how wrong it would be for me to take my own weakness for the measure of other people's duty, or as the standard that I should teach! But it is certain that I ought provide others with example as well as precept, and not make myself like the scribes and pharisees who load others with burdens too heavy to carry, which they would not touch themselves.[1] Yes, my son; yes, my brother; the errors of those in authority are more often known to others than to themselves. If you know of occasions when cowardice or respect for the things of this world have led me to neglect my duty, tell me so frankly, make me correct myself. Thus, where an example has been sought in vain, a confession may at least be

1. See Matthew xxiii, 4. – Translator's note.

found in its place. Reproach me freely with my weaknesses; for then the words I utter will carry more weight, because you will feel more vividly that they are not my words but those of one who can give both of us the strength to carry them out.'

What a holy man he is! thought Don Abbondio. But how he torments you! And himself too! He'll torture himself as well, as long as he can search hearts, and dig up old stories, and criticize, and investigate.

'Oh, Your Grace!' he said aloud. 'You must be making fun of me! Everyone knows about your powerful courage and your unshakable zeal.'

(All too well! – he added to himself.)

'I did not ask you for that word of praise, which makes me tremble,' said Federigo. 'Only God knows all my failings, but those that I know are themselves enough to confound me. But I would have preferred, and I would still prefer, that you and I should both be confounded at once in his presence, so that we might find a common trust. I would like you to understand – for your own sake – how contrary your conduct has been, how contrary your language still is, to the law that you preach, and according to which you will be judged.'

'All the blame falls on my head,' said Don Abbondio. 'The people who told you this story did not go on to say that they got into my house by a trick, and tried to cheat me and conclude an irregular marriage.'

'They did tell me that, in fact, my son ... But the thing that hurts me and depresses me is that you are still trying to make excuses, that you think you can excuse yourself by accusing others, and that you use something which ought to be part of your own confession as material for accusing them. For who was it that led them into the ... not the necessity, but the temptation to do what they did? Would they have taken that irregular road if the right road had not been closed to them? Would they have thought of laying a trap for their shepherd, if he had received them with open arms, and given them help and advice? Would they have forced his door, if he had not barred it against them? And do you blame them? And are you indignant with them because, after so many misfortunes – nay, in the

480

midst of their misfortune – they relieved their feelings by telling the shepherd, in whose flock both they and you have their being, what had happened? The appeal of the oppressed, the complaint of the afflicted, are odious to the secular world, because the secular world is like that; but are we to follow its example? And what good would it have done you if they had stayed silent? Could you not see that their case would go forward in its entirety to the judgement of God? Is it not yet another reason for you to love them (for you had reason enough before) that they have given you the chance to hear the sincere voice of your bishop, that they have given you the means of seeing more clearly the great debt that you have towards them, and of beginning to pay it off? Why, if they had challenged you, insulted you or tortured you, I would still bid you – but surely there is no need for me to say this – I would still bid you to love them for doing so. Love them because they have suffered, because they still suffer, because they are your children, because they are weak, because you need forgiveness and you know how much their prayers could help you to gain it.'

Don Abbondio said nothing; but this was not the strained and impatient silence of a little earlier. Now he looked like a man who has more on his mind than he knows how to put into words. The speech he had just heard was full of unexpected conclusions and novel applications, but they all followed from a doctrine which had long been rooted in his mind and which he had never gainsaid. The sufferings of others – from which his attention had long been distracted by the fear of having to suffer himself – now appeared to him in a new light. And though he did not feel all the remorse that the Cardinal's sermon was meant to produce – for that same fear was still there to protect him from some of its effects – he did feel some remorse none the less. He felt a certain dissatisfaction with himself, a compassion for others, a mixed sensation of tenderness and embarrassment. He behaved like the damp and battered wick of an old candle, if we may be permitted the comparison, when it is offered to the flame of a great torch. At the beginning it smokes, drips, crackles, and will have nothing to do with it; but finally it catches fire and burns passably well. He would have accused himself openly, he would have wept, had it not been for the thought of Don Rodrigo. But even as it was, he looked sufficiently moved for the Cardinal to see that his words had not been without effect.

'And now', continued the Archbishop, 'the young man is a fugitive from his home, and the girl is about to leave hers. Now both of them have all too pressing reasons for staying far away from this village and little prospect of reunion here; they are content to hope that God will bring them together again somewhere else. Now, alas, they have no need of you, and you have no opportunity to help them. Nor can our short-sighted view see any such opportunity in the future. But who can say whether God in his mercy is not preparing one for you? If so, do not let it escape! Search it out, be ever vigilant to seize it, pray that he may grant it to you!'

'I will not fail to do so – I will be true to my word!' said Don Abbondio, in a voice which, at that moment, came straight from the heart.

'Yes, yes, my son!' cried Federigo; and with a dignity full of affection, he concluded: 'Heaven knows I would rather have had a very different talk with you. Neither of us is young, and Heaven knows how unwelcome a task it is to me to load your grey hairs with reproach, how much more willingly I would have spoken to you in mutual solace of our common cares and sorrows, and in joy of that blessed hope towards which we have both now travelled so far. God grant that the words I have said may be of profit to you, and also to me. Do not let it be reckoned among my faults on the last day, that I left you in possession of an office in which you had so lamentably failed. Let us recover the time we have lost! Midnight is near; the Bridegroom will not now be long; let us keep our lamps lit! Let us offer our poor hearts to God, empty, so that he may fill them with that charity which rectifies the past and which assures the future; which fears and trusts, and weeps and rejoices, all in due season; which converts itself in every case into the virtue that we most need.'

He moved away, and Don Abbondio followed him.

Here our anonymous author mentions that this was not their

only conversation, and that Lucia was not the only subject that they discussed. He has confined himself to this one, he says, so as not to digress too widely from the main theme of his story. For the same reason, he does not propose to speak of other noteworthy things that Federigo Borromeo said in the course of his visit; nor of his acts of generosity; nor of the disputes he settled, and the ancient hatreds between individuals, families and whole communities to which he brought permanent reconciliation, or at least temporary peace – which was, alas, necessarily the commoner result. Nor does he mention the taming of bullies and of petty tyrants, whether for the rest of their lives, or for a shorter period. But we know that all these things came to pass, to a greater or less extent, on every visit of any length which that excellent man made to places in his diocese.

Our author goes on to tell us that the following day Donna Prassede arrived, as arranged, to fetch Lucia and to pay her respects to the Cardinal, who praised the girl warmly to the lady, as he recommended her to her care. Lucia tore herself away from her mother, with many tears, and left the cottage. She bade her village farewell for the second time, with that double feeling of sadness with which we leave a spot that has had a special place in our hearts, which it can now never have again. But this was not to be Lucia's final farewell to her mother, for Donna Prassede had said that she proposed to stay a few more days in her near-by country house, and Agnese promised Lucia to visit her there, for a yet sadder leave-taking.

The Cardinal was also about to leave the village, to continue his tour of duty, when the curé of the parish which contained the Unnamed's castle arrived and asked to speak to him. He was admitted, and gave the Cardinal a purse and a letter, in which the nobleman asked him to give Lucia's mother the hundred gold *scudi* which were in the purse, to serve as a dowry for the girl, or for any other purpose that the two women might prefer. He added that if they ever thought that he could assist them in anything, the poor girl knew all too well where he lived, and he would count it the best of good fortune to be able to help them.

The Cardinal sent for Agnese at once, and gave her the message, which left her equally amazed and delighted. Then he gave her the money, which she accepted without too much ceremony.

'God reward the gentleman!' she said. 'And please thank him very much for it, Your Grace. And please don't tell anyone else about it, because this is the sort of village where ... Oh, I'm sorry, Your Grace; I know very well that a gentleman like yourself isn't going to go gossiping about this sort of thing. But ... you know how it is.'

She went home very quietly, and shut herself up in her room. She unwrapped the roll of coins, and, though she was prepared for what she saw, she was still astonished at the sight of so many of those gold coins, all in a heap and all belonging to her. She had probably never seen more than one of them at a time before, and that but rarely. She counted them and laboriously stacked them up again so that she could hold them all together in her hand, though they kept on bulging out and escaping from her inexpert fingers. Finally she got them back into the tidiest stack she could manage, and wrapped it into a sort of bundle with a piece of rag. She tied it all round with a piece of twine. Then she stuck it into a corner of her straw mattress. For the rest of that day, she did nothing but turn things over in her mind, make plans for the future, and long for the following day to come. When she went to bed, she lay awake for some time, thinking of the hundred *scudi* on which she was lying. Finally she went to sleep, and saw them in her dreams. She got up at dawn, and hurried straight off to Donna Prassede's house, to see her daughter.

Though Lucia still felt the same revulsion at the thought of speaking of her vow, she had resolved to overcome her reluctance and to confide in her mother during the coming conversation, which would be their last for a long time.

As soon as they could be alone together, Agnese's face lit up, while her voice dropped as if there were someone present who she did not wish to overhear her words.

'I've great news for you!' she said, and she told her about the unexpected stroke of luck.

'Why, God bless the gentleman, then!' said Lucia. 'Now you'll be well off yourself, and be able to help others as well.'

'What?' said Agnese. 'Don't you see all the things we can do ourselves, with all that money? Listen now! I've got no one but you, Lucia; or I should say no one but the two of you, for ever since Renzo began courting you, I've thought of him as a son. The main thing is to be sure that nothing's happened to him, since he hasn't sent us any news of himself – but why should everything always have to turn out badly? Let's hope he's all right. If it were just myself, I'd like to leave my bones in my own village; but now you can't stay here because of that bully, and the thought of having him for a neighbour spoils the place for me as well. If I can be with you two, I don't mind where it is. Ever since the time that trouble started, I've always been willing to go anywhere in the world with you two, and I still am; but without money, how could we have done it? Do you see now? That poor boy had got a little money together, with great labour and saving, but the police came and whipped it all away; but now the Lord has sent us this bit of luck to make up for it. So when Renzo finds the right way to let us know how he is, and where he is, and what he means to do, I'll come and fetch you from Milan – I'll come myself. At one time I'd have thought that would be too much for me; but even bad luck can teach you a thing or two. I've been as far as Monza now, and I know a bit about travelling. I'll bring some sensible man along with me, one of our relations, as it might be Alessio at Maggianico, for strictly speaking there isn't anyone suitable in the village; I'll come with him. We'll pay for everything, and ... do you follow me?'

Seeing that Lucia, instead of cheering up, was looking more and more upset, with a face that expressed plenty of emotion but no joy, Agnese broke off in the middle, and said,

'What's wrong, then? Don't you agree with what I'm saying?'

'Poor mother!' cried Lucia, throwing one arm round Agnese's neck, and hiding her face in that maternal bosom.

'What is it, then?' asked Agnese anxiously.

'I ought to have told you before,' said Lucia, raising her face, and wiping away her tears, 'but I hadn't the heart. Have pity on me!'

'Tell me what's happened, then?'

'I can't ever marry that poor boy now!'

'Why? Why?'

Lucia's head was low, and her bosom heaved; but though the tears ran down her face, her voice was steady as, with the air of someone announcing an unwelcome but immutable fact, she told the story of her oath. With clasped hands, she again implored her mother to forgive her for not having spoken before, and begged her not to tell anyone else about it, and asked her to help her keep her promise.

Agnese was astonished and dismayed. She would have liked to show indignation at her daughter's long silence; but the seriousness of the event smothered her private resentment. She would have liked to say: 'What on earth have you done now?' – but she felt that this would be to quarrel with the will of Heaven; all the more so when Lucia again vividly described the terrible night, the black despair and the totally unexpected deliverance that had formed the background to the vow that she had so explicitly and solemnly taken.

Agnese could not help remembering various examples of the consequences of broken vows – stories of strange and terrible punishments, which she had often heard, and had indeed related to her daughter herself. After a few moments of dazed silence, she said,

'And what are you going to do now?'

'That's for the Lord to decide,' said Lucia, 'for the Lord and for the Madonna. I put myself in their hands, and they haven't abandoned me yet. They won't abandon me now that ... The one thing that I ask the Lord to grant me, the only thing I ask except for the salvation of my soul, is that he should bring me back to live with you – and he will grant me that, I know he will. On that terrible day ... in that coach ... with those terrible men, Holy Mother of God! ... who would ever have thought that they were taking me to a man who would bring me back to you the very next day!'

'To think of you not telling your mother about it at once!' said Agnese, the love and pity in her voice almost hiding the touch of pique.

'Don't be angry with me; I hadn't the heart ... What good would it have done to distress you before I had to?'

'What about Renzo?' said Agnese, shaking her head.

'Poor lad!' said Lucia with a jump. 'I mustn't even think of him now. You can see it wasn't meant to be. You can see it looks as if the Lord wanted to keep us apart. Besides, the poor boy may be ... but no, God will have preserved him from danger, and will make him happy after all, happier than he would have been with me.'

'Well,' said her mother, 'if it wasn't that you've committed yourself for ever like that, I could have found an answer to all the other problems (provided Renzo's all right) with the help of this money.'

'But would we ever have had the money if I hadn't had to live through that terrible night?' said Lucia. 'The Lord must have wanted all this to happen: his will be done!'

The last words were almost drowned in a flood of tears.

At this unexpected argument, Agnese fell into a gloomy silence. A few moments later, Lucia choked back her sobs and went on,

'Now it's happened, we must make the best of it. Poor mother, you can help me, first of all by praying to the Lord for your poor daughter, and then by ... well, that poor lad must be told about this. Do that for me, do me that kindness, for you can do it. When you know where he is, get a letter written to him, find a man to do it – your cousin Alessio now, who's a kind and sensible sort of man, and has always been fond of us, and won't talk about it. Get him to write and say what's happened ... where I was taken and all I suffered ... and that it's God's will, and that he should try to find peace of heart, and that I can't marry anyone now. And put it to him as nicely as possible; make him understand that I've promised, that I've made a vow. Once he knows I've made a promise to Our Lady ... he's always been a God-fearing man. And when you get some news of him for the first time, have a letter written to me, just to say that he's well. Then, after that, don't tell me anything more at all.'

487

Deeply touched, Agnese assured her daughter that everything would be done as she wished.

'And another thing,' continued Lucia, 'if that poor boy hadn't had the bad luck to fix his heart on me, none of this would have happened to him. Now he's wandering God knows where on the face of the earth, they've taken away his livelihood, they've taken away all his belongings, and the money the poor boy had saved up because ... because ... you know why – and now we've got so much ourselves! Oh mother! Since the Lord has sent us so much wealth, and it's quite true that you've always looked on the poor fellow like a son, like your own son – oh, let's give him half of it! The Lord won't let us go hungry! Find someone you can trust, and send him the money! God knows how he may stand in need of it!'

'Why, of course,' said Agnese. 'I'll send it to him, then! The poor fellow! Why do you think I was so pleased to get the money in the first place? Oh, I was really happy, as I was coming here today ... Never mind, I'll send it to the poor boy ... Poor Renzo! I know what I'm saying, now – money's a fine thing when you're in need of it, but it isn't this lot that'll make Renzo jump for joy.'

Lucia thanked her mother for her prompt and generous kindness with an emotional gratitude from which an observer might have guessed that her heart was still occupied with Renzo, perhaps more than she realized herself.

'And what's your poor mother going to do without you then?' said Agnese, beginning to weep in her turn.

'But what shall I do without you, mother? In someone else's house too! And in that fearful place Milan! But the Lord will be with both of us, and will bring us together again in the end. In eight or nine months we'll see each other again, and by then, if not before, he'll have arranged things so that we can stay together. We'll leave everything to him. And I'll keep praying to Our Lady to grant me that favour. If I had anything else to offer her, I'd do it, but she's so full of mercy, I expect I'll get it for nothing.'

With many repetitions of these and similar words of sorrow and of comfort, of regret and resignation, with many pleas for silence and assurances that it would be observed, with many tears and with long and repeated embraces, the two women finally parted, each promising the other that they would meet again the following autumn at the latest – just as if the fulfilment of their hopes depended only on themselves! But that is what we all do in such cases.

Then a long time went by without Agnese being able to get any news of Renzo. No letters or messages from the young man arrived; and there was no one she could ask in the village or the surrounding country who knew any more than she did.

Agnese was not the only person who was making inquiries of that sort without any result. The Cardinal had meant what he said when he told the two poor women that he would make inquiries about the poor young fellow; and he had in fact written off for information about him at once. When he had returned to Milan after his tour, he had received the answer that no trace could be found of the individual in question. He had indeed spent some time with one of his relations, in such and such a village, and had done nothing out of the way while he was there. But one morning he had unexpectedly vanished, and even his host did not know what had become of him, but could only repeat various contradictory rumours that were in circulation, such as that the young man had enrolled for service in the East, or gone to Germany, or had been drowned while fording a river. But a sharp look-out for him would be maintained, and if any more definite news came to hand, His Grace would be informed immediately.

Later on these rumours, and others, reached the territory of Lecco, and consequently came to Agnese's ears. The poor woman did all she could to find out which of them was true, and to get back to the source of the various tales; but she never found any more solid basis than the words 'they say', which even nowadays often do duty to substantiate a story. Sometimes she had hardly finished listening to one of these rumours before someone arrived to tell her that it was totally untrue, and to tell her another, equally strange or sinister, to replace it.

But this was all idle gossip; now for the facts.

The Governor of Milan and Captain-General of the Spanish forces in Italy, Don Gonzalo Fernandez of Cordova, had lodged a noisy complaint with the Resident of Venice in Milan, on the ground that a malefactor, a common thief, a promoter of looting and murder, none other than the infamous Lorenzo Tramaglino, who when in the very hands of the police had stirred up a riot in order to escape from custody, had been received and harboured in the territory of Bergamo. The Resident replied that he knew nothing of the matter, but would write to Venice for a proper explanation of the case which he could give to His Excellency.

At Venice they made it a rule to support and encourage any inclination that the Milanese silk-workers might show towards emigrating to the territory of Bergamo. They therefore offered them many advantages when they got there, including the indispensable one of personal safety, without which other advantages are worth nothing. When two great powers clash, there is always some benefit, however small, to be gained by a third party. So Bortolo was privately warned, we cannot say by whom, that Renzo's presence in that village was ill-advised, and that he would do better to go and work in another factory, and perhaps change his name for the time being. Bortolo understood at once, asked no questions, and hurried off to tell his cousin what had happened. He took Renzo with him in a trap, and drove him to another spinning mill, about fifteen miles away, where he introduced him to the owner under the name of Antonio Rivolta. The owner, himself a Milanese, and an old acquaintance of Bortolo, did not need to be asked twice, though it was a bad year, before taking on a worker who was recommended as competent and honest by a decent fellow who knew what he was talking about. And in fact he had no reason to regret his decision in the weeks that followed; though at first he thought the young man might be a bit dull-witted, because when anyone called 'Antonio!' he quite often did not reply.

Soon afterwards, the captain of police at Bergamo received a letter from Venice, instructing him, in terms which suggested no special urgency, to investigate and report whether the individual in question was in the area under his jurisdiction, and more particularly, whether he was in the village where Bortolo lived. The captain performed his duty in the manner he understood to be expected of him, and made a negative report, which was passed on to the Resident in Milan, who passed it on to Don Gonzalo Fernandez of Cordova.

Various inquisitive people later asked Bortolo why the young man had left, and where he had gone. To the first question Bortolo replied with the words: 'He's just vanished!' To satisfy the more insistent, without giving them any idea what had really happened, he thought it best to present them with one or other of the various stories mentioned above; saying, however, that these were doubtful matters, and that he himself was only repeating what he had heard from others, without any proof.

One of these questioners was in fact inquiring on behalf of the Cardinal; but the man did not state his master's name, merely letting it be understood, with a certain air of mysterious importance, that he was acting for a person of great consequence. This made Bortolo more suspicious than ever. He thought it safest, to give his usual reply, except that, as it was for a person of great consequence, he let him have all the stories together, which he had been previously giving out one at a time to the various inquirers.

It must not be thought that a nobleman in Don Gonzalo's position was personally angry with a poor silk-worker from the hill-country; or that he had heard about the lack of respect Renzo had shown and the rude words he had used towards the Moorish king with the chain round his throat, and wanted to make the lad pay for them; or that he thought Renzo so dangerous a man that he must be hunted down even in exile, and must not be allowed to remain alive even in a far-off land (as the Roman Senate once thought of Hannibal).

The matters on Don Gonzalo's mind at that time were so many and so important that he could hardly trouble himself to that extent about Renzo's affairs. If he did none the less appear to trouble himself about them, that was because of a singular combination of circumstances, through which the poor wretch was connected with those many and important matters – without desiring it in any way or even realizing it, either then or later – by a tenuous and invisible thread.

Chapter 27

THE war that was raging over the succession to the states of the late Duke Vincenzo Gonzaga, the second of that name, is a subject that we have already had occasion to mention more than once, but always at moments when we were preoccupied with other matters, so that we have only touched on it in passing. But rather more detailed knowledge of the subject is now necessary for the proper understanding of our story. These are things which are doubtless familiar to readers of history. But as a proper sense of our own quality leads us to think that our present book will only be read by the unlearned, perhaps we had better provide enough information to satisfy those who may need it.

We mentioned that, when Vincenzo Gonzaga died, the first candidate for the succession was Carlo Gonzaga, the head of a cadet branch of the family, which had moved to France, where he held the duchies of Nevers and Rhétel; and that Carlo Gonzaga had taken possession of Mantua. We must now add that he had also occupied Montferrat – a point which we left out last time in our haste. The court of Madrid wanted to get the new prince out of those two states at all costs, as we also mentioned. But it needed a good reason for getting him out of them, because a war made without good reason would be an unjust war. So it declared its support for the claim to Mantua of another Gonzaga, namely Ferrante, Prince of Guastalla, and for the claims to Montferrat of Charles Emmanuel I, Duke of Savoy, and of Margherita Gonzaga, the Dowager Duchess of Lorraine.

Now Don Gonzalo was of the same family, and bore the same name, as the Great Captain. He had already fought a war in Flanders, and he was very anxious to fight another in Italy. He probably did more than anybody to get this one under way. In the meanwhile, interpreting the intentions and anticipating the orders of Madrid, he had concluded a treaty with the Duke of Savoy for the invasion and partition of Montferrat. He got the Count–Duke to ratify the treaty without difficulty, by persuading him that it would be quite easy to get control of Casale, which was the best-defended point in the zone reserved for the King of Spain. But Don Gonzalo protested in His Majesty's name that he had no wish to occupy any territory, except to hold it in trust until the Emperor had given his ruling in the matter. Partly because of outside influence, however, and partly for his own reasons, the Emperor had meanwhile refused to sanction the investiture of the new duke, and told him to leave the disputed states in imperial hands for the moment; he himself would hear both sides, and hand the states over to the rightful owner when he had done so. This was something that the Duke of Nevers would not accept.

The duke also had powerful friends on his side – Cardinal Richelieu, the senators of Venice, and the Pope (who was then Urban VIII, as we mentioned before). But Richelieu was then busy with the siege of La Rochelle and with a war against England, and was opposed by the party of the Queen Mother, Marie de' Medici, who had her own reasons for disliking the House of Nevers; so that he could contribute nothing but promises. The Venetians would not move, nor even declare their support, until a French army arrived in Italy. They helped the duke secretly, as well as they could, making representations of various kinds – protests, suggestions, peaceful or threatening exhortations, according to circumstances – to the Court of Madrid and the Governor of Milan. The Pope recommended Nevers to his friends, interceded on his behalf with his enemies, and put forward proposals of compromise. But he would not hear of putting any troops in the field.

So the two aggressive allies could begin their campaign in safety. The Duke of Savoy, for his part, had entered the territory of Montferrat. Don Gonzalo had enthusiastically formed the siege of Casale; but he did not find the operation as satisfactory as he had imagined; for it must not be thought that war is a bed of roses. The Court did not give him the support he wanted; in fact it left him short of the most basic necessities.

His ally gave him more help than he cared for. For the Duke of Savoy not only took his own portion, but began to encroach on that allotted to the King of Spain. Don Gonzalo was furious; but the Duke of Savoy was just as distinguished for skill in negotiation and for changeability in the matter of alliances as for bravery on the field of battle; and Don Gonzalo was afraid that if he made any fuss his ally would call in the French. So he had to shut his eyes to what was going on, swallow his wrath, and say nothing.

Meanwhile his siege was going badly. It was taking too long, and from time to time the besiegers were driven back; both because the defenders were brave, vigilant and determined, and because Don Gonzalo had too few troops. Some historians say that he also made a lot of mistakes. We will not claim to know the truth of this matter; but if it were really so, we would be inclined to regard it as a very good thing, provided that it led to a smaller number of soldiers being killed, mutilated or crippled in that siege – or even, other things being equal, if it merely led to slightly less damage being done to the tiled roofs of Casale. While Don Gonzalo was in these difficulties, he received the news of the riots in Milan, and hastily returned there in person.

Among the things reported to him on arrival were the rebellious and noisy escape of Renzo, and the real and imaginary events that had caused his arrest. Don Gonzalo was also told that he had taken refuge in the territory of Bergamo. This point attracted the Governor's attention. He knew from other sources that the Venetians had been much encouraged by the riots at Milan; that they had at one time believed that he would have to raise the siege of Casale as a result; and that they still thought he must be bewildered and worried – all the more, because of a second piece of news, welcome to Venice but dreaded by Don Gonzalo, which followed soon after the riots: La Rochelle had surrendered. Very indignant, both as a man and as a politician, that the Venetians should have such an opinion of him, he was on the lookout for any opportunity of giving them proof, by implication, that he had lost nothing of his previous confidence. (By implication, because to say explicitly, 'I'm not afraid!' is quite meaningless.)

A good way of furnishing such proof is to show bad temper, to quarrel and to make demands. And so one day, when the Resident of Venice came to see the Governor, to pay his respects and also to judge from his expression and behaviour the state of his inner feelings – this is all worth noting, as an example of the old subtle diplomacy – Don Gonzalo first of all touched lightly on the riots, speaking like a man who has already taken all the necessary steps; but then he went on to make a considerable issue, as you have already heard, of the story of Renzo. The result is also known to you.

Afterwards he did not concern himself any further with an affair of so little weight, which was all over, as far as he was concerned. When the reply reached him, a good deal later on, he was back in camp before Casale, with his mind on other things. He lifted his head and gazed around him, like a silk-worm looking for a mulberry leaf; he stood still for a moment, trying to bring his shadowy memory of the facts back to life. He recalled the episode, and a confused idea of the man concerned passed through his mind; then he went on to something else, and thought no more about it.

From the little that Renzo had been able to put together, he had no reason to expect anything like that benevolent indifference – quite the contrary. For some time he had no thought or care for anything but preserving his incognito. It can be imagined how impatient he was to send news of himself to Lucia and Agnese, and to hear news of them; but there were serious difficulties here. One was that it meant trusting his secret to a letter writer; for the poor fellow could not write. He could not even read, in the full sense of the word. The reader may recall that when Dr Quibbler asked him if he could read, he replied that he could. That was not from any wish to boast, or to show off; he could read printed material, given time; but handwriting is another matter. So he had to tell a third party about his affairs, about that vital secret. It was not so easy to find a man who could both wield a pen and keep a confidence in those days; especially in a place where there was no one whom Renzo had known for any length of time.

The second difficulty was to find a messenger – a man who was going to the right place, would agree to take the job on,

495

and would really carry it out – another set of virtues that could not easily be found in a single person.

Finally, after much searching, he found someone to write the letter. But as he did not know whether the women were still at Monza, or where else they might be, he thought it best to enclose the letter for Agnese in another addressed to Father Cristoforo. The letter-writer took on the job of arranging delivery as well. He gave the envelope to a traveller whose journey took him near to Pescarenico. The man left it with an inn-keeper, as near as possible to its destination, asking him most earnestly to forward it. As the letter was addressed to a monastery, it was in fact delivered there, but what happened to it after that has never been discovered.

As Renzo received no reply, he had another letter written, in much the same terms as the first, and enclosed it in a message to some friend or relation of his at Lecco. Another messenger was sought and found, and this time the letter reached its destination. Agnese hurried to Maggianico and got her cousin Alessio to read it and explain it to her. With his help, she concocted a reply, which he wrote out for her. Then they found a way of sending it to Antonio Rivolta at his place of residence – though not as quickly as this brief account might suggest. Renzo received the letter, and had another written in reply. In fact a correspondence began between the two sides. It was neither swift nor regular, it proceeded by fits and starts, with long gaps; but it went forward none the less.

To have an idea of what this correspondence was like, we need to know how that sort of business was transacted in those days – or rather how it is still transacted today, for we doubt if there has been much change.

The peasant who cannot write, and needs something written, turns to someone who has learned to use a pen. He chooses him, as far as he can, among those of his own class; for he is either shy of approaching others, or does not trust them sufficiently. He tells the man what has gone before, with such clarity and logical order as he can muster, and then tells him, in the same style, what he wants to say. The literate friend understands part of what he says, and misunderstands another part; he advises him, suggests a couple of changes, and then says 'Leave it to me!' He takes up his pen, and puts the first man's thoughts in literary form, as best he can; corrects them or improves them, adds emphasis or takes it away, even leaves bits out, as seems best to him. For there's no getting away from it – a man who knows more than his neighbours does not care to be a passive tool in their hands, and once he has become involved in their affairs, wants to give them a little guidance.

Moreover the literate friend may not always succeed in saying what he means. Sometimes he says something quite different. (We professional writers of books have been known to do the same.)

When such a letter reaches the other correspondent, who is equally ignorant of his ABC, he takes it to another learned man, of the same calibre, who reads it and explains it to him. Then doubts arise over what the letter really means. The interested party, with his knowledge of what has gone before, maintains that certain words must mean one thing; but the man who is doing the reading, from his knowledge of the written language, claims that they must mean something else. In the end the man who cannot write must put himself in the hands of the man who can, and must charge him with the task of replying. The answer will be composed in the same fashion as the first letter, and will be submitted to the same sort of interpretation.

But if the subject of the correspondence happens to be a little delicate; if private matters are involved, which must not be intelligible to a stranger, in case the letter should go astray; if, for those reasons, there is a deliberate attempt not to put things too clearly ... why, then the correspondence cannot go on for very long before the two sides are at the same stage of mutual understanding as two medieval scholars might once have been after four hours of argument about the entelechy. (We have not taken a more modern example, for fear of getting a rap over the knuckles.)

Now the case of our two correspondents was exactly like the one we have just described. The first letter written on behalf of Renzo covered a number of subjects. First of all there was an account of his escape – more concise than the one in this book, but also more confused; then a description of his present circumstances, from which neither Agnese nor her interpreter could get any clear or complete picture. Secret warnings, false names, the idea of being in no danger but having to remain in hiding were all unfamiliar concepts to the readers, and expressed in veiled terms in the letter. Then came desperate, passionate inquiries about Lucia, with obscure and sorrowful hints about the rumours that had reached Renzo on this subject. Last came doubtful words of distant hope, plans for the remote future, promises that he would keep faith and appeals to Lucia to do the same, never to lose patience or courage, always to wait for better times to come.

After some time, Agnese found a trustworthy messenger to take a reply to Renzo, together with the fifty *scudi* that Lucia wanted him to have. When he saw all that money, Renzo did not know what to think. His mind was too full of amazement and suspense to have any room for pleasure, as he ran off to find his literate friend, so that he could have the letter explained to him and get to the bottom of this strange mystery.

In this letter the writer had complained somewhat about the obscurity of the one he was answering, before going on to relate, in almost equally obscure terms, the horrifying story of the *person in question* (to use his own words), and to explain the matter of the fifty *scudi*. Then he went on to speak of the vow, with a good deal of circumlocution. Lastly, in much more direct and intelligible terms, came the advice that Renzo should try to find peace of heart and forget the past.

Renzo nearly came to blows with the reader. He trembled, shuddered and raved, both at the things he had understood and the things he had failed to understand. He had the terrible document read over to him three or four times. At one moment he thought he was beginning to understand the situation better; at another, things which had seemed clear the first time became doubtful. In a fever of passion he made his literate friend take pen in hand at once and answer the letter. After the strongest possible expressions of pity and horror at Lucia's experiences, he went on to say: 'Now write this: I don't want to find peace of heart, and I never shall; and they shouldn't have said that sort of thing to a young man like me; and I won't use any of that money; I'll put it away and keep it safely, to go towards the girl's dowry; for she's got to marry me; and I don't want to know about any vows; and I've often heard of the Madonna helping folk in trouble and granting people favours, but I've never heard of her causing unkindness and broken promises before; and it can't be right; and with all this money we could set up house here; and if I'm in a bit of trouble at the moment, it's a storm that'll pass over before long' – and more to the same effect.

Agnese duly received that letter, and had another written in reply, and so the correspondence went forward in the manner we have already described.

Then Agnese got a message through to Lucia, though we are not told how, to inform her that a certain friend was alive and well, and had had the news. Lucia felt very relieved, and now asked for nothing further except that he should forget her – or rather, to be quite accurate, that he should try to forget her. For her own part, she made a similar resolution about Renzo a dozen times a day, and employed every possible method to keep it. She worked hard and long, and tried to devote all her thoughts to the business in hand. When Renzo's image rose before her eyes, she would recite or chant various prayers that she knew by heart. But his image seemed to show a certain cunning; for it did not often come forward openly, but crept in behind some other figure, so that she did not notice it until it had been there for some time.

Lucia often thought about her mother, naturally enough; and the imaginary Renzo would come quietly in and join the party, just as the real one had so often done in the past. Whatever person or scene came to mind, he intruded into all her memories of the past. And when the poor girl let her mind wander to thoughts of the future he appeared again, if only to say: 'I shan't be there, anyway.'

But though it was impossible to give up thinking about him altogether, Lucia did her best to think of him less often and less fondly than she wanted to, and managed to do so up to a certain point. She would have had more success if no one had tried to help her; but Donna Prassede was there, all agog to expel Renzo for ever from Lucia's heart, and unable to think of any better way of doing so than to talk to her about him all the time.

'Well?' she would say, 'You're not still thinking about him, are you?'

'I'm not thinking about anyone,' Lucia would reply.

But Donna Prassede was not satisfied by that sort of answer; she would reply that deeds, not words were needed. She spoke at length about the natural disposition of girls in general.

'Once they've got some ne'er-do-well into their heads, as they generally do,' she said, 'there's no getting him out again. If it's a proper, sensible engagement, to a decent, steady sort of man, that gets broken off by some accident, they resign themselves to it easily enough. But if it's some useless young blackguard, they never get over it at all.' And then she would launch into a diatribe against poor Renzo, who was not there to defend himself – the ruffian who had come down to Milan to plunder and murder. She would also try to get Lucia to admit that he had played various dirty tricks earlier on in his own village.

Lucia's voice trembled with shame, grief, and as much anger as was consistent with her gentle nature and her humble position, as she assured and promised Donna Prassede that the poor boy had never caused any talk about himself in the village, except in the way of praise.

'I only wish there were someone from those parts here now, to bear me out!' she said.

And though she knew very little about what had happened in Milan, she defended him there too, on the strength of what she knew about him and his behaviour ever since childhood. She defended him – or tried to defend him – out of the duty to be charitable, out of love for the truth, and finally, to use the words she employed herself to explain her feelings, out of kindness to her neighbour. From these excuses Donna Prassede drew fresh arguments by which to prove to Lucia that she was still in love with Renzo. And to tell the truth, I would not like to say exactly what the facts of the matter were at that moment.

Donna Prassede's unworthy portrait of the young man brought fresh colour and life, by a process of opposition, to the picture of him which had been formed in Lucia's mind by so long an acquaintance. The memories that were suppressed by these forcible means came flooding back; Donna Prassede's aversion and contempt for Renzo recalled many long-standing reasons for respecting him. Her blind and violent hatred against him strengthened the girl's feelings of pity. With all these emotions, who can say how much there may or may not have been of that other feeling which so easily finds its way after them into all hearts – let alone a heart whose owner was already having difficulty in holding it off? But, however this may be, the conversation could never be a prolonged one on Lucia's side for the tears always soon came to drown her words.

If Donna Prassede had been induced to treat Lucia in this way by some ingrained feeling of hatred towards her, perhaps the girl's tears would have touched her and made her stop. As it was all in a good cause, she went inexorably on; for groans, screams and supplications can turn aside the sword of an enemy, but not the scalpel of a surgeon. But when Donna Prassede had done her duty in this respect for the time being, she would pass on from criticism and reproof to exhortation and advice, which she tempered with the odd word of praise, designed to mingle the sweet with the bitter, and so to obtain the best possible effect by working on the girl's mind from several angles at once. These disputes, which always had very much the same beginning, middle and end, did not leave the good-natured girl with any resentment against her stern moni-tress, who treated her with great kindness in everything else, and whose good intentions could be seen in this as well. But Lucia was left with a disturbance, an agitation of ideas and emotions, which it took much time and much effort to reduce to the degree of calm she had achieved before.

It was just as well for the girl that she was not the only object of Donna Prassede's good works. This meant that their disputes could not be all that frequent. For there were the other servants – all disordered minds whose thoughts needed redirecting to a greater or lesser extent; there were plenty of further opportunities to provide the same service out of pure goodness of heart to people towards whom she had no special obligation at all – she sought such opportunities out if they did not occur naturally. And then there were her five daughters. None of them was now living at home, but they gave her even more worry than if they had been. Three of them were nuns, and two were married, which of course meant that Donna Prassede found that she had to superintend three convents and two households. This was a vast and complicated task, made all the more laborious by the attitude of two husbands, backed by their fathers, mothers and brothers, and of three abbesses, flanked by other authorities and by a good number of nuns. None of them wanted to be superintended by Donna Prassede. She had a war on her hands – five wars in fact. It was secret warfare, and conducted with a certain amount of courtesy, but active and unceasing none the less. On all five fronts she came up against constant efforts to avoid her loving care, to shut out her opinions, to elude her requests, and to keep her in the dark as far as possible in every matter. I need not mention the resistance and the difficulties she encountered in the conduct of other affairs which were even less her proper business than these; for it is generally known that doing good to people often involves the use of compulsion. The place where her zeal found its freest expression was her own home. There everyone was completely under her thumb, in every possible way, except for Don Ferrante, with whom things were on a very special footing.

He was a studious man, who had no wish either to command or to obey. He did not mind his wife being the absolute mistress in all household matters, but he was not prepared to be a servant. If she asked him, he would in case of necessity lend her the services of his pen; but that was only because it suited him. He would refuse to do even this when he was not satisfied with what she wanted him to say. 'You'd better put your own mind to it,' he'd say in such cases. 'Do it yourself, since it seems so clear to you.'

For a long time Donna Prassede had unsuccessfully tried to draw him out of his shell, and to persuade him to play a more active part; but now she confined herself to grumbling at him frequently, and calling him lazy, and fixed in his ideas, and a literary man – the last phrase being uttered with mingled annoyance and pride.

Don Ferrante spent long hours in his study, where he had a considerable collection of books – little less than three hundred volumes. They were all carefully chosen, all leading works in their various branches, in every one of which he had some learning. In astrology he was regarded as more than a mere dilettante, and rightly so. For he had not only mastered the vague notions and the widely known vocabulary relating to influences, aspects and conjunctions, which were common knowledge, but could also talk relevantly, and with professorial authority, of the twelve houses into which the heavens are divided, of great circles, of degrees of lucidity and tenebrosity, of altitudes and depressions, of transits and revolutions and, in a word, of all the surest and most recondite principles of the science. For about twenty years he had been supporting Cardan and his system of houses, in long and repeated disputes with another scholar who was passionately attached to the system of Alcabitius – out of mere obstinacy, according to Don Ferrante, who was willing enough to acknowledge the general superiority of the ancients, but was repelled by this refusal to admit that the moderns could be right even in the most obvious cases. Don Ferrante also had more than a common knowledge of the history of the science. When necessary, he could quote the most famous examples of predictions that had come true; and he could also speak with subtlety and learning about other famous predictions that had gone wrong, showing that the fault lay not with astrology, but with those who had not understood its proper use.

Of ancient philosophy he had learned as much as he needed, and was continuing to improve his knowledge by the study of Diogenes Laertius. But beautiful as the old systems are, one cannot adopt all of them at once. A man who wants to be a philosopher must choose one author to follow, and Don Ferrante had chosen Aristotle, who, as he used to say, was neither an ancient nor a modern – he was *the* philosopher. Don Ferrante also possessed various works of the wisest and subtlest followers of Aristotle among the moderns. But he said that he would not waste time on reading authors who attacked the great man, nor money on buying their books. He made one exception, however, and found space in his library for the twenty-two volumes of Cardan's famous *De subtilitate*, and for a couple of other anti-Aristotelian works by the same author, as a tribute to his great worth in astrology. No one could write books like the *De restitutione temporum et motuum coelestium* or the *De duodecim genituris* without deserving to be given a hearing even when he went astray, said Don Ferrante; and the great defect of Cardan was an excess of genius. There was no knowing, he would continue, how far Cardan would have gone in philosophy as well, if he had only kept on the right path.

But though other scholars regarded Don Ferrante as a consummate Aristotelian it still seemed to him that he did not know enough. More than once he modestly observed that essence, universals, the soul of the world and the nature of things were not such simple matters as one might suppose.

Of natural philosophy he had made little more than a hobby. He had merely read, rather than studied, the works of Pliny, and even those of Aristotle himself, on this particular subject. But thanks to that reading, together with information picked up incidentally from works of general philosophy, from a passing glance at the *Magia naturale* of Porta, the three chapters '*De lapidibus*', '*De animalibus*', and '*De plantis*' of Cardan, and the treatise on herbs, plants and animals of Albertus Magnus and various other works of less importance, he was always able to keep up a conversation on the subject of the strange virtues and curious features of many simples; and he could give an exact description of the appearance and habits of sirens and of the single phoenix. He could explain how the salamander can stay in the fire without getting burnt; how that little fish the remora has the strength and the cunning to bring a great ship under full sail to a sudden halt; how dew-drops turn into pearls within the shell of a mollusc; how the chameleon feeds on air; how rock crystal is formed from ice, as it slowly hardens over the centuries; and many other wonderful secrets of nature.

He had gone rather more deeply into the secrets of magic and witchcraft, which, as our anonymous author remarks, is a science at once more fashionable and more necessary, and one of which the effects are of far greater importance, and nearer at hand, so that they can easily be verified. We need hardly add that Don Ferrante's sole object in undertaking this line of study was to increase his knowledge and learn all about the evil arts of witches, so that he could ward them off and protect himself from them. With the help, above all, of the great Martino Delrio (the leading authority in this field), he could talk most magisterially about the casting of love spells, sleeping spells and injurious spells, with the countless variations of those principal types of witchcraft, which, alas, to quote our anonymous author once more, are still to be seen at work every day with such tragic effects.

Equally wide and deep was Don Ferrante's knowledge of history, and more particularly universal history, where his favourite authors were Tarcagnota, Dolce, Bugatti, Campana, and Guazzo – those of most reputation, in fact.

But what is history without politics? – Don Ferrante would often ask. It is a guide who walks on and on, without anyone to follow him and learn the road, so that all his efforts are wasted – just as politics without history is like a man who seeks his way across strange country without a guide. So there was a section of his library that was reserved for the political writers. There Bodino, Cavalcanti, Sansovino, Paruta, and Boccalini stood out among many other books of less bulk and secondary import- ance. But there were two volumes which he esteemed far above all others in this branch; two volumes that he had long put jointly in the first place, without being able to decide which of them deserved to have it for his own. One contained the *Prince* and the *Discourses* of the Florentine Secretary[1] – a blackguard, of course, said Don Ferrante, but a deep thinker for all that. The other contained the *Ragion di stato* of the equally cele- brated Giovanni Botero – a decent fellow, of course, Don Ferrante would add, but keen-witted for all that.

But just a short while before the time of our story, a book had appeared which settled the question of primacy for ever, for it excelled the works of even those two *matadors*, to use Don

1. Machiavelli. – Translator's note.

Ferrante's own words. This was a book which contained every kind of cunning trick in distilled form, so that you could easily recognize them, and also all the virtues, so that you could practise them. It was a short book, but of pure gold; in a word, it was the *Statista regnante* of Don Valeriano Castiglione, that most famous man, of whom it could be said that the great scholars vied with one another in his praise, and the greatest statesmen vied with each other for his services. Pope Urban VIII honoured him with a magnificent panegyric, as is well known. Cardinal Borghese tried to persuade him to describe the deeds of Pope Paul V, and Don Pedro of Toledo, the Viceroy of Naples, urged him to write of the Italian wars of His Catholic Majesty – and both in vain. King Louis XIII of France, at the suggestion of Cardinal Richelieu, appointed him his historiographer, and the Duke Charles Emmanuel of Savoy gave him the same honour. Not to prolong this list of splendid recommendations, let us end by saying that the Duchess Christine of Savoy, the daughter of the Most Christian King Henry IV, granted him a diploma in which, among many other distinctions, she felt able to include 'the certain glory of the fame he has won in Italy of being the greatest writer of our day'.

But though Don Ferrante could claim to be well versed in all the sciences we have mentioned, there was just one in which he both deserved and enjoyed the reputation of a leading authority, and that was the science of the laws of chivalry. Not only did he speak of this subject with perfect knowledge, but he was often asked to intervene in questions of honour, and was never at a loss to give a verdict. He had the works of the most highly esteemed authors in this branch of learning in his library, and, we may add, in his head. He had Paride dal Pozzo, Fausto da Longiano, Urrea, Muzio, Romei and Albergato, together with the first *Forno* and the second *Forno* of Torquato Tasso. He also had the last author's *Gerusalemme liberata* and *Gerusalemme conquistata* always by him, and could quote from memory, if necessary, all the passages they contained which had a bearing on questions of chivalry. But the supreme authority, in his view, was our famous Francesco Birago, with whom Don Ferrante sometimes found himself jointly consulted in questions of honour. For his part the author always spoke of Don Ferrante with particular esteem. From the moment that this distinguished writer's *Discorsi cavallereschi* were published, Don Ferrante prophesied without any hesitation that the new work would destroy the prestige formerly enjoyed by Olevano, and would remain, together with the other noble issue of the same pen, as a code of ultimate authority for future generations.

Anyone can see how fully that forecast has been proved true, adds our anonymous author, who goes on to discuss the works of pure literature on Don Ferrante's shelves. But we are beginning to doubt whether the reader really wants to accompany him on this further review of the library. In fact we begin to wonder whether we have not already won the title of servile copyist for ourselves, and a half share of the title of long-winded bore which belongs to our afore-mentioned anonymous friend. For we have naively followed him into matters which are remote from the main thread of our story, and which he probably treated at such length only to show off his own learning and to demonstrate that there was nothing out of date about his views . . . We will leave in as much as we have already written, so as not to waste the work we have put into it, but we will omit what follows, and get back on to the main road again – all the more so because we have a good way to travel before we meet any of our characters again, and a still longer way to go before we find them engaged in the matters that must surely interest the reader most, if indeed he is interested at all in what we have to say.

Up to the autumn of the following year, which was 1629, all of them, whether of choice or necessity, remained in much the same state as we have left them. Nothing happened to any of them, and nothing could be done by any of them, which is worth reporting. Autumn came, and this was the time when Agnese and Lucia had planned to meet again. But an event of great public importance swept their plans away and this indeed was one of the least of its effects. Other great events followed, but did not bring any noteworthy changes into the lives of our characters. Last of all, fresh developments of a more extreme, overwhelming, and universal kind reached out towards them, reached down to even the humblest of them in terms of worldly values – just as a great whirlwind, wandering and trampling through the countryside, breaking down or uprooting trees, wrecking roofs, stripping the tops off bell-towers, smashing walls, and strewing wreckage here and there, will also suck up the twigs hidden among the grass, and seek out the light, withered leaves that a lesser wind has blown into a corner, and whirl them away, 'prisoned in the blowing wind'.

And now, if the private affairs which we still have to relate are to be clearly intelligible, we have no alternative but to preface them with some sort of account of public events, though without going into them very closely.

Chapter 28

AFTER the rioting on St Michael's Day and the day that followed it, it seemed as if times of plenty had really returned to Milan, by some miracle. There was ample bread in all the bakeries, at the same price as in years of good harvest; and the same was true of flour. Except for the small number of men who had been arrested, the people who had shouted, or done more than shout, during those two days now had reason to be pleased with themselves. Nor should it be thought that they kept quiet about it, once the first effects of the arrests had worn off. In the squares, at the street corners, in the taverns there was open rejoicing, and self-congratulatory, defiant boasting over the discovery of a method of bringing down the price of bread. But amid all the festivity and bluster, there was inevitably an uneasy undercurrent, a feeling that this state of affairs could not last. The people besieged the bakers and the flour merchants, as they had done during that other spurious and short-lived period of abundance produced by Antonio Ferrer's first tariff. Everyone consumed what he could, without any thought of saving. Those who had some money put by invested it in bread and flour, storing them in cupboards, tubs or coppers. By vying with each other to take advantage of the low prices, they not only made a long continuance of them impossible (as it would have been anyway), but made it steadily more difficult to maintain them from day to day. And so on 15 November Antonio Ferrer published a proclamation, *De orden de Su Excelencia*,[1] according to which no one who had grain or flour in his house was allowed to buy any more; and no one was to buy more than two days worth of bread at a time, with *financial and corporal penalties at the discretion of His Excellency*. There followed an order to report offenders against this regulation, addressed both to the competent officials and to the general public; and an

1. 'By order of His Excellency'. (In Spanish)

order to the magistrates, to conduct searches at premises where hoarding had been reported. There was also a fresh order that the shops must be kept well supplied with bread, *under pain of five years in the galleys, or such greater penalty as might be determined by His Excellency.*

Anyone who can suppose that such a proclamation could be carried out must have enviable powers of imagination. If all the new regulations published in Milan at that time had been put into effect, the duchy would have had more men at sea than England has today.

However that might be, if they were going to command the bakers to produce all that bread, they had to take steps to see that the raw materials were available. In times of shortage the authorities always busy themselves with methods of making bread out of foodstuffs which are normally eaten in other forms; and so in this instance it had been decided to start using rice as an ingredient in the so-called 'mixed loaf'. On 23 November there was a proclamation that reserved, for the disposal of the commissioner and tribunal of provisions, one half of whatever quantity of unpolished rice (or '*risone*', as it was then called, and still is, in Milan) that each individual might have in his possession, with penalties for anyone disposing of the same without the permission of the said authorities of confiscation of the goods in question and a fine of three *scudi* per measure. Nothing could be fairer than that, as we must all agree.

But that rice had to be paid for, at a price out of all proportion to the price of bread. The task of filling this enormous gap had been imposed on the city itself; but the council of decurions, which had assumed responsibility on the city's behalf, resolved, on that very same 23 November, to represent to the Governor the utter impossibility of carrying the burden any longer. And the Governor published another proclamation on the 7 December, fixing the price of the afore-mentioned rice at twelve *lire* the measure. Anyone who asked a higher price, or refused to sell, was to lose the goods in question, to pay a further fine of equivalent value, and to suffer greater financial penalties, and corporal penalties up to service in the galleys, at the discretion of His Excellency, and according to the gravity of each case and the rank of the person involved.

A fixed price for polished rice had been imposed before the riots began. And most probably a tariff, or 'maximum', to use a word that has become famous in more recent times, had also been fixed for wheat and other grains by more proclamations, which we have not been able to trace.

Since the prices of bread and flour were kept so low in Milan, the natural consequence was that processions of people from the country came into town to buy those goods. To put a stop to this 'inconvenience', as he called it, Don Gonzalo published another proclamation on the 15 December, according to which no one was allowed to take bread out of the city to the value of more than 20 *soldi*, under penalty of the confiscation of the bread itself, and a fine of 20 *scudi*. *And in case of inability to pay, two strokes of the lash, to be administered in public, or any greater penalty*, in the usual way, *at the discretion of His Excellency*. On the twenty-second of the same month – the delay is hard to understand – he published a similar order relating to flour and grain.

The mob had thought it could create times of plenty by looting and incendiarism; the government thought it could prolong them by the threat of the lash and the galley. These two systems were perfectly compatible with each other; but how far they were compatible with the object in view is a question we can leave to the reader – who will see in few minutes how they worked out in practice. It is easy to see, and may be useful to remark, that there is in fact a necessary connection between all those strange provisions. Each was an inevitable consequence of the one before, and all followed logically from the first, which fixed a price for bread which was so far removed from the real price – by which we mean that which would have resulted from the relationship of supply and demand.

To the multitude such measures have inevitably always seemed no less fair in themselves than easy and simple to carry out. It is therefore natural that, when confronted with the deprivations and the sufferings of a famine, the multitude should desire them, beg for them, and indeed impose them by force, if it can. But as soon as the consequences begin to make themselves felt, one after another, the authorities have to cope with them, by a series of edicts each of which forbids people to do the very things which the previous one impelled them to do.

At this point we may be permitted a passing observation on a singular coincidence. In a neighbouring country, and during a recent period – the most stirring and noteworthy of modern history[2] – when circumstances arose similar to those we have just described, recourse was had to similar measures – identical measures, we might almost say, in substance, with some difference of emphasis, but in almost exactly the same order. All this in spite of far-reaching historical changes, and of the advance of knowledge throughout Europe, and more especially in the country concerned. The reason for this was that the great mass of the people, to whom the new knowledge had not penetrated, was able to make its judgement prevail for a considerable length of time, and so force the hand (as they say in that country) of those who were making the laws.

Returning to our own story, there were two important results of the riots, when all was over. During the riots themselves, there was great wastage and effective loss of foodstuffs; and during the period when the tariff was in force there was excessive, thoughtless, unreasonable consumption – and all at the expense of the small amount of grain which had to see them through until the next harvest. Besides these general effects, there were also four poor devils hanged as leaders of the rioting: two in front of the Bakery of the Crutches, and two at the end of the road where the house of the commissioner of provisions stood.

In point of fact, the historical records of those days are so imperfect that we cannot even discover how or when that ferocious tariff came to an end. If we may be allowed to put forward a conjecture, in the absence of definite facts, we are inclined to think it was abolished within a day or two, one way or the other, of the 24 December, which was the day of the hangings. As far as the proclamations are concerned, we cannot find any more that deal with victuals after the last one we have

2. The French Revolution. – Translator's note.

quoted, which was dated 22 December. They may be irretriev-
ably lost, or it may merely be that we have failed to find them;
but it is also possible that the government, though not learning
any wisdom from its failures, was so discouraged by the in-
effectiveness of its measures, so overcome by the force of events,
that it left them to take their own course.

The historians of those days were more given to describing
great events than to tracing their cause or development; but we
do find, in the works of more than one of them, a clear picture
of the countryside, and a still clearer one of the city, in the late
stages of that winter and in the following spring. At that time
the cause of the trouble, which was the disproportion between
the size of the stocks of food and the demand for them, had not
been removed by the remedies which had temporarily masked
its effects – and in fact those remedies had made things worse.
Nor could the cause of the trouble be removed by the import of
adequate quantities of foreign corn, to which there were obstacles such as the lack of private or public funds for the
purpose, the poverty of the surrounding territories, the small
volume and leisurely pace of trade at that time, and the restric-
tions applied to it, and the very regulations that tended to
produce and maintain low prices. The true reason for the
famine was continuing to operate without any restraint and
with undiminished vigour – indeed, we may say that the famine
itself was continuing to do so.

Here is a copy of that tragic picture.

Shops were closed everywhere, and the workshops were nearly
all deserted. The streets were a terrible sight – a parade-ground
for passing miseries, and a dwelling place for the miserable who
could no longer move on.

Among the beggars, the professionals were now in a minority, confused and lost in the crowd of newcomers, and reduced
to disputing for charity with people from whom they might
formerly have received it. There were boys and young men who
had been dismissed by the owners of shops, and had lost part or
all of their daily earnings; they were now living with difficulty
on what they had left over, or on their capital. Some of their
employers were there too, for whom the interruption of their

business had meant failure and ruin. There were workmen and their masters from every type of manufacture or craft, from the most ordinary to the most refined, from the most necessary to the most sophisticated; and all wandering from door to door, from street to street, leaning against the corners of buildings, lying huddled on the paving-stones, by houses and by churches, either pleading pitifully for alms or silently torn between cruel necessity and still unconquered feelings of shame; lean, exhausted, and shivering with cold or hunger in their scanty, ragged clothing, which often still showed traces of their earlier prosperity – just as some signs of the confident, productive worker could still be detected on many a face marked by inactivity and humiliation.

Mingled in the pathetic throng, and indeed forming a substantial part of it, were servants dismissed by masters who had recently sunk from a middle position in life to a state of actual want, or by masters who, though extremely wealthy, still found it impossible to maintain their usual splendid train in a year like that one. And to all the indigent in these categories must be added many others who were normally more or less dependent on them and their earnings – women, children and old people, either huddling close to those who had formerly been their breadwinners, or scattering through the streets to beg separately.

There was a large number of others, distinguished by their tousled quiffs, by the gaudiness of their ragged clothes, by something in their gait and gestures, and by the imprint which is often stamped on a man's face by long habit – all the more clearly if the habit is a strange one. These were bravoes, who had lost the wages of their infamous calling in the common disaster, and were now begging the bread of charity. Tamed by hunger, not competing with the others except in the pathos of their appeals, terrified and bewildered, they slouched through streets where they had so long paraded with heads held high, with fierce and angry look, clad in rich and outlandish liveries, with long feathers in their hats, equipped with expensive weapons, over-dressed and scented. Now they humbly held out their hands for alms – hands that had so often been raised in insolent threat, or drawn back to deliver a treacherous blow.

But the most ghastly, and at the same time the most pitiful sight was provided by the peasants, whether in pairs, alone or in whole families. There were husbands, there were wives with babies in their arms or strapped on their backs, there were older children being led by the hand, and there were old men following on behind. There were people whose houses had been invaded and despoiled by soldiers who had been billeted on them, or by soldiers who had merely been passing that way, so that they had fled from their homes in despair. Among these were some who tried to inspire more pity, and to achieve a sort of pre-eminence in misery, by showing off the bruises and wounds they had received in defending their last few possessions, or in escaping from the blind and brutal frenzy of their attackers. Others had been spared that particular scourge, but had been affected by two others which had penetrated into every corner – the unfruitfulness of the earth and the weight of taxation, now heavier than ever in order to meet what were called the necessities of war; and so they had come to the city, which they regarded as the ancient home and last refuge of wealth and of pious generosity. The most recent arrivals could be known by their uncertain gait and unfamiliar look, and still more by their amazed and indignant expression when they found themselves in such a crowd, with so many rivals in their misery, in the very place where they had hoped to be unusual objects of compassion, and to attract immediate attention and help.

The others, who had been tramping the streets of the city, and living on them too for a fair length of time, keeping themselves going with what help they could find, or with whatever chance brought their way, in times of such disproportion between what was needed and what was available, had in their faces an expression of gloomier and more exhausted dismay. There was much variety in the clothing of those who could be described as clothed at all, and great differences in the men themselves as well. There were pallid faces from the lowlands, bronzed faces from the higher plains, and ruddy faces from the hills. But all had sharpened and distorted features, hollow eyes, and a fixed stare, sullen or crazy; tousled hair and long, ragged beards; bodies which had grown up and grown strong amid the labours of the field and were now weakened by hardship, with the skin hanging on their emaciated arms and fleshless shins and chests, which could be seen through the gaps in their rags. And alongside the sight of ruined physical strength was another sight, different in kind but no less distressing – the more easily conquered resistance, the more hopeless languor and exhaustion, of the women and children.

Here and there in the streets, up against the walls of the houses, lay small heaps of trodden, broken straw, mixed with all sorts of dirty rubbish. Yet this filthy stuff had been given out in kindness and charity, to serve as litter for some of the unfortunates, where they could rest their heads at night. And sometimes even during the day figures would be seen lying or sprawling there who were too weak with fatigue or hunger to remain on their feet. Sometimes too there might be a corpse lying on that grisly couch; or again a standing figure would suddenly crumple up like a rag and fall lifeless on the pavement.

Standing by one or other of those wretched sleeping places, and bent over it in sudden compassion, might be a passer-by, or someone who lived near at hand. Here and there were signs of help organized by more far-sighted generosity, evidently set in motion by someone with wealth at his disposal which he was accustomed to employ in large-scale benefactions. This was none other than Federigo Borromeo. He had selected six priests, whose lively and persevering love for their fellow-man was backed by great physical strength; he had divided them into three pairs, and had given each pair one third of the city to patrol, followed by porters carrying solid food of various kinds, with more delicate and quick-working forms of restorative nourishment in reserve, and also carrying clothing. Every morning, the three teams set out in different directions. They went up to those whom they found lying abandoned in the streets, and gave to each according to his need. Those who were already dying, and unable to take any nourishment, received the final consolations and comforts of religion. The hungry received soup, eggs, bread and wine; those who were exhausted by more prolonged starvation were served with broths, essences, and stronger wines. If necessary, they were revived in the first place with spirits. At the same time clothing was distributed to the more painful and unseemly cases of want.

Their help did not stop there; for the good archbishop intended that, as far as his arm could reach, his assistance should bring not merely temporary relief but permanent benefit. The poor folk who were restored by that initial help to a state where they could stand up and walk were then given a little money, to ensure that the return of hunger and the absence of other succour would not swiftly drag them down into the same condition once more. For those in a worse state, the priests tried to find board and lodging in some near-by house. Well-to-do householders generally took them in out of charity, and on the Cardinal's recommendation; householders who had the good will but not the means to help would be asked by the priests to take the poor wretches in against payment; a price would be fixed, and an advance paid over at once. Then the priests gave the curé of the local parish a list of the names of those who had been lodged in this way, so that he could visit them; and the priests returned to visit them again as well.

Needless to say, Federigo Borromeo did not confine his pastoral care to these extremities of suffering, and had not waited for things to reach that pass before being stirred to compassionate action. His love of mankind was so warm and so adaptable that it was bound to turn to pity for every misfortune, to offer every helpful effort that it could muster, to hasten to fill the breaches that it had been unable to foresee, and to take on whatever varied forms might be demanded by circumstances. The Cardinal summoned up all his resources, imposed yet greater frugality on his household, drew on savings which he had earmarked for other benefactions that were now of secondary importance, and, in a word, tried every possible way of raising money, in order to use all of it for the rescue of the starving. He had bought up a substantial amount of grain, and sent a large part of it out to the parts of his diocese which needed it most. And as the supplies fell very far short of the need, he also sent them salt, 'with the aid of which', says Ripamonti,[3] as he tells us the story, 'the herbs of the meadows and the bark of the trees can be converted into wholesome food.'

The Cardinal had also distributed grain and money to the various parishes in Milan. He himself toured the city, quarter by quarter, distributing alms; and he secretly came to the rescue of many poor families. We read in the *Ragguaglio*[4] of a doctor named Alessandro Tadino – a contemporary work which we shall often have occasion to quote as our story progresses – that every morning two thousand bowls of rice soup were distributed from the Archbishop's palace.

But though these charitable efforts were truly remarkable, when we consider that they were the work of a single man, and came wholly out of his resources (for Federigo Borromeo refused, as a matter of principle, to act as steward for another's generosity); though they were backed by the offerings of other private citizens, less effective than his individually, but significant by their number, and though they were accompanied by the supplies decreed by the council of decurions, and distributed by the tribunal for provisions, they were still little enough compared with the need that faced them. While one lot of hill-folk were being rescued by the Cardinal's generosity from imminent death by starvation, another lot were rapidly reaching the same desperate state. The first lot slipped back into it again, when those modest supplies were exhausted.

In other districts, which had been ... not forgotten, but left till later as less urgent by a charity compelled to choose its objectives, the famine meanwhile reached mortal proportions. Death was everywhere, and from every side more people flocked into the city.

Two thousand men, perhaps, who were either stronger than the others or more skilled at overcoming competition and at carving their way through a crowd, had won themselves a bowl

3. *Historiae patriae*, Fifth Decade, Book VI, page 386.
4. *Ragguaglio dell'origine et giornali successi della gran peste contagiosa, venefica et malefica, seguita nella città di Milano.* Milan, 1648, page 10.

of soup apiece, enough to keep them alive for the day. But more thousands remained behind, envying those more fortunate rivals – but can we call them fortunate, when we remember that their wives, children or parents were often among those left behind? And while in certain parts those who were totally abandoned and reduced to extremity were raised up from the ground, brought back to life, and given lodging and food for a time, there were a hundred other places where their brothers fell, languished and died without any help or comfort.

All day long a confused murmur of imploring voices could be heard in the streets. All night there was a chorus of groans, interrupted at times by sudden outbreaks of loud lamentation, or howls of pain, or voices calling out in deep-felt supplication of their Maker, often ending in shrill screams.

With people in these desperate straits, with so many different grounds for indignant complaint, there were, strange to say, no attempts at rioting; the cry of revolt was never raised – or at least we can find no trace of it in the records. And yet, among those who were living and dying in those conditions, were many men who had been schooled to anything but patience. There were hundreds of the very men who had been so conspicuously active on St Martin's day. Nor can it be thought that the example of those four poor devils who had paid the price for all the others was a sufficient reason to keep the rest of them so quiet. For how could even the presence of the gibbet, let alone its memory, have had that effect on the minds of a mixed yet united crowd which could see that it was already condemned to a slow death by torture, and was in fact already beginning to suffer its pains? But we human beings are like that – we rebel in furious indignation against moderate evils, and bow our heads in silence beneath extreme ill-treatment. Stunned rather than resigned, we put up with twice the load which we had declared to be unbearable earlier on.

Death created many vacant places in that pitiful crowd every day, but they were promptly filled, and more than filled. People flooded in all the time, first of all from the neighbouring villages, then from the surrounding districts, then from the other cities of the duchy, and finally from towns outside its frontiers.

Meanwhile long-standing inhabitants of Milan were leaving the city every day; some to escape from the sight of so much misery, others because they found their places taken by competitors in the begging trade, and wandered off in a last desperate attempt to find help elsewhere, wherever it might be, so long as it was away from dense, trampling crowds and rival claimants for alms. Wanderers inwards passed wanderers outwards on the roads, and each were a sight of horror to the others, a bitter foretaste, a sinister omen of what might lie at the end of their respective journeys. But each continued on their chosen way, not so much hoping to find better luck, as unwilling to return to a place they had learned to hate, to look again on the scenes that had driven them to despair. Sometimes, indeed, one of them would feel his last vestige of strength ebbing away at that moment, and fall down in the road and die – a still sadder sight for his wretched fellow-travellers, and an object of horror, perhaps also of reproach, to other passers-by.

'I myself', writes Ripamonti, 'saw the corpse of a woman lying in the road that girds the walls round about ... half-chewed grass was dropping out of her mouth, and her lips were still twisted as if in an expression of angry effort ... on her back was slung a bundle, and on her chest was slung a baby in its swaddling clothes, weeping as it sought for the breast ... some compassionate people came by, who picked the poor little creature up, and carried it away, thus fulfilling in the mean-while the first duty of a mother.'

The old contrast between rags and rich clothing, between superfluity and destitution, which is so normal a sight in normal times, had completely vanished. Rags and destitution were to be seen almost everywhere, and when something else came to view, it was no more than a look of very modest well-being. The nobles could be seen walking in the simplest and plainest of clothes, sometimes indeed in mean or worn-out garments – perhaps because the common causes of universal impoverish-ment had really reduced their fortunes to that point, or given the final blow to family finances that were already tottering; perhaps because they were afraid of provoking the indignation of that desperate populace by a display of splendid luxury;

perhaps because they were ashamed to triumph in the midst of public disaster. Tyrants who had inspired both hatred and respect, accustomed to walk the streets with a train of bravoes behind them, now went about almost unaccompanied, with head held low, with an expression that seemed both to offer and to beg for peace. Other nobles, who had shown a more humane disposition, and had conducted themselves with more modesty, even in times of prosperity, seemed to be confused, dismayed and overcome by the continual sight of a misery whose magnitude went not only beyond the bounds of what could be remedied, but also, one might say, beyond the bounds of what could be pitied.

Anyone who had the means to give alms still had to make an agonizing choice between emergency and emergency, between hungry mouth and hungry mouth. And as soon as a charitable hand was stretched out towards a poor victim, other victims all around began to compete for attention. Those who still had some strength left thrust their way forward to lodge a more forceful appeal; the exhausted, the old and the children held out their fleshless hands; weeping babies, too weak to sit up, and clad in scanty rags, were held up in their mothers' arms, so that they could be seen from farther away.

Winter and spring went by in this way; and for some time the commission of public health had been drawing the attention of the tribunal for provisions to the danger of an epidemic which now overhung the city because of the growing destitution that had spread through every part of it. The suggestion was made that the beggars should be concentrated into special places of refuge. While this proposal was being discussed and approved, while ways and means were being found, and suitable places selected, the corpses continued to pile up in the streets day by day, and all the other accumulation of miseries grew in proportion. In the tribunal of provisions a slightly different plan was suggested, as simpler and quicker. This was that all the beggars, whether sick or well, should be gathered together in a single place, namely, the lazaretto, where they would be fed and looked after at public expense. This proposal was adopted, against the advice of the commission of public health, which pointed out that so vast a gathering would increase the danger they were trying to avert.

I had better describe the lazaretto of Milan, in case this story ever falls into the hands of someone who has neither seen it nor read about it. It is a rectangular enclosure, almost square in fact, outside the city proper, to the left of the East Gate, and separated from the city wall only by the width of the moat, by a road which follows the line of the wall, and by a water-course which runs round the lazaretto itself. The two longer sides of the rectangle measure about five hundred paces each, the two shorter ones perhaps fifteen paces less. Each side is divided into a series of small rooms, in a single storey, towards the outside of the whole building. Inside the enclosure a vaulted arcade, supported by small and slender pillars, runs round three sides of the courtyard.

At that time the rooms numbered 288, or perhaps a few less – the recent creation of a large new opening in the middle of the side facing the main road, and a smaller one at the corner, has removed a certain number of rooms, but we cannot say exactly how many. At the time of our story there were only two entrances, one in the middle of the side towards the city wall, and the other exactly opposite. In the middle of the courtyard was a small octagonal church, which still stands there today. The construction of the lazaretto had begun in 1489, with money from a private legacy, and had been continued with the help of public funds and of other bequests and gifts. Its original function had been that implied by its name – the provision of shelter, as occasion might arise, for those stricken by the plague. For a long period both before and after that time the plague used to appear two, four, six or even eight times a century, now in one country of Europe, now in another, now in several at one time, and sometimes spreading over the full length and breadth of the continent. But at the time of which we are speaking, the lazaretto was used only for the storage of goods that were subject to quarantine.

In order to get it cleared out as quickly as possible, the authorities did not enforce the health regulations with full rigour. The prescribed fumigations and tests were hurried through, and all the goods were released at once. Straw was put down in all the rooms, supplies of food were arranged, of the quality and in the quantities that were available, and all the beggars in the city were invited by public edict to take refuge there.

Many of them went in voluntarily; all those who were lying sick in the streets and squares were taken in. In the first few days more than three thousand of those two categories arrived at the lazaretto. But the number that remained outside was much larger. Some may have waited in the hope that when the others had gone the small number left behind would get more benefit from the charity of the city, some may have felt a natural reluctance to be locked up. Others may have felt that mistrust which the poor often feel towards any proposal that comes to them from the possessors of wealth and power – a mistrust which is always proportionate to the common ignorance of those who inspire it and those who feel it, to the total number of the poor and to the stupidity of the laws. Others again may have known what the true nature of the benefits offered was. Some, too, may have been affected by all those factors at once, or by others that we have not mentioned – in any case, the fact is that most of them took no notice of the invitation, and continued to drag themselves painfully around the streets.

So it was thought best to pass on from invitation to compulsion. The police were sent round to despatch all the beggars to the lazaretto, and to take those who resisted there in chains. For each one of these last they were paid ten *soldi*; which shows that even in the greatest crises public money can always be found for a really stupid purpose. A certain number of beggars did indeed leave the city, to go and live or die far away, but at least in freedom – as the commission of supply had thought they might, and in fact intended that they should; but the round-up was still so effective that it was not long before the number of people in the lazaretto, counting both guests and prisoners, had risen to nearly ten thousand.

It is to be hoped that there were separate quarters for women and small children, although the memoirs of the period say nothing about it. There must surely have been rules and regulations for the maintenance of good order; but what sort of good order could be established or maintained at that time and in those circumstances, in so vast and varied a throng, whose voluntary members rubbed shoulders with the forcibly interned, and where those for whom beggary was a shameful and odious necessity stood alongside those for whom it was a normal profession, while those who had grown up amid the honest toil of field and workshop had to associate with others who had learnt the arts of idleness, cheating, mockery and violence in the streets and taverns of the city and in the palaces of bullying nobles?

We could make a shrewd but gloomy guess how they all got on for board and lodging, even if we had no definite information on the subject, as in fact we have. They slept heaped up in lots of twenty or thirty in those tiny cells, or huddled in the arcades; lying either on a little rotten and stinking straw or on the bare ground. Orders had indeed been issued that the straw should be sufficient in quantity, fresh, and frequently changed; but in fact it was wretched stuff, in scanty supply, and was never changed at all. There was equally an order that the bread supplied should be of good quality – and what administrator has ever given instructions for the manufacture or distribution of inferior material? But good bread could hardly have been obtained for a much smaller number in normal circumstances; so how was it to be procured for that multitude, in that situation? It was commonly said at the time (as we read in the contemporary memoirs), that the bread issued in the lazaretto was adulterated with various heavy, unnourishing materials; and that, alas, may well have been no unfounded rumour. There was even a shortage of water – of pure and wholesome water, that is to say. The water-course that flowed round the outer wall of the lazaretto was a shallow, slow-moving stream, muddy in places, and soon reduced to the state one might expect with so vast a multitude, of so lamentable a character, camped just by it – but it had to serve as their common source of water.

These causes of high mortality were all the more effective because they were operating on sick or sickly bodies; and to them was added a strange perversity of the weather. First came persistent rains, and then a still more persistent drought, accompanied by a violent heatwave, much earlier in the year than usual. To the real discomforts of the people were added a general feeling of ill-being, the boredom and restlessness caused by being shut up, the memory of earlier habits, grief for dead relations, uneasy thoughts of the absent, the revulsion and spite the members of the crowd inspired in each other, and countless other feelings of humiliation or rage which they had either brought with them to the lazaretto or acquired since they arrived there. Another factor was the constant apprehension and frequent spectacle of death – so common a sight for so many different reasons, and now itself a potent cause of further mortality.

Nor is it surprising that the number of deaths in that enclosure rose to such a level that it began to look like a pestilence, and indeed to be called one by many people. Perhaps the combination of all the factors we have mentioned, and their increasing severity, did no more than accentuate the activity of a simple epidemic of influenza; or perhaps, as seems to happen even in much less serious and prolonged famines than this one, some other infection was involved which found in those pitiful bodies, afflicted and weakened by hardship, bad food, foul weather, dirt, suffering and humiliation, the ideal material and time for its operations – the conditions, that is to say, which it needed to be born, to nourish itself and to multiply (if a writer without special knowledge may be permitted to set down these words, following a hypothesis put forward by several scientists, and most recently reformulated, with a wealth of supporting argument and with all due reserve, by a most diligent and talented man of learning).[5] Again, the infection may have broken out in the first place in the lazaretto itself, as seems to have been the opinion of the doctors on the health commission, to judge by a report (admittedly obscure and inaccurate) which has survived; or the infection may have already been in existence in a latent form (which seems more likely, when we re-

5. Dr F. Enrico Acerbi, *Del morbo petecchiale. . . ., e degli altri contagi in generale*, Chapter III, paragraphs 1 and 2.

member that the general hardship was both long-standing and widespread, and the death-rate already high), so that once it obtained a footing in that permanently overcrowded building, it spread with new and terrible rapidity. Whatever the truth of these conjectures may be, the daily death-rate in the lazaretto was soon above one hundred.

Inside that building debility, anguish, lamentation and cries of agony were the order of the day; while in the tribunal for provisions it was all shame, bewilderment and uncertainty. They argued, they consulted the views of the commission of public health, and the only answer seemed to be to undo what had been done with such pompous deliberation, such expense and such inconvenience. The lazaretto was opened, and all the poor folk in there who were not yet ill were allowed to leave. They came out with frantic joy and haste. The city again resounded with the cries of the poor, though not so loudly nor so constantly as before. The same crowds reappeared in its streets, less dense now, and inspiring all the more pity, says Ripamonti, by the very fact that they were so much smaller than before. The sick were taken to Santa Maria della Stella, which was then a hospice for the poor; and most of them died there.

Meanwhile the blessed earth began to grow yellow with ripening corn. The beggars who had come into the city from the country went back again, each to his own place, for the long-awaited harvest. The good Cardinal sent them off with a final proof of his kindness, and an original expression of it – every peasant who presented himself at the archepiscopal palace was given a *giulio*,[6] and a sickle to reap with.

The harvest finally brought an end to the famine. The mortality, whether epidemic or contagious in origin, dropped from day to day, though it did not cease until the autumn. It was approaching its end when a new disaster struck.

Many important events, of the sort which we specifically call historical, had happened in the meanwhile. Cardinal Richelieu had captured La Rochelle, as already mentioned, and had then patched up a peace with the King of England. In the council of the King of France he next proposed that effective help should

6. A coin worth about half a *lira*. – Translator's note.

be given to the Duke of Nevers, and his powerful eloquence carried the day. At the same time he persuaded the King to lead the expedition in person. While the necessary preparations were being made, the Count of Nassau, as imperial commissioner, appeared in Mantua and notified its new ruler that he must give up the states in dispute to the Emperor Ferdinand, who would send an army to occupy them if he failed to obey.[7] Even in more hopeless circumstances the duke had already evaded these harsh and alarming terms; and, now that French support was near at hand, he was even more determined to evade them; though he did so in language so involved and wordy that it sounded as little as possible like a refusal, and with counter-proposals of acts of submission that would be even more impressive, though less dangerous, than what he was asked to do. The commissioner went off swearing that bloodshed would be the result of his attitude.

In March Richelieu did in fact move against Italy, with the King at the head of the French army, and asked the Duke of Savoy to grant the force free passage. Inconclusive negotiations followed; there was an armed clash in which the French came off best; and finally an agreement was reached. The Duke of Savoy stipulated that Don Gonzalo of Cordova must be made to raise the siege of Casale, promising in return that, if Don Gonzalo refused to do so, the forces of Savoy would join the French in the invasion of the Duchy of Milan. But Don Gonzalo thought that even so he was getting off lightly, and he did raise the siege of Casale, the garrison of which was at once strengthened by the entry of a French contingent.

It was on this occasion that Achillini wrote his famous sonnet to King Louis, which begins with the line,

'Sudate, o fochi, a preparar metalli,'[8]

and also another sonnet in which he urged the King to proceed at once to the liberation of the Holy Land. But it is the fate of poets that no one ever takes their advice. If history contains a record of any acts which appear to follow the suggestion of a

7. See pages 492–4. – Translator's note.
8. 'Sweat, fires, and let the metals be prepared!' – Translator's note.

poet, we may be quite sure that the decision to perform them had been taken before the advice was given. Richelieu in fact decided to go back to France, to attend to affairs that seemed to him to be more urgent. It was in vain that Girolamo Soranzo, the Venetian envoy, brought forward reasons to the contrary; for the King and the Cardinal paid no more heed to his prose than to the verse of Achillini, and went home with the main body of the French army, leaving only six thousand men in Susa to hold the pass and guarantee the treaty.

While the French army withdrew in one direction, the army of the Emperor was advancing from another. It had invaded the Grisons and Valtellina, and was preparing to descend on the duchy of Milan.[9] Apart from all the other disasters that might be expected to follow from their passage, definite news had reached the commission of public health that this army was carrying the plague with it. In any body of German troops there was always a sprinkling of cases of plague in those days, as Varchi tells us when writing about the pestilence that they had brought with them to Florence a century earlier.

The commission of public health in Milan had a president and six other members – four magistrates and two doctors of medicine. They delegated one of their number, Alessandro Tadino (as we read in his *Ragguaglio*, which we have already quoted) to call on the Governor and inform him of the appalling danger which hung over the territory if those troops passed through it on their way to besiege Mantua, as it was rumoured that they were about to do.

From all the actions of Don Gonzalo's life he seems to have had an overwhelming passion to feature in the pages of history, from which he could indeed hardly be altogether excluded. History, however, either did not know or did not bother to record the most memorable of all his deeds – a typical lapse on her part. We refer to the reply which he gave to Tadino on the occasion just mentioned. He said that he did not know what could be done about it; that the reasons of interest and prestige which had set the imperial forces in motion were of more weight than the considerations mentioned by the doctor; but

9. See map on page 16, and notes on facing page. – Translator's note.

that anyway they must take the best precautions they could, and trust in Providence.

By way of taking the best precautions they could, the two doctors on the commission of public health, namely Tadino himself and Senator Settala, the son of the famous Lodovico Settala, proposed to their colleagues that a regulation should be passed with very strict penalties, forbidding the purchase of any articles whatever from the soldiers who would be passing through. But it proved impossible to persuade one man of the necessity of such a rule; and this was the president of the commission. 'Though a very good-hearted man,' writes Tadino, 'he thought it impossible that the deaths of many thousands of people could follow from mere contact with those men, or with their belongings.'

We quote this event as one of the most remarkable of the time. Since commissions of public health were first thought of, there can surely never have been another occasion when such a thought – if thought is the right word – crossed the mind of the president of one of them.

A few days after Don Gonzalo gave that memorable answer to Tadino, he left Milan. The reasons for his departure were unfortunate, and so were the actual circumstances of his going. He was removed from office because of the ill success of the campaign which he had initiated and commanded; and the people of Milan blamed him for the famine they had suffered under his rule. (No one knew about his efforts in the matter of the plague, or at least no one was concerned about them, as we shall see later – with the exception of the commission of public health, and especially the two doctors.)

He left his official residence in a travelling coach, surrounded by a guard of halberdiers, with two trumpeters riding in front of him, and other coaches behind containing nobles of his suite, and was greeted with much hissing by a large number of boys, who had assembled in the Cathedral Square, and now followed him in a mob. When the procession entered the road which leads to the Ticino Gate, by which it was to leave the city, it found itself hemmed in by a crowd of people, some of whom had been waiting since earlier in the day, while others were still arriving; all the more so because the trumpeters, those strict observers of procedure, sounded their instruments all the way from the palace to the gate.

During the investigation that followed this disturbance, one of them was accused of having made things worse with his incessant trumpeting, and he replied,

'That's our profession, your Honour; and if His Excellency didn't want us to blow our trumpets, he should have told us to be quiet.'

But Don Gonzalo had given no such order, whether out of reluctance to show the white feather, or out of fear that it might make the mob more reckless, or because he was a little bewildered by events. The guards were unable to disperse the crowd, which surged along before, behind and around the carriages, shouting,

'Good riddance to famine! Good riddance to the scourge of the poor! Away with him!' and even worse slogans.

As they approached the gate, the people began to throw stones, bricks, cabbage stalks and vegetable refuse of every kind – the usual ammunition of such gatherings, in short. Some of them hastily climbed on to the walls, and discharged a final volley at the carriages as they went through the gate. Then they quickly dispersed.

Don Gonzalo was replaced by the Marquis Ambrogio Spinola, who had already won in Flanders the military glory which still distinguishes his name.

Count Rambaldo di Collalto, another Italian condottiere, of lesser but still considerable fame, was in supreme command of the German army, and had now received definite instructions to proceed with the campaign against Mantua. In September he entered the duchy of Milan.

Armies at that time were still largely made up of soldiers of fortune, enrolled by professional condottieri – sometimes to serve a particular prince, but sometimes on the commander's own account, so that the whole contingent, with its leader, could be sold to the highest bidder. Men were attracted to the profession of arms not so much by the pay as by the hope of booty and the prospects of every other kind of licence. There was no firm overall discipline; and indeed it would have been hard to reconcile anything of the kind with the largely independent authority of the individual condottieri. They too were no great sticklers for discipline; nor can we see how they could have established or maintained stricter control even if they had wanted to, for soldiers of that type might well have mutinied against an innovating commander who tried to abolish looting: they would certainly, at the very least, have left him to guard his standard by himself.

Moreover the princes who hired these bands were more concerned with having a large force, to ensure victory, than with having one the size of which corresponded with their ability to pay, which was often very limited. So the soldiers' pay often arrived late, or in the form of small sums on account, or a little at a time. The loot of places that happened to get looted came to be tacitly regarded as a supplement. There is a saying of Wallenstein's which is almost as famous as its author – that it is easier to maintain an army of one hundred thousand men than an army of twelve thousand. And the army of which we are now speaking was largely made up of the men who had laid Germany waste under Wallenstein's command, in that most famous war – famous both for itself and for its results – which was later named after the thirty years of its duration; at the moment, however, it was only in its eleventh year. Wallenstein's own regiment was in fact serving in the invading army under the command of one of his lieutenants. Most of the other condottieri in that army had served under him, and among them were several of those who helped to cause his tragic death four years later, the story of which everyone knows.

There were twenty-eight thousand infantry and seven thousand cavalry. On their way from Valtellina to the territory of Mantua they were to follow the course of the Adda, as it flows in through one narrow branch of Lake Como and out through another, and then on again as an ordinary river down to its confluence with the Po; and then they were to do a good further stretch along the banks of the Po itself. In all it came to eight days' journey through the duchy of Milan.[10]

10. See map on page 16 and notes on facing page. – Translator's note.

A large part of the inhabitants of the area through which they passed fled up into the mountains, carrying with them all their most precious possessions, and driving their livestock in front of them. But some remained behind, in order not to abandon a sick relative, or to save their house from being burnt, or to keep an eye on valuables which they had hidden or buried. Others remained because they had nothing to lose, or even thought they might gain something.

When the first contingent arrived at a village selected as a halting-place, the men quickly spread out over it and into the neighbouring hamlets, and literally put them to the sack. Whatever could be consumed or carried off vanished at once and everything else was ruined or destroyed. Furniture became firewood; cottages became stables; not to speak of beatings, woundings and rapes. The ingenious inventions and clever tricks that people had thought of to save their property generally proved useless, and sometimes worse. The soldiers were well versed in the stratagems of this sort of campaign too; they searched every cranny of the houses, knocked down walls, dismantled buildings, and quickly identified the spots in the gardens that had recently been dug. They went up into the mountains to steal the cattle. Guided by some treacherous villager, they searched the caves and pulled out the few rich people who were hiding there; they dragged them back to their own homes, and tormented them with threats and blows until they revealed their hidden treasure.

Finally they went; at last they were really gone. The sound of drums and trumpets died away in the distance, and a few hours of terror-stricken peace followed. Then another accursed rolling of drums and shrilling of trumpets announced the arrival of another contingent. Not finding any booty, the newcomers put all the more passion into wrecking what was left. They burnt the wine barrels that their predecessors had emptied, and the doors of the rooms that no longer had anything in them. They even set fire to the houses. They also put all the more rage into their ill-treatment of the villagers. And so it went on, getting worse and worse, for twenty days; for that was the number of contingents into which the army was divided.

Colico was the first place in the duchy to be invaded by those devils; then they hurled themselves against Bellano. Next they entered and spread out over Valsassina, from which they passed on into the territory of Lecco.

Chapter 29

SOME old friends of ours were among the poor terrified inhabitants of the district of Lecco.

News that the army had marched, that it was near at hand, and of its behaviour all arrived together; and to miss seeing Don Abbondio on that day was to miss a fresh insight into the nature of perplexity and terror.

'They're coming!' – 'Thirty thousand of them!' – 'Forty thousand!' – 'Fifty thousand!' – 'They're fiends!' – 'They're heretics!' – 'They're antichrists!' – 'They've sacked Cortenuova!' – 'They've burnt Primaluna!' – 'They're destroying Introbbio, Pasturo, and Barsio!' – 'They're in Balabbio already!' – 'They'll be here tomorrow!'

Such was the news that passed from mouth to mouth, with much dashing here and there, much buttonholing of neighbours in the street, much hasty consultation, much hesitation between running away and staying in the village, much assembling of women on corners, much tearing of hair.

Don Abbondio made up his mind to run away, made it up more quickly and more firmly than anyone else; but he saw insuperable obstacles and appalling dangers in every alternative refuge and every alternative route.

'What can we do?' he exclaimed. 'Where can we go?'

The mountains, apart from the difficulty of getting there, were far from safe. Everyone knew that German soldiers could climb like goats, when they had any indication, or any hope, that there was booty to be had in the hills. The lake was stormy, with a high wind blowing; and moreover most of the boatmen had already taken their vessels over to the other side, being afraid that they would be pressed into carrying soldiers or their equipment. The few boats that were left sailed off later overloaded with passengers; and between the storm and the weight

534

they were carrying they were thought to be in danger of sinking at any moment.

It was impossible to find a trap, a horse, or any other means of transport for a longer journey, to take you right off the army's route; and Don Abbondio was not up to a very long journey on foot. Besides, he was afraid of being overtaken on the road. The territory of Bergamo was not so far away that his legs could not have got him there in one march; but it was known that a contingent of *cappelletti*[1] had been hurriedly sent down from Bergamo to patrol the frontier and protect it against the imperial troops, and the *cappelletti* were fiends in human shape, just like the Germans, and were behaving as badly as possible on their side of the border.

Poor Don Abbondio trotted from room to room, with rolling eyes, beside himself with fear; he followed Perpetua around the house, hoping to reach some conclusion with her assistance. But she was busy sorting out the best things in the building and hiding them in the attic or in various dark corners; breathless and preoccupied, she would dash past him with handfuls or armfuls of stuff, and reply,

'I've nearly finished getting all this put safely away, and when I have we'll just do the same as everyone else.'

Don Abbondio wanted to stop her for a moment and discuss the various alternatives with her. But Perpetua, what with all she had to do, and the little time she had to do it, and the terror in her own heart, and her fury at the terror in her master's, was now in a less tractable mood than ever before.

'Other people are managing, and we'll manage too!' she said. 'Excuse me, sir, but you don't seem able to do anything but get in the way. Don't you realize that other people have skins to save as well as yourself? Do you think the soldiers are coming here to make war on you in particular? You might give me a hand, at a time like this, instead of whining and getting under my feet.'

With these and similar replies, she kept him out of her way. She had already decided that as soon as she had completed the urgent and confused business in hand she would grab him by

1. Foreign cavalry in the service of Venice. – Translator's note.

the arm, like a small boy, and drag him up to the top of the nearest mountain.

Left to himself, Don Abbondio looked out of the window, and watched and listened. When he saw anyone go by, he called out in a half-whining, half-reproachful voice:

'Do your curé the kindness of finding him a horse, or a mule, or a donkey. Can it really be that no one will help me? What people there are in this place! Wait for me anyway; wait till I can come with you! Wait till there are fifteen or twenty of you, and then you can take me with you, and I won't be left alone. Do you really want to leave me to the mercy of those swine? Don't you realize that most of them are Lutherans, who regard it as a meritorious action to cut a priest's throat? Do you want to leave me here to martyrdom? What people there are here; Heaven help me!'

But to whom were these words addressed? To men who were going past bent under the weight of their poor belongings, thinking about the things they had had to leave in their houses, driving their poor cattle before them, leading children who were also laden to the limit of what they could carry, and wives holding in their arms children who were too young to walk. Some strode on without replying or looking up. Some said: 'Why, your Honour, you'll have to do the best you can, like the rest of us; you're lucky not to have a family to worry about. You'll have to look after yourself, and find your own solution.'

'Heaven help me then!' cried Don Abbondio. 'What people these are! What hard hearts! There's no true charity in them at all. Each of them thinks of himself, and not one of them thinks of me!'

He began to look for Perpetua again.

'By the way!' said the housekeeper. 'What about the money?'

'What are we to do?'

'Give it to me, and I'll go and bury it in the back garden, with the best silver.'

'But . . .'

'No buts about it; let me have it now. Keep a little in your pocket for emergencies, and leave the rest to me.'

Don Abbondio went obediently to his money-box and got out

his little hoard of cash. He gave it to Perpetua, who said, 'I'll bury it in the garden, then, at the foot of the fig-tree,' and went off.

She came back presently with a flat basket containing food for the journey, and an empty pannier into which she quickly packed a little of her own linen and her master's.

'There's one thing you can carry yourself,' she said, 'and that's your breviary!'

'But where are we to go?'

'Where's everyone else going? Let's get on the road, first of all, and then we'll hear what they've got to say, and see what's the best thing to do.'

Just then in came Agnese, with a small pannier slung on her back, and with the air of someone who has an important suggestion to make.

Agnese had soon resolved not to await the arrival of those unwelcome guests in her own home, alone as she was, and still in possession of some of the *scudi* provided by the Unnamed; but at first she had been puzzled where to take refuge. The remains of that stock of gold coins, which had been so useful to her during the months of famine, were in fact the main cause of her perplexity and indecision; for she had heard that those who had money had been the most shockingly ill-treated of all in the villages through which the soldiers had passed – exposed both to the violence of the invaders and the treachery of the local inhabitants.

It was true that she had told no one but Don Abbondio about the wealth which had, as she said, fallen from Heaven into her lap. When she wanted to change a *scudo*, from time to time, she had asked the curé to do it for her – always leaving him part of the proceeds to give to someone poorer than herself. But hidden money generally keeps its owner in a constant state of worried suspicion about the possible suspicions of other people – especially if he is not used to handling a lot of cash. She too had gone round hiding away as best she could the things that she could not carry with her, and as she thought about the *scudi*, which were sewn into her bodice, she remembered that the Unnamed had sent her, together with the money, the most generous offer of any kind of help he could render. She remembered all she had heard about his castle, and how it was in such a strong place that you'd need wings to get in there if the owner didn't want you to; and she decided to go and ask the Unnamed for shelter. Then she wondered how she could prove her identity to the gentleman; and she at once thought of Don Abbondio, who had been very friendly to her ever since he had had that talk with the Archbishop – all the more genuinely friendly because there was no risk now of such an attitude getting him into trouble with anyone, and because Renzo and Lucia were both far away, and so unable to make any demands on his services, which might have put his friendliness to a severe test. Agnese reflected that the poor curé would probably be even more perplexed and terrified than herself in this embroiled situation, and thought that he might well be very pleased with her plan; and so she had come to tell him about it. She found him with Perpetua, and made the suggestion to both of them together.

'What do you say to that, Perpetua?' asked Don Abbondio.

'I say it's an inspiration straight from Heaven, and don't let's lose any time, and let's get moving!'

'But then later on . . .'

'But then later on, when we get there, we shall be very well off. We know about that gentleman, how all he cares about now is doing good to his neighbour; and so he'll be glad enough to give us shelter. Right on the frontier like that, and halfway up in the sky, you won't find any soldiers there. And then, later on, we'll have something to eat; while in the mountains, once we'd finished this small gift of God,' said Perpetua, putting the food into the pannier on top of the linen, 'we'd have been in trouble for sure.'

'Yes, yes, that wonderful conversion . . . but is it a genuine conversion?'

'How can you doubt that, after all that we know has happened, and after what you've seen with your own eyes?'

'And if we were to walk into a trap?'

'A trap, sir? What trap? With all these if and buts, we'll never get anywhere, sir, if you'll pardon my saying so . . . Well done, Agnese! It was a good idea that came into your head.'

Perpetua put the pannier on a table, stuck her arms through the straps, and got it up on her back.

'Couldn't we find a man who'd come with us, to act as escort to his priest?' said Don Abbondio. 'If we happened to meet a ruffian – and there are plenty of them around unfortunately – what help could you two give me?'

'There's another trick for wasting time!' cried Perpetua. 'Going to look for a man at a time like this? You won't find one who hasn't plenty to do at the moment looking after his own affairs. Take heart, sir! Get your breviary and your hat, and let's go!'

Don Abbondio disappeared, and came back a moment later, with his hat on his head, his breviary under his arm, and his staff in his hand. All three of them went out by a side door, which opened on to the square. Perpetua locked it behind her, more as a formality than for any faith she had in that lock or that woodwork, and put the key in her pocket.

Don Abbondio cast a glance in passing at the church, and muttered to himself – It's for the villagers to protect it – it's there for their benefit. If they care about their church, they'll do something about it; if not, so much the worse for them.

They set off across the fields, very quietly, each of them thinking his own thoughts. They looked round them cautiously, especially Don Abbondio, to see if any suspicious figures would appear, or anything else out of the ordinary. But they met nobody; those who were not indoors guarding their houses, packing up, or hiding their valuables, were already on the roads that led directly to the mountains.

Don Abbondio sighed and sighed again, let out an exclamation or two, and then began to grumble in a more connected manner. He complained about the Duke of Nevers, who could just as well have stayed in France and lived like a prince (which he was); but nothing would suit him but to be Duke of Mantua as well, against the wishes of the whole world. He complained about the Emperor, who ought to have shown more sense on behalf of the others, and to have let things take their course, and not to make such an issue of minor points, since he'd still be Emperor at the end of the day whether Tom, Dick or Harry were Duke of Mantua. But most of all Don Abbondio grumbled at the Governor, whose job it was to keep the common scourges of mankind away from the duchy, and who did all he could to attract them there, just for the pleasure of having a war.

'It's a pity those fine gentlemen aren't here now, to see and feel what the pleasures of war are like!' he said. 'They have much to answer for. But meanwhile the people who suffer are the innocent.'

'Oh, leave those Governors and Emperors of yours alone, for you won't find them coming to help you!' said Perpetua. 'It's just a lot of your talk, sir, if you'll excuse me saying so, which doesn't do any good at all. Now what worries me is this...'

'Yes? Yes? What is it?'

They had now gone far enough along the road for Perpetua to think over at leisure the efforts she had made in such haste to hide everything, and she began to bemoan the fact that she had forgotten one item and only half hidden another; here she had left a clue that might help the robbers, there she had...

'Bravo, Perpetua!' interrupted Don Abbondio, who was now sufficiently sure of his personal safety to begin worrying about his possessions. 'Splendid! So that's what you did! You must have lost your head completely.'

'What!' cried Perpetua, stopping for a moment and putting her hands on her hips, as well as the pannier on her back would let her. 'Are you going to say it was my fault, when it was you who made me lose my head, instead of helping me and encouraging me? Why, I took more trouble over the things that belonged to the house than over my stuff. I had no one to help me; I had to play the parts of Mary and Martha at once. If anything goes wrong, I can't help it. I've done my duty and more than my duty.'

Agnese interrupted these disputes with remarks about her own troubles. It was not so much the personal inconvenience and the damage to her property that she minded, as losing all hope of an early reunion with Lucia. For, as the reader may

540

remember, the two women had arranged to meet again that very autumn; and it was not to be thought that Donna Prassede would come up to that district for the country holiday season in those circumstances. In fact, if she had been there already, she would certainly have left her country seat in a hurry, as the other gentry were doing.

The sight of the places through which they passed made these thoughts more vivid, and increased Agnese's unhappiness. They had left the byways now, and were on the main road along which the poor woman had travelled when she brought her daughter home – for so brief a stay! – after the time they had spent together in the tailor's house. And now the village where he lived was already in sight.

'We must go and see those good people,' said Agnese.

'And we must have a bit of a rest; I'm beginning to get tired of this pannier,' said Perpetua. 'We'll have something to eat as well.'

'So long as we don't waste too much time,' added Don Abbondio. 'Remember that we're not travelling for pleasure.'

They were received with open arms. Their hosts were genuinely glad to see them, because they were the living reminder of a good deed. Be kind to as many people as you can, says our anonymous author, and you'll find faces you are glad to see wherever you go.

As she embraced the tailor's wife, Agnese broke out into a flood of tears, which did her a great deal of good. She could reply only with sobs to the questions about Lucia from both man and wife that followed.

'Lucia's better off than we are,' said Don Abbondio. 'She's in Milan, out of danger, and far away from this work of the devil.'

'So you've had to run for it, you and these good people, have you, your Reverence?' said the tailor.

'We certainly have!' said master and servant together.

'I'm sorry for you then.'

'We're on our way to the castle of . . . ,' said Don Abbondio.

'A very good idea; you'll be as safe there as you'd be in church.'

'But aren't you afraid to stay here?' said the curé.

541

'Well, sir, I'll tell you what I think. The soldiers won't come here for enlodgement (which is the correct term, as you realize, of course); it's too far off their route, thank God. At the very worst, we might get a passing raid – pray Heaven we don't! But there's time enough; and first we must hear some more news from the unfortunate villages where they're going to stop for the night.'

So the three travellers decided to stop there for a little and get their breath back. As it was dinner-time, the tailor said: 'Well, good sir, good ladies, you must honour my poor table, such as it is; pot luck, you know, and good will the main dish!'

Perpetua replied that they had brought something to eat with them. After a little ceremony on each side, they agreed to pool their resources and dine together.

The children joyfully gathered round their old friend Agnese. But the tailor quickly gave them their instructions. One little girl (the same who had taken the food round to the widow and her children, if you remember the episode) was told to get four of the early chestnuts which had been put away in a corner to remove the spiny outer husks, and to put them on to roast.

'And you, now,' he said to one of the boys, 'go out into the garden and give the peach tree enough of a shake to bring down four peaches, and bring them here – all of them mind! And you', he added, turning to another boy, 'get up the fig-tree and pick four of the ripest figs. You know how to do that – a bit too well, I should say.'

The tailor went off to tap a small barrel of wine that he had, and his wife went to fetch some table linen. Perpetua got out her provisions, and the table was laid, with a napkin and a majolica plate in the place of honour for Don Abbondio, and with cutlery that Perpetua had brought in her pannier. They sat down to their meal; and if they were not an outstandingly cheerful gathering, they were at least more so than any of them had expected to be on that particular day.

'What do you say about all this turmoil, your Reverence?' said the tailor. 'I feel as if I were reading the story of the Saracens in France.'

542

'Why, what can I say about it? As if I hadn't had enough bad luck already!'

'But you've chosen a good place to go; no one will ever be able to force his way into that castle. And you'll have company, for we've heard of a lot of people taking refuge there, and more on the way.'

'I hope we shall be well received. I know that worthy lord; and last time I had the honour of his company he behaved like a perfect gentleman,' said the priest.

'And he sent me a message through His Grace the Archbishop,' said Agnese, 'to tell me that if ever I needed help, I had only to go and see him.'

'Yes, yes! A wonderful conversion indeed!' said Don Abbondio. 'And permanent, I'm told. No signs of backsliding, eh?'

The tailor began to talk at length about the holy life that the Unnamed was now leading, and how he was now a benefactor and an example to the neighbourhood, instead of being its scourge, as before.

'And what about the people he had with him – all those retainers of his?' said Don Abbondio, who had heard a good deal about all this before, but could never have enough reassurance.

'Most of them have gone,' said the tailor, 'and those that are left have changed their ways, more than you'd believe possible. That castle has turned into a real Thebais;[2] you know what I mean, sir.'

Then Agnese had something to say about the Cardinal. 'What a great man!' she exclaimed. 'What a truly great man! It's a pity he passed through in such a hurry that I didn't have time to do anything to show my respect for him. How I'd love to have another chance to speak to him, more at leisure!'

When they got up from table, the tailor showed her a picture of the Archbishop, a print which he had tacked on to one of the doors, out of admiration for the man, and also so that he could say to his visitors, 'It's a very poor likeness, as I can tell you,

2. The area near Thebes in Egypt, which was a great place for hermits in the early days of the Church. – Translator's note.

since I've had the opportunity to see the Cardinal himself, as near as I am to you, in this very room.'

'Why, is that really meant to be His Grace, that thing there?' said Agnes. 'The robes are like enough, but . . .'

'It's not a good likeness at all, is it? said the tailor. 'That's just what I always say myself. And we know, don't we? But at least it's got his name on it; so it is something to remember him by.'

Don Abbondio was anxious to get on with the journey. The tailor promised to find a cart to take them to the foot of the slope that led up to the castle. He went off to look for one, and came back in a few minutes to say that it was coming. Then he turned to Don Abbondio, and said,

'You know, your Reverence, if by any chance you'd like to take something to read up there with you, to pass the time, I could help you, though I'm a poor man, for I read a bit myself, for my own amusement. They aren't really books for the likes of you, of course; nothing in Latin. But if you'd like one of them . . .'

'Thank you, thank you,' said Don Abbondio, 'but at times like this it's all I can do to get through the reading I have to do as a duty.'

Thanks were offered and politely turned aside; farewells and good wishes were exchanged; the travellers were invited to come back and promised to do so on their return journey; and meanwhile the cart had arrived and was standing outside the front door. They put in their panniers and climbed up themselves, and began the second half of their journey with rather more comfort and peace of mind than the first.

What the tailor had said about the Unnamed was perfectly true. From the day on which we last met him, he had continued to follow the course he had chosen – compensating people for the harm he had done them, seeking peace with all men, helping the poor, and always doing good as opportunity offered. He had once demonstrated his courage by attacking others and defending himself; now he demonstrated it by doing neither of those things. He went about alone and unarmed, open to every sort of retaliation for his many past acts of violence. He was convinced that it would be a further act of violence to use force in his own defence, when he was so deeply in the wrong with so many people. Any wrong that might be done to him would indeed be a wrong to God, he said, but in relation to himself it would be an act of just retribution; and he had less right than anyone to punish such a wrong.

But for all that, he remained as free from attack as he had been when his safety was protected by so many weapons, so many strong arms – including his own. The memory of his previous ferocity and the sight of his present meekness might have been thought to provide both motive and opportunity for revenge; but in fact they combined to win him a lasting admiration which was his main safeguard. This was the man whom no one had been able to humble, and who had humbled himself. Old rancours, originally caused by his contempt for others and their fear of him, vanished at the sight of that new humility. His victims had obtained, against all expectation and without any danger to themselves, a satisfaction of a kind which they could never have hoped for from the most successful act of vengeance – the satisfaction of seeing a man of that stamp repent of the wrongs he had done, and, in a sense, join in the indignation he had caused. There were many whose keenest and bitterest grief, endured for many years past, had been the absence of any prospect of ever being stronger than their tyrant so that they could exact retribution for an injury – but when they met him walking alone, unarmed, and clearly unprepared to resist attack, they felt no inclination to do anything but applaud.

In his voluntary humiliation his expression and bearing had, quite unknown to himself, taken on a fresh distinction and nobility; for his contempt for every kind of danger was even clearer to see than before. Even the most brutal and most furious of his enemies was restrained and controlled by the public veneration for that repentant and kindly figure. Often, indeed, he found some difficulty in avoiding embarrassing demonstrations of public enthusiasm. He had to be careful not to let his inner feelings of repentance show too clearly in his face or bearing; not to humble himself too far, for fear of being too greatly exalted. He had taken the lowliest seat in the church for his own, and there was no risk that anyone would take it from him; that would have been like usurping a place of honour. To insult that man, or even to treat him with disrespect, would have been regarded as not merely insolent and cowardly, but sacrilegious. Even those who were mainly restrained by public opinion shared these feelings to some extent themselves.

The same reasons, among others, saved him from retribution at the hands of the forces of public justice, and won him safety – though he cared little enough about that – from that quarter too. His rank and the power of his family had always had some protective value for him, and were all the more effective now that the praise earned by his exemplary conduct and the glory of his conversion were added to that celebrated but infamous name. The magistrates and the most eminent nobles had shown their pleasure at the conversion just as openly as the common people, and it would have been a strange thing if they had gone on to take harsh measures against the object of so many congratulations. Besides this, authorities which were occupied with a perpetual and often unsuccessful war against rebellions which were still full of life, or breaking out afresh, might well be glad enough to find themselves rid of the most dangerous and uncontrollable of all those revolts, without going on to look for more trouble; all the more so since that conversion led to reparation being made such as the authorities were often unable to enforce, and indeed seldom demanded.

To persecute a saint hardly seemed the best way to wipe out the shame of failing to get the better of a criminal; and the effect of punishing him could only be to dissuade others from following his example. Probably the part played by the Cardinal in the conversion, and the association of his revered name with that of the convert, served the Unnamed as a consecrated shield. The state of public affairs and the climate of thought at that time were such that there was a strange relationship between Church and State, which often came to blows, yet never aimed at each other's destruction. They always mingled expressions of gratitude and protestations of deference with their acts of hostility. They often in fact pursued a common aim without ever making peace with one another. And so it could well be that a man who had reconciled himself with the Church might find his offences deliberately forgotten, if not formally forgiven, by the State, in cases where the Church had acted alone to secure an end desired by both of them.

If the Unnamed had been brought low by some external force, nobles and people would have raced each other for a chance of trampling on his prostrate form; but as he abased himself voluntarily, he was spared by all, and honoured by many.

There were of course many others who could hardly be pleased by that amazing conversion – all his paid servants in crime, all his companions in crime, who lost powerful support on which they had come to rely; all who suddenly found that the threads of a long-prepared net were broken, perhaps at the very moment when they expected to hear that the trap had closed. But we have already seen how the thugs who were with him at the time of his conversion had reacted on hearing the news from his own lips. They had shown astonishment, pain, depression, rage – every possible response, in short, except contempt or hatred. The same was true of the agents he kept here and there, and of his accomplices in high places, when they heard the unwelcome news; and for the same reasons in every case. There was a great deal more hostility towards the Cardinal, as Ripamonti tells in the chapter already quoted. They regarded him as a man who had interfered in their plans with the sole object of disrupting them; whereas the Unnamed had at least wanted to save his own soul, and no one could complain about that.

Most of the bravoes in the castle had been unable to settle down under the new régime; and as there was no prospect of it changing, they gradually drifted away. Some must have looked for a new master, perhaps among the old friends of the man they were leaving; some must have enrolled in one or other of the units then being raised by Spain, or Mantua, or one of the other belligerent states; others must have taken to the highways and waged war on society in a small way on their own account, or contented themselves with other kinds of freelance petty crime. And much the same must have happened to those who had served him in various other places. Most of those who had reconciled themselves to the change – or perhaps welcomed it – were natives of the valley; they went back to work in the fields, or to the trades that they had learnt in their youth and then abandoned. Others, who came from farther afield, stayed on in the castle as servants. Of those who stayed, all alike seemed to have been rebaptized at the same time as their master, and went about their business as he did, neither giving nor receiving offence, unarmed and treated with respect.

But when the Germans came, fugitives from villages which had been invaded or threatened with invasion began to arrive at the castle in search of shelter; and the Unnamed was delighted to find that his fortress could be regarded as a desirable refuge by the weak, who had for so long gazed at it from afar in abject terror. He received the exiles with expressions of gratitude rather than mere courtesy. He let it be known that his house was open to all who wished to take shelter there, and at once set himself to the task of putting not only the castle, but the whole valley into a state of defence, in case the German soldiers or the *cappelletti* tried to break in and treat it in their usual way. He summoned the servants that had stayed with him, who were few in number but of great worth, like the verses of Torti,[3] and addressed them on the subject of the wonderful opportunity that God had sent to them, and to himself, to help their neighbours, whom they had oppressed and terrorized in the past. With that natural tone of command which expresses full certainty of prompt compliance, he told them in general terms what he intended them to do, and instructed them especially how they should conduct themselves so as to ensure that the refugees would see them as friends and protectors and nothing else.

He sent up to the attic where all the fire-arms, the swords and daggers, the halberds and pikes had been lying piled up for some considerable time, and had them brought down and distributed. He announced to the tenants and the other peasants down in the valley that all those who wished might come up to the castle and bring their weapons with them; and he gave

3. A poet who was a friend of Manzoni. – Translator's note.

weapons to those who had none. He chose some of the men to be captains, with others under their command, and appointed them to hold various points in the valley, at its entrance and elsewhere; and at the doors of the castle and on the slope leading up to it. He gave them regular periods of guard duty and times for relief, as in a camp – as had also been the custom in that very castle in his unregenerate days.

In one corner of the same attic lay the Unnamed's own weapons, apart from the others – his famous carbine, and various muskets, rapiers, heavy swords, pistols, daggers and poignards, either lying on the ground, or leant against the wall. None of the servants would touch them, but they all agreed to go together to their master and ask him which of the weapons they should bring down for him now.

'None,' he replied.

Whether he had taken a vow, or merely a resolution, the fact is that he remained permanently unarmed, at the head of what amounted to a military garrison.

At the same time he had set a number of other servants and retainers, both men and women, to work to provide lodging in the castle for as many people as possible: making up beds, laying out straw mattresses and quilts in the rooms and halls that were to serve as dormitories. And he ordered in large stocks of provisions, to take that burden from the guests that God might send him, and who were in fact arriving in increasing numbers every day. He himself in the meantime was never still; he was in and out of the castle, up and down the slope, touring the valley, establishing, reinforcing and inspecting defensive posts; seeing everything and letting himself be seen; setting things in order and keeping them so with a word, with a look, or by his mere presence. At the castle or in the streets he always had a word of warm welcome for new arrivals – all of whom, whether they had seen him before or not, looked at him in happy astonishment, forgetting for the moment all the sufferings and terrors that had made them come so far. And they turned and gazed after him when he left them and continued on his way.

Chapter 30

ALTHOUGH the main influx was not along the route used by our three fugitives, but from the other end of the valley, they began to find travelling companions, who were also companions in misfortune, and who had emerged or were just then emerging on to the main road from side turnings and lanes. In such circumstances people who meet each other for the first time behave as if they were old acquaintances. Every time the cart overtook a pedestrian, there was an exchange of questions and answers. Some had made good their escape without waiting for the soldiers to arrive, as our friends had done; others had heard their drums or trumpets in the distance; others again had actually seen them, and described them in the terms that the terrified always use.

'We've been lucky,' said the two women. 'Thank Heaven for it! Never mind about the property; at least we're safe ourselves.'

But Don Abbondio found less cause for cheerfulness in the situation. He began to worry about the size of the crowd that seemed to be going their way, and still more about the larger throng that he heard was coming from the other end of the valley.

'Oh, what a business!' he muttered to the two women, at a moment when no one else was near. 'What a business! Don't you see that gathering so many people together in one place is as good as compelling the soldiers to come? Everyone is hiding their treasures, or taking them away with them – there's nothing left in the houses. So the soldiers are bound to think that there's a real El Dorado up here in the castle! They're sure to come now! Heaven help me! What have I let myself in for?'

'Why, they'll have other things to do besides coming up here after us,' said Perpetua. 'They've got to get to Mantua some time, you know! And I've always heard that when there's danger about there's safety in numbers.'

'In numbers?' said Don Abbondio. 'In numbers? My poor Perpetua, don't you realize that one German soldier can eat a hundred of these people for breakfast? And then, if they want to be silly about it, we shall find ourselves in the middle of a battle, and shall we enjoy that, do you think? Heaven help me! It would have been better to go up into the mountains. Why do they all have to dash off to the same place? What a nuisance these people are!' he went on, in a lower voice. ' "This is the way!" says one of them, and off they go, one after the other, like sheep, and with no more sense than sheep.'

'If it comes to that,' said Agnese, 'couldn't they say just the same thing about us?'

'Let's have a bit less chatter about it,' said Don Abbondio, 'for this gossiping doesn't help at all. What's done is done; here we are, and here we've got to stay. The will of Providence must be done; and Heaven send that it turns out well for us.'

But it was worse still at the entrance to the valley, where he saw a fine detachment of armed men, some of them standing outside the door of a house, and some looking out of the ground-floor windows; it was like a barracks. He watched at them out of the corner of his eye. These were not, in fact, the same faces that he had seen during that agonizing previous journey to the castle – or if there were one or two of the same men, they had changed a great deal in appearance – but the sight of them distressed him more than we can say.

'Heaven help me!' he thought. 'So they are going to be silly about it, and fight! It could hardly be otherwise; what can you expect from a man like that? But what can he be after? Is he going to declare war? Does he think he's an independent monarch? Heaven help me! Here we are, in circumstances where a sensible man would want to hide somewhere underground; but not that one – he does everything he can to make himself conspicuous, to catch everyone's eye. It's as if he were sending them an invitation!'

'Now, sir, just look at the brave men here,' said Perpetua. 'They'll defend us! The soldiers can come if they like, now, for

551

these people aren't like our frightened villagers, who don't know how to do anything but run away.'

'Be quiet!' said Don Abbondio, in a low but angry voice. 'You don't know what you're talking about. You should pray to Heaven that the soldiers may have no time to come here, or that they may never hear what's going on in this place – how it's being turned into a fortress. Don't you realize that taking fortresses is their profession? There's nothing they like better; for them going into the attack is like going to a wedding, because then they can keep all the booty they can lay their hands on, and cut everybody's throat. Heaven help me! I must just see if there's any way of getting up these cliffs to a place of real safety. I'm not going to get caught up in a battle! Not me, not in a battle!'

'Well, sir, if you're going to be afraid of protection and help as well as . . .' began Perpetua; but Don Abbondio interrupted her waspishly, though still in an undertone.

'Be quiet, Perpetua! And mind you don't tell anyone what we've been saying. Remember to keep a smile on your face all the time we're here, and pretend to approve of everything you see.'

At the inn of the Ill-Starred Night they found another detachment of guards, to whom Don Abbondio took off his hat, saying to himself, Oh dear! Oh dear! Here I am in the middle of an armed camp!

The cart stopped, and the passengers got out. Don Abbondio paid the driver off as quickly as he could, and went up the slope with his two companions in complete silence. Each scene brought back to his imagination the sufferings he had endured on his previous visit, and mingled them with his present distress.

Agnese had never been there before, though she had a fanciful picture of the place in her mind, which swam before her eyes whenever she thought about Lucia's terrible journey to the castle. Now that she saw it all as it really was, a new and more vivid idea of that cruel experience came over her.

'Oh, your Reverence!' she exclaimed, 'to think that my poor Lucia came up this road!'

'Will you be quiet, you stupid woman!' hissed Don Abbondio in her ear. 'That's not the sort of thing to say here. Don't you realize that this is his house? Fortunately no one heard you this time. But if you go on like that . . .'

'But surely,' said Agnese, 'now that the gentleman's turned into a saint . . .'

'Be quiet!' said the priest. 'Do you think a saint's a man to whom you can say anything you like, without any consideration at all? You'd do better to think of thanking him for the kindness he's done you.'

'Good heavens, I wouldn't forget to do that, your Reverence. Do you think I don't know my manners at all?'

'Good manners means remembering not to say anything disagreeable, especially to people who aren't used to it. Now listen to me, both of you – this isn't the place for your gossiping, or for saying everything that comes into your heads. This is the house of a great nobleman, as both of you know. You can see what sort of company we've got around us – people of every possible sort are trooping in. So be sensible, if you can. Weigh your words, and don't talk too much, and only when it's strictly necessary. No one ever said the wrong thing through keeping his mouth shut.'

'You're the worst of the lot, sir, with all your . . .' began Perpetua. But Don Abbondio said 'Be quiet!' in a ferocious whisper, taking off his hat at the same time and making a deep bow; for he had looked up the hill a moment before and seen the Unnamed coming down towards them. He, too, had seen and recognized Don Abbondio, and quickened his pace as he approached him.

'Your Reverence!' he said as he came closer, 'I would rather have offered you the freedom of my house on a happier occasion; but in any case I am always happy to be able to help you in anything.'

'Trusting in your illustrious lordship's kindness,' replied Don Abbondio, 'I have ventured to come here and trouble you, in these tragic circumstances; and, as you see, I have taken the liberty of bringing company with me. This is my house-keeper . . .'

'She is welcome here!' said the Unnamed.

'And this is a woman who has already experienced your lordship's kindness – the mother of the girl who . . . who . . .'

'Lucia,' said Agnese.

'Lucia's mother!' exclaimed the Unnamed, turning to Agnese, with head held low. 'And he speaks of my kindness! No, no; it is you who do me a kindness by coming to me . . . to this house. You are most welcome. You bring the blessing of Heaven with you.'

'Why!' said Agnese, 'I'm afraid I'm bringing you a lot of trouble, sir. And another thing,' she added, coming closer to his ear, 'I must thank you for . . .'

But the Unnamed interrupted her, asking her most tenderly for news of Lucia. He heard her out, and then turned to accompany his new guests up to the castle, in spite of their protestations. Agnese gave the priest a glance which meant: Does it really look as if we need you to come interfering between us with your advice?

'And have they reached your parish?' asked the Unnamed.

'No, my lord; I didn't wait for the ruffians to arrive,' said Don Abbondio. 'If I had, there's no knowing if I would ever have got out of their hands alive to come and trouble your lordship.'

'Well, you can set your mind at rest now,' said the Unnamed, 'for you're in a safe place. They won't come up here; and if they want to try, we're ready for them.'

'Let's hope they won't come!' said Don Abbondio. 'But they tell me that over there', he added, pointing to the mountains that walled the valley in on the other side, 'there's another lot of terrible fellows, too . . .'

'That's true enough,' said the Unnamed, 'but don't worry; we're ready for them too.'

'Between two fires!' said Don Abbondio to himself. 'Caught right between two fires! I've let myself be talked into coming to a fine place this time by those two chattering women! And this one seems to be right in his element. What people there are in this world of ours!'

When they entered the castle, the Unnamed had Agnese and

Perpetua taken to a room in the part of the building allocated to the women, which took up three sides of the second courtyard, in a section towards the back of the castle, standing on a projecting, isolated crag, with cliffs falling away below on both sides. The men were lodged in the first courtyard, along the side which looked out over the level space before the castle and along the two sides adjacent to it. A wide passage, exactly opposite the main entrance, gave access from one courtyard to the other through the block that separated them, which was used partly as a store for provisions, and partly as a place of safety for the refugees' valuables. In the men's quarters there were a few rooms reserved for any priests who might arrive. The Unnamed personally conducted Don Abbondio to this section, of which he was the first occupant.

Our friends spent about twenty-three days in the castle, in the midst of continual bustle, and among a numerous company, which grew steadily larger during the earlier part of their stay. But nothing extraordinary happened. Hardly a day went by without an alarm of some kind. German soldiers had been seen approaching from one direction, or *cappelletti* from another. At each report the Unnamed sent out patrols to investigate. If it was necessary, he called out a party which he kept in readiness for the purpose, and led them out of the valley to the place where the danger had been reported. It was a strange sight to see that body of men, in good military order and bristling with weapons, but led by an unarmed man. Most times it was only a matter of stray raiders or foragers, who made off so quickly that there was no chance of surprising them. But one day, as the Unnamed was chasing a small party of this kind, to discourage them from coming back, he received the news that a near-by hamlet was being invaded and sacked. German soldiers from various units, who had stayed behind in search of loot when their companies moved on, had formed themselves into an irregular band, and were making sudden raids on the hamlets near villages where the army was quartered. They were robbing the inhabitants, and subjecting them to every kind of ill-treatment. The Unnamed made a short speech to his men, and led them to the hamlet.

Their arrival was unexpected. The ruffians had no thought of anything but easy booty, and when they saw a disciplined, battle-ready force approaching, they left their looting half-finished and ran for it, without waiting for each other, along the road by which they had come. The Unnamed followed them for a certain distance, and then halted and waited awhile to see if anything further would happen. Finally he turned and went back. The troop of liberators and its leader were received with more applause and blessings than we can say, as they passed through the hamlet they had saved.

The castle now contained a multitude of people, brought together by hazard, of different classes, habits, age and sex; but there was no disorder of significance. The Unnamed had stationed guards at various points, who saw to it that nothing went wrong, with the scrupulous care that everyone put into the performance of tasks for which he had to answer to the master of the castle.

He had also asked the priests, and the other men of authority among the refugees, to go around and help to keep an eye on things. As often as possible the Unnamed went around himself, and let himself be seen in every part of the castle; but even in his absence people remembered whose house they were in; and that served as a salutary check on those who needed it. But, apart from that, they were all people who had recently escaped from danger, and that in itself was a sobering influence on most of them. Thoughts of their houses and their property, and in some cases thoughts of relations and friends left in danger, together with the news that came in from the outer world, depressed their spirits, and maintained a steadily growing desire for tranquillity.

But there were also less serious people there, men of stouter mettle and bolder hearts, who tried to pass those days in a more cheerful manner. They had indeed abandoned their houses, because they were too weak to defend them; but they took no pleasure in sighing and weeping over something that could not be remedied, nor in imagining and brooding over the damage which they would all too soon be seeing with their own eyes. Families who were friendly with each other had gone up there together, or had joined forces after their arrival, and new friendships had been formed as well. The company split up into groups, according to people's dispositions and habits.

Those who had enough money and enough discretion went down into the valley for their meals. New hostelries had quickly sprung up there, in these special circumstances. In some of them every mouthful was followed by a sigh, and it was not thought proper to speak of anything but misfortunes. In others misfortunes were hardly mentioned, except to say that there was no point in thinking about them.

For those who either could not or would not pay for their food outside, there was a distribution of bread, soup and wine in the castle. There were also tables where meals were served every day to certain guests whom the Unnamed had specifically invited; and our three friends were of this number.

Agnese and Perpetua wanted to do something for their keep, and volunteered to help with the extra work arising from hospitality on so vast a scale. This kept them busy for most of the day, and they spent the rest of it gossiping with some new friends they had made, or with poor Don Abbondio. The priest had nothing to do, but that did not mean that he was bored. He had fear to keep him occupied. Fear of an actual assault on the castle had probably faded from his mind; or if traces of it remained, they were among the least of his troubles, because a moment's reflection showed him how unfounded they were. But his mental picture of the surrounding country, overrun by brutal soldiers on all sides; the sight of all the weapons and the armed men that were constantly around him; the fact of being in a castle – and, worse still, in that particular castle; the thought of all the unpleasant things that could happen from moment to moment in such circumstances – all these factors combined to keep him in a state of continual, indeterminate, general terror, apart from the anguish he felt at the thought of his poor house.

In all the time the priest spent at the castle, he never moved as much as a musket-shot from its walls, and never set foot on the slope that led down to the village. His only exercise was to walk on the open space at the top of the slope, and to go from one side of the castle to the other, peering down the cliffs and into the gulleys to see if there was any way down, anything that could be called a path, which might lead to a hiding place he could use in case of trouble breaking out. He greeted all his fellow refugees with deep bows and other formal salutations, but got into conversation with very few of them. He spoke chiefly to the two women, as we mentioned above. It was to them that he turned when he wanted to get things off his chest, though there was the risk that Perpetua might cut him short, or that even Agnese might say something that would embarrass him.

News of the progress of that terrible invasion would reach him at table – though he sat there as little as possible and spoke hardly at all. There was fresh news every day, sometimes passed up through the villages from mouth to mouth, and sometimes carried all the way by a single messenger – someone who had at first intended to remain in his house, but had finally had to run for it, having saved none of his possessions and perhaps been beaten up into the bargain. Every day there was a new tale of disaster. Some of the people in the castle seemed to be professional story-tellers. They collected every rumour, sifted through every report, and then retailed the best of the material to everyone else. There were arguments about which regiments were the biggest blackguards, and whether the infantry were better or worse than the cavalry. People repeated the names of certain condottieri as well as they could, and sometimes described their past exploits, or gave details of their marches and halting places. A certain regiment was spreading out that very day to invade such and such villages; the following day it would pass on to certain other hamlets, where in the meantime a certain other regiment was doing the devil's work, or worse. Above all, people sought for news and kept accurate count of the various regiments as they gradually passed over the bridge at Lecco, for after that they could be considered as having finally departed from the territory. Wallenstein's cavalry passed over, and the infantry of Merode, followed by the cavalry of Anhalt, the infantry of Brandenburg, and the cavalry of Montecuccoli and Ferrari. Altringer crossed the bridge, and Fürstenberg, and

Colloredo. The Croats went over, and Torquato Conti, and others, and yet others. When Heaven finally willed it, Galasso passed over the bridge, and he was the last. The patrols of Venetian cavalry also withdrew in the end, and the whole district was free again on both sides.

The refugees from the districts which had been the first to be invaded and abandoned by the troops had already left the castle, and more people left every day – just as after an autumn rainstorm we see the birds that have taken shelter in a great tree fluttering away from their leafy perches on every side. I believe that our three friends were the last to leave – at the wish of Don Abbondio, who thought that if he went back home too early he might still find stragglers from the army prowling about. Perpetua pointed out that the longer they waited the more opportunity they gave to local criminals to clear out what was left, but it was no use; when it was a matter of saving one's skin, Don Abbondio could always be relied on to make his views prevail, unless a really imminent danger had made him lose his head completely.

On the day fixed for their departure, the Unnamed had a coach brought round to the inn for them, which contained a complete set of new linen for Agnese. He also took her on one side, and made her accept another purse of *scudi*; though she protested, tapping her bodice as she spoke, that she had not yet finished the last lot.

'And when you see your poor, good Lucia . . .' he finally said to her, 'I'm sure she prays for me, seeing how much harm I've done her; so tell her that I thank her for that, and trust that God will make her prayer a blessing for her as well as for me.'

He insisted on accompanying his three guests down to the coach. We leave it to the reader to imagine the humble and abject thanks that he received from Don Abbondio and the compliments he received from Perpetua. So they set out; and though they did make a brief halt at the tailor's house, as they had promised, they did not stay long enough even to sit down. They heard a great deal in that short time about the invasion: the usual tales of robbery, beating up, vandalism and all kinds of filth. But mercifully that village had been spared all this; no soldiers had been there.

'You know, your Reverence,' said the tailor, as he helped Don Abbondio into the coach, 'someone ought to make a printed book about this business!'

When they had gone a little further, the travellers began to see with their own eyes some of the things they had so often heard described. The vines were stripped, not as they normally are in time of harvest, but as if hailstorms and whirlwinds had passed that way together. The stems of the vines were lying on the ground, leafless and tangled; the supports had been pulled up and the ground trampled and strewn with splinters, leaves, and shoots; fruit trees were split or reduced to stumps. Gaps were torn in the hedges, and gates had been carried away. And in the villages they saw doors that had been broken in, windows from which the coverings had been ripped, and straw, rags and all sorts of rubbish strewn or heaped in the streets. The air was heavy and unpleasant, and wafts of a stronger stench came out of the houses. Some of the villagers were busy clearing the filth out of their homes, or repairing their shutters as best they could, while others stood in groups lamenting their fate. As the coach passed through, outstretched hands appeared at the windows, begging for alms.

With such pictures before their eyes, or fresh in their memories, the travellers made their way on towards their own homes, where they expected to find the same conditions. They arrived, and it was as they had feared.

Agnese's bundles were put down in a corner of the courtyard, which was cleaner than any part of the house. She began to sweep out, and to gather together and set in order the few things the soldiers had left her. Then she sent for a carpenter and a smith, to repair the more serious damage to the cottage. Finally she looked over her new set of linen, piece by piece, and counted her new set of coins. 'I've fallen on my feet,' she said to herself. 'Thanks be to God and the Madonna and to that kind gentleman, I can really say that I've fallen on my feet.'

Don Abbondio and Perpetua needed no keys to enter their house. With every step they took along the passage, they became more conscious of an odour, a poisonous smell, a pestilential stink, which almost seemed to push them back again. Holding their noses, they made their way to the kitchen door, and went in on tiptoe, placing their feet with care to avoid the filth which covered the floor. They looked around. There was nothing left in one piece, but remains and fragments of what had been in that room, and elsewhere, could be seen in every corner. There were down and wing-feathers from Perpetua's hens, torn linen, leaves from Don Abbondio's calendars, bits of broken pots and plates; some heaped up and some scattered around. The fireplace alone contained many signs of widespread plundering, all jumbled together – like the many implied ideas in an allusive period penned by an elegant writer. They saw the charred remnants of large and small pieces of burnt wood, still recognizable as the arm of a chair, the leg of a table, the door of a cupboard, a plank from a bedstead, and a stave from the barrel where Don Abbondio had kept the wine that he drank for his stomach's sake. The rest was all ashes and charcoal; and with that same charcoal the despoilers, as if in compensation, had covered the walls with hastily scribbled pictures of great ugly faces. Efforts had been made, by the addition of birettas, tonsures and starched bands, to make them look like priests. Care had also been taken to make them repulsive and laughable – an object in which such artists could hardly fail.

'The dirty swine!' cried Perpetua. 'The blackguards!' cried Don Abbondio. To escape the smell, they went out of the other door which opened into the garden. They drew a couple of deep breaths, and went straight to the fig-tree; but before they reached it they could see freshly dug earth, and both cried out at the same time. And sure enough, all they found there was an empty grave. And here the trouble began. Don Abbondio accused Perpetua of not hiding the things properly; and the reader can imagine whether she took the criticism in silence. When they had had a good shout, both standing there with arms outstretched, each with one forefinger pointing towards the hole, they grumbled their way back to the house.

And wherever they looked they found much the same thing.

They had untold trouble getting the house clean and whole-some again; all the more so because it was almost impossible to get any help at that time. For many, many days they had to camp out, as it were, in their own home, settling in as best they could, which was not very well, while doors, furniture and household utensils were slowly replaced with the help of money borrowed from Agnese.

As if that were not bad enough, some very tiresome further developments followed the first disaster. By inquiry and ques-tioning, by spying and sniffing out, Perpetua discovered that some of her master's valuables had not been destroyed or carried off by the soldiers, as they had supposed, but were safe and sound in the houses of certain of the villagers. She pressed her master to assert himself, and demand the return of his property. No more unwelcome suggestion could have been made to Don Abbondio; for his things were in the hands of bullying ruffians, who were the very class of person with whom he most desired to remain at peace.

'I don't want to know about that sort of thing at all!' he said. 'How many times must I tell you that what's gone is gone? I've been robbed; and now must I be crucified as well?'

'You'd let anyone steal the very eyes out of your head, sir – I can't help saying it!' replied Perpetua. 'It's a sin to rob anyone else, but it's a sin not to rob you!'

'But just see what nonsense you're talking!' said Don Abbondio. 'Why won't you be quiet?'

Perpetua did calm down, but not straight away; and she would use anything as an excuse for starting up again. Poor Don Abbondio reached the stage of being afraid to complain that anything was missing when he wanted it, because when he did so Perpetua would often say: 'Well, then, go and get it back from So and So, who's got it, and wouldn't have hung on to it for such a long time if he hadn't been dealing with a simpleton.'

A further and more vivid disquiet came to Don Abbondio with the news that every day soldiers were continuing to pass through, as he had all too rightly foreseen that they would, though only one or two at a time. So he lived in fear of finding one of them, or perhaps a group, beating on his door – which had been the first thing that he had had mended, in great haste, and which he kept locked, with much care. But by the mercy of Heaven that never happened.

Before these terrors had fully died away, a fresh one was approaching.

But here we must leave poor Don Abbondio on one side; for now we have to pass on to something very different from the private fears of a country priest, the misfortunes of a few villages, or a mere passing calamity.

Chapter 31

THE commission of public health had feared that the plague would come to the duchy of Milan with the German troops; and so it did, as is well known. It is also well known that the plague did not stop here, but went on to invade and depopulate a large part of Italy. Following the thread of our story, we must recount the main events of that disaster, as it affected the duchy, that is to say. The duchy, we may add, virtually means the city of Milan itself, for the memoirs of the time deal almost exclusively with the capital – as is nearly always the case in all periods and in all countries, for various reasons, some good and some bad. And to tell the truth, our object in relating this story is not only to set the stage for our characters, but also to give an adequate picture – to the best of our ability and within the limits of our space – of a period in our country's history which, although famous enough in a general way, is very little known in detail.

Of the many contemporary descriptions, there is not one that gives a clear and orderly account of events by itself, though there is also not one of them that cannot contribute something to such an account. Every one of them leaves out essential facts which others record – this is true even of Ripamonti,[1] who is the best of the lot as a gatherer and selector of facts, and even more for the system of observation which he uses – every one of them contains material errors, which can be recognized and corrected with the help of one of the others, or of the few official documents that have come down to us in published or unpublished form. Often one writer gives us the cause of effects which we have already seen floating unconnectedly in the pages of another. All alike show a strange confusion of times and

1. *Josephi Ripamontii, canonici scalensis, chronistae urbis Mediolani, De peste quae fuit anno 1630, Libri V. Mediolani, 1640, apud Malatestas.*

events. Their stage is full of figures who come and go quite haphazardly, with no general pattern to be seen – no pattern even in the details. This is, in fact, a common and striking feature of most of the books of that period, especially those written in the vernacular – at least in Italy. Whether it is the same elsewhere in Europe (as we suspect), only the learned could tell us.

No writer of more recent times has ever attempted to examine and collate those memoirs, or to extract from them a connected series of events which could serve as a history of the plague. And so the popular idea of it has necessarily been very indefinite and somewhat confused. It has been a vague picture of great misfortunes and great mistakes (both of which did indeed occur, on a scale which can hardly be imagined) – a picture based more on opinions than on facts. For those facts were scattered thinly across the pages of the memoir writers, and frequently divorced from the circumstances that gave them their character; there was often no proper reference to the time they happened, and so no feeling of cause and effect, of movement, or of progression.

We ourselves, with great diligence if nothing else, have examined and collated all the printed memoirs and several unpublished ones, and most of the few official documents that have survived; and we have attempted, not to give the material the final form that it deserves, but at least to do something with it which has never been done before. We do not intend to report all the official documents, nor even all the events which are in one way or another worthy of being recorded. Still less do we claim to have made the study of the original reports unnecessary for those who want to have a more perfect understanding of the matter – we are very well aware that documents of that sort, however they may be conceived and put together, still have a vivid force of their own which cannot be transferred to another work. We have merely tried to distinguish and to verify the most widely significant and most indispensable facts, to arrange them in the order in which they happened, as far as their causes and nature will permit, and to observe their interaction. Thus we hope to offer, provisionally and until someone produces a better version, a brief yet connected and authentic account of that great disaster.

Throughout the whole strip of territory where the army had passed, corpses had been found here and there in the houses or on the roads. Soon afterwards people began to fall ill and die in one village or another – sometimes individuals, sometimes whole families – from strange and violent attacks of sickness, with symptoms quite unfamiliar to most of the survivors. But there were a few who had seen them before – the handful of people who could remember the other plague which, fifty-three years earlier, had devastated a large part of Italy, and especially the Duchy of Milan, where it was known at the time, and is in fact still known, as the Plague of San Carlo. Such is the strength of the spirit of true charity! Among all the varied and appalling recollections of a general calamity, it can make the memory of one man stand out, because it inspired that man to thoughts and actions more unforgettable even than the pains people suffered; it can imprint his name on all minds as a symbol of that terrible period, because it led him to appear and intervene in every sort of individual disaster, as guide, helper, example, voluntary victim. It can convert a public catastrophe into a challenging task for such a man, so that it is ever afterwards known by his name, like a victory or a discovery.

The physician Lodovico Settala had not only seen that earlier plague, but had been one of the most active and courageous of the doctors engaged in combating it – one of the most highly regarded too, though he was still very young at that time. And now, much alarmed at the prospect of a new outbreak, he was on the alert for news about it. On 20 October he reported to the commission of public health that the pestilence had undoubtedly broken out in the village of Chiuso – a remote hamlet in the district of Lecco, right on the border with Bergamo. But the commissioners failed to reach any decision on that date, as we learn from the *Ragguaglio* of Tadino.[2]

Next, similar reports came in from Lecco itself and from Bellano; and then the commissioners did take a decision, though only to send off a representative, who was to pick up a

2. *Ragguaglio*, page 24.

doctor at Como and go on with him to visit the places indicated. But both of them, to quote Tadino,[3] 'either through Ignorance or some other Cause, did let an old ignorant Barber of Bellano persuade them that such maladies were not the Plague', but rather in some places the normal result of autumnal vapours from the marshes, and in others the effects of the privations and torments caused by the passage of the German troops. This reassuring message was taken back to the commission, and seems to have set their minds at rest.

But as more and more news of deaths continually came in from various places, two delegates were sent out to make the necessary observations and provisions. One was Tadino himself, and the other a judge from the commission. When they arrived, the disease was already so widespread that the proofs of it were plain to see, and there was no need to search for them. They travelled through the territory of Lecco, through Valsassina, along the banks of Lake Como, and the districts known as Monte di Brianza and Gera d'Adda; and everywhere they found barricades across the entrances to villages, or villages that were almost completely deserted, their inhabitants having run away and set up tents in the surrounding fields, or wandered further from home.

'And they seemed to us like so many Savages,' says Tadino, 'one with a sprig of Mint in his hand, one with Rue, and one with Rosemary; and another with a flask of Vinegar.'

The delegates inquired about the number of deaths, which was horrifying. They examined the sick and the dead, and everywhere found the hideous and terrible marks of the plague. They immediately reported the sinister news to the commission, which received their letters on 30 October, and forthwith set to work, to quote Tadino again, 'to draw up the Orders to exclude from the City all those who came from Places where the Contagion had manifested itself; and, while the Proclamation was prepared, they gave some brief advance Instructions to the Watch on the Gates.'

Meanwhile the delegates quickly took the measures that seemed best to them at the time, and returned to Milan, un-

3. *Ragguaglio*, page 24.

happily conscious that what they had done could not possibly cure or even halt an affliction which had already gone so far and spread so widely.

They reached Milan on 14 November, and reported to the commission, both verbally and again in writing. They were then delegated to attend upon the Governor and tell him how things stood. They went to the palace and reported back to the commission: that the Governor had been deeply grieved at the news, and shown himself keenly sensible of the situation, but that he was occupied with the weightier affairs of war: *sed belli graviores esse curas*.[4] So Ripamonti tells us, after going through the records of the commission and talking to Tadino, the special envoy to the Governor. As the reader may recall, it was the second time Tadino had carried out an errand with this object, and with the same result. Two or three days later, on 18 November, the Governor issued a proclamation, in which he decreed public festivities for the birth of Prince Carlos, the first-born son of King Philip IV, oblivious or uncaring of the danger of a great public gathering in those circumstances – just as if the times had been normal, and no one had mentioned the plague to him at all.

This Governor, as we mentioned before, was the famous Ambrogio Spinola, who had been sent to Milan to get the war going again on the proper lines and to correct the mistakes of Don Gonzalo, and, incidentally, to administer the territory. We may, incidentally, here record the fact that he died a few months later in that same war which meant so much to him; and he died not of wounds received on the field of battle, but in bed, of sorrow and distress, at the reproofs, injustices and general ill-treatment that had been heaped on him by those whom he served.[5] Historians deplore his fate, and blame the ingratitude of his employers; they describe his military and political exploits with great care, and praise his foresight, vigour and constancy. They might also inquire what use he made of all his good qualities at the time when the plague was

4. The sense of the Latin is given in the previous eleven words. – Translator's note.

5. He was an Italian general in Spanish service. – Translator's note.

threatening, and actually invading, a country and a people that had been placed in his care, or rather in his power.

But there is one thing which must temper our amazement at his conduct, though not our condemnation of it, and that is the behaviour of the population itself, which can only cause us a further and even stronger astonishment. The people of Milan were still untouched by the contagion, which they had the best of reasons to fear. The villages that were so tragically afflicted formed a rough semi-circle around the city, no more than eighteen or twenty miles distant from it at certain points; and when news of their troubles began to come in anyone might suppose that there would be a general stir of disquiet, a clamour for precautions of some kind (whatever their real value) to be taken – or, at the very least, an ineffective but widespread apprehension. But one of the few points about which all the memoirs of the time agree is that there was nothing of the kind. The famine of the previous year, the cruelties inflicted by the soldiers, and the general distress of mind that followed these things, seemed to everybody to be more than enough to account for the deaths. Anyone who mentioned the danger of the pestilence, whether in the streets, the shops or in private houses – anyone who even mentioned the word 'plague' – was greeted with incredulous mockery or angry contempt. The same disbelief, or rather blind obstinacy, prevailed among the senators, the decurions and all the magistrates.

We learn that as soon as Cardinal Federigo Borromeo heard of the first cases of the contagion, he sent out a pastoral letter to the parish priests, instructing them, among other things, to impress on the people as often as possible the importance of reporting all cases of the kind, and the strict obligation to hand in any infected or suspect personal effects for destruction.[6] This too may be counted among his more unusual and praiseworthy actions.

The commission of health begged and pleaded for cooperation, but with little or no result. And in the commission itself far too little sense of urgency was shown. As Tadino several

6. Francesco Rivola, *Life of Federigo Borromeo*, Milan, 1666, page 582.

times remarks, and as appears still more clearly from the whole context of his story, it was the two doctors who realized the seriousness and the imminence of the danger, and proceeded to stir up their fellow-members, who then had to stir up the other authorities.

We have already noted how half-hearted the commissioners had been over taking action, or even gathering information, when the pestilence was first reported. Here is yet another portentous example of their dilatoriness – though it may have been forced on them by the obstructive attitude of the higher magistrates. The proclamation restricting entry to the city, which was the subject of a resolution by the commission on 30 October, was not finally drafted until the twenty-third of the following month, and not published until the twenty-ninth. By then the plague had entered Milan.

Tadino and Ripamonti both thought it important to record the name of the man who first introduced it into the city, with other details of the person concerned and the circumstances. In any discussion of the origins of a vast calamity, where the dead, far from being distinguished by name, can only be reckoned up approximately by the round thousand, a strange curiosity often arises to know the names of the first few victims, if they are recorded in documents that have survived. This unusual distinction, this grisly precedence, seems to confer a fateful and memorable quality on those names, and on associated details which would otherwise be even less significant.

Both of our historians blame an Italian soldier in the service of Spain, but they do not agree about much else – not even about his name. Tadino says that it was one Pietro Antonio Lovato, from the garrison of Lecco, while Ripamonti says that it was one Pier Paolo Locati, from the garrison of Chiavenna. They also disagree about the date on which he entered Milan, the first putting it at 22 October, and the second exactly one month later. Neither of these dates can be accepted, however, for both of them are inconsistent with other and much better established facts. And yet Ripamonti was writing on the instructions of the council of decurions, and must have had ample means of obtaining the necessary information; and Tadino, from the nature of his employment, was in a better position than anyone to get facts of this sort right.

In any case other information is available which seems to us far more accurate, as we mentioned above, and it indicates that the real date must have been before the publication of the proclamation restricting entry into the city; and if required we could also prove almost conclusively that it was in the first few days of the same month. But the reader will undoubtedly excuse us from doing so.

Be that as it may, the unhappy, doom-laden soldier entered the city carrying a great bundle of clothing which he had bought or stolen from the German troops. He went to stay with relations in the East Gate quarter, near the Capuchin monastery. He fell sick almost as soon as he arrived, and was taken to the hospital. A bubonic swelling was discovered in one of his armpits, which made the doctors suspect the truth; and four days later he died.

The commission of health isolated his family, and confined them to their house. The soldier's clothes and the bed on which he had lain at the hospital were burned. Two nursing orderlies who had been looking after him, and a good friar who had given him spiritual comfort, also fell sick a day or two later, all three of them with the plague. In the hospital the nature of the disease had been suspected from the outset, and special precautions had been taken, so that there were no more cases there.

But the soldier had sown the seeds of destruction outside the hospital, and it was not long before they began to germinate. The first to go down was the owner of the house where he had stayed, a lute-player of the name of Carlo Colonna. Then all the tenants in that house were moved to the lazaretto, on the orders of the commission of health, and most of them were taken ill. Several of them died shortly afterwards, and there could be no doubt that their trouble had been an infectious one.

The infection that had already been distributed by those victims – not to mention their clothing and other belongings, which their relations, tenants or servants had concealed from the commission's investigations and saved from its bonfires – was reinforced by the fresh infections that kept on coming into

571

Milan because of defects in the regulations, of the slackness with which they were administered, or of the skill with which they were evaded. It wound its way slowly and secretly through the city for the rest of the year and the first few months of 1630. From time to time, now in this quarter and now in that, the contagion would choose its victim, and someone would die. The rarity of the cases itself diverted most minds from the truth, and progressively strengthened the public's stupid, fatal belief that there was no plague in Milan, and never had been. Many doctors, echoing the voice of the people (but hardly, in this case, the voice of God), ridiculed the sinister prophecies and gloomy warnings of the minority. They had various names of ordinary diseases ready to describe all the instances of plague that they were called on to treat, whatever signs or symptoms they might exhibit.

When the news of these cases reached the ears of the committee of health at all, it did so belatedly, and in an uncertain form. The fear of quarantine and of the lazaretto sharpened everybody's wits. Cases of sickness were not reported, and the grave-diggers and their superintendents were bribed. Even the subordinate officers of the commission, delegated by that body itself to inspect the corpses, could be paid to make false declarations.

Whenever it did succeed in discovering a case, the commission of health isolated houses, had their contents burned, and sent off whole families to the lazaretto – and so it is easy to imagine what angry complaints arose against it from the public at large, 'from Nobles, from Merchants, and from the common People', in the words of Tadino; since all of them were convinced that these were mere unreasoning and pointless acts of harassment. The main odium fell on the two doctors – Tadino and Senator Settala, the son of the Chief Physician – and it reached the point where they could not cross the squares of the city without being assailed with curses, or even stones. The situation of those two men during the next few months was certainly strange, and worthy of record, as they saw a terrible catastrophe coming nearer and nearer and did everything they could to avert it; and at the same time encountered obstacles where they looked for help, became the butt of popular indignation and were regarded as enemies of their country – *'pro patriae hostibus'* in the words of Ripamonti.

A share of that odium fell on certain other doctors who were also convinced that this really was the plague, and consequently suggested precautions and tried to convince everyone else of the appalling truth. The more discreet of their fellow-citizens accused them of nothing more than credulity and obstinacy; the others regarded it as a blatant imposture, a conspiracy designed to make capital out of the fears of the public.

The Chief Physician Lodovico Settala was then nearly eighty years old. He had been professor of medicine at the University of Pavia, and then of moral philosophy at Milan; he was the author of many books which enjoyed a very high reputation at that time; he had been offered chairs at many other universities – Ingolstadt, Pisa, Bologna and Padua – and had refused them all; his authority stood very high among the men of that period. His life inspired no less respect than his learning, and he was loved as well as admired, because of the charity he showed in treating and otherwise helping the poor. There was indeed one thing about him which from our point of view must qualify and diminish the respect to which his merits entitle him, though it can only have strengthened the general admiration for him in those days – namely, the fact that the poor man shared many of the commonest and most lamentable prejudices of his period. He was ahead of his contemporaries; but he had not opened up a real gap between himself and them, which is what generally leads to trouble and loses a man the authority he has won in other ways. And yet the very great authority which he then enjoyed was not enough to overcome the views of the vulgar herd, as the poets call it, though stage prologues prefer the term 'gentle public'. In fact it was not enough to protect him from the hatred and the insults of that section of the public which passes most rapidly and lightly from unfavourable opinions to hostile demonstrations and actions.

One day, when he went out in his chair to visit his patients, a crowd began to gather round him, shouting that he was the ringleader of those who wanted there to be a plague at all costs, and that he was the one who was terrifying the whole city, with that scowl of his, and that great ugly beard – and all to improve business for the doctors. The crowd quickly grew larger and angrier, and the chairmen realized the seriousness of the situation, and took him into the house of some friends of his, which was luckily not far away. This was his reward for having judged things correctly, spoken the truth, and tried to save many thousands of people from the plague. On another occasion he gave a truly lamentable professional opinion, which contributed to the result of a poor unfortunate woman being tortured, torn with red-hot tongs, and burnt alive as a witch, because her master suffered from strange pains in his stomach and a former employer had fallen passionately in love with her;[8] and then, no doubt, he won fresh praise from the people as a man of learning, and also, repugnant as the thought may now appear, fresh renown as a public benefactor.

But towards the end of March the cases of illness and the deaths began to grow much commoner, first of all in the East Gate quarter and then throughout the city. There were strange attacks of spasm, palpitation, lethargy and delirium, accompanied by those sinister livid patches and bubonic swellings. Death was swift and violent, sometimes striking unexpectedly, without any previous symptoms of illness. The doctors who were opposed to the idea that this was the plague were unwilling to admit the truth of a view which they had ridiculed, but still had to find a name for this supposedly new disease, which was now too common and too well known to do without one. So they christened it 'the malign fever', or 'the pestilent fever' – a wretched evasion, in fact a mere fraudulent play on words. And yet it did great harm; for, while admitting half the truth, it still concealed the fact which it was most important for everyone to believe and understand, namely that the disease was transmitted by contact.

Like men awakened from a deep sleep, the higher magistrates began to give a little attention to the representations and proposals of the committee of health, to give force to its regula-

7. Count Pietro Verri, *History of Milan*, Volume IV, Milan, 1825, page 155.

tions, and to carry out the isolation of infected houses, and the quarantine arrangements it had recommended. The commission kept on asking for more money, to supply the rapidly growing daily expenses of the lazaretto, and all the other services. It applied for these funds to the council of decurions, pending a decision whether they were rightly chargeable to the city or to the Crown. (This decision, so far as we know, was never taken, except on a *de facto* basis.) The Great Chancellor was also pressing the decurions for money, on the orders of the Governor, who had gone off to renew the siege of the unfortunate town of Casale. The senate was also pressing them, both to see to the proper provisioning of the city, before the contagion spread further and caused the neighbouring states to break off all commerce with Milan, and to see to some means of maintaining the large part of the population that had lost its work.

The decurions tried to raise money by loans and taxes. Of what they were able to collect, some went to the commission of health, some to the poor, and some was spent on grain. They were able to supply a part of what was needed. And this was only the beginning ...

In the lazaretto, where the total population rose every day, despite the daily toll of deaths, there was the further difficult problem of maintaining the necessary services and the necessary discipline, of keeping the different categories of inmates properly separated – of preserving, or rather of creating, the orderly administration decreed by the commission of health. From the very beginning there had been much confusion in the lazaretto, both because of the disorderly character of many of the inmates and because of carelessness or connivance on the part of the staff. The commission of health and the decurions, not knowing where to turn, finally thought of applying to the Capuchins. They appealed to the Father Commissary of the province – then performing the duties of the Provincial, who had died not long before – and asked him to provide them with someone capable of taking on the government of that unhappy realm. For the post of superintendent, the Commissary recommended one Father Felice Casati, a man of mature age, who enjoyed a high reputation for charity, diligence, and both gentleness and strength of character – a reputation which the event showed to be fully deserved. To accompany him and serve under him, the Commissary recommended one Father Michele Pozzobonelli, a man who was still young, but of a grave and severe aspect, which reflected his character.

The proposal was most gladly accepted, and the two fathers entered the lazaretto on 30 March. The President of the commission of health took them round the building, as if to let them take possession. Then he called together the orderlies and the staff of all ranks and announced to them that Father Felice was now in charge of the place, with the fullest authority over everybody there. As the numbers in that unhappy place continued to grow, other Capuchins arrived, to serve there as superintendents, confessors, administrators, nurses, cooks, distributors of clothing, washermen, and in any other capacity required. Father Felice was always on the move, by day and by night, walking round the arcades and the rooms and the vast internal space with busy speed; sometimes carrying a staff, sometimes with his hair-shirt as his only badge of office. He inspired and controlled everything; he calmed riots, solved disputes, threatened, punished, reproved and comforted; he dried the tears of others and shed tears of his own. He caught the plague at the beginning of his ministry, recovered from it, and went back to his duties with renewed vigour. Most of his colleagues in the lazaretto died there with uncomplaining cheerfulness.

This strange dictatorship was certainly a most extraordinary device for the magistrates to adopt – as extraordinary as that calamitous emergency, as the times themselves. Those in possession of such vital authority could think of nothing better to do than to hand it over to someone else, and could find no one for the purpose but members of an institution for which the exercise of power was an alien concept. Even if we knew nothing else about the history of the period, that fact would be enough to serve as proof of a primitive and ill-organized society – indeed as a good example of such a society at work. But it is also a good example of the strength and ability which the spirit of true charity can confer on men in any walk of life and in any

576

period, when we see how stoutly the Capuchins bore that burden. There was beauty in their acceptance of the task, for no other reason than because there was no one else who would take it on, with no other object but that of serving their fellow-men, and without any hope in this world but that of a death which few men would envy, though it could truly be called enviable. There was beauty, too, in the way that the task was offered to them, solely because it was difficult and dangerous, and they were thought to have the energy and calm courage which are so necessary and so rare on such occasions. And so the great-heartedness and the good works of those friars are worthy of remembrance, admiration, affection and that special gratitude which is due as of right to great services to humanity – all the more so to those who do not expect it as a reward.

'For if those Fathers had not been there', says Tadino, 'the whole City would surely have been destroyed; for it was truly miraculous to see how many things in how short a space of Time they did for the public Benefit; and how, without any Help, save very little, from the City, they were able with their Industry and Wisdom to maintain so many Thousands of poor Folk in the Lazaretto.'

The number of people who found shelter there during the seven months that Father Felice was in charge was about 50,000, according to Ripamonti, who truly remarks that he would have had to give the good father just as much space if he had been writing a book about the most noble passages in the history of Milan, rather than about its greatest miseries.

The obstinate reluctance of the public to admit that there was a plague naturally began to weaken and fade away, as the disease spread more and more widely by an obvious process of infection through contact; especially when the scourge, after some time of being confined to the poor, began to strike at men of more note. The most famous of these certainly deserves special mention here; for it was the Chief Physician Settala. Did they at least admit that the poor old man had been right from the beginning? We cannot say; but he and his wife, two sons, and seven of his servants fell sick of the plague. He himself and one of his sons recovered; the rest died.

'Such Cases occurring in great Houses gave the Nobles and the Plebeians cause to think,' says Tadino. 'The incredulous Physicians and the rash and ignorant Populace began to tighten their lips, grit their teeth, and raise their eyebrows.'

But when obstinate folly is finally overcome its evasions and contortions – its dying acts of revenge, so to speak – are often of such a kind that we can only wish it had held out to the end, unconquered and unshaken, against the evidence and the facts. And this was a case in point. The men who had fought so long and so resolutely against the view that a seed of disease had from the beginning been near at hand, or in their very midst, which could multiply and spread by natural means to cause a disaster – those men were no longer able to deny that the disease was in fact spreading through the city. But they could not admit that it was due to natural causes without also admitting that they had completely misled the public and done great harm thereby. This disposed them to find some other reason, and to accept any explanation of the sort that might offer itself.

Unhappily one was ready to hand among the ideas and traditions that were common at the time, not only in Italy but throughout Europe. Poisonous arts, diabolical operations, conspiracies of people bent on spreading the plague by contagious venoms or by black magic ... Similar theories had been maintained and believed in many previous pestilences; and not least in the same city of Milan, during the epidemic of half a century earlier.

It should be added that a despatch signed by King Philip IV had reached the Governor the year before, warning him that four Frenchmen had escaped from Madrid who were wanted there on suspicion of having used poisonous unguents to spread the plague. The Governor was instructed to be on the alert, in case they appeared in Milan. He communicated the despatch to the senate and to the commission of health, and no one seems to have paid very much attention to it at the time; but now that the plague had broken out, and been recognized as such, memories of that message may have reinforced certain vague suspicions that monstrous treachery was at work – may indeed have been their first cause.

But it was two other events, one caused by blind, uncontrolled panic and the other by a strange impulse of spite, which converted those vague thoughts of a hypothetical outrage into a fear which for many people would soon become a certainty – the fear of a real outrage, of an actual plot.

In the cathedral, on the evening of 17 May, some men thought they saw someone anointing the screen that separated the men's section of the congregation from the women's. That very night, they had the partition and the benches attached to it carried out of the building. The president of the commission of health, with four experts, quickly came to see; and when they inspected the partition, the benches and the holy water stoups, they could find nothing to support the ill-informed suspicion of an attempted poisoning. But as a sop to the imaginary terrors of others, *rather to exceed in caution than compelled of necessity*, they decreed that the partition should be washed down, as a wholly adequate measure.

But the sight of that mass of woodwork had a very frightening effect on the crowd, which is always so apt to take a physical object for a logical argument. It was generally said and believed that all the benches in the cathedral had been anointed, all the inner walls and even the bell-ropes. Nor was this a mere passing rumour, for all the contemporary memoirs which mention the story speak of it with equal certainty; and so do some others that were written a number of years later. We ourselves should have had to guess at the truth of the matter, if it had not been recorded in a letter from the commission of health to the Governor. This document, from which the words printed above in italics are quoted, is preserved in the archive known by the name of San Fedele, where we found it.

The following morning another sight, stranger still and more significant, struck the eyes and minds of the citizens. In every part of the city doors and walls were extensively marked with a strange sort of yellowish or whitish filth, which seemed to have been daubed on with a sponge. It may have been a silly trick, meant only to produce more general and noisier fears; or it may have been a wicked plot, meant to make the public chaos even worse than it was; or there may have been some other explanation about which we know nothing. But the story is so widely confirmed, that we can only regard the theory of a strange illusion of the many as even more improbable than a strange action by the few. Such an action would not, in any case, have been either the first or the last of its kind.

When he comes to the subject of these alleged anointings, Ripamonti often mocks at the credulity of the public, and still more often deplores it; but he confirms that he saw this daubing of the walls himself, and describes it.[8] In the letter quoted above, the gentlemen of the commission of health also describe it in much the same terms as Ripamonti. They speak of various inspections, and of tests carried out with the material on dogs, without any ill-effect. They add that, in their opinion, '*this outrage did proceed rather from insolence, than from any intention to harm*', which shows that they were still cool-headed enough to prevent them from seeing things that were not there.

When the other contemporary memoirs tell the story, they too imply that in the beginning many people thought that the daubing had been done for a foolhardy joke. They do not speak of anyone denying the fact that it occurred – as they surely would if anyone had really done so, if only to tax him with extravagant folly.

(It does not seem to me to be out of place to put together and report these little-known details of a famous outbreak of public madness, for the most interesting and instructive aspect that we can study, when considering human errors – especially those of the crowd – is their mode of progression, the shapes they take on and the methods they adopt to obtain entry into the minds of men and dominate them.)

The city had been agitated before, but now it was in utter turmoil. The owners of houses went around with torches of straw, burning off the patches of unguent; passers-by halted to watch in fear and trembling. Foreigners were suspect as such;

8. '. . . and we ourselves went to see this sight. The stains still had a scattered, irregular dampness about them, as if someone had used a sponge to sprinkle and daub the dirt on to the wall; and the doors and entrances of the buildings were everywhere visibly contaminated with the same sprinkled filth.' Ripamonti, op. cit., page 75.

and as they were easily recognizable by their dress in those days, they were often arrested in the streets by the people and taken to the police. All were examined and interrogated, accused, accusers and witnesses alike. No one was found guilty, for the minds of men were still capable of entertaining reasonable doubt, of looking at facts and understanding them.

The commission of health published a proclamation promising rewards and protection in return for information leading to the conviction of the author or authors of the outrage. *'Since it in no wise seems proper to us'*, said those gentlemen in the letter we have quoted before, which was dated 21 May but was evidently written on the nineteenth, which was the date affixed to the proclamation, *'that this crime should remain unpunished, especially in times of such danger and suspicion as the present, we have today, to console and pacify the people, and to establish the facts, made public a proclamation that ...'* – etc. But the proclamation itself contains no hint – no clear hint, at least – of that most reasonable and comforting theory which they had put forward for the benefit of the Governor. This omission is evidence both of insane prejudices in the public mind and of a dangerous respect for those prejudices on the part of the commissioners, which must be strongly condemned in view of its disastrous potentialities.

While the commission investigated, many members of the public had already reached their own conclusions – as happens sometimes. Of those who believed that the daubed material was really a poisonous unguent, some held that it was an act of revenge by Don Gonzalo Fernandez of Cordova for the insults he had suffered at the time of his departure; some that it was a trick of Cardinal Richelieu to depopulate Milan, and so to make himself master of it without difficulty; while others again, for no known reason, held that the Count of Collalto, or Wallenstein, was to blame, or this or that member of the Milanese nobility. There were also those, as we have already mentioned, who saw nothing in the whole affair except a silly joke, which they attributed to schoolboys, or to the gentry, or to army officers who were bored with besieging Casale.

No universal infection in fact followed, no general slaughter of the population such as must have been feared; and this was probably why the initial panic quietened down, and the whole thing was forgotten – or appeared to be forgotten.

There were also still people who did not believe that there was a plague at all. Both in the lazaretto and in the city there were some cases of recovery, and 'it was asserted by the Plebeians, and also by many prejudiced Doctors, that this could not truly be the Plague, or All would have died'.[9] (The final arguments of an opinion defeated by the evidence always have a certain curious interest.)

To remove all doubts on this point, the commission of health hit on a method suited to the needs of the occasion, a visual method such as might be demanded or suggested by the spirit of the times. It was the custom of the citizens of Milan, on one of the Pentecost feast-days, to flock to the Cemetery of St Gregory, to pray for the souls of those who had died in the previous plague and were buried there. Taking the opportunity to combine devotion, amusement and spectacle, everyone went there in all the finery he could muster. On that very day, among the other victims of the plague, a whole family had died. At the time of day when the crowd was at its thickest, in the midst of the throng of carriages, riders and people on foot, the corpses of that family were carried, by order of the commission of health, to the same cemetery. They were borne naked on a cart, so that the crowd could see the manifest signs of the plague on their bodies. Cries of disgust and terror arose wherever the cart passed; a long murmur followed in its wake, and another went before it. There was more belief in the existence of the plague after that; but in any case it was winning credence more and more every day by its own efforts, and that particular reunion must have done a considerable amount to spread it still further.

In the beginning, then, there had been no plague, no pestilence, none at all, not on any account. The very words had been forbidden.

Next came the talk of 'pestilent fever' – the idea being admitted indirectly, in adjectival form.

Then it was 'not a *real* pestilence' – that is to say, it was a

9. Tadino, op. cit., page 93.

pestilence, but only in a certain sense; not a true pestilence, but something for which it was difficult to find another name.

Last of all, it became a pestilence without any doubt or argument – but now a new idea was attached to it, the idea of poisoning and witchcraft, and this corrupted and confused the sense conveyed by the dreaded word which could now no longer be suppressed.

I do not think that it is necessary to be deeply versed in the history of words and ideas to see that many of them have followed a route similar to that just described. Fortunately, however, there are not many words of comparable type; not many that are of such importance, or that win acceptance at such a price, or that have accessory ideas of such a kind tacked on to them. But in small and great matters alike, it would often be possible to avoid travelling that long and tortuous route, if people would only follow a method which has been recommended to them for long enough – the method of observing, listening, comparing and thinking before they begin to talk.

But talking – just talking, by itself – is so much more easy than any of the other activities mentioned, or all of them put together, that we human beings in general deserve a little indulgence in this matter.

Chapter 32

As it grew steadily more difficult to meet the painful demands of this tragic situation, the council of decurions passed a resolution on 4 May to appeal to the Governor for help. And on the twenty-second two of their number were sent off to his field headquarters, to lay before him an account of the miserable and straitened circumstances of the city – enormous expenditure, empty coffers, the income of future years mortgaged, taxes for the current period unpaid because of the general poverty, to which many causes contributed, but most of all the damage done by the soldiers. They reminded him that expenditure arising from the plague ought to be met from Crown funds, according to old customs and laws which had never been abrogated, and also according to a special decree of Charles V. They mentioned that during the pestilence of 1576 the Governor, who was then the Marquis of Ayamonte, had not only waived all the taxes payable to the State, but had given the city a subvention of forty thousand *scudi* from State funds. Finally they made four requests:

That the taxes should be waived, as on the previous occasion.
That the State should make a subvention, as before.
That the Governor should inform the King of the miseries of the city and of the whole province.
That the Governor should grant exemption from any further billeting to the countryside which had already been devastated by the passage of the troops.

The Governor wrote a reply full of condolences and fresh exhortations. He said that he was sorry not to be able to stay in the city and devote all his energies to the relief of its troubles, but hoped that the zeal of the decurions would be enough to provide for everything. This, he said, was a time to spend freely, to use every resource to the full. As for their specific

584

requests, *'proveeré en el mejor modo que el tiempo y necesidades presentes permitieren'*.[1] Under these words came a hieroglyph, as clear as his promises, which evidently stood for 'Ambrogio Spinola'.

The Great Chancellor, Antonio Ferrer wrote to tell him that this answer had been read by the decurions *'con gran desconsuelo'*.[2] There were further comings and goings, requests and answers; but I cannot trace that any definite conclusions came of them. Some time later, when the plague was at its height, the Governor transferred his authority to Ferrer by letters patent, being himself obliged, as he wrote, to give all his thought to the war.

That war, we may note, caused the death from pestilence, quite apart from military casualties, of at least one million people in the territories of Lombardy, Venice, Piedmont, Tuscany and a part of Romagna; it made a desert of the places through which the troops passed, let alone those where they fought; it culminated in the capture and the horrifying sack of Mantua; and the upshot of it all was that everybody recognized the new Duke of Mantua, to exclude whom the war had been undertaken in the first place. But it must be added that he was obliged to cede a part of Montferrat, with revenues of fifteen thousand *scudi*,[3] to the Duke of Savoy, and a certain other piece of territory, with revenues of six thousand *scudi*,[3] to Duke Ferrante of Guastalla; and that there was also a very secret separate treaty, whereby the Duke of Savoy ceded Pinerolo to the French. This last agreement was carried out a little later, under other pretexts, with every kind of chicanery.

Together with their first resolution, the decurions passed another – to ask the Cardinal Archbishop for a solemn procession to be organized in which the body of San Carlo[4] would be carried through the streets.

1. 'I will provide in the best manner that these times and necessities permit.' (In Spanish)

2. 'With great dismay'. (In Spanish)

3. The point of these sums of money is that they are ludicrously small, in the context. – Translator's note.

4. St Charles Borromeo, Cardinal Federigo Borromeo's cousin and predecessor. – Translator's note.

The good prelate refused for many reasons. He disapproved of people putting their trust in so arbitrary a means of deliverance, and foresaw that if, as he feared might happen, the result did not correspond with their hopes, that trust would be converted into a cause of scandal.[5] He also feared that, '*if these anointers really existed*', the procession would give them all too much scope for their wickedness; while '*if there were no such men*', the gathering together of so great a multitude could only spread the contagion, '*which was a far more real danger.*'[6] For the fear of the anointers, which had been assuaged for a while, had now come to life again, more widespread and more furious than before.

People had again seen – or imagined, perhaps, this time – patches of unguent on walls, on the gates of public buildings, on the doors of private houses, and on door-knockers. The news of these discoveries passed from mouth to mouth with lightning speed. As often happens when people are very anxious, they were as impressed by what they had heard as if they had seen it. Embittered by the presence of disaster, excited by the immediacy of their danger, they were all the more willing to embrace that pernicious belief; for angry men always wish to inflict punishment. And a man of genius[7] has acutely observed on this very point that they prefer to blame disasters on to human wickedness, against which revenge is possible, rather than to attribute them to a factor which can only be met with resignation.

'A subtle, instantaneous, most penetrating poison' – such were the words that were found sufficient to explain the violence of the disease, and all its most obscure and extraordinary symptoms. That poison was said to be made from toads, from

5. *Memoria delle cose notabili successe in Milano intorno al mal contagioso, l'anno 1630, racolte da D. Pio La Croce*, Milan, 1730. This book is clearly drawn from an unpublished work by an author who lived at the time of the pestilence – the editor seems to have reproduced an old book rather than compiled a new one.

6. '*Si unguenta scelerata et unctores in urbe essent . . . Si non essent . . . Certiusque adeo malum.*' Ripamonti, op. cit., page 185.

7. P. Verri, *Osservazioni sulla tortura*. See *Scrittori italiani d'economia politica*, modern section, Volume XVII, page 203.

snakes, from the spittle and pus of victims of the plague, from yet worse ingredients – from the most filthy and atrocious materials that a savage and distorted imagination could invent. With the addition of black magic, anything became possible, every objection lost its force, every difficulty vanished. If no results had followed immediately after the first anointings, the reason was obvious – that had been an unsuccessful attempt by poisoners still in their apprenticeship; but now the art had been brought to perfection, and the determination of the criminals to carry out their diabolical plans had hardened. Anyone who might still have maintained that the thing had been a joke, or might have denied the existence of a plot, was regarded as obstinately blind to the facts – if indeed he did not fall under suspicion of being a man with an interest in diverting public attention from the truth, of being an accomplice, an *anointer*! That word was soon in common use, a resounding word, a word of terror. With such general confidence that anointers did in fact exist, some were bound to be discovered, almost inevitably. Everyone was on the look-out; every act could inspire suspicion. Suspicion soon turned to certainty, and certainty to fury.

In proof of this, Ripamonti quotes two particular cases. He tells us that he chose them not because they were the worst of the daily outbreaks of this sort, but because he personally had the misfortune to be an eye-witness of both of them.

In the church of St Anthony, on a feast-day of some kind, a man of more than eighty years old knelt down to say his prayers; and when he had finished and wanted to sit back on the bench, he dusted it with his cape.

'That old man is anointing the benches!' cried several women with one voice. All the people in church (in church, I repeat!) dashed at the old man, seized him by the hair, white as it was, and loaded him with blows and kicks. Some pushing, some pulling, they hustled him to the door. If they spared his life for the moment, it was only so that they could drag him in that battered state to prison, to judgement, to the torture.

'I saw him as they dragged him along the street,' says Ripamonti, 'and heard no more about him afterwards. I do not think that he can have lived more than a few moments longer after I lost sight of him.'

The other case, which happened the following day, was equally strange, but not equally tragic. Three young Frenchmen – a scholar, a painter and an artisan – had come to Italy to study the relics of antiquity, and to look for opportunities of making money. They approached the cathedral, and stood looking attentively at some external feature of the building. A passer-by saw them and stopped. He pointed them out to another man, and then to others as they came up. A crowd formed, observing and watching over the three men, whose clothing, hair and baggage proved them to be foreigners – and, what was worse, Frenchmen. As if to make sure that it was really marble, one of them reached out his hand to touch the stone. That was enough. They were surrounded, seized, beaten up, and driven into custody with a hail of blows. Fortunately the Palace of Justice was not far from the cathedral; and, more fortunately still, they were found innocent and released.

Nor was it only in the city that such things happened. The madness propagated itself as fast as the plague. Any traveller who was found by the peasants off the main road, or who loitered on the road to look around, or who lay down for a rest; any unknown person with anything strange or suspicious about his face or clothing, was an anointer. The first word of his arrival from anyone, even a child, was enough to set bells ringing and crowds gathering. The unhappy stranger would be stoned, or dragged off to prison by the mob. Prison, in fact, was a haven of safety for him, for the moment at least. We have all this on the authority of Ripamonti himself.

The decurions were not discouraged by the refusal of the wise prelate, but kept on repeating their request for a procession, which was loudly backed by the public. Federigo Borromeo resisted a little longer, and tried to dissuade them. This was all that the good sense of one man could do against the spirit of the times and the insistence of the crowd. In that state of opinion people had very confused and contradictory ideas of the nature of the danger, and were quite unable to see the matter in the clear light in which it appears to us now. So it is not difficult to understand how the Archbishop's excellent reasoning was overcome, even in his own mind, by the bad reasoning of others. Whether there was an element of weakness in his change of mind is a mystery of the human heart which we cannot plumb. But if there is ever a case in which we can blame the head and acquit the heart, it is when we have to judge one of the few men whose whole life is a record of resolute obedience to the dictates of conscience, without any regard for temporal interest whatever. And Federigo Borromeo was certainly one of those few . . .

The requests for a procession were repeated time and again, and he yielded in the end. He agreed not only that the procession should take place, but also, in response to a general, urgent plea, that the coffin containing the mortal remains of San Carlo should be exposed for eight days afterwards on the great altar of the cathedral.

I cannot trace that the commission of health or anyone else made any sort of protest or opposition. The commissioners merely ordered a few extra precautions, which showed some apprehension of the consequences, while doing very little to avert them. They laid down stricter rules to control entry into the city, and closed the gates to ensure compliance. They also tried to exclude victims and suspected victims of the pestilence from the procession, as far as possible, by nailing up the doors of the houses affected by isolation orders. There were five hundred such houses, if we can trust the unsupported word of one writer[8] – and a seventeenth-century writer at that.

Three days were spent in preparations. At dawn on 11 June, which was the appointed day, the procession set out from the cathedral. In front went a long file of the common people, mostly women, with their faces covered by heavy shawls; many of them barefoot and clad in sackcloth. Then came the guilds, each preceded by its own banner; then the confraternities in clothes of various styles and colours; then the orders of friars and the secular clergy, every man bearing the insignia of his rank, and carrying a candle or a torch in his hand. In the centre

8. C. G. Cavatio della Somaglia, *Alleggiamento dello stato di Milano*, c., Milan, 1653, page 482.

of the procession, amid the brightness of more closely serried lights, amid a louder singing of hymns, under a richly embroidered canopy, came the coffin, carried by four canons, dressed in their most splendid robes, who were relieved at set intervals. The body of the venerable saint could be seen through the glass sides of the coffin, clad in magnificent episcopal robes, its skull crowned with a mitre. Amid all its disfigurement and decay, traces could still be seen of the saint's original noble appearance, as it had been recorded in pictures and could still be remembered by the few who had seen him and honoured him in life.

Behind the relics of the dead shepherd (to quote Ripamonti, who is our principal source for this description), and nearest to him in person as in merit, blood and dignity, came the Archbishop Federigo Borromeo. Then followed the rest of the clergy; then the magistrates in their most stately robes; then the nobles, some dressed in their most magnificent clothes as a solemn gesture of respect to religion, while others wore black as a sign of penitence, or went barefoot, in capes with the hoods pulled down over their faces. All of them bore torches. The procession ended as it had begun, with a long, confused train of the common people.

The whole route was decked out as if for a festival. The rich had brought out their most precious belongings. The fronts of the poorer houses had been decorated by their wealthier neighbours, or at the public expense. Here leafy branches took the place of decorations; there they hung above them. Pictures, placards, mottoes hung everywhere. Vases, antiquities and rarities of all kinds stood on the window-sills, and there were lights on every side. From many of the windows sick people who were in quarantine looked out at the procession, and accompanied it with their prayers. The other streets were silent and deserted except for a few heads sticking out of the windows, listening to the shifting murmur of the crowd. There were others, including some nuns, who had climbed on to the roofs in the hope of catching a distant glimpse of the coffin, the cortège, or some other part of the procession.

The procession passed through every quarter of the city. Th

principal streets of Milan end, as they reach the outer parts of the city, in crossroads, or rather little squares, then still known by the ancient name of '*carrobi*', which now only one of them retains. At each of them the procession halted, and the coffin was set down beside the cross which San Carlo had caused to be erected in every one of these spaces during the previous pestilence. (Some of them are still standing today.) It was after midday when they returned to the cathedral.

A presumptuous confidence that the procession had put an end to the plague – in many cases a fanatical certainty that it was so – reigned everywhere the following day; and that very day the death-rate increased in every part of the city, and in every social class, to such an excessive level, with such a sudden jump, that no one could fail to see that its cause, or at least its occasion, lay in the procession itself.

But see what astonishing and lamentable powers a universal prejudice can wield! The majority did not attribute that disastrous effect to the gathering together of so great a multitude for such a long time, nor to the tremendous increase in chance contacts that resulted. They attributed it to the facility that the anointers must have found on that occasion to practice their nefarious art on the grand scale. It was said that they had mingled with the crowd and infected with their unguent every person that they could reach.

But this did not seem a sufficient or appropriate reason for so vast a mortality, so widely diffused in every class of society. Nor does it seem to have been possible even for the eye of fear (so intent to see yet so apt to see wrongly) to detect any unguents, or indeed marks of any kind, on the walls or elsewhere on this occasion. In order to explain the event recourse was had to another legend, which was no longer new at that time and was generally accepted in all Europe as a fact. This was the legend of maleficent and poisonous powders. It was said that powders of this kind had been scattered along the roads, and especially at the stopping-places, and that they had been picked up by the trains of people's clothes, and also by their feet – all the more so since large numbers had gone through the streets barefoot on that day.

'So on the very day of the procession,' says a contemporary writer,[9] 'pity could be seen in battle with cruelty, perfidy with sincerity, and loss with gain.' But it was really only the poor minds of men in battle with the phantoms they had raised up themselves.

From that day forward the infection raged on ever more terribly. Soon there was hardly a house untouched; soon the population of the lazaretto rose from two thousand to twelve thousand, according to Somaglia, whom we have already quoted. Later, according to almost all our authorities, it rose to sixteen thousand. On 4 July, as we see from another letter addressed to the Governor by those responsible for the public health, the daily death-roll rose above five hundred. Later on, at the height of the plague, it reached 1,200 or 1,500, according to the most commonly accepted figure; or 3,500, if we prefer to believe Tadino. He also states that, 'from inquiries made with all diligence' after the pestilence, it was found that the population of Milan had shrunk from 250,000 to little more than 64,000. Ripamonti says that the previous population had been only 200,000 and that 140,000 deaths were recorded in the city registers, apart from those which remained unnoted. Others give higher or lower totals, but on flimsier grounds.

We can imagine the distress of the decurions, whose shoulders had to bear the responsibility of providing for the needs of the city, of doing what could be done to mitigate the effects of so great a disaster. Every day replacements and reinforcements had to be found for public servants of various kinds, such as *monatti, apparitori* and *commissari*.

The *monatti* were employed on the most unpleasant and dangerous of the duties arising from the plague. They collected corpses from houses and streets, and from the lazaretto, carted them to the graveyards, and buried them; they carried or led the sick to the lazaretto, and kept them in order. They burnt or purified infected or suspect belongings. The word *monatti* comes from the Greek '*monos*', according to Ripamonti; Gaspare Bugatti, in a description of the previous plague, derives

9. Agostino Lampugnano, *La pestilenza seguita in Milano l'anno 163*, Milan, 1634, page 44.

592

from the Latin '*monere*', though at the same time he hesitantly, yet more plausibly, suggests that it may after all be a German word, since most of the men were enrolled in the Grisons or in other parts of Switzerland. And in fact it might quite conceivably be a truncated form of the word '*monathlich*', or monthly; for no one could know how long these men's services would be needed, and so it seems probable that the agreements under which they were employed would only have been for one month at a time.

The special task of the *apparitori* was to walk in front of the carts, ringing a bell to warn passers-by to keep out of the way.

The *commissari* were in charge of both the categories mentioned above, and came under the immediate orders of the commission of health.

The lazaretto had to be kept supplied with doctors, surgeons, medicines, food and all the equipment of a hospital. More accommodation had to be found and got ready for the fresh crowds of the sick who arrived every day. So huts of wood and straw were set up in the courtyard of the lazaretto; and a new lazaretto, consisting entirely of huts, was also created; it was surrounded by a simple fence, and had a capacity of four thousand persons. As this was not enough, the construction of two further establishments was decreed, and the work was begun; but the means to complete them were lacking and they were never finished. As the community's needs grew more desperate, the supply of the materials, the men and the courage required to deal with them dwindled away.

It was not only that the achievement constantly lagged behind what had been planned and ordered, not only that many cases of need were covered by provisions that were inadequate even in theory – things reached the extreme of impotence and despair where many types of case, including some of the most urgent and most pitiful had no provisions made for them whatever. A large number of babies were dying of neglect after their mothers had died of the plague. The commission of health proposed that a special home should be set up for those babies, and for destitute mothers-to-be; but they could get nothing done.

'Nevertheless', says Tadino,[10] 'you could not but feel Pity for the Decurions of Milan, who were afflicted, brought to Sorrow and injured by the Soldiery, that knew no law nor restraint; still less in the other parts of the unhappy Duchy, seeing that no Provision or Help could be had from the Governor; except for Messages that a War was being waged and that the Troops must be well cared for.'

Such was the importance of taking Casale! So fair is the praise that victory wins, irrespective of the cause or the objects for which we fight!

Near the lazaretto a large communal grave had been dug – but only one. When it was full of bodies, the corpses of the newly dead began to remain unburied, not only in the lazaretto, but everywhere in the city, and there were more of them every day than the day before. The magistrates searched in vain for labour to employ on the dismal task, and were finally reduced to a declaration that they did not know what to do next. It is hard to see what could have happened, if help had not come from a most unexpected quarter. The president of the commission of health, in despair, with tears in his eyes, went to see the two good friars who were in charge of the lazaretto. Father Michele undertook to have the city cleared of corpses in four days, and in eight days to have enough graves dug to take care not only of present requirements, but of the worst disaster that could be foreseen for the future. Accompanied by another friar, and by some representatives of the commission of health, who were appointed by the president, he went out into the country to look for peasants. Partly with the authority of the commission, and partly with that of his cloth and his own eloquence, he recruited two hundred of them, and got them to dig three huge communal graves. Then he sent out the *monatti* who were in the lazaretto to gather in the dead; and his promise was fulfilled on the appointed day.

At one stage the lazaretto was left without any doctors. Slowly and with difficulty, with promises of great rewards and high honours, some replacements were found, but not nearly as many as were needed. Several times the place nearly ran out o

10. op. cit., page 117.

food, so that there was ground for fear that people would die there of hunger as well as disease. More than once, when no one knew which way to turn to find desperately needed provisions, abundant supplies suddenly appeared as a gift of private charity. For in the midst of the general confusion, and the stupor and indifference for others which so often results from continual fear for one's own safety, there were still people whose hearts were always alive to charity, and others whose hearts were awakened to charity by the loss of all mortal happiness. Of those whose duty it was to supervise and provide for others, many died and many fled; but there were always some whose health and courage held out, so that they stayed at their posts. There were others who were moved by pity to take on duties which were not their responsibility, and to discharge them most nobly.

The most general, prompt and constant response to the harsh requirements of the situation came from the clergy. Both in the lazarettos and in the city itself, their succour never failed. They were to be found wherever there was suffering. They were always in the midst of the sick and the dying, even when they were sick or dying themselves. They did their utmost to provide temporal as well as spiritual help; they offered every service that the circumstances might require. In the city itself more than sixty parish priests died of the infection – about eight out of every nine of them.

Federigo Borromeo, as was to be expected of him, gave encouragement and example to everyone. When nearly all the members of his archepiscopal household had died, he was urged by his relations, by the highest magistrates, and by the princes of neighbouring territories to seek refuge from the danger in some country estate. But he rejected that advice, and resisted all pressure, with the same spirit in which he had written to his parish priests: 'Be ready to leave this mortal life rather than to abandon this our family, these our children. Go out with love towards the pestilence, as if towards your reward, towards a new life, when there is a chance of gaining a soul for Christ.'[11]

He was scrupulous in observing those precautions which would not interfere with the carrying out of his duties, and

11. Ripamonti, op. cit., page 164.

issued instructions and rules on this subject to his clergy. Yet he cared nothing for danger, and there was no sign that he was even aware of it when it stood between him and an opportunity to do good. He insisted that his door should always be open to anyone who needed him, and not only to the clergy – although he was ever ready to praise and regulate the zeal of the priests, to urge on any of them who might be lukewarm about their duties, to send replacements for those who had died. He visited the lazarettos, to console the sick and to put fresh heart into the staff; he hastened through the streets of the city to bring help to the poor wretches who were quarantined in their own houses, stopping at their doors or under their windows to listen to their lamentations, and to give them words of consolation and courage in return. He sought out the pestilence and lived in its midst; so that he himself was amazed, at the end of it all, to find himself unscathed.

In any public misfortune, in any long disturbance of whatever may be the normal order of things, we always find a growth, a heightening of human virtue; but unfortunately it is always accompanied by an increase in human wickedness, which is commonly far more widespread. And so it was this time. Criminals who neither suffered nor feared the effects of the plague found fresh scope for their activities, and a new confidence of impunity at the same time, in the general confusion and the universal slackening of the forces of order. In fact the powers of law and order often fell into the hands of the worst of those criminals. The tasks of the *monatti* and *apparitori* attracted in the main those men for whom the allurements of robbery and licence were stronger than the terror of infection, stronger than all natural feelings of revulsion. Strict rules with severe penalties were drawn up for their guidance, their areas of activity were carefully defined, and *commissari* were appointed to control them, as we mentioned previously; and in every quarter of the city magistrates and nobles were appointed as delegates to exercise a higher supervision, with authority to deal in summary fashion with anything affecting public order. This system continued to operate effectively for a certain length of time. But as the numbers of those who died, ran away or lost their heads increased from day to day, the lower officials reached the stage of having no one to control them. The *monatti*, in particular, assumed absolute powers. They entered people's homes as masters – or as enemies. We need not ask what robberies they committed, or how they treated the poor wretches whom disease betrayed into their hands. But those infected, villainous hands were also laid on the healthy, on the patients' children, parents, wives or husbands, who were threatened with transportation to the lazaretto if they did not ransom themselves, or get someone else to ransom them, with large sums of money. On other occasions the *monatti* would demand payment for their legitimate services, refusing to take away putrefying corpses until they had received so many *scudi* for each one.

There were other stories, which it seems equally unsafe to believe or to reject, in view of the frivolity of some and the wickedness of others. It was said, and even Tadino asserts it as a fact, that the *monatti* and *apparitori* used to drop infected clothes off the carts on purpose, in order to maintain and spread the pestilence, which had become their livelihood, their domain, their pride and joy.

The *monatti* wore a small bell attached to one ankle, as a badge of office and as a warning of their approach. Various other wretches adopted this as a disguise, with which they obtained entry into people's houses to commit all sorts of crime.

Houses that had been left unlocked and unoccupied, or inhabited only by the desperately sick or the dying, were freely invaded and robbed by bands of thieves; others were unexpectedly attacked by members of the police force, who were doing the same, or even worse.

With the increase in general wickedness came an increase in public folly. The absurd beliefs which had previously dominated men's thoughts to a greater or less extent now acquired extraordinary power from the universal turmoil and agitation, and were able to produce quicker and more far-reaching results than before. All those effects contributed to the growth and to the reinforcement of that special fear of anointers – a fear which, as we have already seen, often amounted to a special

597

form of wickedness in its own right, if we judge by the ways in which it expressed itself and by its results. The idea of that imaginary peril obsessed and tortured men's minds far more than the real danger with which they were surrounded. To quote Ripamonti again:

'While the corpses scattered or heaped up in the streets were constantly before our eyes or under our feet, making the whole city one vast charnel house, there was something yet uglier and more sinister to be seen in this mutual savagery, these unbridled and monstrous suspicions... It was not only neighbours, friends or guests who inspired these fears; for those names which are the very links of human affection, the names of husband and wife, of father and son, of brother and brother, became words of terror. Horribly and unworthy of humanity as it may seem, the family dining-table and the marriage bed were feared as ambushes, as lurking places for poison.'[12]

The outlandish nature and the vast scale of the supposed conspiracy clouded all judgements, and corrupted every source of mutual trust. At first it was supposed that the alleged anointers were motivated solely by ambition and greed. But later it was imagined and believed that there was a fiendish delight in the act of anointing, the attractions of which could dominate the wills of men. The ravings of the sick, some of whom accused themselves of committing the crime they had feared to suffer from others, had the effect of revelation, and made it possible for anyone to believe anything.

And the actions of the sick may well have been even more convincing than their words, if it happened in some cases that delirious victims of the plague themselves went through the motions which their poor imaginations had attributed to the anointers. Such a development seems to be probable in itself, and also to provide a better explanation of the general belief in anointers, which was reaffirmed by so many authors.

In the same way, during the long and tragic story of prosecutions for witchcraft, the confessions of the accused, not always made under pressure, contributed greatly to the establishment and maintenance of the popular belief in witches

12. Ripamonti, op. cit., page 102.

When an opinion has been held for a long period over a large part of the earth's surface, it will always end by expressing itself with every appearance of conviction, and by infiltrating through every gap in men's minds and invading every level of their beliefs. And when everyone, or nearly everyone, is fully persuaded that a monstrous thing has been done, it is almost certain that someone will be found who is convinced that he has done it.

Among the various stories inspired by this mad belief in anointings, one deserves special mention both for the credence it gained and for the wide circulation it achieved. People related – with some differences of detail, since we must not expect too much of the forces of legend, but with a fair degree of consistency none the less – that a certain citizen of Milan, on a certain day, had seen a coach and six arrive in the cathedral square, inside which sat, among others, a great nobleman, with a dark and fiery face, burning eyes, bristling hair and menacingly curled lips. The onlooker gazed with interest at the coach, which stopped in front of him; then the coachman invited him to get in, and he found himself unable to refuse. The coach drove off on a winding course through the streets, and put its passengers down at the door of a certain palace. The onlooker went in with the rest of the company, and found himself amid scenes of beauty and terror, desolate wastes and lovely gardens, ugly caves and splendid halls, in which ghosts sat at council. Finally he was shown great boxes of money, and told to take as much as he liked – on condition that he would also take a jar of unguent and go through the city anointing the walls. He refused, and in the twinkling of an eye he found himself back at the place where he had been picked up . . .

This story was generally believed by the common people of Milan, and, according to Ripamonti, was never sufficiently ridiculed by men of more weight.[13] It circulated widely in Italy, and abroad as well. In Germany it even became the subject of a broadsheet and the Archbishop-Elector of Mainz wrote to Cardinal Federigo Borromeo asking him how much he could

13. Ripamonti, op. cit., page 77. '*Apud prudentium plerosque, non sicuti debuerat irrisa.*'

believe of the astonishing stories that were being told about what was happening in Milan. The Cardinal replied that they were all dreams.

The dreams of the learned were not identical with those popular delusions, but they were equally unfounded, and equally pernicious in their effects. Most educated people saw both a prophecy of the pestilence and its cause in the comet which had appeared in 1628, together with a conjunction of Saturn with Jupiter. 'For the above-mentioned Conjunction', writes Tadino, 'has so clear a Bearing upon this Year of 1630, that anyone could understand it. *Mortales parat morbos, miranda videntur.*'[14] This prediction, which came, it was so said, from a book entitled 'The Mirror of Perfect Almanacks', printed at Turin in 1623, was quoted by everybody. A second comet, which appeared in the month of June during the year of the pestilence itself, was taken as a new warning, or rather as a manifest proof of the anointings. Old books were searched (and not, alas, in vain) for examples of 'artificial' pestilences, as they called them. They quoted Livy, Tacitus and Dion – even Homer and Ovid, together with many other ancient writers who have recorded or hinted at similar events. There was an even greater plentitude of modern sources. Dozens of more recent authors had written authoritatively about poisons, spells, anointings and powders, or mentioned them incidentally. They included Cesalpino, Cardan, Grevino, Salio, Pareo, Schenchio, Zachia, and finally we must add the disastrous name of Delrio. If the fame of authors were proportionate to the sum of good or evil caused by their works, Delrio would be one of the most celebrated writers of all time. His literary labours cost more human lives than the military campaigns of any conqueror. His 'Magical Disquisitions', a summary of all the nonsensical dreams that men had entertained on this subject from the earliest times up to his own day, had become the most authoritative and incontrovertible of texts, and provided both the procedure and the motivating force for more than a century of horrifying, continuous legal slaughter.

From the inventions of the crowd, educated men borrowed

14. 'It produces mortal illnesses, and marvellous things are seen.'

all that they could reconcile with their own ideas; from the inventions of the educated, the crowd borrowed as much as they could understand, as well as they could understand it. Out of all this emerged a confused and terrifying accumulation of public folly.

But the most astonishing thing of all was the behaviour of the doctors – even those who had believed in the reality of the pestilence from the first, even Tadino himself, who had foretold its coming, and seen it arrive, who had been a witness of its progress, who had stated and maintained that this was the plague and that it was transmitted by contact, and that it would infect the whole country unless proper measures were taken. For Tadino later extracted from the same events conclusive proof that poisonous anointings and witchcraft were to blame for everything. In the case of Carlo Colonna, the second victim to die of the plague in Milan, Tadino had described delirium as a typical result of the disease, and yet later on he was capable of treating the following story as proof of anointing and of diabolical conspiracy. Two witnesses, he says, swore that a sick friend had told them that unknown visitors had come into his room one night and offered to cure him and make him rich if he would promise to anoint the neighbouring houses; but when he refused, they vanished, their places being taken by a wolf lying under the bed and three great cats on top of it, 'which did remain there until the Break of Day'.[15]

If it had been just one man who drew such conclusions, we would only have to remark that his mind worked in a strange way; indeed, we would hardly need to mention the matter at all. But as these views were common, in fact almost universal, they enter into the history of human thought, and provide an opportunity to observe how an orderly and reasonable series of ideas can be thrown into disarray when another series of ideas strikes across its path.

It should be remembered that Tadino bore one of the highest reputations in Milan at that time ...

Two worthy and distinguished authors have stated that Car-

15. Tadino, op. cit., pages 123 and 124.

dinal Federigo Borromeo was sceptical about the anointings.[16] We would like nothing better than to add this additional touch of perfection to our portrait of that illustrious and well-loved figure, and to represent the good prelate as superior to most of his contemporaries in this, as in so many other respects. But alas! we are compelled to observe in him a mere further instance of the power that a generally held opinion can wield over even the noblest minds. We have already seen what real doubts he had on this subject at the beginning of the plague, according to Ripamonti at least. Later on he continued to maintain that a large part was played in people's ideas about the anointings by credulity, ignorance, fear and the wish to excuse themselves for having been so slow about recognizing the infectious nature of the disease, and about taking the appropriate steps. But though he thought that there was much exaggeration in the public view, he also believed that there was some truth in it. In the Ambrosian Libary is preserved a short work about the plague written by his own hand, which several times hints at the opinion we have just mentioned, and on one occasion states it explicitly.

'It was the common view', he says (we translate freely), 'that these unguents were concocted in various places, and that there were many different devices for setting them to work; some of which seem to us to be genuine, and others invented.'[17]

But there were some men who believed right up to the end of the plague, and indeed to the end of their own lives, that the whole idea of the anointings was a fantasy. We do not know this from the men themselves, since none of them was bold enough to proclaim so unpopular a view to the public. We know it from the writers who ridicule, reprove or refute this opinion as the prejudice of a minority, as an erroneous theory that dared not come to public discussion, and yet did not die

16. See Muratori, *Del governo della peste*, Modena, 1714, page 117; and P. Verri, op. cit., page 261.

17. Here are his exact words: '*Unguenta uero haec aiebant componi conficique multifariam, fraudisque uias esse complures; quarum sane fraudum, et artium aliis quidem assentimur, alias uero fictas fuisse commentitiasque arbitramur.*' See his *De pestilentia quae Mediolani anno 1630 magnam stragem edidit*, Chapter V.

out. We also know of these doubts from people who had heard of them later through oral tradition.

'I have come across intelligent people in Milan', says the worthy Muratori, in the passage mentioned above, 'who had had a clear account of the matter from older members of their families, and were not very convinced of the truth of the stories about poisonous unguents.'

This was clearly a secret disclosure of the truth, a family confidence. Good sense was not lacking, but it was in hiding from the violence of general opinion.

The magistrates grew fewer in number and more and more dazed and confused as day followed day. They used all the little resolution they could still command in the search for anointers. Among the papers from the time of the plague which are preserved in the archive mentioned above is a letter (without any accompanying documents) in which the Grand Chancellor reported to the Governor, as a most serious and urgent matter, that he had heard that poison was being concocted in a country house belonging to the brothers Girolamo and Giulio Monti, members of the Milanese nobility, in such quantities that forty men were employed *en este exercicio*,[18] with the help of four nobles from Brescia, who were importing materials from the territory of Venice, *para la fábrica del veneno*.[19] He added that he had taken all the necessary measures, in the utmost secrecy, to arrange for the mayor of Milan and a legal member of the commission of health to go to the house with a force of thirty cavalry; but unfortunately one of the brothers had been warned of the raid (probably by the legal member, who was a friend of his), and had been able to smuggle away all traces of the crime; also the legal member had made a number of excuses to delay the departure of the expedition; but none the less the mayor had taken the soldiers and gone on *a reconocer la casa, y a ver si hallará algunos vestigios*,[20] and to gather information, and arrest all suspects.

18. 'In this task.' (In Spanish)
19. 'For the production of poison.' (In Spanish)
20. 'To reconnoitre the house, and see if he could find any traces.' (In Spanish)

This case must have petered out without any result, since the contemporary documents which mention the suspicion that fell upon those two nobles do not speak of any action being taken. But there was, alas, another occasion when it was really believed that the guilty parties had been discovered.

The trials which followed were certainly not the first of their kind, and cannot even be considered as a rarity in the history of jurisprudence. Even if we pass over the ancient examples of similar cases, and confine ourselves to those nearer the period we are discussing, there were trials in Palermo in 1526, in Geneva in 1530 and 1545, and yet again in 1574, in Casale in 1536, in Padua in 1555, and in Turin in 1599 and again in this very year of 1630, in all of which trials poor wretches were brought to judgement, in greater or smaller numbers, and condemned to die, generally by most horrible deaths, as guilty of having spread the plague, by means of powders, unguents, witchcraft or all those things together. But the affair of the so-called anointings at Milan is not only the most famous of all, but also probably the one where the facts are most clearly available. At least it offers us a wider field for study, because the documents are more detailed and reliable than in the other cases.

It is true that an author of whom we have spoken warmly above has already written about the Milanese trials; but his object was not so much to give a historical account of them as to draw from them a supply of supporting arguments for a thesis of greater, or at least more immediate importance. We therefore feel that the story could well provide the material for a further study. But it is not a subject that can be dealt with in a few words; and this is not the place to treat it at the length it deserves. And besides, if the reader were delayed by a full consideration of this matter, he might well lose interest in the remainder of our story. Reserving the subject for description and discussion in another work,[21] we now at last return to the characters of our main story, whom we shall not leave again until the end of the book.

21. *La storia della colonna infame* by Alessandro Manzoni. It appears as an appendix in the later editions of the present work which were published in the author's lifetime. – Translator's note.

Chapter 33

ONE night towards the end of August, at the height of the pestilence, Don Rodrigo was making his way back to his house in Milan, accompanied by the faithful Griso, one of the three or four members of his household who were still alive. He was returning from a gathering of friends who were accustomed to pass their time together in debauch, to overcome the melancholy of the times. At every meeting there were new faces to be seen and old faces missing. On that day Don Rodrigo had been one of the gayest men there. Among other things he had made the company laugh long and loudly with a sort of funeral oration on the subject of Count Attilio, who had been carried off by the plague a couple of days earlier.

But as Don Rodrigo walked along he began to feel a discomfort, a fatigue, a weakness in the legs, a difficulty in drawing breath, and a feeling of internal burning which he would have been only too happy to attribute to the wine he had drunk, the lateness of the hour and the time of the year. He did not open his mouth, all the way home, and the first word he uttered when he arrived there was to tell Griso to light him up to his room. When they got up there, Griso looked attentively at his master's face, which was distorted and inflamed, with eyes glistening and standing half out of his head. Griso kept his distance; for by this time every ruffian had to some extent the trained eye of a doctor.

'I'm all right, dammit!' said Don Rodrigo, who could see what Griso was thinking. 'I'm very well, in fact, but I've been drinking. I've drunk a bit too much probably. One of those sweet, white wines! But a good night's sleep will soon put that right. I'm very sleepy ... But shift that light away, will you? It's blinding me ... it's very uncomfortable ...'

'That sort of wine does play tricks,' said Griso, still keeping well away. 'You should go to bed at once, sir; sleep'll be the best thing for you.'

'Yes, yes; you're right ... provided I can get to sleep ... But anyway I'm all right. Put that bell there next to me, to be on the safe side, in case I need anything in the night – and pay attention, mind, in case I ring it. But I won't need anything really ... And take away that damned light, quickly now!' he repeated, as Griso carried out the order, keeping as far away as he could.

'To hell with it!' said Don Rodrigo. 'I don't know why the light should get on my nerves like that!'

Griso took the candle, wished his master a good night, and went hastily out, while Don Rodrigo quickly got into bed.

But the blankets seemed to weigh a ton. He threw them back, curled up and tried to doze off, for he was half dead with the need for sleep. But his eyes had only been shut for a moment when he woke up again with a jerk, as if someone had spitefully given him a shake. He felt himself growing hotter and more restless. He brought his thoughts back to the season, the wine he had drunk, his debauched existence, and he would have been only too glad to blame them for everything. But these ideas were spontaneously replaced by a thought which in those days was associated with all of them, which invaded his mind from every direction, which had cropped up in every speech made at the wild party he had just left, because it was easier to joke about it than to ignore it – the thought of the plague.

After much tossing and turning, he finally got to sleep, and began to dream the ugliest and most tangled dreams in the world. As they went on, he seemed to find himself in a great church, right in the middle of it, among a huge crowd. He stood there, without any idea of how he had got there, or of what could have possessed him to visit such a place, especially at that time; and this infuriated him. He looked at those who were around him. All of them had yellowish emaciated faces, with dazed, unseeing eyes and hanging lips. The rags in which they were clad were falling off them, and through the gaps he could see the bubonic swellings and discoloured patches that were the symptoms of the plague.

'Out of my way, you swine!' he cried in his dream, looking at the door, which was a great way off. Though he accompanied the words with a threatening scowl, he did not raise his hand, but rather shrank into himself, to avoid further contact with those filthy bodies, which already pressed upon him all too closely from every side. But none of those crazy figures showed any sign of wanting to get out of his way, or even of having heard him. In fact they crowded in upon him more tightly than ever, and one of them in particular seemed to be jabbing him with something, perhaps an elbow, in the left side, between heart and armpit. Don Rodrigo felt a painful pricking sensation there, a feeling of heaviness. And when he twisted away, to try and free himself from it, something else at once seemed to prick him in the same spot.

Angered by this, he felt for his sword; but it seemed to have been jostled half out of its scabbard by the crowd, so that it was its hilt that had been pressing against his side. But when he put his hand there, there was no sign of the sword, and he felt a yet sharper stab. He shouted; he was all out of breath; he was trying to shout louder still; and then it seemed as if all those faces suddenly turned to look in one direction. He glanced that way too, and saw a pulpit, over the edge of which appeared something round and smooth and shining. Then a bald cranium rose clearly to view, followed by a pair of eyes, the rest of a face, and a long white beard. A friar stood there, visible from the waist upwards above the edge of the pulpit. It was Father Cristoforo. His threatening gaze passed all round the whole audience, and finally seemed to fix itself on Don Rodrigo. The friar's hand was raised in the same attitude as when he had denounced Don Rodrigo in one of the great rooms of his palace.

Then Don Rodrigo raised his own hand quickly, and made a violent effort, trying to leap forward and grab that outstretched arm. Words which had been choking in his gullet burst forth in a terrible scream, and he woke up. The arm which he had really raised fell back by his side. He had some difficulty in fully regaining consciousness and in opening his eyes, for the light of the sun, which was already high in the sky, gave him as much discomfort as the candle had done the night before. But he recognized his own bed and his own room, and became aware that all had been a dream. The church, the crowd and the friar had vanished, with all the other details – except for one, which was the pain in his left side. At the same time he felt a violent, stifling palpitation of the heart, a constant buzzing or whistling in his ears, a burning in his body and a heaviness in his limbs, worse than when he had gone to bed. He hesitated a little before looking at the site of his pain. Finally he uncovered it, and gave it a terrified glance. Before his eyes was a filthy bubonic swelling, of a livid purplish colour.

He gave himself up for lost, and the terror of death overcame him, accompanied by another and perhaps a stronger fear – the fear of falling a prey of the *monatti*, of being carried off and cast into the lazaretto. As he tried to think of ways of avoiding that hideous fate, he was aware that his mental processes were growing darker and more confused, and felt the approach of the moment when he would have no thought left in his head except the thought of abandoning himself to utter despair. He seized the bell and rang it violently. Griso had been expecting the call, and appeared at once. He halted some distance from the bed, looked carefully at his master, and saw the confirmation of what he had suspected the night before.

'Griso!' said Don Rodrigo, sitting up with difficulty, 'you have always been a faithful servant.'

'Yes, sir.'

'And I've always been good to you.'

'You've been very kind, sir.'

'You are the one man I think I can trust.'

'I should hope so, sir!'

'I'm not well, Griso.'

'I thought not, sir.'

'If I get better, I'll do even more for you than I have in the past.'

Griso made no reply, but waited to see where these preliminary remarks would lead.

'I don't want to trust myself to anyone but you,' Don Rodrigo continued. 'I want you to do me a favour, Griso.'

'At your Honour's command,' said Griso, making a conventional reply to the most unconventional words of his master.

'Do you know where Dr Chiodo lives?'

'Yes, of course, sir.'

'He's a good fellow, who keeps quiet about his patients' illnesses, if they pay him well. Go and fetch him; tell him I'll give him four *scudi* for each visit, or six, or more if he likes – so long as he comes at once, and does the thing properly, so that no one knows about it.'

'That's a good idea,' said Griso. 'I'll go at once, and come straight back.'

'But listen, Griso; give me a glass of water before you go. I've got a burning inside me that's more than I can bear.'

'No, sir,' said Griso. 'You'd better not have anything without the doctor's approval. These are awkward illnesses to deal with; and there's no time to lose. You be patient, sir, and I'll be back with the doctor in a moment.'

He went out, closing the door behind him.

Don Rodrigo lay back under the blankets, and accompanied Griso mentally all the way to Dr Chiodo's house, counting every step, and calculating how long the whole thing would take. Every so often he had another look at his bubonic swelling, but quickly averted his head in disgust. After a short time he began to listen carefully for the arrival of the doctor; and that effort of will made him less conscious of his pains, and calmed the agitation of his thoughts. But suddenly he heard the tinkling of a bell; it was a distant sound, but it seemed to him to come from somewhere in the building, and not from outside in the street.

He listened attentively, and heard it again, louder and at shorter intervals now, and accompanied by a shuffling of feet. A hideous suspicion formed in his mind. He sat up, and listened even more carefully than before. He heard a faint thud in the next room, as of something heavy being gently set down. He swung his legs off the bed, as if to get up; he looked at the door, and saw it open. Two dirty, torn, red uniforms appeared in the gap and came on in; two faces damned beyond redemption – in a word, two *monatti*. He could also see part of another face, which belonged to Griso, who was watching the scene from behind the half-open door.

609

'Why, you dirty traitor! Get away, you scum! Biondino! Carlotto! Help! Murder!' cried Don Rodrigo. He thrust his hand under the pillow in search of a pistol; he grabbed it and pulled it out. But the *monatti* had made a dash for the bed at his first cry. The quicker of the two got to him before he could do anything, seized the pistol from his hand, and threw it across the room. Then he flung Don Rodrigo back on the bed, and held him there. With an ugly mixture of anger and contempt, the man shouted 'Why, you blackguard! What a way to treat the *monatti*! The officers of the commission of health! The ministers of mercy!'

'Hold on to him until we're ready to take him away,' said his colleague, walking over towards a cabinet. Just then Griso came in, and began to help him to smash the lock.

'You bastard!' howled Don Rodrigo, glaring at Griso from where he lay pinned down by the first man, and struggling in those powerful arms.

'Just let me kill that traitor!' he said to the *monatti*. 'Then you can do whatever you like with me.'

Then he began shouting again, as loudly as he could, for his other servants.

But it was no use; for the unspeakable Griso had sent them all out, alleging orders from Don Rodrigo himself, before he went off to make his proposition to the *monatti*, that they should come with him and divide the spoils.

'Be good, now, be good!' said the ruffian who was holding the unfortunate Don Rodrigo down on the bed. Then he turned to the other two, who were ransacking the room, and called out: 'Fair shares, now, mind!'

'Griso! Griso!' roared Don Rodrigo, as he saw his servant busy breaking open chests, hauling out money and other property, and dividing out the shares. 'You! After all I've done ... Ah, devil take it! I'm not dead yet, Griso! I may still get better!'

Griso said nothing, and kept his back turned towards the source of the noise as far as possible.

'Hold him tightly,' said the second ruffian. 'He's out of his mind.'

What he said was now true. After the last shout, after a final and yet more violent effort to free himself, Don Rodrigo had suddenly collapsed, exhausted and stunned. But he still watched what was going on in a dazed manner, and quivered or groaned from time to time.

The *monatti* picked him up, one holding his feet and the other his shoulders, and put him on the stretcher which they had left in the adjoining room. One went back to collect their share of the spoils, and then they picked up their unhappy patient, and carried him away.

Griso stayed behind to make a further rapid choice of whatever might be useful to him; then he packed everything up in a single bundle and went off.

He had been very careful not to touch the *monatti*, nor to let them touch him. But in that last rapid search, he had picked up the clothes which Don Rodrigo had left by the bed, and had given them a shake, without any other thought except that of seeing if there was any money in them. The following day, however, he did have occasion to give the matter some further thought; for as he sat guzzling in a tavern, he was suddenly overtaken by a trembling fit, his eyes were dazzled by the light, the strength left his limbs, and he fell to the floor. His companions deserted him, and he fell into the hands of the *monatti*, who stripped him of what clothes he had on that were worth having and threw him on to their cart. He died on the way to the lazaretto where they had taken his master.

Leaving Don Rodrigo in that place of torment, we must now pick up the traces of another character, whose story would never have become entangled with his own, if he had not willed that it should be so. In fact we may be sure that otherwise neither of them would have had a story at all. This other character is Renzo, whom we last saw working at the spinning-mill – not his cousin's, but the other one – under the name of Antonio Rivolta.

He had stayed there five or six months, in fact. Then hostilities had broken out between Venice and the King of Spain, which meant that there was no further danger that the Milanese authorities would try to have Renzo traced and extradited. So

Bortolo at once went off to fetch Renzo, and took him back into his own mill, both because he was fond of the young man, and because Renzo was a great asset in the mill, from the point of view of the factotum. For he was a bright lad, and skilled in his trade; and also he could never aspire to take Bortolo's place, because of that troublesome misfortune of not being able to write. As this last consideration did play a part in the matter, we have no alternative but to mention it. If the reader wants a more perfect specimen of a Bortolo, we can only say, 'Produce him from your own resources!' The real Bortolo was as we have described him.

From then on Renzo stayed where he was and worked for his cousin. More than once, especially after getting one of those infuriating letters from Agnese, he felt the urge to enlist as a soldier and have done with it. There were plenty of opportunities to do so, for the Republic of Venice was in need of men at that very time. The temptation was all the stronger for Renzo at times when there was talk of invading the territory of Milan; for he naturally thought it would be a fine thing to return home in the guise of a conqueror, and see Lucia again, and have it out with her properly. But Bortolo always managed to talk him out of it in a friendly manner.

'If they're going to conquer the duchy,' he said, 'they'll do it all right without your help, and you can go there later on, whenever you feel like it. And if they are driven back with broken heads wouldn't you rather have stayed here anyway? There's no shortage of desperate fellows to go in first and clear the road for you. But think what they've got to do before they can get in there at all! I'm a man of little faith, myself. They talk big, of course; but the State of Milan isn't such an easy mouthful for anyone to swallow. With Milan, after all, it's a question of Spain, my boy, and you know what that means. St Mark may be powerful in his own land, but more than that is going to be needed this time . . .

'Try to be patient, Renzo; aren't you well off here? I know what you have in mind, of course; but, if it's heaven's will that the thing should succeed, it'll succeed all the better if you're sensible about it, believe me. One of the saints will help you . . .

And soldiering's not the job for you. From spinning silk to slitting throats! How would you get on with people like that? It takes a special sort of chap to do that job!'

At other times Renzo made up his mind to go off secretly, in disguise, under an assumed name. But here again Bortolo was able to get him to abandon his plans every time, with arguments which the reader can easily guess.

Later, when the plague broke out in the Duchy of Milan, it started right on the frontier of the territory of Bergamo, as we mentioned before. It soon crossed that frontier, and ... But there is no cause for alarm; I am not going to tell you the story of the pestilence of Bergamo too. Anyone who is interested can find that story in a book, written on official instructions by a certain Lorenzo Ghirardelli. The work is rare and little known, although it contains more solid information than all the more celebrated descriptions of the plague put together. The celebrity of books depends on so many different factors ... But all I was going to say was that Renzo himself caught the plague, and cured himself of it. In other words, he took no special steps at all, and nearly died of it, but his strong constitution overcame the disease, and in a few days he was out of danger.

As life came back to Renzo, the memories, desires, plans and hopes associated with life came crowding back more vigorously than ever into his mind. In other words, he thought about Lucia even more constantly than before.

What would become of her in times like these, when mere survival was an unusual feat?

To be so near her, and yet to know nothing!

To see no end to that uncertainty! And even if the uncertainty did come to an end, even if the danger of the plague were to pass away and news of Lucia's survival were to arrive, there would still be that other unsolved mystery, that tangled affair of her vow.

'I'll have to go myself; I'll go and get everything straightened out, once and for all,' he said to himself – and this was while he was still too weak to stand. 'As long as she's still alive, if it's a matter of finding her, I'll find her all right. I'll hear about that promise of hers from her own lips, and I'll show her that it can't be allowed to stand. Then I'll bring her away with me, and her poor mother too, if she's alive, for she's always been fond of me, and I'm sure she still is. And that matter of the warrant out for my arrest? Well, they've got something else to think about now, those that are still alive. Even here, you can see people walking freely about, who've ... surely it can't be only the real crooks who are safe for the moment! And they say the confusion is even worse in Milan than here.

'If I miss this fine opportunity,' he went on, meaning the plague (for our incurable habit of subordinating and referring everything to ourselves sometimes leads us into a strange choice of words), 'I may not get another one like it.'

(And just as well, Renzo, we must add.)

As soon as he could drag himself around again, he went off to see Bortolo, who had managed to avoid the plague up to that time, and was very careful. Renzo did not go into his house, but called out to him from the street until he appeared at a window.

'So there you are!' said Bortolo. 'You've got away with it. Good for you!'

'I'm still a bit shaky, as you can see; but I'm out of danger, all right.'

'I envy you. At one time it was a fine thing to be able to say "I'm well," but now it's not worth much. When you can say "I'm better", that's really good news.'

Renzo wished his cousin good luck, and told him what he had decided.

'Well, you'd better go this time,' said Bortolo, 'and the blessing of heaven go with you. You try to dodge the police, and I'll try to dodge the plague. If God is good to both of us, you and I will meet again.'

'Oh! I'll be back again all right, and not alone this time, please God! Well, I can only hope.'

'If you bring the others with you, they'll be welcome. If heaven wills, there'll be work enough for everybody, and we'll be good company together. So long as you find me still here, and this infernal epidemic over.'

'We'll meet again – we must – we've got to!'

'If heaven wills – as I said before!'

For several days Renzo exercised his muscles, to try them out and to increase their strength. As soon as he felt able to make the journey, he got ready to leave. Under his clothes he wore a money-belt, containing the fifty *scudi* that Agnese had sent him, which he had never touched. He had never spoken about them to anyone, even to Bortolo. He also took a further small sum, which he had put aside from day to day, saving on everything he could. He tucked a bundle of clothes under his arm, and put a letter of recommendation from his second master in his pocket, which he had had made out in the name of Antonio Rivolta. A big knife, which was the least a good citizen could be expected to carry in those days, went into its special trouser pocket; and he set off. This was at the end of August, three days after Don Rodrigo had been taken to the lazaretto. Renzo took the road for Lecco, since he did not wish to rush off blindly to Milan, but rather to visit his own village first, where he hoped to find Agnese alive and well, and to ask her some questions about many things he so desperately needed to know.

The few people who had had the plague and got over it were really like a privileged class among the general population. Of the others many were desperately ill or dying, and those who were still untouched by the infection lived in continual terror of it. They walked along cautiously, keeping themselves to themselves, with measured pace and suspicious air, in a way which suggested haste and hesitation at the same time; for everything they saw was a potential deadly weapon which might be turned against them. But those who had recovered were reasonably sure of their own safety, since to have the plague twice was not merely rare, but almost unheard of. They went about in the middle of the epidemic with the utmost boldness and resolution, rather like the knights of a certain period in the Middle Ages, who were encased in all the armour their bodies could accommodate, and mounted on chargers protected, as far as possible, in the same manner, while they sauntered from place to place aimlessly, wherever fate might lead them – whence their splendid title of 'Knights Errant' – amid a poor pedestrian rabble of citizens and serfs, who had nothing but rags on their backs to ward off or deaden the force of the blows they received. What fine, wise, useful fellows those knights were! Their profession was worthy of full treatment in the first chapter of any book about political economy.

Such was the confidence that Renzo felt, though it was tempered by the private uneasiness mentioned above, and saddened by the recurrent sight and the constant thought of the general calamity, as he made his way towards his home. It was a fine day, and a beautiful countryside; but there were long tracts of dreary solitude, and in between them he met only poor wandering shadows with hardly the semblance of living men, or corpses being borne to the graveyard without any decent ceremony, no hymns being sung, no mourners following them.

At about midday he stopped in a small wood to eat the bit of bread and other food that he had brought with him. There was plenty of fruit available – more than he needed, in fact – along the way. He saw all the figs, peaches, plums and apples he could ever have wanted. He had only to step off the road and pick them, or gather them from the ground under the trees, where they lay like hail after a storm. For this was a year of wonderful harvest, especially of fruit, and there was practically no one to give a thought to it. The grapes too were so thick that they almost hid the leaves on the vines; and all this was left for the first comer to take.

Towards evening his own village came into view. Though he should have been prepared for the sight, he still felt a tug at his heart-strings. He fell prey to a host of sorrowful memories and presentiments. The sinister tolling of the alarm bell, which had accompanied, or rather pursued him when he fled from those regions, still seemed to be ringing in his ears; at the same time he was conscious of the deathly hush that hung over the place now. When he came out on to the little square before the church, he felt even more disturbed; and worse still awaited him at the end of the journey, for his destination was the cottage that he used to call 'Lucia's house'. Now it could at best only be Agnese's house, and his one prayer was that he would find her there, alive and well. He was planning to ask if he could stay in that house, for he guessed that his own cottage would now be a fit dwelling only for mice and weasels.

Not wishing to be seen, he went round by a field path – the very path he had travelled, in the best of all company, on that same night when he had set out to trick the curé into marrying him. About halfway along the path lay Renzo's own cottage, with his vineyard on the other side, so that there was nothing to stop him paying them both a brief visit, to see the state of his property.

Renzo walked on, staring straight in front of him, at once hopeful and fearful of seeing somebody. After a few paces he did see a man, wearing only a shirt, and sitting on the ground, with his back against a jasmine hedge, in a crazy-looking attitude. This last detail, and the cast of the man's features, made Renzo think that it was the poor half-wit Gervaso, who had come along with that unhappy expedition to serve as second witness. But as he came nearer, he was forced to realise that this was none other but Tonio, the quick-witted young man who had brought Gervaso with him that evening. Stripping him of both his bodily and his mental vigour, the plague had brought out in his appearance and actions a previously small and unsuspected element of resemblance to his poor dazed brother.

'Tonio!' said Renzo, stopping in front of him. 'Is it really you?'

Tonio raised his eyes, but did not move his head.

'Why, Tonio, don't you know me?'

'When your number's up, your number's up,' said Tonio. His mouth hung open when he finished speaking.

'You've got it badly, then, poor Tonio; but can't you recognize me?'

'When your number's up, your number's up,' repeated Tonio with a strange, stupid grin. Renzo could see there was nothing more to be got from him, and went on, even sadder than before. Suddenly something black came round a corner, and advanced towards him. He recognized Don Abbondio at once. The priest was walking very slowly, carrying his stick as if it were carrying him. With every step he took, it became clearer from his pale, thin face and from all his movements, that he too had had his

617

attack of the plague. He stared back at the young man, uncertain whether it was really Renzo or not. There seemed to be something foreign about the boy's clothes; but then, yes, there was no doubt about it, it was the sort of thing they wore in Bergamo.

'It *is* Renzo!' he concluded, raising his hands towards heaven in a gesture of unhappy surprise, with the stick still dangling from his right hand. His poor skinny arms wavered about inside his sleeves, which had formerly been quite a tight fit. Renzo quickened his pace as he approached the curé, and made him a low bow. For though they had parted on the terms we remember, Don Abbondio was still his parish priest.

'Are you here, then?' the curé exclaimed.

'Yes, I'm here, as you see. Is there any news of Lucia?'

'What news do you expect there to be? There's no news at all. She's in Milan, if she's still in this world. But you . . .'

'And her mother, is she alive?'

'She may be, but how can we know? She's not here. But you . . .'

'Where is she, then?'

'She's gone to stay in Valsassina, with her relations, at Pasturo, you know; for they say that the plague's not so bad there as it is here. But you, as I was saying . . .'

'I'm very sorry to hear that. And Father Cristoforo?'

'He went away some time ago. But . . .'

'Yes, I knew that, they wrote to me about it. I was just asking in case he'd come back.'

'Heavens, no! We haven't heard another word about him. But you . . .'

'That's bad news, too.'

'But you, as I keep trying to say, what are you doing in these parts, for the love of heaven? Haven't you heard about that trifling matter of a warrant being out for your arrest?'

'What does that matter now? They've got other things to think about. There's no reason why I shouldn't come here like anyone else, to see to my own affairs. And so there's no news . . .?'

'What affairs have you got to see to? There's nobody here

now, nothing. But as I was saying, with that little matter of the warrant out for you, you come here, back to your own village, into the lion's mouth – what sense is there in that? Take the advice of an old man, who can't help having more sense than you, and who's speaking solely from natural affection for you. Tighten your boot-laces well, and be off with you, before anyone sees you; go back to wherever you've come from. If anyone has already seen you, that's all the more reason to hurry. Do you really think that this is a healthy climate for you? Don't you know that they've been here to look for you, that they searched your house and searched it again, turned everything upside down . . .?'

'Yes, I know that all too well. The swine!'

'Well, then, for heaven's sake!'

'But I keep telling you, I'm not worried about that. And that man, is he still alive? Is he here?'

'I tell you that there's no one here; I tell you not to think about what happens here; I tell you that . . .'

'But I want to know if that man is here or not.'

'For heaven's sake! Don't talk like that! How can you still be so hot-headed after all that's happened?'

'But is he here, or isn't he?'

'No, no, he's not here. But what about the plague, my son, the plague? Is this a time to travel around the country?'

'If the plague were the only trouble in the world . . . well, I've had it, anyway, so I'm all right.'

'Why then! Why then! Isn't that a sign from heaven? When you've had an escape like that, it seems to me that you ought to thank God . . .'

'And I do thank him, Sir.'

'. . . and not go looking for other sorts of trouble, I was going to say. Do the same as me . . .'

'You've had it, too, your Honour, I think.'

'I certainly have! A most vicious and disastrous attack; it's a miracle I'm still here. I needn't say any more, except that it's left me in the state in which you see me. And now I was just feeling like a bit of peace and quiet, to get myself right again . . . in fact I was just beginning to improve a little . . . But in heaven's name, what have you come here for? You'd better go back . . .'

'You keep on talking about me going back, sir. If I go back to Bergamo, I might as well have stayed there in the first place. And why do you ask me what I've come here for? It's a strange question! I've come home, like anyone else.'

'Come home. . . ?'

'But tell me, sir, have a lot of people died here?'

'I should say so!' cried Don Abbondio. Starting with Perpetua, he reeled off a long list of names of individuals and of whole families who had perished. Renzo had of course been expecting something of the kind; but when he heard so many names of people he knew, of friends and relations, he was overcome, and stood with bowed head, repeatedly exclaiming. 'Poor fellow!' – 'Poor woman!' – 'Poor people!'

'So you see!' continued Don Abbondio. 'And that's not the end of it. If the ones who are left don't begin to show some intelligence, and get all the nonsense out of their heads, the next thing can only be the end of the world.'

'Don't you worry, sir; I don't mean to stop here.'

'Well! Thank heaven you've got that much into your head, at least. And then, of course, you mean to go back to Bergamo?'

'Don't concern yourself about that, sir.'

'What? You're not going to land us in more trouble with some other piece of folly worse than the first one?'

'Don't you bother about that, sir, as I said just now. It's my business; I'm not a child; I've reached years of discretion. But I hope you won't tell anyone you've seen me. You're a priest, and I'm one of your flock – I'm sure you won't want to betray me.'

'I see how it is,' said Don Abbondio, with an angry sigh. 'I see it all very well. You want to ruin yourself, and ruin me too. The trouble you've had isn't enough for you, and nor is the trouble I've had. I see it all . . . I see it all . . .'

Continuing to mutter the last words between his teeth, he walked on.

Sad and discouraged. Renzo was left to consider where he should go for shelter. In Don Abbondio's casualty list there was one family of peasants who had all been carried off by the plague, except for one young man, who was just about Renzo's age, and had been his companion from early childhood. Their house was only a few yards outside the village, and Renzo decided to go there.

On his way he passed in front of his vineyard. Even from the outside, he could guess what a state it must be in. Of the vines and fruit trees he had left there, not a twig, not a leaf showed above the wall. Whatever could be seen over it was stuff which had grown up in his absence. Then he stood in the gap where his gate had been – not even the hinges were left there now – and looked around. What a pitiful sight! For two winters the villagers had come and cut firewood in 'the poor young fellow's place', as they called it. Vines, mulberries, fruit trees of every kind, had been roughly torn down, or cut to the root. But there were still traces of previous cultivation. The devastated rows where the vines had been were still marked by broken lines of new growth. There were fresh twigs or shoots growing from the stumps of mulberry, fig, peach, cherry and plum trees. But even this growth was thin, and half choked by a new, thick, varied vegetation, which had been sown and had grown up without the aid of man. It was a mass of nettles, ferns, tares, couch grass, quaking grass, wild oats, amaranth, dandelions, sorrel, panic and other similar plants[1]; plants, that is to say, which peasants everywhere have always classified in their own fashion in a single large category, calling them dirty weeds, or words to that effect. It was a tangle of stalks vying with each other to see which could rise highest in the air, or crawl furthest along the ground – to steal one another's territory by one means or another, in fact. It was a confusion of leaves, flowers and seeds, of a hundred different colours, shapes and sizes. There were seed-heads like those of wheat or millet; there were flowers growing in spikes or umbels, or as individual dots of white, red, yellow or blue. Amid the mass of plants were some that were taller and showier than the others, but none the better for that in most cases. The poke-weed was the tallest of all, with its wide-reaching, reddish branches, its large, stately dark-green

1. See the last sentence of the Introduction to this edition. – Translator's note.

leaves, some already edged with purple, its curved clusters of berries, shading from a violet colour at the base through purple to green with little whitish flowers at the tips. The large, downy leaves of the mullein hung on the ground, while its stalk stood high and straight, topped by a long spike sprinkled with bright yellow stars, the tall thistles were well armed with prickles on their stems and leaves, and even on the calyces, from which tufts of white or purple petals peeped out, or silvery, light thistledown floated away on the wind.

In one place a mass of bindweed had climbed up and wound its stems round the new shoots growing from the stump of a mulberry-tree, covering them with its wayward leaves, and decorating their tips with its soft, white, dangling blossoms. In another a white bryony, with its scarlet berries, had entangled itself with the new growth of a damaged vine; and the vine, lacking more solid support, had responded by clasping the other plant in its tendrils. Intertwining their feeble stems and their not dissimilar leaves, they weighed each other down – as often happens when the weak rely on each other for help. Brambles were everywhere, growing across from one tree to another, climbing up or climbing down, spreading their branches wide or turning them back upon themselves, as opportunity offered. They also crossed over in front of the entrance, as if to bar the way, even to the owner of the vineyard.

But Renzo had no wish to enter such a place. He probably spent less time on looking at it than we have taken over its description. He went on again; his house was only a few yards away. He crossed the courtyard, knee-deep among the weeds with which it was covered and overrun, like the vineyard.

He went and stood on the threshold of one of the two downstairs rooms. The sound of his footsteps, and his appearance at the door, caused a disturbance among the rats that were there, a criss-cross scampering for safety, a diving beneath the filth that covered the floor where the soldiers had slept. He looked at the walls, and saw patches stripped of their plaster, patches smeared with dirt, and patches foul with smoke. He looked up at the ceiling, and saw a hanging tapestry of cobwebs. Apart from that, there was nothing...

This too was no place for him. Tearing his hair, he went back along the path he had himself made through the weeds a couple of moments earlier. A few yards further on, he took another track off to the left, out into the fields. He neither heard a human voice nor saw a human face until he reached the cottage where he had decided to seek shelter. It was already beginning to grow dark. His friend was sitting on a wooden stool outside the front door, with arms crossed and eyes cast up to heaven, like a man dazed by misfortune and reduced to the level of a savage by solitude. Hearing footsteps, he turned to see who it was. Addressing the dim figure which was all he could see through the screen of leafy boughs in the dusk, he cried:

'Is there no one left at all but me, then?' He got up and raised both arms. 'Didn't I do enough for you yesterday?' he went on. 'Leave me in peace for a bit, will you? That'll be a real act of mercy!'

Renzo had no idea what all this meant, but replied by calling his friend by name.

'Renzo?' exclaimed the young man, questioningly.

'Yes, it's me!' said Renzo, and they ran towards one another.

'So it is really you!' said his friend, when he was close enough to see his face. 'How good it is to see you! Who would ever have thought it? I took you for Paolino the grave-digger, who's always coming and pestering me to give him a hand ... and did you know that I'm left all alone in the world? As lonely as a hermit?'

'Yes, I had heard, and I'm very sorry,' said Renzo.

Rapidly exchanging greetings, questions and answers, all jumbled together, they walked into the cottage side by side. Then Renzo's friend, without interrupting the conversation, bestirred himself to do the honours for Renzo, as far as he could at such a time, and without prior warning. He put the pot on to boil, and began to make the polenta. But then he handed the wooden spoon to Renzo, to stir it with, while he went off, saying 'I'm on my own here; I'm really on my own.'

He came back a little later with a small bucket of milk, some dried meat, two small goat's milk cheeses, and some figs and peaches. He put everything down, and ladled the polenta on to

623

a dish; after which they both sat down at the table, and both expressed their gratitude, Renzo for his reception, and his friend for the visit. After a separation of perhaps two years, they suddenly found themselves far greater friends than they had ever realized they were during the time when they met almost every day. For both of them (to quote from our manuscript) had experienced things in the interval such as make men know what balm can be brought to the mind by benevolence, whether it be a man's own benevolence or that of his friend.

Of course, there was no one in the world who could serve as a substitute for Agnese at that moment, or console Renzo for her absence, both because of the long-standing and special affection that linked them, and because she alone possessed the key to one of the problems which he desperately needed to solve. He hesitated for a little while whether to set off for Milan at once or to go and see Agnese first, since she was not far away; but then he reflected that Agnese could have no recent news of Lucia's state of health, and reverted to his first plan of going straight on to find out how she was, to hear what she had to say to him, and to come back to Agnese with the news afterwards.

His friend was able to tell him many things that were new to him, and to clarify many points on which he was imperfectly informed, regarding Lucia's adventures and the harsh official proceedings against Renzo himself. He also told him about Don Rodrigo, and how he had slunk off with his tail between his legs, and not shown his face in those parts again – the whole complicated story, in fact. From the same source Renzo also learned the correct version of Don Ferrante's surname, which was a matter of considerable importance to him. (Agnese had indeed tried to give him the name through her letter-writer, but heaven knows what he really wrote down; and when Renzo's letter-writer read it out to him he made such an odd word of it that if Renzo had gone to Milan and looked for Don Ferrante's house on the strength of that version of his name, he would have been hard put to it to find anyone who could guess what he was talking about; and yet up to that moment that had been the only clue he had which might lead him to Lucia.)

As far as the police were concerned, Renzo's friend confirmed that danger from that quarter was too remote for him to concern himself greatly about it. The mayor of Lecco had died of the plague, and there was no knowing when a new one would be appointed. Most of the police were no longer there, and the few that remained had plenty to think about without raking up old cases.

Renzo told his friend about his own adventures, and heard many tales from him in return – tales about the passage of the army, about the plague, about the anointers, about all sorts of marvels.

'It's been an ugly business,' said Renzo's friend, showing him into a bedroom made vacant by the pestilence. 'Yes, an ugly business – things you'd never have dreamt of, things that'd stop you laughing again for the rest of your life. And yet it's a comfort to talk them over between friends.'

At daybreak they were both up and in the kitchen. Renzo was dressed for his journey, with his money-belt hidden under his doublet and his knife in its special trouser pocket. Wanting to travel as lightly as possible, he left his bundle of clothes in the care of his host.

'If all's well,' he said, 'and I find her alive, and if ... well, never mind about that ... I'll come back this way, and then hurry on to Pasturo and tell her poor mother the good news, and then ... But if it's bad news, God forbid ... why, I don't know what I'll do then, nor where I'll go, but you certainly won't see me in these parts again.'

As he spoke, he was standing at the front door, with head thrown back, watching the sun rise over his native village, as he had not seen it rise for so long, with mixed feelings of tenderness and melancholy.

His friend said, as people do on these occasions, that they must hope for the best, and insisted on him taking some food for the journey. He accompanied Renzo a short way, and said good-bye to him with renewed good wishes.

Renzo did not force the pace, since all he wanted was to reach the neighbourhood of Milan before nightfall, so that he could enter the city early the following day and begin his search at once. The journey was uneventful, with nothing to distract

Renzo from his own thoughts, except the usual scenes of misery and despair. As he had done the day before, he stopped at a convenient point to rest and eat his meal in a wood. In Monza, he happened to pass a shop which was open, and had bread set out for sale. He asked for two loaves, so that he would not have to go hungry later on, whatever might happen. The baker signed to him not to come in, and held out a small dish filled with water and vinegar on the blade of a shovel, telling him to drop the money in there. Then he passed the two loaves over to Renzo one after the other, with a pair of tongs. Renzo put one in each pocket, and went on.

Towards evening he arrived at Greco, though he did not know the name of the place when he got there. But with the help of memories of his earlier journey, and a calculation of the distance he had come from Monza, he reckoned that he was now not far from Milan; and so he left the main road and went off into the fields to look for some hut where he could spend the night. He did not want to get involved with inns.

In fact, he found something better than he had hoped. He noticed a gap in the hedge that surrounded the yard attached to some buildings, and went in to see what he would find. There was no one there; but on one side was a big open barn containing stacked hay, with a light ladder leant against it. He looked around, and climbed up, hoping for the best. He settled down to sleep in the hay, and did not wake up again until the sky began to grow light. Then he crawled to the edge of that vast bed and looked out. There was still no one there, so he climbed down the same way he had climbed up, went out the same way he had come in, and set off through a maze of field paths, using the cathedral as his guiding star. After a very short walk, he came face to face with the city wall, between the East Gate and the New Gate, which was not far away.

Chapter 34

As for getting into the city, Renzo had heard, in a general way, that there were very severe orders that no one should be allowed in without a certificate of health, but that in practice you could get in quite easily, if you used a little resource and chose the right moment. All this was true. Apart from the general reasons which led to orders being commonly neglected at that period, and apart from the special reasons that made the strict enforcement of that one so difficult, Milan was then in such a state that it was hard to see to what advantage the city could be guarded any longer, or against what. In fact anyone who went there might be regarded as careless of his own health rather than as a danger to the citizens.

Working from the information he had, Renzo had decided to try the first gate he came to; if there was any obstacle to his entry, he would merely walk round the outside of the walls until he came to one where it was easier. (Heaven knows how many gates he thought Milan had.) So when he reached the walls, he stopped and looked around, as people do when they do not know which way to take, but seem to be waiting for an indication, and searching everywhere for one. Whether he looked right or left, however, he could see nothing but two curved stretches of road; in front, there was only the wall; and no sight of human life anywhere, except that a column of thick black smoke was rising up from a certain point on the fortifications, widening out as it gained height and billowing out into spherical masses, which dispersed slowly in the grey, motionless air. Infected clothing, bedding and other household goods were being destroyed. These dismal pyres were burning all the time, not only at that point, but at several others along the walls.

It was a close day, the air was heavy, and the sky completely covered with an even, lifeless layer of cloud or haze which hid the sun without promising the blessing of rain. The countryside around the city was largely uncultivated, and wholly parched by drought. The foliage had all lost its colour, and there was not even a drop of dew on the faded, drooping leaves.

The silence and the loneliness of the scene, so close to a great city, added fresh consternation to Renzo's troubled mind, and made his thoughts yet gloomier. Having stood there for a while, he decided, for no special reason, to turn to the right, which took him towards the New Gate, though he was not aware of the fact. Near as it was, the gate was out of sight behind a bastion. When he had gone a few yards, he began to hear a tinkling of bells, which periodically died away and started up again, and then the sound of men's voices. He went on round the corner of the bastion, and the first thing he saw was a wooden sentry-box, before which stood a guard, leaning on his musket with a weary and negligent air. Beyond was a palisade, and beyond that the great gateway itself, flanked by two solid masonry structures, with a roof across the gap to protect the double gate, which was open. So was the small gate in the palisade; but right in front of the opening was a grisly obstacle – a stretcher, on which two *monatti* were placing a poor fellow, to take him away. It was the head exciseman of the post, who had been discovered to have the plague a short time before. Renzo stopped and waited until they had finished. The procession moved off; and as no one came to close the gate in the palisade he thought this was the time to go, and walked briskly towards it. But the guard called out to him to stop, with an ugly gesture.

Renzo halted again. Then he caught the man's eye, pulled out a half-ducat, and showed it to him. Perhaps the guard had already had the plague, or perhaps his fear of the disease was less than his love of half-ducats; in any case, he motioned to Renzo to throw him the coin, and as soon as he saw it land at his feet, he whispered,

'Go on then; but be quick!'

Renzo did not wait for a second invitation. He walked through the palisade, and then through the main gate itself, and strode on without anyone noticing him or bothering about him at first – but when he had gone perhaps forty paces, he heard himself hailed from behind by one of the excisemen. This time he pretended not to hear, and quickened his pace without turning round.

'Hoy! Come back!' cried the exciseman again; but his voice suggested annoyance rather than any real determination to get his orders obeyed. Seeing them ignored, he shrugged his shoulders and went back into his hut. He evidently cared more about avoiding close contact with passers-by than about discovering their business.

The road which Renzo had taken led straight to the canal called the Naviglio, as it does today. On either side were garden walls or hedges, and churches and monasteries; there were not many houses. At the junction of this road with the one that ran along the bank of the canal there was a column, with a cross dedicated to St Eusebius. And, however hard Renzo looked along the road in front of him, there was nothing to be seen except that cross. When he reached the intersection, which divided the street into two roughly equal parts, he looked along it in both directions. To the right, in St Teresa's Street, as it is called, he saw a citizen who happened to be walking straight towards him.

'A human being, at last!' thought Renzo, and quickly turned in that direction, meaning to ask him the way.

The man had noticed Renzo – obviously a stranger to Milan – coming down the street, and was already running a suspicious eye over him when they were still some distance apart; all the more so when he realized that the newcomer, instead of minding his own business, was coming straight towards him. As he drew close to the man, Renzo took off his hat, like the well-mannered young hillman he was; he held it in his left hand, and happened to put his right hand in the crown as he walked more directly towards the citizen. But the man jumped back, with wildly staring eyes, and lifted the knotty stick he was carrying so that its iron tip pointed straight at Renzo's body, shouting: 'Get away! Get out!'

'Why, what's this?' cried Renzo, replacing his hat. As he put it himself later when telling the story, the last thing he wanted to do at that moment was to get mixed up in a quarrel; and so he turned his back on the eccentric fellow, and continued on his way – or rather went further along the road to which chance had directed his footsteps.

The citizen went his way, trembling with passion, and looking over his shoulder every few moments. And when he reached his home he told them how he had been approached by an anointer with a humble, gentle manner and an infamous, hypocritical expression, who had got his box of unguent (or perhaps his packet of powder – there was some doubt upon this point) with him, hidden in the crown of his hat; and how the villain had been all ready to play him a dirty trick, if he had not had his wits about him, and kept him off.

'If he'd come a single step closer to me,' he added, 'I'd have run him through before he could do anything to me, the blackguard. The worst of it was that it happened in such a lonely place. If it had been in the middle of the city, now, I'd have called for help, and we'd soon have got hold of the wretched fellow. I'm certain he had that filthy stuff in his hat. But as it was, with just the two of us there, all I could do was to frighten him off, without risking my neck. For it doesn't take long to throw a bit of powder at someone, and those fellows are well trained. Besides, they've got the devil on their side. He must be still doing his round of Milan now; and I shudder to think what slaughter he's causing.'

For the rest of his life, which was a long one, he repeated this story whenever the conversation turned to anointers. 'And I understand that there are some people who don't believe in them!' he would add. 'They'd better not come here and tell me so, for it's another matter when you've seen something with your own eyes.'

Renzo was far from realizing what a narrow escape he had had. Angry rather than frightened, he tried to think as he walked along, what that strange meeting could mean. He made a good guess at what had been in the man's mind, but the thing seemed so outrageously unreasonable to him that he came to the conclusion that he had been dealing with a lunatic.

'Things are beginning badly,' he thought. 'Milan seems to be an unlucky place for me. I get in easily enough each time; but once I'm there, every sort of trouble seems to be ready and lying in wait for me. But never mind ... If Heaven helps me ... if I can find ... if I can only manage to find her ... why, I shan't care about anything else.'

When he reached the bridge, he at once turned to the right, into St. Mark's Street, which he rightly thought would take him towards the centre of the city. As he walked on, he looked right and left in search of humanity, but could see nothing except a bloated corpse lying in the narrow ditch which runs between one section of that street and the few houses that border it. (They were fewer still in those days.) He went on past the end of the ditch, and then suddenly heard a voice cry: 'Help! Help me, young man!'

He looked round, and saw a poor woman, with a flock of young children gathered about her, who was standing on the balcony of a small, isolated house, nor far away. She called him again, and beckoned to him with her hand. He ran over to the house.

'Listen, young man,' said the woman, 'I beseech you, for the sake of your own dead, to go to the commission of health and tell them that we've been forgotten. They locked us up in this house as plague suspects, because my poor husband died, and they nailed up the door as well, as you can see yourself. And since yesterday morning, no one has brought us anything to eat. For all the hours we've been here, not one decent Christian has been past who'd do me that kindness; and these poor innocents are dying of hunger.'

'Hunger!' cried Renzo. He put his hands in his pockets. 'Here you are!' he said, pulling out his two loaves. 'Lower a basket down to me on a bit of string, and I'll put them in for you.'

'God reward you!' said the woman. 'Wait there for a moment.'

She disappeared for a minute, and came back with a basket, which she let down to Renzo on the end of a cord.

Meanwhile he began to think about those other loaves, which he had found at the foot of the Cross of St Denis, when he had come to Milan for the first time. 'You could say I'm returning that first lot of bread,' he thought, 'and it's better than if I'd returned it to its proper owner, for this is a real work of mercy.'

'But I don't know about that commission of health you mentioned just now, madam,' he said, a moment later. 'I'm a foreigner myself, and I don't know my way around here at all. But if I happen to meet a decent, kindly looking sort of man, that I feel I can talk to, I'll tell him about it.'

The woman begged him to do so, and told him the name of the street, so that he could pass that piece of information on as well.

'Now I'll ask you to do me a kindness – a real act of charity that won't be any trouble to you,' said Renzo. 'I'm looking for a noble family's house – one of the great families of Milan. Their name is . . . – can you tell me where it is, now?'

'I've heard of them, all right,' said the woman. 'But I don't know exactly where they live. If you go on in that direction, you'll find someone who can tell you. And don't forget to tell him about us.'

'I won't,' said Renzo, and walked on.

With every step he took he could hear a noise, which he had first noticed during his recent conversation, growing louder and coming nearer. It was a sound of wheels and horses' hoofs, a ringing of hand-bells, with a cracking of whips from time to time, accompanied by much shouting. He looked ahead, but could see nothing. When he reached the end of the road, where it comes out into St Mark's Square, the first thing he saw in that open space was a pair of upright beams, fitted with a rope and various pulleys. He soon recognized the abominable instrument of torture for what it was, for that was a familiar sight in those days. Similar equipment had been set up in all the squares and all the wider streets of Milan, so that the deputies for each quarter, who had the most arbitrary powers for its use, could immediately stretch out upon it any unfortunates who seemed to them to deserve punishment; it might be plague suspects who had left their quarantined houses, or subordinates who had failed in their duties, or virtually anyone else. It was one of those curious remedies, excessive yet ineffectual, which were employed in so spendthrift a fashion at that period, and especially at that particular time.

Now while Renzo was looking at the instrument of torture, and wondering why it had been set up at that point, he heard the noise grow yet nearer, and then saw a man come round the corner of the church ringing a hand-bell. This was an *apparitore*. Behind him came two horses, stretching out their necks and digging in their hoofs as they strained their way forward; and then a cart laden with dead bodies, and another, and another, and another, with *monatti* walking alongside the horses, urging them on with fists, whips and oaths.

Most of the bodies were naked, though some were carelessly wrapped in a few rags. Piled up and interwoven together, the dead looked like a cluster of snakes slowly reviving in the warmth of spring, for those grisly heaps stirred and slithered horribly at every jolt. Heads wagged, maidens' lovely hair fell this way and that, arms freed themselves from the tangled mass of limbs and dangled and beat against the wheels.

And so the horrified spectator might learn how the most terrible of sights can be made yet more agonizing and hideous to look upon.

Renzo had stopped at the corner of the square, not far from the canal fence, and was praying for the souls of those unknown dead. A terrible thought suddenly flashed into his mind : 'She may be there, among the others, or hidden under them . . . dear God, don't let it be true ! don't let me think about it !'

When the dismal procession had gone by, Renzo set off again across the square, and took the road to the left along the canal, for no other reason than that the carts had gone the other way. Having walked a few yards between the side of the church and the canal, he saw the Marcellino Bridge to his right, crossed it and came out into the Borgo Nuovo. Still looking for someone to tell him the way, he scanned the road in front of him, and at the end of it he saw a priest, dressed in an ordinary doublet, with a stick in his hand, standing by a half-open door with his head bowed and his ear to the crack. Then he saw him raise his and in benediction.

Renzo rightly guessed that the priest had just heard a confession, and said to himself: 'That's the man for me. If a priest, engaged in his regular duties, hasn't charity, love of mankind and the grace of God in his heart, we might as well admit that there's none of those things left in the world.'

Meanwhile the priest had left the doorway, and was walking towards Renzo, very careful to keep exactly in the middle of the street. As he came closer, Renzo took off his hat, and indicated that he wanted to speak to him. At the same time he halted in his tracks, to show that he did not intend to come any closer. The priest halted too, and prepared to listen; but he stuck his walking-stick into the ground in front of him, as if to make a protective barrier. Renzo asked his question, and the priest not only told him Don Ferrante's address, but gave the poor lad the other details he obviously needed, telling him where to turn left and right, and where to look out for churches and crosses, so that he could find his way through the six or seven streets that still separated him from his destination.

'May God bless you and keep you well, now and always,' said Renzo. As the priest began to move away, he quickly added: 'But do me another kindness, sir.' Then he told him about the poor woman who had been forgotten. The good priest thanked Renzo for giving him the opportunity to perform such an essential good deed. He promised to go straight off and pass the message on to the right quarter; and went his way. Renzo moved on too, and as he walked along, he kept repeating his directions as best he could, to avoid having to ask the way again at every street corner. The reader will scarcely imagine how difficult he found it, not because the directions were complicated in themselves, but because of a new disquiet that had suddenly arisen in his heart. It was that address, those directions for finding it, that had disturbed him so deeply.

He had wanted that information, and had gone to some trouble to get it, for without it he could do nothing; and the priest had said nothing that could be taken as an ill omen. But that made no difference – he now had a distinct idea in his mind of a rapidly approaching moment when his great uncertainty would be resolved, when he would either hear the words 'She alive!' or the words 'She's dead!' That idea hit him so hard that for a moment he felt that he would rather have still been wholly in the dark – rather have still been at the beginning of the journey which was now almost ended. But he pulled himself together. – If I start behaving like a child now, he said to himself, what will happen later on? – Having got his courage back as well as he could, he walked on again, going further into the heart of the city.

And what a city it was! The state to which the famine had reduced Milan the year before was nothing to this.

Renzo's way happened to take him through one of the most squalid and desolate areas, around the crossroad known as the Carrobio of the New Gate. (There was a cross in the middle of it then, and opposite the cross, next to the site where the church of St Francis of Paola now stands, was an old church dedicated to St Anastasia.) The fury of the plague in that neighbourhood, and the stink of the unburied bodies, had been so fearful that the few survivors had had to move out. To the feelings of sadness which that desolate and abandoned scene inspired in the passer-by were added the horror and disgust caused by the debris and the other signs of recent habitation. Renzo quickened his pace, encouraging himself with the thought that his destination was not after all so very close at hand, and the hope that he might find the scene to some extent changed for the better before he got there. And in fact he did quite soon reach an area which could still be called a city of living men. But what a city, and what living men! Such was the universal suspicion and terror that every single front door was locked, except for those that were flung open because the houses were uninhabited, or had been broken into. Other doors were nailed up and sealed, because people had either died or fallen sick of the plague there; others again were marked with a charcoal cross to show the *monatti* that there were dead bodies there for them to take away. It was all very haphazard, according to which houses chanced to be visited by some *commissario* or other official who happened to feel like carrying out his orders, or making a nuisance of himself.

Rags lay everywhere, and, more repulsive than the rags, filthy bandages, infected straw, dirty sheets which had been thrown out of the windows. Here and there lay dead bodies. Some were those of people who had collapsed and died in the street, and been left there for a passing cart to pick up later; others had fallen from the cart that was carrying them; yet others had been flung from the windows like the bedding – such was the savagery with which the long continuance and increasing severity of the plague had filled men's hearts, making them lose all sense of family affection and of obligation towards society.

The usual clatter of shops, and din of coaches, and shouting of hawkers, and chatter of passers-by, were no more to be heard; and the deathly silence was seldom broken except by the rumble of carts bearing the dead, the lamentations of the destitute, the complaints of the sick, the screams of the delirious, the shouts of the *monatti*. At daybreak, noon and sunset one of the great cathedral bells gave the signal for the recital of certain prayers appointed by the Archbishop. The call was taken up by the bells of the other churches; and then you might have seen many faces appear at the windows as people made ready for a common act of supplication, and might have heard a confused murmur of words and sighs, which breathed a sadness that yet had something of comfort in it.

Perhaps two thirds of the citizens of Milan were dead by this time, and a good part of the rest had fled or been taken sick. The influx of people from outside the city no longer amounted to anything. You could probably have gone for a long walk through the streets without seeing a single person, among the few you met, who had not something strange about him – something suggesting a tragic turn for the worse in his affairs. Men of the highest qualifications were to be seen without either gown or cape, which was then a most essential part of the dress of a citizen. Priests were to be seen without their cassocks, and some of the clergy wore ordinary doublets. In fact nothing was worn which could billow out and sweep against the objects its wearer had to pass, or give an opportunity to the anointers, who were feared more than anything else. But though all were careful to dress in the shortest and tightest clothes they could, their appearance was untidy and neglected in every other way. The bearded now wore their beards very long, and those who were normally clean-shaven were growing beards too. Hair was also commonly worn long and untidy at that time. This was not only because of the carelessness that comes from a long period of depression, but also because suspicion had fallen on the barbers, since one of them had been arrested and condemned as a notorious anointer. This was Giangiacomo Mora – a name which for a time enjoyed a local celebrity as an example of turpitude, and deserves permanent and universal fame as an example of a most pitiable fate.

Most citizens carried a stick, or even a pistol, in one hand as a warning or threat to anyone who might try to get too close to them; in the other hand they would have sweet-smelling pastilles, or a perforated ball of metal or wood containing a sponge soaked in medicated vinegar. One man would apply a remedy of this kind to his nose every few yards, while another would hold it to his face all the time. Yet another would carry a phial of quicksilver, which was believed to absorb and retain all pestilential exhalations, on a string round his neck; and this would be carefully renewed every few days.

Noblemen not only went out without their usual train of retainers, but could be seen setting out with basket in hand to do the shopping.

When two friends happened to meet on the road, they greeted each other from a distance, with hurried, wordless gestures.

It was only with great difficulty that walkers in the streets could avoid treading on the repulsive and deadly objects with which the ground was scattered, or indeed heaped, in some places. Everyone tried to keep in the middle of the road, for fear of filth or worse falling from the windows, for fear of the poisonous powders which were said to be often dropped from upper storeys on to passers-by, and also for fear of the walls themselves, which might be anointed.

Ignorance often inspires courage at a time for caution, and caution at a time for courage. Now it added distress to distress, and filled men's hearts with unfounded terrors as a poor compensation for the sensible and beneficial alertness to danger of which it had robbed them at the beginning of the pestilence.

And these were the least ugly and least pitiful of the sights to be seen in Milan, involving only the healthy and the prosperous. For after describing so many scenes of misery, and bearing in mind the yet more terrible scene towards which we must now lead the reader, we do not intend to stop here to record the spectacle presented by those sufferers from the plague who were crawling or lying in the streets – the poor, the women, the children. But it was so terrible that the onlooker might almost find a desperate consolation in the very fact which makes the strongest and most painful impression on ourselves, who are far away in time or space – the fact, that is, that the living were reduced to so small a number.

Renzo had already completed a large part of his journey through this wilderness, when he heard a loud, discordant noise, amid which he could distinguish that horrible tinkling of bells. It came from a side-road still some way ahead, down which his directions indicated that he should pass.

When he reached the corner of the street, which was a very wide one, he saw four carts standing in the middle of it. If the reader thinks of a corn merchant's shop, with people coming and going, and sacks being loaded and turned over, it will give him an idea of the movement in that place. There were *monatti* trooping into the houses and other *monatti* coming out with a load on their shoulders, which they piled on to one or other of the carts. Some were wearing the red uniform, others had no such special dress. Many had a yet more odious distinctive sign, being decked out with feathers and tassels of various colours, which those wretches wore like a symbol of gaiety in the midst of so much public grief. First from one and then from another window came a melancholy call of 'Here, *monatti*, here!' Then a yet more sinister sound would emerge from that grisly bustling throng – a harsh voice saying 'Coming! Coming!' And again some of the tenants would begin to grumble and to urge the *monatti* to be quick. The *monatti* replied with curses . . .

As Renzo turned into that street, he quickened his pace, and tried not to look at the obstacles it contained, except so far as was necessary to avoid them. But then his glance fell on a most pitiful scene, so pitiful that it compelled attention. He stopped, almost against his will.

A woman was stepping out of one of those doors, towards the carts. She was young, though no longer in the very first bloom of youth, and there was still beauty in her face, a beauty veiled and dimmed but not destroyed by unbearable emotion and a deadly weakness – the soft yet majestic beauty that goes with Lombard blood. Her step was tired but firm; she shed no tears now, though she had clearly shed many before. There was something calm and profound about her grief, which bore witness to a heart that felt its sorrows deeply and constantly. But it was not only her own appearance which singled her out amid all the surrounding wretchedness as so special an object of pity, reviving a feeling which had become generally dulled and exhausted in men's hearts.

In her arms she bore a little girl, perhaps nine years old, dead, but very neatly attired, with her hair carefully parted in the middle, and a spotlessly white dress, as if loving hands had adorned her for some special occasion, some long-promised reward. The woman was not holding her in a lying position, but sitting upright on one arm, with her chest leaning against the woman's bosom, just as if she had been alive – except that one small hand, of waxen pallor, hung down by her side, heavy and lifeless, and her head rested in an abandonment deeper than that of sleep on her mother's shoulder – we say 'her mother's', since even if it had not been for the similarity of those two faces, the expression of the one that could still show feeling left no doubt of the fact.

A loathsome *monatto* went up to take the child from its mother's arms, though his bearing showed an unusual degree of respect, and an involuntary hesitation. The woman drew back, though without any sign of anger or contempt.

'No!' she said. 'You must not touch her yet. I must put her in that cart with my own hands. Here! Take this.'

She showed him a purse which had been hidden in her hand, and dropped it into his outstretched palm.

'Now promise me this,' she went on. 'Not to touch a stitch of her clothes; not to let anyone else dare to do so; and to lay her in the earth exactly as she is.'

The *monatto* laid his hand upon his heart. His manner was solicitous, and might almost have been called deferential – more because of the unfamiliar feeling which had overcome him than because of the unexpected reward – as he quickly made room on the cart for the little body.

Her mother kissed her on the forehead, and laid her down as if on a bed, as comfortably as possible, put a white sheet over her, and said:

'Good-bye, Cecilia! and sleep well! Tonight we shall be with you in the place where you are going, to stay with you for ever. Until then, pray for us, and I will pray for you and for the others.'

Then she turned to the *monatto* and said, 'When you come back this way tonight, you must come in and take me away too ... and not me alone.'

She went back into the house, and appeared at a window a moment later, holding another little girl in her arms, younger than the first, who was still alive, but had the marks of death in her face. She stood there and watched the unworthy obsequies of her daughter; watched until the cart moved off, until it went out of sight; and then she vanished from the window. And what could she do then but lay her one remaining child on the bed, and lie down beside her so that they could die together, as the flower already blossoming on its stem falls together with the bud beside it, at the passing of the scythe which lays low grass and flowers alike?

'Dear God, hear her prayer!' cried Renzo. 'Take her to yourself, together with the little one! They have suffered enough!'

When he had recovered from that strange and moving sight he tried to recall his directions and remember if the next cross road was the one he had to take, and whether he should turn to the left or the right when he came to it. But he suddenly heard a loud, confused noise coming from that direction too – a mixed sound of shouted orders, feeble laments, the weeping of women, and the sobbing of children.

Renzo went on, with his heart full of a familiar vague foreboding. When he reached the crossroad, he saw a confused multitude advancing along one of the side streets, and stopped to let it go by. These were sick people who were being taken to the lazaretto. Some were being thrust along by force, vainly resisting and crying out that they would rather die in their own beds, and replying with useless imprecations to the orders and the oaths of the *monatti* who were herding them along. Others went silently forwards, without any show of sorrow, or of any other feeling, as if benumbed. There were women who had babies in their arms; there were children more terrified by the shouting, the orders, the fearsome company, than by their vague and indistinct ideas of death, as they cried out for their mother and her comforting embrace, and for the security of their home. Alas! Perhaps the mother that they thought they had left asleep on her bed had collapsed there, overcome by a sudden attack of the pestilence, and was now lying there unconscious, ready to be taken away on a cart to the lazaretto, or to the common grave, if the cart did not come so soon. Or perhaps the mother had been smitten by a yet bitterer stroke of fate, and was so overwhelmed by her own sufferings that she had forgotten everything, even her own children, and had only one thought left, that of dying in peace.

And yet amid all that turmoil there were still some instances of courage and respect for the bonds of family. There were fathers, mothers, brothers, sons, husbands and wives who helped their loved ones, and accompanied them with words of comfort; and not only adults, but little boys and girls who led their smaller brothers along, wise and compassionate as if they had been grown up, telling them to be obedient, and assuring them that they were going to a place where there were people who would look after them and make them well again.

Among all these tragic and pitiful scenes, there was one thought which touched an especially tender spot in Renzo, and agitated him greatly. The house he was seeking must now be near at hand; one of that wretched crowd could so easily be . . . but the whole procession filed past, and that fear faded. Renzo turned to a *monatto* who was walking at the back, and asked him in which street he could find Don Ferrante's house.

'Damn you for an ignorant yokel!' was all the reply he got.

Renzo did not bother to give the man the answer he deserved. He saw a *commissario* a couple of yards away, who was bringing up the rear and had a face with a little more Christian kindness in it, and asked him the same question. The man pointed with his stick in the direction from which he had come, and said, 'The first road to the right, and then the last big house on the left.'

With a new and stronger fear in his heart, the young man followed these instructions. Soon he was in the right street; he rapidly picked out the right house from the others, which were less lofty and less opulent-looking. He went up to the outer door, which was shut, and grasped the knocker. His hand remained motionless there for a moment, as if in an urn from which he must draw a slip of paper which would determine whether he lived or died. Finally he lifted the knocker and brought it down with a resolute bang.

After a moment or two a window opened a couple of inches, and a woman peeped out to see who it was. Her distrustful expression seemed to say:

'What's this? *Monatti*? Tramps? *Commissarii*? Anointers? Or devils from hell?'

'Oh, madam!' said Renzo, looking up, with a tremor in his voice, 'is there a young woman from the country in service here, by the name of Lucia?'

'She's not here any longer; and now be off with you!' said the woman, making as if to shut the window.

'Just a moment, for pity's sake! "Not here any longer!" Where is she, then?'

'In the lazaretto.'

And again she was going to close the window.

'But wait a moment, for the love of God! Has she got the plague, then?'

'Of course she has. What's so strange about that? Be off with you!'

'Why, God help me, then! But wait! Was she very ill? How long ago was it?'

But by this time the window was really shut.

'Madam! Madam! Just one more word, for pity's sake! For the sake of your own poor dead! I'm not asking you to give me anything of your own. Madam! Madam!' But he was speaking to the wall.

Appalled at the woman's words, and angered by her manner, Renzo leaned against the door and grasped the knocker again. He tightened his hold on it, twisted it, and raised it as if to knock again, louder and more desperately, but then held it poised without actually doing so. In his agitation he looked around to see if there were any neighbour in sight from whom he could get some more exact information, some hint, or some mere glimmer of light ... But the first and only person he saw was another woman, standing perhaps twenty yards away. Her face expressed terror, hatred, impatience and malice. Her eyes twisted this way and that in an effort to watch Renzo and look away into the distance at the same time; her mouth gaped wide as if to shout with all the force of her lungs, and yet she was holding her breath. Her long, skinny arms were raised, and her wrinkled hands, crooked as talons, were moving in and out as if clutching at something. You could see that she was trying to summon help without attracting the attention of some particular person. As her glance met Renzo's, her look grew even grimmer, and she jumped as if detected by an enemy.

'What on earth ...?' began Renzo, raising his arms towards the woman. But she now lost the hope of having him taken by surprise, and let out the scream that she had been holding back until that moment.

'Anointers!' she cried. 'Get him! Get him! Get the anointer!'

'Is it me that you mean? Why, you lying old witch! Be quiet!' shouted Renzo, and dashed at her, meaning to frighten her into silence. But he soon saw that there was no time to think of anything but his own safety. In answer to the woman's cries, people came running from all directions. It was not the crowd that would have responded to that call three months earlier, but it was still more than enough to do whatever it liked to one man on his own.

Just then the window opened again, and the same wretched woman who had spoken to him before reappeared, and shouted:

'Grab him! Grab him! He must be one of those blackguards who go around anointing decent people's doors.'

Renzo did not stop to think about his next move; he saw at once that it would be better to get away from those people than to stop and argue with them. He looked right and left to see where the crowd was least dense, and set off in that direction. He shoved aside the first man who tried to stop him, and gave the next a great punch in the chest which sent him reeling back for several paces. Then Renzo ran for it, with his clenched, strong-knuckled fist poised ready for anyone else who might get in his way.

The road before him was empty; but behind him he could hear the trampling of the crowd, and above it those hateful cries of 'Get him! Get him! Get the dirty anointer!' He had no idea how far they would follow him, nor where he could find refuge. His anger turned to blind fury, his anguish to desperation. Beside himself, he seized the hilt of his knife and drew it out of its sheath. He stopped short, and swung round to face his pursuers, with the grimmest and ugliest look that his face had ever worn. With his arm outstretched, brandishing the shining blade in the air, he shouted:

'Come on, you scum, if you've got the guts, and I'll anoint them properly for you with this!'

But then he saw, with amazement and a confused feeling of relief, that his pursuers had already halted, and seemed overcome by hesitation. Yelling as before, they were waving their hands in an odd, frenzied gesture, which seemed to be addressed to someone coming up behind him in the distance. He turned round, and saw something which he had failed to notice a moment before in his distress. A cart was approaching, or rather a procession of those familiar funeral carts, with their usual escort. Beyond the carts was another group of people, who also evidently wanted to catch the anointer, and were hoping to shut him in from that side as well; but they were held back by the same fear of the carts and their contents.

Caught between two fires, Renzo was struck by the thought that the very thing which terrified them so much could well be his salvation. He realized that this was no time to be squeamish. He sheathed his knife, stood back a little, and took a run at the carts. He went past the first one, but spied a useful empty space on the second, took aim, and jumped. He landed on the cart, and stood there on one foot for a moment, with the other leg and both arms waving in the air.

'Well done! Good lad!' cried the *monatti* as if with a single voice. Some of them were accompanying the procession on foot, others were sitting on the carts, and others again, to tell the horrible truth, were sitting on the corpses, swilling wine from a big bottle which was going the rounds. 'Well done indeed! Smart lad!'

'So you've come to put yourself under the protection of the *monatti*!' said one of the two who were sitting on Renzo's cart. 'That's as good as taking refuge in a church.'

The enemy had for the most part turned their backs at the approach of the procession, and were now moving off, still shouting: 'Get him! Get the anointer!' One or two of them were retreating much more slowly than the others, and stopped every so often, turning with threatening grimaces and gestures towards Renzo, who replied by shaking his fist at them from the cart.

'Leave them to me!' said one of the *monatti*. He pulled a filthy, hideous rag off one of the corpses, and quickly tied a knot in it. Then he took it by one corner, and raised it like a sling, pretending to throw it at those obstinate pursuers, shouting 'Catch this, you scum!'

At this they all fled in horror, and Renzo saw nothing more but the backs of his enemies and their flying heels, working up and down like paddles in a fuller's mill.

A howl of triumph, a stormy burst of laughter, a lengthy booing arose from among the *monatti*, as an accompaniment to their rout.

'Ha! ha! See if we don't know how to protect a decent lad!' cried one of the *monatti* to Renzo. 'One of us is worth a hundred of those cowards.'

'There's no doubt about it, I owe you my life,' said Renzo. 'I thank you with all my heart.'

'There's no need for thanks,' said the *monatto*. 'You deserve our help; anyone can see that you're a fine young chap. You're quite right to anoint those bastards. You get on with it, and kill them all off, for they're not worth anything at all, except when they're dead. Why, do you know what reward they want to give us for doing this dirty job? They curse us, and say that when the plague's over they're going to string us all up! But mark my words, there'll be an end of them before there's an end to the plague, and the *monatti*'ll be left alone to sing their victory song and have a fine time in Milan.'

'Long live the plague, and to hell with the dirty rabble!' exclaimed his colleague, and with this cheerful toast, he put the bottle to his lips, and held it there with both hands. He took a good swig, for all the jolting of the cart, and passed the bottle to Renzo, saying 'Now drink to our health!'

'I wish you good health, with all my heart, every one of you,' said Renzo. 'But I'm not thirsty just now. I just don't feel like having a drink at the moment.'

'You seem to have been badly frightened,' said the *monatto*. 'You look a poor-spirited fellow to me. You haven't the sort of face to make a proper anointer at all.'

'Everyone has to do the best he can,' said the other.

'Let's have the bottle then,' said one of the *monatti* who were walking alongside the cart. 'I'd like another swig of that wine too; and I'll drink to the health of its owner, who's somewhere in this noble company ... yes, there he is, I think, in that handsome carriage there.'

With a horrible, evil smirk, he pointed to the cart in front of the one where poor Renzo sat. Then he composed his features into a yet more perverse and criminal-looking expression of mock-seriousness, bowed in the same direction and said,

'Pray forgive a poor *monatto*, my lord, for sampling the contents of your cellar. You see how it is, everyone has to make a living as he can. And who but ourselves had the honour of helping you into your coach, to take you down into the country? And besides, you gentlefolk are so easily upset

646

by wine, while we poor *monatti* have much stronger stomachs.'

Amid the laughter of his companions, he took the bottle and raised it to his lips. But before he drank, he turned to Renzo, stared him straight in the eyes, and said, with an air of contemptuous pity,

'When you sold your soul, it must have been some poor prentice devil that bought it. If we hadn't saved you, you wouldn't have had much help from him.'

Amid another burst of laughter, he applied the bottle to his lips.

'Hoy! What about us?' cried several voices from the cart in front.

The ruffian quickly swallowed as much as he could, and held the bottle out with both hands to his mates, who passed it round until it reached a man who emptied it completely; after which he grabbed it by the neck, whirled it round his head, and threw it away to shatter on the paving-stones, shouting 'Long live the plague!'

Then he began to sing one of their repulsive songs, and all the other members of that hideous chorus joined in at once. The hellish sing-song, accompanied by the jangling of the bells, the creaking of the carts, and the trampling of the horses, resounded in the silence of the empty streets, and echoed through the near-by houses, causing a bitter disgust in the hearts of their few remaining inhabitants.

But is there anything which never has its comforting side? anything which can never give pleasure in the right circumstances? The danger in which he had found himself a few minutes earlier had made the company of those grisly bodies and their grisly companions more than acceptable to Renzo; and now the singing of the *monatti* was music, we might almost say heavenly music, in his ears, because it relieved him of the unpleasantness of taking part in their conversation. Still slightly out of breath and very confused, he thanked God as best he could in his heart for allowing him to escape from that predicament without either being hurt or hurting others. He prayed to him also for a speedy deliverance from his rescuers;

while for his own part, he kept his wits about him, watched his companions carefully, and looked along the street in the hope of finding an opportunity to slip unobtrusively away, without giving them a chance to make a disturbance or to create a scene that would get him into trouble with the passers-by.

As they went round a corner, he suddenly felt that he had been there before. He looked again, and was sure of it. He was in the avenue leading to the East Gate – the very road along which he had entered the city at leisure, and left it in haste, about twenty months before. He at once remembered that this was the direct way to the lazaretto. To find himself on the right road without taking thought about it, or asking the way, seemed to him to be a special kindness of Providence, and a good omen for what lay ahead.

At that point a *commissario* came up to the head of the procession, and shouted to the *monatti* to halt, with some other indistinct instructions. The convoy stopped, and the music changed into a noisy dispute. One of the *monatti* on Renzo's cart jumped off. Renzo said to the other 'Thank you for your kindness to me; may God reward you for it!' and jumped down on the other side.

'Be off with you then, you poor little prentice anointer!' said the man. 'You'll never be the one to destroy Milan!'

Luckily there was no one to hear his words. The procession had halted on the left side of the avenue; Renzo quickly crossed over, and kept close to the other wall as he trotted on towards the bridge. He crossed it and went on through the outer part of the city, recognizing the Capuchin monastery as he passed it. Soon he was close to the gate, and could see the corner of the lazaretto. He passed through, and the whole scene outside the enclosure opened up before his eyes – no more than an indication or sample of what lay beyond, and yet a vast, varied and almost indescribable scene in itself.

Along the two sides which were visible from that viewpoint, there was a constant stir. There were sick people going to the lazaretto in droves; there were others who sat or lay on the banks of the ditch that surrounded it, whether because their strength had failed them before they could get into the refuge or its walls, or because they had left that refuge in desperation and their strength had failed them before they could get any further away from it.

Other poor wretches wandered here and there at random, as if stupefied; and indeed some were really out of their minds. There was one feverishly recounting some imaginary nonsense to a poor soul who was already half dead with the plague; another was in a frenzy of rage; another was gazing here and there with a bright little face, as if witnessing a very happy spectacle. But the strangest and noisiest sign of that sort of tragic gaiety was a continuous high singing, which did not seem to come from anyone in that miserable throng, and yet could be heard above all the other noises. It was a country song, a happy, playful love-song, of the kind known as *villanelle*. And those who followed the sound to its source, to see who could be so happy in such a place, at such a time, found a poor fellow sitting calmly at the bottom of the ditch, with his head thrown back, singing away with all the force of his lungs.

Renzo had gone only a few yards along the south wall of the building when an extraordinary noise arose among the multitude, with distant cries of 'Look at that! Stop him!' Renzo stood on tiptoe, and saw a great brute of a horse galloping by, urged on by a strange rider. It was a lunatic who had noticed the animal standing by a cart, unharnessed and unguarded, and quickly jumped up to ride it away bareback. Hammering its neck with his fists, and spurring its sides with his heels, he drove it along at a furious speed. The *monatti* were after him in a moment, with loud cries. Soon all that could be seen was a flying cloud of dust in the distance.

Already dazed and wearied by the sight of so much misery, the young man arrived at the doors of the building where more misery was heaped together in one place than he had seen in all the journey which had brought him there. He drew himself up and walked in under the archway. Then he stood motionless there for a moment in the middle of the portico.

Chapter 35

Now the reader must imagine the enclosure of the lazaretto, with a population of sixteen thousand sufferers from the plague; the whole internal space crammed with sheds and hutments, with carts and with people; those two endless colonnades on either side full and overflowing with the desperately sick and the dead, lying together without distinction on palliasses or on the bare straw. Throughout that vast compound, a stir, a movement, a sort of undulation could be seen. Here and there people came and went, stopped or sped on, bent over patients or straightened up again; those moving figures might be convalescents, or lunatics, or attendants. Such was the sight that suddenly filled Renzo's field of vision, and kept him standing there, amazed and overwhelmed.

We do not propose to offer a complete and detailed description of that sight, nor would the reader wish it. But we shall follow Renzo as he makes his painful round of the place, and shall stop where he stops. Of the sights that he saw, we shall relate enough to explain what he did, and what came of it.

From the doorway where Renzo stood to the central chapel, and past it to the opposite doorway on the other side, ran a sort of avenue which had been kept clear of huts and other such permanent obstacles. When he looked again, Renzo saw carts being shifted and things dragged away to clear a proper path along that line. He saw Capuchins and lay brothers directing the operation, and moving on bystanders who had no business in that place. Fearing that he might be moved on in the same way, right out of the lazaretto, he made his way straight into the thick of the huts, setting off in the direction he happened to be facing, which was to the right of the path.

He picked his way forward from hut to hut, as he found room to place his feet, and peeped into each in turn. He also examined the beds which stood outside in the open. He looked searchingly into faces exhausted by suffering, faces contracted in agony, and faces calm in death, seeking that one face which he so feared to find. He went on some way, and repeated that painful examination a number of times, without seeing any women; and it struck him that there might be a separate place reserved for them – as in fact there was. But he had no idea where it might be, and no means of finding out. He met officials every so often, who differed from each other in appearance, manner and dress as much as might be expected from the two different reasons which gave men the strength to live on in that service, and under those conditions – in some the extinction of every feeling of pity, in others a pity of more than human quality. But Renzo did not feel inclined to ask members of either group the way, for fear of creating obstacles in his own path. He decided to go right on until he came to the place where the women were. As he went forward he continued to look about him; but from time to time he had to turn his eyes away, saddened and almost dazed by so many ghastly sights. But where could he look, without his gaze falling on sights almost equally ghastly?

If anything could increase the horror of the spectacle, the weather and the aspect of the sky were calculated to do so. The haze had grown gradually thicker and had built up into great billowing clouds which grew darker and darker, giving the impression of the approach of a stormy night, except that in the middle of the lowering, overcast heaven the pallid disc of the sun could be seen, as if through a thick veil, spreading a feeble colourless glow around it, and radiating a deathly, oppressive warmth. Every so often, amid the continual murmur of that confused multitude, the threatening voice of the thunder could be heard in deep, broken, hesitant rumbling tones. The listener could not tell from which direction it came, and might have taken it for the sound of carts being driven along some distant road with many sudden stops.

In the countryside around not a leaf stirred on the trees; not a bird flew in or out of the branches. Only a swallow suddenly appeared over the roof of one side of the courtyard and swooped down with outstretched wings to skim low over the ground;

but it was terrified by the hubbub and quickly soared up again and vanished.

It was the sort of weather when a company of travellers will go for miles without one of them saying a word, when the hunter walks sadly through the woods with his gaze bent on the ground; when the peasant girl hoeing in the fields lets her song die away all unawares – the sort of weather that goes before a storm, when nature seems outwardly motionless and inwardly troubled, bearing down oppressively on every living thing, and adding a strange heaviness to every task, to leisure, to existence itself ... But in the lazaretto, which was destined to be a place of suffering and of death, men who were already hard hit by the plague quickly succumbed to this new oppression, beneath which you could see hundreds of them rapidly sinking; and at the same time it made their final struggle with death more chokingly bitter, stifling the victims' groans as the pain became more unbearable. Even in that place of sorrows, there had probably never been so cruel an hour as the one which was now passing.

After Renzo had been fruitlessly wandering through that maze of huts for some time, his ear began to pick out a curious mixture of wailing and bleating sounds from the general background of varied lamentations and confused mutterings. Soon he arrived at a splintered, broken-down fence, from behind which those strange noises were emerging. He looked through a large crack between two planks. Inside was an enclosure with huts scattered here and there. But this was not the usual spectacle of disease; for in the huts and in the open space between them were babies; lying on little mattresses, or pillows, or sheets spread on the ground, or quilts. Wet-nurses and other women were looking after them; but the goats were what caught and held the eye most of all: nanny goats mingling among the women, and serving as their assistants. It was a refuge for innocents, such as the time and the place could afford. But it was a strange thing to see one of those beasts standing over a baby and giving him her teat, and another run off in response to a hungry wail, as if prompted by a truly maternal instinct, and stop by her little foster-child and try to get into the right position for him, bleating and wriggling as if to call someone to come and help both of them.

Nurses with babies at the breast were sitting here and there. The attitudes of some of them showed such love for their charges that the onlooker might well wonder whether they had been attracted to that place by the promise of payment, or by the spirit of charity which spontaneously seeks out the needy and those in pain. One of them remorsefully pulled a poor weeping little wretch away from her empty breast, and went off to look for a goat to take her place. Another looked proudly down at the baby that had gone to sleep as it sucked, kissed it lightly, and took it into a hut to rest on a mattress. But a third woman, as she gave her breast to a thirsty little stranger, sat staring up in the sky, with an air not of indifference but of preoccupation. And what could she be remembering, in that attitude and with that look, if not another baby, born of her own body, that had perhaps lain at that breast not long before, perhaps died there?

There were older women there as well, performing other services. One ran to a crying, hungry baby, picked him up and took him to a goat that was grazing at a near-by tuft of grass. She set his mouth to the goat's teat, scolding the unpractised animal and stroking it at the same time to make it perform its duty gently and well. Another ran to pick up an unfortunate child that was being trampled by a goat that was busy with another baby. A third walked up and down with her charge, crooning over him and trying to sing him to sleep, or to soothe him with affectionate words – calling him by a name she had given to him herself.

Just then a snowy-bearded Capuchin friar arrived, carrying two squalling children, one in each arm; he had just taken them away from their dead mothers. A woman ran up and received them from him, and went off with them, searching among the women and the goats for a foster-mother who could accept them at once.

The first and dominating idea in Renzo's mind several times impelled him to leave the crack in the fence, as if to go on; but each time he came back and put his eye to the gap again for another look.

When he finally got away, he walked along the fence, until he came to a small group of huts built right up against it, which made him turn aside. He skirted the huts, with the idea of getting back to the fence, and following it along to see what lay at the far end. But as he looked ahead to see where he was going, a sudden, passing glimpse of an unexpected figure caught his eye, and filled his heart with amazement. It was the distant figure of a Capuchin, which crossed the gap between two huts and vanished again – a Capuchin who, even when seen from so far away and for so short a moment, unmistakably had the walk, the action and the shape of Father Cristoforo.

With the desperate haste that the reader can well imagine, Renzo ran forward to find him. He reached the place, and began to search amid that maze of huts, round and round, to and fro, indoors and out, until he again saw, with redoubled joy, that form again, the very same friar he had seen before. This time he was not far off, walking away from a great cooking-pot towards one of the huts, with a bowl in his hand. The friar sat down in the doorway of the hut, made the sign of the cross over the bowl on his lap, and began to eat, glancing around meanwhile like a man who keeps constantly on the alert.

It really was Father Cristoforo.

The good friar's story since we last saw him can quickly be told. He had not stirred from Rimini, nor thought of doing so, until the outbreak of the plague at Milan offered him an opportunity he had long desired: that of giving his life for his fellow men. He begged, with great urgency, to be given his marching orders for Milan, so that he could help and serve the victims of the plague. Don Rodrigo's noble uncle had died by this time; and in any case nursing ability counted more than political considerations at that moment. His request was granted without difficulty. He went straight to Milan, straight into the lazaretto, and he had been there for about three months.

But the pleasure Renzo felt at seeing the good father again was a mixed one from the very beginning. In the same moment that he made sure that it really was Father Cristoforo, he could not but notice how greatly he had changed. His back was bent, his posture strained, his face emaciated and deathly pale. His exhausted body, broken by labour and ready to drop, was supported and kept going from moment to moment only by his indomitable will.

Now he too was staring at Renzo. Not liking to raise his voice as he walked towards the friar, the young man was trying to attract attention and gain recognition by his gestures.

'Oh, Father Cristoforo!' he finally exclaimed, when he was near enough to be easily heard.

'You, here!' said the friar, setting down his bowl, and standing up.

'Yes – but how are you, father? How are you, yourself?'

'Better than all the poor folk you see around us!' said the friar. His voice was hoarse and dull, changed like his appearance. Only his eyes were unchanged; indeed they seemed somehow keener and more brilliant than before. It was as if the spirit of charity, refined and ennobled by the extremity of its labours, and rejoicing to find itself drawing nearer to its divine source, had replaced the natural fire, which physical infirmity was slowly extinguishing, by a purer and more ardent flame.

'But you, Renzo,' he went on, 'what are you doing here? Have you come on purpose to catch the plague?'

'I've had it, thanks be to God. I'm looking for . . . for Lucia.'

'Lucia! Is she here?'

'Yes, sir; at least, she was here, and I pray she still may be.'

'And is she your wife, now?'

'Oh, Father Cristoforo! No, she's not my wife. Don't you know anything about all that's happened to us?'

'No, my son. Since God took me away from you, I've heard nothing; but now that he has sent you back to me, I will admit the truth, which is that I long to hear all about it . . . But what about your banishment?'

'You've heard about what they did to me then?'

'But what had you done, Renzo?'

'Why, father, if I said I hadn't done anything silly, that day in Milan, I'd be telling a lie; but I didn't do anything wrong at all.'

'I believe you, and that's what I believed before.'

'And now I can tell you the whole story, then.'

'Wait a moment,' said the friar. He took a few paces forward from the door, and called, 'Father Vittore!'

In a couple of moments a young Capuchin appeared, and Father Cristoforo said:

'Be so kind, Father Vittore, and do my share of the work as well as your own for a little. Look after our poor people while I retire and attend to something else; but if anyone particularly asks for me tell me at once. And especially the one that you know about; if he shows the slightest sign of regaining consciousness, inform me at once, for the love of Heaven!'

'I will, I will,' said the young friar, and the old one turned back to Renzo.

'We'll go inside here,' he said. Then he stopped, and quickly added:

'But you look half dead, my boy; you need something to eat.'

'You're right, father,' said Renzo. 'Now that you remind me of it, it's a long time since I had a meal.'

'Stay there,' said the friar. He took another bowl, and went and filled it from the cooking-pot. He added a spoon, and gave it to Renzo, making him sit down on the straw mattress which served him for a bed. Then he went to the barrel that stood in the corner of the room and drew a glass of wine, which he set on a little table in front of his guest. Lastly he picked up his own bowl again and sat down next to him.

'Oh, Father Cristoforo!' said Renzo. 'Is it right for you to do that sort of thing? But you'll always be the same, I know; and I thank you with all my heart.'

'You need not thank me,' said the friar. 'This food belongs to the afflicted. But you are one of them, at the moment. And now tell me what I still do not know – tell me about that poor girl. And don't be too long about it; for we've plenty to do here, and not much time to do it in, as you can see for yourself.'

Between one mouthful and another, Renzo began to tell the story of Lucia; how she had been given sanctuary in the convent at Monza, how she had been abducted . . .

As he heard about all the sufferings and dangers through

656

which she had passed, and remembered how it had been himself that sent the poor child to Monza in the first place, the good friar held his breath. But he soon breathed more easily again, when he heard how wonderfully she had been delivered and returned to her mother, who had then found a new refuge for her with Donna Prassede.

'And now I'll tell you about myself,' Renzo went on. He gave a brief account of his day in Milan and his escape; of his long absence from his village, and how finally, in the general confusion, he had taken a chance and gone there, but had failed to find Agnese; how he learned, after his arrival in Milan, that Lucia was in the lazaretto.

'So here I am,' he concluded. 'Here I am to look for her, to see if she's still alive, and if ... if she still wants me ... because sometimes ... sometimes, you know ...'

'But haven't you any idea at all where they put her when she arrived here?'

'No, father – all I know is that she's here somewhere – if she still is, as I pray to God she may be!'

'My poor boy! What have you done about finding her so far?'

'Why, I've gone round and round looking for her. But one thing I've noticed is that it's nearly all men in the places where I've been. I thought the women must be in a seperate place. But I can't find it. If that's right, I expect you could tell me where it is.'

'But don't you realize, my son, that no men are allowed in there unless they have some duty to perform?'

'What can happen to me if I go in all the same?'

'The rule is a just and holy one, my dear boy, and even if the numerous and grievous afflictions of these times prevent it from being enforced with full strictness, is that a reason for a decent man to break it?'

'But Father Cristoforo!' said Renzo. 'Lucia should have been my wife long ago. You know how we came to be separated. I've had this sorrow in my heart for twenty months, and I've borne it with patience. I've taken all sorts of risks, one worse than the other, to get this far, and now ... !'

'I don't know what to say,' the friar went on, answering his own thoughts rather than Renzo's words. 'You'd go there with good intentions, and I wish to Heaven that all the men who have free access to that place would behave as I believe you will. God must surely bless this persevering love of yours, the faithfulness with which you desire to search after the woman he has given you. God is stricter than man, but also more indulgent, and he will not regard too closely any irregularities in the way in which you seek her. But remember this – you and I will both have to render account for your conduct in that place; perhaps not before man, but most certainly before God. Come here, my son.'

Father Cristoforo stood up, and so did Renzo. While listening carefully to the friar's speech, he had also been thinking things over, and had decided not to mention Lucia's vow, as he had previously intended to do.

'If Father Cristoforo hears about that,' he thought, 'he's sure to raise more difficulties. Either I'll find her, and we'll still have time to talk about that; or else I shan't . . . and what'll it all matter then?'

The friar took him towards the door of the hut, which faced towards the north, and went on,

'Listen now. Today Father Felice, who is in charge of the lazaretto here, is taking away the few people who have recovered from the plague, to complete their period of quarantine elsewhere. Do you see that church there in the middle. . . ?'

He lifted his trembling, fleshless hand and pointed over to the left, towards the dome of the chapel, which towered above the wretched tents in the murky air.

'That is where they are gathering,' he went on, 'to move off in procession through the gate where you must have come in.'

'Yes, I see. That must have been why they were clearing a path over there.'

'That's it – and I expect you heard the bell toll a couple of times, as well.'

'I only heard it once, father.'

'That was the second time, then. When the third one goes, they'll all be assembled; and then Father Felice will give them a little talk and go off with them. When you hear it, go to the assembly point, and try to find a place behind the others, to one side of the path, where you won't be in the way or attract any attention, but can watch them all as they go by, and see ... and see if she's one of them. But if it's not God's will that she should be there ... well, you see that part of the building,' he went on, raising his hand to point towards the side of the lazaretto which stood opposite them. 'That bit over there, and part of the ground in front of it, is reserved for the women. You'll see that there's a fence dividing it from this section, but there are gaps and openings in it, so that you won't find it too hard to get in. And once you're inside, if you don't do anything to annoy anyone, they probably won't say anything to you. But if you do run into any difficulty, say that Father Cristoforo of — knows you, and will vouch for you. Search for her there; and let your heart be full of faith, but also full of resignation to the will of Heaven. For you must remember that what you ask is not a small thing. You are asking the lazaretto to give up not the dead, but the living! You do not know how many times I have seen my poor folk here completely replaced by newcomers, how many I have seen carried away, how few I have seen walk out! Go, my son; but go prepared to make an offering of all ...'

'Yes, father, I understand,' interrupted Renzo. His eyes began to roll strangely in his head, and his face took on a quite different look. 'I understand as well as anyone could. I'll go; I'll look for her, up and down, and to and fro, all through the lazaretto, from end to end and from side to side. And if I don't find her ... why... !'

'What then?' said the friar, in a serious, questioning manner, and with an admonitory glance.

But Renzo was beside himself with a rage which the idea of not finding Lucia had rekindled in his heart. 'If I don't find her,' he went on, 'there's someone else I'll look for. Whether it's in Milan, or in his cursed palace, or at the end of the world, or at the gates of hell, I'll find that swine who separated us; for if it wasn't for him Lucia would have been my wife these last twenty months, and, if we'd had to die, at least we could have died together. If he's still alive, I'll find him, and ...'

'Renzo!' said the friar, seizing him by the arm, and looking at him yet more severely.

'And if I find him,' said Renzo, now quite blind with rage, 'if the plague hasn't already done justice on him ... why, the time's past when a cowardly blackguard with a train of bravoes at his back could reduce people to desperation and laugh at the consequences. It's a time now for men to meet each other face to face ... and then justice'll be done – by me!'

'Miserable sinner!' cried Father Cristoforo, in a voice which had recovered all its old full sonorous power. His head had been bowed, but now it lifted itself proudly erect again; his cheeks regained their old colour, and a strange and terrible light came into his eyes.

'Look around you!' he went on. He held Renzo fast, and shook his arm with one hand, while he swept the other round in front of him to take in as much as possible of that terrible scene. 'Look and see who it is that chastiseth mankind, who it is that judgeth and is not judged, who layeth on sore strokes and who granteth men his pardon! And you, worm that you are, crawling on the face of the earth, *you* want to administer justice! *You* know what justice is! Go, wretched sinner, leave my sight! And I hoped – yes, I had hoped that before I died, God would have granted me the happiness of knowing that my poor Lucia was still alive, perhaps even of seeing her again, and of hearing her promise to offer up a prayer over my grave. Go! for you have robbed me of that hope. I know now that God has not left her in this world for you. And you for your part cannot dare to hope, to think yourself worthy that he should have any care for your happiness. He will have taken thought for her, because she is one of those souls that are destined to eternal felicity. Go! I have no more time to waste on listening to you!'

He pushed Renzo's arm away from him, and walked off towards one of the huts where the sick lay.

'Ah, Father Cristoforo!' said Renzo beseechingly, following the friar. 'Are you really going to send me away like this?'

'What!' said the Capuchin, his voice no less severe than before. 'Do you dare to ask me to rob these poor people of the time I might give them, as they lie and wait for me to come and speak to them of the mercy of God, just so that I can listen to you, and your words of wrath, your plans for revenge? I listened to you when you asked for consolation and help, for that was but leaving one work of charity for another; but now you have revenge in your heart. What can you want from me? Go!

'I've seen men die here forgiving those who had injured them,' he went on, 'and I've seen those who had injured others die grieving that they could not humble themselves before their victims. I've wept with the first lot and I've wept with the others as well; but what have I to do with you?'

'I'll forgive him now! I really forgive him! I forgive him for ever!' cried the young man.

'Renzo!' said the friar with calmer earnestness. 'Think for a moment; and then tell me how many times you have uttered those words before.'

There was no reply for some time. Father Cristoforo suddenly bowed his head.

'You know why I wear this habit,' he said in a slow, grave voice.

Renzo hesitated.

'You do know why!' said the old man.

'Yes, I do,' said Renzo.

'I too hated a man. Though I've reproved you for a mere thought, a mere word, what did I do to the man I'd hated with all my heart for many years? I killed him.'

'Yes, but he was a bully, he was one of those . . .'

'Be quiet, my son!' interrupted the friar. 'If there were a good reason for what I did, don't you think that I would have thought of it myself some time in the last thirty years? Ah, Renzo, if I could only fill your heart with the feeling I've had in mine for my enemy, from that day on, and right up to today! But why do I say "If only I could do it"? I can do nothing. But God can do it, and I pray that he will. Listen, Renzo: He loves you more than you love yourself. You can make plans for your revenge; but he has strength enough and pity enough to prevent you from taking it. He shows you a mercy of which someone we both know was found unworthy . . .

'You know', continued Father Cristoforo, 'that God can hold back the hand of a bully, and you've said so yourself many a time; but remember that he can also hold back the hand of an avenger. And because you're a poor man, because you've been wronged, do you think that God cannot protect a man – a man whom he has made in his own image – against your vengeance? Do you think he'll let you do whatever you please? Never! But do you know what you can do? You can hate your neighbour and lose your own soul. By indulging that one feeling you can lose all hope of God's blessing. For however things go with you hereafter, whatever fortune may befall you, you can be sure that everything will be as a punishment to you, until you forgive him to such good purpose that you can never again say, 'I'll forgive him now!'

'You're right, father, you're right!' said Renzo, touched and embarrassed. 'I see now that I really hadn't forgiven him at all; I see I've been talking like a brute beast and not like a Christian; but now, with the grace of God, I do forgive him. I forgive him with all my heart!'

'And if you should see him again?'

'I'd pray God to give me patience, and to touch his heart.'

'And would you remember that the Lord did not bid us to forgive our enemies, but to love them? Would you remember that he loved your enemy, enough to die for him?'

'Why, yes, father; with his help, I would.'

'Well, then, come with me. You said that you'd find him, and find him you shall. Come now, and see the man you found it so easy to hate, the man to whom you wished ill and whom you would so gladly have harmed yourself, the man whose life you desired to hold in your power.'

He took Renzo's hand in a grasp as firm as a healthy young man's, and moved off. Renzo followed him without venturing any further questions.

They went a few yards, and the friar stopped by the door of a hut. He gazed at Renzo with a look of grave tenderness, and led him inside.

The first thing the young man saw as he went in was a

sick man sitting on the straw that covered the ground. He was not desperately ill, however, and looked as if he might soon be convalescent. When he saw Father Cristoforo, he made a little sign, as if to say that there had been no change. The friar bowed his head in sorrowful resignation.

Renzo looked round the room with uneasy curiosity. He noticed three or four invalids, and especially one who was lying a little to one side on a mattress, with a sheet around him and a rich cape on top of it to serve as a blanket. He looked again carefully, saw that it was Don Rodrigo, and started back. But Father Cristoforo tightened the grasp of his left hand on Renzo's wrist, and drew him to the foot of that wretched bed. He stretched out his other hand over it, and pointed with one finger towards the figure that lay there.

The unhappy man was stretched out motionless. His eyes were wide open, but unseeing, his face pale and covered with dark blotches. His lips were black and swollen. It might have been the face of a corpse, except for a violent contraction of the features which bore witness to a tenacious will to live. His chest heaved from time to time in a painful struggle for breath. His hand lay outside the cape, pressed against the region of his heart with a claw-like grasp of the bloodless fingers, which were black at the tips.

'You see!' said the friar, in low, solemn tones. 'Who knows whether it is a punishment or a mercy? But the feeling that you now have in your heart for this man who has wronged you is the very feeling that God (whom you have wronged) will have for you in his heart on the last day. If you bless this man, you too will be blessed.

'He has been here for four days in the state you see him now, without a sign of consciousness. Perhaps God is ready to grant him an hour in which he can make his peace, but awaits a prayer from you, Renzo. Perhaps a prayer from you and that poor innocent girl, perhaps a prayer from you alone, in the affliction and resignation of your heart. Perhaps this man's salvation – and your own – depend on you at this moment – on an impulse of forgiveness and pity from you ... yes – an impulse of love!'

He said no more, but put his hands together, bowed his head, and began to pray. Renzo followed his example.

They had been in that position for a few moments when the chapel bell tolled again. As if at a pre-arranged signal, they both started up and went out together. Father Cristoforo asked no questions and Renzo made no protestations; their faces spoke for their hearts.

'Go now,' said the friar. 'But go prepared either to receive a boon or to offer a sacrifice; prepared to praise God whatever the result of your search may be. And, whatever it is, come back and tell me. We will praise him together.'

They parted without further words. The friar went back to the place from which he had come, and Renzo went on towards the chapel, which was not many yards away.

Chapter 36

Who would ever have believed, a few short hours before, that at the very height of Renzo's search, and just at the point where it was entering its most doubtful and critical stage, his thoughts and feelings would be divided between Lucia and Don Rodrigo? And yet so it was; as he walked along, with his mind full of the alternating images of happiness and terror which were born of his hopes and his fears, that appalling face kept on appearing in their midst, and the words he had heard at the foot of that bed kept recurring amid the ideas of optimism and despair between which his heart was torn. He could not finish a prayer for the success of his great enterprise, without adding on to it that other prayer which he had begun in the hut, and which had been interrupted by the bell.

The octagonal chapel stands in the middle of the lazaretto on a platform reached by a short flight of steps. When it was originally constructed, it was open on all eight sides, and supported only by columns and pillars – a perforated building, so to speak. Each side contained an arch flanked by two pairs of columns; next came a portico that ran right round the church proper, which in its turn was composed only of eight arches corresponding to those outside, with a dome on top. The altar set up in the centre was visible from every window that overlooked the courtyard, and almost from every point in the whole enclosure. Now the building is used for a totally different purpose, and the clear spaces in the sides have been walled up; but the bones of the original structure are intact, and show plainly what its appearance and use must have been in the old days.

Renzo had only gone a few yards when he saw Father Felice appear in the portico of the chapel, and take up his stand in the arch at the centre of the side which looks out towards the city. His audience was assembled in front of that arch in an open space, along the central path. Soon Renzo could see from the father's stance that the sermon had begun.

He made his way round through the maze of alleys towards the back rows of the audience, as Father Cristoforo had suggested. When he got there, he stood very quietly, and looked around at the crowd; but there was nothing to be seen but a dense mass, we might almost say a solid block, of heads. In the middle were some which were indeed covered with veils or with shawls, and he looked at them with particular attention. But as he could see nothing of their owners' faces, he looked away from them and up in the same direction as everyone else. He was impressed and touched by the sight of the venerable preacher, and gave him all the attention he had to spare at that moment of anxious expectation. And so he heard the following part of that solemn discourse.

'Let us give thought to the many thousands which have left this place by that road,' said the Capuchin, pointing over his own shoulder to the gate that leads to the cemetery known by the name of St Gregory, which was then one vast newly dug grave. 'Let us give heed to the many thousands who must remain here today, and who do not know by which road they will leave this place when their time comes. Let us take heed for ourselves, so small a band, who leave it in safety. Blessed be the Lord! Blessed in his justice, and blessed in his mercy! Blessed in death and blessed in health! Blessed in the choice that he has made in saving us! And why did he make that choice, my children? Was it not to keep for himself a small nation chastened by affliction and fired by gratitude? Was it not to make us feel more keenly that this life is a gift of his hands, to be cherished as a thing given by him, to be used in works which we can offer up to him? Was it not so that the memory of our own sufferings might make us compassionate and helpful to our neighbours?

'Think now of those others, in whose company we have known pain, and hope, and fear; among whom we leave friends and relations, and all of whom are our brothers. Those of them who see us pass through their midst will perhaps be cheered to see someone get out of here alive; but let them also be edified by our conduct and bearing. God forbid that they should see in us a noisy gaiety, an earthly rejoicing at having escaped from that death with which they are still wrestling. Let them see us go forth thanking God for our safety, and praying God that they too may be saved. Let them say to themselves: "Even when they are outside, those people will not forget us, and will still pray for us."

'Let us begin a new life from the first moments of this journey, from the first steps we take along this road – a new life which shall be all charity! Let those of us who have got back all their strength give a brotherly arm to the weak! Let the young help the old! You who have lost your children, see how many children around you have lost their fathers. Take the place of those lost parents! And as your charity cancels out your sins, so it will soften your grief!'

A low murmur of weeping, broken by sobs, had been mounting from the audience; but there was suddenly complete silence as they saw the preacher put a cord round his neck and fall on his knees. There was not a sound as they waited for his next words.

'I speak both for myself and for all my companions,' he said, 'who, without any merit of our own, have been chosen for the high honour of serving Christ by serving you, when I beg your forgiveness most humbly if we have failed in so great a mission. If idleness or the rebellion of the flesh have made us inattentive to your needs, or slow to come to your call; if unrighteous impatience, or blameworthy intolerance have made us appear before you with a severe or angry expression; if ever the wretched, unworthy thought that you needed us has led us to treat you with less humility than was seemly; if our human frailty has led us into any action that has been of scandal to you – forgive us! And so may God forgive you all your debts, and bless you.'

He made a great sign of the cross over his audience, and rose to his feet.

We have been able to report, if not the exact words of his sermon, at least the theme and the sense of what he said. But the manner in which he spoke is not to be described. It was the manner of a man who called it a privilege to serve the victims of the plague, because he really thought of it as being one; who confessed that he had failed in his duty because he really felt he had done so; who asked for forgiveness because he really considered that he needed it. But those people, who had seen the Capuchins constantly busy about them, with no other thought but their service, and had seen many of them die; who had seen the man who was now speaking to them always the first in effort as he was the first in authority, except when he had been at the point of death himself – it can be imagined with what sobs and tears they answered his words.

Then the admirable friar took a great cross, which had been leaning against a pillar, and raised it high in front of him. He left his sandals at the edge of the outer colonnade, and went down the steps. The crowd respectfully made way for him, and he passed through to his place at its head. Renzo felt tears in his eyes, as if that strange request for forgiveness had been addressed to him. He moved out of the way and stood at the side of a hut. He remained there waiting, half-hidden, with only his head peeping out. His eyes stared and his heart thumped; but at the same time he felt a certain strange and special faith in his heart, which I believe came from the tender warmth that the sermon had infused into his soul, and the sight of a similar emotion in the crowd around him.

First Father Felice came by, bare-footed, with the cord still round his neck, and the long, heavy cross held before him in both hands. His face was pale and emaciated, and breathed courage and compunction at the same time. His step was slow but resolute – the step of one concerned only with sparing the weakness of others. His whole aspect was that of a man who finds in an excess of labour and discomfort the strength he needs to bear the necessary and inevitable fatigues of his task.

Next came the older children, many bare-footed, some in their shirts, and very few completely dressed. Then came the women, almost all of them leading a small child by the hand, and taking it in turn to sing the *Miserere*. The feeble sound of their voices, the pallor and weakness in their faces, were enough to leave room for no thought but pity in the heart of anyone who might have been there as a mere spectator. But Renzo looked intently at every row, at every face, without missing a single one; for the procession went by so slowly that there was no difficulty about this. The column went on, and he continued his inspection, always to no effect; his eye darted quickly from time to time at the ranks of women who were still to pass. Soon there were not many more of them to come; soon the last of all approached and went by; and all were unknown faces.

He let his arms swing and his head droop to one side as he watched the women walk on away from him, while the men went by in their turn. But then there was a renewal of hope and a renewal of attention as he saw some carts follow the men into sight – carts that carried the convalescent who were not yet able to walk. This time the women came last; and the train went at so slow a pace that Renzo was again able to look carefully at all of them, without exception. But alas! he scrutinized the first cart, and the second, and the third, and those that came after, always with the same unhappy result, until he came to one which was followed only by another Capuchin, with a serious expression and a stick in his hand, to supervise the train. This was Father Michele, who had been appointed to help Father Felice in the administration of the lazaretto, as we mentioned earlier.

And so that precious hope vanished altogether. As hope often does, it not only took away with it all the comfort it had brought, but left him in a worse state than he had been in before. Now the very best that could be looked for was to find Lucia on a bed of sickness. But the ardour of that remaining hope was so reinforced by the increase in his fears that poor Renzo clung to that miserable, fragile thread with all his strength. He came out into the middle of the way which had been cleared, and walked back in the direction from which the procession had come. When he reached the chapel, he knelt down on the lowest step, and put up a prayer, or rather a mixture of broken words, unfinished phrases, exclamations, laments, supplications and promises. Such appeals are never addressed to men, for men lack the penetration to understand them and the patience to listen to them, and have not the stature to respond to them with a compassion unmixed with contempt.

He felt a little better when he rose to his feet. He walked round the chapel and into the other path, where he had not been before, and which led to the opposite gate. When he had gone a few yards, he saw the fence which Father Cristoforo had mentioned, with the gaps in it, just as he had said. Renzo went through one of them, and found himself in the women's quarters. Almost immediately he saw a bell lying on the ground, of the sort which the *monatti* wore tied to one foot. It struck him that this might well serve him as a sort of passport while he was in there. He picked it up, looked round quickly, and attached it to his foot in the usual way.

Then he began his search – a search which would have been onerous enough from the sheer number of objects among which he had to find what he sought, even if those objects had not been so heart-rending in themselves. His glance now passed over – or rather dwelt upon – a fresh series of tragic sights, in some ways very like those he had seen in the men's section, in other ways very different. The nature of the scourge was the same; but here the suffering and the debility were of another sort, and so were the complaining, the patience, the sympathy and the mutual help. The onlooker felt a different pity and a new sense of horror.

Renzo had walked quite a long way without incident and without finding what he sought, when he heard a loud shout behind him, which seemed to be addressed to himself. He turned round and saw a *commissario* standing some way off, who raised a hand in a gesture clearly meant for him, calling out:

'Go over to that building there, where they need your help. We've finished the job of clearing up here for the moment.'

Renzo realized at once what the man had taken him for, and that the bell was the reason for the misunderstanding. He cursed himself for having thought only of the troubles that the bell would save him, and not of those it might cause. At the same time he quickly thought of a plan for getting out of the immediate difficulty. He nodded rapidly several times, to indicate that he had understood and would obey, and got out of the man's sight by diving in among the huts, away from the path.

When he thought he had gone far enough, he decided to get rid of the cause of the trouble. In order to complete the operation without being seen, he got into the little space between two huts that had been built back to back. He bent down to untie the bell, and as he stood with his head touching the reed wall of one of the huts, he heard a voice inside the building...

'Dear God! Can it really be her?' he thought. All his being was concentrated in that listening ear; he held his breath. Yes! It was her voice!

'Afraid?' said that gentle voice. 'Why should I be afraid? We've passed through worse things than a storm of rain before this. He who has protected us for so long will protect us now.'

If Renzo did not shout for joy, it was not for fear of discovery, but because he could not find the breath. His knees gave way, and the world grew dark before his eyes. But that was only for the first moment; in another second he was standing upright again, more fully awake and stronger than before. Three quick strides took him round the hut and into the doorway; he saw the owner of the voice, up and dressed, and bending over a bed where someone lay. She turned round at the sound of his coming and looked at him; she thought that her eyes were playing her false, or that she was dreaming. Then she looked again and cried: 'Dear God! Dear God!'

'Lucia! So I've found you at last! So you're here! It's really you! You're alive!' cried Renzo, trembling in every limb as he advanced towards her.

'Dear God!' repeated Lucia, trembling even more. 'Is it really you, then? What's happened? How...? Why...? And what about the plague?'

'I've had it already. What about you?'

'Yes, I've had it too. Do you know anything about my mother?'

'I haven't seen her, because she's gone away to Pasturo; but I believe that she's well. But you! how pale you are! how weak you look! But you've got over it, haven't you? You're all right now?'

'It's the will of God that I should stay in this world for a bit longer. But Renzo! Why have you come?'

'Why?' said Renzo, coming closer still. 'Do you ask me why? Why I had to come to you? Do I really have to tell you? Who else have I got to think about? Isn't my name Renzo? Aren't you Lucia?'

'What are you saying, Renzo? Whatever are you saying? Didn't my mother have a letter written to you...?'

'Yes, she sent me a letter all right. Fine stuff to write to a poor fellow down on his luck, in trouble, all on his own...! to a man who at least had never done anything to hurt you.'

'But, Renzo! Renzo! If you knew ... why did you come here? Why?'

'Why, Lucia? can you really ask me that? After all our promises? Aren't we still the same people we were before? Have you forgotten everything? What more could we have done to bind us to each other?'

'Dear God!' cried Lucia sadly, clasping her hands and looking up to heaven, 'why did you not have mercy on me and take me to yourself? Oh Renzo! What have you done? Just when I was beginning to hope that ... with time ... I might be able to forget ...'

'That's a fine hope to have! and a fine thing to say to me! A fine smack in the face!'

'But what have you done? And in a place like this, too, amid all this misery, these frightful sights! In a place where nearly everyone's at the point of death, how could you dare...?'

'Those that die ought to have our prayers; we must pray to God that they may go to a good place; but that doesn't mean that the rest of us are bound to live the remaining part of our lives out in misery.'

'But Renzo! You can't be thinking what you are saying. It was a promise to the Madonna! A vow!'

'What I'm saying is that some promises don't count for anything.'

'Dear God! What a thing to say! Where have you been all this time, and who have you been with, to talk like that?'

'I'm talking like a good Christian; and I think more of the

Madonna than you do; for I believe that she doesn't want people to promise to hurt those that are near to them. If the Madonna had spoken to you, that'd be another matter. But it was all your own idea . . . I'll tell you what promise you ought to make to the Madonna – promise that we'll name our first daughter after her; for I'm here to join you in that promise. That's the kind of thing that does far more honour to the Madonna – that's a kind of tribute that makes far more sense, and doesn't hurt anybody.'

'No, no; don't say things like that. You don't know what you're talking about. You don't know what it is to make a vow. It wasn't you that had to do it; you haven't felt what it's like. And now go! for Heavens sake, go!'

And she moved brusquely away from him, turning toward the bed.

'Lucia!' said Renzo, not moving, 'tell me one thing. If it weren't for that vow, would you still feel the same about me?'

'You cruel man!' said Lucia. She turned back to him, hardly able to restrain her tears. 'When you've made me say something that can't do any good, and that'll hurt me, and may even be a sin, I suppose you'll be satisfied! Go, now, go! Try to forget me! It's clear enough that it wasn't meant to be . . . We shall meet again in Heaven; this life is not so long. Go, now and try to let my mother know that I've got over the plague, that God's helped me in this as well. And tell her that I've found a kind woman here, the one you see with me now, who's looking after me like a mother. Tell her that I pray that she may be spared from getting the plague; say that we'll see each other again when and where it's God's will that we should. And now go, and don't think of me again . . . unless it's to remember me in your prayers.'

Like someone with nothing further to say, and no wish to hear any more, like someone trying to escape from danger, she moved away from him, even closer to the bed in which lay the woman of whom she had spoken.

'Listen, Lucia, listen!' said Renzo. But he did not move towards her.

'No, no! Go now, for pity's sake!'

'Listen: Father Cristoforo . . .'

'What? What was that?'

'Father Cristoforo's here!'

'Here? But how do you know? Where is he?'

'I was talking to him just now; I spent quite a long time with him. And a holy man like that, I'd have thought, might be able to . . .'

'So he's in the lazaretto! He'll have come to help the poor folk with the plague, no doubt. But what about him? Has he had it himself?'

'Oh, Lucia, I'm afraid . . . I'm very much afraid . . .'

While Renzo was hesitating over words that were so painful for him to utter, and must be so painful for her to hear, she came away from the bed, and moved closer to him again.

'I think he's got it now!' said Renzo.

'Poor man! Poor, good man! But it's ourselves we should be sorry for, if he goes. And is he in bed? Is someone looking after him?'

'He's up and dressed, and going round helping other people; but if you could only see him, Lucia! His colour and the way he stands! After all the cases we've seen before, you can't mistake it, more's the pity!'

'Why, Heaven help us then! To think of him being in this place!'

'Yes, he's here, all right, and quite close at hand. Hardly further than from your cottage to mine, if you remember . . .'

'Holy Mother of God!'

'Not much more than that, then. And what a talk we had about you! I wish you could have heard him. And who d'you think he . . .? – but I'll speak about that in a minute; first of all I must tell you what he said to me at the beginning, what I heard from his own mouth. He said I'd done well to come and search for you, and that it's pleasing to God for a young man to act as I've done, and that he'd help me to find you, as he did . . . and he's a saint, mind you! So what have you to say to that?'

'But if he did speak like that, it can only be because he doesn't know . . .'

'How do you expect him to know about things that you've done all on your own, without any advice and without any rhyme or reason? When it's a fine man like that, and a man of sense, and ... why, it wouldn't even cross his mind! But that wasn't all! Just listen ...'

And he went on to describe his visit to that other hut. And though Lucia's mind and feelings must have become accustomed to the most violent shocks during her stay in that place, she was still filled with horror and pity by what she heard.

'And there too he spoke like the saint that he is,' Renzo went on. 'He said that perhaps the Lord has it in mind to show mercy on that poor devil (for I can't call him anything else now), and that he's waiting for the right moment to have pity on him ... but that first of all he wants you and me to pray for him together! ... "together" was the word he used. Do you understand?'

'Yes, yes; we'll pray for him, each of us where it's the Lord's will that we should be. He'll know well enough how to put our prayers together.'

'But I'm telling you the good father's very words!'

'But, Renzo, he doesn't know ...'

'But don't you see that when a saint speaks, it's the Lord himself that speaks through him? He'd never have said that if it wasn't right ... And what about that poor fellow's soul? I've prayed for him, and I'll pray for him again. I've prayed for him as sincerely as if he'd been my own brother. But how do you think he'll be placed in the world to come, poor man, if things aren't put right in this one – if the wrong he's done isn't righted? If you'll listen to reason now, his slate'll be wiped clean. What's done is done, and he's already suffered enough to pay his debt in this world ...'

'No, Renzo, no – God doesn't want us to do wrong just so that he can show mercy afterwards ... We must leave everything to him; our only duty is to pray. If I had died on that fearful night, do you think God couldn't have forgiven the man who'd wronged me? And since I didn't die, since I was set free ...'

'But what about your mother then?' interrupted Renzo. 'Poor

woman, she's always been so fond of me, and so anxious to see us man and wife. Didn't she tell you that you were all wrong about this? I know she's put you right several times before, because in certain things she's got a lot more sense than you have.'

'My mother! Do you think that my mother would advise me to break a holy vow? Renzo, you're out of your mind!'

'Do you want me to tell you the truth? These aren't things that you women can understand at all. Father Cristoforo told me to go back and let him know if I found you. I'm going now, and we'll hear what he's got to say!'

'Yes, yes! Go and talk to the good father! Tell him I'm praying for him, and ask him to pray for me, for I've such need of it. But for the love of Heaven, for your own soul's sake, and mine, don't come back here to cause me more pain and . . . and temptation. Father Cristoforo will know how to explain it all to you, and bring you back to your senses. He'll help you to find peace of heart.'

'Peace of heart! You might as well forget that! Those stupid ugly words came in one of those letters you had written, and you've no idea how unhappy they made me. And now you can find it in your heart to say them to me! But I'll tell you loud and clear that peace of heart is one thing I'll never find. You may want to forget me, but I don't want to forget you. And I'll tell you one thing – if you drive me into going off the straight and narrow path, I'll never come back to it. To hell with my trade, to hell with trying to behave decently! You want to make me live in desperation for the rest of my time, and it's a desperate life I'll lead!

'And that poor devil!' he went on. 'The Lord knows I'd forgiven him with all my heart; but now look what you've done! Do you want me to go through life with the thought that if it hadn't been for him . . .? Lucia! You've told me to forget you – but how can I do it? Who do you suppose I've been thinking about all this time? After all that we've meant to each other, after so many promises! What harm have I done you since we last met? Is it because I've had a bad time that you're treating me like this? Because I've been down on my luck?

676

Because the folk of this world have persecuted me? Because I've been away from home so long, so miserable, and so far away from you? Because I've come to look for you the first moment I could?'

When Lucia's sobs allowed her to speak she joined her hands once more, raised her tearful eyes to heaven, and exclaimed:

'Most holy Virgin, help me! For you know that ever since that fearful night there hasn't been a time when I've needed you like I need you now! You helped me then; help me again today!'

'Yes, Lucia,' said Renzo, 'you're right to call on the Madonna! But what makes you think that the Madonna, who's kindness itself, the Mother of Mercies, can find any pleasure in tormenting us – tormenting me, at least – for the sake of a few words which passed your lips when you didn't know what you were saying? What makes you think that she'd have helped you then just to see us both in a mess like this later on? ... But if it's an excuse, if you don't like me any more, you'd better say so now and say so plainly.'

'For the mercy of Heaven, Renzo, and for the sake of your own poor dead, stop it! You'll kill me, and ... and it's not a good time for me to die. Go to Father Cristoforo, and ask him to pray for me, and don't come back – never come back again!'

'I'll go all right; but you needn't think I won't be back! I'd be back if it meant travelling to the end of the world!' He vanished.

Lucia sat down, or rather collapsed, by the bed. She leant her head against the blankets and continued to weep bitterly. The woman who lay there had been watching and listening in complete silence; but now she asked what that sudden apparition had been, and what that argument had been about, and the reason for all those tears. Meanwhile the reader will perhaps be asking who she was; and we can satisfy him in a few words.

She was a wealthy merchant's widow, about thirty years old. In the course of a few days she had seen her husband and all her children die around her in her home. Then she too had been struck down. She had been taken to the lazaretto and put in the hut where Lucia lay. The girl had been there for some time; she

677

had got over the crisis of that terrible disease without knowing anything about it, and the bed alongside hers had had several changes of occupant, also without her knowledge. But now she was beginning to regain her health and the awareness of her surroundings which she had lost at the beginning of her illness, when she was still in Don Ferrante's house, and had never recovered until now. There was only room for two people in the hut, and these two, so afflicted, deserted and terrified, alone in the middle of so great a multitude, soon began to feel an affection for each other and an intimacy which years of living together in normal times could hardly have produced. Soon Lucia was well enough to help her companion, who was in desperate straits. Now that the older woman was also out of danger, they took it in turns to guard and comfort and encourage each other. They had sworn not to leave the lazaretto until they could leave it together, and had also agreed to stay together after that. The widow had left her house, her shop and her till, all well stocked, in the safe keeping of her brother, who was a *commissario*. She had every prospect of finding herself the sad and lonely mistress of far more than she herself needed to live in comfort; and so she wanted to keep Lucia with her, as if she had been her daughter or sister.

Lucia had agreed to stay with her, with the utmost gratitude both to her friend and to Providence; but only until she could get news of her mother, and (as she hoped) find out what Agnese's wishes were. In her reserved way the girl had said nothing to her friend about her engagement, and nothing about her other extraordinary adventures. But now her feelings were in such turmoil that she was as anxious to pour out her heart as the other woman was eager to hear the story. Lucia grasped one of her friends hands tightly in both of her own, and answered all her questions without any restraint except that imposed by her sobs.

Meanwhile Renzo was running towards Father Cristoforo's hut. With a little difficulty, and after a couple of false starts, he finally found the place. There was the hut; but the good father himself was not at home. Renzo searched around for him, and after a little found him in one of the shelters, bent double and in fact almost prostrate by the side of a dying man, whom he was comforting. Renzo stood and waited in silence. Presently he saw Father Cristoforo close the poor man's eyes, and kneel in prayer for a few moments before rising to his feet. Then the young man went up to him.

'Ah!' said the friar, catching sight of him. 'What news have you?'

'She's here! I've found her!'

'Is she all right?'

'Yes, she's cured . . . or at least she's out of bed!'

'May the Lord's name be praised then!'

'But, father,' said Renzo, when he was near enough to the friar to be able to speak in an undertone, 'father, there's another difficulty.'

'What is that?'

'Well, you see . . . you know what a good girl she is, but she does get a bit fixed in her ideas sometimes. After all our promises, after all the rest of it, which you know about, she says now that she can't marry me, because she says that on that night, when she was so frightened, and half out of her mind, she made some sort of vow to the Madonna. It doesn't really make sense, does it, father? A very good sort of thing to do for anyone who's got the learning and knowledge to do it properly; but for ordinary folk like us who don't know what they're about . . . isn't it right that it can't really mean anything?'

'Tell me, Renzo; is she far from here?'

'No, father; just a few yards beyond the church.'

'Wait here a few moments for me,' said the friar, 'and we'll go there together.'

'So you'll tell her, will you, father, that . . .'

'I don't know, my son, I don't know. I'll have to hear what she has to say.'

'Yes, I understand,' said Renzo. He stood there looking down at the ground, with his arms crossed, no less troubled with doubts about the future than he had been before. The friar went off again to find Father Vittore and to ask for his further help. When he returned, he went back into his own hut, and came out again in a moment with a basket on his arm.

'Come, Renzo,' he said. He led the young man back towards that other hut which they had both visited a little earlier. This time Father Cristoforo went in alone. He came out a few seconds later, saying: 'There's no change! We can only pray, and pray we must!'

'Now you show me the way, my son,' he went on; and they set off without another word.

The sky meanwhile had continued to darken, and there could be no doubt now that the storm would soon break. Frequent flashes of lightning broke across the gathering darkness, shedding a fitful light over the immensely long roofs of the main buildings, the arches of the porticoes, the dome of the chapel, the low roof-trees of the huts. The sudden, noisy claps of thunder seemed to run right across the sky. Renzo walked in front, intent on finding the way. Though impatient to reach Lucia's hut, he was careful not to go too fast for Father Cristoforo, who was exhausted by his labours, oppressed by the stifling atmosphere, and weighed down by sickness, so that he walked with difficulty, raising his pallid face to heaven every few yards, as if to seek for air that he could breathe.

When Renzo caught sight of the hut, he stopped and turned round.

'There it is!' he said in a trembling voice.

They went in.

'Here they are,' cried Lucia's companion. The girl looked round, jumped to her feet, and came forward towards the old man, crying:

'Father Cristoforo! Is it really you?'

'Lucia! From what perils has the Lord delivered you! You should indeed be happy that you placed your trust in him!'

'I am! I am! But what about yourself, dear father? Heaven help us, how changed you look! Tell me how you are!'

'I'm as God wishes me to be, and, thanks to his grace, that's what I wish for myself too,' said the friar, looking calmly at her. Then he drew her to one side, and said:

'Listen, Lucia; I can only stay here for a few minutes. Do you want to put your trust in me, as you have before?'

'Why, I think of you as my own father, just as I always have!'

'Well, then, my daughter, what's this Renzo tells me about a vow?'

'It's a vow I made to the Madonna in a time of great anguish – a vow that I'd never get married.'

'My poor child! But did you think at that time, about the promise you'd already made?'

'Why, this was different! It was the Lord ... the Madonna. No, I didn't think about my promise.'

'Our sacrifices are pleasing in the sight of the Lord, my daughter, when what we offer is our own. They must come from the heart, from the will; but you could not offer him the will of another – the will of a man to whom you were already betrothed.'

'Did I do wrong, then?'

'No, my poor child, don't think that. I believe that the impulse of your afflicted heart may well have been pleasing in the sight of the Madonna, and that she may well have offered it up to God for you ... But tell me: haven't you asked anyone's advice about all this?'

'Well, father, I didn't think it was a sin, so I didn't say anything about it in confession; and when we do manage to do a little good we're not supposed to talk about it.'

'Is there any other reason that might hold you back from keeping the promise you made to Renzo?'

'As far as that goes ... why, for my part ... what reason could there be? ... I couldn't say ...' replied Lucia. It was clear that her halting speech was caused by anything but inner uncertainty. A sudden bright flush came into her cheeks, which were still pale from her illness.

'And do you believe,' the old man went on, lowering his eyes, 'that God has given his Church the power to remit or confirm the debts and obligations that men may have undertaken towards him, as may be for the greater common good?'

'Yes – I do believe that.'

'Then I will tell you that we who have been deputed to the care of the souls in this place have in our hands the widest powers of the Church, for those who come to us. I can therefore free you, if you ask me to do so, from every obligation that you may have taken upon yourself when you made that vow.'

'But isn't it a sin to turn back and repent of a promise made to the Madonna? When I made that vow, I made it with all my heart,' said Lucia, deeply stirred by the upsurge of a feeling which we can only describe as hope, and by the fears which rose up to counter that hope – fears fortified by many considerations with which her mind had been busy for a long time.

'A sin, my daughter?' said Father Cristoforo. 'A sin to have recourse to the Church and to ask her minister to use the power that he has received from her, which she has received from God? I have seen how you two were brought together in the intention to marry; and if ever two young people seemed to me to be brought together by God it was you. Now I can't see for what reason he should wish you to be set apart. And I bless him for having given me the power, unworthy as I am, to speak in his name, and to free you from your vow. And if you ask me to declare you free I shall do it without the slightest hesitation. In fact I hope you will ask me to do so.'

'Well then! I do ask you to!' said Lucia, whose face now showed no other confusion except that caused by her modesty.

The friar beckoned to Renzo, who had been standing in the farthest corner of the hut, a fascinated observer (since he could play no other part) of the dialogue which meant so much to him. After the young man had come up to them, the friar raised his voice a little and said to Lucia:

'By virtue of the authority which the Church has given me, I declare you free of your vow of virginity, setting aside any steps you may have undertaken without due thought, and cancelling every obligation that you may have taken upon yourself.'

The reader can imagine the effect that those words had upon Renzo. He gave Father Cristoforo a glance of heartfelt thanks, and then quickly tried to catch Lucia's eye, but without success.

'And now you must return in safety and in peace to the thoughts that filled your mind before,' the Capuchin went on. 'You must pray again for the divine grace that you prayed for in the beginning, to help you to be a holy wife. You must have faith that he will grant you that grace in even fuller measure, after all that you have suffered. And you, Renzo,' he went on, turning towards the young man, 'remember this: if the Church now gives you back this companion in life, she does not do so to provide you with a temporal and earthly happiness, which, even if perfect in its kind and without any admixture of bitterness, must still finish in a great sorrow when the time comes for you to leave each other; she does so to set you both on the road to that happiness which has no end. Love each other as fellow-travellers on that road, remembering that you must part some day, and hoping to be reunited later for all time. Give thanks to the Power that has led you to this blessed state not by the path of turbulent and passing pleasures, but by the path of toil and affliction, to bring you to a steady and tranquil gladness of heart. If God grants you children, you must endeavour to bring them up for him, and to instil in them the love of him and of all men; for if you do that you will surely guide them well in all else ... Lucia! Has Renzo spoken to you of someone else that he has seen in this place?'

'Yes, father, he has!'

'Then pray for that man! Do not tire of praying for him! And pray for me too ... My children! I want you to have something to remind you of your old friar.'

He put his hand into his basket and took out a box, made of ordinary wood but shaped and polished to the degree of perfection commonly associated with the work of the Capuchins.

'In here', he said, 'is what remains of that bread ... the first bread I ever begged; you know the story. I leave it to you. Keep it carefully and show it to your children. They will be born into sad times, in a sad world, among proud and overbearing men. Tell them they must forgive ... always forgive, no matter what it may be ... and tell them too to pray for the poor old friar!'

He held the box out to Lucia, who took it with the respect due to a holy relic. Then he went on in a calmer voice:

'But now tell me, Lucia; what help can you hope for in Milan? Where are you going to stay when you leave this place? And who will take you back to your mother, if she is still in health, as I pray God she may be?'

'This kind lady is looking after me like a mother in the meantime. We shall leave here together, and then she will take care of all that needs to be done.'

'God bless her for it!' said the friar, coming closer to the bed.

'First of all I must thank you, father,' said the widow, 'for the happiness you have given to these two poor souls; though I'd been hoping to keep the dear girl with me for ever. Well, I'll keep her with me for the meanwhile, and later on I'll take her back to her village, back to her mother.'

She paused and went on in an undertone:

'And I'm going to give her her trousseau. I've got more worldly goods than I need, and no one to share them with me.'

'In that way', said the friar, 'you can make a fine sacrifice to God, and do good to your neighbour at the same time. I won't recommend Lucia to your care, for I can see that she's like a daughter to you already. We can only praise the Lord, who shows himself a loving father even when he chastises us, and has shown so clearly his love for you two by bringing you together in this place . . . – and now, come on my boy,' he said, turning to Renzo, and taking him by the hand. 'You and I have nothing further to do here, and we have been here too long already. We must be off!'

'Dear Father Cristoforo!' said Lucia. 'Shall I see you again? It's hard that I should be cured, though I'm no use at all in this world, while you . . .'

'It's a long time now,' said the old man in grave and gentle tones, 'since I first asked the Lord to grant me a favour – and a great favour at that – to be allowed to finish my life in the service of my neighbour. If he is going to grant me my prayer, everyone who cares for me must help me to thank him. And now, if you have any messages for your mother, give them to Renzo.'

'Tell her what you've seen,' said Lucia to her betrothed. 'Tell her I've found a second mother here, and that she and I will come to the village as soon as we can, and that I hope and pray to find her well.'

'I've got all the money that you sent me; I've got it here,' said Renzo, 'so if you need any . . .'

'No, no,' said the widow. 'I've got more than enough.'

684

'Let's go, then,' repeated the friar.

'Good-bye, then, Lucia; and may we meet again soon – and you, too, God bless you, madam,' said Renzo, not finding the words he needed to express his feelings properly.

'Perhaps the Lord will give all of us the happiness of meeting again!' cried Lucia.

'God be with you both always, and bless you,' said Father Cristoforo to Lucia and her companion; and then he led Renzo out of the hut.

It was almost evening, and the weather seemed closer to breaking than ever. The friar again offered to put Renzo up for the night in his hut. 'I can't offer you much in the way of company,' he said, 'but at least you'll be under cover.'

But Renzo felt an overpowering need for movement; and he had no wish to stay any longer in a place like that if he could not see Lucia, and could not even spend any more time with the good father. As far as time and weather were concerned, we may say that day and night, sun and rain, gentle breeze and howling gale were all one to him at that moment. So he thanked the friar, and said that he wanted to go off and find Agnese as soon as possible.

Father Cristoforo and Renzo walked back along the central path. The friar grasped the young man's hand and said:

'If you find our good Agnese, as I pray to God that you will, give her my greetings. Tell her, and anyone else who still survives and still remembers Father Cristoforo, to pray for him. And now God be with you, and bless you always.'

'Dear Father Cristoforo! When shall we meet again? When?'

'In Heaven, I hope.' The friar turned and walked away. Renzo watched him out of sight, and then walked quickly towards the gate, glancing left and right with a final look of compassion at that place of sorrows. There was an unusual bustle going on. *Monatti* were running here and there; people's possessions were being shifted here and there; coverings were being put over the windows of the huts; convalescents hobbled towards the nearest portico to shelter from the coming storm.

Chapter 37

RENZO passed through the gates of the lazaretto, and turned to the right to look for the path which had brought him through the fields to the city walls that morning. No sooner had he begun to do so than a few big drops began to fall, looking almost like hailstones, as they struck and bounced along the dry, white surface of the road, each kicking up a minute cloud of dust. In a few moments it was raining heavily, and before Renzo reached the path he wanted, it was coming down in buckets. But Renzo was far from being disturbed by the rain; he revelled in it in fact, enjoying the freshness, the rustling, the stirring of grass and foliage, as the trembling, dripping leaves recovered their shining greenness. He drew in great deep breaths of the good air, all the more freely and vividly aware of the happy break in his luck because of the simultaneous break in the weather.

His joy would have been even fuller and more unmixed if he had been able to foresee what followed a couple of days later. The rain literally washed the pestilence away. Though the lazaretto could not return to the land of the living all of the patients who were still alive at the time of the storm, it would swallow up no fresh victims afterwards. In another week there would be no more nailed-up doors, the shops would be open, and almost all the talk would be of quarantine. Of the pestilence itself only a few odd cases would still appear – the aftermath which a plague of that sort always leaves behind it for time.

So Renzo trudged on happily enough, without any plan when, how or where he would seek a night's lodging, nor indeed whether he would do so at all. All he cared about was getting on with his journey, getting back to his village as soon as possible to find someone he could talk to, and tell his story to, and above all to be able to set off again as soon as possible

Pasturo, to find Agnese. As he walked on, his memory was full of confused pictures of the day's events; but amid the scenes of misery, horror and danger that thronged his mind, a cheerful voice kept on breaking in with the words, 'I've found her! She's out of danger! She's mine!'

And then he would cut a caper, and shake off a shower of drops all round, like a dog that has been for a swim; or again he would merely rub his hands for a moment, and stride on more ardently than before.

The scenes he passed as he went along the road reminded him of the thoughts that he had, so to speak, left there that morning and the previous day, on his way into Milan. He was especially glad to recognize the ideas which he had then tried hardest to banish from his mind – the doubts, the difficulties, the improbability of finding Lucia at all – let alone of finding her alive – amid so great a multitude of dead and dying.

'But I did find her! And she is alive!' he concluded.

Then he began thinking about the worst moments of the day; he imagined himself standing there with the door knocker in his hand, thinking 'Will she be there, or won't she?' And then that dismal reply, which he had not even had time to take in properly before that pack of crazy brutes went for him. And then the lazaretto, that morass! Talk about needles in a haystack! But he had found her!

His mind went back to the time when he had watched the last of the convalescents file past – what a moment that had been! What heartbreak not to find her among them! But now that did not matter at all . . . And then the women's section of the lazaretto! And then, at the moment when he least expected it, he stood behind that hut, to hear her voice! Her very own voice! And then to see her, to see her recovered from the plague! But even then there had been the obstacle of the vow, more insoluble than ever . . . But that difficulty had vanished too. And the hatred he'd felt for Don Rodrigo, that continual, gnawing hatred which had made all his burdens heavier and poisoned all his pleasures, had gone as well.

In fact it would have been difficult to imagine livelier feelings of complete happiness, but for his uncertainty about Agnese, his sad forebodings about Father Cristoforo, and the fact that the pestilence was still all around him.

He reached Sesto towards evening, and there was still no sign of an end to the rain. But Renzo was feeling fuller of energy than ever. He knew how difficult it would be to find lodging, especially in that soaked condition, and he did not try. The only discomfort he felt was caused by the pangs of hunger, for all that happy activity had long ago absorbed the small bowl of soup Father Cristoforo had given him, and would indeed have absorbed a lot more than that. So he looked round to see if there was a baker's shop open in Sesto. He found one, and bought two loaves, which were passed to him with a pair of tongs, amid all the usual ritual. He put one in his pocket and munched the other as he went on.

When he reached Monza, night had fallen; but he still managed to find the gate which led out on to the right road. But though the road was the right one, which is always a great advantage, its condition in other respects can easily be imagined, and was getting worse every moment. It was deeply sunken between two banks, like a river-bed – for all main roads were like that at the time, as we must have mentioned in an earlier chapter. At that moment the road itself really looked like a river, or perhaps an irrigation channel; and it had pot-holes every so often which were enough to have the feet off you, not to mention your shoes . . . But Renzo got on as best he could, without an oath, without an impatient gesture, without regretting his decision to continue his journey. For he reflected that each step, no matter what effort it cost, took him further along the road; and that the rain would stop when it was the will of Heaven; and that sooner or later day would break; and that when it broke the bit of road he was then travelling would be behind him.

And I would go so far as to say that he did not even think about all that except at the moments when he could not help. These were distractions from the main theme with which his mind was busy. This was a long recapitulation of the events of the miserable couple of years that had just gone by – all the complications, all the adversities, all the moments when he had been on the point of losing hope and giving up entirely, with which he contrasted the images of a future which would be so different from the past ... Lucia's home-coming and the wedding, and setting up house together. They'd have time to tell each other all their adventures, and they'd stay together for the rest of their lives.

It is hard to say how he managed when he came to a fork – whether his little knowledge of the road was enough to help him to find the right way in the darkness, or whether he left it to chance. Later on Renzo used to tell the story himself in very great detail, taking a long time over it – and everything goes to show that our anonymous author had heard it from him more than once – but even Renzo used to say that he could remember no more about that night than if he had spent it asleep in bed. At all events, when dawn came, it found him on the banks of the Adda. The rain had never stopped; but at one point it had turned from a deluge into an ordinary downpour, which had later become a fine, noiseless, steady drizzle. A layer of high, thin cloud covered the sky with an unbroken but tenuous and translucent veil, and the morning twilight enabled Renzo to see the countryside around him. His own village formed part of that landscape, and I cannot express what he felt as he saw it again. I can only say that those mountains, the near-by ridge of the Resegone, and the territory of Lecco, all seemed to belong to him personally at that moment.

Then he took a look at himself, and thought that his appearance was a little odd, as indeed he had expected it to be, from the way he felt. All his clothes were ruined, and clung tightly to his body. From head to waist he was soaked and dripping; from waist to toes he was all mud and slime. The clean bits showed up as streaks and patches on a background of dirt. And if Renzo had seen himself in a full-length mirror, with the brim of his hat limp and flopping, and his hair hanging down and stuck to his face, he would have been even more disgusted with himself. As far as fatigue was concerned, he quite possibly was tired, but he did not feel it. The coolness of dawn following on the chill of the night air and of the soaking he had had merely put new spirit into him, and made him want to walk faster.

He reached Pescate, and walked along the bank of the Adda for that final stretch, looking sadly at Pescarenico. He crossed the bridge, and quickly made his way along roads and field paths to the house of his friend and host, who had just got up, and was standing at the door looking out to see what the weather was like. He raised his eyes and saw that soaking, muddy, not to say filthy figure, which at the same time looked so gay and unembarrassed. In his whole life he had never seen a man in a worse state or in better spirits.

'Well!' he said. 'You're bright and early this morning! And in this weather too! What happened then?'

'I found her!' said Renzo. 'She was there! I found her!'

'And she hasn't got the plague?'

'She's had it and got over it, which is better still. I'll thank God and the Madonna for it as long as I live. It's a wonderful story, a tremendous story; I'll tell you all about it later on.'

'And aren't you in a mess!'

'Why, yes; I must be a really good-looking fellow now!'

'To tell you the truth, we might as well use the top half of you to scrub down the bottom half. But wait there a minute, and I'll light a good big fire for you.'

'I won't say no to that. Do you know where I was when it started to come down? I was just coming out of the lazaretto! But don't let's worry about that; the weather can mind its business, and I'll mind my own.'

Renzo's host went off and came back presently with two armfuls of brushwood. He put one lot on the floor and the other on the hearth, and with the aid of some hot coals left over from the previous evening he soon had a fine blaze going. Meanwhile Renzo had taken off his hat, shaken it a couple of times and thrown it on the floor. Then he got his doublet off, which was more difficult. Finally he took his knife out of its special trouser pocket; the sheath was as wet as if he had put it to soak over night. He laid the knife on a stool, and said:

'My poor knife has had a bad time too; but it's only water, thank God! And I was just going to ... but never mind; I'll tell you later.'

He rubbed his hands. 'And now do me another kindness

he went on. 'Go and get me that bundle I left with you; for it'll be a long time before the clothes I've got on are dry.'

His friend got the bundle and said 'I should think you must be pretty hungry. I can see that there must have been plenty to drink on the road, but I don't know about food.'

'I did get a chance to buy a couple of loaves yesterday evening, but to tell you the truth I didn't even feel them as they went down.'

'Leave it to me,' said his host, and put some water in a pot, which he hung up over the fire. 'I'm going out to do the milking,' he added. 'By the time I get back, the water will be boiling, and we'll make a good polenta. Meanwhile, you can make yourself comfortable.'

When he was alone, Renzo got off the rest of his clothes, with some difficulty, for they seemed to be glued to his skin. Then he dried himself and put on fresh clothes from head to foot. Later his friend came back and went to attend to the pot; Renzo sat down at the table and waited.

'Now I can feel that I'm tired,' he said. 'But it's a good long way that I've come. That doesn't matter though. I could talk to you all day about what I've seen. You can't imagine the state Milan is in! The horrible sights you can't help seeing, the horrible things you can't help touching! It's enough to make you feel disgusted with yourself for ever having had anything to do with them! I really feel it was just as well I had that thorough wash in the rain on the way here. And the things those gentlemen in Milan wanted to do to me! But you can hear about all that later on.

'If you could only see the lazaretto!' he continued. 'The misery there is enough to drive a man mad. But I'll tell you the whole story presently. Anyway, that's where Lucia is, and she's coming here as soon as she can, and she's going to marry me, and you'll be one of the witnesses at the wedding, and I want everyone to be happy, plague or no plague, for an hour or two at least.'

Renzo was as good as his word in the matter of being willing to talk all day about what he had seen – all the more so as it continued to drizzle, and his friend spent the whole day indoors, some of it just sitting with Renzo, and some of it tinkering with a small wine-vat that he had, and a cask, and various other jobs connected with the next vintage, in all of which Renzo did not fail to give him a hand, for he was one of those people (as he said himself) who find it more tiring to do nothing than to work. But he could not resist the temptation of going off to pay a visit to Agnese's old house, where he gazed up at one particular window, and rubbed his hands again. He made his way back without anyone seeing him, and went straight to bed.

He got up before dawn. The sky was still overcast, but the rain had stopped, and he set off for Pasturo.

It was still early morning when he got there; for he was as anxious to reach his journey's end as certain of our readers may be. He asked after Agnese, and was told that she was in good health. His informant pointed out the isolated cottage where she was living; he went up to it, and shouted to her from the road. At the sound of his voice she hurried to the window, and stood there open-mouthed, trying to say something, to utter some sound at least; but Renzo got in the first word, saying 'Lucia's had the plague and got over it; I saw her the day before yesterday. She sends her love and will soon be here. And I've many more things to tell you.'

What with her surprise at the unexpected apparition, and her pleasure at the news, and her eagerness to hear more, Agnese got out the beginning of an exclamation, and then half a question, without being able to finish either of them. Then, forgetting all the precautions that she had been taking for so long, she cried out,

'I'll come down and let you in!'

'Just a moment, though – what about the plague?' said Renzo. 'I don't think you've had it, have you?'

'No; have you?'

'Yes, I have. But that means you ought to be careful. I've just come from Milan, and, as you'll hear in a moment, I've been in the infection right up to my eyes. It's true that I've changed all my clothes; but it's a filthy thing and sometimes goes on hanging round you like a sort of witch's curse. And since the Lord

692

has spared you, I want you to take care of yourself until it's all blown over; for you're like a mother to both of us, and I hope we'll all live happily together for a good long time yet, to make up for all that we've suffered, or all that I've suffered anyway.'

'But . . .' began Agnese.

'There's no "buts" about it,' said Renzo. 'I know what you're going to say, but I'll tell you what's happened, and you'll see that the time for "buts" is past and gone. Now let's go and find an open space, out of doors, where we can talk comfortably, without any danger, and I'll tell you all about it.'

'Go in the garden behind the house,' said Agnese. 'You'll find a couple of benches there, facing each other, that might have been put like that on purpose for us. I'll be there in a moment.'

Renzo went round and sat down on one bench, and before long Agnese was sitting on the other. If the reader, knowing what had led up to this conversation, had been able to be there himself, and see with his own eyes the lively way they spoke, and hear with his own ears the tales they had to tell and the questions they had to ask; the explanations, the cries of astonishment; the expressions of sympathy and of delighted relief; the story of Don Rodrigo and Father Cristoforo and all the rest; the descriptions of the future, just as clear and definite as the narrative of the past – why, I am sure that he would have enjoyed every minute of it, and stayed until the very end. But whether he would like to have the whole conversation put before him on paper, without the sound of their words, and without a single new fact being presented to him, is more doubtful, and I think he would rather imagine it for himself.

The end of it was that all three of them should set up house together in the village in the territory of Bergamo where Renzo had a good job waiting for him. When they would do so could not be decided yet, because it depended on the plague, and on certain other circumstances. As soon as the danger was over, Agnese would go back home and wait for Lucia, unless indeed she found Lucia already waiting for her. Meanwhile Renzo would come back to Pasturo from time to time to see Agnese and tell her how things were going.

Before he left, he offered her some money, as he had to Lucia, saying, 'I've got all that cash you sent me, you know; I swore I wouldn't touch it until things were cleared up. If you need it now, bring me a dish of water and vinegar, and I'll drop those fifty bright new *scudi* into it and leave them for you.'

'No, no,' said Agnese. 'What I've got left is still more than enough for me. You keep your share, and it'll come in useful for setting up house.'

Renzo went back to his village with the further consolation of having found another person who was dear to him safe and in good health. He spent the rest of that day, and the following night, in his friend's house. The next morning he was off on his travels again, but in a different direction – towards the village which had provided him with a second home.

There he found Bortolo, who was also in the best of health, and less fearful of losing it than he had been before. For in the last few days things had taken a marked turn for the better in those parts too. Very few people were being taken ill now; and the illness was much less serious. Those deathly blotches on the skin, that violence in the symptoms, were things of the past, and the patients suffered only a slight fever, intermittent more often than not; if they had any bubonic swellings, they were small affairs, with no abnormality of colouring, which could be treated like an ordinary boil. The village had begun to take on quite another appearance. The survivors had started to come out into the open, to count their numbers and exchange condolences and congratulations. People were already talking about getting production going again, masters were thinking about finding and taking on new workmen, especially in the trade where there had been a shortage of labour even before the plague – and the silk-working trade was one of these.

Meanwhile he got on with the most important preparation. He found himself a larger house – which was a task that had become all too easy and relatively inexpensive. He fitted it out with furniture and household equipment; and this time he did dip into that store of *scudi*, though without making a very big hole in it. For everything was cheap, since there was more stuff to sell than people to buy it.

694

After a certain period, he went back to his native village, which he found still more notably changed for the better. He hurried over to Pasturo, and found that Agnese had quite taken heart again, and was ready to go back home whenever it might be. So he escorted her there – and we shall not attempt to describe their feelings or their words as they returned to those scenes together. Agnese found everything just as she had left it. She could not help exclaiming that the angels must have guarded her cottage because it belonged to a poor widow and her poor daughter.

'That first time,' she went on, 'when we might have thought that the Lord was thinking about something else, and had forgotten us, and he let everything we had be carried off – well, then he showed us that it wasn't like that at all, by sending me that wonderful money, so that I was able to replace everything I'd lost. I mustn't say everything, though, because Lucia's trousseau, which they carried off all fresh and new with everything else, was something I hadn't been able to replace; but now that's being sent us too from somewhere else. What would I have thought, if someone had come and said to me, while I was working my fingers to the bone on that first lot, "Why, you poor thing! You think you're working for Lucia, but you're really working for someone you've never met! Heaven knows what sort of creature will end up wearing that piece of material, or those clothes! But Lucia's real trousseau, the one that'll really be used by her, will be provided by a kind soul you've never even heard of!"'

Agnese's first thought was to prepare the best accommodation she could in her modest cottage for the kind soul just mentioned; then she went off to look for some silk to spin, and so while the time away by doing something useful.

Renzo also felt no wish to remain idle during a period when the day's seemed all too long in any case. He was fortunate enough to know two different trades; and now he went back to farming. Some of the time he helped his host, who was very lucky to have an extra pair of hands to call on at a time like that, and luckier still to have someone as capable as Renzo. Some of the time he cultivated Agnese's garden, or rather broke the ground there, for it had been totally neglected during her absence. But he did not try to do anything about his own property, saying that it was in too much of a mess, and needed more than one pair of arms to put it straight. In fact he would not set foot in his vineyard, nor in his house, for it would only have distressed him to see all that desolation, and he had already decided to get rid of everything, for what it would fetch, and to make use of the money in his new home across the border.

If the survivors of the plague seemed to each other like men risen from the dead, Renzo appeared to his fellow-villagers like a man who had been resurrected twice over. Everyone greeted him and congratulated him; everyone wanted to hear him tell his story. And what about the warrant out for his arrest, you may ask? That troubled him very little; in fact he hardly thought about it now, supposing that those who could have carried it out had stopped thinking about it themselves – and he was quite right. That was partly because of the plague, which had swept so many things away; but there was another reason too. As the reader will have noticed in other parts of the story, it was a common experience at the time that decrees of all kinds, whether directed against classes of people or against individuals, often had no lasting effect. If a decree led to a definite result immediately after it was promulgated, that was another matter; or if some powerful private resentment intervened to keep it alive and operative. But otherwise the decrees were like musket balls, which, if they missed their target in the first place, lie peacefully on the ground and harm nobody.

And indeed that followed naturally from the generous way in which the decrees were strewn abroad. There are only twenty-four hours in the day, and the extra time spent on issuing new orders meant that there was correspondingly less time to ensure that the old ones were carried out. What you spend on ribbons cannot be spent on lace.

If anyone wants to know how Renzo got on with Don Abbondio during this interval, I must inform him that they kept away from each other. Don Abbondio did so for fear of having to listen to more about weddings – at the very thought of which Don Rodrigo rose up before his eyes on the one sid with his bravoes, and the Cardinal on the other with his arguments. Renzo had decided not to speak to the priest until the last moment, because he did not want to make him take fright before the time came, to stir up some unforeseen difficulty, or to confuse things by a lot of unnecessary gossip. The gossiping he did was done with Agnese. 'D'you think she'll soon be here?' one would ask the other. 'I'm sure she will!' the other would reply; and often it would not be long before the one who had answered the question was asking it again. And with tricks like this they managed to get through a period of waiting that seemed to get longer instead of shorter as the days went by.

But we can make that period pass in a flash for our readers, by relating briefly how, a few days after Renzo's visit to the lazaretto, Lucia and her kind friend the widow came out, and went through the period of quarantine prescribed for everyone in their position, remaining shut up together in the widow's house; how part of the time was spent in preparing Lucia's trousseau, a task with which the girl, after some polite protestations, lent a hand herself; and how, when the quarantine was over, the widow left the shop and the house in the charge of her brother the *commissario*, and they began to get ready for the journey.

We could go on to say with equal brevity that they left Milan and arrived in the village, and so with the rest of the story; but much as we wish to second the reader's laudable haste, there are three things relating to that interval which we would not like to pass over in silence. As far as two of them are concerned at least, we think that the reader will agree that it would be a mistake to leave them out.

First, when Lucia began to tell the widow again about her adventures in a more detailed and connected manner than she had been able to achieve in the excitement of her earlier confidences, she spoke more particularly about the Signora, who had given her shelter in the convent at Monza. The widow replied with some information about the Signora which explained many things that had been puzzling Lucia, and which filled her with sorrow and timid astonishment. The wretched woman had fallen under suspicion of having committed the

697

most abominable actions, and had been transferred, on the Cardinal's instructions, to a nunnery in Milan, where after much fury and many struggles she had finally come to her senses and confessed her crimes. She had now chosen so agonizing a course of voluntary penance that no one could have devised anything harsher without endangering her life. If anyone wants to know more of the detail of this tragic story, he will find it in the same section of the same book which we have quoted before in connection with this unhappy woman.[1]

Secondly, Lucia asked all the Capuchins she could find in the lazaretto for news of Father Cristoforo, and finally heard, sadly but without surprise, that he had died of the plague.

Thirdly, before leaving Milan, she went to find out what had happened to her previous protectors, and to perform her duty, to use her own words, by taking leave of them. She and the widow went to Don Ferrante's house, where they learned that he and his wife had both gone to join the great majority. As far as Donna Prassede was concerned, to say that she was dead left nothing more to say; but as Don Ferrante was a learned man our anonymous author felt that he ought to go into rather more detail. Entirely at our own risk, we propose to transcribe his words very much as they have come down to us.

He tells us that when people first began to talk of there being a plague, Don Ferrante rejected the idea as resolutely as anyone, and that he maintained his opinion to the end with great constancy; not in a noisy, ignorant manner like the common people, but with a series of arguments whose logical connection, at least, could be denied by no one.

'In the nature of things,' he would say, 'there are only two kinds of entity – substances and accidents. If I prove that contagion cannot be either the one or the other, I shall have proved that it does not exist, that it is a mirage. And here I am to do that very thing.

'Substances must be either spiritual or material. That contagion can be a spiritual substance is so great a folly that no one

1. Ripamonti, *Historiae patriae*, Fifth Decade, Book VI, Chapter III. (And see also the bibliography on page 15 of the present edition. – Translator's note.)

would defend it, and it is therefore pointless to discuss it.

'Material substances must be either simple or compound. Now contagion cannot be a simple substance, and this can be shown in half a dozen words. It is not an aerial substance, for if it were, instead of passing from one body to another, it would fly straight up to its sphere. Nor is it a watery substance, for then it would appear as a dampness and be dried up by the winds. It is not a fiery substance, for then it would burn away. It is not an earthy substance, for then it would be visible.

'Not yet can it be a compound substance, for then it must at least be perceptible to either sight or touch – and who has seen the contagion, or who has touched it?

'We still have to consider if it can be an accident. But that is worse still. These distinguished doctors tell us that the contagion is transferred from one body to another; for this is their argument of arguments, this is their excuse for issuing so much silly advice. So, if it is an accident, it must be a transferable accident. But these are two words which clash horribly, for in all philosophy there is nothing clearer or more perspicuous than the fact that an accident cannot pass from one body to another. And if they try to avoid this Scylla by saying that it is a produced accident, they fall into the maw of Charybdis – for if it is produced, it cannot be communicated or propagated, as they foolishly maintain.

'These principles having been established, what is the use of these gentlemen coming to us with their talk of livid blotches, exanthemata and carbuncles . . .'

'Just a lot of meaningless words, in fact!' one of his listeners exclaimed on one occasion.

'No, no!' replied Don Ferrante. 'I don't say that at all! Science is science; it's all a matter of making the right use of it. Livid blotches, exanthemata, carbuncles, parotitis, purplish abscesses, blackish pustules, are all perfectly respectable words, that have their own good and legitimate meanings. What I do say is that they have nothing to do with the question. No one can deny that these things may exist – that they do exist, in fact. The thing is to be able to see where they come from.'

But here Don Ferrante himself began to get into trouble. As

long as he confined himself to attacking the idea of an infection in general terms, he found willing and receptive hearers everywhere, for there is no limit to the authority a man of learning can command when he sets about proving something which his fellow-men already believe. But when he went on to draw his distinctions, and to show that the error of the doctors did not lie in their statement that a general and most terrible malady was abroad, but in the reasons to which they attributed it – that was when things went wrong. (We are speaking now of the early days, when no one wanted to hear the word 'plague' mentioned.) He soon began to find himself confronted not with willing ears but with rebellious, intractable tongues. It was no longer possible to deliver a proper lecture on the subject, and his learned message could only be put forward in bits and pieces.

'There is unfortunately a genuine reason for all this,' he would say, 'and it cannot be denied even by those who support that other vague nonsense. I'd like to hear them deny the existence of that fatal conjunction of Saturn with Jupiter! When, I'd like to hear, has anyone ever maintained that planetary influences can be propagated? And are those gentlemen going to deny the existence of planetary influences? Are they going to deny the existence of the heavenly bodies themselves? Or to tell me that they just stay up there in heaven without doing anything, like so many pin-heads sticking out of a pincushion? But the thing I can't get over is the attitude of those medical gentlemen. They admit that we're living under the threat of a fearful conjunction like that, and yet they have the nerve to come to us and say: "Don't touch this, and don't touch that, and you'll be all right!" As if avoiding the material contact of earthly objects could impede the powerful working of the heavenly bodies! And all that wasted labour of burning rags! Poor wretches! Can you burn Jupiter? Can you burn Saturn?'

His fretus – or, in other words, basing himself on these fine suppositions – he took no precautions whatever against the plague. He caught it in due course, took to his bed, and died, like a hero of Metastasio, quarrelling with the stars.

And that famous library of his? It may well be still lying around on the secondhand bookstalls.

Chapter 38

ONE evening, Agnese heard a carriage stop at the door. 'That must be Lucia!' she cried, and this time it really was Lucia with her kind friend the widow. We will leave the reader to imagine how they greeted each other.

Early the next morning Renzo arrived, not knowing what had happened, but intending to have a good grumble with Agnese about the length of time it was taking Lucia to get there. How he looked, and what he said, when he found himself face to face with her, is another thing that we will leave to the reader's imagination. But Lucia's behaviour on that occasion was of a kind which we can describe in a few words. She kept her eyes lowered and did not lose her composure, as she said,

'Good day to you, Renzo; and how are you?'

And it must not be thought that Renzo found her manner too formal, or that he was offended by it. He took it exactly in the spirit in which it was meant. Just as educated people know how to discount the flattery in a compliment, so Renzo knew how to allow for the fact that those words did not express all that was passing through Lucia's heart. Besides anyone could see that she had two different ways of saying them – one for Renzo and one for everyone else.

'I'm all the better for seeing you,' said the young man. Though the phrase was an old one, he would have invented it himself at that moment in any case.

'Poor Father Cristoforo!' said Lucia. 'You must pray for his soul, though it's as good as certain that he's already up there in heaven praying for us.'

'It's what I expected, more's the pity,' said Renzo.

And that was the only sad note they touched during their conversation. But whatever they talked about, it was still a most delightful conversation to Renzo. If we think of a nervous horse, that jibs and refuses to go on, and lifts one hoof after another, always putting them down in the same place, and goes through dozens of tricks before it will budge an inch, and then suddenly is off like the wind – that is how time seemed to have been behaving to Renzo. Until that moment the minutes had seemed like hours, and now the hours seemed like minutes.

The widow did not spoil the reunion; in fact she fitted into the company very well. When Renzo had first seen her in that bed in the hut, he had never dreamt that she could be so good-humoured and sociable. But then the lazaretto is a different matter from a country village, and death is a far cry from weddings. By this time she had made friends with Agnese; and it was a joy to see her with Lucia – such affection, such gentle banter, rallying her so tactfully; never going too far, but just far enough to make the girl show all the happiness that was in her heart.

Renzo finally remarked that he had better go and see Don Abbondio and make the arrangements for the wedding; and off he went to the priest's house.

'Well, your Reverence,' he said, in a joking yet respectful manner, 'I expect that by now you'll have got over that head-ache you told me about which prevented you from marrying us before? Now we're all ready; the bride's here too, and I've come to ask you when it would suit you to perform the cere-mony. But this time I will ask you not to be too long about it.'

Don Abbondio did not refuse; but he began to shilly-shally, to find certain fresh excuses, and to make certain fresh insinu-ations. Why should Renzo want to appear in public, and have his name shouted abroad, with that warrant for his arrest still outstanding? The wedding could just as well take place some-where else ... and so on.

'I understand,' said Renzo. 'That headache of yours hasn't quite cleared up yet. But now let me tell you something else.' And he began to describe the state in which he had last seen the unfortunate Don Rodrigo, and said that he must most certainly have departed this life by now.

'We must hope that the Lord has been merciful to him,' he concluded.

'But that has nothing to do with it!' said Don Abbondio. 'Did I say I wouldn't marry you? I'm not saying I won't. What I'm saying is ... is said for the best of reasons. And anyway, you know, while there's life there's hope ... Look at me now; I'm one of the weaker vessels, all right, and I've been more than halfway into the valley of the shadow myself, yet here I am. And if more troubles don't overtake me, I may hope to stay here a bit longer. So what about people with constitutions like ... but, as I was saying, all this is beside the point.'

After a few more thrusts and parries, no more conclusive than what had gone before, Renzo bowed deeply and went back to his friends. He told them the story, and finished with the words:

'And then I came back, for I'd had enough of it, and I didn't want to lose my temper, and show him less respect than is his due. But some of the time he was exactly the same as he was a couple of years ago – the same stuck-up look, and the same old arguments. I'm sure if I'd stayed just a little bit longer he'd have started talking Latin to me again. I can see that it's going to be another of these long-drawn-out affairs. The best thing'll be to take his advice, and get married in the place where we're going to live.'

'I'll tell you what,' said the widow, 'why shouldn't we women go and try our hand with him, and see if we get on any better? Then I shall have the pleasure of meeting your Don Abbondio, and seeing if he's really like you say he is. Let's go after dinner, for it wouldn't do to attack him again straight away. And now, while Agnese is busy, perhaps the bridegroom will take Lucia and myself for a walk. I'll look after Lucia like a mother; and I want to have a better look at your hills and your lake, which I've heard so much about, and which seem to be so beautiful from the little I've seen of them so far.'

Renzo started by taking them to the house of the friend with whom he had stayed. More greetings and rejoicings followed, and they made him promise to come and have dinner with them, not only on that particular day, but whenever he could.

After the walk was over, and the dinner, Renzo went quietly off without saying where he was going. The women sat and discussed the matter a little further, and decided what would be the best way to get Don Abbondio to do what they wanted. Finally they went off to the attack.

'It never rains but it pours,' were the words that passed through the priest's mind when he saw them. But he put a bold face on it, with congratulations to Lucia on her escape from death, polite greetings to Agnese, and compliments to the stranger. He had chairs brought for them, and at once began talking about the plague. He wanted Lucia to tell him all about what had happened to her in those terrible conditions; mention of the lazaretto enabled him to get the widow to tell him her story as well; and then, as was only fair, Don Abbondio told them about his own illness. Then came expressions of happy wonder that Agnese had escaped the contagion completely. It seemed as if all this would never end. The two older women had been on the alert from the beginning for an opportunity to introduce the all-important subject, and finally one of them did succeed in bringing it up. But what could anyone expect? That was Don Abbondio's deaf ear.

It was not that he said 'no' in so many words; but he began zigzagging again, and fluttering, and hopping from twig to twig.

'First of all,' he said, 'we must find a way of getting that wretched warrant cancelled. Now you, madam, living in Milan as you do, must know the way these things go to a greater or lesser extent. You probably have influential friends, some powerful nobleman perhaps, and that's the way to overcome any difficulty. Or if you want to do it the quickest way, without going to such lengths, why, since the young couple, and our good Agnese here, are thinking of leaving the country – and I can't blame them, for it's a true saying that a man's country is where he's well off – it seems to me that you might as well do the whole thing on the other side of the border, where the warrant isn't valid anyway.

'I can't wait to see this match finally concluded; but I want it to be concluded properly and peacefully. I'll be quite frank with you now: to do it here, with that warrant still out, and still valid; to proclaim that famous name of Lorenzo Tramaglino from the steps of the altar – why, it's something I wouldn't like to do at all. I'm too fond of him; I'd be afraid of doing him a bad service. You can see it for yourself, madam; you can all see it for yourselves.'

Agnese and the widow joined forces to refute those arguments; and Don Abbondio reintroduced them one after another in a different form, and so on from the beginning again, until finally Renzo came in, with firm tread and a look of important news in his face.

'The Marquis of — has arrived!' he announced.

'What do you mean? Arrived where?' said Don Abbondio, jumping up.

'He's arrived in his palace, which is the one that used to belong to Don Rodrigo. The marquis has inherited it by entail, as they say, so there's no doubt about what's happened. For my part, I'd be pleased enough, if I could be sure that poor man had made a good end. Well, anyway, I've been saying Paternosters for him up to today, and now I'll say the De Profundis ... The marquis is a very good man, they say.'

'That's certain enough,' said Don Abbondio. 'I've heard of him many a time as a very fine gentleman, and one of the old school. But is it really true ...?'

'Would you believe the sexton?'

'Why do you ask?'

'Because he's seen the marquis with his own eyes. I've only been in the neighbourhood of the palace, and to tell the truth the reason I went was because I thought they'd know more about it down there. And I met several people who all told me the same thing. And then I met Ambrogio, who'd been right up to the palace and had seen the marquis there as the new master of the estate. Would you like to speak to Ambrogio? I've got him waiting outside, just in case.'

'Yes, let's hear what he has to say,' said Don Abbondio.

Renzo went out and fetched the sexton, who confirmed all that had been said, and added further details, so that there could be no doubt about it. Then he went home.

'Ah! So he *is* dead! He's really gone!' exclaimed Don Abbondio. 'See, my children, how Providence does in the end overtake people like that! Why, this is a wonderful thing! A great relief for this poor countryside! For he was a man you really couldn't live with. The plague has been a great scourge; but we may fairly say that it has also functioned as a broom, and swept certain individuals away, my children, who seemed to be there for ever. Men who were young, strong and in the best of health, so that we might have thought that the priest who would bury them was probably still in the seminary, learning his Latin grammar. And now, in the twinkling of an eye, those individuals have vanished, dozens of them at a time. We shan't see Don Rodrigo stalking around again with his bravoes at his heels, and his arrogance, and his airs and graces, and that look as if he'd swallowed a ramrod, and that way of gazing at people as if we were all in this world by his special grace and favour. Well, he's gone and we're still here. He won't send any more of those messages of his to decent people. He gave us all a lot of trouble, a lot of misery; and now we can say so freely.'

'I've forgiven him with all my heart,' said Renzo.

'And you did your duty when you forgave him,' said Don Abbondio. 'But we may also thank Heaven for freeing us from his presence ... But now, coming back to our own affairs, let me repeat what I was saying just now. You others must do whatever you want to. If you want me to marry you, here I am; if you'd rather do it some other way, you're free to do so. As far as the warrant is concerned, I too can see that now there's no one watching out for a chance to do you a bad turn, we needn't worry so much about that – especially as we've had that gracious and merciful decree on the occasion of the birth of the royal prince. And then there's been the plague, which has wiped so many things off the slate. So if you like ... let me see. Today's Thursday. I'll call your banns in church on Sunday; I know I called them once before, but that was so long ago that it doesn't count any more. And then I'll have the pleasure of marrying you myself.'

'Why, sir, you know very well that's what we're here for!' said Renzo.

'Excellent! Excellent! And I'll do what you ask. I must report all this to His Eminence as soon as I can.'

'Who's His Eminence then?' asked Agnese.

'His Eminence,' replied Don Abbondio, 'is our Cardinal Archbishop, may God preserve him.'

'Oh! You must pardon me there,' said Agnese, 'for though I'm only a poor ignorant woman, I can assure you that that's not the right way to address him; because the second time we had the chance to talk to him, just like I'm talking to you now, one of those clerical gentlemen took me on one side, and told me how to speak to him, and that I must always say "Your Grace" or "Monsignore".'

'And now, if he were going to give you a second lesson, he'd tell you to call him "Your Eminence". Do you understand, now? The Pope, whom God preserve also, has given instructions that from June of this year the title of "Eminence" should be given to Cardinals. And do you know why His Holiness decided on that step? Because the title of "Your Grace", which used to be reserved for Cardinals and certain princes – why, you can see for yourselves what it's become, how many people it's given to – and how they love it! So what was the Pope to do? Tell them to stop using it? That would have meant grumbling, requests for exemption, ill will and general trouble, and wouldn't have made any difference – they'd have gone on using it just the same. So he's found a very good way out of the difficulty. Later, of course, they'll start calling bishops "Your Eminence"; and then abbots; and then provosts. For human beings are like that, and always want to climb a little higher. Then it'll be the canons...'

'... and the parish priests,' said the widow.

'No, no,' said Don Abbondio quickly, 'parish priests will munch hay and pull between the shafts till the end of time. You needn't worry about anyone killing them with kindness. "Your Reverence" is all that they'll be called until the last day. But what wouldn't surprise me at all would be if the noblemen who've got used to being called "Your Grace" like the Cardinals were formerly, should want to be called "Your Eminence" now. And if that's what they want, mark my words, they'll find people to do it. And the Pope who's in office then will have to find something newer still for the Cardinals. But let's get back

707

to our own affairs. I'll call your banns on Sunday, then; and do you know what I've just thought of to make you happier still? In the meantime we'll ask for a dispensation for the second and third times of asking. They must be pretty busy down in the consistory, giving out dispensations, if it's the same everywhere else as it is here. I've got one . . . two . . . three . . . couples on my hands for next Sunday, without counting you two, and I shouldn't be surprised if some more come along as well. And you can see what it's going to be like, from now on – everyone's going to pair off. The biggest mistake Perpetua ever made was to die when she did, for this is just the moment when she'd have found a customer herself. And I should imagine, madam, that it's much the same in Milan.'

'You're quite right there! In my parish alone there were fifty lots of banns called last Sunday.'

'That's it! That's it! This world isn't in a hurry to put up the shutters. And what about yourself, madam? Haven't you had some busy bees buzzing around you?'

'No, no; I'm not thinking about that, and don't want to think about it.'

'Naturally, naturally, if you prefer the single life. But there's Agnese, too, isn't there? There's Agnese, too . . .'

'Why, you must be trying to make us laugh!' said Agnese.

'That's true enough; for it seems to me that the season for laughter is with us now, and none too soon at that. We've seen some ugly times, my dear young people, ugly times in plenty . . . we may fairly hope for better things during the few years that still lie before us in this world. But all of you are in luck, for if all goes well you should have quite some time to spend talking over your past troubles. But the hands of my clock stand at a quarter to twelve, and . . . well, scoundrels may die; people may have the plague and get better; but there's no cure for anno domini. *Senectus ipsa est morbus,*[1] as they say.'

'Now, sir, you may talk all the Latin you please, and I shan't mind at all,' said Renzo.

'So you're still against Latin, are you? Well, I'll see to you when you come before me with this young woman to have a

1. 'Old age itself is a disease.'

few words of Latin pronounced over your heads. "Be off with you!" I'll say, "for I know you've no use for Latin!" Will that be all right?'

'I'm clear enough in my own mind about all that,' said Renzo. 'That's not the sort of Latin I'm afraid of. That's an honest, holy sort of Latin like you get at Mass; and besides, you clerical gentlemen have to read what's written in the book in those cases. No, no; I was talking about that blackguardly, out-of-church Latin, which creeps up behind a man in the middle of a conversation. For instance, now that we've reached this point and it's all over – you must remember all that Latin you dug up a long time ago, in this very room, in that corner over there, to tell me that you couldn't marry us, and that all sorts of other things needed to be done first, and so on. Why don't you tell me plainly now what all that meant?'

'Be quiet now, you stupid fellow, and don't stir all that up again, for if we were to make up our books properly, I don't know who'd be better off. I've forgotten and forgiven everything now, and don't let's say anything more about it, but you certainly played some tricks on me. I'm not worried about you, for we all know what a young rascal you are; but what about Miss Still-Waters-Run-Deep here, this demure young lady, this little plaster saint, who'd make you feel you'd committed a sin if you didn't trust her? But there, I know who put those ideas in her head, I know very well.'

With the last few words he switched his accusingly pointing finger from Lucia to Agnese; and it would be hard to describe how pleasantly and jovially he delivered his reproof. The news he had heard had given him an easy manner and a chatty flow of conversation which he had not displayed for a very long time; and we would still have a long way to go if we were to report the remainder of this talk in full. For Don Abbondio kept on drawing it out, holding his guests back more than once when they tried to leave, and making them stop again for a few minutes at the front door while he talked some more nonsense.

The following day Don Abbondio had a visit, quite unexpected but all the more welcome for that, from the very marquis of whom they had been speaking. He was a man in late middle age, whose face was like a certificate of all that people said about him – frank, courteous, calm, modest and dignified. There was also something about him which indicated a resigned sorrow.

'I have come to bring you the greetings of the Cardinal Archbishop,' he said.

'Ah, what noble condescension – on both your parts!'

'When I went to take my leave of that admirable man, who honours me with his friendship, he mentioned two young people of this parish, who were going to be married, and had a good deal of trouble with the unfortunate Don Rodrigo. His Grace wanted to have news of them. Are they still alive, and have their problems been solved?'

'Yes, sir, all's well with them now. In fact I was about to write to His Eminence about them; but now that I have the honour . . .'

'Are they in the village here?'

'Yes, sir, and they'll be man and wife as soon as it can be arranged.'

'Then I must ask you if there's anything I can do for them, and what the best way of helping them would be. In this terrible calamity I've lost my two children, and their mother; and at the same time I've inherited three considerable estates. As I had more than I needed before, you can see that giving me a chance to use some of it, especially for a purpose like this, is to do me a real favour.'

'God bless you, sir! It's a pity there aren't more like you among the . . . but never mind that; I thank you from the bottom of my heart on behalf of these children of mine. And since your noble Lordship is so kind as to encourage me, why, yes, there is a way of helping them that I could suggest, and which might meet with your approval. I must explain that these good people have decided to sell up the little bit of property they have in the village, and go off and set up house somewhere else. The young fellow's got a small vineyard, one and a half acres, I suppose, but very neglected at the moment, so that the value is just that of the land; and then he's got one cottage, and his bride's got another – very humble affairs, both of them.

'Now a gentleman in your Lordship's position can't realize what happens to poor folk, when they have to sell up. Their property always ends up in the hands of some cunning ruffian, who's probably had his eye on those few square yards of land for years, but when he knows that the other poor folk have got to sell, he backs off, and pretends not to be interested. So the poor seller has to run after him, and let him have it for a song; and all the more so at times like these. Your Lordship can see what I'm getting at. The most splendid act of kindness you could do to those poor folk would be to get them out of that difficulty, by buying their bit of property.

'I must admit that it's not exactly disinterested advice that I'm giving here, for I'd dearly like to have your Lordship for one of my parishioners. But anyway, you'll decide as seems best to yourself; I've done my duty in replying to your Lordship's question.'

The marquis had nothing but praise for the suggestion. He thanked Don Abbondio, and asked him to fix the price, and to fix it at a generous level. Then he amazed the priest by suggesting a visit to the bride's house, where, as he remarked, they might quite possibly find the bridegroom as well.

On the way there Don Abbondio, all jubilant, as the reader can well imagine, had another idea, which he also mentioned to the marquis.

'Since your Lordship is so interested in doing good to these people, perhaps I may mention another thing that could be done for them. The young man's got a warrant out for him, a sort of summons – it's because of some silly tricks he got up to in Milan, two years ago, on the day when there was all that trouble; he got involved somehow, without any malice on his part, out of pure ignorance, like an animal falling into a trap. It wasn't anything serious, you know – some stupid, boyish prank. He couldn't do anything really wrong – and I should know, for I've baptized him and watched him grow up. And if your Lordship has a fancy to hear these poor folk talk in their artless way, you can get him to tell you the story himself, and you'll see. At the moment, since it's ancient history, no one is giving him any trouble about it. And, as I mentioned, he is planning to settle across the border anyway. But later on, if he comes back here, or something, you never know what may happen. I'm sure you'd be the first to tell me that he'd be better off not to have his name written down in that particular book. Now in Milan, my lord, you have the influence that rightly belongs to a great noble, and a great man, such as you are ... but no, sir, let me finish, for truth will out, after all. A recommendation, just a couple of words from a man like your Lordship, is more than enough to get him a free pardon.'

'So there are no serious charges against this young fellow?'

'No, sir, I think not. The whole thing was greatly exaggerated to begin with; but now I believe it's just a matter of a simple formality.'

'In that case it won't be a difficult matter, and I'll gladly accept responsibility for it.'

'I can't think why your Lordship objects to being called a great man. I said it before, and I'll say it again, with or without your permission. And even if I didn't, it wouldn't make any difference, because other people will talk, and *vox populi, vox Dei*.'[2]

The three women and Renzo were all there. You can picture how astonished they were; for I think the bare rough walls, the primitive curtains, the stools and the crockery must all have been amazed too to see such an extraordinary visitor in their midst.

The marquis set the conversation going; he spoke of the Cardinal and the other matters with unaffected cordiality, and also with the most delicate tact. Then he went on to put forward the proposal which was the object of his visit. He invited Don Abbondio to fix the price. The priest came forward, and, after making some ceremonious protestations, and saying that it wasn't really his line of country, and that he was quite in the dark about that sort of thing and would only speak from a sense of duty towards his Lordship, and that he would rather be excused from making a suggestion, he finally named a figure which in his eyes was absurdly high.

The buyer said that he, for his part, was very pleased with the

2. 'The voice of the people is the voice of God.'

bargain. But when he came to repeat the sum, there seemed to be some mistake, for the figure was now double what it had been before. The marquis would not hear of any correction to what he had said, and brought the discussion to an end by inviting the whole company to dinner in his palace for the day after the wedding, and saying that the papers could be signed then.

'Why, now,' said Don Abbondio to himself when he was back at home, 'if that were the sort of result we could expect the plague to have every time, everywhere, it would be very wrong of us to complain about it. It would be almost worth having one every generation, even if one had to catch the disease oneself – provided one got over it, of course.'

The dispensation came, and so did the free pardon; and last of all came the happy day itself. The betrothed couple went triumphantly and safely to their very own church, and were married by none other than Don Abbondio. It was an additional triumph for them, and a far more extraordinary one, to go up to the marquis's palace; and I leave it to you to think what things must have passed through their minds as they climbed the slope, and went in at the great door, and what they must have said, each in his or her own style. I will only say that, in the midst of all their happiness, first one of them and then another mentioned that the party was not and could not be complete without poor Father Cristoforo.

'But then there's no doubt that he's in a better place than we are,' they added.

The marquis greeted them most warmly, and took them to a fine room in the servants' quarters, where places were laid for bride and groom, and for Agnese and the widow. He saw them seated at table, and before taking Don Abbondio off to dine with him in another room he stayed for a little to chat with his guests, and went so far as to help serve them.

I hope none of my readers is going to have the brilliant idea that it would have been simpler all round if they had all sat down together. I have described the marquis to you as a good man, and a fine man, but not as what people might nowadays call an eccentric. I have said that he was a modest man, but not

713

that he was a portent of humility. He had enough of that quality to put himself below those good folk, but not enough to put himself on a level with them.

After both tables had been cleared, the contract was drawn up by a lawyer, who was not Dr Quibbler, for he was at Canterelli, where he still is now – his bones, that is to say. For the benefit of anyone who does not come from those parts, I can see that I should add a word of explanation.

About half a mile above Lecco, and almost alongside another township called Castello, there is a place known as Canterelli, where two roads intersect; and at one side of the crossways you can see a mound, a sort of artificial hillock, with a cross on top of it; and this is nothing but a great heap of those who died during that pestilence. To be absolutely truthful, tradition calls them merely 'the people who died in the plague', without specifying which one; but it must be the one we have been discussing, which was the last and the most murderous out-break of which memory remains. Besides we all know that traditions, unless someone lends them a hand, never give you the full story.

On the way back the only trouble was that Renzo was slightly inconvenienced by the weight of the money he was carrying. But he had carried worse burdens than that, as we know ... I will not mention the mental exertion, which was considerable, of trying to decide which was the best way of putting the money to work. The visions, the reflections and the projects which passed through the young man's head, and the argu-ments for and against, the reasons for preferring agriculture and the reasons for preferring industry, might have made you think that you were listening to a dispute between two learned societies during the eighteenth century. And for him the diffi-culty was of a much more serious kind; for since the discussion was going on in a single man's brain, there was no possibility of anyone coming along and saying, 'But why do you have to choose at all? Why not do both? The resources involved are basically the same in both cases, and having a pair of occupa-tions like those two is like having a pair of feet – you'll get a lot further with both of them than you would with just one.'

When they got back to the village, their one thought was of packing up and getting moving: the Tramaglino household to their new home across the border, and the widow back to Milan. There were many tears at parting, many expressions of gratitude, many promises of future visits. Equally heartfelt, though not so tearful, were the farewells which Renzo and his family took of the friend who had been his host. Nor must it be thought that their leave-taking from Don Abbondio passed off in chilly indifference. Those good folk had always retained a certain respectful affection for their curé, and he, in his heart, had always been fond of them too. It is so often questions of business that spoil our natural affections for each other . . .

And did they feel no sorrow at leaving their native village, and the mountains around it? They did indeed; for everything that happens brings some sorrow with it. But in this case it cannot have been a very strong feeling, since after all they could have avoided it by simply staying where they were, now that the two great stumbling-blocks, namely Don Rodrigo and the warrant, had both been removed. But all of them had become accustomed to think of the place where they were now bound as their new home. Renzo had told the two women about the advantages the place offered to a skilled workman, and endeared it further to them by a host of details about the fine life people led there. And anyway they all had plenty of bitter memories of the village on which they were turning their backs; and such memories in the long run always spoil our ideas of the place which recalls them to our mind. And if the place happens to be the one where we were born that probably gives those recollections a still more harshly unpleasant quality.

Even a baby, to quote from the old manuscript, though he will rest gladly enough on the bosom of his nurse, and will suck with avidity and trust the breast which has sweetly nurtured him for so long, yet if she rub her nipple with wormwood in order to wean the child, then will he turn his mouth aside; and though he will return and make further trial of it, yet will he leave it for ever in the end; he will leave it with tears, but for ever.

But what will the reader think when he hears that they had

715

no sooner reached their new home and settled in, than Renzo ran into a new lot of trouble, which seemed to be ready and waiting for him? They were trifles, really; but it takes so little to disturb a state of happiness!

This, in brief, is what happened: The people in that village had heard about Lucia long before she arrived there; they knew how much Renzo had had to suffer for her, and with what firmness and fidelity he had endured to the end. Perhaps some friend who had Renzo and his affairs very much at heart may have added something to the story. All this had caused a certain curious interest in Lucia's appearance, and a certain anticipation that she would be beautiful. Now anticipation is an odd thing, as we all know – imaginative, credulous, and sure of its facts before the event; difficult to please and overcritical when the time comes. Reality never seems enough to it, because it has no real idea what it wants; and it exacts a bitter price for whatever sweets it may have mistakenly supplied on credit.

When the famous Lucia finally arrived, there were many people who expected that her hair would really be of gold, and that her cheeks would really be roses, and each of her eyes more star-like than the other; and they began to shrug their shoulders and wrinkle up their noses, and say: 'What? is this really her? After all this time, and so much talk, we might have expected something better. What is she after all? A country girl like any other! You'll find girls as good-looking as that, or better, wherever you go.'

And when they came to look her over in more detail, one of them noticed one defect, and one another. There were even some people who said she was positively ugly.

But as no one went along and told Renzo all this to his face, there was not much harm done to begin with. The harm came later, when certain third parties came and told him what other people had been saying. Renzo, naturally enough, was cut to the quick. He began to turn it all over in his mind, and to complain about it bitterly, first of all to his informants, and later on to himself.

'What's it got to do with all of you?' he thought. 'Who told you to expect anything out of the way? Did I ever come and tel you about her? Did I ever say that she was beautiful? And when you started talking to me about her looks, did I ever say anything in reply except that she was a fine young woman? She's just a country girl! When did I ever tell you that I was going to bring a princess to your village? If you don't like her, you needn't look at her! You've got some pretty girls of your own here; why don't you look at them?'

Here we may note that sometimes a silly trifle can determine the whole course of a man's life. If Renzo had happened to spend the rest of his days in that village, as had been his intention, he would not have been at all happy. He had taken offence so often that he had become offensive himself. He was unpleasant to everyone, because anybody might be one of Lucia's critics. Not that he specifically broke the rules of good manners; but we all know how far a man can go without breaking them – far enough for someone to get a knife in the belly.

There was something sarcastic about everything he said, and he constantly found cause for criticism in everything that happened. If it rained two days running, he would say,

'Well, what can you expect in a place like this?'

By this time there were quite a lot of people who had taken a dislike to him, including some who had been friendly enough to begin with. If he had stayed there, one thing would have led to another, and he would have ended up at war with the whole village, though he might have been hard put to it to say how the whole thing had begun.

But it seemed as if the plague had assumed responsibility for rectifying all Renzo's errors. It had carried away the owner of another spinning-mill, which was situated almost at the gates of Bergamo. The heir was a young rake who could see nothing likely to amuse him in any part of the mill, and had decided to sell it – could hardly wait to do so, in fact, even if he only got half what it was worth. But he wanted immediate payment in cash, so that he could get on with spending it on less productive business. When Bortolo heard about this, he went off at once to see what the position was, and entered into negotiations without delay. He could not have hoped for a better bargain; but the demand for ready money spoilt everything, because the savings he had slowly and laboriously accumulated fell a long way short of what was needed.

Bortolo left the matter open, and hurried back to his village to tell Renzo about it, and to suggest that he should come in for a half share. The proposal was so attractive that it solved Renzo's investment problem in a flash. He decided in favour of industry, and accepted at once. So they went off together and concluded the deal.

When the new owners took possession, Lucia found herself in a place where nothing special was expected of her. There were no criticisms, and in fact it can be said the people there liked the look of her. It came to Renzo's ears that several people had said,

'That's a pretty young cloth-head[3] who's come to live here!'

The adjective more than made up for the noun.

And in fact the trouble that he had experienced in the other village had taught him a useful lesson. Up till then he had been a bit free in expressing his views, and had often allowed himself to criticize other people's womenfolk, and that sort of thing. But now he realized that certain words make one effect when they go out of the mouth, and quite another one when they come in at the ear; and he got a lot more into the habit of listening to the sound of his remarks inside his own head, before he opened his lips.

But of course there were some minor troubles even in the new place. You may have noticed that our anonymous author has rather an odd taste in similes, but perhaps you will allow him one further example, which, as it happens, will be the last. As long as a man stays in this world, says the manuscript, he is like an invalid lying on a bed which is always more or less uncomfortable. Around him he sees other beds, with the bedclothes to outward appearances very neatly arranged, smooth and level and he concludes that those who lie there must lie very well indeed. But if he should contrive to change, no sooner is he in his new bed, and letting his weight rest on it, than bristles in the mattress begin to prick him, and bumps begin to bruise him, so that the last state of the patient is very much like the first. An

3. The local nickname for a citizen of the Duchy of Milan. See page 33

this shows us, our author concludes, that we should think less about lying well and more about doing good; and this, he says, will make us lie more comfortably into the bargain.

What he says is a bit far-fetched, in his usual seventeenth-century style; but at bottom it is perfectly true.

And thereafter, he tells us, those good people had no more confusions or sufferings to endure that might be compared with those that have already been described.

From that point on, in fact, they led the most peaceful, happy and enviable of lives; so much so that if I told you about it you would be bored to death.

Their business affairs went magically well, though there was a little difficulty to begin with because of the shortage of workers, and because of the bad habits and high wage claims of those who remained. Edicts were published fixing maximum wages; but in spite of that well-meant intervention things got going again, because sooner or later that is what things have to do. Then another edict arrived from Venice, a rather more sensible one this time, giving ten years exemption from all personal taxation and taxes on property to all foreigners who came to live in the territories of the Republic. For our friends it was as if the golden age had returned.

Within twelve months of the wedding a fine baby was born to them. As if to give Renzo an early chance to keep a certain noble promise that he had made, it was a girl; and you may be sure that she was christened Maria. As the years went by, other children arrived, some boys and some girls – I forget how many. Agnese was kept busy carrying them here and there, one after the other, telling them they were naughty children, and planting great kisses on their cheeks, which left a visible imprint there for several moments. They were all good, sensible children, and Renzo insisted that they should all learn to read and write.

'Since this scoundrelly business has come to stay,' he said, 'they might as well have the benefit of it.'

But the best thing was to hear him tell the story of his adventures, which always ended with a list of important things he had learned, to enable him to do better in future.

'I've learned not to get mixed up in riots,' he would say. 'I've learned not to preach at street corners; I've learned not to raise my elbow too often. I've learned not to hold door knockers in my hand too long when there are people around who jump to conclusions; I've learned not to tie bells on my ankles without thinking what it might lead to.' And so on.

But Lucia was less than satisfied with his teaching – not that she found it wrong in itself; but she had a confused feeling that there was something missing there. She heard the same homily a number of times, and thought it over carefully on every occasion; finally she answered the family moralist one day, and said,

'What about me? What am I supposed to have learned? I didn't go out of my way to look for trouble; troubles came to look for me ... Unless you'd like to say,' she added with her sweet and gentle smile, 'that I did make a mistake after all – the mistake of being fond of you, and promising to marry you.'

Renzo did not know what to say for a moment. But after a long debate, and much heart-searching they came to the conclusion that troubles very often come because we have asked for them; but that the most prudent and innocent of conduct is not necessarily enough to keep them away; also that when they come, through our fault or otherwise, trust in God goes far to take away their sting, and makes them a useful preparation for a better life.

This conclusion may have been reached by humble folk, but we find it so just, that we have decided to place it here, as the very essence of our whole story.

If the story has given you any pleasure, think kindly of the man who wrote it, and also try to find a little kindness for the man who has rearranged it for you.

But if on the other hand we have only succeeded in boring you, please believe that we did not do so on purpose.